DAYSTAR

KATHY TYERS

MARCHER
LORD
PRESS

DAYSTAR by Kathy Tyers
Published by Marcher Lord Press
8345 Pepperridge Drive
Colorado Springs, CO 80920
www.marcherlordpress.com

MARCHER LORD PRESS and the MARCHER LORD PRESS logo are trademarks of Marcher Lord Press. Absence of ™ in connection with marks of Marcher Lord Press or other parties does not indicate an absence of trademark protection of those marks.

This is a work of fiction. Names, characters, places, and incidents are products of the author's imagination or are used fictitiously. Any similarity to actual people, organizations, and/or events is purely coincidental.

Cover designer: Chris Gilbert, www.studiogearbox.com
Editor and typesetter: Jeff Gerke

Library of Congress Cataloging-in-Publication Data
An application to register this book for cataloging has been filed with the Library of Congress.
International Standard Book Number: 978-1-935929-50-5

Printed in the United States of America

For Matt and Anneloes
Together in each others' hearts
And in mine

Caldwell Lineage

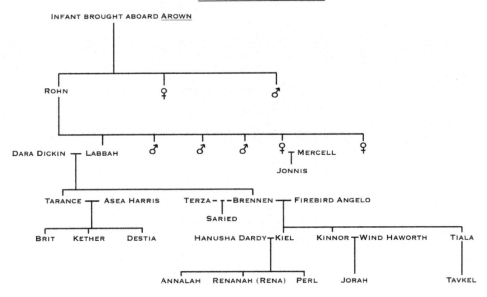

CAST OF CHARACTERS

* DENOTES MAJOR ROLES

*High Commander Brennen Caldwell: Recently retired Head of
    Intelligence, Elysia

Commander Cort Harris: Captain of the cross-space shuttle *Daystar*

Major Tewana Kirzell: Systems officer on board *Daystar*

Captain Danton Harris: Pilot on board *Daystar*

Lieutenant Dijka Gardner: Engineer on board *Daystar*

*Meris Cariole: Fourth year medical student at Elysia General,
    disciple of the Collegium for Human Learning

Willin Prescott: Security Sentinel at Hesed House, the Sentinels' Sanctuary

*Medical Specialist (MedSpec) Saried Kinsman: Psi medic in
    residence at Hesed House; daughter of High Commander
    Caldwell and Terza Shirak

*Lady Fi Caldwell: High Commander Caldwell's wife

*Annalah Caldwell: Meris's room-partner at medical school; High
    Commander and Lady Caldwell's granddaughter, Kiel and
    Hanusha Caldwell's eldest daughter

*Sanctuary Administrator ("Minster") Wind Haworth-Caldwell:
    High Commander and Lady Caldwell's daughter-in-law,
    serving at the Sentinel Sanctuary on Procyel II. Kinnor
    Caldwell's wife

*Lieutenant Jorah Caldwell: Newly vested Special Operations
    Sentinel in Federate Service; Kinnor and Wind Haworth-
    Caldwell's son

*Air Master Kinnor Caldwell: Special Operations Sentinel in
    Federate Service; High Commander and Lady Caldwell's
    son, Wind Haworth-Caldwell's husband

*Chancellor Piper Gambrel: Head of the Collegium for Human Learning, based on the Regional capital world of Tallis

*Colonel Ottar Zeimsky: Chancellor Gambrel's medical research colleague

Colonel Cora Claggett: Special Operations Oversight Committee member

Colonel Artur Mercell: Special Operations Oversight Committee member

*Shamarr Kiel Caldwell: High priest of the Holy Path; High Commander and Lady Caldwell's son

Hanusha Caldwell: Kiel Caldwell's wife

Perl Caldwell: Kiel and Hanusha Caldwell's youngest daughter

Rena Caldwell: Kiel and Hanusha Caldwell's middle daughter, a sekiyr at the Sentinel College on Thyrica

*Tavkel Caldwell: High Commander and Lady Caldwell's grandson; Tiala Caldwell's son

Terza Shirak: Elderly Mikuhran resident of Hesed House; Saried Kinsman's mother

Pieters Keeson: Sekiyr on Sanctuary rotation at Hesed House

Colonel Reg Harris: Defense commander, Hesed House

Lieutenant Colonel Kirck Spieth: Arrives at Hesed House with Jorah Caldwell

Gini Spieth: Colonel Kirck Spieth's wife

Madam Kudennou Kernoweg: Head of the Federate Regional Council on Tallis

Colonel Pelson Urnock: Non-Sentinel Tallan, Covert Operations; appointed to Special Operations Oversight Committee by Federate Regional Council

Captain Mel Anastu: Sentinel recently based on Netaia, Minster Wind's office aide

Major Heryld Ryken: Sentinel, recently based on Caroli, Jorah's guard

Captain Jamee Mattason: Intelligence Sentinel

Tiala Caldwell: High Commander and Lady Caldwell's daughter, cloistered at Tekkumah settlement on Procyel II; Tavkel's mother.

Rava Haworth: Wind Haworth-Caldwell's clan aunt

Prince Tel Tellai: Netaian nobleman, friend to High Commander and Lady Caldwell

MAJOR LOCATIONS

Federacy: A government unifying twenty-three worlds in the local Whorl of star systems. Its two major regions are governed at Elysia (High Command) and Tallis (Regional Command). Other Federate worlds include Thyrica, Tallis, Procyel, Netaia, Caroli, and Lenguad. The Sentinel kindred is sworn to serve the Federacy.

Mikuhr: A non-Federate world, formerly home to another genetically modified people group, the renegade Shuhr, who were descended from the same genetic stock as the Sentinels

Procyel, also called Procyel II: The Sentinels' sanctuary world, location of Hesed House sanctuary and Tekkumah prayer retreat

Sabba Six-alpha: A variable star lying between the Federacy's Elysia and Tallis regions, responsible for a Whorl-wide catastrophe about three centuries before this story takes place. Data storage and technology were lost on Whorl worlds, space travel became impossible, and civilizations declined.

Thyrica: The Federate world where the Sentinels' ancestors arrived as refugees more than ten generations ago

Whorl: An eddy of stars that trails the galactic arm. Rich in habitable worlds, it was widely settled during the great wave of human expansion.

ACKNOWLEDGMENTS

I never would have tried to write this novel before my time at Regent College in Vancouver, BC. I send deep gratitude northward, to friends and advisors too numerous to list again. Their wisdom and example made an impact that I hope will last for a lifetime.

Sincere thanks to my editor, Jeff Gerke. If Procyel is visible at all, it's because of him. Thanks also to my agent, Steve Laube, for bringing the project to fruition.

I want to thank my friends, Rev. Bob and Pat Baker and Rev. Jeff Hamling, for reading the manuscript with theologically grounded eyes. To Dr. Len and Cindy Ramsey, friends of a lifetime, who offered medical suggestions, encouragement, and Kenyan tea. To fellow writers Mel Anastasiou, Dr. Beverly Greenwood, Dr. Sue Geske, Paul O'Rourke, Susan Pieters, Jamie Upschulte, and Marci Whitehurst, for guidance along the long path. Thanks to Kerry Nietz for excellent technical assistance.

And in the place of honor, I wish to thank my friend and assistant Jamie Upschulte. Jamie faithfully kept me moving forward, sane enough to finish this project on time. Special thanks to Jamie for all of the typing and the invaluable web help, but also for the many other ways she has been letting people know about the *Firebird* series.

As always, I must take responsibility for all inconsistencies, impossibilities, and weak wordings.

PART ONE

. . . In Him shall perfect peace, true atonement, be fully accomplished.
In Him is your covering swept away, made unnecessary,
and drowned with your offenses in the depths of forgiveness
. . . the ocean depth of your tears turned to the blood of unending life.

II CHOTER 31, 32B

He was only expected to live a few hours. I saw the readouts! I'll send another
Procyel Eyewitness Report as soon as there's more to tell.

ANNALAH CALDWELL

Only the light is real. And I am the light, and I go to rejoin the brilliant light.
Only the light is real. And I am the light, and I go to rejoin the brilliant light.
Only the light is real. And I am the light . . .

LITANY 8, AGAINST PREOCCUPATION WITH THE PHYSICAL

PIPER GAMBREL, CHANCELLOR

COLLEGIUM FOR HUMAN LEARNING

PROLOGUE

High Commander Brennen Caldwell rushed upship from his sleeping cabin. A tightly closed service hatch vibrated visibly as a metallic bell rattled bulkheads. The starboard deck seemed to be sinking, which meant the *Daystar* had to be turning hard. In all his trips across this quadrant of Federate space, Brennen recalled no such maneuver.

This alarm bell was no drill.

The service corridor ended in a hatch. Brennen pressed his palm to a side panel, and the hatch slid aside. The alarm jangled even louder in the passageway beyond.

He stepped in. A guard in Sentinel midnight blue stood beside a wider hatch. Between one stride and the next, Brennen scattered his mental shields and saluted. The guard was shielding his thoughts heavily. Not even emotion seeped through.

Brennen restored his mental shields. "Permission to enter, Lieutenant."

The guard slapped a control panel. It gave off a sweet piping sound as the wide hatch slid aside. "High Commander on the bridge," the guard called.

Brennen strode through. The guard followed. The hatch slid shut behind them, muffling the klaxon's metallic shriek.

Very well, Holy One. Brennen sent the words subvocally out into the universe. Trying to alter chain-of-command could cost lives, and he'd been a warrior since his youth—but just now, for only the sixth time in his long life, he'd heard a distinct holy Voice. *I'm here,* he prayed. *Use me!*

Daystar's six-station bridge was shaped like a blunt wedge surrounding a black acceleration chair. To starboard, he recognized Major Tewana Kirzell sitting at Systems—her grandfather had flown under his command at Netaia—but he did not know the equally young shields officer seated beside her. The main sensors screen dominated the wedge's apex, and a startlingly young man sat beneath that screen. Beyond Sensors were Pilot and Engineering.

For the moment he kept his eyes on those personnel, not the sensors screen high on the bulkhead, nor the nav monitor below it. Six crew members, plus the guard: seven imperiled lives. *I see, Holy One. I will do what I can.*

Brennen paced straight to the Commander's acceleration chair. Passing Shields and Systems, he resisted the temptation to check those officers' status boards or their emotional state.

Commander Cort Harris spun the central chair. His chin tilted upward. *Sir,* Harris subvocalized directly to Brennen's mind, *we want you and Lady Fi in Secure.*

Not this time. Brennen took a few seconds to explain subvocally to Commander Harris what the Voice had told him to do. As he subvocalized, the pilot and the engineering officer—two more Sentinels in their late twenties—called off numbers to each other.

"Line twelve, eight six percent."

"Eight six, confirm."

"Execute." Commander Harris turned back around. Brennen felt his reluctance. Apparently Commander Harris wasn't shielding his emotions in Brennen's direction. *Only if you're sure, sir.*

Brennen dipped his chin. *More than sure.*

Commander Harris spun the chair away. *Carry on, then.*

Forty-six years ago, Brennen had also occupied a command chair. Today they faced no human enemy, which made some choices easier. This bridge didn't need to be fully staffed.

Brennen turned and saluted the guard who had piped him in. "Sentinel, I relieve you. Get to Secure."

It was harder than it used to be to sense others' emotions. Still, through Brennen's thinned shields he felt the guard's surge of gratitude and a sudden wave of fear. Obviously, the guard had controlled himself on duty. He hesitated a moment, looking Brennen up and down.

Brennen squared his shoulders, knowing the young Sentinel saw a body still trained and taut but unmistakably eighty years old—his white hair thick, his shoulders thinning. "Go," Brennen murmured.

The hatch slid aside. For a few horrendous seconds, clanging filled the bridge again. Bootsteps pounded away, and the hatch slid shut.

Next, Holy One? Pilot and Engineering kept singing off numbers behind him, a syncopated bass-soprano duet.

Sensing no clear reply, Brennen fell back upon common sense. He strode forward to Systems Officer Tewana Kirzell. "Major Kirzell, I relieve you. Get to Secure."

Without even glancing at the command chair—after all, Commander Harris hadn't countermanded Brennen's previous order—Major Kirzell unbuckled and stood. "Thank you, sir."

He returned her salute and gestured her toward the hatch.

She too fled. The horrendous clanging rattled the deck and again fell silent.

Brennen eyed the slanting systems board as he sat down and buckled in. On the display, half the gleaming status lines blinked cautionary yellow, one shone orange, and two had already gone red. Emergency power was on line.

Systems wasn't his specialty, and he couldn't run this station as well as an experienced systems officer, but for one watch, that wouldn't be necessary. He switched off a nonessential grid and linked another to timed sweep, and he double checked everything Major Kirzell had done. Once *Daystar* had passed the threat up ahead, Major Kirzell could fix anything Brennen had botched.

Finally, satisfied by the stabilized readings, he stared up and forward, into the main sensors screen.

At the enemy's eye.

The star designated Sabba Six-alpha did look eerily like a gold-rimmed eye, focusing its brilliant pupil toward *Daystar's* external sensors. The main monitor would normally be split into six quadrants. At this moment, a composite image filled the array.

Coronal mass ejection, the physicists would call it—a black blaze headed directly toward them. After a century of relative stability, Six-alpha was flinging out a spray of radiation and charged particles that would have dwarfed Brennen's homeworld.

Below that display, the sensors officer spoke softly. "No outrunning that, is there, sir?"

"No." Brennen also spoke aloud, out of courtesy. "And if it takes down our shields, every one of our civilian passengers will be dead in minutes." His wife and granddaughter's faces appeared in his mind. Tenderly he dismissed the images and returned to his task. Military ships carried powerful slip, particle, and energy shielding, and military grade shields might have easily deflected this assault. The group aboard this shuttle had been denied a small cruiser, though, since Elysia-to-Tallis was a passenger route. *If only . . .*

In light of the current political situation, Brennen hadn't pressed.

And not even full shields would completely protect them, up here in the crew cabin.

His right hand trembled. He stilled it, seeing a dark irony: That deadly sun was a natural object, the Holy One's creation, while in every cell of his body he was a genetically altered human, the only Thyrian Sentinel in history to sit on the Federate High Command.

Frowning, he pushed up onto his feet. He reached the forward station in a few strides—it was strange how the aches vanished when there was a job to do—and he grasped Sensors's backrest, looking down over the young man's shoulder. Unfortunately, in the shock of sudden retirement and evacuation, he'd never bothered to learn the younger crewers' names.

Sensors's boards looked grim. Half the ship's external eyes had blinked out in the ejection's first wavefront. The other half gave impossible readings—to be expected, as they crossed this unusual region. Physicists had predicted more major activity here within ten to twenty thousand years.

But not this soon. On the nav monitor, along the graphed vector that *Daystar* would travel—they had too much momentum to significantly change it—bubble-like wavefronts pulsed like coals, fanned by solar wind gusts.

Even in quasi-orthogonal slip space, this storm could kill.

Brennen cudgeled his memory, trying to bring up Sensors's name. He couldn't even address the young man by rank. No Sentinel, not even a High Commander, wore any rank insignia other than the small gold star on one shoulder.

Sensors glanced up at him.

Brennen frowned. "Wavefront. We're going to fly straight through one." He raised his head and looked aside.

Pilot and Engineering sat staring back at him. "Yes, sir," Sensors answered. He looked no older than Brennen's eldest granddaughter.

She should have reached the secure cabin by now. Firebird Mari would take care of her.

Commander Harris spoke. "We've altered pitch and initiated a turn. We can use the particle stream for extra broadside propulsion. It should drive us into that shadow lane fairly quickly." He pointed toward the main display. "If we don't lose thrust."

Brennen narrowed his eyes, focusing an excellent pair of lens implants, his only physical concession to age. Six-alpha's dwarf companion star cast a conical shadow on the monitor, a narrow safe zone that pointed north-spinward into the Federacy's Tallis region. He looked over his shoulder at Commander Harris. "How long will we be critically exposed?"

"Best guess: two point six hours. Peaking eighteen minutes, six seconds from now."

Brennen's certainty wavered. Service didn't always require martyrdom. "Is there anything more we can automate for three hours?" He would've liked to see his family's prophecies come true. His own children hadn't fulfilled them, but his grandchildren were reaching their twenties.

Assuming the Federacy didn't—

He cut off the thought. No time for it. "Can't we automate for twenty minutes?"

Commander Harris waggled a hand. He gripped a sideboard on his chair with his other hand, his shoulders slightly rounded. Brennen didn't envy the load he carried right now. "Auto systems are fluttering. Tricky course."

Brennen understood. If Harris could have emptied the deck of personnel, he would already be commanding this ship from its hardshielded secure cabin.

Brennen saved regrets for later. In sickbay. "Good." He turned back down toward the young man at Sensors, the most vulnerable position on this bridge in a radiation event. "Then I relieve you."

The face looking back up at him had lost all color. "Sir, you—"

"Sentinel." Brennen let his voiced interruption deliver the threat of authority. Then he sent privately, *We've seen all we need.*

Sensors glanced at the command chair. This time, Commander Harris frowned deeply before he swiveled away—but again, he did not object.

Sensors glanced down at his armrest panel. Every crew member had one of these. It recorded vital signs, including cumulative radiation exposure. That light still shone green. "Sir." He unbuckled hastily, stood, and paused to salute. "Thanks."

Brennen seized his upper arm and leaned close. "Don't panic the passengers. Control your emotions." Better than anyone else on the bridge, Sensors knew what would shortly wash through this ship.

"No, sir."

Dispersing his mental shields again, Brennen felt the young man strengthen his ayin static cloud. "You may inform them that this is no drill, if they don't already know. Tell them we're on the safest course, but don't frighten the civilians. Remember, there's an outsider on board." Unfortunately, Annalah had brought a friend.

"Yes, sir." Sensors touched his eyebrow again. He glanced at the hatch.

"Go," Brennen ordered. "And switch off that alarm."

The hatch slid aside and shut again.

In the silence that fell, Commander Cort Harris stared his direction and raised an eyebrow.

Brennen subvocalized, *We can't change course now. Can we override the failsafes?*

Negative. Civilian shuttle—

Right. There must be human hands on Pilot's and Engineering's controls. *Anyone else?*

Harris flicked a glance to starboard. *Tully has a sick son at Tallis, but we need Shields.*

Yes, we do. Brennen let Harris feel his regret. He might still relieve the young pilot, but at Shields, as at Engineering, he didn't feel even marginally competent. If the oncoming surge took down slip-shields, there'd be nothing left of the *Daystar* but quarks. For the next 2.6 hours, even life support—completely automated—would remain secondary to the shuttle's civilian rated slip, particle, and energy shields. Balancing them would take trained oversight.

Very well, Commander Harris's subvoice said at the back of Brennen's mind. Commander Harris pushed out of his acceleration chair and strode aside. "High Commander, the *Daystar* is yours. Shields, I relieve you. Get downship. I am about to seal the bridge."

Shields didn't pause to salute. As the hatch opened and shut one last time, the pilot gripped his steering rods. Engineering shifted a hand on her own board.

The four of them would ride into the storm together. *I'm sorry.* Brennen wanted to send them all that thought—especially the pilot, whom he might have saved—but he knew better than to distract them now. There were civilians to protect, including his wife and one of their granddaughters, and Annalah's friend Meris. The other Sentinels also had family aboard. Brennen kept two beloved faces in his mind's eye as he sank into the command chair. Commander Harris buckled into the acceleration seat nearest the sealed hatch.

Staring up at the enemy on screen, Brennen recalled a hymn that had sustained him years ago, on another desperate flight:

Holy Speaker, Shaliyah,
With your own hands lift us past sorrow
To your land before time, where you are the light,
And there is no darkness at all . . .

He glanced down at an armrest, called up a duty roster and identified the pilot and engineer: Sentinel Captain Danton "Dusty" Harris, Sentinel Lieutenant Dijka Gardner. Was it still possible that they might not all take fatal doses? *Please, Holy One. They could still live for decades.* "Sentinel Harris, Sentinel Gardner." He swiveled his chair slightly to port. "It's an honor to serve with you. Thank you for remaining on station."

"You too, sir." How could such a young looking man have such a deep voice? Just beyond his station, Lieutenant Gardner nodded and pressed her lips together. Perhaps she'd been tempted to bolt for Secure.

Brennen swiveled the chair starboard again. Beyond the empty systems station, Commander Cort Harris—*our pilot's father, uncle, cousin?*—sat staring back at him. Realizing he'd let his mind's ayin shields thicken again, Brennen dispersed them in that direction. Commander Harris had the slightly uneasy savor of a man wanting to ask questions. *What is it?* Brennen subvocalized privately. *Might as well ask. We're staring down death.*

Commander Harris's shoulders relaxed a few degrees. *I've just been wondering, sir. Very unprofessional, I know—but you were Head of Intelligence. Did you get the evac order any more pleasantly than I did?*

Brennen compressed his lips and swiveled the command seat forward once more. As he locked it down, he shot a thought in Commander Harris's direction. *Probably. A handsome but firmly worded request that I take retirement, so that my well-trained Assistant Head could move smoothly into my office. Mari and I will be glad to be closer to the grandchildren. I'm sorry if you were summarily dismissed.*

About exactly that.

Unable to see the nav board beyond Sensors's empty chair, Brennen flicked a finger toward one of his sideboards. A miniature display appeared over his tri-D projector. *Daystar* was visibly closer to that wavefront.

I wondered if Elysia was getting as uncomfortable for you in your office as for me at my command. Commander Harris's tone, normally disciplined and firm, felt oddly mournful. *All those years of service. Nearly all of us, doing all we could for the Federacy. They're turning on us anyway.*

They're afraid of us. For good reason. Brennen kept scrolling through primary displays. Had he missed anything?

Commander Harris's subvoice continued. *With you and Lady Fi gone from High Command, there's not one of us left. Not even the students in school. Annalah among them.*

Brennen nodded. It had been good to have his granddaughter close enough for visits, these three years.

What's next, Commander Harris added. *Mass murder?*

Brennen glanced back up at the screen. The cosmic eye had started to cloud. The wavefront was upon them. *We know one thing,* he sent Commander Harris. *A holy promise is at stake. We will not die out until Boh-Dabar comes.*

Maybe all those prophecies just pointed to you, sir. You burned out the Shuhr at the Golden City. And I can't see the Whorl turning to one of us. Commander Harris's tone sounded dubious. *Not anymore.*

Brennen also had doubts. Politics were getting ugly. Still, he answered as calmly as possible. *We don't know the future.* A yellow warning light appeared on his right armrest: *Daystar's* automated life support system was diverting power to the gradually strengthening shields.

Commander Harris, manning those shields, subvocalized again. *And your granddaughter's friend onboard—she has powerful parents. If Meris Cariole is hurt or killed along with us, there could be repercussions for our . . . survivors.*

That's also out of our control, Brennen returned firmly. *How are shields?*

Commander Harris glanced down. *Holding.*

A red light appeared on Brennen's armrest. Beneath the yellow life-support warning, a radiation alert now glimmered.

Daystar was well shielded for normal space.

But not for this situation.

Save us, Holy One!

CHAPTER 1

Body, relax. Mind, be still. I fear what I only imagine.

Meris Cariole sprinted up an empty passway and shifted her internal focus to a more powerful Collegium litany. She must not dwell on the danger. *Mind, you are calm. Body, you are strong.*

A falsely tranquil, androgynous voice drifted down from the bulkhead: "Passengers, report to shelter area. Please walk. Do not endanger yourself or others by running. Passengers, report . . ."

She careened around a corner and was absorbed by a crowd plodding along in soft shipboard slippers. A green light flashed up ahead. Someone shouted. Heads turned right and vanished through a hatch. Breathing hard, Meris let the flow carry her through the doorway.

The secure cabin was barely adequate for thirty passengers, as she'd learned in yesterday's shelter drill. Grey metal containers lined the bulkheads. Ventilation fans hummed softly, but it smelled close anyway. Blue striplights high overhead cast an eerie light on stressed faces. Since nearly everyone on board the *Daystar* could speak mind-to-mind, it seemed weirdly quiet. She'd gotten used to people around her acting strangely, cocking their heads or staring as if listening to voices she couldn't hear. In this moment, it felt freshly ominous.

She paused just inside the door, heart thumping. Where was Annalah?

"Meris!"

She spun around. Several people knelt around something down on the deck, including her college room-partner Annalah Caldwell. Annalah straightened and waved. "Meris!"

Meris guided on Annalah's coppery hair and a glimpse of something redder—blood?—as she shouldered between two older people. "Med student. Let me through." Was Annalah hurt? They might all die of radiation, but maybe not—and here was an immediate crisis.

A youngster lay on the textured black deck, a boy of maybe ten or eleven. Face shocky, blood spurting from his thigh. Jagged bone poked through his pant leg. Meris swallowed, her throat suddenly thick. Fractures weren't her school specialty, nor Annalah's. Still, that bleeding had to be stopped, and there was no medspec on this shuttle's passenger manifest. She shoved aside her fear of radiation as she reached the group. Swiftly twisting her hair into a rope, she knotted it at the back of her neck. "Tell me what to do. Is there a styptix kit?"

"I just sent for . . . Here it comes!" Annalah's river of red hair was already tied back. "Simple fracture, thank the Holy One." Annalah scooted aside, and a man wearing a midnight blue uniform tunic wedged himself into the kneeling circle and sank down. He pushed a red metal container at Annalah. Annalah plunged both hands into the box and tossed Meris a sterile wipe. Then she went back to digging.

The injured youngster whimpered. A black-haired woman knelt beside him, gripping his hand and trying to turn his head away. She plainly didn't want him to look at the ugly injury. Since he wasn't screaming, she probably was doing something mental against his pain too.

Lucky child.

Or maybe not. Meris scrubbed her hands with the wipe, wondering how in the starry Whorl a child could have broken a femur in this small space. High above this deck, the stacked containers looked climbable. Had he been playing up there?

If he hadn't been lying there bleeding, she might have envied his freedom. She focused on the moment's need instead, eyeing her room-partner's progress. Step one always was to treat for shock. Someone had covered him with a grey blanket. Next, stop bleeding—would they need a tourniquet? No, Annalah had a stypix kit. Third, reduce the fracture. That would be next.

Actually, it was good to think about something other than having her chromosomes cooked. Femoral fractures required major traction. It looked like they would have plenty of strong help.

Still, that looked like a lot of blood. Meris addressed the black-haired woman holding the boy's hand. She couldn't be many years out of school herself. These Sentinels married so young! "Can you do anything special to slow down that bleeding too? It looks like the bone nicked an artery."

"Wait!" Annalah donned pale blue exam gloves. "This should do it." She tucked a hand into the wound, spread its edges, tucked some tiny objects inside, and sprinkled white powder. Welling blood crusted rapidly.

Absorbable sponges, styptix powder—just like in school at Elysia Central.

Except this time, they were light-years from Elysia and about to be bathed in hard radiation—

Don't think about that! Meris commanded herself. *Mind, you are calm. Body, you are strong.*

Annalah hadn't stopped talking. "They can't put him in t-sleep until the fracture's reduced. He might need to be transfused too."

She dug deeper into the red box. "Marta, Kason, one of you might need to donate."

"Of course." A man kneeling beside the black-haired woman nodded, his face almost as pale as the child's.

"All right." Annalah straightened. "We'll try the reduction. I want our biggest and strongest holder on his shoulders. Kason, you don't weigh enough. Take the uninjured leg. Marta, keep cutting his pain." She looked around the circle.

Meris did too. "Come on. Move. Somebody heavy, take the shoulders. One hand under each arm."

The others rearranged themselves. Meris scooted into a position opposite Annalah, careful not to jostle the patient. The black-haired woman sprang up and made room for a burly man wearing snug grey shipboards. Really, it was impressive how these people rallied together.

She mustn't envy them either.

"Okay." Annalah glanced left, then right. "Count of three. One." The burly man leaned forward. "Two." The father and another man tightened their hands around the boy's ankles. "Three. Pull!"

Meris closed both hands around the leg just below the break. She must angle the broken end toward his pelvis . . . Someone cried out, close by . . . Annalah would push and manipulate the upper stub . . . Once the injured leg muscles were pulled taut, releasing pressure from the femur, those bone ends ought to move easily . . . She felt disoriented, trying to aim one jagged end toward the other . . .

There! A distinct relaxing of muscle tension. Annalah had rejoined the ends. "Don't stop pulling," Meris ordered the traction team. "I'll anchor. Annalah, how's the artery?"

"Bleeding's stopped. Getting ready to fuse and brace it." Annalah reached into the kit again. "You're doing great, Rex. Just another minute."

Meris relaxed slightly. With standard shipboard med gear, they should be able to immobilize the break. Then, these people could . . . they could make sure he rested.

She shied away from that thought and kept both hands firm on the crusted wound, one above and one below the break. The child's face had relaxed, showing no sign of pain. They hadn't used a drop of anesthetic, and his nerves ought to be screaming. The black-haired woman's mind powers were obviously strong. Shortly, his father would put him into . . . into tardema-sleep. After all, there were no stasis crypts on board.

A sweat droplet trickled down Meris's temple. As if traveling in tandem, a tear dribbled along her nose. How ironic that these strange and unpopular people had such caring families.

Annalah leaned in again, brandishing an osteo fusion light like a weapon. She trained it over the wound for half a minute. Meris kept her hands steady. Annalah slid the metal bands of a Ramsey brace around the injured boy's leg. "Hold on," she muttered, closing the brace's first latch. "Almost done."

Meris's shoulders ached. Still, she'd seen worse fractures at Elysia General. The boy would be fine, provided they all didn't die here in deep space, cooked by radiation or smeared across space like so many bloodstains, if the slip-shields failed—

Body, relax. Mind, be still.

"Okay." Annalah gave the Ramsey brace a last click of pressure, and she reached into the red box once more to pull out a palm-size scanner. "Blood pressure's low, but he's within normal range. All right for t-sleep, Kason."

Meris backed away hastily.

The young father leaned across his son's body. "Rex. Eyes here."

The boy looked up. He inhaled a long breath and coughed once. Then he lay utterly still.

Tardema-sleep. In memory, Meris heard her physiology profes-sor: "Tardema-sleep is a unique variety of deep hibernation, almost as quiescent as cold stasis. The procedure is never recommended for normal individuals, except in situations where death is otherwise inevitable and imminent. Non-Sentinels have been known to die in tardema-sleep. Conventional cold stasis is nearly always available."

Cold stasis was Meris's medical specialty. It wasn't available here, though. She got to her feet and backed away, trying to keep her crusted hands from touching anyone and hoping the Sentinels hadn't sensed how badly tardema-sleep unnerved her. This time, she guessed, they were listening to their own fears. Not hers.

Annalah flung her a wiping cloth.

"Thanks." Motion mid-cabin caught Meris's eye. A small, grey-haired woman sidled toward her, carefully stepping over and around passengers who'd sat down on the deck. Meris hadn't given any of them a moment's thought. Annalah's grandmother, the High Commander's wife, looked like an aged little bird under the strip-lights. Maybe it was the blue light's reflection in her bright eyes, or the way it shimmered in her hair as she cocked her head to one side. She had admitted that "Lady Fi," as these people called her, was a shortened form of "Firebird."

She was one of exactly three people in this secure room with no Sentinel powers, which had made her an instant friend. Meris had already enjoyed talking Federate politics and culture with her.

She reached Meris. "Anything I can do?" She shot a glance toward Annalah. "Looks like you two controlled the crisis very competently."

Meris stretched her aching shoulders. "Thanks. His dad just put him into . . . t-sleep." She avoided saying *tardema*. The very word repelled her. Thank goodness Lady Fi wouldn't be able to read her mind or emotions.

The Lady's loose grey shipboards blended with her hair. Here and there, a faint streak of its former reddish brown shade shone through the silver. These people didn't use anti-aging implants, so their elders looked *old*. "I think your parents would have been proud, if they could have watched that."

"Oh." Meris gave her hands a final hard wipe and tossed the cloth back to Annalah, who tucked it into a debris bag. "No." She took a deep breath. "No, they still wouldn't approve. Inferior minds can set bones, they'd say."

Lady Fi cocked an eyebrow. "Even your mother? She's a—"

"She's a researcher, not a practicing medspec."

"Hmm." Something clattered near the main door. Frowning, Lady Fi turned around. Nothing else happened over there, and she faced Meris again. "I know how badly that hurts, Meris. Move on. Your future lies along a different path. Someday, they'll understand you."

Meris doubted that Lady Fi grasped the depth of her private pain. Surely, no one else in the history of the Whorl had ever been so thoroughly betrayed. By her own parents, no less!

Lady Fi looked straight up into her eyes. "We all admire you for wanting to help people, Meris."

Meris glanced away. "Wasn't it supposed to be safe, crossing this region of space?" No world near Sabba Six-alpha was settled, but commercial shuttles traveled it regularly.

"Of course." There was more noise near the door, and this time the uniformed door guard beckoned toward Lady Fi.

Lady Fi nodded. "Excuse me. Please tell Annalah we're proud of you both." She turned carefully and stepped back in the direction she'd come from.

Meris flicked a wisp of hair out of her face. Lady Fi's husband was up on the bridge, taking the worst of the radiation storm. For Lady Fi, waiting to learn his fate would be awful.

Someone moved on Meris's other side. She too turned in place, careful not to step on outstretched hands or legs. Other people were mopping the deck and tossing cloths into the debris bag. The boy and his parents had retreated into a corner. Meris spotted Annalah springing up to take a seat on a large, grey metal container. It looked as if people had made enough room for them both up there.

Very well, then. Meris shuffled forward. Was she imagining things, or did she feel slightly strange, as if radiation were washing through her? Or was that simply the normal buzz of slip-shields, turning everything onboard sideways to real space?

She made it to the inner row of containers and sprang up to sit beside her room-partner. "Your grandmother says to tell you she's proud of us."

"Thanks." Annalah smiled for an instant. Her long, waving red hair still was tied back, and the prominent widow's peak over her forehead, her delicate cheekbones, and her fine chin made her face look oddly heart-shaped. "Has she had any updates?"

"Not yet. She could be getting one right now." Over by the door, Lady Fi conferred with the door guard. The cabin still seemed unnaturally quiet. Meris wouldn't have wanted to travel with these people, except that Annalah had offered passage—gratis!—to Tallis for their practicum year. It had seemed like a stellar solution to her sudden financial squeeze.

And her father, the senator, had liked the political implications well enough to answer her query. He'd written back, "You never know what you might learn from them, before they die out."

But he had not sent love. He hadn't wished her a safe trip or shown any other sign of affection. To him, she was already dead. Her chest ached, as if someone had stepped on it. Fear and grief were getting the upper hand again. Polluting her thoughts. *Mind, you are calm . . .*

Abruptly Annalah rocked forward off the container. "We should be praying." She raised an arm and started to sing. Meris didn't recognize the language or the weird, vaguely minor key. The woman sitting on Meris's other side joined in. So did the parents of the injured boy. He now lay perfectly still in the nearby corner.

Meris frowned and scooted back on the container, resting her shoulders against the hard metal behind her. She had no prejudices. She was liberal-minded enough to know that these people really weren't the abominations that some people called them. Still, that music had all the comforting quality of a sob. If they all didn't die in the next few minutes, she'd teach them some Collegium litanies. She had dozens of them filed on her handheld.

Stars swam in front of her eyes. Hyperventilation. *Body, relax—*

The overhead light faded to orange and winked out.

Meris gasped. The big engines' thrum sounded loud in her ears.

Had they lost shields? Was this the end?

Body, relax. Mind, be still. Body, relax—

The fans started again. Striplights came back on, dimmer than before, giving upturned faces a darker blue cast. The left wall seemed to have sunk. The ship must have been turning hard this whole time.

Near the doorway, the man in the uniform tunic still leaned toward the wall panel. What was he hearing?

He turned toward the cabin's center. "Attention." He didn't raise his voice, but he did speak aloud. "*Daystar* has lost some onboard systems. However, shields and life support are intact."

A young voice cheered. Heads turned, clothing rustled. Meris shut her eyes as relief fluttered through her veins.

The door guard crossed his arms. "They're requesting that any of you who can t-sleep would please do so. They're going to try and get us down out of slip-state in ten or twelve hours. We do have adequate onboard air for that length of time, plus passage afterward. Still, we'd like to retain a safety margin."

Tardema-sleep! Meris didn't dare look at Annalah. It would save oxygen if they all tardema-slept, but surely they wouldn't make her risk it. It was safe for *them*.

"Please," she whispered to Annalah. "I'd rather not."

"Of course not. They'll be glad to have one of us conscious, since there isn't a real medspec this trip. I'll see you when we get . . . wherever we end up."

Meris straightened, not particularly reassured. Would they finish this trip stranded on some low-tech Federate world? Who would fly the *Daystar* if everyone on the bridge succumbed to radiation poisoning?

Annalah stretched out atop the container. Meris scooted down onto the deck. She pulled off her slippers and the pullover she wore over her shipboard suit, wrapped them together, and made a lumpy pillow.

Straightening carefully, she lay down. She never would be able to sleep, but at least she wouldn't have to make small talk with strangers. She could concentrate on her litanies.

The woman who'd been sitting next to Annalah leaned over her, covered Annalah's forehead with a hand, and stared down at her face.

Meris rolled away. *Body, relax. Mind, be still. I fear what I only imagine.* Already most of her shipmates lay squeezed down onto available surfaces, head to head or foot to foot like a school of psychotic fish. A few of them walked back and forth, helping the ones who couldn't reach tardema-sleep on their own. Soon Meris lay alone, wide awake in blue half-darkness near her immobilized friend. It seemed pathetic, now, that she'd feared instant death. She would have simply become nonexistent. Reabsorbed into the Infinite Divine, free from pain and fear.

Since the shields seemed to have held—so far—it had become likelier that they'd all die over the next weeks or months. Radiation sickness generally set in long after the exposure, in cancers or other debilitations that required bothersome treatment . . . or killed slowly and inescapably.

The cabin smelled distinctly sweaty. Someone's stocking foot lay close to her nose. She tried to breathe slowly.

A low rustle came from near the door. Meris pushed up on both straightened arms. Uniform Man backed toward that bulkhead panel again, looked around, cleared his throat, and raised a hand toward Meris.

She pushed up onto her knees and finally dared look at Annalah, who lay with her eyes closed and face relaxed. If she were alive, Meris saw no sign. She got to her feet and gingerly stepped over several sleepers.

Lady Fi had also stood. She was probably staying awake until she heard from her husband. They both pressed close to Uniform Man, and Lady Fi spoke first. "Well?"

"Mostly good news, ma'am." He spoke softly. "We've got major systems back on line and a new course calculation. The rad counters in this cabin show no significant exposure to passengers."

Unspeakably relieved, Meris blurted, "But the crew?" As soon as she'd said it, she wished she hadn't.

Lady Fi winced.

Meris tried to look apologetic. "I'm sorry, I didn't mean—"

"Somebody had to ask." Lady Fi stood stiffly, her chin high. "Well?"

"They're seriously dosed, ma'am."

Wrinkles deepened between Lady Fi's darkening eyes. Almost without thinking, Meris laid a hand on her shoulder. Lady Fi nodded slowly. Plainly, the bridge crew had sacrificed themselves to protect their families. They were the ones who would die slowly, over the next days and weeks.

"There's some good news, though." Uniform Man spoke hurriedly. "We're overshooting the Tallis system, so they've set a course for a safe drop point from slip state and then steady deceleration within towing range of the Procyel system."

Lady Fi's eyes brightened. "Well done, Brenn," she said softly. "Our most gifted psi healer is right there at the Sanctuary."

Their special private world? A whole planet, reserved by Federate law for a handful of Sentinels and nobody else—was *that* where they would end up? Meris had heard terrible things about outsiders who had tried to go there. She tried to push another new fear away. "Your husband. He . . . That is, I hope . . ." Meris faltered, remembering all she had heard about radiation sickness. "I'm sorry. He's very brave." Her own voice sounded awkward. How could she comfort Lady Fi, with the prospect of ending up on Procyel added to her troubles?

But it would be perfect for the crew. For everyone on board except Meris Cariole.

Lady Fi looked down at the deck. "When a second shift relieves them, they'll all be put into t-sleep. Quickly. That should arrest any damages, until they're reawakened at Sanctuary."

This was no time to remind Lady Fi that Procyel II was off limits to normal persons. "That will be a good place for them." *To die.* Meris thought it but didn't speak. It was a relief to know Lady Fi, like Annalah, couldn't hear her thoughts.

A new question occurred to her: Why not? What had happened to those two, out of everyone onboard?

"Yes. The best. Go on, sleep if you can. Or shall I . . . Are you ready to let someone help you?" Lady Fi glanced toward Uniform Man.

"No! But thank you." After all, the offer had been meant as a kindness.

Lady Fi's mouth twitched. "I didn't grow up around these people either. I would have refused at your age. Now I know better."

Rather than answer, Meris turned and stepped back toward Annalah.

Procyel! Sentinels never let outsiders land on that forbidden world. The planet was blockaded with some kind of mind-destroying technology. Obviously, they had reasons for keeping ordinary people away. They wouldn't want her running loose down there, spying on their private place. Rumors abounded: military stronghold, genetics research center, a location for secret breeding programs—

But they didn't seem to be bad people. Furthermore, they wouldn't want to make an enemy of her father by mistreating her. They would undoubtedly put her in stasis if they had a good med center, but she'd experienced stasis as part of her training. It was nothing to dread.

She found her place and lay down again. There on the deck, the loneliness caught her. All her life, her father had assumed she would intern for his Senatorial position. Through three years of med school he'd pursued her, insisting this was why he and Mother had given her life in the first place.

Two weeks before her scheduled departure from Elysia, he'd made a public announcement: Since his only offspring could not be persuaded to accept the coveted internship in his department, that position would go to someone he barely knew—so far, it had all been fine with Meris—but then he and her mother had officially disowned her as well, cutting off all contact and financial support.

Originally, she would have been able to afford commercial transport to Tallis. She wouldn't have been Annalah's suddenly impoverished friend. She wouldn't be a charity case, the only normal person on a genetically altered passenger list. She wouldn't be headed where they didn't want her and she didn't want to go.

Surely, the Sentinels would put her on the first shuttle off Procyel. They would want to get rid of her too.

She glanced into the corner. The young family lay together, as motionless as if they all had died, the father on one side of the injured boy, the mother resting her arm on his other shoulder.

Meris shut her eyes and tried to sleep.

CHAPTER 2

Shipboard days dragged after the disaster. Decelerating into the Procyel system provided a few exciting hours, but then Meris had to wait in the stinking galley while a ten-seat landing shuttle took groups offship. Annalah left on the first shuttle down, since her specialty was regeneration therapy. Lady Fi left too, naturally.

The radiation-sick crew members had been wakened from tardema-sleep and were barely upright. They would need immediate regen at the very least. As they boarded the landing shuttle, each leaned on the arm of a younger officer—those whose lives they'd saved, Meris guessed. All the members of that honor guard wore dress-white uniforms. So did a cordon of others who stood at attention along the main corridor.

Meris boarded the third and final ride down, leaving a dead and darkened ship behind her. She felt lonely and mousy, and she hoped they would let her bathe before putting her in stasis.

Stasis, not t-sleep!

The landing shuttle's cabin air had a sharp, sweet odor that was delicious after what she'd been breathing. She settled into a comfortably padded passenger seat next to a round window, wriggled her shoulders . . . and abruptly, she found the shuttle's cabin tilted for deceleration. Could she actually have slept, or might they have done something to her?

Slept seemed likelier. She stretched her back.

Her middle-aged seatmate leaned away from the window. "Oh, good. You're awake. Look! Isn't it beautiful?"

Meris stared down and out, expecting to see laser-cannon installations. Instead, they seemed to be descending toward a broad valley. Her window gave her a view off to the left. Rugged hills rose toward a country of jumbled, jagged mountain peaks.

She stretched her shoulders again. How nice, that they were letting her get a look from the air. This planet seemed to have been thoroughly ecologized, unlike her homeworld. Elysia was primarily urban. Here, it looked as if oxygenation was maintained not by vast algae farms but a dark green fabric of trees spread over the hills—and paler green plant life of some sort, down in the valleys.

"Looks like late spring," her seatmate remarked.

Seasons. How quaint. Meris kept staring. The mountains ahead seemed to grow larger, each jagged peak reaching into the sky as if it wanted to grab any aircraft that flew too low.

The shuttle swooped lower into that valley. A river below her branched and then meandered off toward the distant mountains. The shuttle's nose tipped up, and Meris flattened her back against the seat. Wherever these people were headed, it might be the only settlement on the whole world.

They bumped to a landing. Everyone around her unharnessed. Meris stood, shuffled up the aisle, and fished her duffel out of a forward compartment, determined to see as much as they would let her. What was it about this place that made it such a tightly guarded secret?

She ducked out a hatch and descended a short ramp. Planetside air smelled almost unbearably sweet. It was heavy with leafy scents and a musty smell it took her a moment to recognize: soil, like her father sometimes poured from a bag into flower pots. Here it was everywhere. Beneath her feet, even. This landing strip was covered with genuine mowed grass, where previous landings hadn't dug up long brown furrows of the musty-smelling dirt.

She saw two big metal doors in the hillside to her left, but the people in her group trudged straight ahead up a short slope instead, toward a grove of trees that were all covered with small pink and white flowers. Plainly, these people had all been here before. Every one of them grinned. It was as if simply by standing on this world, they left anxiety behind.

Meris wished she could feel that way. She paused a moment and peered up the hill ahead. Several laborers were perched on ladders amid the flowering trees, doing something—she squinted—were they actually picking those flowers? Not one of them even bothered to look in her direction. She supposed that was a good sign. Apparently they weren't *too* concerned about her being here.

She plodded uphill with her group. Where the grassy slope leveled off, they all turned left. It looked like they were headed toward a small white building. It stood alone, between this grassy hillside and a long, flat field that looked like bare dirt. Those jagged peaks made a formidable backdrop behind that field.

Where were all the buildings? Where was the housing complex, and where were the military defenses? Underground? She glanced to her right again. Farther up the long slope stood several wooden barns. They looked like they were made of wood . . . wood that had been allowed to turn grey, exposed to the elements.

How odd.

They reached the small white building. It was surrounded by low-growing plants with spearlike leaves and fat stalks that supported floppy purple flowers. The building's double doors looked as if they were rimmed in real gold.

Everyone crowded inside. Meris shouldered into the middle of the group. At least these people knew her. They were used to her. She'd helped save a child they all loved. . . .

The floor dropped beneath her, confirming her guess. Below ground, someone was surely waiting for her. *I fear what I only imagine.* She hadn't seen any hostility, though. Just the other passengers' very normal relief to be off the *Daystar*. She mustn't accuse them of any ill will. Surely, they would let her wait out her time here in cold stasis.

She could use a good long rest. She silently recited a Collegium litany for exhaustion: *The eternal is in me. I cannot know defeat. The eternal is in me . . .*

The doors slid open. Meris stepped with the others into a soaring underground chamber. It seemed to be jammed with hurrying people. Quite a few wore their midnight blue uniforms, but no one seemed to be waiting for her. Younger adults were all dressed in incongruous pale blue gowns or fitted tunics, and they too all seemed to be headed somewhere.

Off to her right, in what looked like an open-air dining area, a mixed-age group sat at wooden tables. Their clothing was as rough and brown as the rustic furniture. Muddy overcoats hung over several chairs. Swishing and splashing noises seemed to be coming from somewhere.

Meris's shuttle-mates all turned toward the dining area. At its near end, a group milled around a table littered with writing paper. She pushed forward with them. The floor under her feet was white stone. So was the wall ahead of her.

It was one of the young gowned women, not a uniformed Sentinel, who appeared beside her and tapped her shoulder. "Meris?" she asked. "Meris Cariole?"

Meris raised her head. *Body, relax.* "Yes, that's me."

"Good day. My name is Shari. Please, would you follow me?"

Several strangers who hadn't been on board the *Daystar* turned to stare as she followed Shari out of the dining area and got another good look at her surroundings. This chamber was probably two full stories in height. After so many days confined shipboard, she felt oppressed by its immensity.

Still, she appreciated a chance to look. All the chamber's squared walls and its ceiling appeared to be white stone. And . . . oh, my.

Straight ahead, dominating the artificial cavern, an enormous pool—more like an underground lake—lay rippling under broad strips of skylights in the ceiling of the cavern high overhead. Large, roughly conical trees seemed to grow out of the water, stretching toward those skylights. A path of large, square white stepping stones crossed the water from where she stood. Two uniformed Sentinels, who appeared to be walking across the pool from right to left, were undoubtedly treading on more stepping stones.

Well. This world defended by mind-destroying technology was nothing like Meris had imagined.

But of course, she was not seeing all of it. Just what they were allowing.

"Please come, Meris." Her young guide swept a hand left along the poolside, indicating what looked like a broad stone walkway. A white metal railing surrounded the pool, broken only where the stepping stone paths led out over the water.

She stood still, took another deep breath, and followed her guide along the waterside walkway. *Mind, you are calm. Body, you are strong. I fear what I only imagine.* The first Collegium litany she ever had learned—against fearfulness—was her own sanctuary today. She caught herself fiddling with the ends of her hair. Not wanting to look as nervous as she felt, she knotted it back. "Have you been here long?" she asked.

The young woman's freckled face was framed by closely cropped brown hair. She held up her right hand to display a thin gold ring. "Most of a year. It's part of our College rotation. We all spend a year here, on Sanctuary duty. I'm due to be rotated home in a few weeks, but I'll miss the place."

Meris looked down. They were walking on more of the white stone, with faint grey veins. "It is beautiful."

"Thank you." Her guide stopped in front of an unmarked arch built of more white stone. "Here you are. The Administrator will speak with you."

Meris stepped through the stone arch. Beyond an impressively broad data desk—the first sign of high tech Meris had seen, she realized—a tall woman stood waiting. Then she saw the woman's long oval face, pure black eyes, and greying black hair.

Meris controlled a sudden urge to turn and run. She'd seen people who resembled this woman, but only in historical tri-Dramas. Just one people group in the Whorl unnerved her worse than the Thyrian Sentinels: the Mikuhran Shuhr, who'd been the Federacy's worst villains. These truly evil, genetically modified people had spent 100 years raiding, robbing, and murdering on all twenty-three Federate worlds.

Supposedly, the Mikuhran Shuhr had been defeated and absorbed by the Sentinels. They had never dared show those long faces on Elysia. To Meris's relief, there hadn't been any on board the *Daystar*. But this woman had absolutely classic Mikuhran features. Meris swallowed, her throat suddenly tense.

"Come in, Meris. Sit down." The woman indicated a wooden chair near one end of her data desk.

This room was also walled and floored with white stone, with stone benches around its edge. Strangely, fabric streamers dangled from the ceiling. Meris sidestepped to the chair, wondering whether that arm gesture signaled the woman's intention to voice-command her—to force her to do things she did not want to do. It was one of these people's more frightening abilities.

"Meris, I'm the Sanctuary Administrator, Wind Haworth-Caldwell." As Meris sat, the woman lowered her arm and sank onto a large black desk chair. "And I'm sorry you've been caught in this situation. I understand that my niece Annalah invited you to travel with the *Daystar* group."

Niece? "Yes. Annalah has been my room-partner for three school terms." The safest approach was honesty. These people could also detect deception. One false word might land her in tardema-sleep. Instantly.

Still, the administrator didn't need to know about her family troubles. "My parents encouraged me to accept Annalah's offer." Before the tall woman could speak again, Meris squared her shoulders. "My specialty at Elysia General has been medical stasis, and I would be glad to assist here. I'm sure some of the radiation sick crew members will need stasis care, not just regeneration."

"Yes." The administrator spoke blandly. "Our medical specialist is extremely capable."

"And stasis should be redundantly monitored." Dread squeezed Meris's gut. This was their Sanctuary, their secret place, fully authorized by the Federate government. The fact that it wasn't what she expected did not change her status here.

The administrator looked down at her desktop's reflective dark surface. A gold Sentinel's star gleamed on the shoulder of her formal brown coat. "Meris, tardema-sleep is perfectly safe for periods up to forty days, but we don't like imposing it on anyone who's unwilling. I must stress that in all our history, we never have allowed outsiders on this world. We have nothing against you personally."

Meris leaned forward. "Surely medical stasis is a better option. If cost is a factor, I . . . My parents . . . That is, I will repay you. As soon as I can." And how would she do that? Never mind. She pressed on. "I honestly would like to assist your medspec, if I may. I owe your people my life. The crew—they were terribly brave, up there on the bridge." If they'd altered the *Daystar's* flight path enough to bring it down out of slip-state within towing distance of this place, could she criticize?

The administrator's mouth looked stern, and her black eyes seemed to bore into Meris's subconscious. If Lady Fi hadn't assured Meris that mind-access created a distinct, prickly nauseous sensation, Meris would have suspected her mind was being read. "Please, Administrator—"

The administrator's mouth softened slightly. "*Minster,* please. I did not feel qualified to take the same title as my gifted predecessor. And I understand why my appearance unsettles you. I also know how it feels to be an outsider. I was born on Mikuhr, but I grew up on Thyrica. Imagine that, if you will." She raised a hand and touched the shoulder star. "Their acceptance didn't come easily. I have tried to serve the Federacy faithfully, by maintaining this Sanctuary in safety and security."

Buoyed by a faint hope, Meris followed the shift in the conversation. "You have the same surname as Annalah. And her grandfather."

"Yes. I married her grandfather's other son. Annalah calls my husband 'Uncle Kinnor.'"

"Oh." Meris had never asked about Annalah's family. It would have felt . . . nosey . . . given these people's declining popularity.

She braced herself. "I'm quite willing to be put in medical stasis, Minster. I experienced stasis as a student."

The administrator—*Minster*—slowly shook her head. "I'm sorry, but we will need all our available stasis units for those radiation patients."

As Meris sat groping for some other argument, part of the broad data desk lit with a moving image. Meris couldn't tell for certain from this angle, but it looked like the head and shoulders of another woman—another black-haired woman, almost as long-faced as this one, apparently wearing medical yellow. "Wind?" A deeper voice spoke out of the desktop. "Are you with Meris Cariole? Lady Fi just told me that Meris has been offering to assist me. And I certainly need help. For the next few hours, at least."

Meris's breath caught. This was her chance. "Yes." She spoke slightly louder. "I would be happy to—"

The Minster raised a hand. She addressed the image on her desktop. "Unfortunately, security is a higher concern." Meris caught motion back at the arched entry and saw that a uniformed Sentinel had stepped inside. The Minster glanced at him and nodded.

Body, relax. Meris tilted her head for a better look at the woman in the image, her best remaining hope. This woman, also plainly Shuhr-descended, wore her black hair in a braid that accentuated her long features. "I was already short-handed, and now the center's overwhelmed. If Meris is headed for t-sleep, may I at least take her up on that offer for a few hours?"

The Minster folded her hands on the desktop. She stared back at Meris, who tried to keep her emotions under control. She'd heard that feelings could be sensed, even if one's mind wasn't being read. Did she really want to stay conscious, surrounded by these people?

Yes, I do! Given another hour, she might convince the medspec to keep her around. As those thoughts flitted across her mind, she wondered whether the man standing under the door arch had been called specifically to put her in tardema-sleep.

The Minster glanced up at Meris and back down at the desk. "Saried, please assure her that medically, t-sleep is nothing to fear."

"I will," the voice said.

The Minster shrugged. "All right. I'll send her with a guard. Please keep her close, until she's safely asleep."

The desktop went dark.

Meris got a deep breath. "Thank you, Minster. If I can repay even one of those crew members by helping, I'll be glad." It sounded sycophantic, but she meant it.

"Mm." The Minster got to her feet, walked around the broad desk, and sat down on one corner of its surface. Did she wear brown, instead of the ubiquitous midnight blue, because she was Shuhr—or because she wasn't military? "I promise, we'll send you to Tallis as quickly as possible. We're not on a commercial route, so if no one heads there before the safe limit for t-sleep approaches, I promise we'll bring you out for a recovery period."

That cold, invisible hand squeezed Meris's gut again. She needed to convince these people not to do that to her, nor to subliminally change her feelings about it. "I've already missed the start of term."

A hint of humor warmed the Minster's voice. "We'll do our best. I'm truly sorry this incident gives you the impression we're unreasonable. Our own safety is simply paramount. Would you go with Lieutenant Prescott, please?"

Meris stood. She bowed slightly toward the Minster and followed the uniformed man back out onto the waterside.

CHAPTER 3

The Sentinel led Meris straight up the pool's end. Daylight filtering down through those skylights felt warm and inviting. Fewer people jostled and hurried up at this end than down near the elevator. Aware she was being watched (*Me, a security risk?*), Meris kept looking straight ahead. A puff of breeze off the water chilled her eyes. *I'm guilty of nothing,* she thought at the guard. Nothing but accepting a ride on a shuttle that hadn't reached its original destination.

They passed an arch on the left, its door made of wood and shut tight beneath another white stone arch. A uniformed woman stood guard beside it. She wore midnight blue, anyway. She saluted Meris's guard as they passed. Maybe that arch led to secrets. A broader arch lay ahead, wide open with no wooden door in evidence. Brilliant lights shone out from inside. It looked medical.

Sure enough, her guard headed for it. Meris braced herself to face another Shuhr-Sentinel authority figure and strode through.

This corridor also was floored and walled in white stone, though its surface was smoother than out by the pool. Just a few steps inside, a gowned young woman sat at what looked like an admissions desk: wood that had been painted white, but with several inset data panels. "You must be Meris Cariole. Welcome to Hesed House. MedSpec Kinsman is waiting for you down the left hall, in the stasis suite. You should enter through the third door on your left."

"Left, then third door left. Thank you." Their med center had to be fairly large. Annalah had said most of their old people came here to spend their last years, and so the Sanctuary might need dozens of final care suites.

Meris glanced over her shoulder, realized that her guard had remained at the desk, and was struck by the urge to run . . . hide . . .

Where? Her best chance of avoiding tardema-sleep was to make the medspec into an ally. Somewhere else in this medical corridor, her only other shipboard friends—Annalah and the elderly Lady Fi—were undoubtedly busy.

She raised a hand and made sure her hair wasn't coming untied. If only she'd had time to unpack her own medical tunic. She'd brought it from Elysia for her practicum year on Tallis. She shifted to another litany from the Tallis Collegium. *I am the spark of undying light. I shall see. I shall know.*

The third door on her left lay across the passway from a large, open general use station that was also lined in white stone. Meris glanced through that third left door into a smaller room, with its gowning closet and several lockers built into the walls. There was a deep spray sink for scrubbing. What looked like a sanitizing arch led into the stasis chamber itself. She was shifting her balance to walk through that door when she spotted a glowing visual monitor out in the passway.

It appeared to display the actual stasis room, where the medspec would be. Meris stepped closer.

On the room display, an open stasis crypt rested on a wheeled cart under a tank that had been suspended from the stone ceiling. Meris recognized the crypt's brown metal surface and rounded corners as the most common form of current Tallis crypt designs. Standing next to it was the woman whose long face and braided hair had looked up out of the monitor on the Minster's desk. The woman who looked like another Mikuhran Shuhr.

Meris planted her feet in front of the intercom panel. "Hello."

"Good morning, Meris." The medspec's placid voice filtered through the wall 'com, and her image shifted to face the monitor squarely. She walked closer. "For your information, I'm only half Mikuhran, but I look more than that. They're used to me here. I work here on Procyel for obvious reasons, instead of elsewhere. I look much more like my mother than my father."

"Good . . . morning," Meris returned, embarrassed that the woman had sensed her disquiet. The Minster probably had too. She hoped too late that she hadn't offended. "Please, let me apologize."

"No need. I studied on Tallis. I understand." The front of the woman's yellow tunic bore Tallis General's med school crest and the name KINSMAN.

I fear what I only imagine. Meris raised her eyes back to that long face. The woman had weary eyes, and her head drooped forward. She was a medical specialist, to whom people came for help, just as Meris hoped people would come to her someday. Meris had paid dearly for that hope.

Behind the medspec, beneath tubes that dangled from the perfusion tank, the stasis crypt's lid lay open. On its underside, a row of red lights showed that the medspec had just begun processing a patient. Some *Daystar* crew member undoubtedly lay inside.

Those crewers had sacrificed themselves for the sake of their families. And for her. *Body, relax. Mind, be still.* Feeling poised again, Meris spoke. "What would you like me to call you? 'MedSpec Kinsman'?"

"Yes, or *Saried* is all right." The medspec rested a hand on a counter that looked laser-scrubbed. "We're terribly busy today. Even with your friend Annalah's help, I am short an aide. The crew members who needed emergency regen are settled, and Annalah's up the hallway with them. Now . . ." She looked back at the crypt. "I have a less seriously irradiated patient to bring up out of t-sleep and put into stasis. You can scrub up next door, if you're still willing." She smiled wryly. "Now that you've had a good look at me."

"I would be glad to assist you." The Shuhr had ceased to exist before Meris was born. She just didn't want anyone diving into her mind and shutting off her autonomous nervous system, stopping her heartbeat, and overriding the breathing reflex. Blood clots could form in tardema-sleep. Toxins could accumulate, blood vessels could dysfunction . . . "I'll scrub and be right with you."

"Thank you, Meris."

She slipped into the prep room, found a clean tunic and hair tucker, and pushed the knot of her hair up into the tucker. With nothing to leave in the locker, she stepped straight to the spray sink and thrust her arms in. The bracing, familiar smell of chemicals rejuvenated her.

One, two . . . Disinfecting by the book required a seventy count. *I fear what I only imagine.* Actually, if they put her in t-sleep, the odds were still better than what she'd already survived on board the *Daystar.* And if she'd died on board, it would've happened so fast that she simply would've become nonexistent. Unaware. No pain, no fear, her own spark of life reabsorbed into the eternal flame.

So she had no cause to worry.

If only she could believe that.

Sixty-nine, seventy. She stepped into the sterilizing arch and raised her hands. Here, it was just a ten count.

It had been frightening to see Annalah lie there on the metal container, sleeping more deeply than medical stasis, closer to death than to unconsciousness.

I am the spark of undying light. I shall see. I shall know!

Meris elbowed a control panel. The door ahead of her slid open, and she stepped into the stasis room.

Beyond the crypt lay another uncluttered counter. This floor also looked like smoothed white stone. Other than that counter and the stasis equipment, including a monitor mounted on the stone headwall over the crypt, the procedure room was bare. The long-faced woman stood over the crypt's head end, reaching down with both hands and staring eerily without blinking. Meris froze in place.

MedSpec Kinsman's eyes looked wearier by the moment. Was she waking the crewer out of t-sleep? Sure enough, a soft groan came from the crypt. "Hello, Cort." The medspec leaned away, stretching her back but obviously maintaining eye contact. "I apologize for the chilliness, but you're all safe at Hesed House, and you're headed for stasis. You're going to make it, Cort. I'll see you again, probably in a few weeks. Any messages, anyone you wanted me to contact?"

Meris heard nothing, but the medspec nodded. They must have communicated telepathically. "I will." She pressed a hypospray against his forearm. "All right, Meris. I've inserted all the cannulas and administered the anesthetic. I just need a redundant monitor."

Meris took up the monitor's position, down at the crypt's foot. From here, she could see inside. The patient was a middle-aged man with short, dark hair and blunt features—the ship's commander, if she recalled correctly. Adjustable bracing inside the crypt cradled his head, pre-cooling the brain. A miniature life signs transmitter lay on his chest. In just a few moments, non-aqueous cryoserum from the tank hanging over that crypt would begin to replace his blood, which would drain into the crypt's fractionation and storage unit.

Her own stasis experience hadn't been unpleasant, except for the deep, awful cold just before she lost consciousness. Perfusion hadn't hurt, as her veins flooded with oxygenated cryoserum. She had only felt eerily light, and she had gone under with Chancellor Gambrel's words on her lips.

Over the patient's head, the wall display showed his vital signs—blood oxygen, hemoglobin, and so forth. "Initial check," the medspec called.

"Initial check, confirm." Apparently Tallis General's signals were the same as the ones she'd studied on Elysia, since the medspec hadn't corrected her. That was good.

Now it came down to waiting, as cryoserum slowly replaced the patient's blood.

The medspec turned toward her. "You're a fourth year?"

Meris nodded. "They tell me the dull classes are finished and the terror of responsibility is about to begin."

"That's what I remember, from Tallis." The MedSpec smiled as she kept looking down, and hope tickled Meris's gut, as if she'd swallowed a feather. "We were terribly worried when we heard that the *Daystar* was passing through a coronal mass ejection. It must have been a harrowing experience. All praise to the Eternal Speaker, and to the crew."

Eternal Speaker? "Yes. I . . . leaned on my litanies. I'm a member of Tallis Collegium."

"Chancellor Gambrel's organization?"

"That's right." How delightful, that they'd heard of the Collegium even here in isolation . . . and yet had the medspec's eyes narrowed slightly?

The medspec settled onto a tall metal stool. "Sometime, you'll have to tell me more about the Collegium. What I've heard has been . . . unsettling."

"Oh?"

The medspec shrugged. "Our spiritual understandings are quite different. I suppose you heard that from Annalah."

Meris stretched her memory. "No. But she never came to Collegium meetings with me, if that's what you're asking."

"We aren't allowed to proselytize. If you didn't ask questions, she was right to say nothing." On the string of red lights inside the stasis crypt's open lid, the left light turned blue. "Ten percent," the medspec said.

It always went quickly at first. "Ten percent, confirmed." How should she answer? She needed this woman's support! "Annalah did say her father was some sort of priest."

The medspec's smile broadened. "He is."

Apparently this was a safe topic. "During the crisis, there was praying and singing in your special religious language. Annalah started it."

"Good for Annalah," the medspec murmured.

Meris took another slow look around, ending at the crypt. "Why," she started, but she changed her mind and shook her head.

"Go ahead, ask questions if you're curious. And no, I can't override Minster Wind's policies on your behalf. But I do need additional staff, and I will keep asking for you."

That was something. Meris folded her arms. "Why bother to stase this patient if he's just waiting for treatment? Why not just keep him in . . . t-sleep? Is there a time limit, even for you people?"

"Yes. Toxins can build up in our bloodstreams too. Stasis is actually safer. They all took a risk t-sleeping, sick as they already were. But it was that, or else die before they could reach a med center."

"I see." Meris leaned against the stone wall. It felt cool against her back. "They were very brave," she said softly. "The whole crew. I don't know if I could have done it." She hadn't dared to even think about leaving the secure room.

The medspec's features softened, her eyes more mournful than weary. "I agree. There's such a thing as doing one's duty. Still, it can be hard."

"True. How are the other crew members?"

"The two more seriously injured are under regen with Annalah. They're still in their physical prime, and I think their systems will respond well."

That didn't jibe with what Meris had seen. "Three crew, total? I thought there were four."

"Yes," the medspec murmured. "There is a fourth. But he's not expected to live, so he has declined treatment. We're simply keeping him comfortable. He wants our limited resources allotted to people that he already expected to outlive him."

"Annalah's grandfather. Lady Fi's husband."

The medspec nodded. Small talk seemed inadequate, so Meris fell silent too. Long before this trip—back when she first had known Annalah—Meris had asked her mother which historical biolog of High Commander Brennen Caldwell's life was accurate. Had he been the military intelligence celebrity who had coordinated the Federate invasion of Netaia, or the hero who had nearly died bringing down the Mikuhran Shuhr, or the half-alien menace frequently caricatured in contemporary politico-animations?

Her mother, objective as always, simply had said, "They're probably all half true."

Mother! Meris had hoped that even if her father never approved her chosen profession, her mother might come around. Someone had to apply the researchers' discoveries to actual patients, all those new protocols and techniques. Otherwise, it all would be for naught.

It took roughly an hour to perfuse an adult, and they seemed to have exhausted casual conversation. Soon Meris caught herself yawning, as she stood resting her left hand on the foot of the crypt. Its smooth brown metal felt cool under her palm. Eventually, just one light remained red on the lid's underside. Ninety percent of the patient's preservative cryoserum had been administered, and outflow fluids—visible inside the crypt through tubes inserted into veins on his lower legs—looked appropriately dilute.

The yellow standby light came on. "Holding for stage three," Meris announced.

"Holding." The medspec bent over some display on her counter. They'd spent an hour together, and it seemed acceptable to stare for a moment. As the medspec straightened her shoulders, room light flickered off her gold Sentinel's star.

Meris frowned and adjusted her hair tucker. It had slid down over her eyebrow. She'd known people who were virulently anti-Sentinel. After all, just look at this: Sentinels were actively training Shuhr and half-Shuhr survivors. What if the Shuhr mindset prevailed, and they decided to seize the Federacy together? Given their unusual abilities . . . Well, the thought would be truly disturbing, if she let herself linger on it. Surely she wasn't the only intelligent person who had imagined that future. It probably had been why they were all ordered off Elysia in the end.

Focus, she told herself. She should be mentally counting seconds, anticipating the moment when the last light in the string turned color. Six . . . five . . . "Perfusion complete." She stepped away as the light turned blue. The medspec touched a control. By now, the patient would have lost consciousness. Meris didn't remember this part at all. The crypt's lid swung down and sealed with a soft whoosh. Meris announced, "Ready for stage three."

"Initiating." The medspec reached down out of Meris's sight. From inside the crypt came the expected snap and clang, and a frigid whine. Shivering in sympathy, Meris watched the cooling indicator fade from deep blue, through ice blue, to white.

MedSpec Kinsman stood up and slowly arched her back, twisting it. Her long braid flicked out from behind her for a second. "There. I can't help wondering what the Whorl will be like for us, by the time some of my patients wake up." She turned toward the counter. "Stasis storage is at the hall's end. Would you take him down there, please?"

"Certainly." Being trusted alone seemed like a good sign. Meris unlocked the cart wheels under the humming crypt, activated its servos, and steered the bulky unit back out through the prep room and left, down the corridor to another white stone arch. Through it she saw the foot ends of two crypts. She slid this cart into the last available parking spot at the chamber's far end. Here, the ship's commander would wait for his turn at tissue regen treatment.

Meris stood a moment, rubbing her hands in the chamber's warmth. Stasis Storage had actually been her preferred retreat back at Elysia General. For the last two years, she'd spent almost as much time with silent stased patients as her study group. For one thing, it was easier to relax when she was alone. And she always got a sense of waiting-for-rebirth from those crypts.

She'd spoken with several newly awakened Elysian patients. Some had dreamed, while others remembered only the chill before sedation. In both cases, Meris had felt deeply satisfied to have helped them through their crises.

If MedSpec Saried Kinsman couldn't countermand the Minster's orders, then Meris had just one hope left: Lady Fi. Still, her husband was dying, and Meris must not intrude—

Yes, she must! She returned up the corridor and found the med-spec sitting at a data station in the triangular all-purpose room. Her right shoulder rose as she reached up to her touchboard. Again, Meris stared at the star on that shoulder. Stories of Shuhr piracy had peppered her grandmother's reminiscences. Unfair, that events had stranded Meris here of all places, when all she'd wanted—all she had needed—was to get to Tallis General!

Deep creases had appeared between those black eyes. "Meris, it's natural that you feel uncomfortable with us. I hope you understand that we must use our stasis crypts for our injured, instead of for you. Otherwise, you certainly might have been allowed to sleep through your stay here that way. You must understand that we never allow outsiders to see this place."

"I'm not sure that I do." She might as well admit it. "It doesn't look anything like a top-secret installation. Not like I've seen in tri-Dramas, anyway."

The medspec barely smiled. "We just need a place where we aren't considered unusual. Here, we renew our ties to the natural universe."

Meris wanted to correct her. There were no "natural" planets. All worlds, except one that was lost, had been ecologized by an ancient wave of human settlers. Instead she said stiffly, "Of course."

"We will not harm you, Meris. I promise."

Meris squelched her fearfulness again, hating that part of her imagination. "I see." She glanced out toward the bright central cavern. On the breeze blowing in from that pool, she caught a whiff of something tantalizingly meaty.

The medspec's brow furrowed, drowning her blue-black eyes even deeper in what looked like grief. "Now I need to assist my fourth patient, since the others are settled."

"High Commander Caldwell." Meris reminded herself not to react. Still, hope prickled again. "May I help you?" Lady Fi would be there. Here too was a chance to meet Annalah's famous grand-father, who'd retreated to his cabin to sleep out the last part of the voyage. A chance to thank him, and see more of the unusual medi-cine they practiced here.

The medspec waved a hand across her touchboard. Its viewing display winked off. "You'd like to observe, I assume?"

Meris went stiff. Had the medspec been reading her mind? No, she realized. Annalah had always insisted that she drew a lot of conclusions simply by watching people's gestures and facial expres-sions—and Annalah was no mind reader. MedSpec Kinsman simply knew that anything delaying t-sleep would be welcome.

"Very little of we do here is actually secret, Meris. You might even want some of our help some day."

Was that mind manipulation? No . . . she felt just as anxious after hearing it. "I would like to join you, if I may." But Lady Fi had insisted she'd been born outside the kindred. She knew how it felt to be an outsider. Surely, a High Commander's spouse outranked the sanctuary administrator.

She might speak up for Meris.

MedSpec Kinsman raised an eyebrow knowingly. "Walk with me, then."

CHAPTER 4

Meris followed the medspec past several patient rooms, deeper into the corridor. A second short hallway branched off to the right. Meris wondered fleetingly whether they'd found all this white rock *in situ* or brought it in from somewhere. The polished surfaces in this corridor would be easier to sterilize than the rougher stone out in the big central chamber.

MedSpec Kinsman stepped into a treatment room, where something hummed at a low pitch. A man lay on the bed before them, one side of his face and neck striped with biotape. A feeding tube vanished beneath the coverlet, and headwall monitors showed that they were providing substantial life support.

As expected, High Commander Brennen Caldwell's initial prostration was resuming. Soon, there should be a short respite that most meds called latency and others called walking death. After a few comfortable days, his interior organs would begin to collapse in a massive disintegration.

He looked surprisingly calm. Sedated, she guessed, or resigned to his fate. Lady Fi sat on the stool beside him, propping her arm against a bedrail and letting one of his hands rest on her palm.

She turned her head. Although she sat upright, her forehead looked more deeply wrinkled than Meris remembered. "Meris," she said softly. "What a nice surprise to see you here, assisting."

That was not auspicious. "Hello, Lady Fi. I'm . . . so sorry."

The medspec strode straight to the bedside. "May I ease you, Lady Fi?"

"Please. And some energy for this arm would be good."

MedSpec Kinsman rested a hand on Lady Fi's right shoulder. Meris saw nothing happen, but Lady Fi straightened immediately and gave her head a sharp shake. The lines crossing her forehead looked shallower. "Better. Thanks."

To Meris's surprise, the old man's lips and the skin under his closed eyes crinkled with the slightest smile. He was at least somewhat awake.

The medspec turned to Meris. "There. That was psi medicine. Since they are pair bonded, the stronger and more comfortable Lady Fi feels, the more it eases his discomfort. They feel emotions together, to a certain extent. Together we're hoping to get him through the acute phase quickly, to a good long latency."

Pair bonded. Annalah had claimed this was part of what held Sentinel families together. Meris swallowed, nodded, and took a short step closer to the elevated bed. "Thank you, sir. For the lives you saved. Including mine."

That slight smile stretched just a bit. He had to be in considerable discomfort, even if they were medicating him.

"Now," the medspec murmured. "Father. Look here, please."

Meris's stomach somersaulted. MedSpec Kinsman was this man's daughter? But . . . wait, if the woman was half Mikuhran . . . Meris's imagination tossed up several unsettling possibilities, but the others present showed no sign that they'd sensed her shift in emotion. The High Commander looked steadily up at the medspec. A tear crept down her lined face.

Lady Fi backed away from the bedside and touched Meris's arm. "They'll be busy awhile. Let's go out in the passway."

The man pulled in a labored breath. "Stay. Please."

"You won't disturb me." The medspec kept staring down at him as she spoke. "It's all right. Stay here. Tell her."

The High Commander managed another word. "Yes."

Meris wanted to hide. How humiliating to get her curiosity satisfied at the man's deathbed. She would've rather asked Annalah privately: When, why, and by whom had the High Commander fathered a half-Shuhr daughter? Back *then?*

She didn't dare to offend any of them. Stalling, she studied the head-wall lifesigns monitor. Linked to a small transmitter on his upper arm, it painted a grim picture in gleaming lights. The man's blood chemistry had gone insane. Though he couldn't see the monitor, plainly his wife and daughter knew they could hope for only a few good days.

His *daughter . . .*

Meris backed up to stand beside Lady Fi.

"Old story, really." Lady Fi pursed her lips, looking more than ever like a little bird. "Back in the old days, when we were at war with the Shuhr and they were trying to wipe out his family, they tried to entrap him by taking genes from his skin cells and impregnating Saried's mother. Saried wasn't meant to survive, of course. Brennen managed to save them both."

"Oh my." Again Meris recalled quizzing her parents about the man, back in the happy days when they shared her world. Maybe all the stories about him really were true.

"Not alone," the man murmured.

Lady Fi puckered her mouth into a smile. "I was locked down under a regen arch, you may recall."

"Not alone," he repeated.

Lady Fi shrugged. "Terza—Saried's mother—still lives here. We visit her when we're on site. I'd ask Saried how she's doing now, but Saried's working."

Meris glanced back at the bed. Apparently, whatever psi medicine involved, MedSpec Kinsman—Saried—was busy doing it. She hadn't even seemed to notice when Lady Fi had mentioned her name. "She'll . . . certainly come by to . . . greet you both, then." *And to say goodbye.* It would have been unkind to say that, though. Meris wondered how long the medspec would wait—how long she would let her father slide toward internal disintegration—before taking the mercifully obvious step. Perhaps they would wait for other family members to gather.

A moment after that thought crossed her mind, she felt vaguely ashamed, like a voyeur. Whatever else the people in this room might be, plainly they were family to each other.

Meris couldn't imagine either of her parents traveling cross-space just to visit her, even if she were dying. They would have correctly called it a pointless extravagance, even . . . before.

"What is it?" Lady Fi asked.

Meris glanced at her, startled. Hadn't everyone said that Lady Fi couldn't even read emotions?

Oddly, Lady Fi was smiling. "Remember, I didn't grow up around these people either. I remember how strange and threatening it all seemed. At your age, I would've refused t-sleep too. I know better now."

This was her chance. "But won't you speak to the Minster on my behalf, please? I've gotten top grades. I'll be a competent assistant, and I'll be glad to earn my keep. Including . . . I know about . . ." Should she offer?

Of course she should! Every possibility was worth trying. "Down the years, I've learned some very useful litanies. Chancellor Gambrel's meditative techniques are a great help and comfort. I've got dozens of them on my handheld." Unfortunately, she'd left it in her duffel, along with her yellow tunic. "Maybe over lunch sometime?" If she was still awake to teach them! She held her breath.

"Thank you for offering." Lady Fi drew away, frowning. "I know you mean that very generously."

Meris glanced at the door, recalling too late that the med-spec had had a similar reaction to the Tallis Collegium. Had she heard footsteps? "I meant it with more than kindness. And please tell . . . Saried . . . that I would be honored to work with her. In any capacity."

Lady Fi nodded, already scooting her stool back toward the bedside.

A soft rap came at the door. Meris spotted her guard. He saluted. "Excuse me, but Meris Cariole is to come with me."

Meris's pulse accelerated as the medspec turned around. "Thank you for assisting, Meris. I truly am grateful. You'll be fine. Don't worry."

Heart sinking, Meris followed the Sentinel back up the corridor and along the waterside. She'd run out of options. The immense cavern felt close now. Suffocating. *I fear what I only imagine. I fear what I only imagine. I fear what—*

They reached the administrator's door arch. But before Meris could step inside, the guard raised a hand. "Wait."

Meris thought she heard another male voice behind the arch. However, when the guard finally motioned her inside, she saw only the Minster sitting at that huge desk. "Come, Meris. Sit. Let me put your mind at rest."

Startled, Meris hustled forward. She took the wooden side chair again.

"You will not be asked to tardema-sleep."

"I . . . Thank you! Why?" Meris gripped the chair's edges, leaning hard forward. On second thought, questions could be risky. "No, never mind. Thank you, Minster. I don't need to know why."

"As soon as you left, I sent a DeepScan transmission to my husband's brother, our highest spiritual leader. I had a suspicion that asking you to t-sleep against your will might be against our

Privacy and Priority Codes in this unprecedented situation." The Minster barely shrugged. "Kiel just replied, and he agreed with me. We all need mercy from time to time, Meris. I must ask, in return for this freedom, that you will conduct yourself with absolute trustworthiness."

Meris wanted to dance with relief. "Of course."

The Minster glanced toward Meris's guard and then back at Meris. "Any door you see open, you may walk through it. Please comply with anyone in uniform, though."

She could stay. She could learn to be useful. She could not have asked for more, for the moment. "Yes. Yes, I shall. Thank you, Minster. And I sincerely don't want to impose any longer than necessary. As soon as possible, I will be on my way."

The Minster smiled faintly. "We already agreed on that. Meanwhile, Medical Specialist Kinsman is an excellent teacher, and you may go on working with her."

"Yes," Meris repeated, "thank you." She would not get credit for taking a practicum anywhere but on Tallis, so any time she spent as Saried's assistant wouldn't count toward her certification—but she could fret about that some other time. For now, she felt only relief.

"We are honorable people," the Minster said. "I hope that helps us to recognize someone else who might be trusted."

A puff of air wafted in from the big chamber, smelling oddly sharp and . . . green. Meris nodded. And hadn't she just been hoping to share Collegium teachings with a wider audience? It would be worth finding out why these people reacted to her suggestions without enthusiasm. "I mean to earn that trust, Minster Haworth-Caldwell."

"Excellent. Your parents have been notified that you arrived safely, by the way. I'm a parent too, Meris. I can only imagine how worried they've been."

Meris blinked. Didn't the staff here know she'd been disowned? This felt like an invitation to casual conversation, though. Meris snatched it. "How old are your children?"

"Kinnor and I have a son." The Minster pulled a tri-D portrait off an office shelf. Meris took the small, thick rectangle by its edges and looked into a serious face framed by short black hair. The Minster's son had a pointed chin like Annalah's, and the portrait showed him wearing a Sentinel star on his shoulder.

Naturally.

The Minster laced her fingers on the desktop. "We had that taken last month, just after Jorah took his vesting vows." That note of pride in her voice reminded Meris of her own mother and the way she used to speak, years ago.

Meris handed back the portrait without looking closer. She was unlikely to meet this clan member. "What would you like me to do now, Minster?"

"I will enter your name in the task rotation, and a sekiyr will guide you wherever you're needed."

"Sekiyr?"

"Student-apprentice. The young people, nicely dressed, like the one who brought you here when you landed. For now—" She looked up. "Lieutenant Prescott will escort you to the commons for something to eat. Annalah will join you there. You may dine at any time, day or night. There will always be sekiyrra on duty to serve you."

"Thank you." Meris rocked forward and stood, feeling like a different person from the woman who'd sat down on that chair.

The Minster swept a hand up the desktop. Another panel lit. "When you leave to finish your schooling on Tallis, we hope you'll tell people—your parents, particularly—that Hesed House hides nothing sinister. It's simply a place of rest and retreat. It's unlikely that you will observe anything that falls under our minimal security precautions."

"I won't open any closed doors." On the other hand, might accidentally tumbling into any of their secrets get her memory disabled? She still knew too little about what they could do to people, and when they might do it. She kept her tone polite. "Thank you again." She turned, stepped out the stone archway, and paused on the waterside pavement. She was free! Free to explore, free to wander . . . though she would be watched more closely than ever in her life.

That was all right, compared with the alternative. She looked out at the pool and took a deep breath of amazingly fresh and damp air. Far off to the right, in that open-air dining commons, Annalah already sat at a table. She was easy to spot, thanks to the red hair and medical tunic.

"This way," her guard said.

"Yes, thank you. I see Annalah."

Meris picked up her pace. From this angle, she saw that the big trees grew in clumps, planted between several stone benches on what looked like a square stone island. Really, she wouldn't have minded staying awhile if it hadn't been imperative to reach Tallis.

Annalah sprang up and ran a few steps to intercept Meris. She threw her arms around her shoulders. "This is amazing! I'm thrilled for you. And it was my dad who gave you the go-ahead, did you know? I hope you're still here when he arrives with the Sentinel College group. You've just got to meet him . . ."

On she rambled, as Meris sat down. Meris's guard took a seat at another table, with several other people in uniform. A young person hurried toward Meris, set down bowls of soup and a small loaf of nut-laden bread, said "Welcome," and scooted away without introducing himself. Another speedy young server offered steaming pottery mugs of something that didn't smell like kass.

Meris could feel her apprehension melting away by the moment. She busied herself with the soup as she waited for Annalah to finish talking. It was mellow with spices and thick with brilliant green, orange, and red vegetables. Annalah's high cheekbones did make her look extremely young and slightly aristocratic. Maybe she resembled that minor royalty on Lady Fi's side.

Meris had never quite understood why Annalah had attached herself so firmly to her, back at Elysia General. She'd proved a loyal friend.

Eventually she said, "Aunt Saried said you were a great help this morning." Then she fell silent.

Meris had learned to leap into Annalah's pauses. This time, she simply wanted to eat. Her stomach had unclenched, and now she realized she'd been famished. "Thank you for telling me that. Your Aunt Saried is an interesting woman." That should be good for another short discourse.

Annalah tossed her head. "She's one of our most gifted psi medics. She just doesn't feel she can work anywhere else without frightening people. It's a shame." Off she went again, telling the medspec's life story. Meris had already heard all she needed to know. She kept spooning up fragrant soup, stealing glances up the waterside as she ate. A huge open doorway apparently led to the kitchen, because servers kept hustling through in both directions. Beyond that big open door, an even larger door—double—was closed by two pale, polished wood panels.

"The Sanctuary's crowded," Annalah finished.

Meris swiveled her head. Another mixed-age group emerged from the elevator, wearing rough brown clothes similar to what Meris had seen an hour ago. They walked straight to two tables.

More people came and went from the medical corridor at the pool's far end, through the guarded doorway, and from several other stone arches. The big double doors remained shut.

"But Aunt Wind is moving you in with me, into a room all to ourselves. You're an honored guest now. I get to show you around. And don't worry. I won't talk the *whole* time."

Aunt Wind . . . Yes, the Minster also was part of Annalah's family. Smiling wistfully, Meris tore a hunk of bread off the loaf and used it to wipe her soup bowl clean. Annalah's soup was only half gone. "But we won't be here long, right?" No matter what the Minster had said, Meris felt the threat of tardema-sleep still hanging over her. She glanced aside. Her guard sat with his arm around a woman, also uniformed.

Annalah sipped from her mug, which was pale green with an abstract leaf design. "Well, actually, I've decided to stay. When you travel on, I'll certainly miss you. It's been nice to have a friend who also lives in the silence."

Silence? Annalah? Meris was careful not to smile. Maybe she understood Annalah better now. Among a community of mind-speakers, Annalah had to feel excluded. Maybe she really should ask about it. Maybe this was the time.

Then Meris realized what else she'd said. "You aren't coming to Tallis? You'll have to take another practicum year!"

Annalah toyed with her mug handle, her forehead a wavefront of wrinkles. "Aunt Saried needs me. I do want to apologize for all you've just been through. It's my fault, in a way."

"How do you figure that?"

Annalah leaned over the table. "Remember that delay before we left Elysia? We stayed two extra weeks because my family wanted to see me get the Greenwood Award."

"Don't blame yourself for the weather unless you're on the control committee." That was another Collegium litany. "I'm sure they all wanted to say some extra goodbyes too." Meris frowned, reluctant to sympathize with Annalah's guilt feelings. The Greenwood Award was a high honor for innovative treatment protocols. Annalah's specialty, regeneration therapy, was a fiendishly complicated healing regimen that approached each organ system differently. Stasis didn't constantly need refinement, so there were no awards. Every step simply had to be done right, or else the trusting patient—deep in frozen slumber—didn't wake up. "So you're putting an award-winning career on hold . . . for what?"

"They told me the awards ceremony was important, like Grandfather being on the High Command. To show others that we're hardworking, moral people. But in the end, I guess it didn't make much difference. We're becoming unpopular out there. We walk a narrow road, and the price of survival has been severe discipline. Aunt Saried's going to need staff. I want to help her."

Meris shook her head, and she felt her hair coming loose at the back of her neck. She twisted it hard and anchored it again. "Sensible people out there still respect your people. Even if they prefer to keep a distance."

Annalah smiled faintly.

"And I really am sorry about your grandfather. That was very brave, what he did. I'm sure they won't let him suffer."

"Of course not." Tears formed in Annalah's eyes. "Aunt Saried will keep him comfortable when the latent phase ends."

Meris set down her spoon and her last hunk of bread. "That's all? Just . . . palliative care?" These people had inexplicable customs. MedSpec Kinsman, for example, would have been aborted without hesitation under normal circumstances—but it sounded like High Commander Caldwell had taken heroic measures to save her. "Annalah, you know what's normal. He gets a final cool, tasteless drink when cell death sets in, and he goes peacefully away. He's had a good life. Why put both him and Lady Fi through horrors," she asked, realizing that their pair bonding and emotional linkage had a truly dark aspect, "since there are people triaged for treatment, who need your meds' attention?"

Annalah shook her head. "We say that Elysian gentle-death practice is 'off the holy Path.' There's a waiver in my school file stating that I can't be required to participate in euthanizing a patient. And Grandmother will be glad to keep Grandfather with her as long as possible. It's terrible for the pair bonded to suffer together, yes. But it's worse when they're bereaved. Aunt Saried lost her husband, my Uncle Nebb, about eight years ago. She won't have forgotten. It's awful, Meris."

Bereavement. Yes, perhaps she could sympathize. Losing family was devastating. She pushed back her chair. "Are you ready? I'd like to see where we'll sleep."

CHAPTER 5

The lounge in the main civilian spaceport on Tallis, capital world of this Federate region, was a virtual blast zone of competing conversations. Not even the dull grey shortweave carpet could dampen the noise. Debarking passengers emerged through eleven doors along a curved wall, and beyond an enormous glassite window wall, a civilian landing shuttle accelerated skyward.

Jorah Caldwell stood with his back to another glassite wall on the lounge's far side, resting one shoulder against a cold sandstone pillar. This was the local debarking area's brightest corner. A thin shadow stretched away from his feet on the carpet.

He'd never seen so much grey in one place. Federate military forces all wore local uniforms and insignia. In most places, Tallan grey was just one of the uniforms he saw. Here on Tallis, the number of soldiers seemed out of proportion for a civilian spaceport. This was Tallis's holiday season, though. Probably most of them were home on leave.

Jorah glanced down at his sleeve. He wore the midnight blue of his own homeworld, Thyrica, but without any of the usual non-Sentinel Thyrian sleeve insignia. No, he'd just won the only insignia he ever would display, the coveted star on his right shoulder. He was a fully vested Sentinel in Federate service, even if they had stuck him with backing up his father the first time out.

There, he heard at the back of his mind. The single subvocalized word, sent without audible speech, had a familiar tang.

Air Master Kinnor Caldwell stood on the pillar's far side, positioned like Jorah with the sun at his back. They weren't invisible to the civilian crowd, but people were unlikely to stare at them for long.

One of the first skills everyone learned—Jorah had been taught by his parents, before leaving home—was to constantly surround himself with a cloud of static at the special energy frequency that he produced deep in his brain. This shielding cloud protected him from the barrage of emotional noise he would constantly feel otherwise. On duty, Jorah kept his shields dispersed so all his senses would be as sharp as possible.

As he stood unshielded in an emotional maelstrom, his father felt like a keenly whetted knife. He was ready to plunge into the herd and cut out the individuals he suspected of illegal intent.

Seven civilians had just walked out of a shuttle corridor near mid-wall. They shuffled along in a formation that looked too defensive to be casual: One pair of Lenguans—two men, muscular—paced in front while another pair—man and woman, similar in height and build—came behind, as if defending the ones in the center—three men, slightly built. Their brown and muddy green clothing, a little looser than shipboards, was only slightly less drab than the ubiquitous Tallan grey.

Jorah sent a subvocalized thought back to his father. *Hard to believe they arrived with so few guards.*

Jorah caught a slight nod with his peripheral vision as he peered through a gap in the debarking crowds. He'd also been ordered to keep a grey-suited trio of local military people under surveillance, although he suspected that his father simply wanted to test his powers of observation.

One Tallan, apparently off duty, sat sipping from a steaming cup while the others looked over her head and out the far viewport. Those Tallans were Federate military.

Jorah was Federate too, technically. A generation ago, he and his father might have expected deferential salutes if the two groups passed.

This was Jorah's generation, though. It was time to earn back the Federacy's respect.

One of the lead Lenguans slowed slightly. He turned his head toward the Tallans and back toward his partner. The group stepped out more quickly.

According to Sentinel Special Ops intelligence, it was a dissident trade delegation. They'd come to attack their own representative to the Federate Regional Council, Madam Kudennou Kernoweg. They had traveled passenger class to avoid attention. This was exactly the kind of situation Sentinel operatives handled best, a quiet and conclusive intercept, with no one harmed and suspects safely delivered for justice.

Jorah crossed his right hand over his left and gently cracked his knuckles. He would love to complete one successful mission— which would surely please Grandfather—before hustling back to Sanctuary for the death watch. He'd gotten the awful news just this morning.

He caught the stab of his father's light monitoring probe. *Your grandfather's lucky to be dying a hero at his age,* his father's crisp subvoice said. *The last thing he'd want is your pity.*

Air Master Kinnor Caldwell pushed away from the window wall. Second Lieutenant Jorah Caldwell followed several paces back, feeling incongruously visible in his midnight blue tunic and particularly aware of his new gold star. He'd been taller than his dad for three years now, but it still felt odd to look down on him.

They're going to walk right past that privacy lounge, Jorah sent. *This is going to be easy.*

Always suspect a trap. Watch for other Lenguans. His father took a few steps left, apparently eyeing an array of overpriced snacks on a dispenser wall. Jorah paced toward the opposite wall. As a knot of mixed travelers swarmed between them, he used the cover to turn fully around and sweep the crowd. He stretched out with his inner senses for suspicious intent. Mostly, the debarking travelers had the usual nervous buzz of relief, trying to relax after long flights. A few walked in a slight fog, having self-tranquilized.

Ahead, though, the Lenguans were overreacting to minor stimuli, obviously defensive. They'd nearly reached the secure lounge that Kinnor and Jorah had inspected an hour ago.

Clear, Jorah sent over his left shoulder.

The midnight blue shadow beyond the crowd pressed forward, staying close to the left wall. *Close up,* his father ordered.

Jorah sent a steadying burst of energy through his nerves and walked quickly. He was less than four meters out when the secure lounge's door slid aside. Jorah felt a surge of broadcast mental energy suddenly surround his father, strongest in the direction of one of the middle Lenguans. Plainly, he'd singled out the leader for voice command. The others would either follow or scatter.

Taking a few last strides, Jorah closed with the back of the group. He stretched out with his own abilities and nudged the two Lenguans in back. "Hands away." He put command harmonics into his voice. "Follow."

Just short of reaching under their clothes for weapons, the Lenguans' hands sprang open. His father herded them all into the lounge. It took mere seconds. Jorah came behind. He waved at the door's locking panel and secured it.

A stun pistol's whine caught his attention. It was a Lenguan who went down, stunned. His father stood raising his left hand in command and covering the other Lenguans with a stun pistol.

Jorah felt their barely controlled panic. *Situation managed,* he told himself, and he let his habitual shields spring back up.

Now his father gave a short, sharp laugh. *Keep them still. This'll take just a minute.* Jorah leaned forward with his epsilon sense and felt his father pull his own energy back, and they managed a smooth command transfer. He couldn't help smiling now. After all those months and years of education and practice, it looked like this was going to be a by-the-book interception.

His father turned to the Lenguan leader, who stood wide-eyed, palpably angry and afraid. Jorah kept both his own hands slightly raised. He'd spent five years learning to use them as focal points for energy flow.

The closest Lenguan stood motionless, staring furiously at Jorah over his shoulder. Jorah knew he'd inherited his Mikuhran mother's long, oval face and black eyes—and some of her height. He reached up to meaningfully touch the star on his shoulder, reminding the Lenguan that he, his father, his father's father, and all the Caldwells back to the family's arrival on Thyrica had been sworn to Federate service. "If you cooperate," he said softly, "you'll make this much less unpleasant."

About three meters away, his father's voice had a more menacing tone. "And where are the weapons?" Few people would be able to resist thinking of the answer. His father would take that information directly from the man's mind. Madam Kernoweg would be safe.

Something moved behind him. Jorah spun around, still maintaining mental contact with the immobilized Lenguans. One of the "off duty" Tallans had burst through the door, sweeping the room with a stun pistol and firing. Jorah recognized the weapon's whine as a light burst. He found himself crumpling to the lounge's floor along with the Lenguans and his father.

He'd been stunned? Ridiculous! He and his dad already had the situation under control. Was this how Tallan forces operated?

Did they stun everyone and then sort out the ones they wanted in custody? *Amateurs.*

Another Tallan stepped in through the door, speaking into a wrist unit. "They're down. Will transport in enclosed stretchers." The man's head turned. Jorah guessed he was listening on an aural implant. "Copy," the Tallan said. He called to the woman who'd done the stunning, "Half charge. Not just down but unconscious."

Jorah couldn't raise his head, but he heard a lower pitched whine from the lounge's other side, close to where his father had disabled the Lenguan leader. Apparently the Tallan commander was taking no chances, taking the Lenguan into custody.

The Tallan in the doorway walked into Jorah's limited field of vision. "Just following orders, I suppose." Her voice sounded cold. To Jorah's shock, she swung her bulky weapon around and pointed it straight at Jorah. From this angle, it hid most of her face.

It was *his father* they'd stunned? Jorah tried to raise a hand, to command the Tallan to drop her weapon—

Too late. The lounge seemed to go black as he fell backward down a dark, silent tunnel.

• • •

Through the cold darkness came a single subvocalized word, with the knife-edge quality Jorah associated with his father. *Jorah.*

He blinked, but the darkness remained. What was this—had he been blinded?

The word came again. *Jorah.*

His head seemed to be spinning. He focused a thought onto the standing carrier wave and sent, *I'm here.*

You've got to recover from stun faster than that.

True. If he'd been more alert, he might have shut down his nervous system before the full charge hit. He just hadn't expected the Tallan to fire on him. Those fake trade delegates should have been targeted.

He'd been cocooned, then. Almost certainly.

Don't trust the Feds, his father's voice said in his mind. *You've heard for years that they're turning on us. Now you've seen it. Whatever happens, pay attention. Trust nobody. Get back to SO as fast as you can.*

Why are they—

If you need to defend yourself, his father interrupted, *you were just following orders.*

Jorah bristled. He was loyal to Special Operations, the Sentinel kindred, and particularly to his father. And he'd done nothing wrong.

Appreciated, the voice said. Jorah hadn't subvocalized those thoughts, but his father had always been able to read him without provoking the usual prickly mind-access nausea. *Anyway,* he heard, *we probably need you here on Tallis.*

Jorah might have frowned if he could move. The Sentinels' military Special Operations branch in Federate service had shrunk, within his father's lifetime, from an elite organization active on all twenty-three Federate worlds to just a few individuals, mostly here on Tallis, occasionally called for emergencies. And yes, Jorah had been following orders. But he would be proud to share responsibility with his father, if someone would just explain the problem.

Retreating into the emotional control he'd learned, he considered the darkness itself. They'd been cocooned, all right. The Feds must not have wanted to haul unconscious uniformed operatives through the spaceport.

But why had they been stunned? He'd heard the talk about debudgeting Special Operations. This shift in Federate attitudes supposedly lay behind his grandparents' departure from the Federacy's other regional capital too. With the renegade Shuhr threat neutralized, the surviving Sentinels were no longer needed so desperately.

And they still were feared, especially after intermarrying with the few remaining Mikuhrans—including his mother. But none of that explained the stunning. Were they starting to persecute Sentinels from mixed marriages?

His parents had strong and contradictory beliefs about how to keep peace in the Federacy. If they'd known how things would turn out, maybe they wouldn't have—

That's none of your business. The thought sliced through Jorah's mind. His face felt hot, since capillaries weren't affected by stun pulses. Those reflections had taken him just seconds, but he ought to be thinking about—

Strategy. He heard the word clearly. *What must you do in the face of overwhelming odds?*

A quote sprang to mind. He formed the words subvocally: *There's no shame in retreating to regroup.* All the Federates on twenty-three worlds were their theoretical allies, though. Tallans, Lenguans, and Thyrians—especially the small subgroup of Thyrian Sentinels— should be working together.

Good. Remember— After a moment's silence, the subvoice's timbre hardened. *They're coming. Remember. Following orders. This is a fall I'm ready to take, if someone has to go down.*

Jorah made the mental equivalent of a nod, but he wanted to protest. Neither Air Master Kinnor Caldwell nor his father, High Commander Brennen Caldwell, had ever retreated when faced with overwhelming odds. Something had gone wrong with this mission.

At least Madam Kernoweg—head of the Regional Council— was safe from potential Lenguan assassins.

Light flooded in from his right side. High above, textured tiles made random-looking patterns. The ceiling looked institutional. Sensation returned too, with a rush of small aches and a cold surface pushing against his back and skull. "Get up, Lieutenant," a brusque voice said.

Jorah used both hands against the transport cart's guardrails, acting weaker than he felt. He might need to surprise someone later. He swung around to sit up and look around. Five meters square, the room had a comm table pushed to one side. Four people sat behind it. He blinked and stabilized his balance. In training, he'd been stunned and then forced to defend himself. Obviously, being *ready* for stun made a difference.

The shining black lid of a second transport cart blocked his view to his right. It looked disturbingly like a coffin. His father already stood at stiff attention in front of it, and on his father's right side, the armed Tallan woman who'd stunned Jorah stood back several steps, in the arresting officer's position.

Jorah turned to the black comm table. Behind it, two people wore Tallan grey and—to Jorah's shock—the other two were senior colonels from Sentinel Special Operations.

What were they doing here? Was something wrong inside Special Ops? He consciously thickened his shielding cloud of mental static and stepped into position beside his father.

"This is a disciplinary meeting of the Special Operations Oversight Committee," one of the seated Tallans said, and Jorah's insides curdled. The man had an angular face. Jorah didn't recognize him, but above the Federate slash on his grey uniform's left breast, he wore the triangular collar insignia of a Tallan field general. "Air Master Caldwell, I have before me a record of your specific orders for the Lenguans' arrival. You will quote them to me."

Staring straight ahead and shielding himself, Jorah couldn't see or feel his father's anger. His father's voice was unnaturally deep, though. "The delegation is to be allowed to land unmolested." He clipped the words as if mocking them. "Other arrangements have been made for their interception."

Jorah's throat tightened. *Those* had been their orders? Suddenly he knew exactly what had gone wrong, and what his father meant about taking a fall.

One of the Sentinel colonels pointed down at a gleaming patch on the black table. She leaned left, toward her fellow Sentinel.

"Yes." The Tallan general stared at Jorah's father. "Air Master, that was a clear order. Did you not understand?"

• • •

Overlooking that chamber, Chancellor Piper Gambrel sat motionless, watching the feed from a monitor embedded in one corner of its ceiling. The two Sentinel operatives plainly were related, despite the younger one's long, interesting face.

One of Gambrel's collegiate employees, a high-ranking medical researcher with a Security I clearance, sat beside him. "That lieutenant would be perfect."

Gambrel agreed. "He's young enough, of course. I would have preferred recruiting him as a student, not an experimental subject."

"The protocol must be tested, though—"

"Yes." Gambrel cut him off. This was also an unexpected assist from the Special Operations Oversight Committee. Thanks to SOOC, Gambrel's Collegium might not have to demand volunteers after all.

The Chancellorship sat heavy on his shoulders at times such as this. However, before his Collegium could take the Sentinels' place in the Federacy as negotiators who couldn't be deceived, the Sentinels must cease to exist as a people. *Compassionately,* he had always insisted. An exciting new Collegiate communication technology would shortly make such transhuman go-betweens and negotiators unnecessary.

Gambrel studied the young lieutenant. Yes, he decided. He would honor that request from his medical colleague, Colonel Ottar Zeimsky. The young lieutenant's soul would not be altered, which was all of him—all of anyone—that really mattered. Only one part of his body, a part already changed by illicit science, would be affected if the treatment succeeded.

And they would obtain his consent, of course.

"Can he be detained?" Zeimsky asked.

Piper Gambrel reached for a touchboard set into his armrest.

• • •

"I researched those other intercept arrangements," Jorah's dad said. "They were ineffectual."

With his eyes fixed straight ahead, Jorah still couldn't see his father well. Ten years ago, the edge on that voice would have meant serious trouble for young Jorah. Still, he could plainly see the officers seated behind that table. One of the Tallans stared for a few seconds, probably hearing some message Jorah could not.

"Maybe." Colonel Sentinel Cora Claggett of Special Operations Intelligence had the steady stare of authority. Jorah didn't think he remembered such dark circles under her eyes the last time he saw her. "However," she said, "that decision was not yours to make. SOOC now is forced to deliver a formal apology to Madam Kernoweg, as well as those delegates from her homeworld. Tallan Security will provide guards for the remainder of their residence here on Tallis."

Colonel Artur Mercell, the other Sentinel officer, added, "Sentinel Caldwell, we particularly respect commanding officers who do not share our abilities. This is not the first time you have ignored such orders."

"May I respond?" Jorah's father spoke without emotion.

Colonel Claggett opened a hand. Jorah felt his body tense. Though she granted permission, Jorah imagined—or did he sense it?—that she simply was letting his father incriminate himself.

As Jorah knew he would.

"Wing Colonel Anastis is a diplomat." Jorah heard both respect and disdain in the way his father named the non-gifted Special

Ops liaison. "He believes that we're living in times that call for restraint. So he called for a non-Sentinel intercept. But NSIs can be messy. Stopping Sentinels from saving Tallan officers' lives just makes no sense. We have to act. To remind people that we can do difficult jobs well. Madam Kernoweg is safe now. That was always our objective."

Jorah wanted to groan. Orders were to be obeyed, not second-guessed. Especially orders from Wing Colonel Anastis! His dad had been ordered to do something entirely different.

The officers behind the table shared glances. One man reached for his touchboard. The others looked down into shining zones on top of the comm table. Colonel Claggett nodded. "Sentinel Caldwell, other Federates are afraid of us. Terrified, some of them. By disobeying a superior officer, you endangered your own life— and your subordinate's," she added, glancing in Jorah's direction, "and us all. You came perilously close to actions that could be construed as capricious or selfish."

"Never!" Jorah's father exclaimed. "I put myself and my son in danger, sparing your people."

"Silence." Colonel Claggett glared.

A shudder leaped across Jorah's shoulders. A Sentinel convicted of "capricious or selfish" use of ayin abilities suffered the death penalty, regardless of age or rank. He realized he'd relaxed his shields when he caught a blast of his father's fury. At the back of his mind, Jorah heard his father's subvoice. *Regional Ops is panicked. They're turning our own SOOC committee against us. Remember where your loyalty lies.*

One of the Tallans caught Colonel Claggett's attention. He pointed over the table at the two Sentinel operatives. "Shouldn't Air Master Caldwell be access questioned?"

As the intelligence officer stared down at her tabletop, Jorah imagined the humiliation of baring his mind for examination. He wanted to shout, *Access me, look at my motives. All I wanted, all I*

have ever wanted, is to make a difference for good. We all feel that way!
Sentinels can protect the Federacy from all this unrest!

Colonel Claggett shook her head. "No. We all know what happened. Air Master Caldwell, step forward."

Jorah finally could see his father clearly, his wide shoulders squared in an attentive brace.

"To our deep regret," the woman said, "for the offense of insubordination we find it necessary to dismiss you from Federate service. For your own safety as well as disciplinary reasons, you are remanded into protective custody and isolation at our Sanctuary on Procyel II, where you will spend the next year on probation."

Jorah's first reaction was relief. A dismissal could be reversed, and after all, his mother was stationed on Procyel as Sanctuary Administrator. His father would be able to update the rest of the kindred about these unsettling developments inside Special Ops.

Still, the whole situation was plainly Kinnor Caldwell's fault.

It took hard concentration to keep from thinking about the questions Jorah wanted to ask. He remained at attention, shields lowered and listening hard. Maybe there'd be more explanation.

A Tallan escort grabbed his father's elbow and steered him toward the door.

His father had shielded his thoughts and emotions. *Against me,* Jorah wondered, *or against them?*

As soon as the door closed and his father would no longer pick up his thoughts, Jorah finally let those questions rise into his conscious mind. *Dad, why didn't you follow orders? . . . And what about me?* He suspected his father had already explained the first question: because he disapproved of those orders.

Jorah centered his weight over both feet, holding his spine stiff and straight. He'd obeyed his immediate superior. No one had been harmed in the incident, and not even the Tallan military wanted a furor right now. He hoped not, anyway.

The Tallan field general rested both forearms on the comm table and leaned forward. "Lieutenant, when you are given an order that plainly contradicts Federate policy, your responsibility is to report your superior to his own commanding officer."

"Yes, sir." Jorah answered without hesitating. Finally, he stood on firm ground. "However, sir, I was unaware of the previous order." He glanced at Colonel Claggett and added, "I offer access to my memory, ma'am." He had heard about his father's old reputation as a loose cannon, but Father had avoided official discipline for years. Anyway, there was plenty to respect in Kinnor Caldwell. Jorah wanted to show Colonel Claggett the father whose daring dedication inspired him.

"That won't be necessary." Her voice was oddly stiff. The Codes prohibited him from trying to probe a superior officer, so he didn't dare try to find out what she was thinking. "Your case will be reviewed at a later date, Sentinel Caldwell. Until then, you will remain here in custody. And until then," she said, frowning up into his eyes, "you will remain medicated to prevent the use of your special abilities."

The conference room seemed to go cold, but Jorah stayed at attention. They probably wanted to wait until after the Lenguan delegation got offworld, and to placate Madam Kernoweg. When that happened, he should be cleared in short order. "Yes, ma'am." He tried not to sound reluctant. He wished his emotional control felt less ragged.

"That's all, Lieutenant." The Tallan general flicked a finger against the tabletop, and his monitor's light flickered on the underside of his chin. "Corporal, process him into Detention."

The corporal guided him up a corridor and into an elevator, where Jorah finally recognized the secured directional panel and concluded that he'd been transported to the maximum security complex in Tallis's primary city. Most Federate business was conducted here. After a long drop, there was a brief wait in a bright, bleak room with metal wall panels. Then the humiliation of having his skin scraped and DNA checked.

A med aide walked toward him with an injection, and he struggled not to panic. Once he was dosed, the aide and the corporal stared down at him as he waited on a hard chair for the drug to take effect. Slowly, like a blanket that gradually suffocated his most delicate sense, a dense silence fell.

The med aide crouched down to look into his eyes. "Gone?" she demanded.

He nodded, but she reached aside for something he couldn't see. She made a flinging motion. Something sharp—something he couldn't anticipate anymore—hit his right knee. He stifled a grunt of pain.

The med nodded at the corporal, who stepped backward and rested a hand on his holstered stun pistol. "This way, Lieutenant Caldwell," he said.

Brilliant overhead lights lined the corridor, but Jorah felt like he was shuffling in darkness.

• • •

An hour later he sat on a narrow bed, cracking his knuckles and glad to be left alone. He'd spent a listless time staring at a newsnet display inset at eye level on the narrow back wall. It was playing the same story about haves and have-nots that he could have heard back at College on Thyrica, so it felt like an hour wasted. He waved a hand through the control zone and shut off the screen. Clenching his hands, he got up and paced to the far corner, then along the transparent metal door at mid-cell. Pale blue security lights in the door frame winked slowly off, then on. Off, on.

The corridor remained empty, of course. They didn't need to bother to set guards. Also, no one would want to risk being seen chatting with him.

He turned slowly, careful to glance at the viewing door instead of the security monitor. Maybe his father was right. Maybe it was time to slip out of Federate constraints and try to restore some justice to the Whorl. Maybe—

He froze. In his cell's far corner, something shone like dust specks in a pulsating sunbeam. His first thought was that it was some odd midair reflection of the security lights. It didn't blink in their rhythm, though. He watched it for several seconds, trying to make out what it was. He had the strangest sense that it was alive, but when he tried reaching out with his inner sense, he felt nothing—of course. He'd been drugged. He couldn't even shield himself against it. What good was five years of training if someone could render him helpless with a hypospray?

He stepped toward the glimmer, wondering whether he should try speaking to it. If this was simply some new form of surveillance, he would be incredibly embarrassed. He knew something about security measures, though. This was nothing he'd ever seen. Was his father trying to get in touch?

It spoke. "All hail, Jorah." The voice shimmered, barely audible.

Jorah set his back to the security monitor he had spotted and did his best not to move his lips. "Who are you?" he asked softly. "What are you?"

"All hail, Jorah," the voice repeated. "I come to pay homage and help you escape."

Stunned, Jorah tried for a moment to make sense of "all hail" and "homage." Then that last word sank in. Escape? If he'd been imprisoned by enemies, his responsibility always would be to escape. Nothing in his training had mentioned being taken prisoner by his superior officers, though. He still was completely innocent.

But if he tried to escape custody, they could justifiably lay charges. "What do you mean?" He sat back down on the narrow bed and tried to look like he was simply staring at the wall.

"Jorah, you are growing wise and courageous." The speckled swirl moved out of its corner, nearly a meter closer. The speckles danced in midair . . . too close, actually. "Perhaps you have begun to guess your high destiny. The question is whether you are brave enough to begin to fulfill it."

Jorah drew his hands across the rumpled blanket's rough surface. Destiny? He recalled reading and rereading the family prophecies, in Chapter worship and in his private study. He'd wondered if any of them could possibly refer to him. Also—supposedly—supernatural news could arrive via a bright messenger.

Was *that* what this was?

"I'm Jorah Caldwell," he said. "Second Lieutenant, Sentinel Special Operations, and I hope my destiny is to go on serving the Federacy. Like my father and grandfather," he added, in case he was being monitored.

"And so much more." The sparkling motes trembled, and he had the impression of laughter. "All hail, Jorah Caldwell. Your people have waited for you for so very long."

He frowned, but he couldn't help wondering, *Really?* Could he be the singular person he'd read about all his life? He wanted to ask the sparkling creature, but—but surely someone was listening! How could *he* be the human exhalation of One who'd spoken everything into existence—the predicted Boh-Dabar, who was supposed to make an immolation of all evil? Boh-Dabar would somehow present a purified creation back to its Creator.

No. It could not be him. Jorah's Path instructor had told him, gently, that if he really were That Person, he probably would have known from an early age.

Still, this shimmer sharing his cell was clearly supernatural. Bright Ones had appeared to Mattah, the prophet and priest who had led the exiles off Ehret to Thyrica—right?—but not even Shamarrs like his uncle Kiel usually spoke with them.

According to ancient holy books, Boh-Dabar would be gifted beyond the Sentinels' imagining. The culmination of human history.

"That's not me," he muttered.

"Your skills already are solid," the shimmering voice said.

It was true. He'd almost tested in the "exceptional" range.

"In a new role, you might receive more power."

Jorah tried not to move. Just one of the prophecies was unambiguous: Boh-Dabar would be born into his own family. Other, more obscure predictions were scattered among historical and prophetic chapters of *Dabar* and *Mattah*. His people had argued for centuries about what they really meant.

But no one ever argued against the Caldwell lineage. The Shuhr had tried several times to wipe them out. That had to prove something.

No. If it were him, he would have known by now. What was this creature?

"In you," the voice whispered, "finally, all the scattered Ehretan peoples are reunited. Your father's father preserved the name. Your father's mother brought in the Netaian unknowns. And from your mother, you inherited the genes of the unbound Mikuhrans. Father to son, you are the only offspring who joins all three lines of your heritage."

Jorah reached over and cracked his knuckles. This had actually occurred to him before he'd started training. And he'd wondered—back then—whether *this* was why his proud father had married a Mikuhran woman. Had destiny brought them together simply to produce a son . . . to produce him?

Well? Was it possible after all?

No mere human could handle that much responsibility. Still, no one got to choose the call on his own life. Jorah imagined hearing people speak his name with the reverence they usually reserved for his grandfather. He couldn't help smiling.

Then he erased that smile from his face. No. It was impossible.

"I can restore your abilities right now, Jorah, and help you escape. Your people need you, but even at full ayin capacity, you are still too weak to help them. I will take you and train you, and reveal everything you need to know."

Jorah frowned. Too weak to help them? Whatever happened to "all hail"? Was this messenger condescending, now, or was it humbling him so that later, he could be trained to move in truly supernatural circles? "I do want to help them." It was hard to speak without moving his lips. "After all we've done for the Federacy, for them to treat us like—like terrifying trash," he added, liking the expression he'd invented on the spot, "is completely unjust."

"Come, then." The sparkling cloud drifted across his cell toward the metal door. Surely it wouldn't be doing that if anyone was watching them. It had to be blinding the security eye. "Come with me and restore justice. They will not see you."

"Wait," Jorah exclaimed.

The shimmer halted between him and the transparent door. Through it, he saw that the corridor was still empty.

In order to be Boh-Dabar—as he understood the predictions— he had to achieve perfect virtue, didn't he? What would a perfectly virtuous man do with this opportunity to escape?

And wait, wouldn't Boh-Dabar have the authority to command supernatural messengers?

Probably! Jorah cleared his throat and spoke, without trying to be unheard. "I need to clear myself with my supervisors. I can't do that if I leave this cell before my hearing. They'll give me an antidote and release me. Speak with me then, when I'm fully myself."

There was an uncanny hiss. The voice spoke once more. "All hail, then, until I come again." The sparkling motes fled upward, leaving Jorah alone with blinking security lights and a head that spun with possibilities.

CHAPTER 6

In another civilian spaceport on the world of Thyrica, several travel days away from Jorah on Tallis or Meris on Procyel II, Shamarr Kiel Caldwell watched his youngest daughter step onto a moving walkway. It would carry her through a transparent security tunnel, to be observed by local Thyrian police before being allowed to board. Kiel waited beside his wife and their middle daughter and wreathed the family in prayer. He was a priest, after all. *Keep them safe, Eternal Speaker. Don't let them be challenged. Let this go smoothly.*

Young Perl stood with one foot on each of the "juvenile rider" stripes and one hand on each moving handrail. His youngest was practically a woman now, and plainly she was nervous. He had unshielded in her direction. Her anxiety felt like a sharp, jabbing pain.

This was Perl's first time through port security. In troubled times, security officers sometimes took advantage of their authority to confiscate beloved belongings or conduct harsh interviews.

The Shamarr's high-priestly position, for which Kiel felt woefully underqualified, was a special hindrance today. Civilian

Security would be watching for him to do anything they considered suspicious.

The odds of Perl—or Rena, or even his wife, Hanusha—being pulled off that walkway for questioning were slight. Kiel would come last. He was the one they would intercept, if they stopped anyone. The port authority might even decide not to release this sekiyr flight—or, if their suspicions centered on Kiel himself, the college students on board could theoretically take off for their Sanctuary term without him.

Still, Kiel had the strongest feeling that either of those options would be catastrophic. He must see his father again. He felt the urge as clearly as a holy call, although he'd heard no voice.

Kiel reached out with his mind to calm Perl. None of them carried anything illegal, of course. To Kiel's way of thinking, the most questionable things he carried today were his fears for the Sentinel kindred and his queasy suspicion that he might not get offworld.

From a newsnet monitor near the waiting area's ceiling, he heard his own voice. Startled, he glanced up to see his face and the subscript *Kiel Caldwell, Shamarr of the Sentinel faith.* He'd been interviewed yesterday.

What execrable timing! Why did they have to broadcast that awful conversation just now?

"Yes," his mouth onscreen said, "it could be time for the Sentinel kindred to build a generation ship and leave Thyrica—leave the Federacy entirely. My ancestors arrived here as refugees twelve generations ago. We might leave on the same terms, trusting the Eternal Speaker to carry us wherever we might still serve Him." The image paused.

Kiel cringed, recalling that next, he'd deviated from his prepared remarks. Perhaps the interviewer had edited them out?

"Then," said the image, "our nervous Thyrian hosts might not have to make difficult choices on behalf of the Federacy."

"Oh, Kiel." Hanusha stood tall enough to look him in the eye, and he was a tall man. Some called her thin—he preferred "willowy"—and she had her mother's aquiline nose. She'd passed it to Rena and Perl. He found them all utterly lovely.

"I know," he said. He should have stuck to his script.

The near end of the transparent arch glimmered green, creating strange green lights in their middle daughter Rena's light brown hair. "Go on, Rena," he said gently. "Your turn."

Rena stepped onto the walkway.

As she reached for the handrails, he smiled at the sekiyr's ring on her left hand. Just one year into her Sentinel studies, already she hoped to become a teacher.

She'll be a fine one, he heard at the back of his mind.

He turned to smile at Hanusha. They were so closely linked on the pair bond, and over the years she had become so keenly aware of the way his thoughts shaped themselves, that nine times out of ten she could tell what he was thinking—without conscious mind access.

Yes, Kiel returned subvocally, *if the Federacy will let us keep teaching our children our ways.*

Hanusha nodded.

Kiel straightened his back, watching and waiting as Rena passed through the security tunnel. He'd been quietly contacting young families all year, suggesting they travel offworld. He'd even agreed to let them hide the insignia, if they swore not to use their abilities. Chapters of faith had been established on other worlds. Expatriates could go on worshipping, following the ancient Path.

There'll be lots of friends for the girls on Procyel, he reminded Hanusha. Few families had chosen to vanish, but several had gone to the Sanctuary on Procyel and refused to leave.

Therefore, Hanusha returned, *Thyrica steps up security whenever a College shuttle leaves here for Procyel. They're herding us together.*

Kiel frowned. One of his friends had recently asked, *What do they want us to do? Die out?*

The security archway went green again. Hanusha stepped onto the walkway. The silver streaks in her hair flickered as she turned aside and stared up into the transparent arch over the moving walkway. From this angle, Kiel couldn't see what had caught her eye. Again, no one moved to stop her.

Other than Rena, who'd insisted on staying with young Perl, all the student-apprentice sekiyrra on this shuttle flight had also passed the security area. All second year sekiyrra served at the Sanctuary, and Kiel's family had simply been summoned for a death watch. By deciding to board this flight, Kiel did risk having it detained. Thyrian officials had recently turned back several high-ranking Sentinels who had tried to leave for Sanctuary.

Hanusha walked out the tunnel's far end and into a corridor. Kiel took a deep breath. He stepped on, quieting his thoughts for the emotional scan. His dark grey ministerial tunic's sleeves dangled over the railing. He glanced up, in the direction Hanusha had looked. A midnight-blue shadow with several sleeve insignias stood staring back. A local Thyrian soldier who plainly was not one of his people.

Kiel focused his thoughts on spiritual matters. If not for the ayin, which Ehretan scientists had created in their physical brains, his people already might have brought genuine peace to scattered humanity. According to prophecies older than the Whorl settlements, priestly leadership had been promised to them. Soul-deep purification for all of humanity. Everywhere.

In Boh-Dabar.

Instead, they had been required to serve unaltered humankind. They now lived to prove their obedience by serving others with their impressive mental abilities, until the Eternal Speaker decided the time was fulfilled.

This would be a good time, Holy One.

Brilliant yellow lights appeared at the arch's end. They shone into his eyes. He stepped off, blinking. A voice said, "Shamarr Caldwell, please come with us for a few minutes."

Three soldiers stood there, all armed with stun pistols and wearing Thyrian midnight blue with sleeve insignia. His brother, Kinnor, might have read each one's rank and commendations off those sleeves, but to Kiel they were just mysterious glyphs. He would have called his own calling "higher" than the military until Kinnor had saved his life some years ago. Kiel finally had understood that each branch of the Sentinel kindred needed all the others: military, medical, diplomatic, spiritual.

The diplomatic branch was already all but gone. Regional Command, Tallis, had dismissed its last Sentinel negotiators two years ago.

Guide me, he prayed. *Protect Perl and Rena, and Hanusha. Annalah too.* His eldest would be at Sanctuary already, having been on board the *Daystar* with her Elysian friend, Meris Cariole.

Kiel took deep, slow breaths as the Thyrians escorted him into a small room. One walked ahead of him and two of them fell behind. He prayed for the soldiers' well-being as the room's door slid shut. Worrying was pointless.

The room plainly was used for security interviews, with three unadorned metal chairs under its brilliant lights. It smelled like meat and spices, as if someone had ducked in here to eat a savory lunch.

A fortyish soldier backed against the wall. He wore twice as many sleeve decorations as the others.

A younger man stepped forward, his pale blond hair shorn so short that his scalp reflected glints from the overhead lights. "Why are you going offworld, Shamarr Caldwell?"

"My father is gravely ill." He smoothed his words with the calming subvocal overtones that the Privacy and Priority Codes allowed. "I've been called to ask a blessing before he dies. Even if they hadn't sent for me, I would want to go. I'm sure you understand." The news had arrived yesterday, via DeepScan II technology, from both Tallis and Procyel.

The short-haired young man frowned. Speaking with confident arrogance, he pronounced, "Your place is here with your community, Shamarr Caldwell. If you leave, who's going to keep them in line? Who's going to protect the rest of us—the *humans?*"

Kiel resisted the urge to bristle. Most of his people were exemplary citizens. It staggered him to hear them referred to as inhuman. Had it really come to that?

He calmed himself. "There is a line of authority on the Path of faith, even as in your military service, sir." He named several Sentinels, including his in-laws, who were remaining. Hanusha's parents had decided to stay on Thyrica. Come what may, they would fight to keep the College open.

The young man motioned Kiel toward the chair, and he sat down. "Why did you suggest a general Sentinel evacuation, Shamarr?"

So he'd heard the newsnet interview. "To keep peace in the Whorl, my friend. We use our skills to serve others, not to menace them. However, if even our Codes don't allay others' fears, perhaps we should become refugees again. Perhaps that is our fate."

"You do have a violent history." The same guard spoke again. "Are you organizing that evacuation now, Shamarr?"

"No. I am not." Ominously, his attempts to purchase a cross-space freighter—which might have been converted for generational travel—had fallen through. Decisively. Neither Thyrica nor the Federacy had offered financial assistance.

"And why take your entire family offworld?"

Kiel crossed his legs, willing himself to look casual. "As I said, sir, my father is dying. The girls wish to say goodbye to their grandfather."

"And when do you plan to return?"

"Probably after conducting his Shekkah memorial service."

Standing near a wall, that fortyish soldier leaned forward over crossed arms. Kiel sensed chilly suspicion streaming off the man. There, Kiel guessed, was the real hostile force in the room, with authority to cancel the shuttle flight. *Help,* he prayed again. *Is there anyone nearby who outranks him, who could release us?*

As questions kept coming, light appeared through the doorway. A heavier man strode in. All three soldiers snapped to attention. Kiel held his breath. "At ease," the newcomer said. "What's the issue here?"

The fortyish supervisor stepped around his aides. "Sir, Shamarr Caldwell is high on the watch list."

"Of course," the heavier man snapped. Kiel kept his hands in his lap and eyed the newcomer, whose hair had gone grey at the temples. Sentinel families couldn't use anti-aging implants, but this man probably had one. Non-gifted people rarely looked their true ages. "Shamarr Caldwell, what's your reason for making this trip?"

"My father, sir." Kiel avoided staring at the man's eyes, hoping to make it clear that he was not using Sentinel skills to influence anyone. "Radiation sickness, after—"

"Yes, I heard." The officer turned back to the suspicious Thyrian. "Major, I served with High Commander Brennen Caldwell when you were a pup, before public opinion tarnished everyone who wears their insignia. I would not want to know that his equally respected son was not allowed to see him before he died."

Kiel held another breath. His prayers were rarely answered so decisively.

The oldest officer reached for a panel near the door arch. The door slid open. "Get on board, Shamarr Caldwell. If you reach him in time, tell your father that there are many of us on Thyrica who remember him gratefully."

Tempted to sprint from the room, Kiel stood slowly. He raised his right hand in blessing. "I will, sir. Thank you. Go with the Eternal Speaker."

"Not yet, I hope," the officer said in a wry voice.

Kiel hurried to rejoin his wife and daughters.

Two hours later, he peered over Perl's round head into the upper corners of a shipboard viewport. The blue and white world he'd called home for two decades shimmered against a black starfield.

His father would not see that watery jewel ever again. And while Kiel did hope to return, under these circumstances he couldn't hope to come back soon.

• • •

Five days after her arrival on Procyel II, Meris had settled into a routine. Each morning, she assisted Medical Specialist Saried Kinsman or one of her aides. Her shipboard friendship with Lady Fi had gone on hold, so she spent afternoons on administrative detail. She took the time to explain Collegiate philosophy to every sekiyr who would listen, and a few of them seemed intrigued. The Collegium offered deep self-awareness, empowerment, and self-control.

One youngster kept chattily comparing these techniques with their "Path" doctrines, which were oriented toward a frustratingly supernatural theme that couldn't be monitored or proved. New ideas delighted most of them, though.

This particular morning, Meris had been awakened before dawn to assist with an emergency. *Seizures,* she read off her handheld.

She dressed and hustled to the med center, where she hastily consulted her handheld again before she filled a care tray: injection-ready seistat and sucrin, two disposable electrodes, and a rolled towel that might double as a padded restraint. She strode up the medical corridor, its brilliant lights creating an illusion of daylight.

Saried was easy to spot from behind by the long, graying braid that dangled down her back. She sat on a treatment room stool, directly in front of a large, deeply padded chair. On a counter beyond that chair, a single black box had a numerical readout. Meris didn't recognize it. It could be almost anything. Something to do with their "epsilon" mental energy, maybe.

A white-haired woman wearing a thin blue nightrobe over shapeless pajamas sat sighing in the padded chair. Meris walked silently behind the chair and laid her tray on the countertop.

"Thank you." Saried didn't take her eyes off the elderly woman. "I'm sorry to have bothered you. I think she's going to be all right. Simple matter of a waning epsilon shield."

Torn between curiosity and the urge to back away, Meris took a step forward. "How's that treated?"

The medspec still did not move. It looked as if she were maintaining eye contact. "Stimulate the ayin. Part of my training. Many of us lose our abilities after seventy."

"Hmm." So MedSpec Saried's domain doubled as a geriatric center, and the world's solitude helped protect their elders' sanity. Meris now understood one reason why they kept outsiders away. "Calmatives can also ease seizures."

"Yes, if the conventional brain is to blame. This is an ayin issue. And . . . hold."

Abruptly, the white-haired woman's forehead wrinkles became shallower. On the black box, glowing red numbers melted into each other. Ten . . . twelve . . . fifteen. "Ayin static at two meters," Saried explained. "How's that, Daphna?"

"Better," the elderly woman squeaked. "Much better. Calm. I can find myself amid the noise."

"That's all we ask." Saried leaned away, staring at the ceiling. As when Meris had last seen her use psi medicine, now too her eyes had gone dark. Weary.

The old woman stood up, smiling. Freshly appalled by how *old* these people looked in their later years, Meris promised herself a youth implant as soon as she got to Tallis. "Thank you, Saried. And you too, Meris."

That startled her. "I didn't do anything."

"Oh, but you did. I felt you come into the room. And when I felt you vanish, I knew my shields were back. Saried, you've got a valuable assistant here."

Valuable . . . because she had none of their strange abilities? That was a new thought. She should tell the Minster.

The patient left the room, and Meris slid off her stool. "How is your father this morning?" Saried often slipped into his room between other patients.

"He had a good night. Slept soundly."

"I'm glad. Do you think his sons will make it in time?"

Saried shrugged and shook her head. "We can still hope so."

If his condition hadn't been so delicate, and if these people had owned enough stasis crypts, he might have been stased and sent to Tallis General. Perhaps he simply wanted to die here. Annalah had said that their dead waited together for a change in the universe. It had seemed an odd hope.

To Meris's surprise, this morning she found herself sympathizing. No loneliness, no dissolution . . . not even in death?

Wish fulfillment! She gave herself a mental shake. "Are you finished with me, Saried?"

"Yes." Saried stood keying something onto her handheld, her face still wrinkled and weary. "Go get some breakfast. Thank you again."

Meris strode out of the med center and turned left under pale blue skylights. It felt good not to need Annalah to guide her. If any Sentinels had been tasked with watching her, they were doing it invisibly. This morning, the aromas drifting across the pool from the dining commons were spicier than usual. She'd eaten a lot of plain food for five days. Some of the fruit they'd raised here had surprisingly complex flavors, even after a full winter in storage.

A few energetic children clustered around the tabletops, close to a pair of big double doors. Meris peered over their heads at the nearest table. A large, twiggy basket full of brown sandwiches gave off the spicy scent. Beside the basket lay stacks of earthenware plates and bowls of sliced white fruit. Annalah had called them snow apples. Why so much food, so early?

Oh, yes. Annalah had said they were expecting a large group of arrivals late this morning. The college shuttle, including Annalah's parents. It would be landing here, since it was atmosphere capable.

Meris backed away from the tables and spotted Annalah coming toward her. This morning, she had pulled on a long dress like the sekirra's duty gowns, but while theirs seemed to float around them, hers was the heavy local weave. "Why do the sandwiches smell so odd?" Meris asked.

"Winter cheese." Annalah's grin turned her cheeks into round little pillows. "The milk's been undrinkable all winter because the kipreta ate hay instead of green grass, but the cheese is excellent. There are several varieties—"

Meris glanced up at the brightening skylights. "Can we take a breakfast topside?" That would be an exotic experience!

"Sure. But it's chilly. Let's go back to the room and bundle up."

Ten minutes later, encased in a borrowed white coat that scratched at the neckline, Meris was riding an elevator with Annalah and a garden shift supervisor who wore the ubiquitous brown work clothes. The doors finally opened. She blinked at the relative brilliance and then they hurried uphill, away from the crop fields.

One side of the sky glowed purple. The distant toothy peaks reflected back that shade of the light. Down at her feet, veritable puddles of tiny yellow flowers had opened amid the short grass.

Gorgeous! She broke into a run, trying not to step into any of the flowery puddles. Soon her legs started to tire, and she turned around to make sure Annalah followed with the smaller twig-craft basket they'd borrowed. Above the valley, thin clouds were turning pink and white. So were the jagged mountains. *Spectacular* was the word that came to mind.

If these people were smart, Meris decided, they might start letting normal folks come here for exotic vacations. The Sentinels might earn some genuine goodwill that way, from people who really mattered out in the Federacy. And income too. With that incredible skyline, and snowfields starting to gleam as the rising sun hit them, not to mention the contours of that big glacial valley on the river's west side—well, this place looked almost too magnificent to be real.

But it *was* real. It was more real than anything she'd ever seen, growing up on urban Elysia.

And that bothered her, since according to all she'd been taught, the physical world had no lasting value. No reality at all. It was merely a shadow of the Infinite Divine.

Annalah led across the grassy hillside overlooking the landing strip, to a boulder that stuck out of the ground. Meris lowered herself onto its flat, chilly surface as Annalah unloaded the basket. Banging noises already drifted up from beyond the crop fields. Down there, workers swung long-handled axes, lopping branches off newly cut trees and piling debris into pyramids. She'd heard they were expanding their planting area.

"How's your grandfather?"

"He's been so strong, for so long, that it breaks my heart to know how soon we're going to lose him." Annalah spoke softly as she spread the food between them. "He had about sixty visitors yesterday. All the elders are coming in by twos and threes, so not to stress him or themselves."

Meris couldn't help sympathizing. Yet how could they let that poor, brave old officer die in misery? "Annalah, the man's body is ruined. He has lived a good long life. They should set his spirit free before he starts to really suffer. Whether or not," she added firmly, "your father and your uncle get here in time. It's only compassionate."

"Father's going to be here in less than an hour." Annalah bit into a quartered sandwich and chewed slowly as Meris sniffed a sandwich of her own. "And I disagree with this line that you draw between body and spirit. It's as if you don't think physical life matters. Physicality is important."

"How could it be?" Meris blurted. "How can you believe you survive after death, if the body's so vital? The spirit dissolves at death. It rejoins the Infinite Divine. Really, it is so simple." She took a small bite. The cheese had a sharp, piquant flavor that was much nicer than it smelled.

Annalah squinted up over the compound, toward the peaks. "Father says we sleep on the far side of a vast Crossing, peacefully enjoying the presence we're created to adore and waiting to be re-bodied. He says that the resting will be full of joy, but that really, we're fully human only as ensouled bodies—or you could say embodied spirits. At the end of time-as-we-know-it, we'll be fully ourselves again, healed and restored and transformed."

Meris had not forgotten that Annalah's father was some sort of priest, and that she owed him a fervent thank-you for keeping her out of tardema-sleep. "But those bodies might be scattered throughout an ecosystem, or even launched into a sun. And what about people who died in wars, blasted apart? How will *their* bodies get into an afterlife?"

Annalah shook her head. "Complicated, isn't it? Not even Father claims to know all the details. But we believe. Maybe when Boh-Dabar comes, he'll explain. It's predicted that he'll purify all of creation. . . ."

Annalah kept talking, but Meris rolled her eyes as she rolled sharp cheese paste off her lower teeth with her tongue. Annalah had already mentioned this exalted leader they claimed to expect. It was crazy to think that people long ago might have predicted events yet to come. Even Chancellor Gambrel's complex calculations of socio-psychological upheavals could forecast only general trends. The Collegium itself probably would give rise to massive political changes in the near future.

By comparison, Annalah's understanding did seem primitive. "Primitive" didn't necessarily mean "wrong," though. Obviously it gave her comfort right now. Meris decided not to confront her too severely.

When Annalah paused to inhale, Meris interrupted. "Your Boh-Dabar event might not happen for another thousand years. Your concept of human existence," she added carefully, "well, would you be offended if I called it primitive and individualistic?"

"I'm not offended." Annalah shrugged. "It is ancient. And we are individuals." Uncharacteristically silent, she stared into the brightening sky. Maybe she was hoping her father, the high "Shamarr," would get here quickly. Not just for her grandfather's sake, but to argue with Meris.

Meris might enjoy repaying her debt to him that way. She glanced downhill. Something had moved, down on the landing area. It was the only truly ugly part of the compound. Each small ship or landing shuttle dug a long scar and scorched even longer strips of grass. The gouges dug by their own multiple landings were barely turning green again at the edges.

People milled around the strip's near end, probably getting ready for that big Sentinel College group. "Is it all right to be up here?" Meris asked, alarmed. "Are we in a blast zone?"

"We're fine, but you wouldn't want to be outdoors under the flight path." Annalah turned her head and squinted into the southern sky. "There. Dark spot. High." She flung out an arm and pointed south.

Meris squinted and spotted it, growing larger and darker and lower. Its whining roar arrived just as she realized how small its atmospheric wings were. She covered her ears and shouted, "That's a mighty small shuttle." Its stubby nose tilted up for the last drop. It looked like a rocket, or an enormous missile. Out of the hillside at the strip's end, which evidently covered hangar doors, a small dual-tread vehicle lurched forward. The ship dug new tread tracks into the ground before it fell silent. Meris uncovered her ears.

Annalah stood. Her hair streamed behind her. "That isn't the shuttle. I think it's one of the old *Brumbee* messenger ships. Special Operations keeps a few at Tallis. I wonder if it's my Uncle Kinnor!"

Tallis? Meris sat up straighter. "Do you think they might send it back any time soon?"

Annalah laughed softly. "You wouldn't want to travel in a messenger ship. They date to back before DeepScan Two, when the messenger service was bigger. The passenger cabin is, well, about an eighth as big as the room we're sharing here."

Meris imagined sharing a space that size with a Sentinel pilot. It wasn't a pleasant thought. They'd probably make her travel in t-sleep. "I see. But I'll talk to the Minster." That might be worth the risk.

A pilot in a dark blue tunic jumped out of the little craft and gestured toward its back end. As he did, the ship slid toward the dual-tread vehicle, apparently pulled by a catchfield.

"Is that your uncle?" Meris asked.

"I can't tell . . . um . . . No, that man looks too tall. Normally, small ships offload out here on the landing field. But these people are hurrying." She squinted south again. "Look, there's why! They just beat the College shuttle!"

Meris scanned the sky and finally saw another dark speck. "That one's coming in a lot lower." Lights appeared to the left and right of the speck, probably wingtips. Annalah bent down, gathered up what was left of their breakfasts, and swept it all into the twig basket. "They're going to need help processing the arrivals. As soon as they're down, we'll head indoors. I haven't seen my parents in almost a year."

CHAPTER 7

"Shamarr?"

Half an hour before Meris saw that shuttle glide toward Hesed House, a woman's voice had filtered into Kiel's mind. He pushed up through the shreds of tardema-sleep and struggled toward wakefulness.

She stood in the Sentinel College shuttle's aisle, bending toward him. The main cabin lights had already been brought back up, and he felt no slip-shield vibration, so they must be decelerating toward Procyel II. Close by him, Hanusha slept on. So did the girls.

Kiel craned his neck toward the shuttle's student section. The other young people t-slept too, reclining in the shuttle's seats. The shuttle was decades old but still utterly spaceworthy, and it showed only the slightest wear. Traditionally, coming to Sanctuary on College rotation was a sekiyr's first t-sleep experience. Only the brownbuck seats, with their thin edges and cracked cushions, hinted at the use this shuttle had seen.

Kiel focused on the woman who'd awakened him. "Did something happen while we were in slip-state?"

She straightened and leaned away from him. He had come up out of t-sleep with his shields intact, out of habit. He let them thin out and sensed her uneasiness. "It's your brother, sir. He's been sent off Tallis."

Kiel glanced around. Plainly, he'd been awakened first to hear the news privately. "Off Tallis? What happened?" How much trouble was Kinnor in this time?

"He was arrested there for insubordination and brought up before SOOC. Apparently, it was all done very hastily. They declared him guilty. They dismissed him from Federate service."

Kiel shut his eyes and exhaled.

"They sent him to Sanctuary in stasis. Officially, he's under Minster Wind's protective custody." She glanced forward, toward the crew compartment. "In fact, we're having to stand out slightly. His craft is just now on landing approach."

Kinnor! Kiel clenched his armrests. His brother had been in and out of trouble all his life. Why couldn't Kinnor simply follow orders?

He knew the answer: Because he was Kinnor Caldwell. No other reason was necessary.

The woman still stood in the narrow aisle, lightly resting a hand on a seat back. "Regional Command, Tallis, is acting more and more like an enemy to us."

"No!" Kiel had heard too much of this kind of talk. "Tallis is not the enemy. Tallis is never the enemy. We serve Tallis. We must all remember that."

"Very good, Shamarr. Now, if you'll excuse me . . ."

She and another staff member worked their way through the passenger cabin, waking people. He focused an epsilon probe and soothed Hanusha back to consciousness. She blinked at him.

Kinnor's in trouble again, he subvocalized to her. *I must pray.*

She nodded and reached out toward Rena.

He shut his eyes and spent the landing approach in prayer.

Once the shuttle glided to a halt, he touched Hanusha's arm again. *Assist the young people, please. And greet Annalah for us both. I'll be needed in the Minster's office.*

Hanusha offered a citrene to Perl, who popped it into her mouth. *Of course. Greet Wind for me.*

He unbuckled, strode up the aisle and down the ramp onto welcoming grass. Early morning sun lit up the peaks he loved.

He barely spared them a glance.

The shortest route indoors, used only by Sanctuary staff, led straight through the main hangar and up a staff stairway. He took that route.

In the Minster's office, he found his brother's wife sitting in her desk chair. Wind wore one of the long sekiyr gowns and smelled faintly floral, plainly looking forward to seeing her husband as soon as Saried revived him. Kiel noticed her fidgeting, though.

"Thank you for hurrying." She rose to give him a quick sisterly embrace. "Are you all right? Did you have any trouble leaving Thyrica?"

"A bit." Kiel recalled the heavyset Thyrian who had rescued him from interrogation. He stared into Wind's eyes while pointing to his own, inviting a quick probe. After the nauseous moment, she looked away. "How is Father?" Kiel asked.

Wind's black hair had recently grown a grey streak that framed her face. In every way that mattered, the passing years had made her only lovelier, and he felt honored to call her "sister." She sat back down at her desk, near the ceiling streamers. She shook her head. "You're just in time. He's upright again today, but . . ."

Grief twisted his gut. "Not much longer?" It was hard to imagine a Whorl without his father.

"This morning's blood counts are ominous." Wind raised her chin. "Saried can tell you more when we get to the med center. She's already initiating Kinnor's stasis revival. Are you ready to counsel him?"

Whether or not Kiel felt qualified for his post, he wore the Shamarr's responsibility. Even for his brother. "Yes. How far along is the resuscitation?"

She picked up her handheld and eyed it. "Re-infusion's about half done. Saried's sedating him pretty heavily, since he's Special Ops. He's likely to bounce out of the crypt ready to attack someone."

Kiel nodded. He guessed that it also would be humiliating to be remanded into his wife's custody. Apparently the reason he'd been sent here wasn't yet general knowledge.

Wind's gown and perfume were plainly a special effort to welcome Kinnor back, but her eyes looked shadowy. He thinned his shields and sensed the achy tension of sleep deprivation.

He rested a hand on her shoulder. "Wind, the real question is whether you're ready for him."

She hesitated, smiling with eyebrows arched. He'd often thought she was likely the only woman in their generation with the grace to handle his brother. If the kindred assembled here one day to flee the Whorl, she'd be among its leaders. "I'm as ready as I can be," she said. "I've done all the calming exercises I know. And Kiel, I dearly love that man."

"As he loves you," Kiel murmured. "Maybe now, there'll be a goal that you can give your best united effort. By the way, where's Jorah?"

She shrugged and crossed her legs. "Still on Tallis, I assume. My DeepScan alert said to only expect Kinnor. I'm sure he'll explain."

He turned to leave, but a thought struck him. "Are things all right with our outsider? The one who's not t-sleeping?"

She stood. "There've been no problems so far."

"Good." Kiel rubbed his chin. "And I had a few second thoughts. The Collegium has always seemed like fertile ground for dark spirits. Shadows. She could be under their influence." He had glimpsed Chancellor Gambrel years ago. The man was not to be trusted.

Wind raised her head. "But a shadow's influence can be overcome. You did, didn't you, Kiel?"

Silent, he nodded. She did not need to say another word about that.

"All right." She stepped around the desk. "I'll make sure you're introduced to her. But let's go to Father."

They walked out of her office and along the water, to the left on the stone walkway. At the pool's far right end, a noisy mob had gathered around the breakfast tables. The familiar smell of winter cheese hung in the air as he scanned the crowd for his eldest daughter.

Ruefully ignoring his rumbling stomach, he turned up the medical corridor. Wind stepped aside as his parents appeared in a doorway.

He'd steeled himself to see a badly altered appearance, but the sight of so much biotape on his father's neck, vanishing under the open neckline of a med center tunic, and that beloved face without eyebrows or the thick white hair over it, clawed his heart. He clamped down on his emotional control, even though he knew that his father would be politely shielding against that first response, letting Kiel adjust to the changed appearance.

At least he was on his feet.

"Mother." He bent down to embrace her and reached out simultaneously with his mind, sending a warmth she would feel plainly. *I'm here for you,* he subvocalized.

His mother smiled. For a moment, she resembled the old tri-Ds he'd seen—defiant, even regal.

He released her and stretched out both arms, opening his mind fully too. From his father he received a stronger caress, the sense of controlled but unmistakable dread, and the understanding that soon, the family he'd led like a flagship would face the continuing crisis without him.

This exchange took only seconds. Wind led them all into a side room where a stasis crypt lay open on a tabletop. From this angle, Kiel could not see inside. Wind stopped next to his half-sister Saried near the crypt's head, and she looked down with a rueful smile. Kiel pressed close to her, guessing she'd need extra support.

Now he too peered into the crypt. His brother looked angry, with a furrowed forehead and compressed lips. He'd been stased in uniform instead of hospital garb. That confirmed the hasty arrest, hearing, and dismissal.

The room fell silent. Saried touched her handheld to the life-signs board, which was mounted on the wall. "You can keep talking. Reinfusion's complete, but he's sedated. You won't disturb him. I'll let you know when we're going to bring him up."

"Thank you." Kiel glanced at their mother, who stood close to Kinnor's feet. Today, the smile lines around her eyes were less pronounced than her forehead wrinkles, and those grief lines over her nose looked like stab marks. In bereavement shock—soon—the loss of her spouse would debilitate her. She would need Kiel's full support. His parents had been deeply and obviously in love for fifty years, working in tandem like well-matched dancers.

To Kiel's surprise, he heard his father's strong subvoice. *You don't think we'd have shown you when we were arguing, do you?*

Kiel smiled before answering. *I overheard more than one fire fight. And you aren't supposed to be in my mind without my permission, are you?*

No. At the crypt's other end, his father looked up. His mouth twitched. *The Codes still apply. But when was the last time I could speak with you this way instead of over DeepScan?*

To Kiel's embarrassment, it had been more than two years. His father's work on Elysia and his own on Thyrica had kept them apart. *I've missed you,* Kiel answered.

And we have missed you. We're terribly proud, Kiel. I still have to remind myself not to refer to "Shamarr Dickin" but "Shamarr Caldwell." You are a credit to the family.

Thank you. Kiel suppressed his self-conscious disquiet and focused on his father's vividly blue eyes. The eerie appearance of final illness no longer bothered him. Besides, this man had faced death before. *You probably should be resting,* Kiel sent.

Kiel's father barely smiled, and he tucked an arm around his mother's shoulders. *If I overexert, all I lose is a few miserable hours. Get ready for fireworks, though. This might be the last time I can get between your mother and your brother and calm them down. It's good,* he added wistfully, *to have all of you in the same room.*

His father was including Saried, of course. Kiel made a mental note to visit her aged mother, Terza, in the elders' quarters while he was here. *I nearly didn't get to leave Thyrica,* he sent gravely. He relayed the old officer's message, which provoked another faint but sincere smile. Kiel continued, *It might be wise to imitate Mattah at this point. Gather up the young people. Get them out of harm's way. Leave the Whorl, start over.*

Sometimes I wonder, he heard in a regretful tone, *whether it did any good, all those years on the High Command keeping peace and maintaining good relations. And I won't be able to hand off the job. No one came up through Special Ops to succeed me.*

Kiel understood that regret. Kinnor might have succeeded their father in the military hierarchy, if he'd been less of a rebel. Kiel subvocalized, *You followed the call on your life. That's all anyone is responsible to do. I suspect there's a grand reward waiting for you, especially after you saved all those younger officers on board the* Daystar.

He thought he saw his father wince. *Please, Kiel. Take care of your mother.*

I will.

"Ready, everyone?" Saried brandished her handheld. "We'll cut off Kinnor's sedative and administer the stimulant simultaneously."

She seemed to be addressing all five of them, including the Sentinel aide who'd stood almost unnoticed behind Kiel's mother. However, Saried immediately turned to Wind for the official order.

Kiel slipped an arm around Wind's shoulder from the other side. Wind nodded.

"Administering," Saried said.

Silence fell again. Wind leaned out from under Kiel's arm and reached for Kinnor's hand. Kiel completely dispersed his shields. He immediately sensed that all the others except Wind had shielded heavily, giving her and Kinnor privacy. Kiel was a priest, though. His duty was to assist. So he felt Kinnor's moment of returning consciousness, the slightly sick bafflement, and the chilly irritation.

Wind leaned closer. "Kinnor, you're at Hesed House," she said aloud.

"The room's full of people." Kinnor's voice rasped.

She answered, "The family's here to welcome you."

Kinnor groaned. "Can't a man be sick in private?"

Kiel glanced at Saried, who shook her head slightly and nodded toward a vitals display on the wall. Kinnor had come up out of stasis smoothly, without any sign of the normal gastric misery, thanks to his Special Ops training.

"You won't be sick." Kiel stepped forward also. "Hello, brother. It's good to see you."

Kinnor pulled his hand out of Wind's, grabbed both of the crypt's edges, and pushed himself into a sitting position. He looked back and forth across the crypt. "How about giving me some time alone with my dying father?"

Kiel felt hurt and disappointment stream from Wind.

"We need to talk about getting Jorah off Tallis," Kinnor said. "And then there'll be time to socialize. There's a showdown coming. We need Jorah here." He glanced up at Kiel and then back to their father. "We need everyone who's trained in defense. We've got to stand together, or we'll be wiped out."

Kiel frowned. Kin had come out of stasis in a military state of alert, ready to enlist their father's expertise.

Wind leaned down and spoke gently. "Isn't that up to Jorah's commanding officer?"

"I was his CO." Kinnor spared her a glance. "Not anymore."

"Then who's he been transferred to?" Father asked, and Kiel had an uneasy qualm.

Sure enough, his brother's shields turned thick. His eyes narrowed. "They're detaining him, pending a hearing."

Now it was Wind who shielded heavily. In her icy stare, Kiel saw the unvoiced question: *What kind of trouble did you get our son into?*

"We'll send an envoy to Tallis," his mother said in a surprisingly firm voice, "and demand his release. In fact, I suspect that if anyone should have been released, it was Jorah. Following his CO's orders, was he?" She frowned at Kinnor.

Kiel glanced across at Father. *Do you want to get between them?* Kiel sent quickly, *or should I?*

Kinnor craned his neck toward Saried and scowled. "Get me out of this box, would you?"

Father shook his head at Kiel. *I think Wind is going to take charge.*

Saried's aide hurried forward. She offered Kinnor a hand. Wind grabbed his other hand again. "Are you hungry?" she asked, her voice steady. "There's breakfast in the commons for the sekiyrra, and we could have a private meal brought to Saried's office. Hanusha's here too, and Annalah, Rena, and Perl, and of course Saried can join us. Your father and mother would cherish having a . . . reunion meal."

Kiel didn't miss the way Wind almost called it a *last* meal.

"Kiel will pray for Jorah." Wind shot a glance toward Kiel. "And we'll talk about sending an envoy, but we'll do it on full stomachs."

Saried turned to stare at Father. If Kiel hadn't been standing between them, he might not have caught her subvocalization: *That's an excellent idea, Father. And you can eat anything you want.*

Because it won't make any difference. That answer came in a calm, strong tone, but Kiel winced. When cell death set in, the digestive system generally disintegrated first. They would take this meal as a sacrament—all of them but Jorah, who probably was being held as a hostage against Kinnor's good behavior.

Kinnor spun around, glaring, and Kiel guessed that his brother knew exactly what he'd been thinking. As adult twins, they'd sometimes passed information without trying. *When Father's gone,* Kinnor sent him, clenching his jaw, *you and I will be the heads of this family. Work with me or get out of the way.*

Kiel nodded soberly, crossing his arms under the ministerial tunic's loose sleeves. *As we leave the Whorl, we'll need to defend the young people and the Sanctuary. You'll have my full support.*

Kiel felt Kinnor's anger surge again. *You want to leave the Whorl? Without having kept all our family promises?* Before Kiel could compose an answer, Kinnor continued, *If we have to fight the Federates for our right to exist, then the war has already begun. And we don't leave people behind enemy lines.*

CHAPTER 8

Meris exhaled hard, relieved to see the last newly arrived sekiyr in her lineup turn and walk away, taking bites from his breakfast sandwich and striding toward the housing corridors. She enjoyed helping with administrative work. Annalah still sat beside her, giving housing and chore directions to the final student in her own line. The boy bending over the table looked frighteningly young, too young to be learning to do the uncanny things the Sentinel College had to be teaching him.

Finally, Annalah finished. "Good thing we ate early." She stared out over the water, wearing a wistful look.

Meris had an epiphany: Annalah's parents had been on board that shuttle, but until someone summoned her, she was supposed to stay on task. She found she could sympathize. "I'm sure your parents are busy with your grandfather," Meris said. "They'll probably join you soon."

Another sekiyr hurried toward the table. Meris thought he looked vaguely familiar. Was he one whom she'd told about the Collegium?

He bent toward Annalah. "Your family's going to eat together down in the med center. Go on over. I'll relieve you here."

Annalah sprang up. "Oh!"

"Wait!" Meris seized her hand. "Thank your father for me. Please."

"Yes, all right." She hurried off along the pavement, headed toward the medical corridor.

Meris pressed her lips together. Hard. *Only the light is real. And I am the light . . .*

Across the way, Annalah made it as far as the housing corridor before a tall, slender woman and two younger girls converged on her. All four of them wrapped their arms around each other, creating an eight-legged being that rocked back and forth. The littlest girl had to jump up and down to maintain her grip.

The sekiyr chuckled, seated next to Meris. "You'd think they hadn't seen her in years, wouldn't you?"

Years. Would it be that long before she saw Mother or Father, or would she see them again . . . ever? Meris stared at Annalah and her family, jealous pain scalding her. Unfair, unfair!

She pushed up from the table and shoved back her chair, ignoring the sekiyr's startled protest, and fled toward the elevator. She needed to get away from these people. For a few hours, at least. She must concentrate on her litanies! The Sentinels wouldn't miss her. They hadn't wanted her here, had they? Nor was she wanted back home on Elysia. Her vision blurred. *Only the light is real. And I am the light . . .*

To her relief, no one stopped her and nobody followed. She rode topside, wiping tears from her eyes. In cool sunshine she jogged away from the small elevator building. A shift of young people was scattering into the crop fields inside the tall wire-chain fence. As usual, they wore rough brown clothes and broad-brimmed hats.

Midmorning light and fragrant wind made her loneliness seem less awful. Chasing that wind's wordless comfort, she ran across the landing strip and found another graveled path. She didn't normally take chances, but this felt safe enough. A wooden bridge crossed a clear little river. That river was apparently the compound's boundary, since she'd been asked to stay on the near side.

She crossed and kept running. Over here the trail continued, but it was plain hard dirt instead of gravel. It led through tall bushes, at least three meters high. She couldn't see far ahead, but that also meant no one would see her—not until they came looking for her, and they probably wouldn't look for awhile. It felt downright reckless. It felt wonderful.

The trail emerged from the bushes into shin-high grass. Distinctly warm and slightly sweaty, she plodded up the valley's opposite side. She pumped her arms in a satisfying rhythm, silently reciting in cadence with her strides. *The mind rules the body. I choose to continue. The mind rules the body—*

At a bend in the trail, a soft *crack* in the trees off to one side startled her. She froze. *I fear what I only imagine!* The Sanctuary's defensive fielding team famously watched space for intruders from out in the Federacy, right? So there shouldn't be any human intruders . . . other than herself. And she hadn't heard any tales of wild animal attacks here. Really, she ought to be perfectly safe. Still, she stood motionless, breathing hard. There were no further noises. She pushed on up the stony dirt trail.

At the top of this rise, the trail dropped slightly. Now she could see that it led through another clearing. On either side, the trees cast short shadows under the warming sun. She hustled down into that clearing and up the next hill. It rose even higher, into bare, skinny trees. For awhile, it wandered—still plainly leading upward. Curiosity, not pain, impelled her on now, and she walked on and on. Short twiggy bushes were breaking out with green buds beneath the trees.

By now, maybe they had missed her. Maybe Minster Wind would send out a searcher.

Or maybe they were too busy taking care of their own people to even notice she'd left the compound.

She marched on into the morning.

Dim light filtered down between the treetops. Finally, the trail leveled out. The last turn had been to the right, and she followed along the edge of a blunt hilltop. Ahead, brighter sunlight shone down into the trees. Were they thinner up there? She might able to see farther. Maybe into the mountains. She quickened her pace.

Sure enough, she walked out of the forest and found herself looking down into a long valley. It ran due west for quite a distance, and the immensity of the peaks on both sides—especially the jagged ones to her right—made her breath catch. A shining stream meandered down its center. She picked out the thin brown thread of a trail that followed the water, and she congratulated herself again. That was where she would end up, if she kept walking. Just to make sure she wasn't technically out of touch with the Sanctuary, she pulled out her handheld and randomly touched a key.

The panel lit. Satisfied, she was about to slip it back into her pocket when she recognized the information she'd accidentally called up. It looked like some kind of Sanctuary roster. She flicked the screen, and names scrolled past.

An unusually long name caught her eye, and she was startled to recognize a greatly expanded title for her sometime shipboard friend, Lady Fi: Firebird Mari Caldwell, neé Lady Firebird Elsbeth Angelo—cross referenced *Casvah*—all subtitled with the heir name (whatever that meant) *Domita*. Amused, Meris touched the name. What kind of data did these people keep on each other?

She speed-read, oblivious to her surroundings. Evidently the Lady had been born on the minor but wealthy Federate world of Netaia before it had covenanted to the Federacy. Her aristocratic family had tried to sacrifice her in the name of its local religion. Could that possibly be right? Furthermore, she'd been trained—

really?—as a combat pilot, sent out on a suicide run to an already Federate world.

She'd been sent to attack a *Federate* world. "I wasn't raised among these people, either." Meris's lips moved as she repeated the statement Lady Fi had tossed off back in the *Daystar's* secure cabin. Plainly, she'd experienced the dark side of religion before even leaving her homeworld.

She might be interested in the Collegium! Meris skipped an information link regarding Netaian customs and stayed with this biographical page. Lady Fi had accepted amnesty under then-Field General Brennen Caldwell. *There's a story,* Meris observed . . . But that story was ending tragically. On the other hand, Meris had decided some time ago that all human stories ended tragically.

What kind of scars would it inflict on a person, to be raised as a human sacrifice—no matter how many luxuries they gave her to enjoy? The woman seemed fairly normal on the surface, but if bereavement shock was as awful as these people claimed, Lady Fi stood at the brink of a plunge back into misery. She was a prime candidate for the help Meris could offer.

And at least Meris's parents hadn't tried to *kill* her—

She glanced up from the screen and back down into the valley.

A dark shape was moving on that trail. How far off? Two klicks away? Four? Without city blocks to establish perspective, she couldn't tell. One thing was plain: It was coming this way.

Predators? She could alert the Sanctuary via this handheld—but before taking that potentially embarrassing step, she squinted and looked again. Actually, even from this distance, the figure couldn't be mistaken for an animal. It walked upright, and she caught the occasional swing of a walking stick . . . or was that a weapon?

Meris straightened. Sanctuary staff seemed to be busy, processing the expected shuttle's arrivals. This had to be an outsider. But was there some other place on Procyel for a walker to have come from? Wasn't this whole world supposedly secure?

She raised her handheld. She would call the Minster, and—

No. She lowered her hand again. The Minster was busy at a special family meal. Meris especially didn't want to embarrass herself by bothering her. The walker would have to struggle up the far side of this hill, and for Meris, it was downhill all the way back.

This was her chance to make them glad she wasn't in tardema-sleep. She whirled around and started to run.

• • •

Wind Haworth-Caldwell wiped crumbs from her fingers with a cloth square. Miraculously, the meal had gone peacefully. Maybe her father-in-law's condition had kept everyone from picking arguments in front of the granddaughters.

Annalah's reunion with the family had washed everyone in delight; there'd been a brief, mutually respectful visit from Saried's aged mother Terza; and Kinnor hadn't verbally criticized Kiel's intention to gather the kindred and leave the Whorl. He was probably saving that for later, along with his umbrage about their admitting an outsider to the Sanctuary . . . just as she was waiting for her maternal anger to subside before pressing him about Jorah.

If their son were being detained as a hostage, they would have to proceed cautiously. Current reports from Tallis were ominous. Between frantic worry for Jorah and the exquisite sensation of sitting in the same room with her husband, she felt downright dizzy. Sensing Kinnor's emotions on the pair bond did not steady her. Most of his emotional flickers were frustrated or aggrieved.

The long dining table filled Saried's medical conference room. Kiel sat close to Hanusha. Their middle daughter, Rena, reached for a third sandwich as Hanusha delicately dipped a frozen garnet-berry into a bowl of fresh cream. Both Rena and Hanusha looked as slender as ever.

It was good to see Annalah sitting between her younger sisters, regaling them with stories about life on Elysia. Through no fault of her own, Annalah had always been a bit of an outsider. Kiel was still plainly on good terms with kitchen staff, for he'd spread his bread slices with last fall's precious *latchem* preserves. Wind could smell its delicate perfume from her place farther up the table.

Her father-in-law laughed softly at one of young Perl's rejoinders to Annalah. Father—she'd called him that for years, never having known her gene-father—and Lady Fi plainly were overjoyed to sit among so many grandchildren. If only Jorah could have been here!

Father pushed his plate away. The gesture made Wind uneasy.

Sure enough, he stood less than a minute later. He thanked them all for the unexpected gift of this hour and asked Kiel to pray a benediction for the family's future. As Kiel prayed, he and Lady Fi left the room. MedSpec Saried and an aide followed. After the prayer ended, Hanusha sent their daughter Rena to rejoin the sekiyrra as she took little Perl in hand. Annalah headed back out to the commons, probably to check on her friend Meris.

Wind waited.

Finally, Kinnor pushed back his own chair. Wind got up and caught his hand. She tugged him into an empty treatment room. Alone, finally! She wrapped her arms under his shoulders and pulled him toward her. Pressing the side of her head against his uniform tunic and his man-scented chest, she murmured "Kin" and stretched out a tendril of ayin energy.

He responded instantly, his mental touch gratifyingly tender as it flooded her with the intoxicating potency of menthe liqueur, a secret savor of his inner person as only the connatural could detect it. She sighed. Their spats might be infamous, but surely the rest of the kindred guessed how intense their private moments could be. "I'll be cleaned up," he whispered, "and glad to see you in a few hours." *But you have to understand,* he switched to subvocal speech, *every minute with Father counts now. And I promise, they won't hold Jorah. I'm going back for him.*

She opted not to argue, not yet. And today, after months apart, if they touched minds any deeper than this, it would send them both tumbling toward mindless passion. That would have to wait. "Go, then," she said. "I'll join you in the med center as soon as I can, for as long as I can. If he wants me. And we do have to talk about Jorah."

Someone tapped on the door arch behind her. Wind spun around and saw Lady Fi leaning against the arch stones. "Sorry, Kin, but he's asking for you. Something about the expanded defense force you've got in mind here. He has some ideas."

Wind seized his shoulders once more. "Officially, then," she said, "as Sanctuary Administrator, I'm ordering you to talk with your father, who has spent nearly fifty years in command positions."

He laughed harshly and dropped a kiss on her forehead before he hurried out. Lady Fi lingered in the arch a little longer. Wind bowed her head and stared at her husband's mother. She sent a quick subvocal *How can I help you?*

Lady Fi shook her head and answered aloud. "He's in Saried's hands now. And the Holy One's. I can't hope it will be soon. Still, for his sake . . . I don't want him to . . . linger . . ."

She turned and quickstepped up the corridor.

Wind rubbed her face with both hands, grief and desire scrambling against frustration to dominate her thoughts.

I have nineteen new arrivals to work into the task rotation. Wind walked back to her own office with a spring in her step. Desire might be stronger than dread, she decided. Fresh air flowed into her face, carrying the scent of the spring water that constantly refreshed the central pool. Jorah was smart and well-trained. She would contact Special Ops on Tallis about him, via DeepScan. Unfortunately, the new instantaneous communication Tallis was reportedly developing hadn't become available yet. Keeping the Sanctuary isolated from the rest of the Whorl was vital in some ways, but in other ways it frequently proved inconvenient.

She was sitting at her desk five minutes later, composing a message while a voice at the back of her head whispered *tonight, tonight,* when Meris Cariole pushed through the door, panting. "Sit down," Wind said gently. "There's no hurry—"

"But there is." Meris's forehead shone with sweat. Wind dissipated her shields to taste the young woman's emotions: startled, guarded, but oddly triumphant. Meris inhaled another deep breath. "Your security team doesn't watch the ground, does it? I mean, do they?"

"Primarily," Wind answered mildly, "they watch local space." Her desk's broad surface was a patchwork of data monitors, any one of which could link her with interior or exterior comm—but within the Sanctuary, they preferred not to use subtronic communications. She dimmed the entire desktop with a touch.

"Well." Meris sat stiffly on the edge of the visitor's chair. "Someone's walking toward us from out of the west. Down that big valley."

"You left the grounds."

"Only for . . . a few minutes. I had to get away. I just couldn't bear . . . seeing . . ."

Anguish streamed off Meris, but Wind strengthened her shields. She had important things to think about. "Someone's coming back from a hike," she guessed, but she didn't recall anyone checking out to travel. Anyone who actually belonged here, who pulled *that* stunt, would need to be reprimanded. Meris could be disciplined later, if necessary.

Wind touched a desk panel and keyed for the security display. The fielding team could scan any part of the planet using Procyel's satellite network, from their duty station in the west corridor. It just wasn't generally necessary.

Wind requested a groundside scan and then waited, disinclined to make small talk, thinking instead that the people on fielding duty were undoubtedly showing off for the sekiyrra she'd just sent to assist them . . . and that Jorah was locked up somewhere. His father's fault.

His father . . . Kinnor might be waiting in their small private suite by the time she came off duty tonight. She imagined warm breath on the side of her neck, tasted the secret savor of menthe—

To her shock, a report appeared several seconds later: *Confirm single groundside individual, carrying no energy sources or weapons. Profile does not appear on Sanctuary records. Intercepting.*

Wind blinked down at the display and keyed for a map. From the glacial cirque at the far end of the Khaspis Valley, a seldom used trail crossed a high pass into a higher hanging valley. She'd never been up there, but the Sentinels who had built this sanctuary, calling it Hesed House, had also established a secret prayer retreat. One or two people from each generation had left here to spend a cloistered life at Tekkumah, becoming ground-based spiritual defenders. Children who followed that call were honored with Shekkah funeral services, since they did not return.

Kinnor had mentioned, just once, that he'd lost a young sister to that place. Kiel had told her more about it, obviously having a higher opinion of Tekkumah. Still, within Wind's lifetime she'd never seen anyone called there.

Her first thought was to alert Kiel. He would know what to do with anyone who came back illegally. Her second thought made her shudder. Two decades ago, Kiel had been kidnapped by a shadow-possessed Mikuhran. The shadow had thought Kiel might be the coming One, Boh-Dabar, and had tried to corrupt him. It had actually brought him here to the Sanctuary, to spy on Hanusha and their children.

Had another shadow arrived on Procyel II?

Meris still sat on the visitor's chair, drumming her fingers.

Wind dismissed her thoughts. "Thank you, Meris. Well done. We're dealing with it."

Meris made no move to leave. Wind looked her in the eye, reached out a quick probe, and saw what she was waiting for. "We'll remember that you gave us the warning, Meris. Thank you."

Meris returned a crisp, self-satisfied nod. She strode out, swinging her arms with obvious satisfaction.

Wind grasped the desktop's edge and wondered what to do next. Until the fielding station returned a report, she simply had to wait. Fielding would call an alert first. They would send one of the Sanctuary's few motor vehicles and bring in the stranger.

She crossed her arms and laid her head on them. For seventeen years, her chief role had been peacekeeping: between enthused sekiyrra on the verge of responsible adulthood and waning elders who simply wanted restful days and nights, between instructors who wanted ayin skill drills to fill the sekiyrra's hours and the Sanctuary's need for self-sufficiency, and of course, between military Sentinels whose stressful service qualified them for Sanctuary leave and their overworked superiors back on Tallis, Elysia or Thyrica. Those demands generally had kept her from grieving the closeness she and Kinnor rarely enjoyed.

Now, maybe, it would please him to be sent out to intercept the stranger.

But he was with his dying father. She decided she would serve the community best by handling this situation, not by delegating it away. She straightened and touched that panel again, checking with Security. Data appeared: They'd sent two Special Ops personnel and a permanent staff member, all Sentinels with solid ES ratings. They should be able to protect themselves, even if this were a supernatural intruder.

If it could be supernatural, what about calling Kiel away from the med center?

Wind dismissed that idea too. She lit a second desk panel and ordered her security team, "Lock down all topside access until we cancel this alert."

CHAPTER 9

Two guards in Tallan grey strode into Jorah's cell, and two remained at the door.

Jorah smoothed the baggy grey shipboards they'd issued him to wear and stood at attention. This looked like either an intimidation or an important visitor. If it was intimidation, he was in for a rough time—but he wanted to meet it standing up.

A middle-sized man in business clothes walked through the doorway and paused there, glancing left and right before looking straight at him. "Lieutenant Caldwell."

"Yes, sir." Jorah thought he recognized the man, but he couldn't recall a name. That irritated him. With his abilities intact, he'd had a good memory.

"I want to speak with you, but I don't like the surroundings." The man halted, as if waiting for a response.

Jorah didn't intend to give anything away. "Neither do I, sir."

The man shot him a broad smile—a diplomat's smile, if Jorah read him right. His pose communicated sympathetic assurance: head high and slightly tilted, back straight, but not too straight. The man nodded to the guard on his right, whose sleeve stripe

Jorah read as a first sergeant's. "I want a conference room, with you and your team just outside."

The soldier acknowledged.

The stranger turned back to Jorah. "Come out. This way. They'll follow us."

Jorah strode beside the stranger and kept track of turns in the corridor. The man took him in a different direction from the way he'd come in, so he guessed they were headed deeper into the building's detention section. Pinhole security monitors had been punched in the walls over most doors and at corridor corners. The dull grey walls seemed to suck life and hope out of him. Yet despite his eerie visitor's promise and his own preference, he was not ready to try and escape custody. This man might suggest a legal way out of whatever mess he was in.

Still, knowing his surroundings was a priority. At the back of his mind, on a grid he'd been trained to envision, he recorded each turn in the corridor. They were bearing steadily westward, away from the direction his cell window faced. Based on the sun's angle, he'd concluded that that was east.

"Ah." The stranger stopped in front of an unmarked black door. "Here. This one."

The sergeant waved a code key at the doorway, and the door slid aside. "Please," the stranger said, stepping back.

Jorah preceded him into a windowless room—plainly, they were in the MaxSec tower's interior. The room had grey walls and a dark wooden table that might seat six, but there were just four padded metal chairs, widely spaced. Jorah also spotted two ceiling monitors. He guessed at more devices embedded in the walls or perhaps in the chairs.

The stranger pulled back a chair for himself and gestured Jorah to sit across from him.

He sat down and gave up trying to identify the stranger. "I apologize, sir. I think I recognize your face, but I don't know whether the drugs they've given me interfere with memory."

"Piper Gambrel." The man gripped a handheld close to his chest and extended his other hand over the tabletop. "Chancellor, the Collegium of Human Learning."

Jorah leaned far forward to shake hands, remembering that Uncle Kiel had mentioned the man. Supposedly, Chancellor Gambrel headed a philosophical organization that was "the only real competition with our holy Path for the Federacy's spirit"—whatever that meant. There were other local sects elsewhere, weren't there?

Well, this should be interesting. Jorah liked Uncle Kiel, but as a priest he seemed allergic to new ideas.

Chancellor Gambrel looked at him steadily, his face open and frank, his body language welcoming.

Jorah answered, "I'm honored to meet you, Chancellor."

"No, the honor is mine." Gambrel set down the handheld and folded both hands on the tabletop. "Lieutenant Caldwell, I'll give you the bad news first. Special Operations has experienced numerous reductions in personnel during the past decade. It's stretched even thinner now." He shrugged. "The individual who should have heard your case has unfortunately been assigned offworld. We hope his assignment can be completed in less than a year, but I can't promise a speedy hearing."

Jorah's hands went cold. He tried to imagine spending three hundred days with nothing to do but track newsnets. "I see." But Gambrel had promised better news to follow, so he'd better not flame the man. Not yet. He still heard his father's voice at the back of his mind: *Always suspect a trap.*

"I've been authorized, however," Chancellor Gambrel said, "to have you released into a secure apartment here in the tower, which would be far more comfortable, and from which you would be able to do some supervised traveling. Considering who you are, it is unconscionable for the Federacy to lock you into a cell for any length of time."

"Sir." They'd trained Jorah in appropriate responses to outsiders. "I am a Sentinel in Federate service, sworn to serve you just as much as Madam Kernoweg or . . . or any child playing keepaway with his friends." He waved his right hand. Outside these walls, children had to be playing somewhere.

Gambrel looked down at his own hands, smiling as he barely shook his head. "Oh, Jorah," he said, and Jorah noted that he'd stopped calling him *Lieutenant*. Plainly, the man was playing the role of a rescuing friend. The scent of *trap* became stronger, along with the frustrating realization that this might not be his way out after all.

"Jorah," Gambrel repeated, "your family has served the Federacy for decades, and we both know there is trouble ahead. But some persons within my Collegium have developed a non-surgical cure for the difficulties that beset you people."

His stomach lurched. "Difficulties? Sir, I have special abilities that give me the power to serve you. To serve the Federacy, like my . . . grandfather." He'd probably better leave his father out of it.

Gambrel's right eye twitched, and he almost smiled. "Jorah, admit it: You frighten people. You can look into their minds. You could force them to move against their will. You could make objects move without touching them—"

"Kinetics isn't one of my gifts." Jorah rubbed his chin. "And as for the others, why do you think Sentinel College takes so many years to graduate from? It's not just learning the skills. It's memorizing when we are and aren't allowed to use them."

"Controlling electrical circuits." Gambrel slid a finger across the table. "Eidetic memory." He pointed to his forehead. "Being able to read other people's emotions without even hearing them speak, clear across a room. To say nothing of the things some of you can do over planetary distances, if you have fielding or Remote Individual Amplification equipment. You can block your own pain or inflict it directly upon other people—"

"Sir." Jorah spread his hands. "The Mikuhrans did all these things without regard for other people's freedoms. But we do not. We serve the Federacy. Not all of us can do all those things, anyway. We're evaluated, we're trained, we do our best. Never selfishly. Never capriciously."

Gambrel folded his hands again. "It's an experimental procedure, of course, and it needs to be tested. Would you be willing to serve the Federacy—and your people—in this new way?"

Stunned, Jorah listened hard to the silence where he ought to be hearing Gambrel's emotions. If this was a trap, Gambrel seemed to be telling him exactly how terrible taking the bait would be. Sizing him up, maybe. "You mean as a test subject? I . . . I don't see how this is good news. Not for me, and not for other Sentinels. Not even for the Federacy."

"Think, Jorah." Gambrel pushed away from the tabletop and crossed his arms over his chest, looking casual and sympathetic. "I understand their predicament. It's not their fault that they've inherited something that makes them so dangerous and so frightening to other people. If you had some other physical disfigurement, the possibility of a cure—so that those children playing keepaway wouldn't run away, screaming—that would be welcome news."

"This isn't a disfigurement, sir." Jorah's face heated again. "The Sentinels serve you. We don't threaten you."

"Only because you've organized your entire lifetimes around learning to control this—we'll keep calling it a disfigurement, for now—to keep it from controlling you. Your Shuhr relations had a much more normal attitude regarding unusual power. Forgive me for speaking plainly," he added, "but they were your *personal* relatives."

Jorah squared his shoulders. His mother had willingly converted to Federate ways. He'd been raised to carry his dual heritage proudly.

He glanced over the Chancellor's shoulder at the sergeant, thinking that escape really might be his best option. He hoped he hadn't imagined that sparkling apparition, and that it hadn't been a drug-induced hallucination. Meanwhile, he'd better stall.

He let his shoulders roll forward again, creating a more defeated impression. "What would this procedure involve?"

Gambrel pressed his palms together, almost smiling. "My training isn't medical, but here's how I understand it. It's something they call a 'binary treatment.' A first kind of medication collects harmlessly at several points in the body. We're almost certain that it would accumulate in the ayin but no other brain organs—obviously, though, we haven't been able to confirm that hypothesis, and that's why we need your help.

"If at that stage, we saw any unexpected intracranial collection points, naturally we would halt the test without proceeding. Further research would be done." He flattened both hands on the tabletop. "I promise you, Jorah, no one will damage any other part of your brain, nor the rest of your body."

No, no, no! Jorah tried to sound curious and cooperative. He was determined to refuse, but he needed information—and not just for himself! He resisted the urge to reach for his knuckles. "And the second dose?"

Gambrel pulled back his hands and relaxed against his chair. "That, of course, reacts with the first medication. The combination poisons whatever tissue it adheres to. The second substance has a large molecular profile," Gambrel added, "so it cannot pass out through the blood-brain barrier."

"I see." Jorah stared down at the table. It had a dark but dull finish that didn't reflect Gambrel's face. At the back of his mind, something kept screaming *No!* He was learning to cope with his abilities' absence, but the idea of never getting them back . . . ever . . . mortified him.

Gambrel was right about one thing. He'd organized his adult life around managing his abilities. Every step—each thought—felt unbalanced, now that they were gone. If Gambrel's people had a wider "curing program" in mind, Jorah doubted they would wait to get other people's permission. In that case, asking *him* for permission was a sham, an attempt to convert him, or both.

This was huge. Gambrel essentially wanted the Sentinels wiped out. Jorah had to inform Special Ops. They were headquartered right here in the building. Surely they weren't all in Gambrel's pocket.

"There could be a substantial reward, well beyond simply releasing you, if you helped convince more Sentinels to take this cure." Gambrel spoke casually, and for an instant Jorah wondered whether his thoughts had been read. Surely, this man couldn't do that. "You might even save their lives."

Was that a threat? Jorah shook his head. "I wouldn't feel right taking a reward. My people aren't for sale. I don't like thinking they could be threatened."

"Jorah," Gambrel murmured, "your destiny is spiritual, not physical. You could lose an arm or a leg and still achieve all you were born to be." He paused and tilted his head a few degrees, plainly cuing Jorah. He'd reached the heart of his offer. "Your father, and his father, and his father before him form a line stretching back to the days when predictions were made that even I have heard of. You are—you have to be—potentially the most important Thyrian Sentinel alive. And I," he said, further softening his voice, "and the Collegium—all of us, Jorah—are ready to support your claim to a very ancient title."

Jorah sat upright.

Gambrel wanted his soul, all right. In a vain attempt to protect Jorah's Caldwell ancestors, the prophecies specific to that family had been kept quiet for several generations.

The Shuhr had kept picking off Caldwells anyway, and eventually the old stories got out more widely.

Besides, there were Path adherents on dozens of worlds now. The old stories were being translated by plenty of "normal" people, who didn't bother to keep secrets.

Jorah cleared his throat. "That title, especially, isn't for sale."

"Of course not. But think, Jorah. 'The power to unmake all that His hand once made; unmake the universe and form it again, perfectly, as in the beginning.'" Gambrel spread his hands, as if the idea awed him. "The right to immolate all evil, everywhere. Think of the power that implies! And you want it, don't you?" Gambrel narrowed his eyes. "If not for yourself, for your family. For the rest of your people. The Whorl made whole, at last. Justice restored."

"I don't think I'm that person, sir." Jorah knew that "unmake" passage, from the book of *Mattah*. How could he have been born for such a high destiny without knowing it?

But if he were, it would make no sense to give up his ayin abilities. To make the predictions come true, he would need more power, not less. Wouldn't he?

"How would you know?" Gambrel asked, again seemingly reading his thoughts. "The need is great right now, and our *paths*," he said, stressing the word and lacing his fingers, "could come together. Our spiritual organizations could merge. We might bring the Whorl safely through the briefest possible turbulence into a blessed peace that could last hundreds of years."

And three guesses who meant to lead those merged spiritual organizations! Furthermore, Gambrel wanted Jorah—disempowered—as his Boh-Dabar figurehead. The idea made Jorah sick. "You'll give me time to think this over, of course." After a lifetime of silence and guesses, two unconnected strangers had suggested the very same thing within a very short time.

Unconnected? Or was someone—something—playing on his childhood hopes, his grown-up fears, and his people's expectations?

"Of course." Gambrel stood. "Take all the time you want."

The sergeant escorted him back to his cell, where Jorah sat down with his shoulders blocking the newsnet screen. He gripped his hands between his knees and stared at his feet. How *would* he have known if he'd been born into the role the prophets predicted? Could he singlehandedly restore the kindred's prominence?

His father would be hugely proud, and his grandmother would positively dance with enthusiasm. But how would he know?

He'd always thought of the spiritual disciplines as checks on his abilities, not a real way to approach the supernatural. Apparently, Chancellor Gambrel thought the same thing.

But imagine the power, he reflected. Power to unmake and restore the universe—how could that happen? Physical science had proved that impossible, right? So this ancient prediction had to be symbolic. Maybe it could simply mean remaking the Federate Whorl's political structure. Gambrel seemed to be thinking along that line. Conflicts were brewing between wealthy and less wealthy worlds and even among smaller populations. Soon, it might get harder to shore up the Federate government with fiscal incentives.

On the other hand, if the predictions were real—not just a lot of poetic exaggeration—then Jorah had no right to lay down his abilities. Not in some quasi-noble experiment. Not ever.

He stared hard into the cell's darkest corner. Could his shimmering visitor be waiting, or choosing to be invisible? He formed words in his mind. *Can you hear me? I need to get out of here.*

The shimmering presence seemed to be busy elsewhere.

Jorah's next human visitors arrived within an hour. One wore a med's yellow tunic and took his vitals without asking permission. Another explained the "binary cure" in detail, and Jorah felt slightly sick as they clarified the poisoning protocol. He hadn't said yes, so what were they doing here? He had sworn to defend his loved ones to the death, if necessary. He would rather die here than endanger them by cooperating with these Tallans.

Now he realized that the Tallans might not even let him die. It wouldn't be difficult to stun him again and administer the drugs against his will. They plainly hoped he would cooperate, though.

The third visitor wore Tallan grey uniform pants with his medical tunic, and a colonel's quadruple stripes had been sewn to his sleeves. He had an odd gap in one eyebrow and a nameplate that read ZEIMSKY. Jorah would have saluted him under normal circumstances, but this man didn't salute, didn't even seem to acknowledge that Jorah had recently worn the midnight blue uniform of Federate Thyrica. "What do you think of the Collegium?" the Tallan demanded.

Jorah stared at the man, wondering what connections the civilian Gambrel had in the Tallan military. "I haven't studied it," he said carefully. "I've heard some things about it that I admire, though."

The Tallan was a little less than his own height but a little more than his weight, and he kept glancing side to side as if Jorah made him nervous, even as a drugged prisoner. "Do you think that this 'Path' you've been raised to follow might be reconcilable with Collegiate teachings?"

"It's . . ." Jorah didn't dare speak his mind. He let himself slump slightly, guessing that this man could be dangerous if he felt threatened. "To be honest, sir, I don't know enough to guess."

As the Tallan stepped closer, he flicked his fingers down at his side, and the med workers backed off. Jorah tucked that information away: They answered to this nervous officer. "Your people," Colonel Zeimsky said, "if they were cured of their peculiarity, could command respect in the Federacy. They have created a nearly perfect religion. With a few modifications, it might become a crucial part of our higher understanding of humankind."

In other words, this was one of Chancellor Gambrel's cronies, planning some kind of sedition against the Federacy's political machinery. This was bigger than huge! "That's an interesting thought." Jorah rubbed a sweaty palm against his pant leg, increasingly doubtful that these people would release him. Surely his grandfather wouldn't have placated anyone who had threatened him this way. And as for his father—

Was *this* why the Feds had sent Dad away, to keep him from disabling the trap that had caught Jorah?

The med who'd taken his vitals stepped forward again. "You've got until this time tomorrow. That's when we're going to need your authorization for treatment."

"Wait a minute." Jorah stared across at the officer, not the underling. "Sir, Chancellor Gambrel said I should take all the time I needed."

"Tomorrow," the med repeated. Colonel Zeimsky just stood there, staring back.

Something cold seemed to blow through the cell. "You'd better talk with Chancellor Gambrel, sir," Jorah said firmly. "That wasn't what he told me, and he gave me the distinct impression that he's at the top of your chain of command."

"He does give people that impression." Colonel Zeimsky reached behind him and touched that smooth place on the wall. The door slid open. He motioned the other meds out of the cell and followed them silently.

Jorah turned away from the door, feeling dehumanized. Instantly, the cell's inmost corner glimmered again. The melodious shimmer hissed from midair, and Jorah recognized the eerie voice. "Hail, Jorah."

Infuriated, Jorah balled his right fist against his left palm. "I needed you two minutes ago," he exclaimed before remembering to lower his voice and try not to move his lips. "Did you see what just happened?"

"Be at peace, lord. You cannot be defeated. How now does my offer of escape sound to you?"

The questions that had been roiling in Jorah's mind tumbled out. Forget security. If they could see his lips move, surely they would see the thing in his cell with him. "Who are you? *What* are you? What do you want from me?"

The glimmer brightened and took on an enormous form that was no physical body, though it projected an image of shining militancy. "I am a soldier, like you." The shape lowered itself. Jorah had the impression of a deep obeisance, as if it were sinking down on one knee.

"Chancellor Gambrel told me to take my time." Jorah lowered his voice. "But they just threatened to 'treat' me tomorrow."

It occurred to Jorah that Bright Ones allegedly carried messages from the divine presence. Maybe it would alert someone for him! "I need to speak with . . . my uncle Kiel," he decided, since his father might still be in stasis. "Can you . . . Could you tell him what's happening, and ask him what he thinks I should do?" Uncle Kiel wouldn't hesitate to answer a divine messenger. In fact, Uncle Kiel probably could tell what this person or thing really was.

"Of course. Meanwhile, be courageous. Trust your initiative, and lead your people into a remade Whorl."

The moment it vanished, Jorah realized that he'd forgotten to press the most important question: When could it get him out of here?

He couldn't believe he'd forgotten! *It'll come back,* he reassured himself, sitting again. It might be talking to Uncle Kiel already, at this very moment. He rubbed his palms on the sides of his shipboards. To pass the minutes of waiting, he imagined his uncle staring up at that sparkling, militant image. The messenger was probably saying, "Your nephew needs advice."

Uncle Kiel would be staring in wonder.

• • •

Kiel Caldwell stood at his father's bedside, staying out of his half sister's way as Saried settled a lifesigns monitor on the elder man's chest and re-inserted slender tubes at the sides of his throat. Lightweight bedcovers afforded some modesty, but Kiel and Kinnor had been excluded for several minutes while Saried and her staff had connected other devices.

Kinnor sat on the bed's other side, staring intently into their father's eyes, and Kiel felt certain they were discussing strategies for rescuing Jorah and creating a defense force here.

That was good, since it kept his father distracted from these procedures and their finality. Later, when everything had been said, Kiel would take up the priestly office and comfort his parents by sharing memories, or by providing a stronger emotional linkage, or in any other way they requested.

They might still have a day or two, but judging by the readouts on that wall display over his father's head, he might not last through tonight. It was bitter to hope that his father would pass out of life as quickly as possible, without suffering. For a moment, he wished Hanusha weren't away with Perl and the sekiyrra. Having her here would have been a comfort.

Having slipped out briefly, his mother hurried back in and settled on a chair underneath Kiel's outstretched arm. She tilted her chin up to whisper, "I'm glad you're here, Kiel. Thank you for coming so far."

He rested his free hand on her shoulder and let go of the bed rail near his father's shoulder. Feeling in a pocket inside one of his loose grey sleeves, he made sure he was carrying his tiny vial of holy oil. He would anoint his father a final time before long, to help calm his heart and mind for the last Crossing.

Decades ago, the High Commander had been given another *talas* oil anointing. Kiel's predecessor had marked him as the eldest family survivor, shortly after his brother—Kiel's Uncle Tarance— had been murdered by Shuhr agents.

Kiel had never known that uncle. Now, though, he might face a quandary: Who was older, Kinnor or himself? Kiel had been born first, but on his mother's homeworld, a second-born fraternal twin was considered to be the first conceived. In his father's family, the anointed eldest sometimes had significant dreams or heard the holy Voice.

Since Kiel already had the privilege of dreams and messages from the Voice, he decided to defer the honor to Kinnor. It would be bizarre to anoint himself, anyway.

Something rustled behind him. Tossed out of his thoughts, he turned around. A sekiyr in a blue duty tunic stood in the doorway to the treatment room. She pressed both palms together under her chin in an apologetic gesture. She glanced over her shoulder.

Kiel understood that signal. Frustrated, he squeezed his mother's shoulder again and walked out. This was Kinnor's turn, after all, for a long last conversation. Saried had had time too. It was too bad that Tiala . . .

No, his sister Tiala was separated from them not only by a rugged mountain range but also by a life vow. Not even Wind communicated with the prayer retreat. Not that he knew of, anyway.

The sekiyr led him a short way up the passage.

Wind stood in the arch between medical corridor and waterside walkway, fidgeting against the wall with one hand. A half dozen uniformed Sentinels passed behind her, headed toward the commons end. Judging from that and the brilliant skylights, it had to be after noon. "Forgive me," Wind said. "Of all the times to have to call you away—"

"It's all right." He'd served as a priest for so long that the response came naturally, even if it felt less than sincere.

"Kiel." Wind pushed away from the wall. "There's a young man in my office, claiming to be your nephew."

"Jorah?" But Wind and Kinnor's son had supposedly been detained on Tallis. Had his Federate superiors released him and sent him here?

She shook her head and looked up, lines zigzagging her forehead. *No,* she sent subvocally, and Kiel sensed tension in the way she paced her words slowly and cautiously. *He claims that his mother is your sister Tiala.*

CHAPTER 10

Kiel stared into Wind's wide eyes. He guessed that his own had gone just as large. Tiala had left for Tekkumah, the prayer retreat, more than thirty years ago. If he remembered correctly, a boy had been called out to Tekkumah ten years before Tiala.

Not one Sentinel had been called since then. Had people begun to marry there? If Tiala and that boy had produced a child, the prohibition against returning might not apply. Maybe Kiel's dying father would meet a grandchild he hadn't known about. An unexpected gift. *And the boy would be my nephew.*

"He wants to talk with you." Wind backed toward the reflecting pool. "But Kiel, I remember what you told me, about that . . . that shadow creature, that it transported you here all those years ago. We'll confirm who this person is, genetically. We aren't just going to believe a stranger's story."

"Good." Chilled, Kiel realized Wind's wits weren't as scattered as his own. She was one of the few people he'd told about his travels with Tamím, the shadow-possessed Mikuhran. He hadn't thought it necessary to explain to her—or anyone else—that Tamím, tempting him off the holy Path, had also enhanced his substandard ayin abilities. He made a point to avoid using them, whenever he could.

Guide me, he prayed as they turned toward her office. Really, it made no sense that a person born at Tekkumah would leave there for any reason, unless . . . "Maybe this person was sent with a message." He walked slowly, wanting to get this talked out before they arrived.

"Yes." Wind matched his pace. "But from our people, or from the enemy?"

Kiel gave himself a severe emotional shakedown. "Possible. Although even a person under shadowed influence needs mercy." As far as Kiel knew, Tamím—the real Mikuhran, not his demonic possessor—had died in a state of grace. Kiel hoped never to face another struggle of that intensity.

"Don't worry." Wind kept facing straight ahead, looking toward her office. They passed the defense corridor. "I didn't leave him unguarded. And I had Saried's aides start the gene tests, to see if he's really descended from . . . your mother. . . ." She let her voice trail away.

Kiel frowned. Evaluating this person could be perilous, as Wind was reminding him. His mother's mutated ayin had been incredibly dangerous. Kiel's daughter Annalah had inherited it, and so Sanctuary Master Dabarrah had developed a device to scan epsilon waves' polarity in future generations. Only her prompt ayinectomy had spared Annalah from growing up in deadly peril.

Could it have skipped a generation in Tiala's case too? If this stranger had a mutated ayin *and* had fallen under a shadow's influence, he could have potentially unlimited killing power. He might have already wiped out the prayer retreat. He could have come here to do the same to the Sanctuary.

Kiel's gut twisted. "Do you have an age on him?"

"He says he's twenty-seven."

That placed his birth within a year of Kiel's encounter with Tamím. If Tamím had known about the prayer retreat, he could have violated Kiel's sister—another sickening notion—but he had never mentioned the place. "Who's guarding him?" Kiel tried to stay on track without panicking.

"Three on fielding duty went out and brought him in. They're sticking with him like bindweed."

"Good." They had reached Wind's office. He strode in.

Four people stood to face them, two from the left stone bench and two from wooden chairs. The first man and woman wore the uniform and were plainly Special Ops on Sanctuary leave. Ideal guards for a dangerous guest.

Kiel gave the other pair a glance and recognized the man on the left as Sanctuary staff, gripping an unfamiliar walking stick.

The other was a tanned young stranger with a broad upper body and muscular arms, wearing a rough work shirt and pants. He looked slightly upward at Kiel as they clasped hands. Kiel thought he'd never seen such intelligent dark eyes.

He cautiously dispersed his epsilon shields, careful not to touch the stranger with a mental probe yet. Listening from a safe distance, he felt no agitation or hostile intent, and none of the smug superiority that had characterized Tamím.

He let his shields spring up again.

"Shamarr Kiel Caldwell," Wind said, "our visitor says that his name is Tavkel." She walked behind her desk—all its monitoring panels darkened—picked up her handheld, and raised an eyebrow. "And he is our nephew. Saried's aide has already confirmed your mother's mitochondrial type in his skin cells. We're still waiting on the other results."

Kiel released the rough hand he'd clasped and dispersed his shields again. He still felt no threat coming off the young man, not even a static shielding cloud. Tekkumah probably wasn't equipped to train people in College skills, since they all left Hesed House as untrained children. Still, Tavkel could be under a spirit's control. Shadowed. "Sit down, everyone," Kiel said.

The Special Ops people sank back down on their stone bench, turning slightly toward the intruder. The Sanctuary staffer slid his own chair into the middle of the room. Kiel took it. "You're Tiala's—?" He stopped short of saying *boy*.

Tavkel smiled. Kiel was startled to realize that he was seeing his own mother's eye color, a clear, hot brown, over his father's fine cheekbones. "She is well and happy. She loves her work. You're always remembered."

"Tell me more." Reminded what work they reportedly did at Tekkumah, Kiel shot off a prayer of his own. *This is unprecedented, Holy One. Protect us, guide me.* "Why are you here?"

"I have several messages for you all." Tavkel turned to include Wind. "And a concern. To answer your questions first, I didn't show any of the Ehretan abilities at the usual age, but I've done some unusual things recently. We know that my grandmother's gene line is potentially dangerous."

The sudden arrival of unusual abilities was a danger sign, all right. Still, he'd said "we." Maybe Tekkumah was still standing, and they'd sent him away.

"Ah." Wind spoke in a well modulated, calming tone. "But if you were a danger to them, you are potentially a danger to us as well, and to yourself."

Again, Kiel tasted the young man's emotional state. Completely unflustered, Tavkel raised his chin. He said, "I know about the surgery, Sanctuary Administrator. I need no ayin for what I was born to accomplish. But you know what that is."

Kiel choked on his next breath. Wind's head turned, and their eyes locked. *Is he saying he's Boh-Dabar?*

That shadow wanted me to make the same claim, Kiel answered. *But Tavkel could be. He's from the Caldwell line.*

Be careful!

Yes! What in the Whorl should he do? Sitting calmly on that wooden chair, Tavkel could be a threat they must neutralize instantly . . . or else here, at long last, could be a person who rightfully demanded Kiel's instant and complete obedience. Ironically, Kiel remembered how recently he'd prayed, "Now would be a good time." How many times had he warned people to be careful what they asked for?

But Tavkel had the dangerous Netaian heritage, so Kiel couldn't ask the Special Ops to mentally examine him for outside influences—or to make sure he didn't remember harming anyone at Tekkumah—or even to see how he understood the claim he'd apparently just made. There was a chance that he had inherited the dangerous Netaian ayin. But not everyone who carried the gene had that problem. Kiel didn't.

Tavkel barely nodded, as if he'd tracked Kiel's thoughts without using mind-access. A chilly finger seemed to run down Kiel's spine. "What," Kiel asked, staring into those keen brown eyes, "were you born to accomplish?"

In the brief silence that followed, Kiel heard water splashing from the pool and the pulse in his own ears. If Tavkel were Boh-Dabar, the very stars had to be listening.

"Our people," Tavkel said, "should have brought peace and reconciliation to humankind fourteen generations ago. We should have been a beacon. Instead, people want to extinguish the faint light we've been allowed to give." He paused and sent a short but deliberate glance to each of them, including the guards. "They fear us. They fear our abilities. As a people, we are still self-serving and deeply flawed. That is why I would welcome that surgery."

Again, Kiel felt blindsided. This didn't sound like a demonic power play—but wasn't Boh-Dabar supposed to be a high priest, a warrior lord who would lead them into a blessed era of leadership? "Did they teach you this at Tekkumah?" he asked stiffly. "We assume that the people there defend and cherish us."

"They do," Tavkel said, "but long ago, our people were commanded to serve unaltered humanity and thereby prove our obedience. That puts us under them, not over them—except as that beacon."

It was a good answer. Still, a shadow could quote the holy books. This shadow might be much more subtle than the one who had controlled Tamím. Kiel must use his own experience to assess the threat Tavkel posed.

Threat? Kiel caught himself sliding toward one end of the judicial balance and scrambled back toward the center. If the Eternal Speaker had enfleshed his own words to save Sentinel families from Federate persecution, to unmake and lovingly renew the Federate Whorl, then Kiel Caldwell must not try to stand in his way.

However, it remained possible that Kiel had been allowed to battle one shadow in order to recognize another.

Wind rested her elbows on her desk's darkened surface. Her handheld blinked twice. *Ah,* she subvocalized, *Shari has set up the Dabarrah apparatus.* Out loud, she said, "Tavkel, we can confirm right now, in the next room, whether you have the dangerous kind of *ayin.* Are you willing to be tested again?"

"Of course." As Tavkel got up, Kiel spotted the aide through one of Wind's inner doorways. Tavkel followed her. The guards came after Tavkel.

Relaxing slightly, Kiel reached into his tunic's pocket, nudged the oil vial aside, and pulled out the small red, blue, and green brocade squares that he often used to create a private altar. He spread them on one knee but couldn't decide how to lay them: blue, then green, and red on top would focus his thoughts to pray for someone in mortal danger—but he reversed the first two, reminding himself that creation had been locked in cosmic battle for millennia.

He wondered whether the young man used "Caldwell" as his surname, or the ancient equivalent "Carabohd," or even something different. He hadn't plainly claimed to be Boh-Dabar, had he? Kiel felt oddly reluctant to press the question. If he were That One, Tavkel would prove himself. Questioning would be useless.

How would they deal with him if he were an impostor?

Kiel bowed his head, trying to quiet himself. As Wind busied herself at her desk, making faint taps on her handheld, ancient prophecies sprang into his mind, oblique promises given over many generations. Some of the predictions normally associated with Boh-Dabar seemed to have been fulfilled within the Caldwell family already. Kiel's parents had destroyed a "nest of evil" on Mikuhr, assisted—coincidentally?—by fused energies of their differently polarized ayins. Plus a geologic cataclysm.

The Holy One rarely gave incontestable proofs, though. He seemed to love watching people step toward him as trustful children. According to the holy books *Dabar* and *Mattah,* prophets' special abilities confirmed their authority, and some prophecies' fulfillment was only clear in hindsight.

But wouldn't Boh-Dabar, highest of all, prove himself to anyone who wanted to believe?

Kiel rubbed his tired eyes, realizing he'd last slept on a different day cycle. Even if Tavkel weren't personally dangerous, Kiel mustn't betray all the faithful by delivering them to a prophet of evil.

Tavkel, the aide, and the guards re-entered Wind's office. Saried walked with them. "He has it," she said soberly. "The first Netaian ayin we've seen since Annalah's."

Tavkel extended a hand toward Saried. "MedSpec Kinsman has agreed to perform surgery immediately."

"Good," Kiel said. A fresh possibility occurred to him: What if the ancient prophets had used their ayins to perform those confirming signs? Surgery was irreversible . . . and, come to think of it, Tamím had shown him years ago that if an ayin had abnormal polarity, the operation could prove fatal. "Wait!"

They all turned to look—Wind with her arms extended over her desktop, Saried already stepping out of the office, and Tavkel crossing his arms.

Again, Kiel had the uncanny feeling that his thoughts had been tracked. He knew what mind-access felt like, though, and Tavkel was not using it. "Surely blocking drugs would suffice for now," Kiel suggested.

Saried turned toward Wind's desk. "They can be administered in overlapping doses. Almost indefinitely."

And they took several days to wear off. Kiel crumpled his prayer cloths and eyed his nephew again. "You're untrained?"

Tavkel shrugged. "I'm a trained herdsman. Ask me about breeding, or shearing, or butchering kipreta."

"That's not what I meant."

"But it's what you asked. It was hard training, and it's demanding work."

Disarmed—and charmed despite his reservations—Kiel sent Wind a subvocal burst. *Medication, not surgery. But keep him under guard.*

She nodded. "Saried, use the blocking drugs for now. Surgery is permanent. We don't want to make a mistake."

"Go bring a dose," Saried told Wind's aide, who slipped out of the room. The sound of running footsteps pattered away on the stone walkway.

Kiel could guess why the sekiyr was running. His family had tried to keep that reversed polarity ayin mutation as secret as the Caldwell prophecies, simply to protect the rest of the kindred from worse persecution. Still, dangerous abilities made fabulous rumors, and young people controlled by codes and their elders absolutely loved secret knowledge.

The sekiyr returned in less than two minutes. Kiel dispersed his shields as she administered the injection. The sekiyr's frantic hurry came through clearly, but the young man's mental and emotional state did not change. Whatever else he was, he seemed utterly self-confident. Kiel felt no sense of waning ability, no disappearance of epsilon static. That made sense, if he were untrained.

"I want to talk with you," Kiel said after Wind had timed the standard three minutes. He wanted to have that talk where Tavkel couldn't harm all these young people in any way. He ordered the guards, "Follow us, please," and he led along the water to the upside elevator, out of the crowded Sanctuary and into the long-shadowed end of afternoon on the planet's surface.

CHAPTER 11

Meris was taking a welcome afternoon nap in her shared room, sinking into a dream that wafted her to Tallis—Chancellor Gambrel himself was greeting her—when she heard a sharp rapping. She rolled over.

Someone stood just inside the door, wearing a pale yellow tunic. Medical garb. Meris sat up. "What?"

"One of the regen patients has developed a respiratory infection." The young woman spoke quickly. "They're going to shift him to stasis, and most of the staff is busy in the Caldwell suite or the Minster's office. We need you, if you're willing."

Still only half awake, Meris almost asked why they hadn't just commed her handheld. *Doing everything the old-time way,* she realized. Emergency stasis wasn't exactly old-time, of course.

And yet it was another chance to prove herself too useful for t-sleep. "Okay."

She smoothed the rumples from her tunic and followed the girl back to the med center.

Three doors past the admissions desk, she scrubbed, dressed, and decontaminated. An empty crypt lay in the stasis room. On the now familiar workstation status screen, she found orders for pilot Danton Harris to be moved from regen to this crypt. The screen also displayed tissue type, blood volume, and all the other specs she would need. Whenever a patient developed a runaway infection, the usual strategy was to stase him or her, and then—while the infected body remained inactive—to clone enormous quantities of self-derived antibodies. They then would revive and inoculate the patient with the body's own natural defenses.

Pleased to find herself working unsupervised again, Meris initiated pre-stase. The crypt had to be sterilized, so she closed its lid and activated its flash cycle. Next, she keyed for the serum bank and dialed an order for sufficient units of non-aqueous cryoserum to perfuse according to those vitals. Over the crypt, a clear tank started to fill.

A body frozen with normal aqueous blood in the veins would have been destroyed by ice crystals expanding inside and between every delicate cell. Meris momentarily wondered whether the isolated Sanctuary's med center also manufactured the free radical scavengers and other preservatives that cryoserum contained.

Through the open door came the rattling crescendo of a transport sled being wheeled over a stone surface. Saried preceded the patient, looking slightly harried. She'd plainly been busy elsewhere. She looked up to the work station, where crypt and serum tank's status were displayed. "Good job, Meris."

Annalah arrived next, her red river of hair contained by a close-fitting hair tucker over her duty tunic. Sentinel Harris—not the *Daystar's* Captain Harris, she realized, but a younger man—lay aboard the med sled between them, eyes wide, taking gurgling breaths. Sedating him properly would take several minutes.

Instead, Saried strode straight to his head. She curled her hands around it and spoke in a firm voice. "Dusty." The man looked into her eyes. After another ragged breath, his shoulders went still and his face relaxed. The wrinkles over Saried's eyes got darker and deeper, though.

T-sleep? Or something very similar.

The mind rules the body. I choose to continue. As Meris slipped into the Collegium litany for temporary physical strength, she realized this litany might be a help to the frightened Dusty Harris too. Using their mental abilities obviously tired them. Litanies took no effort, actually linking a person with his or her own inner power. Meris stepped forward. "Saried, if Sentinel Harris is conscious at all, I'd like to help him in another way too. Let me teach him a few words, to focus his mind in a positive direction." She leaned toward the crypt.

"Wait." Saried bent over its head end, probably adjusting the supercooling cradle. "Not yet, Meris. I need to hear it first, and I still might need to have it okayed by Minster Wind."

Frustrated, Meris backed away. What *was* their issue with litanies?

Saried and Annalah transferred Sentinel Harris from med sled to crypt. Annalah stepped away, frowning at Meris. Saried deftly inserted the serum cannulas at venous and arterial access points, to drain normal blood and gradually inject temp-controlled cryoserum.

Then the wait began, and the watching of vital signs on the big wall display next to Sentinel Harris's head. Annalah stood against the opposite wall, crossing her arms and pointedly not looking in Meris's direction. She'd never been this defensive on Elysia, especially about Collegiate philosophy. Had her father, the Shamarr, criticized the Collegium?

Saried twisted her body in a slow stretch. "Meris, I need to set up for the antibody clone and check on the Caldwells' suite. You're on watch for ten minutes. Annalah, you're assisting." Clenching her handheld, the medspec hurried out.

Meris stepped to the crypt's head. Annalah pushed away from the wall and took the aide's position near its foot, tucking a stray lock of red hair back into the hair tucker. "Initial check," she called.

Meris nodded, approving. Her room-partner had received basic stasis training, of course, just as Meris had taken basic regen, Annalah's specialty. "Initial check," she answered Annalah, "confirm." Then she too relaxed and stepped closer to the crypt. Sentinel Harris's eyes had closed. "Is he conscious at all?" Meris asked.

Annalah cocked her head. "No. Aunt Saried's got him nearly asleep."

"But not tardema-sleep."

"No."

"Is that a normal procedure here?"

"No. Did you see how tired it made her? But he must have needed to be stabilized. Aunt Saried's probably going to have to pick up a cup of kass before she does anything else. And especially before she goes back to Grandfather. This is probably one of her last chances to talk to him, now that he's . . ."

Meris pitied them, coping with death without the dependably effective litanies. Annalah had been a stellar student back on Elysia, but she'd occasionally seemed lost and homesick. Meris had tried inviting her to Collegiate affairs. She'd declined politely.

Annalah stared at the line of red perfusion lights and furrowed her forehead. "I'm really sorry you're losing him," Meris said. "And really, the litanies—"

"Stop." Annalah turned suddenly, her voice grating, her eyes narrowed. "Your litanies don't belong in this place, and we don't appreciate your trying to turn any of the sekiyrra into little Collegiates."

Startled, Meris looked back at the crypt's in-lid perfusion display. All ten lights remained red, but the left one should change color in about another minute. That outburst hadn't sounded like the Annalah she knew, not at all. She had to be under intense stress.

Meris tried to keep her voice low. "When I see people struggling, I can't just sit there."

The first light turned blue. "Ten percent," Annalah said. "There are some sweet souls among this group of sekiyrra, and one girl came to me in tears last night. She'd been talking to you. Father says—"

"Ten percent, confirmed." Eventually, Meris would need to hear what Annalah's father had told her about the Collegium. Not yet, though. Up on the wall display, Sentinel Harris's blood hemoglobin had started dropping dramatically. Just as it should. "Annalah, I want to help them! You people don't have a monopoly on wisdom. I suspect this is the first time some of those kids ever talked to someone from outside, someone who knows the rest of the Whorl, what's important out there—"

"That's not true." Annalah's voice rose. "My people who still have their abilities spend most of their lives among non-altered people. I spend even more. When we come here, we bring all we've learned—"

"Dismissed," a voice called from the doorway. Meris whirled around to see who was speaking. There stood Saried, brandishing a pottery mug. "Thank you both," she said firmly. "Please continue your discussion elsewhere."

Meris's cheeks heated. That hadn't been ten minutes! Had she been speaking too loudly? Had other patients overheard? She almost said "I'm sorry" before she realized it would be a lie, and these people could detect lies.

They needed help, though, and they were blind to their need. Meris pushed past Annalah and her half-Shuhr supervisor, and she walked out of the med center at a dignified pace.

● ● ●

The late afternoon breeze carried a hint of rain, with grey clouds gathering over the valley. Kiel didn't want to walk far, anyway. He had a right to feel weary. Hadn't he arrived just this morning?

He and Tavkel had almost reached the fence at the end of the Sanctuary compound, walking silently except for their footsteps crunching on gravel. The Sanctuary staffer had handed the walking stick back to Tavkel, and the armed trio followed. Below them in the crop fields, sekiyrra wielded their guhshes and hoes. Above and to their right, scrubby bushes dotted the hillside.

Kiel wondered what the stranger would say if Kiel kept walking silently, but he felt responsible to guide the conversation.

Responsible? What kind of staggering weight was he carrying up this trail? *Guide me,* he prayed for the tenth time—at least— since they'd stepped off the elevator. Up ahead, the compound ended and the hillside grew steeper. He didn't want to go all the way up to the knob and its fire pit.

He glanced aside. Tavkel's sincerity seemed real. Kiel had seen the raw power of shadow possession, though. He'd been whisked instantaneously across the Whorl and kept alive in hard vacuum. He'd been given full Sentinel abilities after years of limping by, and tempted to use them wrongly.

And he'd fallen. Now he walked with his shields dispersed. "So." His voice cracked in his throat. He cleared it and repeated, "So, you're Tiala's son."

"As I said." Kiel sensed an affectionate warmth in Tavkel's voice, which seemed like another positive sign. Tamím had never shown the slightest affection.

Encouraged, he asked more gently, "Did she marry?"

Tavkel planted his walking stick idly with every other step. "No."

"Ah." Kiel wondered how to phrase the next question respectfully. Even if Tavkel proved to be That One, surely it was all right to simply ask, "Who is your father, then?"

They reached the end of the fence. Tavkel turned uphill, on a narrower path that meandered between tufts of last year's grass. "You could say I had six fathers. I was the only child in the community."

Kiel followed, deciding to let Tavkel keep that secret a little longer. After all, Saried's tests would tell them everything, including whether a Mikuhran such as Tamím had provided any chromosomes.

Tavkel didn't look half Mikuhran, though. He had neither the black hair nor the long face.

He stepped off the narrow trail and let Kiel catch up, then stood alongside him. "I can't tell you any more about Tekkumah," he said. "Some things happen there that most people shouldn't know about, simply for their spiritual health."

"It's a dangerous place?" What had they sent his sister into, all trusting, with her breathtaking spirituality? He barely remembered Tiala, but he had loved her.

Tavkel squinted toward the mountains in the westerly distance. As Kiel followed his gaze, a patch of sunlight swept down from one peak, making a snowfield gleam. "Tekkumah is dangerous in ways you can't imagine," Tavkel said. "But so is this place. So is every place."

It was another good answer. Still, Kiel gave the guards an uneasy glance—they'd fanned out, one below them and one on each side. Might a shadow-infested person know how to circumvent blocking drugs? The fact that Kiel hadn't sensed any change in Tavkel's mental state, as they took effect, now seemed ominous. "You're a student of *Dabar* and *Mattah?*" he asked.

"I understand that your father—my grandfather—had a nearly perfect memory. I seem to have inherited it."

"He trained it to be nearly perfect," Kiel insisted, "as a Master Sentinel."

"He couldn't have trained it if he hadn't had outstanding heritable potential."

Kiel nudged the conversation back in his intended direction: interviewing Tavkel. "You know the classic set of prophecies, of course."

"Yes."

He eyed the stranger. Tavkel was no taller than Kiel's father, and he had the muscular arms and shoulders and tanned face of a man who spent much of his life working outdoors. The hand gripping that walking stick looked strong, and a pale old scar crossed it—more evidence of an outdoor life, as was the closely cropped hair. Brown hair and eyes, which reminded Kiel of his mother, Lady Firebird. An otherwise ordinary face . . .

Except for its intensity. Again he thought he'd never seen such intelligent eyes. Traveling with Tamím all those years ago, Kiel had often sensed an enormous superiority. Compared with that blatant power, Tavkel seemed human and ordinary.

On the other hand, a shadow might have impenetrable shields and unprecedented emotional control.

"You feel you have the power to make and unmake the universe?" That seemed unlikeliest, so it was a good place to start. Besides, time and space had seemed meaningless to Tamím. Worthless, even. If a shadow found them irrelevant, why shouldn't their creator control them?

"Yes," Tavkel answered, "but not yet. And not in an expected way."

This amused Kiel. So the boy really was saying he was the long-awaited Boh-Dabar. All right. Kiel would suggest something that might prove even more difficult. "The restoration of justice?"

"Again, in ways you literally cannot imagine."

"Hmm." The Federacy's billions of citizens were scattered on twenty-three worlds. Kiel had often wondered how real justice might ever be administered to all of them.

And one prophecy, plainly unfulfilled, troubled him more than any of the others. In each generation since the great historical Melauk of Ehret, spiritual leaders had argued bitterly about how to interpret it. "Melauk claimed that only a perfect priest would have, in essence, the power and authority to make a sacrifice of all evil." Kiel could not begin to understand what that meant.

"Ah." Tavkel gripped his walking stick with both hands and leaned on it, facing downhill. The sun had vanished behind the distant peaks. The Sanctuary's long skylights were beginning to glow. "Yes."

Kiel stared. "You're claiming that?"

"I am."

There was no doubt, then, who the young man thought he was. Kiel didn't need to ask any further oblique questions. "You're Boh-Dabar." Kiel said it flatly, trying not to encourage either a "yes" or a "no" with his tone of voice.

This time, Tavkel turned to him with a steady stare of his own. "The time has come. Love will triumph, and the Holy One will reign—though you're not ready to face all the implications."

"You're probably right." Kiel certainly wasn't prepared to talk "reign." First, he needed to pursue that topic of sacrifice. Some people thought that his father and mother had fulfilled some of the Boh-Dabar prophecies, but at what a cost! Shuhr had been genuinely evil, but the Golden City's destruction had been horrendous. That could have been considered an altar.

And Kiel still wept each time he passed along a sacred, sacrificial memory during a new convert's consecration: the bloody slaughter of a kipret beside an altar on the lost homeworld. "The idea of sacrifice troubles me," he said.

"It should disturb anyone." Tavkel stared over the valley. The peak's shadows stretched over it, darkening the greens and browns. "The very need for it is tragic. Shamarr, you guide unloving people toward obedience, loving people toward peace, and gifted people toward service. My calling is different. There is peace beyond the sacrifice. Its purpose is reconciliation. It always has been that way." He paused and turned his head. His eyes flicked up and down. "You have walked with a shadow."

Caught unprepared yet again, Kiel glanced at the closest guard. He hoped the Special Ops man was too far away to have heard. "What makes you say that?" he whispered.

"For one thing," Tavkel said in a low voice, "Tekkumah is always informed. They know who is in danger. They actually participated in the Holy One's promise to protect you on Mikuhr. The event was recorded in our chronicles."

"How did they know?" Kiel forced himself to keep breathing normally.

Tavkel shook his head. "Tekkumah needs to keep its secrets a little longer. But speaking with the dark ones also leaves effects I can see."

Kiel fell silent. Because of that terrible episode, Kiel had long known he was *not* the long-awaited one. Even now, feeling the calm patience beside him through his scattered epsilon shields, he wondered whether he ought to explain why his very abilities were tainted, and that he'd done all that a mere mortal could hope to do.

However, he'd confessed all that to the Holy One years ago. He did not need to achieve perfection. Only Boh-Dabar . . .

Yes. If Boh-Dabar had to be perfect, maybe this was the best test to apply to young Tavkel. If they caught him in any offense against current laws or ancient traditions, then his claim was downright blasphemous. They must impound him and perhaps put him on trial.

But what if he *were* Boh-Dabar? Was Kiel grasping for reasons to condemn someone whose power could change the universe? "Have you ever met one?" He watched Tavkel closely. "One of the shadows?"

Tavkel appeared to wince. "Yes. Yesterday, as I walked here from Tekkumah."

"Did it follow you?" Kiel looked up the valley again. The Sanctuary might be in danger from yet another source.

Tavkel shook his head. "You can't be perfectly safe anywhere, any more than you can be perfectly obedient or give perfect service. You can only turn to the One in faith."

"What did it do?" Kiel pressed.

"I'll tell you, some day." Tavkel planted his stick in the ground. "I appreciate the role you're asked to fulfill, Shamarr, and how much it intimidates you. You are respected and deeply loved, here and elsewhere. Walk carefully, though."

Vaguely offended, Kiel looked up at reddening clouds. Time was passing. Blue-green patches of light shone up out of the sky-lights, and his father lay dying. He needed to get back. "Tavkel, what would you want me to do? What would you see as my role?"

"Leave your own path. Walk mine."

Kiel bristled. "I haven't walked my own path since I was sworn into the priesthood."

"You do," Tavkel said, "and you have. And I would also ask you to give me something."

"What?" Kiel asked, startled by how deeply Tavkel offended him. He'd led a highly disciplined life. He hadn't been able to afford luxuries for his family, because he had followed a profession defined by centuries of believers.

"Give me everything you are, both good and evil, but especially that darkness that made you decide you aren't the Eternal Speaker's Dabar."

The idea overwhelmed him with longing. If only it were possible! "Give it to you? I can't do that."

Tavkel spread his hands. "Our family is full of odd talents, isn't it? This is mine. Ownership can be transferred with just a word."

"But that makes no sense," Kiel said dully. The Sanctuary's young visitor was inventing things. Nowhere in the holy books had *this* been mentioned.

"You are correct. This is new."

Kiel frowned, alarmed that Tavkel seemed to have followed his thoughts again. He stared at Tavkel's tanned face: the strong cheekbones, the brilliant eyes under full, dark brows, the sunburned forehead and nose. *Was* the young man possessed? Did Kiel stand in front of another shadow creature, who hungered for others' inner darkness and fed on their fear?

"The human mind," Tavkel said, "even the altered mind at full power, can't comprehend what the Eternal Speaker intends to do. Federates, Collegiates, and Sentinels could debate this for decades without understanding it any better. What matters is that you are loved, although none of you is fit to stand in front of real perfection.

"In other words," he said, and finally, Kiel felt the other man's emotions shift toward urgency, "you have to trust me to deal with details. Trust the Eternal Speaker you serve, if you don't yet trust me."

Glancing up at the darkening clouds, Kiel wished he could share this baffling responsibility of discernment.

Abruptly he realized that he could. "My father." His thoughts raced. "Your grandfather. He used to be one of the very strongest Sentinels. He was specifically trained to look into other people's minds, at their memories, worldview, and intentions." Kiel hadn't realized the kind of skill and training a *Class Three Intelligence Qualification* implied until he was in College himself. "And he used to be able to control the fused energies of accessing a Netaian ayin. But he's dying. Radiation poisoning."

Tavkel's chin tilted down, toward the strengthening blue-green lights in the roof panels below them.

"Would you be willing—if he's willing," Kiel added, hoping his father would have enough strength left to do this, "to let him examine you?"

Tavkel shut his eyes and leaned on the staff. "Yes."

Kiel studied him again. Would he have agreed so quickly if he were shadow-influenced? Maybe the shadows still hoped to personally kill his father, avenging the Golden City. The idea made Kiel feel sick, but taking Tavkel to him seemed the best test he could think of.

An inner voice reminded him that a quick death in service might actually be merciful. He strangled the thought. "Let's go back."

Kiel plodded straight downhill, toward the graveled trail they had left. If they were going to do this, they would have to arrive before the young stranger changed his mind and before his father died. At the gravel path, he let Tavkel catch up. He hurried toward the elevator building, followed by the guards with their crunching footsteps.

CHAPTER 12

Something shimmered over Jorah's left shoulder. He turned toward it, and impossibly, he seemed to be looking into the duracrete wall— maybe a meter beyond its grey surface. "Did you talk to him?" He glanced left and right. If this visitor had disabled listening devices before, it should be pulling the same trick now. "Uncle Kiel?"

"He is relieved that you are unharmed." Speaking from inside the wall instead of midair, the voice had less shimmer and more of a subaudible growl. "He asks you to greet his colleague, Chancellor Gambrel."

"Oh." Jorah's thoughts tumbled, first toward the startled sus- picion that this creature hadn't spoken to Uncle Kiel at all, but was lying—into fear, that his shieldless suspicion would be read—and finally, he remembered that supernatural spirits allegedly couldn't read minds. His parents had always said mind-access had been the Eternal Speaker's exclusive right, before his people had co-opted it.

Still, Uncle Kiel had never called Gambrel a "colleague." He'd actually accused the man of collusion with dark spirits. "Where is he?" Jorah whispered, increasingly suspicious.

"At Sanctuary, with his father."

It was a terrible reminder. Outside this cell, other people were going on with their lives. And their deaths. Jorah gave his knuckles a crack. "How's Grandfather?"

"He is sinking, Jorah. The fate of all men is upon him."

Jorah slumped. "I won't get there before he dies. Will I?"

"You will do better than that, lord. You will create a new Whorl where his descendants honor his memory." After a pause, the voice added, "Your uncle is delighted, though. He had planned to gather your people and flee from the Whorl, as they previously fled Ehret. Instead, you will be restored to prestige and power."

Maybe. Jorah straightened. "Where's Chancellor Gambrel? And what did Uncle Kiel say about those medical people?"

"The Chancellor is investigating a new communications technology. He is thrilled by its potential for your use. As for the medical people," the voice said, and Jorah thought he caught a hesitation, "he defers to your wisdom."

Jorah stared at the vibrating wall. The blocking drugs hadn't affected his emotional control. He still was able to keep his face strictly passive. He didn't feel any particular wisdom, though. He knew only that none of that "message" had the lofty but affectionate tone he'd expected from Uncle Kiel.

Still, maybe Uncle Kiel hadn't realized until this moment who and what Jorah actually was. Jorah wanted to be alone with these thoughts. "Thank you," he whispered.

Instantly, the wall stopped vibrating and fell silent.

Jorah blew out a breath, relieved to be left alone with his suspicion that the visitor had been shooting thoughts into his mind. And he'd forgotten to ask about escape again! Plainly, the visitor was managing him. In that case, he couldn't trust its reports.

Well, he'd been trained by exceptional people. He perched on the bed, hugged his knees, and tried to think. If he were his people's new spiritual and military leader, that called for a new maturity. Was it possible that the best plan would mean cooperating with Gambrel's cronies? He had to consider that first. From inside their power circles, could he demand better treatment for Special Operations and funding for the Sentinel College? Would it be possible to work alongside sympathetic Tallans and remake the Whorl according to justice and goodness, not financial convenience?

No! To abdicate any part of his humanity and bow to some other person's judgment—it just felt wrong. Even if he couldn't hope to win, he mustn't surrender. He had only two options: escape or suicide.

Escape, then. Preferable. And he would not trust the manipulative sparkle-voice to help him.

Heart pounding, he reached deep inside himself for control over his body and mind. With those controls firmly in place, he ran through a set of motionless isometric exercises to warm his muscles.

He got up and walked to the transparent door.

The hall was empty. He touched the glassy call light, leaned against the wall next to the door, and waited. Within less than a minute, one guard appeared. Cautiously elated, Jorah motioned for him to open the door. The guard reached down toward the locking panel, but instead of sliding the door open, he had apparently activated a speaker circuit. "What do you want?" The voice came from one of the cell walls.

"I'm ready to talk with Chancellor Gambrel's Tallan friend." Jorah kept his own voice low and serious. "Colonel Zeimsky. Would you take me to him?"

"Just a minute." The guard turned smartly and walked away to the left.

Jorah exhaled. It had been unrealistic to hope that the guard wouldn't call for backup. He still had a good chance against two, though.

The guard returned. A partner stood back, stun pistol at the ready. Jorah kept his shoulders slumped and his weight unevenly balanced, trying to look unready and unthreatening. But every muscle was taut. He would get just one chance.

The door slid aside. He barreled through, grabbed the near guard and shifted his weight. Without waiting for that one to hit the ground, Jorah seized the second guard's wrist, dodging stun bursts.

The second guard threw his weight left. Jorah let himself be thrown, but he pulled the guard down with him. He rolled, taking the guard over and under, and grabbed for the wrist again.

This time, he came up with the stun pistol. He fired. Still rolling, he fired again, this time at the first guard, who had almost gotten back upright. That one fell on his belly.

Jorah bolted up the corridor. At its familiar bend, he turned in the direction Gambrel hadn't taken him. He dashed toward a recessed doorway and paused to breathe and get his bearings. There'd been a processing desk and a narrow security corridor between here and freedom. He couldn't hope to get out that way. At any moment, surveillance monitors would alert someone to his empty cell.

Actually, they probably already knew he was loose. He glanced down at the stun pistol, satisfied himself that it was well charged, and hoped for more than one way out. A service elevator, maybe.

He turned to sprint up a side way. Finally, a siren wailed. He kept running. A maximum stun burst could kill an adult at short range. Death still might be his only escape, especially if he threatened his family by surviving.

A second siren started wailing at a hideous, bloodcurdling interval from the first. They were using sonics, sound waves that would build in his brain to drop him like a stone. T-sleep was the standard defense. It was no hope to him without his abilities.

Silently cursing, he spun and charged back toward the processing desk. The walls seemed to be turning to liquid and flowing down toward his feet. His head was swelling, would explode, would kill him—but they wouldn't let it do that.

Gritting his teeth against pain that he simply wanted to end, he gripped the stun pistol two-handed and brought it to his chin. If he died, Chancellor Gambrel couldn't use him against the rest of his people. This was better. Better, he repeated as his vision turned black at the edges. *Better . . .*

● ● ●

He rose painfully back up to consciousness, feeling much sicker than he'd been when they'd stunned him the first time. He tried to dive deeper, to hide from his pounding head in unconscious darkness.

"Won't work, Lieutenant," a voice said. "We know you're awake."

Jorah forced himself to relax, breathe slowly, regather his strength. Whatever happened next, he needed to meet it fully conscious. He opened his eyes. Sure enough, Chancellor Gambrel's medical crony—the one with the colonel's quadruple sleeve stripes—stood close to Jorah's hip, while a brilliant lamp dangled over his chest. Two men and a woman in plain medical attire stood in a group behind Gambrel's friend. He thought he glimpsed more Tallan grey beyond them.

"Thank you," Colonel Zeimsky said wryly, "for getting our research back on schedule. The delays were truly irritating. Don't worry, by the way—you won't remember this conversation, nor trying to escape. You've got a big future ahead, and you'll need to focus on what you're doing, not what we're doing to you. I almost envy you."

Jorah grunted. Memory-modifying drugs were illegal, except when military security was at stake.

Zeimsky raised an eyebrow, the one with the odd gap in it. "Our binary treatment, assuming it works, is going to save your life. Because while we're in there, we're also going to infect you with a new bacillus. It can produce a systemic toxin inside artificially created organelles. It won't harm you at all, since your ayin, as you call it, will be dead tissue by then. But you're going to shed spores with every breath.

"And that," he said, "will be how you remake the Whorl and wipe out something truly evil—a race of nonhuman parasites who have dominated the rest of us far too long."

Jorah frantically searched his memory for ways to beat mind-altering drugs. Every one of them involved using his ayin. He had to remember this!

"The bugs have an incubation period of several weeks, so no one's going to suspect you're the one spreading it. Not until the die-off begins." Nothing in the man's expression or body language gave Jorah any hope he was lying. Grimacing, Jorah tried to flex his left arm. It was cuffed to the table he lay on.

"We'll speak again, Lieutenant." Zeimsky nodded to the med attendants and backed out of the room.

The attendants moved closer.

• • •

Kiel hurried his guest into his half sister's medical corridor. Saried must have been alerted as they re-entered the compound, because she stood just inside the main arch. Before Kiel could take Tavkel to his father's bedside, she waved them into a private conference room and motioned them to wooden seats. "I have the full DNA analysis," she said.

"We can't take long." Kiel remained standing, shifting his weight from one foot to the other. "I'm going to ask Father to inter-view him."

Saried remained close to the door. "We did rerun the mito-chondrial scan. It's clear and conclusive, Tavkel. You're maternally descended from Tiala Caldwell and her mother, Firebird Angelo Caldwell, both of whom have full mitochondrial scans on record."

Tavkel sank into a chair and rested his walking stick against one of his legs. "And then, it gets complicated."

"Oh, yes." Saried pursed her lips. Kiel caught a subvocalized thought. *Complicated doesn't begin to describe it.*

Surely his cloistered brethren hadn't practiced gene tampering at the prayer retreat! Aloud, Kiel said, "Can we save details for later? This is urgent."

She nodded. "Essentially, we still have no idea who contributed the Y chromosome, or the paternal chromosome in any of the other gene pairs. Half of his chromosomes show absolutely no breakage or cross-linkage. Those are markers we normally use to trace inheritance over the centuries.

"And Tavkel," she said, turning aside, "the end sections of those chromosomes—the telomeres—are longer than any newborn's I've ever seen. If no other factors controlled aging, you're theoretically immortal. You could live several hundred years, anyway."

Kiel shook his head, trying to remember what telomeres were. Didn't they have something to do with the number of times a cell could divide before it eventually lost the ability?

"In other words," Saried continued, eyeing Tavkel, "your paternal genes are medically ancient. As I read them, the first human ever born could have been your father."

A chill settled on the room. Kiel shivered. Was Tavkel the spawn of a shadow? If the shadow who'd possessed Tamím could have physically impregnated a woman, the possibility was almost too frightening to consider.

"None of this matters, of course." Tavkel spoke softly.

Saried glanced up as someone hurried past the conference room's door. "Who did they tell you your father was?"

Tavkel spoke toward Kiel, as if he were the one who'd asked the question. "My mother said I had no father in the normal sense. I don't suppose you want to suggest parthenogenesis."

Distracted, Kiel shot a subvocal *What?* at his half sister.

"Woman gives birth to her own clonal offspring, without help." She flicked silvered hair away from her face. "We see parthenogenesis in some animal species. But the offspring is always female, since only a father can donate a Y chromosome."

Kiel considered that. A mysterious birth was suggested in one scriptural prediction. Still, that was a common poetic form among ancient cultures, and not necessarily to be taken literally. He believed that the prediction simply restated Boh-Dabar's mythic importance.

At least the ancient genes and startling telomeres didn't suggest that Tavkel had Mikuhran ancestors—but they did nothing to dispel his darker suspicion. Kiel turned back to Saried. "Thank you. Now, I want Father to do mind access if he's willing. He survived contact with Mother's reversed carrier several times." Kiel would stand ready too, to stop anything that looked too dangerous.

Saried nodded. "I was going to send you to him now, anyway."

Kiel led them up the bright corridor back to his father's room.

As before, his mother sat at the bedside, her face set in a weary smile. His father lay almost upright, leaning on several cushions. His face had less color than at lunchtime, but his eyes retained their blue brilliance.

"Father?" Kiel crossed his arms. "Have they told you Tiala's boy is here?"

"Yes." To Kiel's relief, the voice still was strong. "Wind says that Tavkel has been telling you interesting things." His father's eyes flicked toward Kiel's right, and so Kiel assumed that Saried and Tavkel had entered behind him. "Tavkel, come in. It's good to know I have another grandson."

Saried hung back. Tavkel handed her his staff and took two steps forward, his rough brown work shirt and pants looking out of place in the medical suite. Obviously, Saried wasn't worried about contaminants.

"I'm also told that you're cursed with the reversed-polarity carrier," Kiel's father said, "but they've medicated you." The old man reached leftward. Kiel's mother seized his left hand between both of her own.

Tavkel took the last steps to the bedside and stopped just short of its white railing. "Sir," he said, and Kiel approved of his respectful tone. "My mother has prayed all her life for your wisdom, courage, and safety. Before I left Tekkumah, she asked me to greet you. Both of you," he added. Kiel's mother—Tavkel's grandmother—stared back with a possessive smile.

"Sir," he repeated, looking down at the face on the pillow, "I know what you're being asked to do. May I ask you to change the order?" To Kiel's shock, that sounded more like a command than a question. "Rather than claiming authority over me, are you willing to come under mine?"

Kiel almost stepped forward to rebuff the question.

His father half smiled, though. "Why, Tavkel?"

Tavkel glanced over his shoulder at Kiel. He turned to Saried and inclined his head toward his grandmother. Then he placed both hands on the white bedrail to address his grandfather. "You've lived an exemplary life, and every warrior at Tekkumah would stand at this bedside and salute you. But even you have carried the darkness that plagues humanity. You have acted against higher authority."

Kiel stepped forward. Enough!

His father waved him away. "Of course I have." As Kiel's father looked back up at Tavkel, one eye widened oddly, and Kiel realized that if the radiation hadn't stolen his eyebrows, that gesture would have raised one of them. "Why would that change my authority to access-question you?"

"Not your authority, but your responsibility. That is the change, Grandfather. If I am to make a sacrifice of all evil, then I have a unique authority. I can take away everything that has made you less than perfectly human, if you'll allow it."

Kiel's father gave a short laugh, and his mother sat up straighter. Kiel couldn't guess what had just passed between them on the pair bond.

"It's not necessary," Tavkel added, "if you want to simply do the inquiry. Still, if you decline you'll miss something unique."

None of this made sense. To Kiel's surprise, that very confusion almost convinced him. Some of the canonical prophets made little sense on a first reading, a second reading, or even a tenth. Simple explanations of infinite issues always made him wonder what had been left out.

Meanwhile, his father kept staring at Tavkel. The old man's prodigious abilities had been waning for decades, but he certainly would have been able to tell if Tavkel were trying to deceive him.

Tavkel tilted his face. For an instant, he looked oddly regal. "All your life," he murmured, "you have wielded authority under authority. I have the authority to ask for your loyalty and the ownership of your darkness."

Oddly, his father's eyes widened. He lifted his free hand as if he'd heard something Kiel hadn't.

"Tavkel," Kiel said sternly, "don't waste his time."

Again, Kiel's mother and father shared a long glance. Kiel sensed that whatever Father had asked her subvocally, it had startled her. "Very well," the old man said, "on your terms. Sit down. Close to me, please."

Kiel spotted a metal stool and pushed it toward the bed. Tavkel sank onto it without letting go of the bedrail. Kiel took a short step backward, wanting but not daring to disperse his ayin shields again. If carrier fusion exploded out of the impending contact, almost anything might happen. He admired his parents' courage.

Those familiar blue eyes stared up at Tavkel, but Kiel couldn't see Tavkel's face from this angle. He sidestepped to the bed's foot, getting closer to his mother. If she fell into bereavement shock, he would need to catch her. Some of the elderly actually died of bereavement.

His father's eyes closed. Kiel guessed he was focusing the mental probe. The room fell silent.

Tavkel spoke. "Again and again you offered yourself willingly. Now, be the first to receive."

His father opened his eyes, again staring at Tavkel. He drew a deep breath. Kiel's mother dropped his hand. Kiel lunged for her arm, but she slid away from him and scrambled up onto her feet, gaping at the wall display.

Kiel gaped too. Bloodstream chemicals, cellular debris, gastrointestinal neuron function . . . every danger sign had vanished.

Kiel dared to disperse his mental shields. There'd been no explosion of fusion energy. In fact, there was absolutely no ayin activity in his father's direction, not even a shielding cloud. His mother stood blinking down at the bed, pressing one hand over her mouth. Kiel stepped to the foot rail, daring to probe.

His father had just lost his remaining Sentinel power. All of it.

"He's regained latency!" Saried gaped up at the glimmering vitals board and down at her handheld, as if comparing readouts.

"No." Kiel's mother grabbed the side rail. "No, look." She plucked a strip of biotape off her husband's neck. "Look at this. The burn's gone. That is healthy skin." She stared across the bed into Tavkel's face. "You healed him. You said 'everything that has made you less than perfectly human.' This is exactly what he would have been, without . . . without the ancestors' gene tampering, isn't it?"

Shaking his head, Tavkel reached down to clasp his grandfather's hand. Kiel's father's face was a map of smile lines. "Whatever you did," he said in a gasping voice, "I thank you."

Appalled, Kiel backed away from the bed. Maybe Tavkel didn't think he needed an ayin, but no prophecy had suggested that Boh-Dabar might take power *away!*

• • •

Fi Caldwell grabbed her husband's other hand, assuring herself that he was warm and living. In an instant, she'd lost the second presence that had lived for decades at the edge of her mind. In the emotional resonance of pair bonding, there'd been doubled joys, doubled pains—and yes, doubled embarrassments.

He lay there right next to her, but her Brennen-sense had vanished.

She would've recognized the choking pain of bereavement shock. Instead, they had shared a final, vivid emotion that still ricocheted through her heart and made her hands tremble: He'd felt absolute certainty.

No one else in this room might be convinced that here, finally, stood the one they had waited for—but her Brennen knew.

She'd felt the exact offer Tavkel had made him. Since Brennen lay shackled by medical attachments and couldn't get up, she gently freed her hand from his and stepped around the bed's foot, between her beloved, distracted son Kiel and dear Saried. She eased down stiffly onto her knees, since Brennen could not. "That darkness," she said, "I have no trouble believing it's there. Take mine, please."

She clasped her grandson's free hand. It felt rough and warm. He pulled her onto her feet. "I own it now. Thank you."

Standing unsteadily, she held on to him. It was her grandson. Not one of her sons, after all, but her grandson—after she'd given up hope of seeing Tiala ever again! At the back of her mind soared a melody she'd first imagined years ago, when she had transferred her loyalty from mythical Netaian powers to One she'd learned to call the Mighty Singer.

"MedSpec Saried," Tavkel said, and his voice spoke the same notes that she was hearing, "do I smell dinner out in the commons? Grandfather's hungry."

That was when Fi Caldwell sensed the vague irritation that normally signaled her life mate's appetite. She was feeling Brennen's emotions.

Glory! Had Tavkel healed and restored *her* ayin as she knelt?

She spun around to look at her Brennen. He'd swung his legs over the side of the bed and was sitting upright, pulling the lifesigns transmitter off his chest. His secretive smile told her that everything may have changed, but that it was fine with him.

● ● ●

Feeling unneeded, Kiel touched Saried's shoulder and backed out of the suite. When they stood alone in the white stone corridor, he muttered, "Where's Kinnor?"

Saried still gripped her handheld and Tavkel's walking stick. "Wind would know. I don't."

"Fielding station," he guessed. Kin needed to be told that their father probably wasn't going to die anytime soon. This was incredible news, though it came at a baffling price. He shook his head, grasping at too many bewildering ideas. First, the unusual chromosomes. Now, a spontaneous healing—apparently at the cost of a complete loss of ayin powers—and his father hadn't declared the young man a fraud, which Kiel now realized he'd expected. Instead, Father had watched, smiling, as Mother got down on her knees.

Tavkel had won his first converts. Kiel recalled hearing Tavkel say he'd done some "unusual things" recently. What else might he do?

Saried raised her handheld. "I'll contact Wind and get Kinnor sent in."

"Good." Kiel clenched a hand at his side, deeply uneasy.

• • •

An hour later, Wind stood staring at her father-in-law. He sat upright on a white stone bench on the largest island, stroking his wife's hand. All the biotape was gone from his neck, though he still looked odd without eyebrows. He'd put on a rough brown work shirt. Apparently it wasn't irritating his neck. That skin had *healed.*

Tavkel stood close by. Looking for family resemblances by the dim turquoise glow around the pool's edge, Wind spotted Lady Fi's eyes and the High Commander's facial planes. Saried had quietly told her that there didn't seem to be any of the Mikuhran inheritance she and Wind shared. Still, the mysterious chromosomes remained unexplained.

Seven people had gathered around this bench: Tavkel, his grandparents, Kiel with Hanusha, Wind and her husband Kinnor. Within an hour of the High Commander's emergence from the med center, rumors had flashed through the Sanctuary like an explosion. It was almost midnight. Overhead lights still burned in the dining commons across the water. Out here under darkened skylights, kirka trees overhead gave off a spicy scent. Their stout trunks almost filled the planters on this island. The spiky leaves of a few spring bulbs poked up through the soil in the closest planter's near corner.

Wind breathed deeply, staying calm.

Whether or not he was Boh-Dabar, Tavkel displayed an incredible talent, even with a bloodstream full of blocking drugs. Saried had taken him through the medical corridor, where he'd healed everyone and emptied every bed. Annalah, Meris and other medical staff would spend the rest of this evening reviving stasis patients, and tomorrow, they could all be sent topside with the planting and pruning crews.

Kinnor paced back and forth in front of the senior Caldwells' bench. His excitement—reaching her on the pair bond as a strong scent of menthe—threatened to make her giddy. "What we need is an expanded defense force," he insisted. "Kids who were going to take the medical option won't be needed, now that you're here." He pointed at Tavkel. "We need to defend you until you're ready to take command.

"So," Kinnor said, spreading his hands toward the bench. Wind felt his urgency flicker like uncontrolled heat. "Father, you're our senior officer. You're the obvious leader for a bigger force."

"Thank you," Father said, "but I'm finished with combat. Have you asked Tavkel whether he wants to be trained in military command?"

Wind's cheeks flushed. That was exactly what she'd asked Kin, as they'd crossed the stepping stones to reach this largest island.

Again, Kinnor ignored the question. "I'm sorry. Well, Colonel Harris offered to lead in case you declined, Father. Meanwhile, we need to bring Jorah back from Tallis." He turned around. "Tavkel."

Tavkel stood close by, and Wind glanced past his shoulders at the crowd of late night snackers in the commons. Everyone near the waterside sat with his or her head turned this way. She caught a faint whiff of quickbreads and kass.

"Would you come to Tallis with me?" Kinnor asked.

Tavkel shook his head. "Tallis will send Jorah here, after his hearing."

Wind frowned. Was Tavkel predicting the future—was he a *shebiyl* user? Future gazing was proscribed as evil in the holy books. Those mysterious chromosomes still didn't rule out shadow possession.

She tried to catch Kiel's eye, but he stood frowning at Tavkel. Maybe he'd also caught that apparent misstep.

But was it a misstep? If Tavkel had genuine links with the Eternal Speaker, it might be his privilege and responsibility to foresee things that the rest of them must not.

Her husband turned toward the stepping stone path. "Fine, then. There's a *Brumbee* in the hangar. I'll bring him back."

"Kinnor," Tavkel said. Wind was startled to hear a tone of authority she associated with his freshly healed grandfather. "If you go back to Tallis, you'll die there."

Kinnor's chin came up.

Kiel stepped away from Hanusha, his frown suddenly deeper. "Do you claim to see the future?"

"Do you feel that would be my right," Tavkel answered, "if I am the Boh-Dabar you expect?"

Appalled, Wind waited for Kiel's answer. Whatever the old people thought about Tavkel, her own generation needed to talk this over. Quickly.

Hanusha broke out of the circle. She strode out across the stepping stones, headed toward the commons.

"We will speak again," Kiel said. "Later." He turned and followed his wife.

Wind still stood speechless, torn between competing fears. If Tavkel could predict events, Kinnor mustn't leave the Sanctuary.

Kinnor raised a hand in a salute. He spun around and headed off on another stepping stone path. This one led toward her office and then the hangars.

She recovered the use of her legs a few seconds later and followed him, catching up on the last stepping stone before the main walkway.

"He's cocky," Kinnor said. "I like that."

"Kin." She stepped off the last stone and onto the siding. "If he's a prophet, you can't go back to Tallis. And if he's using the *shebiyl*, then we need you right here."

"Oh, climb down." He spoke loudly in a voice she'd heard too many times. "If he's who he says he is, he hasn't got Shuhr imitation magic. That's the real thing. And if he really is Boh-Dabar, we're about to be front-and-center in the Federacy again."

Wind spread her hands. "Kinnor, he took power away from your father. Think! Do you believe he could be a leader you want to follow, if he does that kind of thing? And if he is real," she added, "you can't go to Tallis. You mustn't."

Kinnor laughed and tugged his uniform tunic straight. "Tavkel might be Boh-Dabar, but he's going to need to be educated. Just because Father lost his abilities, that doesn't mean anyone else will." He glanced back toward the island. "Look at that."

Kinnor's parents lingered with Tavkel, heads bowed as if praying together.

"Tavkel's already got the kind of authority people will follow. My parents have met every minister, diplomat, councilor, and administrator from here to Elysia, and they'd fly into the sun for him already. It's our golden moment, Wind. He'll figure things out. Don't get in the way."

"You've been ordered to stay here, Kin! You're under protective custody!"

He drew up stiffly, almost standing at attention. "The people who gave that order have turned against us. So the order's invalid."

The world seemed to be rocking underfoot. "They'll still enforce it," she said. "Please. Please, don't do this." He could not believe in Tavkel and yet still ignore that prediction . . . could he?

Yes. Yes, he could. Simply because he was Kinnor.

He turned his back and walked away.

Wind remained on the siding and watched his strides lengthen as he hurried toward the hangars.

Icy fingers wrapped around her midsection. She'd been trained to make difficult choices, and she knew her responsibility. To protect Kinnor from himself—and everyone on Procyel from

Federate reprisals—she must follow her own orders and have him put into stasis. He wouldn't go peacefully. She must order her security staff to have him stunned, and the sooner they caught him, the better.

On second thought, he'd be watching for just such a move. He might drop his guard after he got involved in preflight preps.

The thought of seeing him lying stunned and helpless made her weep inside. Still—her mind worked relentlessly—at her desk, she could override any security circuits he set up. Whoever Security sent down to the hangar, they must stun him on sight.

She drew a deep breath that turned to a yawn. Midnight must have come and gone. She would have to thank Tavkel for making her duty clear. If he hadn't made that prediction, she might have been tempted to send Kin away with her wholehearted blessing. No, if he was determined to break arrest, she must protect him.

Still, they could end up exiled here together for life. If any harm came to Jorah, she would blame herself. Kinnor would blame himself too. And her, for preventing him.

So be it. This is the right thing to do. She must trust that somehow, things would work out.

Wind had learned emotional control at the Sentinel College. She focused on an exercise she'd often needed when Kinnor was at the Sanctuary as she hurried toward her office.

• • •

Meris sat resting her forearms on a wooden dining table, staring over the water. Air Master Kinnor Caldwell strode through a door that had always been closed. Minster Wind was headed the other way, toward her office. The elder Caldwells and the mysterious healer were already talking again.

"Meris? Meris Cariole?"

She turned toward the voice. Near her table, the Shamarr and his wife stood towering over her. She sprang up. "Shamarr. Ma'am. I'm pleased to meet you at last."

The Shamarr solemnly clasped her hand.

So did his wife. "Hanusha Caldwell," she said. "I am sorry. We should have met sooner, but I am sure you understand."

Meris nodded and glanced back at the island. Not far from the planter and that huge drooping tree, the senior Caldwells still stood shoulder to shoulder with the newcomer. "It's been a long, bizarre day. I'm sure you've been in the midst of it." A mug of herb tea curdled in her stomach. All around her, exultant Sentinels had been chattering about becoming the Whorl's new rulers—about provoking the Federacy, getting back the respect they'd lost. "You must be delighted by all those instantaneous healings."

They looked at each other. To Meris, those glances did not look delighted. Interesting.

"Plainly," Meris said, "healing people is only a small part of what some of your people think this . . . stranger can do."

"His claims are yet to be confirmed." The Shamarr shook his head slowly. "Even his healing abilities could—must be evaluated."

Very interesting. Meris glanced from the Shamarr to his wife, then back toward the island. No one had moved over there.

The Shamarr bent toward Meris. "True healing, especially of the heart, is more often solemn and slow. If you ever feel the need for counsel and comfort, I am at your service."

What? "Oh," she said. "Oh. Annalah must have told you. About my parents."

"Indeed yes." He gave her a solemn nod.

She raised her head, wishing she could be anywhere else in the Whorl. "Thank you, Shamarr. I have litanies for that. But the offer is appreciated."

Hanusha Caldwell barely frowned. She touched her husband's arm. "It's late. We all need to sleep."

"Yes." Shamarr Caldwell made a quarter-bow toward Meris. "Whether or not you want counsel, Meris, I look forward to getting to know you."

They walked away, arm in arm.

Meris sat down again, not even slightly sleepy. The excited buzz of conversation went on at the tables around her.

" . . . respect, like in the old days . . ."

" . . . Well, my parents, back on Tallis . . ."

She drained the cold dregs of her tea. It wouldn't surprise her if these people brought down a fresh war of annihilation, just like their ancestors had done back on Ehret, as soon as their infamous genes had been altered. What would that mean to her parents—to everyone else on Elysia?

I fear what I only imagine—

And with a miraculous healer around, had medical personnel become extraneous? Would they file her away in tardema-sleep after all?

I fear what I only imagine—

This time, at least, there were stasis crypts available.

She clenched a fist on the tabletop. It was too late for litanies. Even stasis—here—no longer sounded safe. Over the last ten days, these people had almost won her over. Almost.

Now, though, she sat watching events that could lead to a war. She had to get away quickly. Either that, or for the sake of everyone else out in the Federacy, she had to stop these people.

For the moment, though, all she could do was stare.

PART TWO

At the last he walks among us,
so that all humanity might be blessed through us
and the Holy One's promises kept.
He shall not falter until he brings justice to all peoples,
though we be struck down and scattered . . .

SHEBET 134, 135A

True, some people still don't feel that the "classical" prophecies said Boh-Dabar
would heal people's bodies. But the prophet Renanah (78–81) plainly said he
would restore broken souls. That wouldn't be obvious to an eyewitness, would it?
But here on Procyel II, we medically proved that he healed several bodies that
even regen couldn't repair. He says he did it to prove he has power over body
and soul, both—over our whole personhood! He says he has authority to reverse
death and decay of both body and soul. He says that he's here partly to show us
what the Eternal Speaker really is like, and that his miracles are like beacons,
meant to get our attention.

I wish you all could be here to see him. But when distance keeps him from
healing your body, you can still bring him your broken soul, can't you? Give him
your darkness. Do it now, before this window closes. He has flung it open to
everyone throughout the Whorl.

He asks me to say this to you today: "Now the Holy One is Lord not just over time and space, but also Lord within them! Come in sorrow, or come rejoicing. But come."

FROM *Procyel Eyewitness Report #6*
DAY 3 OF HIS COMING AMONG US:
ANNALAH CALDWELL

The mind rules the body. I choose to continue.
The mind rules the body. I choose to continue.
The mind rules the body . . .

LITANY 13, FOR PHYSICAL STRENGTH
PIPER GAMBREL, CHANCELLOR
COLLEGIUM FOR HUMAN LEARNING

CHAPTER 13

Kiel had passed a fretful night since his father's miraculous recovery. He sat on the front bench of the Chapter room, feeling hemmed in by the red stone walls and pressed by a crowd of his people. No matter how he looked at what had happened to his father, there was no word for it but "miraculous."

He gazed around his bench. He'd known this room could hypothetically seat 150, and today he believed it. Sentinels in uniform sat shoulder to shoulder with sekiyrra in gowns or tunics. Thyrian refugee families crowded together in their work or off-duty clothes. Sekiyrra who'd arrived on the College shuttle filled the center aisle, sitting on the floor. Some of the youngest ones, up at the front, peered out from under the brocade altar cloths.

Tavkel sat on the red stone steps that led up to the stage, flanked by sekiyrra and looking very much at home. He'd been speaking for most of an hour, alternately earnest and bantering.

Along the left wall under a candle sconce, ten of the Sanctuary's aged had claimed the ends of two benches. Since they could not shield themselves, they normally held separate services. This morning they rejoined the community.

Was it possible Boh-Dabar had come at last—within Kiel's lifetime?

He gripped Hanusha's right hand with his left. Their three daughters sat on his right. With his shields dispersed, he tasted a simmering emotional stew, heavy with the disquieting spice of apprehension. How could this man be Boh-Dabar, after robbing such a gifted man of the abilities that had made him unique even among the Sentinel kindred?

News out of the med center must have swept the Sanctuary last night via handhelds and whispers. People had been streaming into this room since before sunrise. As if to complete the gathering, a door popped slightly open on the platform's left side. Those private doors were epsilon-locked, requiring a passcode. Who had dared . . . ?

His sister-in-law Wind cautiously stepped out into the press of seated people on the stage, wearing her formal brown jacket and followed by—no, that couldn't be his mother behind Wind.

But it was. She wore her silvered hair loose over an old cobalt blue military uniform. All his life, Kiel had felt keenly attuned to her thoughts and emotions. Now he sensed some of the strongest imaginable afterglow. She and Father must've spent the night celebrating his recovery. A flush spread over Kiel's cheeks. His mother had no cause for embarrassment, but Kiel found it too easy to imagine returning to life and strength in his bond mate's company.

The women must have decided they couldn't get close enough using the main doors. Anyway, everyone else seemed to be looking at Tavkel, who sat silently a few meters from Kiel's bench, listening to a sekiyr's long, convoluted question.

" . . . and so if Boh-Dabar really is the very essence of the Eternal Speaker's unseen nature, then what *is* . . ."

One of the youngsters under the altar giggled.

"No, I'm serious! We've been told . . ."

Kiel craned his neck and looked for his brother. Kinnor rarely bothered with spiritual sessions. He sometimes even missed regular Chapter. He was probably down at the security station, implementing some of the plans he and their father had come up with.

And had their other outsider also come?

Yes . . . Meris stood against the back wall where she could escape quickly, the poor fearful thing. She'd knotted her hair in a severe-looking bunch again.

"Watch me. I'll show you."

A wave of whispers and murmurs rose and fell. On Kiel's left side, Hanusha's emotions—carried via the pair bond—shifted from confused to decisive. Tavkel had apparently given the sekiyr a short, provocative answer while Kiel had been checking the room.

Hanusha stood up off the bench and cleared her throat. "Excuse me, Tavkel, but don't the holy books predict a significant change in physical existence, some cosmic catastrophe?"

"Yes," Tavkel said, "the universe will be renewed. Don't be afraid, though. Keep walking the Path you're called to walk. Not too far behind me, but never ahead."

Two sekiyrra close to Tavkel nudged each other, grinning. Kiel guessed they thought this was a grand apocalyptic adventure. Personally he felt more like the white-haired elder sitting near the first candle sconce, frowning and shaking her head. Could this truly be . . . him?

A young voice came from under the altar. "Sir? So we've finally cleansed ourselves of the genetic sins, right, sir? We've served unaltered humanity long enough. It's time to call them in. Finally."

That was the prediction, more or less, as Kiel had taught it for twenty years: Their kindred would not die out until the Eternal Speaker had conquered and blessed all peoples through them. Until then, they'd been forbidden to proselytize outside Sentinel families. All cross-cultural outreach had been done by non-Sentinels, including his royal cousin on Netaia.

Tavkel craned his neck, smiling with obvious enthusiasm. "Yes and no. You have parts of that wrong," he told the sekiyr. Then he beckoned toward Kiel's mother and Wind. "Let these people through. Scoot aside, please."

Faces turned and sekiyrra shifted, creating an odd oscillation of dipping heads and shoulders. Kiel's mother led the way across the stage. Her posture was markedly straighter than most of the other elders, especially in that old uniform.

Tavkel turned back toward the seated assembly. "You've heard rumors about High Commander Caldwell. Now listen. That man lost only his training. Not his abilities. His ayin is intact."

Startled, Kiel kept monitoring the room. Ripples of excitement and relief started at several spots and spread as people realized that they might not face such a terrible choice. Kiel frowned slightly. Whatever Tavkel was, he had plainly realized that he'd win few converts if people had to permanently relinquish their precious abilities.

But could this be true about his father? Was he simply starting over, with the same prodigious potential? He needed to have Saried run a brain scan.

My father is not going to die today. For that I owe Tavkel my gratitude.

Trailed closely by Wind, Kiel's mother reached the steps. Sekiyrra squeezed closer together to make space for them. His mother sat down first, so Wind ended up beside this young man who might be the very spoken word, "Dabar" in its literal sense, of the Eternal Speaker. Wind's jacket grazed the work shirt he had worn on his trek from the prayer retreat. For one moment, Kiel wished that he too could sit with Tavkel and make up his mind, for himself, alone.

"Listen," Tavkel said again, clasping tanned hands in his lap. "Remember that thick darkness still separates you from the Holy

One. Still, the talents your ancestors developed have now been revealed as part of his design. You will simply learn new ways."

Another rush of whispers swept the room. "And." Tavkel raised a hand, and the whispers faded away. "As you heard, High Commander Caldwell was asked to touch my mind and discern whether I am, in fact, the Dabar. Here sits his bond mate, who witnessed it. What will he tell them, my Lady Grandmother?" Tavkel leaned forward to look beyond Wind.

Kiel was struck by how ordinary that posture made him look. Not supernatural at all, but as human as his chromosomes indicated. As Kiel listened with his inner sense, he also felt that Tavkel was keenly alert. Absolutely confident.

Kiel's mother cleared her throat. She looked straight across at Kiel, as if she'd known she would find him sitting in precisely this place. She called in a strong voice, "Tavkel is one of us, but he is also far more. He is the one." She turned to look out over the crowd. "You people can draw your own conclusions from that observation. Or," she added, regaining a teasing, almost cocky tone, "if you asked him, I think he would let you find out for yourselves."

Kiel felt the oddest pang of loss. All his life, his mother had been his strongest supporter, a homing beacon of encouragement and approval. Had he lost his place to a stranger?

"Yes." Tavkel turned forward again. "All of you may touch me and see for sure. If you do, you will also lose your training, though not your biological gifts." He paused, and Kiel felt the crowd's apprehension rise again. "But if you cannot humble yourselves that completely, I still can take ownership of your darkness. Certainty may be glorious, but a gesture of faith is a precious gift. I'll gladly receive it."

That offer would be inexcusably pompous out of the mouth of anyone but Boh-Dabar himself. Still, a freshly vested Sentinel sitting on the platform's edge in her brand-new uniform broke into a relieved smile. That young woman had just spent five years studying codes and drilling in the appropriate uses of her abilities. Several second-year sekiyrra sitting closer—who still faced most of that training ordeal—shifted their legs as if ready to scramble up and get closer yet.

"My Lady Grandmother," Tavkel said, and as Kiel focused toward him again, he felt a deep, warm gratitude flowing from Tavkel toward Kiel's mother. It made him ashamed. "The people who begin again will need a new training protocol. Would you ask High Commander Caldwell if he would be willing to lead that project?"

Kiel's mother grinned, looking decidedly unmilitary. "I'll ask him. He'll be honored, I'm sure."

"You'll be his first student." Tavkel turned back to the crowd. "For she has also been healed. Restored to her full potential, forty years after her ayin was destroyed."

Time seemed to freeze. Kiel's family had kept Lady Firebird's dangerous mutation as secret as possible for decades. Now, he scanned the assembly and sensed hot spots of sudden fear, and his heart sank even further. Evidently, overnight rumors had blasted away this family secret too. Many of them had just found out she'd been born with an ayin dangerous to herself and everyone else— and had passed it through Tiala to Tavkel.

Kiel reached out to his right and took his daughter Annalah's hand, hoping the poor girl didn't find herself shunned when people realized why she'd been ayinectomized so young.

"Healed," Tavkel repeated, stressing the word. "Fully healed. Her new ayin has a normally polarized carrier."

Annalah's hand tightened on his, clutching fiercely. A moment later, Kiel realized why. If Tavkel could restore her grandmother's mutated and damaged ayin, he could restore hers. Annalah could take a sekiyr's vows and start learning their people's ways, if she submitted herself to this stranger.

He felt Hanusha subvocalize to them both. *Annalah, do not make assumptions! We don't know enough about this man yet.*

Kiel thrust down his own moment of terror. He needed to distract them, if only to keep Annalah from provoking an argument— but also to divert her from taking Tavkel's bait without considering the consequences. He stood slowly, clasping his hands in front of his ministerial tunic.

"Tavkel, thank you for clarifying those situations." Kiel turned to face the crowd seated behind him. "I also thank all of you who have respected our family's confidences for so many years. Now, I thank you in advance for your patience while we sort out what should be done. Please remember that Tavkel's statements have not been certified by your leadership."

Turning toward the platform again, he felt a distinct chill at the back of his mind, not from Tavkel but his mother. He must speak with her alone. Soon. "You are welcome, at present," Kiel told her, expanding a gesture to include everyone in the Chapter room, "to work with him. Still, none of you will be required to offend your conscience, your training, or your understanding of holy Scripture if you do not feel compelled to commit yourself to him.

"Many of you could be wondering whether there will be time enough to retrain between now and . . . whatever catastrophe Tavkel predicts. I would call that a valid concern." Whatever his parents had seen and felt last night, Kiel had sworn to uphold thirteen generations of tradition. He would keep doing so until he was absolutely convinced otherwise.

His mother glared, but Tavkel spoke affably over the crowd's murmur. "You are correct, Shamarr Caldwell. There always is freedom to receive or refuse, to give or hold back."

For several seconds, no one else spoke.

Kiel touched Hanusha's shoulder and sidled along the front row, making his way toward the main aisle. It was time to leave. As he stepped carefully around seated youngsters, he heard Hanusha's subvoice, *I'm coming. I've got Annalah.*

Hold tight, he returned, resisting the temptation to look back. A spot between his shoulders prickled, as if someone had leveled a targeting beam at him.

Tavkel's voice rose. "And some of you want to see for yourselves, whatever it costs. Please, would the rest of you make room? Clear a space."

Kiel made slow headway toward the main doors at the back. He had to step over and around the floor sitters in the aisle as they also stood up.

Wind called behind him, "Everyone, if you are on the morning task rotation, please get a quick breakfast and go to your duties whenever you're finished here."

Off to the side, people were pressing forward under the candle sconces, the aged heading down front *en masse.* Saried's mother, so bent and slender, leaned on Saried's arm.

Actually, Kiel realized, if Tavkel could heal those elders' waning abilities and let them learn to shield again, they'd be able to return to this community. He would love to see that happen. Though he struggled upstream against a crowd that was either standing in place or pushing forward, hope sprouted in his spirit.

What if Tavkel really was That One? His peculiar air of authority and humility, his mysterious statements about sacrifice that no scripture satisfactorily explained, and most of all, those inexplicable healings suggested that he was something—someone—genuinely unprecedented.

Hanusha's sudden anguish stabbed like a dagger. Kiel whirled around. Annalah had broken free to head back toward the altar, carried along by the flow. A mob was gathering up there. Tavkel motioned for people to sit down again.

No! Hanusha shrieked in his mind. *Kiel, I've got Perl. And Rena's following me. Get Annalah!*

Theology was one thing. Watching his daughter walk blindly into something they didn't fully understand was another. Heart pounding, he started to push back toward the stage, pressing against others' shoulders—until his conscience halted him. Annalah was long past the age of discernment. How many priests' children had eventually rebelled? *And I was unsympathetic!* He subvocalized to Hanusha, *Let her go. You have to. We must.*

He felt Hanusha's startled confusion and saw anger flame in her eyes as she seized the younger girls' hands. Annalah hurried on forward, bumping others' shoulders as if the crowd weren't surging forward fast enough for her. He longed to chase her down.

But he must not.

Up front, his half sister Saried had already extended a hand to Tavkel.

Kiel had always loved and admired Saried, partly for the way she'd overcome her dubious beginnings and won everyone's love and trust. She stood eye to eye with the young man, and hesitantly— this felt like an appalling breach of their privacy, but Tavkel was doing this in full view of a room full of telepaths—Kiel lowered his shields again.

Out of Saried blared a wordless cry of joy and awe—and was that relief? Tavkel had offered to take ownership of people's darkness, but what did that *mean?* What had he just given Saried—or taken away from her?

Annalah moved closer to him through the crowd.

Baffled and bereft, Kiel remembered the chilling exclusion Wind had described, growing up a Mikuhran among Sentinels. Had Annalah felt that way, growing up disempowered among the kindred?

A part of him wanted to linger, to see whether Annalah's lack of ayin abilities made her experience any different.

He turned away. At the bottom of his sinking heart, he felt as if she'd just died, and he would not be allowed to grieve. *I have work to do. Information to gather, scriptures to review.* He'd made many mistakes in a lifetime of service. This time, any mistake could doom all his loved ones. For eternity.

As he pushed toward the rear door, his eyes burned with tears he must not shed.

CHAPTER 14

A clamp bit into Jorah's scalp. He lay on his back. He'd exhausted himself struggling against arm and leg restraints. Years ago, he'd been told there were no sensory nerves inside the brain, but now he imagined he could track the needle threading up from the opening at the base of his skull. He *wanted* to feel it. It might help him remember. He must remember.

Only one face in front of him was unmasked: Chancellor Gambrel stood back several meters, occasionally asking about the procedure. His medical man, Zeimsky, was out of Jorah's line of sight. He was probably standing in the well under this table, guiding that needle.

They'd already injected one drug. This second one would poison his ayin. As a tear trickled from his right eye, he particularly wanted to remember that he'd tried to fight them off. If he couldn't remember that, could he ever respect himself again?

Colonel Zeimsky reappeared, his yellow lab tunic worn over Tallan military grey. Jorah wanted to remember the eyes over that pale yellow face mask, brown eyes with darker brown striations. And the odd gap in his left eyebrow.

Zeimsky stared at something Jorah couldn't see and spoke over Jorah toward Gambrel. "Do you want to do the honors?"

Jorah couldn't turn his head, but throughout the procedure, the Chancellor had stayed within his field of vision. "No, but thank you," he said smoothly. Jorah hated him for his clinical calmness, but even more for destroying all that Jorah had done with his life. For substituting another destiny. This was enslavement. This was evil.

"Very well." Zeimsky reached under the table.

Jorah shut his eyes and tried to feel it. He couldn't. They must've been right about the brain's lack of sensory nerves. If they were also right about being able to block those memories, his people were doomed.

• • •

Piper Gambrel watched the small flask drain. If Zeimsky was wrong and this killed the boy, they'd have to find another banner carrier. That could create an irritating delay. Still, Zeimsky hadn't been wrong about anything major, and Gambrel had no trouble taking responsibility for high-level decisions.

After all, he was a man of responsibility. He'd studied the learning process for three decades, finding ways to produce profound self-knowledge and self-confidence. Contemporary research explained many ancient understandings, especially the fact that physical reality merely reflected a higher plane of existence. During these decades, Piper Gambrel had learned to communicate with something he thought of as his own higher self—but he called it his god-voice.

The memory made him smile now. He'd first touched that brilliance shortly after a true turning point in Whorl history, the final devastation of Shuhr-settled Mikuhr. That cancerous world had sent out many metastases. Dealing with them had required the use of those barely human employees, the Thyrian Sentinels.

The last of those barely-humans could now be set aside. Air Master Kinnor Caldwell's insubordination had been one more proof that their powers over humanity needed to end.

The entire Federacy needed massive changes. The Regional Council, once a bastion of idealism, had fallen past bureaucracy into corruption as its aging members grew too comfortable with power. Gambrel had been given a grant, years ago, to study how the Federacy might revitalize itself. He had developed and staffed the Collegium and brought it to Federate prominence.

He had also found his god-voice during that decade. Communing with it left him revitalized, even more so than when he recited the litanies he'd penned early in his career. He sometimes even seemed to sense it as a second presence, like a counselor beside him. Now, for instance, he felt oddly assured that the boy would survive this procedure.

An image gleamed on his handheld. Along one side of the frame, near the curvature of Jorah's inner skull, radio-tagged molecules flowed out of the long, black needle. The flow looked random, but molecules were unmistakably accumulating in the y-shaped target organelle.

Gambrel frowned. This second solution must not pass out through the blood-brain barrier to collect in other organs. He thumbed the handheld for a second display, which monitored veins flowing down through the boy's neck. That display remained unchanged.

Was the boy going to be all right? Zeimsky was only human. All people made mistakes. He took another long look at his hand-held. Would Jorah Caldwell have fulfilled his people's prophecies without Collegiate help?

The answer felt like a tickling laugh. *Does it matter? A few people whose corpses rotted long ago thought they could predict what we're doing today. If they were right, doesn't that simply mean that one random guess out of thousands proved accurate?*

Exactly. The Sentinels' exclusivist religion assumed a personal deity, one that existed outside the space-time it had created and that could reportedly drop prophetic predictions into it. Other spiritual lineages, such as his own, called divinity an impersonal fire that sparked each human mind into existence.

In his opinion, the physically modified Sentinels had needed a belief system that justified their existence. If they had gone on keeping that system to themselves, it would not concern him now.

Unfortunately, it had been spreading among non-altered people during recent decades. Gambrel's intelligence gatherers had fingered Jorah's paternal grandmother, an adult convert, as the chief culprit. Apparently, Firebird Angelo Caldwell had inherited massive wealth from her aristocratic family. She'd invested much of it to train priests who were free of the Sentinels' longstanding ban. *An effective strategist.*

By now, she probably was a deeply devastated widow.

"Ah." Zeimsky interrupted his speculation. "We're seeing the change."

Gambrel raised his handheld again. He eyed the target tissue. Its firmly rounded edges were collapsing.

• • •

Jorah heard that pronouncement too. Already ayin-blind from their drugs, he felt nothing.

A second tear seeped out onto his cheek. In his blurred vision, light shimmered oddly near a corner of the ceiling. Jorah instantly recognized his previous visitor. He no longer cared whether these people thought he was crazy. "Get me out," he cried, wrenching against his restraints. Two burly aides rushed forward and grabbed his shoulders. Struggling, he stared up at the shimmer and pleaded again, "Get me out!"

• • •

Frowning, Piper Gambrel asked Zeimsky, "He can't hurt himself, can he?"

"No. But I could sedate him."

Eyeing the aides and the lieutenant's padded restraints, Gambrel shook his head. "A muscle relaxant, maybe." Really, Gambrel didn't see why it was necessary to torture Lieutenant Caldwell by keeping him conscious. After all, he soon would be drugged to forget it all.

It's important, he felt assured.

For once, his god-voice made little sense. He tried to puzzle this out. The handsome boy would look excellent on the new ITD network, posing as the Whorl's emergent hero. He would be convinced that all this was for the best. Those ancient "prophecies" were pure fool's glimmer, but they gave Jorah a compelling human interest story.

However, it still made no sense to keep the boy conscious. He opened his mouth to order a sedative.

• • •

Before Jorah's blurred eyes, the shimmer flitted across the ceiling like some kind of aurora. It landed on top of Piper Gambrel's head and gave off a thin scream. The aides at his own shoulders seemed not to hear, but kept pushing down on him.

Jorah blinked.

The shimmer had vanished.

• • •

It had been silly to argue with the god-voice, Gambrel realized. The lieutenant was too firmly clamped down to harm himself, and it did somehow seem important, with a super-logical sort of sense, to keep him conscious for this.

An aide held up one more ampoule, filled with Zeimsky's cloudy bacillus culture. The aide stood waiting while Zeimsky checked two handheld scanners. Apparently satisfied, Zeimsky carried the ampoule back down into the well under the lieutenant's head.

As the plague that would reshape the Whorl flowed toward Lieutenant Caldwell's shriveled ayin, Piper Gambrel had the strangest feeling. He imagined himself hovering, watching himself walk forward, crouch down, and stretch a hand toward Zeimsky. "Well done," he heard himself say. Zeimsky pulled off a glove before clasping his hand.

Perhaps finally, after so many years of trying to develop his highest potentials and integrate them with the lower, physical reality, the god-voice had suddenly learned to move his body and speak through his mouth. He saw himself straighten up, rest a hand on the restrained lieutenant's shoulder, and say, "Jorah, you would like to let your family know you're all right, wouldn't you?"

● ● ●

Jorah pushed his lips together and refused to answer. He concentrated instead on every detail of what they'd done to him. He'd been trained to build memory chains, associating important intelligence data with everyday cues. The commonest linking cue was ordinary hunger. He let his gut's aching emptiness flood his mind. He added the deep sense of fear, danger, sickness—and the notion of plague—so that the next time his belly was empty he might remember all this—but when he glanced at the Chancellor, his mind went blank.

Out of Gambrel's eyes flickered the same shimmer he'd seen loose in the room. Except that now, it was inside the Chancellor.

Zeimsky reappeared. Something stung Jorah's arm. "You're going to sleep," Zeimsky said, "and you are now going to forget quite a few things."

No! I'm not. Jorah squeezed his eyes shut. *When I'm hungry, I'm going to remember you. I'm going to remember . . . plague . . .*

His head whirled.

CHAPTER 15

Kiel and Hanusha stepped out of the crowd exiting the Chapter room, and Kiel paused near the waterside.

The moment he had left the Chapter room, a joyous confusion had faded from the edge of awareness. Out here away from Tavkel and his new converts, the general mood passing through his shields was rather sedate.

On a more physical awareness, sizzling sounds came from the kitchen. Apparently pancakes were still being offered.

"Go on," Hanusha told Rena and Perl. "Get some breakfast. We'll join you."

Their two younger daughters melted into the mob headed toward the commons.

Hanusha backed against the white metal railing, arms crossed. Kiel could not shield himself against her fury. It flooded the back of his mind. "Tavkel should be arrested," she said. "For impersonation, if not sacrilege."

He wanted to agree. His own anguish was clearly distinguishable from her fury, despite the pair bond's intensity. And yet— "Still, look at the group who went to him without hesitating. Annalah.

Saried. Terza. All the elders, most of the sekiyrra. Some of the most publicly faithful and the most marginalized of us all." He stared through the big double doors back into the Chapter room. Dozens of people clustered around the altar, each waiting to mind-access Tavkel.

"I always imagined," Kiel continued, "that when Boh-Dabar did appear, those two groups would recognize him instantly— or else need him with the most fervent desperation." So then . . . could it be real?

"Hmm." Hanusha looked very much like her mother, the historian, when she lowered her chin over crossed arms. "This is no time to talk theology. Our daughter—"

Kiel's handheld gave a soft *blat*. "One moment," he said. She would understand. Subtronic communication was rarely used here, so this could be an emergency . . . as if losing their daughter to a possibly false prophet were no emergency!

He raised the device and glanced at it, saw his sister-in-law's origin code and the message, *Need to talk. Urgent. My office.*

"Hanusha, I'll be with you as soon as I can. It's the Minster."

"I'll be with the girls." She strode off.

Kiel couldn't help glancing into the Chapter room one last time before he headed across the pool on the stepping stones. It looked like a quarter of the Sanctuary's population was lingering in there. Half blind with grief for them, he strode onto the stepping stone path. At the pool's edge, water poured into a drainage channel and flowed toward recirculating filters.

Annalah! He should've known how vulnerable she would be, how tempted by the promise of being made whole. She was both faithful and marginalized. He, on the other hand, hauled the chains of position and authority.

The sound of rushing water had no comfort for him today.

Beyond the office's clustered streamers, Wind already sat at her desk again. She leaned forward over two illuminated inset panels.

Kiel hurried forward and scattered his shields. Instantly, her anxiety made his chest ache even more painfully. "What do you need?" he asked.

I found Kinnor, she subvocalized with frantic speed. *He's been off surveillance since just after midnight, and I put Security on it.* She glanced left, then right, then looked back up at him, making eye contact for easier subvocalizing. *They were going to comm me as soon as they got him in custody.*

Alarmed, he thickened his shields again. "Wind, slow down. What has he done, that they'd have to take him—"

He's been prepping a Brumbee *ship. He's determined to leave. For Tallis, for Jorah. I tried to talk him out of it last night, the last I saw him. And I did check the hangars, but his shields are strong. He must've hid down there. I have to enforce his house arrest, now that we've located him.*

Of course you do, Kiel sent subvocally. As he stood staring down at his sister-in-law, his heart bumped against his stomach. Was that where Kinnor had been lurking during that peculiar Chapter session?

Breaking arrest would be only the first charge Tallis leveled against him. There would also be "interfering with an impending hearing" and a risk of the most serious charge, "selfish or capricious" use of his abilities. For decades, the College had prohibited flaunting their ayin skills. "What happened?" he whispered.

She stared without blinking and stuck to subvocalization. *A security officer finally called in. Kin must've slipped up for an instant. But now Security isn't answering either. Something bad must've happened.*

"Don't assume the worst." He leaned toward her and used a calming undertone, soothing her fear. "We're all exhausted. Emotional days like yesterday and today drain a person."

We should have been checking the ships themselves. It didn't occur to me. I was distracted. I did put the hangars on lockdown last night, right away. Your father helped. Kinnor shouldn't have been able to override a lockdown. I tried to tell Security to wait until he lowered his guard again, maybe an hour, then go in and stun him.

"Wind, slow—"

I was going to have Saried put him in t-sleep quietly. Keep him here secretly. Put out some kind of explanation that wouldn't damage his pride. But Security isn't responding.

Kiel turned in place. The ceiling streamers fluttered, revealing air currents he could not see. He'd never heard Wind so frantic. "Maybe you do have to assume the worst."

You know his hair trigger! He's likely to attack anyone I send down there now. I don't think he'd deliberately hurt someone, but Sentinel against Sentinel, you never know what'll happen. Unless— Finally, she paused. *Tavkel predicted . . . he'll die, if . . .*

"Tavkel!" Kiel exclaimed. "You cannot put your faith in his predictions. The *shebiyl* is evil, Wind."

Then maybe he'll listen to us both, if we go together.

He didn't hesitate. "Maybe he won't," he returned, "but we'd better try." And he mustn't let Wind go first. Kinnor did know how to stop people without harming them, and he'd never injure Wind deliberately, but accidents could happen when emotions ran high. He stepped toward the private passage. "Let's go."

Kiel hustled down the tunnel just ahead of her. Small yellow-ish everburners lit the narrow passageway, but they were far apart. As he quickstepped, white stone walls grew darker—brighter—and then darker again. He recalled Kinnor's dark, bitter words from years ago, during an argument. "You and Wind. Always stuck on the rules. Why you two aren't connatural, I can't guess."

He and Wind weren't connatural, though. They merely worked well together, and Kiel hated the idea of taking her side against his brother. Annalah had just shown him how betrayal felt.

Help us, he prayed. *Guide us.*

The tunnel emerged in Hangar One, the largest and most public. Its service door to H-2 was shut. The big launch doors were closed, and the lights were turned off. Down here the walls were metal, the flooring duracrete. The College shuttle was an enormous blocky shape under blue striplights.

He crossed H-1 and touched his personal code into the service door's access panel.

The metal door fan-folded itself into the ceiling. He stepped inside cautiously, wondering whether Kin did have a stun pistol. He braced for a tumble and glanced around the second hangar bay for any sign of those security personnel. A stun burst usually wore off in a few hours.

"Kinnor?" he called softly, dispersing his shields. "I'm unarmed. Are you there?" He thought he sensed one person somewhere ahead.

Something rumbled off to the right. Alarmed, Kiel hurried forward. The mechanical prep for departure took a crew several hours. Launching also required security codes to open launch doors and light the engine, as well as a final code to pass the orbital fielding net. *Stay behind me,* he warned Wind.

He slapped a wall control, and light blasted his eyes. H-2's launch door was rumbling upward. Startup machinery and dangling lines cluttered the smaller bay. A *Brumbee* messenger ship slid forward.

"No!" Wind cried behind him. He spun around. She lunged toward a security panel.

Someone stepped out of the shadows to block the panel, holding a stun pistol down at his side. Someone without hair. It took Kiel fully a second to recognize his father.

"No," his father said firmly. "I can't let you abort the launch."

Kiel stood gaping. *You, Father? You?* The launch door slid fully open with a final crunch. Instantly a deeper, throatier roar shook the ground, the *Brumbee's* starter engine.

"No!" Wind cried again, reaching forward.

His father raised the stun pistol several degrees, still pointing it aside. It would take microseconds to aim and fire.

Kiel forced words out. "Sir, this is direct disobedience of a Federate arrest order." *I thought you were resting!* Plainly Wind had too, since she hadn't tracked him via her desk links.

His father had to shout over the engine noise. "Son. Please. Before your mother and I even married each other, I disobeyed an order that conflicted with my vesting vows. We face a similar situation."

Kiel stood frozen, not out of fear—he'd been stunned before, and he didn't seriously think his father would fire on Wind—but by his onrushing thoughts. His father had made countless *Brumbee* trips as an SO operative. He wouldn't have forgotten procedures, and he had access to highest level security overrides. Plainly, he was the only person at Sanctuary who could have gotten Kinnor away.

"Sir," he shouted back, "are you authorized to make that decision?"

The *Brumbee* cleared the launch door, which started to drop.

Kiel's father shook his head. The brilliant overhead lights cast faint shadows under his eyes. "I just sent away two of my other children with an extremely sober blessing, Kiel. I might not see either one of them alive again."

"Two?" Startled, Kiel stared down into his father's face. The older man could no longer shield his feelings, and grief streamed from him. Beyond the launch door, the engine roar deepened. Kiel asked again, "Two?"

His father looked up, his eyes thick with tears. "The moment Saried went to Tavkel, she had a powerful sense of being called to Tallis. She got here through the private tunnels. She followed you for a little ways, Wind."

"Oh!" Wind's hand went to her chest.

Kiel shook his head. Saried? Tallis? Why?

Wind faced the launch doors. Tears streamed down her cheeks. Kiel had to thicken his shields against the icy pain those two radiated.

His father lowered the weapon to dangle at his side. "I would have liked to go with them. I'd planned to spend some months helping with the Federate downsize, and I might have enjoyed surprising certain people at Special Ops. But," he said, running his free hand over bare scalp, "Tavkel has work for me here. End of discussion." He stepped forward to rest that free hand on Wind's shoulder, keeping his body between her and the security panel.

Still facing the launch doors, she covered her face with both hands. Her shoulders shook.

"What have you brought down on us all?" Kiel barely kept from shouting. "Do you realize what the Federacy could do to us?"

His father spoke softly, with undertones of regret. "Think. Think where I've been for the last decade. I've seen and heard things I can't tell either one of you, even now. Nothing that you, or I, or Kinnor could do will stop what's going to happen anyway. The Federacy preaches respect and freedom for all peoples, but we are being shifted out of that category. We are no longer 'people' but dangerous non-humans."

Remembering his close call at the Thyrian spaceport, Kiel couldn't argue.

"We were born into this time, facing the terrible risk of genocide. If Kinnor triggers it," his father began, but instead of finishing the sentence, he took a deep breath. "Kiel, Wind. We must stand together. Listen, both of you."

Outside the launch doors, the roar of Kinnor's ship faded into unseen distance. Wind lowered her hands and turned around.

"I knew I could stand back and watch my family shatter, with Kinnor staying here, permanently alienated from you, Wind." Kiel's father spoke quietly, with years of authority in his tone. "Or I could help him slip away and try to save Jorah. You know what I chose.

But you did the right thing too. You did it out of love for him, and to protect the rest of us." He set down the stun pistol on a charging console. It made a soft clank.

"How could we both be right?" Wind spoke toward the duracrete floor. Her voice quavered.

"Yes, how?" Kiel demanded. "Why did you do this? And what about Jorah?"

His father's voice became raspy and regretful. "Because Kinnor was also right. If anyone can save Jorah, he can."

"Tavkel . . ." Wind choked as she spoke the name.

Kiel stepped closer to her.

"Wind," his father continued, "I hope that in time, you'll forgive me. If Tavkel is correct, I have sent Kinnor to his death. The Holy One never revokes our freedom, though—and I believe in his mercy. We all do." He glanced at Kiel. "If anyone needs to face charges, I will take responsibility."

Kiel shook his head. Sending personnel on dangerous missions was nothing new for his father. And it was good to see that his father's conversion to Tavkel had not left him mindless.

Wind wiped her cheeks and murmured, "I'm not going to have you charged, Father. Of course not. But what happens next? And—" She craned her neck. "Where are my security people?"

Kiel's father glanced deeper into H-2. "They never expected to see me holding a stunner. Let them sleep."

Wind smiled weakly. *Good idea,* Kiel heard her subvocalize. Had she already decided that all this was for the best? Had some part of her wanted to let Kinnor go?

Maybe so. His own anger softened. *Why?* He sent his father privately. Maybe Wind didn't need any further answer, but he did. *Please answer me. How could you?*

"Jorah is their son." His father responded in a whisper, reminding Kiel that the only Sentinel ever named to the Federate High Command—a Master Sentinel, at that—could hear subvocalization, but he no longer could subvocalize. "Any one of us would gladly die for any one of our children. And they won't necessarily catch him. Pray for mercy, Kiel. We all need it. Especially Kinnor, now."

Silence filled the next several seconds. Kiel couldn't help thinking that Annalah had gone to Tavkel without stopping to consider her own danger. Truly, he would rather die than see her fall into darkness. Should he have stopped her?

But had she actually fallen into light? What about those inexplicable chromosomes and Tavkel's mysterious words, which felt so much like scripture? "Father," Kiel asked softly but vocally. He looked into a face he'd always loved, though it still looked odd without eyebrows. "Do you really think the universe is about to change?"

His father leaned against that charging console, arms crossed. "The Whorl has already changed. And I have read, in the books you teach, that the universe will be renewed by Boh-Dabar. I believe that. So do you."

"Yes. I do." Kiel had argued doctrine with sincere believers before. Never before had it hurt this badly. "But it must be done without calling Federate forces down on the Sanctuary."

"Tavkel is our only hope to survive."

"No. He's not." Kiel glanced into dark Hangar One, realizing that Kinnor's unauthorized trip had also cut into their fuel reserve. "Most of us still could leave the Whorl in the College shuttle, if our engineers can refit it, and if we don't all forget how to t-sleep. And from all you're not saying, we'd better depart soon."

"What will it take to convince you?" His father stepped closer.

"That Tavkel is the Boh-Dabar?"

His father nodded.

What would it take? Kiel turned aside. He'd been present, unshielded, as his parents had become Tavkel's first disciples. And how could he explain that blare of joy he'd sensed in Saried, unless she was completely deceived?

People had been sincerely wrong before, though, and this was no time for theological discussion. There were prophecies that might not line up. One in particular . . . "I don't know," he admitted, suddenly exhausted. Later today—or tomorrow, or the next day—they would deal with the consequences of what his father, brother, and half sister had just done. The family must survive. Plainly, the High Commander remained a force to be reckoned with.

And so did Tavkel, even untrained and dosed with blocking drugs.

Kiel folded his arms under his tunic's sleeves and left his father and Wind behind.

He headed back to the waterside, using the public passway. He did hope—fervently—that Kinnor would bring Jorah back. That would prove Tavkel wrong. And too many Caldwells had fallen in Federate service, or been murdered outright. Jorah was the only young man carrying the name in this next generation.

Other than Tavkel, he realized with a shudder, *if Tiala is unwed.*

CHAPTER 16

Meris spent the rest of the morning and the whole noon hour in her room, fortifying herself with a good long session of Chancellor Gambrel's wisdom. After what she'd just seen in the Chapter room, she wanted to clear her head. Fortunately, she wasn't on morning shift—neither outdoors, nor in the depopulated med center.

Near the noon hour's end, she sat on her bunk and leaned against the stone wall. The wall was white stone, naturally. From a tall wooden wardrobe came a faint scent of Annalah's floral perfume.

The Chancellor's small image was elegant in a cutaway formal coat, of the dark grey-green color all Tallis Collegiates favored. It hovered over Meris's handheld on top of the bunk's white coverlet.

"Every human mind is an eternal spark, valuable and whole." He'd been speaking for more than an hour. Recognizing the opening lines of a litany, Meris knew he would finish shortly. The image turned right and then left. He held one arm outswept in the elegant classical style. "It is fully independent, although it be separated from the body—even although it be severed, if need be, from other divine humanity . . ."

Her focus flickered. What time might it be, back at Jerone City on Elysia? Was her father boarding the morning transport, followed by a discreet bodyguard? Had her mother arrived at the university medical center? Was she bent over a cadaver or standing with eyes pressed to a scanning molecular scope . . . or might she too be en route, checking overnight messages via her own handheld?

Meris folded her arms tightly. Did they ever think about her, or was their attention focused only on the young man who'd taken her place?

She shook her head and blinked up at the ceiling light. *I am an eternal spark, valuable and whole.* She reached for the handheld, wanting to reverse the lecture, back to the point where her mind had wandered.

No. That would be futile. He'd reached the lecture's end. Palms pressed together, his miniature image seemed to stare into her soul. "And so I teach you a new saying. Listen once and then speak it with me. Let it bathe the eternal spark that is your true self. Let it ring in your memory. It is the litany for patience, perseverance, and serenity. Use it to form your soul for eternity.

"It is this: 'Time passes. I endure.' Speak with me, thou eternal spark."

This was his signal. Meris formed the words with her lips, but she didn't speak out loud. She had long ago ceased needing that physical involvement, and she'd watched this lecture before. "Time passes. I endure." She mouthed it once and set it free to reverberate in her spirit. *Time passes. I endure. Time passes . . .*

The image vanished. Once again, Chancellor Gambrel had done excellent work: Feeling steady and strong, she rolled off the bunk. She checked her appearance in a glass reflecting panel and smoothed her hair before heading out into the housing corridor.

Her route turned left at the poolside. She followed the heartening scent of freshly baked bread toward the dining commons, feeling strangely at home in this odd place. If the Minster had decided to have her put into t-sleep, with the med center emptied—or into stasis, with all the crypts suddenly available—surely she would have been summoned by now.

She needed to escape, though. She picked up her pace, swinging her arms. Tavkel's performance and the crowd's reaction had left her even more determined to leave—not simply to protect herself, but to warn the Collegium. Chancellor Gambrel was a wise, merciful man. He would know how to cope with a potential doomsday cult. If someone else started a fight with the Federacy, Chancellor Gambrel could call on an overwhelming force. After all, the Tallis Collegium worked closely with the Federate Regional Command on Tallis.

So she need not panic. *Time passes. I endure.* Still, she didn't want to be here if conflict broke out.

And her allies had joined the cult. Annalah and Lady Fi, both of them.

Should she have stayed on Elysia after all? Accepted that internship—

Rounding the corner at the pool's far end, Meris dodged two young boys who ran past her without slowing down. Many of the commons tables had emptied. Annalah's grandparents sat close to the waterside with emptied plates, two mugs, and a stoneware pitcher arrayed in front of them. Three other people stood close by, looking as if they'd just risen from that table.

Meris narrowed her eyes. Perhaps High Commander Caldwell had not been as sick as everyone thought.

No, of course he had! She'd personally checked his monitors. Then what about Tavkel . . . It was possible these people had staged his arrival, setting her up to spot him on the trail and give the alert. But why?

Unlikely. She could've sworn they hadn't expected him. Maybe his mutant abilities included an unprecedented group of bioelectric phenomena. That might explain his healings.

Right, Mother? She drew close enough to recognize the people standing around the Caldwells' table: the *Daystar*'s Commander Harris, and the two younger bridge officers who'd ridden into the radiation together with High Commander Caldwell. All of them upright again, all of them completely healed. Commander Harris said something she didn't catch. All the others laughed, and then the three of them walked toward the elevator.

Meris hurried to the empty chair next to Lady Fi. "Were you going to stay a little longer? May I join you?"

"Meris." Lady Fi had changed out of her blue uniform tunic into one of those quaint long dresses. "Certainly. Sit, please. I'm sorry we haven't spoken in so long."

"You've had other concerns." Sinking onto a hard chair, Meris stared at the High Commander's plate. The variety of streaks and crumbs on that plate suggested he'd just finished a large meal, and he looked drowsy. Adopting her rehearsed bedside manner, she said, "It's good to see you upright, sir."

"It's good to be upright." He used both hands to raise the pitcher, filled a clean mug from a vacant place at the table, and slid it toward her before refilling his own. "And to see my comrades healthy again."

She took a long sip, careful to avoid self-pity. *The eternal is in me. It cannot know defeat.* She did not need close companionship. And maybe his abilities really had been taken away.

Or maybe not. Meris set down her mug. "Has the entire med center actually been taken off the task rotation?"

"Lieutenant Gardner just came from there." Lady Fi nudged her husband, who topped up her mug too. "She says there's only one care staffer left on duty, and just one patient. It's wonderful." Her eyes widened as she repeated, "Wonderful."

Meris turned her head. Here *he* came, walking along the water-side, still wearing those work clothes. For once, he was alone. "Looks like he's finished in the Chapter room," Meris said. "Finally.

How many people do you think just . . ." What was the term? " . . . joined you as . . . converts?"

"I didn't stay to count."

Hearing Lady Fi's adoring tone of voice, Meris hid a frown behind her kass mug. *The eternal is in me . . .*

"Don't worry," the Lady added softly, "I'm not going to tell you how amazing he is. It's not allowed. I've got a functioning ayin again." She lowered her voice and spoke confidentially, though she glanced aside at her husband. "It's amazing, after all those years pair bonded, to be this much in love with a man who feels so separate from me. So . . . emotionally different."

The old man smiled and sipped from his mug. "Not for long," he murmured.

Was he referring to those other alarming rumors—that Lady Fi's dangerous ayin had been healed? Would they shortly be "pair bonded" all over again? Meris switched litanies. *I fear what I only imagine.* "There's no need to tell me about him anyway," she said lightly, "since here he comes."

By the time Tavkel reached them, the High Commander had filled a fourth mug. "Thank you." Tavkel accepted it in both hands. "Good afternoon." Those broad shoulders looked at home in a dirty work shirt. Mentally comparing him with the refined, highly educated Chancellor Gambrel was an exercise in irony.

Meris didn't miss the reverence in the elders' voices as they returned the young herdsman's greeting, but when they asked him to sit down, he declined. "I've accepted an invitation to spend some time in the shearing shed. I do have a request, though."

They both leaned toward him. It made them look silly, as if they would gladly swim laps in the reflecting pool or swing from the skylights for him. At their age!

A sekiyr hurried up, balancing a plate on one arm. He set it down and picked up the others' empty ones. Meris caught a whiff of fish.

Tavkel shot Meris a lopsided frown before he turned to the Commander. "Grandfather, would you work first with My Lady Grandmother and the elders on shield projection? Your mind's privacy was given at creation. Go ahead and re-establish this, even before you examine their other most natural skills."

Meris didn't understand a bit of that.

Apparently the High Commander did, though. "Yes, of course." He did look slightly pale this morning, except those dark circles under his eyes. Maybe he hadn't slept. "Terza checked into the med center," he told Tavkel. "Right after you spoke to her."

"Yes. She's ready." Tavkel glanced from the High Commander to Lady Fi, smiled at Meris, and then turned to go, carrying his kass toward the elevator.

"Don't you want lunch?" Meris called after him.

He stopped and turned around, flashing a charming grin. "This morning was meat and drink to me. Maybe later."

"I should get to work." High Commander Caldwell kissed his wife's forehead and strode off in the opposite direction, leaving Meris and Lady Fi alone at the table.

"Well." Lady Fi crossed her arms and leaned back in her chair. "My dear patient obviously doesn't need to be watched anymore. And apparently Tavkel made it difficult for you to do much more medical training here."

Instead of agreeing, Meris attacked her plate full of shellfish and spring vegetables. Shipboard, they'd conversed about Federate politics and Lady Fi's cultural exchange. Now, she was tempted to interrogate the woman about the upheavals she'd heard predicted by other Sentinels. *I fear what I only imagine,* she reminded herself, and she kept eating instead.

Lady Fi stared over the water. Meris had nearly finished when Lady Fi abruptly said, "Meris, do you really think you have to perform at a certain level to be valued by others?"

Meris covered her mouth, so her vehement denial wouldn't display a half-chewed bite of vegetables. Where had *that* come from? "No," she managed. "As Chancellor Gambrel says, every human mind is an eternal spark, valuable and whole."

Lady Fi lowered her voice. "I didn't say 'valuable.' I said 'valued.' A person who doesn't know how deeply she is loved has a hard time trusting anyone. Believe me, I know."

Meris stared back at the woman, recalling what she'd read in the Sanctuary roster. Apparently Lady Fi did know how it felt to be betrayed by her family. Sent to her death, even!

"I've had a few of your experiences." Lady Fi stared down at her mug. "The wealthy and powerful family, the attempts to impress them when it really wasn't possible."

"I did read that about you," Meris said stiffly. "They trained you as a suicide pilot." *An offering to the local gods,* she added silently, but that seemed particularly inappropriate at the moment. *The eternal is in me . . .*

"And I went along. Not just willingly, but proudly. Defying anyone to try and stop me." She looked up at Meris, and her eyes softened. "I'm a proud woman."

"Nothing wrong with that."

Lady Fi pursed her lips. "Yes, there is. And for a while, it looked like I'd lost everything. The Eternal One never lost sight of me, though, even when I was utterly blind. He waited for me." She shook her head slowly. "A very long time. He waits for you too."

Finally, something she could easily answer. "You aren't supposed to proselytize."

"Ah." Lady Fi shook her head and rested her wrists on the table. "I'm sorry! Old habit. I see traces of myself in you, but I won't say another word."

Meris didn't believe that. Lady Fi was a woman who spoke her mind. Actually, Meris liked that. "I need to get to Tallis," Meris said, since they were being direct. "I can't train here anymore."

Lady Fi leaned forward and refilled their mugs, using both hands to steady the pitcher. "Don't waste the time you have here, just waiting. You're intelligent, you're responsible, and you're ready to give your life to the right cause. And I see courage starting to blossom in you. Reach out. Listen. Watch."

Meris washed down the last of her midday meal with a gulp of cooling kass. "I do. And I see trouble brewing here, and I want to get out of the way. That was a military uniform you were wearing this morning, wasn't it?"

"Oh, as it happened, I had undressed and . . ." Smiling wryly, Lady Fi went on. "I spotted it among my old belongings, and it seemed like a way to honor him. To give him all that I am, including my somewhat questionable past."

Questionable? For more than forty years, she'd been a respected public figure.

"Meris." Lady Fi dipped her chin and wrinkled her forehead. "Tavkel isn't a fighting man. If you're worried by that talk about raising a defense force, you need to know something. As more people commit themselves entirely to Tavkel, there'll be fewer combatants. All we want is to hear him speak.

"And there probably isn't much time for even that," she added softly, puckering her lips in a smile. "Brennen already worked with me this morning on the shields Tavkel just suggested. It's been a long time since I was a beginner at anything. It's very different this time, without all that dark in the way." She drained her cup and grimaced as if she disliked the taste. "Now I want to get out my old clairsa—my harp—and see if my fingers are as flexible as they feel."

"What's Tavkel planning to do? He can't accomplish much more here."

"Go to Tallis? Maybe Elysia?" Lady Fi shook her head. "I don't know. I hope he tells us soon. I'd like him to stay."

"I want to talk with him."

Lady Fi raised both eyebrows. "We all do."

"Look." Meris spread her hands on the table. "I can't be the only person who thinks Tavkel could be rallying an army. I wish he would just work with Chancellor Gambrel. Together, they could set the Federacy on a new path."

"Tavkel," the old woman said drily, "will be up in the shearing shed, by the sound of it. That shed's full of foul smells and organic dirt. He couldn't be more different from your honorable Chancellor. He knows how important the physical really is. It's the Holy One's beloved creation. So—" She stood up. "I could use help restringing my clairsa."

Meris ignored the jab at Collegiate teachings. "What about that new patient? Terza?" Actually, it would be wise to recite her entire Collegiate focusing sequence before she talked with any self-proclaimed prophet. *I fear what I—*

She still imagined too much, actually. "Does Terza have something Tavkel can't heal?"

"She'll probably be gone within the hour. She just needs to be comfortable."

"Gone? You mean . . . dead?" Startled, Meris also stood. "But Tavkel's the super healer."

Lady Fi firmed her mouth. "I don't think he means to cure extreme old age. When Terza was young, her own people abused and tortured her, mentally and physically. Brennen saved her life decades ago, and Saried's been here with her. Did you know Saried's her daughter?"

Meris nodded.

"Terza never was really whole again, though. We cared for her here, and we've all been amazed she hung on this long. Maybe at first, she was living for Saried. Then maybe Saried gave her extra special care. But I think the Eternal Speaker let her live just long enough to speak with Tavkel. I think it was a reward, of sorts. You can think what you like." She shrugged. "Brenn and I said our good-byes to her just now."

And what had the High Commander's relationship been like with the woman who gave him a half-Shuhr daughter? Had Lady Fi tolerated her? Meris stuck to the subject. "Tavkel was talking about defeating death, right? Maybe he can't do it after all."

"Not yet," Lady Fi answered, "obviously." She reached down and fidgeted with her mug's handle. "The care staffer could probably use a break, if you'd rather work downlevel than up in the fields—"

"Yes." And she could recite part of her focusing sequence as she walked to the med center. "Good day to you." She headed out, swinging her arms.

Apparently she'd found this alleged prophet's limits. By the time she rounded the walkway's Chapter room corner, she was already clearing her mind. *I am the spark of undying light. I shall see. I shall know.*

Less than a minute later, under the cleanup station's bright lights, she performed a simple hand scrub. If this old woman were dying, there was no fear of infection. MedSpec Saried, her daughter, probably was with her already.

In case it hadn't already been done, Meris gathered up a tray of various containers—shaved ice, water, juices—and pushed it into the room.

She didn't see Saried. The bed was draped in white, and two men stood beside it. A young man—barely more than a boy—on the bed's other side wore a pale yellow tunic with no shoulder star. Obviously a sekiyr studying medicine. The other man was Shamarr Kiel, which made sense.

"Thank you for coming, Meris," he said softly. "She's leaving us quickly." He glanced up across the bed.

The younger man frowned. Meris saw tear tracks. Was this a grandson? An apprentice? Where had Saried gone?

The elderly woman who lay on this bed had the longest oval, Shuhr-type face Meris had ever seen. She was still so tall that her feet reached the end of the treatment bed, and her breaths came slow and shallow, but her face was split by an incongruous smile. The Shamarr stood over her, the long, loose sleeves of his grey tunic dangling onto the coverlet.

The lifesigns board over the bed hadn't been turned on, so Meris fished under the bed for the switch and activated it on *silent* mode. She filled a small cup with ice chips and slipped closer. "Would you like to moisten your mouth?" she murmured. "Ice, or a cool swab?"

"No, no." The ancient woman's voice cracked. "I've seen him. That's water in my spirit, and it won't stop flowing."

The sekiyr shook his head, frowning. He had short curly hair and an innocent-looking round face, with eyes so red Meris felt sure he'd been crying. "I'm glad you're so happy." He seized the old woman's hand. "But I wanted to study with you. Your inspiring life, your comeback . . ."

The patient's arm shook as she reached with her whole body to pat his hand. "Thank you, Piet. Don't worry. Study with Tavkel instead."

Shamarr Kiel looked up at the board. Meris followed his gaze. Pulse, blood chemistry, body temp all were plummeting. The Shamarr reached into his left sleeve and pulled out a small vial, unscrewed the cap, and upended it over one finger. "Terza Shirak," he said, making a shiny streak on the woman's forehead, "cross with the blessing of eternal joy, and wait for us in peace."

A sweet, spicy smell drifted across the room. The woman looked up. Her smile broadened again. "Not long," she said.

The young man glanced across the bed at the Shamarr. Again, Meris wondered where the medspec had gone. Wasn't it her duty to attend a deathbed, especially her own mother's?

"What?" asked the young man—Piet, who'd wanted so badly to study with Terza.

Terza rolled her head side to side. "He apologized." Her voice had fallen to a whisper. She stopped for several seconds, inhaled slowly, and spoke again. "That I have to leave this way. He promised, though. It won't be long. Go to him, Pieters. He loves you."

"What won't be long?" The sekiyr leaned toward her. "What, your dying? Or your waiting . . ." A light started to blink on the wall panel. His voice trailed away.

"Soon," she whispered. She inhaled deeply, let out that breath like a sigh, and then simply stopped. On the board overhead, all the levels zeroed.

Meris squeezed her eyes shut. She hated seeing this. It was one reason she'd chosen to specialize in stasis instead of a broader field. Stasis specialists rarely saw death.

Shamarr Kiel turned toward her, probably sensing her horror and distaste. Intellectually, she understood that a human spark had simply ceased to exist and rejoined the Infinite Divine. Still, it was a sobering moment. No matter what the Sentinels said about "crossing" and "waiting," Terza Shirak—with all her emotions, knowledge and memories—was plainly no more.

The sekiyr started to cry. Shamarr Kiel walked around the bed toward him while Meris backed away and left the room. Out in the hall, she leaned against a stone wall.

What was the point of living at all, if even a long life was grieved so painfully? These people claimed the dead were "waiting." Did they really believe some people had been "waiting" for hundreds or thousands of years? If their Holy Speaker existed, why didn't he simply speak spirits into existence on that "crossing's" other side? Billions had died—some peacefully like Terza, but some in agony.

And actually, life made just as little sense from the Collegiate viewpoint. Why would a spark fly off the eternal flame into corruption, neediness, pain, and death?

Maybe life was just random circumstance and molecular motion, as non-Collegiates claimed.

She gritted her teeth. The last death she'd seen had also sent her spinning. The fresh corpse had looked so much like a real person, something that might have moved again momentarily. *Body, relax,* she commanded herself. *Mind, be still.* Still shaking inside, she glanced back into the room. Shamarr Kiel stood embracing young Piet. Why in the world had he let that sekiyr witness this?

The Shamarr turned his head to look straight at her. For an instant, he frowned. *Go ahead,* she thought at him. If he were listening in on her thoughts, maybe he'd hear this—or her agitation, at least. *Do your spiritual job, whatever it is. That precious Tavkel didn't help her much, did he?* She turned aside and busied herself putting the tray away in the prep area.

A few minutes later, Shamarr Kiel joined her. "I decided," he said softly, "to give him a few quiet moments with her. He really was an admirer, and it was the Holy One's last gift to her, letting her know she had one. But are you all right, Meris? I could comfort and calm you, if you'd let me. I'd only touch your emotions, not your thoughts."

"No, thank you." At least it no longer frightened her to hear such an offer. Evidently she now believed that if she declined their so-called help, they would honor her reluctance with polite restraint. She glanced back up the passway. "Where's MedSpec Saried?"

Shamarr Kiel drew up even taller. "Gone." His voice was surprisingly curt.

"What? She isn't dead too, is she?"

He looked up at the ceiling. Squaring his shoulders, he appeared to compose himself. "No. Not yet, anyway. My half sister left Procyel for Tallis this morning after . . . Chapter."

Meris abruptly recalled the shouting match on the stepping stones last night. Half the Sanctuary probably had heard it. "With your brother?" she guessed.

He nodded.

"Breaking house arrest," she blurted, and instantly she wished with all her might she hadn't said it.

The Shamarr stared down at her, eyes narrowed. She hadn't realized before that he was a very tall man. Even if he hadn't had ayin abilities, he could threaten her. As he was, what if he put her under one of their vocal commands, to not speak—or to enter t-sleep against her will? Maybe she didn't believe in their polite restraint after all.

"I'm sorry," she added hastily. "I'm sure you would have stopped him if you could've."

"Thank you for assisting, Meris." His voice was so soft and sincere that she felt briefly convinced—and then instantly suspicious. He was probably manipulating her with his vocal tone. "You may leave now." He turned and plodded back up the corridor toward the patient room.

Meris stood motionless in the passway, but the adrenaline in her veins made her feel like she was vibrating. If MedSpec Saried and the Air Master were both en route to Tallis, these people were about to be in much worse trouble. Surely that pair would be intercepted. Probably prosecuted. Shamarr Kiel plainly knew it.

But they had just lost their medspec. They actually needed her now, awake and alert. Relief washed over her like a deep, warm wave.

Then came a sudden chill. Might they refuse to let her leave?
Body, relax. Mind, be still.

Minster Wind plainly had DeepScan communication capability, there in her office. Maybe it was time to see just how real that polite restraint actually was. So far, Meris had not insisted on sending her own message to Tallis.

That time had come.

She made fists at her sides and headed toward the Minster's office.

CHAPTER 17

An electronic tone chirped in the main room of Jorah's new apartment.

He'd spotted a pin lens on the wall. He stared at it deliberately, ran his hands over his hair. He grimaced for whoever was watching. He glanced at the front room's window. Its sparkling security flecks blurred his view, except when he looked straight out, so he couldn't stare down to see how high they were housing him.

The apartment was sparsely furnished, with a seating L under grey wall panels nobody had bothered to decorate. At least it had separate sleeping and freshing rooms. An untrained occupant might have even thought it was private.

Its door slid open, and Chancellor Gambrel stepped into the main room. His dark green cutaway dress coat was a stark contrast to the uniformed Tallan beside him, whose constellation of Federate decorations made the grey tunic look like a trophy board. "Good morning, Jorah," Gambrel said. "Colonel Zeimsky is one of our experts on brain alteration. I'll escort you to your hearing in just a few minutes, but the colonel wants to check you over first. Assuming everything goes as planned, you'll be leaving us shortly."

Jorah backed out of their way, wondering whether Colonel Zeimsky fit inside the enormous hole in his memory. The man had an odd gap in one eyebrow, maybe an old scar he'd never bothered to have patched. He set a carry case on Jorah's food servo.

Yesterday, some tech had taken Jorah out for a brain scan and confirmed that their treatment had shriveled his ayin like a chunk of dried meat. He couldn't remember how they'd done it. He didn't remember giving permission, either, though the tech had insisted he had.

Surely, the tech was lying or had been lied to. These people might have scarred him deeply—they might as well have branded him, *this man is ours*—but they couldn't change who he was. Jorah Caldwell would've fought anyone who tried this.

He just wished he remembered how they'd beaten him, so next time he might see it coming. It galled him now to roll over and pretend to cooperate. But this was not the time to fight back.

Not yet.

At Colonel Zeimsky's gesture, he sat down on one end of the seating L with his back to his kitchen servo. The colonel ran a specialized handheld over his head. Staring out the sparkling window at a local shuttle soaring past, Jorah remembered a shimmering visitor that had seemed to use dust specks for a body. He hadn't forgotten everything. So where had it gone, with its extravagant promises?

"Low blood sugar," the colonel pronounced. "You should eat before we attend your hearing. It's just a formality. They've already put together a crew and an escort for your departure."

Jorah frowned and straightened, the padded black slab still cold underneath him. He'd awakened with a headache and skipped breakfast, and as the headache faded, he'd blacked out twice in quick succession.

Now, the gnawing in his stomach set up a deep uneasiness. He sat a moment longer, blinking slowly. Memory-lodging tricks had been part of his SO training, with hunger as the primary cue. If these people had taken part of his memory, plainly there'd been something he meant to hang onto. He shut his eyes. "Just a minute." It was fortunate Gambrel had brought up this Tallan, not one of the Sentinel colonels from that sorry excuse for a SOOC board. Special Ops people would have realized what he was doing.

Hunger means what? he asked himself. *What?*

It wouldn't come. He covered his eyes with both hands. *Hunger. Danger?*

Whatever they'd done, it was a thorough job. Maybe they'd had SOOC's cooperation.

Jorah would never trust SOOC again.

"Headache?" The colonel's voice was bland.

"Yes." *Cooperate,* Jorah reminded himself. *For now.* "But it's going away. Tell me what to expect at this hearing." He eyed Gambrel. "You predicted a longer wait, sir."

Gambrel nodded down at him. "Much to my relief, we've been able to put together a group qualified to hear your appeal. You will simply explain that you were following orders. No more, no less."

Jorah nodded back. That had been his plan anyway.

His ayin was gone. And what else had they done? *Hunger,* he pressed himself again. *What?* It still wouldn't come. He had to play along with Gambrel for now, but he needed to access the information that was still lodged somewhere in his memory if he meant to save his people. He needed Sentinel help for that. But not SOOC.

The colonel reached into his carry case and pulled a hinged glass square out of a flexible sleeve. He opened the hinge and stuck one piece of glass in Jorah's face. "Exhale through your mouth."

"Why?" Jorah snapped.

Evidently that was all the colonel needed. He closed the square and slipped it back into the carry case. "Certain chemicals are released into the bloodstream when there's been tissue damage. We're checking your levels." Nothing in that smooth voice or his steady eyes suggested that he was lying. He was, though. Jorah felt sure of it. "Are you reasonably comfortable?" the colonel asked. "Do you feel well enough to travel?"

"I wouldn't object to some painkillers." Tempted to mention the blackouts, Jorah decided against it. He could imagine other parts of his brain swelling into the space his ayin once occupied. He stood up to look the colonel in the eye. "Travel where?"

The colonel glanced at Chancellor Gambrel, who crossed his arms over the front of that dress coat. "We want to introduce you to your people in your new role, of course. They should be glad that they can continue in cooperation with the rest of the Whorl, instead of at cross purposes. They can live without altered abilities. You are proving that."

Jorah did recall that they meant to present him as Boh-Dabar. This was no time to demand to know what they'd made him forget—he must be subtler than that—but he could at least stand his ground. Push back a little. He took a step forward. "Why send me anywhere? There's a worshipping Chapter on Tallis. I could announce myself as Boh-Dabar right here."

The other two exchanged glances. "Some of those worshippers will be leaving Tallis with you," Gambrel said, "so that you can start to indoctrinate them. They will begin to form a core group for you when you reach . . . College."

Gambrel must've realized Jorah was pushing. College wasn't the obvious choice, and he plainly expected Jorah to push back again.

Gambrel was correct. Jorah wanted to go elsewhere. "Procyel," Jorah suggested. There were people there who could give back his memory . . . he hoped.

Gambrel raised his hands in a dismissive gesture. "If you wish. But we want to send a small Tallan force with you on a second ship, as an honor guard, and then retain them close by to protect you. If you go to Procyel, they won't be allowed to land, will they?"

"You just said you were sending some Sentinels from Tallis. They'll do."

But Gambrel could be sending him—and the Tallan escort— as part of an attack force. *Always suspect a trap,* as his father had said. Hadn't he?

Well, Procyel had defenses. Jorah had to get out of this place, and that meant playing along for now.

"Tell them," Gambrel was saying, "that there's a non-surgical cure for their disfigurement. That's why I was going to suggest the Sentinel College on Thyrica. The matter should eventually be taken up there, so that future generations can be treated in infancy."

"Eventually," Jorah echoed, hoping to lead Gambrel back toward what he really wanted to know: What were they up to?

"Still," Gambrel said, "I think you are right. It would look more respectful to send you to Sanctuary."

Jorah was not surprised to hear him agree. So was it a bad idea? Should he look elsewhere for help?

Gambrel continued, "After all, your grandfather has probably passed by now. They will probably delay a memorial service until College people arrive from Thyrica. Important people. They will be glad to get your news. Don't underestimate them, Jorah. They expect Boh-Dabar to bring enormous changes."

Staring back at the Chancellor, Jorah was startled to see something shimmer behind the dark pupils of his eyes. He didn't have time to wonder about it. "Do you really think Grandfather has died?" That just didn't seem possible. The old man had seemed like a force of nature. Always there. Always in charge.

The Chancellor raised his eyebrows, as if the news saddened him. "We did receive an intelligence report from the tug that towed the *Daystar* to the Procyel system. Command deck staff received varying exposures to hard radiation, and unfortunately, your grandfather's dose was highest by far. I'm very sorry, Jorah."

Chancellor Gambrel was still lying, though. He'd straightened his back almost imperceptibly, showing Jorah he liked the idea of Grandfather dying. That death would create a power vacuum to move Jorah into. Jorah was used to taking orders, but feeling manipulated made him hot inside.

Especially by people who'd messed with his mind.

"Unfortunately," Gambrel said, "a device that we would have liked to send with you is not quite ready."

Now they were getting somewhere. Jorah kept his voice calm. "Oh?"

Gambrel smiled broadly. "The lightspeed communication barrier is about to be shattered."

Jorah crossed his arms. "Almost any installation of any size can receive DeepScan II, and many of them can send. That isn't new."

"No," Gambrel said, "but sending those transmissions uses an exorbitant amount of subtronic power, and only a few governmental centers are authorized to transmit. We'll soon introduce something far more efficient: Instantaneous Transceiver Disks. We call them ITDs."

Jorah stood staring back at Chancellor Gambrel and his colonel until the silence got to him. "You're waiting for me to ask what they are. Just tell me."

Chancellor Gambrel flicked a hand down at his side. It looked like a signal to whoever was watching via the pin lens on that grey wall. "You will be polite with me, Jorah Caldwell. I still have the authority to have you charged and executed."

This time, he wasn't lying.

"Tell me, if you would. Sir," Jorah added, keeping derision out of his voice.

Gambrel sat down on the other end of the seating L. The colonel remained standing. "ITDs are platters sliced from a new intelligent-crystal medium that researchers in my Collegium have been developing, based on some ancient artifacts that were found on . . . an isolated world. Somehow, the ancients created a metal-crystal matrix that could grow as if alive. Even after they are sliced, subatomic forces link the disks like a neural network. We can attune them in arrays of one large and several small disks."

"Instantaneous?" Jorah backed toward the window. "Two-way?"

"Two-way." Gambrel smiled. "Stop and think what this could mean for you. For unifying the Whorl behind you."

He could think of dozens of applications, both military and social. "Can they be used for transporting objects? People?"

"They aren't magical, Jorah. No more than this." He pulled something out of a coat pocket, and Jorah's pulse sped up. His crystace! Jorah had been wearing it when they arrested him. He took it back gratefully and buckled it onto his forearm as Gambrel continued. "They will carry a tri-dimensional image. That's all."

But that was a lot. "And your Collegium developed them. So you own a technology that's going to change the Federacy forever."

"We do." Gambrel glanced at the colonel.

Jorah's mind spun forward. "You can transmit anywhere. Everywhere. To anyone who owns a disk. You'll control information flow."

"Eventually. For now, they are under Regional Council sponsorship and planetary governments' controls, like DeepScan II. It takes years to grow the disks and weeks to assemble the arrays. But yes, in time, Federate thinking will equalize and diversify. And the Federacy's spirit and heart must become focused. We need you, Jorah."

"Will you send an ITD to Procyel soon?" If he really was Boh-Dabar, everything would fall into place for his people and others. There would be help from outside space and time. Let the Federates crow for now. Their era was ending!

And he knew, even if Gambrel didn't, that the Sentinel kindred would never submit to Gambrel's "treatment." They would defend themselves—or they'd run, if they faced an overwhelming force. Wouldn't it be ironic if Uncle Kiel had been right about that?

Then again, maybe the One who had promised to empower Boh-Dabar had other plans.

"Oh, yes." Gambrel stood back up. He stepped toward the windows, but he kept his eyes on Jorah. "Procyel will receive one. For one thing, we will need to communicate with you for as long as you're there. For now, though, we aren't telling Procyel that you're coming. We'll let you surprise them." He glanced through the door toward Jorah's small sleeping room. "Are your personal items packed? The hearing will begin as soon as we arrive. But you still haven't eaten."

Really hungry now, Jorah tried once more as he stepped around the food servo. *Hunger. What?*

Nothing came. He might as well give up and eat. Soon he'd be on shipboard rations, headed to Procyel. Sanctuary staff could deal with people like Chancellor Gambrel.

CHAPTER 18

Piper Gambrel's next Sentinel prisoner arrived on Tallis eight days after Jorah Caldwell had departed.

He sat in the small central chamber of his official residence in the Maximum Security Tower. A hover screen glowed in front of him, mid-air, at eye level. This chamber was a highly effective cocoon, with a chair that shifted each time he moved to keep electromagnetic contacts at his vital energy points. This twitch exercised his major muscle groups and freed his mind to compare cost/benefit rations for the new ITD communication units. For some reason, his cocoon's cleaning and disinfection cycle had apparently reset to night function and spritzed a mild chemical odor into the air.

This necessitated using a Collegium litany for focus. *Let me show them truth. Let me show them real humanness.*

Building Maintenance had apologized.

Let me show them real humanness. It should not happen again.

According to the next row of figures on his hover screen, a freshly grown Instantaneous Transceiver Unit had been successfully sliced into twenty-three disks, each precisely four centimeters thick, with a diameter of 137 centimeters—

Oddly, he seemed to be floating over his body. The god-voice, which lived on a higher mental plane than even his exceptional mind had previously achieved, seemed to have taken his place in that chair. He felt himself return to his body bare seconds later, but there'd been no mistaking it this time. He'd had a similar sensation a few days before, right after he sent Jorah Caldwell back to Procyel. That time, he'd thought perhaps he'd imagined it.

He stared at the numbers, suddenly aware of a strong correlation between the four-centimeter thickness and the dimensions of the original seed from which they'd been grown. Even as he grasped at that correlation, it faded.

Why could he not remember? Was he not more brilliant than ever, a true fire in the cosmos? Had the god-voice effect lingered inside his body for just a few moments? Yes, that must be what had happened.

Something new was transpiring. He found it highly satisfactory.

A green patch flashed near the bottom of his hover screen. He acknowledged the comm request by staring and blinking. A human image appeared above his projector, replacing the numerical feed: SOOC Colonel Sentinel Cora Claggett grimaced over her left shoulder, probably making sure her own security measures were in place before saying, "Chancellor, I've been interrogating someone you'll want to interview."

"I have a presentation to write." As soon as he finished reading this report, the Regional Council wanted an update on his ITD project. "Can this wait?"

"No. It will affect your insertion of Lieutenant Caldwell at Procyel."

He narrowed his eyes and gave her his full attention.

"The new detainee is one of the mixed-breed Sentinels," Claggett droned on. "She just arrived from Procyel via a messenger ship."

"Oh?" Glancing left, at a list of messages that aides cleared to reach him, he re-read something else that had been sent via DeepScan from Procyel, just before Jorah had departed from Tallis. It surely had been censored, but its origin code indicated that a non-Sentinel human had apparently penetrated that secret enclave. The sender, one Meris Cariole, had even claimed to be loyal to the Collegium. She had reported some odd religious activity taking place on Procyel II.

He'd sent her a message with Jorah.

Leaning into an isometric stretch, he followed that train of thought just a bit further. Meris Cariole should be immune to the Sentinel-specific plague. As a Collegiate, she could even be asked to cooperate with the mysterious super-Sentinel Jorah Caldwell, who also was going to survive.

Excellent.

"Go on," he told the SOOC woman.

"This prisoner's mixed lineage is relevant, sir. However," Claggett continued, "more important, there was a second passenger who didn't land at the spaceport. Air Master Kinnor Caldwell apparently bailed out somewhere. I sent a team to bring him in."

Where had the god-voice gone? He would like its input. "Our young messiah's father? He's too late."

Colonel Claggett nodded, flattening her lips. "Eight days too late."

By now, Jorah should be more than halfway to Procyel. Gambrel smiled slowly. He hadn't told Procyel to expect the boy. Even if he had DeepScanned, the Air Master couldn't have heard that his son Jorah was en route. Comm was impossible in slip-state.

This was marvelous. SOOC could simply entrap Air Master Caldwell and deal with him. "You'll have legal proceedings prepared," he said.

"Yes. Meanwhile, will you speak with this woman? She's not here on official business, but what I saw in her mind is disturbing."

"Don't be coy, Colonel. I'm busy." It had been years since a new technology had such potential to shift information flow. As soon as Regional released the ITD for general use, Collegiate income would rise dramatically.

Perhaps it would happen sooner than Regional Command expected.

The colonel hesitated. "Sir, you should hear this from her. You'll have further questions. I'll bring her up personally."

"With a second guard," he ordered, resigning himself. "If she's mixed-breed, she could be extraordinarily strong."

Colonel Claggett's image tilted slightly. "That's part of what's strange, sir. She has unusually strong genes from her Sentinel father—and Golden City maternal genes, the strongest of all—but she seems to have lost all her abilities. I want her to tell you how, sir. The explanation is bizarre."

Gambrel sensed a prickle of interest that felt oddly foreign. Perhaps his god-voice was active today after all. "Even under mind access, you felt no ayin activity?"

"Correct."

He shifted his forearm against his chair. Any time a person lost Sentinel abilities, he was interested. "Bring her to me. But stay in mental contact with her. If information surfaces that she doesn't see fit to tell me, key me a message."

He finished framing a draft of his report and then moved to his anteroom, where he seated himself behind a more conventional desk. The anteroom was carefully constructed so that from this elevated desk he looked down at the rest of the room. Visitors always stood on black flooring. The walls were highly reflective. A calm sense of floating alongside himself had settled in by the time his outer door opened, admitting three people.

It did feel as if he were not alone in this physical body. Fascinating!

He recognized SOOC Colonel Claggett, he ignored a broad-shouldered guard in Tallan grey, and he spent several seconds studying the prisoner who stood between them, a tall woman wearing plain blue detention shipboards.

Her long grey hair was braided back from a disturbingly Mikuhran-looking face. She'd also picked up a slight tic under one eye—apparently, she'd resisted at least part of Colonel Claggett's interrogation.

It was good to see these people fight each other.

"Good morning, Chancellor." She gave him a reasonably respectful nod. "My name is Saried Kinsman. I'm sure you are thinking how Mikuhran I look. I'm precisely half, sir."

From this vantage, both women looked somewhat foreshortened. The reflective black tile and glossy black walls gave him an almost full-angle view. No one had tried to carry a weapon into his presence yet, but it was wise to be thorough.

"And your father," Colonel Claggett snapped. "Tell him."

"He is High Commander Caldwell." The woman spoke matter-of-factly.

"Really. Really," Gambrel repeated, wondering whether this was a scandal that could be exploited. He'd waited for years to get something on the High Commander. Even now, with the man probably dead, the Collegium might benefit from inside information. "Data, please." On a hover screen over their heads, Sentinel Saried Kinsman's interrogation data appeared.

He read a few lines and looked back down at the women, disappointed. Apparently the only moral offense had been committed by the woman's Golden City ancestors.

She spoke again. "Thank you for agreeing to speak with me, sir. I have unusual news."

She wanted to speak to him, did she? He opened a hand toward her, gesturing for her to continue.

"I've already spoken with Tallis's Chapter group, you understand," she said. "It was important to tell them my news first."

"That's when we were alerted," Colonel Claggett said.

Gambrel pointed at the half-Shuhr woman, indicating that she was to finish speaking. Then, the colonel could fill in any gaps. The prisoner's omissions could be interesting.

"Chancellor." She raised both hands, as if handing him something precious. "I have spoken with Boh-Dabar." She paused, perhaps hoping for a shocked or delighted reaction.

He stared back, refusing to give any such response, but he paid close attention now. Another Boh-Dabar claimant? A fascinating coincidence.

Eventually, she cleared her throat and spoke again. "I believe he would like to broadcast to the Federacy, sir. Naturally, the Chapter priest here recorded my message. He is in contact with private communication concerns, and he is already disseminating that information. He tells me that your Collegium is developing a new communication medium. So I come to you." She paused again, as if she hoped he would explain.

He waited instead, keeping his own thoughts muted and letting his god-voice lead.

After a plainly calculated silence, she spoke again. "I see the hand of the Eternal Speaker in this, Chancellor Gambrel. This technology is being developed precisely as our Dabar needs it. He hasn't asked me to make this request, but I believe it would be to your advantage to send one of those—disks? Do I have it right?—to our Sanctuary on Procyel. For Tavkel's use."

"Tavkel." He repeated the name softly, and at the back of his mind he felt a bizarre sensation of speaking unintelligibly over a vast distance. Meanwhile, he analyzed the name, *Tavkel*. He'd studied their prayer tongue, since ancient languages intrigued him. Boh-

Dabar, their "word to come," evidently had become "the deity's final letter." It was a play on words, very amusing. Or was it "the deity among"? Either was a possible translation of the name.

Then came a paroxysm of frustration. "One moment," he heard himself say in that barely different other voice. "Tell me how you think you lost your abilities."

"He asked for them. I gave them up gladly, for one glance at his heart and mind."

Gambrel glanced at Colonel Claggett, who was under orders never, ever to touch him subvocally. She said aloud, "Sentinel Kinsman does seem to have lost all her ayin abilities. And that is essentially how the encounter proceeded, although no memory persists of that . . . glance. Only the memory of certainty."

Interesting! Sentinels were giving up their powers willingly?

"Tell him," Colonel Claggett said, "who did it first, and what happened."

"My father, the High Commander. And . . . Chancellor, he was completely healed."

"What?" As a High Commander, Brennen Caldwell had been something of a threat to Gambrel's reorganization plan. His survival—even retired—could be inconvenient.

Then again, it would be temporary. Zeimsky's plague bacilli would kill the elderly first.

A second, unsettling realization hit him next, followed by a delightful implication. "Did High Commander Caldwell lose his abilities, then?"

The woman pressed her palms together. "Yes, of course. But it's short-term, you see. He can retrain. I have chosen to remain as I am."

"What?" Uneasy again, he glared down at Colonel Claggett.

"I . . . didn't have her brain scanned, sir. There simply hasn't been a flicker of ayin activity."

"Tavkel," the Shuhr-Sentinel woman continued, "asked my father to help us all retrain under a new set of codes. Under new authority," she ended wistfully.

"And what," he blurted. For some reason, his god-voice had suddenly turned furious. That made it difficult to speak. "What is this Boh-Dabar supposed to be?"

Her eyes widened. "You don't know? Doesn't your Collegium study all faiths?"

"Humor me. Tell me how you understand it." He rested his elbows on the smooth desktop. This would be amusing, since those people were doomed anyway. Bacteria inside young Lieutenant Caldwell's skull would be multiplying in waves. Each time they built up too much pressure, they died back, forming spores that were gathering in his lungs. He should have already infected his Sentinel shipmates.

And there was more, of course. Piper Gambrel never worked without an alternate plan.

The Sentinel-Shuhr woman kept prattling about a long-promised king of the universe, with power to destroy the Whorl and make a sacrificial immolation of all evil—a speech that was being recorded for later. "Destroy the Whorl?" he asked crisply. "Please elaborate."

She looked down at the flooring, perhaps resting her neck, before facing him again. "He has predicted some kind of catastrophe, but apparently, even he isn't privy to the details."

He smirked. Obviously, someone else also had alternate plans. Whatever happened, this Tavkel could claim he'd predicted it.

Over Colonel Claggett's shoulder, rapidly appearing letters caught his attention. *She's recalling,* they spelled, *that non-Sentinel Tallans are volunteering to go to other Whorl worlds and spread this news, in case you don't send an ITD. And unspecific DeepScan possibilities exist at Procyel.*

The long-faced prisoner continued in a singsong tone that sounded as if she'd been rehearsing. "I could lie to you, sir. I don't expect you to like the idea of catastrophe or sacrifice. But soon, all people will be ushered into a new state of being. It will be bliss for those who have been reconciled with his perfection. I can't bear to imagine what it would be like for people who remain hostile to it."

Gambrel's mouth spoke words he hadn't intended. "Where did he come from? Surely not your Sanctuary."

She shook her head and glanced over her shoulder at the colonel. "We've had a second Procyel settlement for many generations. It's been secret until now. Tavkel was born there. He says it has served its purpose and will be defended until the end."

This was news. *Confirm?* he messaged the colonel.

She nodded slightly again. Another howling frustration boiled up out of him, and with it came the odd sense of distraction over a vast distance. Evidently, it hadn't occurred to Colonel Cora Claggett that he was entitled to this information.

This second mistake was unfortunate, of course. She remained at attention, but he imagined he could sense her sudden fear. Surely, such abrupt terror didn't come from his powerful god-voice.

"You're completely free to disbelieve," the prisoner said. "He calls freedom the greatest gift after life itself. You may focus on yourself, or you may gaze on the One. But when the sacrifice is complete and the Adversary's hold on us destroyed, then the one who has always Spoken will be satisfied. There will be genuine goodness again."

Gambrel felt himself stand up. "She's deranged," he declared. "She's a danger to herself and others, spreading this gibberish. I want her in protective custody. Near Lieutenant Caldwell," he added, staring down at the colonel. If Sentinel Cora Claggett understood his intent, she might redeem herself for a little longer.

Let's see, he observed silently, *what the prisoner does if she thinks Jorah Caldwell is still here.* The thoughts and the declaration left him slightly confused. Which words were his god-voice's, and which came from his prior, slightly less capable self?

The colonel smiled slightly and addressed the guard. "Sergeant, take this Sentinel to housing block thirteen-twelve."

The prisoner and her guard walked out silently. The moment his outer door closed, Colonel Claggett started pacing the black flooring. "You'll want her watched at epsilon frequencies, particularly. To see if she tries to contact Lieutenant Caldwell."

He collected himself, dismissing confusion. *I am the spark of undying light.* "Exactly."

"Consider it done." She reached the reflective wall, turned, and looked up again.

Gambrel leaned against his backrest and glanced at a control. A new current warmed his shoulders. The SOOC colonels still would be useful for awhile. He'd known all along, though, that he couldn't really trust any Sentinels who cooperated with his Collegium. Deep in their minds, they kept secrets from him.

"Excellent," he said in a casual tone. "She'll have no way of knowing he already left here. If she shows any twitch of those allegedly former powers, notify me. And tell me," he added, "what has happened to High Commander Caldwell. Not dead yet?"

"Evidently not." Cora Claggett stared straight ahead. "Apparently this Tavkel restored him to full health. Saried Kinsman was the Sanctuary's medical specialist, and she was in personal attendance when it happened." She looked up. "It apparently convinced her this Tavkel is supernatural, since he'd been injected with blocking drugs."

That was unsettling. "Plainly, the High Commander wasn't as sick as—"

"Excuse me, sir, but he was. His death was expected within hours. Does this information affect our mission en route to Procyel? Do we DeepScan other orders to our RIA escort ship when it emerges from slip-state?"

He rubbed his chin. "Not yet. When these two Boh-Dabars meet each other, only one is likely to survive."

"You expect this Tavkel to kill Jorah, if he turns out to be immune to plague bacilli?"

That hadn't occurred to him, but yes, if the stranger had supernatural healing abilities, he might survive the disease. And if everything went perfectly, he might even eliminate a competitor.

Then again, he might not function so well without Saried Kinsman's medical presence. Maybe he'd been reading MedSpec Kinsman's mind, "healing" by drawing out Shuhr secrets she hadn't previously practiced.

At any rate, Colonel Claggett had not been exposed to the bacilli by Jorah. That could be changed. "I expect you," he told her, "to advise me as ordered and then wait for further instructions."

She pulled her shoulders back into a military brace, as if saluting. At that moment, he thought he heard a voice inside his own mind, this time no plainly "higher self" but someone or something else that was communicating with him. Claggett? Furious, he was about to touch a button that would fire a stun beam, until he realized that the words couldn't have come from her. *I can't get to him, having attached this body, unless we go to Procyel . . . yourself.*

"We" did not belong in the same sentence as "yourself." The odd sense of otherness dissipated, leaving him awed by a new realization: Non-physical creatures could apparently enter reality by occupying a particular human body. He'd actually been co-embodied with another transcendent being! His god-voice was, in fact, a godlike spark of the Infinite. It was poised to save humanity from the Sentinels' clutchings for more power.

The idea both thrilled and terrified him. How did a person cope with such a situation without relinquishing control? "It will be six to ten more days before we can hope to hear that Lieutenant Caldwell's shipmates are ill," he said. "If we hear nothing, we'll do exactly what this Tavkel is asking for."

"Send him an ITD disk?"

"*Take* him an ITD disk. Personally. In force." Plainly, that was what his god-voice—this other distinct intelligence—had meant. Non-Sentinels had been barred from Procyel for a hundred years. However, the Whorl was changing. He loved the idea of exposing their secrets. "And we have a Collegiate already on the ground there."

Colonel Claggett looked down, evidently consulting her handheld. "Meris Cariole. Medical trainee. They're extremely reticent about outsiders there. Minster Haworth-Caldwell probably has her in stasis or tardema-sleep by now." She clipped the handheld to her belt. "I didn't get her status from our prisoner. Apparently it didn't seem important."

Three mistakes, Colonel, he thought toward her, though she would not hear him. He flicked an eye toward a point on his hover screen, brought Meris Cariole's personal information back up, and smiled. "Do that. We need to protect that young woman."

He smiled slowly, and the god-voice cohabiting his body seemed to smile too. The idea of hosting such a being was beginning to delight him. "And our Lieutenant Caldwell can't infect her, since she has no ayin."

Another pleasant thought occurred to him. "Also, when Air Master Kinnor Caldwell surfaces here, I want capital charges and the official sentencing transmission already prepared. I want this finished as quickly as possible."

Why? he wondered. The urgency seemed to come from elsewhere, a sense that Jorah Caldwell's family was particularly dangerous to non-altered humanity. If every person who carried that name were to die, the Whorl would be safer.

He couldn't say why he felt so certain, but he did. He, himself. Not the god-voice.

"We'll be ready." She tucked her handheld into a belt pocket. "Saried Kinsman does appear to be under a deep voice command, probably imposed by Air Master Caldwell."

Two words came to mind, the words Sentinels feared most. "Selfishly? Capriciously?"

She looked up at him again, raising her chin. "Possibly both," she answered without expression.

Plainly, she knew what he wanted and would cooperate. Perhaps he would pardon her offenses of the last hour.

Furthermore, protocol demanded that Regional Command must DeepScan the Sentinel College on Thyrica whenever one of their people faced a death sentence. The College was entitled to request clemency.

This time, they wouldn't dare.

CHAPTER 19

Meris's hopes were fading. It had been more than ten days since she sent Tallis her DeepScan message, and if the Collegium had responded, Minster Wind hadn't said so. No one had needed her medical skills since Terza Shirak's passing, but to her profound relief there'd been no further talk of t-sleep. The only interesting event had been an astrophysics report on Sabba Six-Alpha, which had apparently settled back down to its usual ominous inactivity.

Why us? she grumbled. *Why just then?*

The report—relayed from Tallis—offered no explanation.

This morning, she stood topside in the dirt. The sun shone strongly over the hill on the compound's east side. She'd plunked on a broad-brimmed straw hat to keep her face from burning like Tavkel's. From beyond the tall fence to her left—a fence woven from some kind of thick wire, supposedly to keep animals called cornjackers out of the crop fields—she could hear the Tuva River as a steady rush-swishing. She couldn't see the river for the swath of tall, lacy bushes, but in the clearing between bushes and fence, clusters of pink-spiked blossoms stood almost knee high. They were drawing a swarm of small black bees.

Above the wire mesh fence, the peaks were like jagged teeth, freshly whitened by the spring storm. Small, puffy clouds cast distinct shadows on the mountainsides, sweeping upslope and then vanishing over the crested peaks as the clouds blew past.

She blew out a breath. This was a vast improvement over the last few days, which she'd spent underground. She couldn't believe these people had never installed a weather control system. Nothing steered Procyel's storms but prevailing winds and Coriolis forces, so three stormy days had kept them from hurrying to plant this season's food crops—since they also didn't have hydroponics. During those three days, her work team had been sorting stores in a cellar and moving them up to the kitchens.

It all felt like a full immersion tri-D visit to the distant past. With Annalah assigned to a different work team and then spending most of her free hours following Tavkel around, they rarely even saw each other. Annalah had come back to the room bubbling about how Tavkel had changed her life. "It's amazing, how I can suddenly remember things. Grandfather always had that eidetic memory gift, but I never . . ."

Meris had tuned her out and gone to sleep.

Today, almost everyone was working uplevel, planting the fields or pinching pink blooms off snow-apple trees. It was also some kind of annual festival. According to the woman she'd been partnered with, each year they did a major dirt dig to commemorate the colony's first planting. Meris had now learned the fine points of wielding a long-handled tool they called a "guhsh." Others could say the word with straight faces, but she couldn't.

Other teams' shovels and root rakes had softened the ground, but dirt clods still needed to be broken. She raised the guhsh's bulbous metal end over one such clod, let the guhsh fall, and watched the clod shatter into smaller bits. Satisfied, she pounded them out as well.

Expanding the crop field was apparently part of the Tehillah festival. It made particular sense this year, with a plainly over-crowded situation.

The woman working next to Meris bent down, pulled something brown out of the dirt, and held it between thumb and fore-finger. "Another seed pod. There'll be plenty of wildflowers in this year's greens."

Meris eyed the tiny thing. "Is that a problem?"

The woman laughed as she tossed the pod onto a debris pile. "The Tehillah field is always greens. We harvest them quickly and then do another sweep for weeds. That's how we find all the weed seeds and grass roots."

Meris's back ached. The knot of hair at the back of her neck felt hot and sticky, the sun hat made her forehead itch, and inside her dirty fabric gloves, her hands itched too. Still, it felt good to lean on her guhsh and look back at the smooth, clod-less soil she'd left behind. She liked the cheerful Sentinel too. Shared labor did seem to create an emotional bond—or maybe it was just the warm sunshine that made her feel oddly contented. The cooling breeze smelled of trees and moist soil. Other workers followed her team, re-raking the guhshed ground, marking planting rows, and drop-ping minuscule seeds.

"Your wildflowers can't be weeds," she told the woman. "They're too pretty."

"Anything growing where it doesn't belong is a weed."

Amused, Meris made sure no one else was in earshot. She leaned closer. "So who's the worse weed, me or Tavkel?"

The woman laughed and whacked another clod. "You should be glad I'm not a first-circle."

"A what?"

She shrugged. "Willing to pay for full mental contact by being disempowered. People who've gone all the way inside. I gave him my darkness but kept my abilities, and he didn't seem to mind. I don't know who started the labeling. We're getting called second-circle, though."

Meris snorted. "It just goes to show. People love to argue and compare themselves with each other."

The woman didn't answer that.

"Annalah must be first circle."

"Oh, yes."

"So what do you do, out in the Federacy?"

The woman went silent for several seconds. Finally she looked Meris straight in the eye. "Military intelligence."

Meris felt a chill. "Does that mean you . . . organize it?"

The woman shook her head. "No, I gather."

"You interrogate people? Using your powers?"

The woman leaned heavily on her guhsh. "It's my job, Meris. Here, I'm on leave. Here, I'm just as close to a normal human being as I ever can be."

Meris knew she ought to make small talk, to ask whether the woman had ever worked with High Commander Caldwell. But the realization that she'd worked all morning with a cheerful woman who was trained to break into other people's minds and memories . . . It was overwhelming.

She concentrated on her work with new energy. Obviously, the woman sensed her horror—because she too fell silent.

By the time they reached the row's end, the shovel and root-rake teams were pulling off gloves and laying tools on the path. Meris's team boss shouted, "Guhsh, you're finished as well."

Meris and her partner hiked without speaking to the end of the field and on up the hillside to the graveled path, where they too laid down their tools.

From here, Meris could see past the barns. Above the landing strip, near the end of the orchards, lay a natural bowl in the hillside that the Sentinel woman had called an amphitheater. She had also predicted a midday celebration.

As Meris trudged up the path, she could see that food and drink was being distributed on a table that must've been carried out through the hangars. Off-duty people were trudging uphill from the elevator building, stopping at the table and finding places to sit in the amphitheater, on ground that was part grass, part dirt.

Yesterday another private craft had arrived from Caroli, carrying four more refugee Sentinel families. Apparently they had heard about Tavkel at their Chapter meeting and decided to come here to participate in whatever was going to happen.

Meris and her partner got into the food line. White-haired men and women served them lunch from bowls and baskets, and Meris found herself wondering how many of them had been trained to trespass in other people's thoughts. The table, weighted with food and drinks, was covered with red, green, and blue cloths, like the altar cloths down in the Chapter room. The breeze barely fluttered its heavy brocade.

She didn't spot Annalah, but she escaped her guhsh partner and found a more or less comfortable position halfway up the hill, glad to be wearing the brown, unstainable work pants. Shamarr Caldwell and most of the Sanctuary staff sat down near the front, closer to the table. She didn't see Tavkel.

As she finished settling in, Shamarr Kiel and Minster Wind strode forward. Each rested a hand on the big book that must have been laid out on the table beside an oil lamp while she turned her back and found a seat. The newly placed objects weighted down the fluttering cloths after food bowls and platters had been whisked away.

Meris peered at them from under the brim of her sun hat. She thought the Minster looked weary, with a tendency to flinch when workers walked behind her. After all, Tavkel had predicted her husband's death.

Meris still hadn't seen the infamous bereavement shock that Lady Fi had escaped: not in Minster Wind, nor in anyone else here.

From a medical standpoint she was curious, but as a fellow human, she hoped Minster Wind didn't have to go through it. Still, if it did happen, she knew several litanies that might give Minster Wind hope and comfort.

The Shamarr raised a hand. "Pray with me."

Meris found herself agreeing with much of what he said in his prayer—spring as a time of rebirth, which certainly was going on all around her—how the new season meant nurturing life so it could eventually nourish them, and so forth. He claimed they all were grateful.

I would be, she wanted to answer him, *if there were someone to thank—other than my own work crew. But I would be even more thankful for a ride to Tallis.*

Minster Wind spoke next. "Today's traditional Adoration is from the historical sequence. Our guest Tavkel has asked if he might cantor." Her voice carried just as well as the Shamarr's.

They both backed away from the table and seated themselves off to one side, the Shamarr with his family and the Minster with the elder Caldwells—and there sat Annalah, beside her grandfather. Meris squinted downhill at her room-partner. *Where were you last night?* she wanted to ask.

Nothing happened for several seconds. Maybe they all were praying in silence. Meris ate quickly, eyeing the Shamarr. She'd attended several of his morning sessions during the rainy spell. After all, she'd had to do something in her spare time.

He'd been talking about the infamous Boh-Dabar prophecies and explaining traditional interpretations. It had been undeniably interesting to see how many pieces Tavkel seemed to bring together, assuming there was a puzzle to be solved. In other passages, though, they seemed to be expecting someone much more militant and dangerous.

Hence the talk in the dining commons that night that High Commander Caldwell had been healed. About regaining the Federacy's respect, even becoming the Whorl's new rulers.

Tavkel finally stood up near the crowd's center. He left his walking stick on the grass and strode downhill to position himself in front of the long table. He stared left and slowly turned his head toward the right. For one moment, those brown eyes looked straight at her. Was he reading her mind? He certainly knew how to work a crowd. On Elysia, he could've gathered quite a following.

He lifted his chin and began to sing. He sang from memory, using that other language, the language that Annalah had called "almost incomprehensibly ancient." What a voice! Mellow and soft-edged, it turned a song into something ecstatic. Each melody line rose, did a few turns at the top, and fell to settle on a lengthy low note. After four such lines, everyone else sang a refrain. Phrases followed each other. First came what sounded like a song's verse, then a brief answer that she recognized on the third pass.

She nibbled a perfumy pastry and waited for them to say something she could understand. Meanwhile, she really didn't want to fall under the man's almost hypnotic appeal. She focused her mind. *I am the spark of undying light. I shall see. I shall know . . .*

● ● ●

The *latchem* pastries had been like tasting paradise. As Tavkel sang, Kiel tried to relax his shoulders and maintain a grateful, worshipful mind. He enjoyed letting other people cantor festival services, but he always followed the Adoration carefully.

So far, Tavkel seemed to be sticking to the authorized version. Its lyrics recounted how the Eternal Speaker had preserved their people, as well as some of the terrible consequences of historic rebellions.

He shot his father a sidelong glance, still angry over the high-handed way he had helped Kinnor break custody. If his father really believed in Tavkel, he'd sent his other son—Kiel's brother—to die. Beside Father, Annalah sat with her eyes closed, smiling rapturously.

Kiel couldn't bear the sight. He caught Hanusha's uneasiness on the pair bond, like a thrumming echo of his own. She'd been DeepScanned from Thyrica late yesterday evening. Her parents had moved onto the Sentinel College campus, after a string of petty vandalisms. Patrols and defenses could prevent harassment there, and Mother Ellet and Pa Damalcon would be safer. They had promised to maintain a nexus, passing information among Sentinels scattered to other worlds.

He looked up at Tavkel in time to catch the second stanza's closing phrases.

"*. . . In great deliverance, when they pursued us,*
     You fed us on heavenly bread and restored us to your
land of promise . . ."

Kiel prayed silently. *Where are you taking us now, Eternal One?* Then he sang with the others, "Your mercy is eternal." He'd coached countless sekiyrra to read from *Dabar* and *Mattah*. Tavkel's fluency was impressive.

It struck him that he could actually stay in the Whorl. He might surrender his abilities to Tavkel and choose not to retrain. That would leave him free to proselytize among non-gifted peoples. He could guide them all toward the Holy Path and let them decide whether to align themselves with Tavkel.

Should he?

No. He glanced at Hanusha. As clouds rushed past, she sat frowning. He sensed her uneasiness too. No, the Sentinel families were his responsibility. Shaking his head, he stared at the altar flame. Was he simply reluctant to let someone else lead? Pride was deadly, his mother had always said. *Protect the College,* he prayed, *and Hanusha's parents.*

He broke off another small, delectable bite of the holiday pastry and tucked it into his mouth.

• • •

" . . . And our hearts pursued other gods . . ."

Those two small words, "other gods," had always pained Fi Caldwell when she'd heard this Adoration.

She sat clasping her husband's hand, trying to find a comfortable way to position her sit-bones on lumpy ground. She had literally served other gods, other so-called powers, as a girl. What a privilege to have survived and lived free of them.

From this side of the amphitheater, she could study many of the faces that were turned toward Tavkel, some of them wide-eyed and others dubious, their faces like shuttered blast doors. She closed her eyes, wanting to listen undistracted, but her mind wouldn't settle. Just like in a vision she'd seen decades ago, she was hearing the voice that had sung time and space into existence. The Eternal Speaker's own final Word. His *Dabar.*

Focus, she reprimanded herself. *Listen.* Still, one more thought fluttered wantonly into her mind. She'd known doting grandmothers, women who had virtually worshipped a grandchild.

She'd been given that privilege, since her own grandson was more than merely human. She could actually worship Tavkel.

A breeze tickled the side of her face. She sensed Brennen sitting close by, equally absorbed. He squeezed her hand, but he didn't look away from Tavkel—except when he glanced at Annalah to give her an encouraging nod. She'd shown a startling new gift in memory skills, a gift that had been one of his specialties.

How marvelous to see Annalah using that gift.

• • •

" . . . so you went bound with us into captivity,
Where we transgressed mightily against you.

We stretched out and took power
That in your wisdom you declined to give . . ."

Hearing that line about transgression, Wind Haworth-Caldwell flinched. *Kinnor!* her heart shrieked. *Jorah!* She quickly turned it into a prayer, since it would be inappropriate to distract others by broadcasting grief and fear. *Help them, protect them, bring them back safely!* Would this season of life and color and rejoicing turn to death and agony?

She shifted her seat on the cold, grassy ground and pulled her coat closer around her. People did die during festivals. Still, she believed she could ask for special mercy because of the festival . . . couldn't she? Sentinel mercy had spared her life as a little child, when the very elders sitting close by her today had led the last assault on the Golden City. Many highly placed Sentinels had wanted the Shuhr wiped out, every last one of them, down to the smallest DNA carrier.

It seemed appropriate to remember that dark history today, and that she might have died without ever having met Kinnor.

She took a deep breath. The fields still smelled of the recent rain.

Tavkel had requested and received another dose of DME-6 yesterday. She had to admire that man.

"Your mercy is eternal," she sang.

If anyone could save Jorah, Kinnor could.

• • •

Brennen Caldwell's lips moved as he mouthed lines he'd memorized decades ago. Twice, the Holy One had rained down catastrophe to cleanse his progenitors of their idolatries. First, an asteroid had struck an inland sea near the first land he had given them. For a generation, the Holy One had fed his people heavenly bread. Slowly, civilization had risen again. Humanity had fouled that world but leaped to others, bringing its darkness along with it.

Two worlds lay behind them, both scoured of life. Tragically, the Holy One's image bearers had repeatedly destroyed his creation. The Adversary seemed to have triumphed both times.

Now, the awful cycle might end. Those worlds might become gardens again, and he might live to see it!

He caressed his wife's hand with his thumb. He'd fought battles with weapons and words. He'd sent others to die and labored to repair botched negotiations, saving other lives. He had the sense, now, that it had been work well done.

He would've crossed willingly after the *Daystar* catastrophe, except he was glad that Firebird Mari had been spared that agony. He gladly would spend the rest of this life on the task Tavkel had set him, retraining their returning abilities with a stronger sense of community and a less competitive emphasis. There would be no skill ratings in the new era.

Perhaps in Tavkel's renewal, people outside the kindred would receive similar skills and need training. Maybe he too was being trained.

Like his granddaughter Annalah, his mate was proving an apt pupil. He pressed her hand again. She squeezed back.

"Sustain us until the day when we may be found worthy
To kiss your feet as you walk among us, renewer of worlds . . ."

Brennen straightened his spine, thinking once more about that renewal. If it came soon, did that mean many of the people seated here would not die? Until then, would they suffer loss—possibly including Kinnor, who was as courageous and defiant as his mother? Obedience wasn't easy for such people.

It was not easy for anyone.

". . . Call out your beloved children to yourself, and reign forever . . ."

Hearing the cue to rise, Brennen struggled to his feet. He helped Firebird Mari to stand, and they faced the altar. Above and around them, voices resounded. "Your mercy is eternal. Your mercy is eternal. Your mercy is eternal."

• • •

Kiel shifted his legs to walk forward, but Tavkel motioned everyone to sit down again. Having claimed the podium, Tavkel was entitled to hold it. Kiel didn't want to disrupt the festival by asking the young teacher to stand down. He sat on the hard ground again.

Don't let him teach error, Kiel begged the Eternal Speaker. *But if he does, let me catch it. I'll need to explain tomorrow—to anyone who's still listening,* he finished glumly. Attendance was dropping at his daily prophecy sessions.

"Our history," Tavkel called, "did not end on Thyrica. Listen to a story about this world, about Procyel."

Kiel folded his arms around his bent knees. He shifted his weight and attended closely.

"Water was the issue." Tavkel leaned against the altar's brocade cloths. "Several locations were surveyed. South, on the other side of the mountains, there's a plain with plenty of room but not much rain. What little rain does fall, it soaks down through sandy soil. Any seeds planted there wouldn't even put down a root.

"Some distance west, they found water to spare—too much, in fact. The Tuva River spreads out into a swamp that would have swallowed anything they tried to build, not to mention the seeds they planted." He tucked one hand into a pocket and pulled out a brown speck. At that moment, he glanced in Kiel's direction. Through his shields, Kiel felt several others turn their attention toward him. He nodded agreement, but he understood that Tavkel was not talking about either history or horticulture.

"Much farther north," Tavkel continued, "the Tuva is fresh and clean, but it freezes for half the year. Your seeds would grow well in the long summer days, but winter comes early. Crops would fail.

"Between the swamp and the snowfields," he said, spreading out both arms, "they found this valley. Good soil, good drainage, but you all were warned not to drink from the Tuva, weren't you? There's a large game population upstream. Brownbucks don't care where they relieve themselves."

Kiel's daughter Perl chuckled and looked guiltily over her shoulder at him. Half smiling, he shook his head.

"So the water carries fecal bacteria. Water purification would have required technology they didn't want to depend on. I'm told that they thought about hunting the brownbucks out of the watershed, but that seemed cruel. Wasteful too. Brownbuck is good eating, a valuable resource." He paused for several seconds. "So they were about to move on." He raised his head. "Who knows why they didn't?"

A young voice shouted, "The spring."

Kiel stared up into the amphitheater, trying to identify who'd spoken. The sekiyrra sat scattered among refugee families, elders, and Sanctuary staff.

"Yes." Tavkel smiled. "Just uphill from here, they tapped clean water flowing out of the ground. The reflecting pool is filled from it directly. Gravity sends water into the cistern, the generator, bath heaters, and our irrigation system. Even," he added, "a certain waterfall you couples have enjoyed."

Kiel felt warm pressure against his shoulder. He and Hanusha might both distrust everything Tavkel said, but he hadn't forgotten that night of creating the pair bond in the privacy suite, beside that unending waterfall.

Scanning the crowd again as Tavkel paused for effect, Kiel glimpsed Meris Cariole. He thinned his shields and tried to pick out her emotional state. As far as he could tell, she found the history interesting.

Closer, now that he'd thinned his shields, Annalah appeared utterly rapt. Plainly, she was hearing a layered story. Water and seeds had been used as symbols in the holy books, all the way back to *Negiynah Zamahr.*

He hasn't mentioned Tekkumah, Kiel realized. Thinking of that holy place made Kiel wonder whether he ought to somehow ask the people beyond those mountains for prayer—for help—for advice. And what if they had exiled Tavkel as a false prophet—shouldn't someone here try to find out? How could anyone do that without breaking a holy law, without making the trip illegally?

I could go to Tekkumah, he observed, *if things became desperate. If it looked like all was lost, I would sacrifice myself to save a remnant.*

"So when summer comes, you water these fields," Tavkel said. "The soil holds unpolluted moisture. The seed you saved from last year's crop puts down deep roots. Meanwhile, under slopes farther north, rains and snowmelt collect in an aquifer that will keep refilling this spring until time itself ends."

He performed another one of those silent eye-sweeps. "Some of you understand all that I've said. What you plant here, this year, will still grow in a renewal you cannot comprehend. Ask me, and I will bring you the clean water of life and truth. Give your darkness to me. It stands between you and the true eternal."

With that, Tavkel sat down.

Kiel couldn't spare the time to ponder the story. He hurried up front and dismissed the gathering. As before, through his lowered shields bubbled others' confusion, delight, or hostility. His sister Wind hurried straight to the elevators, while many others returned to the new field, including Hanusha, Rena, and Perl. They'd been honored with places on the planting team.

Others lingered near Tavkel, including his parents and Annalah. Unsurprisingly, a Sentinel who'd just returned from Federate Caroli was already kneeling.

Kiel thickened his shields, knowing what would come next. He was tired of bracing himself to resist it.

He stared at the landing strip instead. From here, he could see that the downhill side was becoming edged with a line of tethered and covered landing craft. Tomorrow after the festival, ten volunteers would start refitting the biggest ship that had arrived here: the College shuttle, parked down in the largest underground hangar. They would replace its recliner seats with stacked berths. It would be the Sentinel kindred's means of escape. If just one of them kept the ability to put others into t-sleep, most of them could travel in near hibernation for rotating shifts. Kiel also hoped to add external pods, expanding its storage capacity.

If Kin and Jorah returned from Tallis safely—possibly in as little as ten more days—he would ask Kin to expand the defense force he'd already suggested, not simply to defend the Sanctuary now, but also to escort the shuttle out-Whorl. This morning Kiel had sent a coded transmission to Hanusha's parents at College. He'd begged them to prep their biggest ship too. They would need to leave Thyrica soon and secretly.

Water, he repeated silently, frowning into the throng that was gathering near the altar. Tavkel might accuse him of having a mind flooded and quenched by tasks and worries.

Other people needed him, though. To Kiel, the reflecting pool had always felt like the very soul of this place. Often when he taught, he compared it to a person's heart. Day or night, a pure heart reflected light and peace.

And the shuttle's water recycling apparatus would be crucial. He didn't yet have a systems engineer for that job. He needed to check the arrival roster.

He felt numb, as if part of his spirit were dying. Glancing left, he made sure that sekiyrra were folding the altar cloths. They were. He headed for the hangar area's small access door, stepping carefully around tussocks of last year's dry grass.

CHAPTER 20

Piper Gambrel hustled out of a midmorning administrative meeting, his wrist monitor shining with the words he'd been hoping for two days to read: "Kinnor Caldwell in custody."

He rode the secure elevator down to SOOC. As the door closed, his handheld already displayed a second message: *Full interrogation?*

That would take three days, so he hesitated. He might have liked to find out all of Air Master Caldwell's dirty secrets, as well as more information on his son Jorah's alleged competitor for the Boh-Dabar title.

Still, Piper Gambrel was a busy man. All he needed was a guilty verdict, so that was the essence of his reply. The god-voice sharing his body wanted this man dead by midnight. The troublemaker's swift encounter with justice should deter the rest of his people from interfering with changes in the Federacy.

Twenty minutes later, Gambrel sat behind an observer's one-way window. It was both fascinating and horrifying to watch Sentinels work against one of their own kind. On the window's other side, restrained in an interrogation chair and drugged to disable his ayin,

Kinnor Caldwell finally stopped struggling. Colonel Cora Claggett and Colonel Artur Mercell sat beside him, one apparently keeping him under voice command and the other digging through his mind for incriminating memories.

While he waited, Gambrel queried the detention area via his handheld. Saried Kinsman, he was informed, still hadn't shown any signs of using Sentinel abilities. She hadn't tried to escape either, but had spent most of her time singing.

Gambrel felt fully alert at both levels of awareness—himself, and his god-voice. He got up and paced the observation room. His own curiosity wanted to know what would happen if real prophecies were coming true. Whether he was challenging a genuine god. Whether such a being could really exist.

The god-voice displayed no such doubts. It was calmly managing circumstances, gathering evidence against half siblings Saried Caldwell Kinsman and Kinnor Caldwell.

On the window's other side, the colonels stepped away from the heavy chair. Air Master Caldwell's restraints retracted into the chair's arms and seat. He stood up and stretched his back, glaring at his superior officers.

"Air Master," Colonel Mercell pronounced, "you have broken house arrest and used voice command against a fellow Sentinel, Saried Kinsman, to not speak about you. You ordered her to create a diversion while you returned to Tallis in order to kidnap your own son, whom you clearly understood to be in Federate custody. You will not deny any of that. It is fact."

Gambrel watched, wondering whether Air Master Caldwell would try to deny it anyway. The defendant couldn't defend himself. There was no arguing with truth they'd taken from his own mind.

Colonel Mercell came to attention. "Sentinel, I pronounce you guilty of capricious, selfish use of your abilities." He frowned at Air

Master Caldwell. "Our vows demand the death penalty for that offense."

Air Master Caldwell finally seemed to wake up. He balled his fists and leaned toward Colonel Mercell. "Does treachery run in your family?" he asked, again arousing Gambrel's curiosity. "I'll appeal to the College, of course."

"Of course you will." Colonel Mercell crossed his arms. "But we're going to demand that their appeal, if it's coming, arrive by midnight. Our time. And I wonder," he added, "just how much credence we can give your report regarding my late brother, now that we know how little regard you show for orders."

What was this? Gambrel paused at the window's end and peered at Air Master Caldwell's face. He consulted the Federate register via his handheld. According to a quick scan, Caldwell had briefly been paired with Artur Mercell's brother. He'd accused him of selling out to the last active Shuhr enclave.

Irrelevant. Today, Kinnor Caldwell's appeal would be purely a formality. Gambrel did want to give the Sentinel College a chance to cooperate with Federate justice. The transmission was perfectly worded, the College's choice clear.

It seemed strange that his god-voice would be so eager to see people die. Perhaps that was actually a higher mercy, since the Air Master would shortly rejoin the Infinite Divine. He would fly free of his deformed, altered body, free of all selfhood and struggle.

Still, the eagerness seemed startlingly intense. *Why?* He had no idea whether the god-voice would answer. *Why would the Whorl be that much safer?*

To his delight, it responded—but the answer was oblique. *That family and I have danced with death for many generations. It is time to silence that tune.*

"I have a question too." The Air Master spoke thickly, interrupting Gambrel's thoughts. Caldwell craned his neck and stared up at the observation window. He was looking at the wrong spot, near its center. "I think I have a right to know where Jorah is."

Colonel Mercell also glanced toward the one-way window.

Delighted, Gambrel spoke toward the sonic panel. "Tell him, Colonel."

The colonel raised his head. "He's already on his way to Procyel. We sent him off Tallis nine days ago."

Air Master Kinnor Caldwell's eyes widened. His mouth dropped open for a moment. He took a step back. "No," he mouthed.

Gambrel let himself gloat for the tiniest instant. He rested a hand on the transparent panel. Not only was Jorah out of his father's reach, but things had been done to him—besides his inoculation—that would guarantee changes in the Federacy. "Oh, yes," he whispered. "You have no idea with whom you are dealing, Kinnor Caldwell."

The Air Master turned away from the window, using a hand to steady himself against the interrogation chair.

Colonel Cora Claggett stood at a touchboard, staring up at the observation window. She was plainly sending a message. Letters appeared on a wall-mounted reader board inside Gambrel's observation room. *High Commander Caldwell is confirmed alive. He abetted the Air Master's departure and can be pronounced guilty of the same crime, if we want to press charges.*

Gambrel's delight seemed to echo back at him from somewhere out in the universe. Apparently the god within really was an age-long enemy of this family. This god was the one who had suggested watch-link, which was illegal except in direst emergency. One of the Sentinels' own RIA apparatuses was aboard the "honor guard" ship. Controlling Jorah from orbit would not be difficult.

Gambrel touched his personal code into one corner of the window and deactivated the security glass. Colonel Claggett met his eyes. He gave her a nod. She'd redeemed herself for the moment.

He checked the time lights at his wrist. If he hurried, he could catch the end of that administrative meeting from which he'd been called.

• • •

Soon Kiel was spending all his waking hours in the College shuttle, overseeing the critical first stages of its refit. One designer's plan was more detailed, but a different plan made better use of materials that could be stripped from arriving refugee ships. The task overwhelmed him. He felt shorthanded.

Laying his handheld on a hangar console, he had a sudden urge to revisit the beautiful privacy suite for some peace and clarity. One didn't walk in without making sure that suite was unoccupied, though, so he called up another roster. What he saw made him smile. Even under these crowded conditions, his sister-in-law was keeping that sanctum vacant. He silently commended Wind and hurried up the private passway.

Along the suite's long inner wall, the watery shimmer rushed from emitters along the ceiling to cascade over veined stone. The very air seemed alive. Maybe it was simply because falling water created ions in the air, but still, he wondered whether the joyful discoveries young couples made in here also lingered, somehow, at this place.

Near the cascade stood a broad bed. He glanced at it and through a familiar archway, remembering a deep bathing pool and a lissome new wife. He'd blessed other couples on their way to this suite, dropping his shields just long enough to confirm their connaturality. Smiling at the memory, he poked a finger into the watery wall and parted the shimmer. Tension washed away in here.

When he caught a faint whiff of barnyard and greenery, he turned calmly.

Tavkel stood at the waterfall's other end. A fresh grass stain marked one knee of his work pants. Something about his manner suggested that this was no chance encounter. Kiel wondered fleetingly whether Tavkel had supernaturally called him to the suite, maybe even to Procyel.

That thought, and his fear of being manipulated, roused all the suspicions Kiel had shoved aside to concentrate on refitting his shuttle. Now, he must confront this terrifyingly talented youngster. He dried his finger on his sleeve and spoke cautiously. "You're probably having trouble getting a moment alone too."

Tavkel seated himself on the bed's foot, resting his walking stick against one leg. "This is supposedly your Sanctuary, a place of rest and refreshment. But you're constantly busy."

Kiel sensed the man's sincerity as a faint, unsullied glimmer, without any of the usual shades of epsilon grey that dimmed most people's emotional state. Tavkel genuinely believed in what he was doing.

So either he was deluded, or he had been deceived by the very shadows Kiel had already faced . . . or else he was speaking the truth.

"Do you even need sleep?" Kiel asked. "Wait. First, tell me why you would heal my mother's reversed-polarity carrier but you never dealt with your own. Is that how you're taking other people's abilities away? Does touching them with your . . . your medicated carrier somehow snuff them out?"

Tavkel touched his forehead with one finger. "Shamarr, I don't need your special abilities. You do, though. As they reemerge, every one of you will use them to either serve or betray the Eternal Speaker and his co-eternal Word."

As usual, the young man sitting so casually on that bed seemed to be saying several things at once, strengthening his claim to that holy title while warning Kiel that he too needed to act decisively.

Tavkel spoke again. "You have been giving excellent doctrinal reviews in your morning sessions. I heard nothing better at Tekkumah."

"I thank you," Kiel answered.

"What they see will confirm what they have heard, if they're willing to really see."

Kiel narrowed his eyes. Tavkel still glimmered with sincerity. "I do what I can for them," Kiel said.

"And for yourself?" Tavkel uncrossed his legs. "Those who teach are also required to respond. You finished your interpretive task this morning." He stood up and walked a few steps away from the bed, casually planting his stick with every other step.

Kiel glanced at the coverlet to make sure Tavkel hadn't left pasture stains. And . . . was that walking stick latchem fruitwood? He thought of the blossoming orchard, the sweet perfumy fruit—his favorite—and realized that a young tree had been cut to make that walking stick.

"Let me take your darkness." Tavkel's voice took on a seductive clarity. "Running away from the Whorl could save your own life, but for the Whorl and the rest of your people, it would resolve nothing. And you're in grave danger."

"It could mean our survival as a people." Kiel's thoughts suddenly seemed to slow. *Running could save your own life*— Tavkel had just predicted Kiel's death, if he didn't flee. The idea seemed surreal.

"I cannot make this easier for you, Shamarr Kiel. In fact, I must make it harder and say plainly that if you turn to me and remain here, your own martyrdom will come here on this world."

Kiel narrowed his eyes. "You don't fight fairly."

"I do. But your adversary does not. Remind me, Uncle." Tavkel's voice grew softer as he looked down at the floor. Kiel might've even called that vocal tone *tender*. "Why was it our people had to survive? Had to?"

A chill breeze seemed to sweep across his shoulders. Kiel stepped away from the cascade. He knew exactly what Tavkel wanted him to say: They'd been preserved so that all of humanity could be brought back to its Creator . . . by Boh-Dabar.

He resisted the twin temptations to take umbrage or let his thoughts loop back to that deadly new prediction. Years ago, Kiel had personally extended the Holy One's mercy to poor Tamím, who'd been shadow possessed and abandoned to die. Mustn't he offer Tavkel the same mercy?

But would the Adversary let Tavkel escape, if he'd taken possession specifically to make such claims? "Would you consider leaving with us?" Kiel asked, embarrassed by the way his voice croaked and betrayed his double-mindedness. "Or are you already planning to travel to Tallis or Thyrica, or Elysia itself? Will you try to convert Chancellor Gambrel?"

Tavkel shook his head. Kiel thought he sensed the faint scent of dread on him now. "Piper Gambrel is dangerous, but even he isn't your real adversary. What I do, I'll finish here. There'll be collateral damage, as your brother would call it. Including," he said, raising his head, "your death, if you stay. Right now, our people are in a kind of bonding shock." He gave the stick a casual swing. "These have been sweet weeks, a foretaste of joy to come.

"But," he said, and through Kiel's shields he felt Tavkel's dread melt away. "Before the crisis that must come, your real Adversary will strike hard. You could leave the Whorl with your holdouts, but that door is closing rapidly, unless you fit every ship here with weapons."

Stung, Kiel clenched a hand and let his epsilon shields spring back up. "Do you predict we'll all die here, like Terza Shirak?" Enough of this!

"Not so peacefully, some of you." Before Kiel could speak his mind, Tavkel planted his stick and leaned on it. "And Uncle, if the crisis comes and you haven't committed yourself to me, you'll be pitted against me, even if you don't want to be."

"You're repeating yourself." Kiel stared into the falling water. "If just a few of us leave the Whorl, there'll be decades of surviving without serving. Just rebuilding our numbers. We will survive, though. For the same reason as ever." He raised his head and answered Tavkel's previous question. "So that all of humanity might be blessed through us, and the Holy One's promises kept."

Tavkel looked solemn as he nodded. "That is the oldest promise. But a remnant that outlived me would not have the same protection you've enjoyed for centuries."

Protection? Kiel recalled whole generations of Caldwells murdered by Shuhr renegades. Time after time, only one Caldwell had survived. Once, the family had been reduced to a single infant. It was a miracle any of them remained.

So yes, they had been protected, in a way. Kiel knew he should pray for wisdom again. He'd been dully repeating that prayer since Tavkel arrived, though. It was becoming rote, and rote prayers were virtually pointless.

It was time to confront. "Tavkel." He took a moment to balance his weight over both feet. "What about Melauk's second prophecy, that Boh-Dabar would shed his enemies' blood in rivers? We've been looking for someone to cleanse the Whorl, making it safe so that peaceful peoples could live in peace. That's one reason we've always offered military training. So we could swear our allegiance to . . . him."

Tavkel stared back. "Your scholars grouped that prediction with the Boh-Dabar prophecies by mistake. It applied only to the time in which Melauk was living. He was a wartime prophet. Be sure of this: I don't come to bring peace. But I will shed no one else's blood."

That was a bizarre new interpretation. "And was Ehret cleansed?" Kiel frowned. "Was the Whorl? Why don't we all live in permanent safety, if that prediction was for Melauk's time?"

"It was fulfilled. Our former homeworld was soaked in blood." Tavkel grimaced as he shook his head. "What was prophesied was the safety of the remnant, not of the entire Whorl, and only if certain people obeyed other terms that Melauk delivered. They did not."

The waterfall kept pouring steadily, but the stones seemed to shift under Kiel's feet. "You pass judgment on all the Shamarrs and nearly all the commentators. Who do you think you are?" It slipped off his tongue unintended.

Tavkel's stare didn't waver. "You know who I am."

Kiel folded his arms. Melauk's was a peripheral prediction, and many teachers chose to ignore it. Still, it was one of the classical group—and so Kiel had to believe he had finally trumped Tavkel. By setting aside any prophecy and its traditional interpretation, he had challenged them all.

Now, finally, Kiel could end the painful days and nights of mental wrestling. He'd known he would end up either worshipping this young man with his last breath or else trying with that same last breath to destroy him. At last, he knew which it would be.

His head drooped. He must try to save his people from this man, this mocker of faith and tradition. But he hated the idea of trying to destroy anyone. Maybe he could send Tavkel back to Tekkumah, or else turn him over to Federate authorities.

Tekkumah. His thoughts snagged there again. After all these years, should he break with tradition and ask the people there for prayer—help—advice? What if they had exiled Tavkel as a false prophet? Wouldn't they want Hesed House to know?

Your martyrdom will come here . . .

He was not simply trying to save himself! He must try—gently, at first—to undo the damage Tavkel had already done, without destroying his loved ones' dignity. If Tavkel had unwittingly given himself over to be possessed, he needed help and pity, not retribution. But other souls were at stake.

Besides, Tavkel had made another fateful prediction, concerning Kinnor. Like Melauk's prophecy, it had not yet come true. *Can you spare my brother,* Kiel prayed, *and thereby reveal what Tavkel is? All I want, all I have ever wanted, is Your truth.* "What did you mean," he asked out loud, "when you said Kinnor would die if—"

His handheld blatted. He untucked it and held it up.

The monitor shone with a code red call from Wind, and a shock shot through him. "Is this about Kin?"

The young man nodded slightly. Kiel was in full pelt up the corridor, robes flapping, before he realized he'd assumed Tavkel would know the answer.

At the moment it didn't matter how he knew, or from what source. *Holy One, you used Kinnor to save my life years ago. Now, I beg you to save his!*

CHAPTER 21

Kiel found Wind in her office, leaning heavily on both arms and staring down at her largest desktop communication panel. An aide stood nearby. Wind wore a white robe that trembled with her shoulders, and he felt her panic simmering just under the surface. "The College just DeepScanned," she blurted, "and I answered."

He sank onto a stool, gathering his own feelings and clapping a lid on them. "Would you run it for me?"

To his surprise, she shook her head. She had to be waiting for their next reply.

"May I take the memory?" he murmured.

"Of course."

Ignoring Wind's room aide, Kiel focused a probe, shut his eyes, and threaded into Wind's conscious mind. At the top of her recall, speaking up out of the desk monitor, his mother-in-law sat under the College seal, an image that carried the vaguely pastel blurring of Wind's own mental matrix.

"Wind," Ellet Kinsman Dardy said, "we were just alerted by Regional Command. Kinnor was caught returning to Tallis, against orders. He stands convicted of the 'capricious and selfish' clause, and they're giving us just two hours to decide whether to request clemency. They're changing protocol. We feel they intend to use any appeal we send as an excuse to prosecute us."

Kiel's stomach knotted.

"We'll reach our own decision," Ellet continued. "We will not betray your Kinnor, Wind. We aren't afraid of threats. There have been acts of vandalism all along, and we simply turn over the perpetrators to Thyrian authority. If we take further defensive measures, that could cause more tension. Tell Kiel that evacuation plans are being discussed, though. And give our regards to young Tavkel. Brennen scanned us about him at some length. Perhaps Kiel could convince him to flee too."

Kiel opened his eyes to see Wind still leaning over that part of her desk. "And you said?" he asked. He detected movement at the doorway and glanced toward it. His mother hurried in and took up a position on Wind's other side. From there, she could also watch the main monitor.

"I asked," Wind whispered, "if they'd heard anything about Jorah. I know they'll send a clemency plea. She's right. They mustn't turn our College into an armed camp."

He caught a horrified glance from his mother as she wrapped her arms around Wind's shoulders.

"Eternal Speaker," Kiel prayed aloud, "protect Kinnor and Jorah, and our loved ones back on Thyrica. Protect Wind." And what about Tavkel's predictions, about the Adversary striking here, an enemy worse than Chancellor Gambrel? The knot in his gut tightened. "Protect us all," he added fervently. "We trust your eternal mercy."

The screen lit again, and he repositioned himself for a better view. This time, both Ellet and her husband, Damalcon, appeared. "No," Ellet said, "we've heard nothing about Jorah. Please notify us if anything changes. Remember who defends us."

Wind sagged onto her chair and reached up to take Kiel's mother's hand. She turned back to Kiel. "They'll probably ask Tallis to remand him into their custody instead of executing him. But the last time I heard directly from Tallis, it was unlike anything I've seen."

. . . Instead of executing him . . .

If you go to Tallis, you will die there . . .

Shadows could predict the future. Tamím had proved it.

"Yes." Kiel's mother stepped back and eyed him, and Kiel wondered what she'd just seen him do. "Brennen and I have spoken with Chancellor Gambrel. He seems to have grabbed the Regional Council with one hand and SOOC with the other."

"What in the Whorl . . . He spoke with you?" Kiel asked.

His mother shrugged. "We've been watching that man for years. His Collegium once tried to absorb my arts program. Ellet and I have our differences, but I agree with her this time. Gambrel just wants the College to draw hostile local attention."

Kiel reminded himself that up until recently, his parents had moved in the highest power circles. His own glimpse of Gambrel had been just momentary. "All right. As Shamarr, I'm also entitled to DeepScan to Chancellor Gambrel. Move away, please."

The women looked at each other. Wind clung to her chair's armrests.

"Wind," he said gently, "I won't provoke him. I'll ask for compassion, as a fellow human being."

She got up slowly. "This isn't . . . There's no precedent, Kiel."

"There's no precedent," he muttered, seating himself, "for too many things that are happening." He touched in the Tallis codes. A recording pickup snaked up out of its desktop recess.

After composing himself, he looked into it calmly. "Chancellor," he said, "you might suspect selfish motives if I request clemency for my brother. Think of the rest of his family, though, who will also be bereaved should you carry out your sentence. I only ask for human compassion. If you would graciously commute his sentence and remand him back into our people's custody, there on Tallis or elsewhere, what concessions might I negotiate?"

He touched the control to end his recording and looked over the desk at his mother and sister-in-law. "I'm open to advice. Send it, or re-record?"

"You're giving him the chance to make demands." His mother frowned, creating deep lines all over her face.

"Only if Kinnor remains alive," Kiel said. "If they execute him, they lose whatever leverage I just offered. Surely we have something they want."

His mother raised an eyebrow. They both looked at Wind.

"Do what's right." She spoke softly. "Kin knew he was breaking arrest when he went back to Tallis, and Tavkel—" She glanced up at Kiel's mother. "He warned Kin not to go, didn't he? Kinnor wouldn't want all the rest of us held hostage to Federate demands on his behalf. He knew he was gambling."

Kiel shielded himself and turned away, needing to hide the pain that surely showed on his face. Denouncing Tavkel in public would cost Kiel dearly.

And what about sending this transmission? he silently begged. Feeling no deep hesitation, he touched another control. It lit momentarily to acknowledge that his message had been sent.

Assuming that Chancellor Gambrel would agree to discuss concessions, Kiel might suggest surrendering Tavkel. He rather liked that idea. Let the Collegium deal with him!

"You still aren't bereaved," he reminded Wind as he rose out of her chair. "Hold on to that. You might not be. They still could show mercy." He stared down at the monitor, wondering how long to wait for a reply. Today, DeepScan II seemed appallingly slow. The only sure, instantaneous way they would know if the Federates executed his brother would be seeing Wind fall into bereavement shock. Hesitantly he lowered his shields again.

Wind had abruptly become calmer, even hopeful. He thought he felt a rising determination. She brushed her eyes with one hand. "You wouldn't know where Tavkel is?"

She wouldn't! "Wind," Kiel said, alarmed. "Tavkel can't help Kinnor."

She straightened her back. "No," she muttered, "I don't think Tavkel can help Kinnor. But maybe he can help me."

Did she think that if Tavkel took her abilities, she might not feel the moment of Kinnor's death? Kiel stepped between her and the door, blocking her way to the waterside. "Wind, if you need prayer, I'm here. Don't give up your abilities out of fear, without thinking. Kinnor wouldn't want that."

She glared and crossed her arms over her robes. "How long have you known me? How many times have I acted without thinking? I've been to your lessons. I know what you say about the prophecies." She glanced past him. "I asked if you know where he is."

He resisted a rising panic. "Wind, the second Melauk prophecy does not line up. I just spoke with the young man. He had the audacity to insist that it isn't a Boh-Dabar prophecy at all." Never mind the fact that a few of the more "liberal" commentators agreed with Tavkel . . .

"Do you see what he's doing? He speaks subtly, with apparent wisdom, but I tell you—I tell you both," he said, shooting his mother a glance, "that young man is not Boh-Dabar. He cannot be, not if he denies the core Boh-Dabar prophecies and calls our entire tradition into question. But he plainly has access to enormous power. That puts us in a desperately dangerous situation."

He didn't need to speak any more clearly. Wind had been with him just after he'd escaped Tamím. She would know exactly what he was suggesting.

His mother groaned softly.

He kept his shields strong, hating Tavkel for dividing his family. "Wind," he said, "you're justly terrified—"

"And he'll have me, even if terror sends me to him. There's nothing evil about that man, Kiel. There's nothing sneaky or proud. Look at all he's done!" As her voice faltered, Kiel's mother shifted a hand to grip her shoulder. "Kiel," Wind said softly, "we're all going to die eventually. If it's Kinnor's time, I have to be ready."

Kiel stepped away from her. If he frightened her any further, that would only drive her to Tavkel. "Wind." This time, he sent a calming undertone with his voice. "You aren't alone. We all love and support you. And Mother," he added, still using his abilities to head off a harsh response, "don't push her into something she could regret."

"Do you see me pushing?" his mother asked sharply. It broke Kiel's heart to hear her use that tone. "You're withholding information, if you know where he is."

This was tragic. Still, they were correct. He preached a faith that emphasized freedom, even the freedom to fall grievously. He raised his hands, feeling helpless. "He was in the privacy suite a few minutes ago."

"Thank you." Wind hurried out the door, robes fluttering behind her.

Kiel's mother followed her. She paused in the archway to glance aside. Did he hear her call Annalah's name?

He looked down at the desktop again, then past it toward the room aide. "Shari, call me instantly if you hear from Tallis or Thyrica." He must prepare for negotiating before Tallis scanned back.

She nodded. Kiel hurried back down to Hangar One.

He managed to fill most of an hour with constructive work, though terrible echoes flitted through his mind. *Your own martyrdom . . . If you go to Tallis . . . That isn't one of the Boh-Dabar prophecies . . .*

Would Wind and his mother go to Annalah first? He tried sending his daughter a message via his handheld. She didn't respond, and he thought he understood: For decades, most people had not carried handhelds here, expecting messages to arrive via sekiyr, and enjoying the rare privacy of being unlinked from instant access. Annalah had probably left her comm device somewhere.

He was reviewing an engine modification suggestion, wishing he could call on his father's experience, when his handheld rebroadcast the soul-grating alarm. This time, the screen message carried his father's code. *Med center. Hurry. Wind's going into shock.*

Kiel sprinted back up the stone steps, blinkering his imagination. Had she not gone to Tavkel after all?

And Kinnor—this meant his brother had to be dead!

Kiel had sudden duties, customary prayers for the newly departed, for the bereaved mate, and for the extended family. It would take most of an hour to get through them. Inside, though, he was shouting denial. His brother, dead? Was this Chancellor Gambrel's "considered response" to his offer of concessions? If so, Gambrel had shown him in the clearest possible way that the Sentinel kindred had nothing he wanted.

Nothing but lives they could lose. Kiel strengthened his shields before striding into the med center's primary treatment room.

Wind lay on the bed, eyes shut and clutching her chest with one hand. He'd seen that body language too many times. This was indeed bereavement shock.

Tavkel stood on the bed's opposite side. Kiel's resentment flared, seeing him there already. He willed away the ill feeling when he spotted Meris standing against the near wall, wide-eyed, plainly needing Saried's directions—but Saried had gone to Tallis with Kinnor. Was Saried also dead? They had no way of knowing immediately, since she had no surviving spouse.

Kiel's mother was also in the room. She stood close, trying to catch Wind's flailing right hand.

Ignoring Tavkel, Kiel stepped close to his suffering sister-in-law. "Wind," he murmured. "I'm here."

She glanced up at him and recoiled, flailing again.

"Sh-h." His mother rested a hand on her forehead and craned her neck to look at Meris. "You'd better sedate her," she said crisply. "Nothing too strong, but the worst of it hasn't hit her yet. We've got to get her through the next few days."

Even shielded from Wind's anguish, Kiel reeled with his own grief. *Kinnor!* Surely his mother was in shock too, and the grief and the anger hadn't hit her yet. Her son was dead. *Holy One, my brother!* When his mother finally found her anger, Chancellor Gambrel had better watch his back.

Meris returned with a hypospray. Kiel backed into the hallway and stood staring at the white ceiling, trying to wrap his mind around the unacceptable truth. His brother had given his life for the kindred, serving in his own inimitable way, bending rules and paying the full price.

Light footsteps approached, a stride he knew well. He felt Hanusha's presence as she rounded the corner into the corridor. All his senses came fully alive. "I just heard," she said. "If you need someone to sit with her—"

Tavkel backed through the door into the corridor. Kiel felt Hanusha's disdain at seeing him, stronger than his own.

"So," Kiel murmured, eyeing Tavkel. "She didn't bow to you after all?"

"She did," Tavkel said softly, "but I can't help her with this. Even without ayin powers, she was pair bonded. She has been torn in two."

Kiel managed to get a deep breath. He couldn't denounce Tavkel while people were struggling to cope with the loss of his brother. "Kinnor is dead." He needed to hear the words.

"But Kinnor is safe in a way that you are not."

Before Kiel could respond, his father's head appeared beyond Tavkel's shoulder. Just then, Wind screamed. Kiel lunged toward his father and embraced him. His father held tightly for several moments before pulling away.

Kiel struggled to focus his mind, to ignore what he couldn't change—including Wind's defection—and concentrate on what he must do. These rooms could be sonically shielded. They'd sheltered many bereaved Sentinels. Someone with bereavement experience should be brought in to guide Meris through Wind's treatment protocol. Who could he call?

He turned to his wife. "Go on in. Sit with her for now."

Hanusha nodded and hurried through the door.

"Kiel." His father broke into his skittering thoughts. "While she's incapacitated, you're next in line to administer the Sanctuary."

This seemed like stating the obvious. Kiel looked down into his father's eyes and diffused his shields. He saw worry mixed with grief's first shock. "Wind has organized this place extraordinarily well," Kiel said. "Her aides are already handling most of the routine work. And," he added, recalling what he heard out on the waterside, "I think she just added Annalah to her staff roster."

"I'm concerned that you'll do something rash. Toward evacuation." His father frowned up at him.

Startled—evacuation hadn't been on his mind—Kiel caught another flicker of his father's grief before thickening his shields again. His father had helped Kinnor leave this place. He probably regretted it.

Then Kiel realized that the Federates could come after his father, if they'd interrogated Kinnor and found out how he'd broken arrest.

Kiel planted his feet. "I will not leave the Whorl without seeing Kinnor buried with our grandparents, without speaking the Shekkah blessings over him. Your forces didn't leave fallen soldiers behind, except in extreme emergency. Neither will I." *But as soon as that's done,* he promised himself, *we can't waste a moment. With or without you, Father, the faithful must run for our lives.*

That also made it urgent to convince more people to evacuate, even if they had accepted Tavkel's claims. Kiel must become a second Mattah and bring a remnant out of catastrophe. He must trust the Holy One to guide them to one more new world. The family would continue in his own faithful daughters, Rena and Perl. The Holy One's promises would not fail.

Maybe Annalah would come too. He had ten days to convince her, to refit and crew that shuttle, since it would take Tallis another ten days to return Kinnor's body.

Before he could turn and head to the hangar again, that hated alarm sounded once more. Thick-headed with shock and dread, he raised his handheld. The origin code was Wind's office aide, the message almost incomprehensible. *Saried too. For collusion. You need to read this, Shamarr.*

Collusion? Saried . . . dead as well?

His father reached out a hand, and Kiel showed him. His father's eyes widened. He shook his head. "Then they executed the wrong collaborator. And they did it without even notifying the College. Kiel, we're at war."

"Then will you help me?" Kiel pocketed the handheld.

Father's head turned. He glanced toward Wind's room and over at Tavkel, who'd backed off a few steps. "Kiel," Father said, "I've been given another post. You've been preparing all your life for this moment, and I trust you will find your way. I trust the Holy One's love for you. But I must also trust him," he finished, his voice catching, "for my other son. And my daughter Saried."

CHAPTER 22

Several hours past midnight, Kiel stood near Wind's bed again. As usual, the med center's air felt warm but smelled cold. Hanusha had come again too. She stroked Wind's hand over the white coverlet, and Kiel was still putting so much energy into his personal shields that the effort tired him. The night tech had sedated Wind. That dimmed her agony, but the only way through bereavement shock was conscious time, so the mind could process the terrible loss. *Help her,* he prayed silently.

Tavkel had left for awhile but now had returned. He stood on the bed's other side as if guarding her from Kiel, just as Kiel vaguely felt he was guarding her from Tavkel. Tavkel rested a hand on her shoulder, his eyebrows drawn up so painfully that Kiel wanted to believe he was also suffering.

Tavkel looked up and met Kiel's stare. He murmured, "Imagine you and Kinnor had been born conjoined, grown up together and then separated without an anesthetic. That's the physical equivalent of what this has done to her spirit."

"So now you're saying that pair bonding is wrong?" To Kiel's mind, Tavkel couldn't answer that without offending. Hanusha's mouth quirked to one side.

Tavkel shook his head. "Marital love is one of the deepest purely human experiences, more sacred than anything short of serving your God. When telepathy was invented, pair bonding became inevitable—but you were created to bond this deeply only with the Eternal Speaker. Pair bonding is as fragile as human life. But your bond with the Holy One cannot be broken by your death. Only by your own free choice."

"We do know," Hanusha said as she stroked Wind's shoulder, "that there are worse things than dying."

Kiel was about to ask what Tavkel meant by calling pair bonding "inevitable" when his handheld sounded again. As the crisis dragged on, they all were falling back on this technological form of communication instead of sending Sanctuary runners.

Wind startled at the noise and went on shaking.

Kiel backed across the room, leaving Hanusha to comfort her and keep an eye on Tavkel. On the device, a message had appeared in red type: *Incoming ships.* "Must go." He showed Hanusha the message, glanced at Tavkel, and let her feel his suspicion on the pair bond. She nodded.

Kiel hurried up the corridor.

Out at the waterside, the only light was what glimmered from panels along the pool's edge. He rounded the stone arch into Wind's office. To his surprise, Annalah sat at one end of the desk. She was rapidly keying a touchpad. A sekiyr, evidently acting as night aide, instantly slid out of the main desk chair and carried her kass mug over to the bench.

"Good morning," Kiel told them both. Technically, it was morning. He sat down.

"Good morning, Father." Annalah extinguished her screen and backed away from the desk.

"You can stay," he told her. "Thank you for helping Aunt Wind while she's disabled."

"Thank you. I'm nearly finished." She touched the desk. Her monitor relit.

He spent a moment just looking at her, sitting there at his sister-in-law's desk. This awkward politeness pained him—and she looked so terribly young. Could she really be an adult now, capable of major life decisions?

Yes, she could. His heart ached for her. "What are you writing?"

She didn't look away from her monitor. "Reports." Her voice wasn't hostile. It would be unlike Annalah to show hostility. To anyone. It was unlike her to not explain, though.

At any rate, Wind would have excellent records to review when she was able to return to work. "Don't forget to sleep, sweet one."

"I won't, Dad."

Smiling, he looked down at the main monitor. His mood instantly shifted. A priority message from the Sanctuary's fielding station filled the screen: A subspace wake had been detected, heading in on the Tallis vector. Fielding's estimate was one or two ships in the large passenger shuttle or small cruiser range. As soon as the ships left slip-state, the fielding team would know much more.

Tallis vector? There'd been no DeepScan announcement when these ships had departed Tallis. That made this look ominously like an attack.

Surely not.

Then he remembered hearing his father say, "We're at war." He quickly called a second fielding defense team out of their beds and sent them to the satellites' downside station in the defense corridor. He cross-programmed the console so he could observe from this office, closer to the med center, whatever the fielding team saw. For Wind, this night was crucial.

Annalah appeared at his left side. She dropped a kiss on his cheek, murmured "Good night," and hustled away before he could bring his mind back to the Minster's desk.

"Good night," he called after her. Then he lowered his voice and softly added, " . . . dear child."

The night aide sipped her kass. He was about to ask her to get him a cup too when more information appeared on the monitor. Two Federate ships had dropped out of slip-state, a lightly armored cruiser and an unarmed deep space shuttle. The shuttle requested permission to send down a landing craft. A heartbeat later, the surveillance team confirmed a roster of seven Sentinels on board the shuttle, including his nephew Jorah.

Finally, some good news! Kiel gladly granted landing authority. Jorah was exactly who Wind needed to see.

Out of habit, he counted back transit days. He recounted. Then he sagged against the desktop. Jorah had left Tallis before Kinnor had arrived there. Traveling in slip-state, neither of them could have known where the other was. Jorah couldn't know that his father had been executed yesterday evening. Kinnor's mission had been doomed even before he'd left Sanctuary.

As Tavkel had predicted.

Kiel clenched a fist. He keyed the primary monitor for visual communication with Fielding. The face that appeared belonged to Reg Harris, the colonel who'd volunteered to command Sanctuary defenses. Kiel mostly saw Colonel Harris's chin and nostrils until the face tilted down.

"Ah," Harris's voice came from the monitor screen. "Good morning, Shamarr. Good news. It's your nephew."

"Yes, thank our Holy One. Why the extra cruiser?"

"My question exactly. It's the *White Squall,* out of Tallis. I'm being told it's an honor escort, and they aren't requesting clearance to land anyone else, but they're using brakes to establish a stable orbit."

The Federates meant to stay there, spying? "Is it in fielding satellite range? Can you scan it?"

"No. The projected orbit is high geosynch."

Kiel frowned. That orbit would keep the ship above one spot on the planet's surface, beyond range of the Sentinels' defensive network. "What's their ordnance?"

"We're seeing relatively light standard defensive armament, primarily ship-to-ship, but we'll continue to try and scan."

"Not ship-to-ground." That was a relief. He stifled a yawn. *I need to sleep, or I'll be no good to greet Jorah when he lands.*

"We don't know for certain," Colonel Harris said. "I'm going to keep Fielding on highest alert until they leave orbit. I'm thinking this is a surveillance ship, though."

Surveillance generally preceded attack. Kiel felt a chill. "I agree. You're authorized to take any necessary defensive action. When can we expect Jorah?"

"The passenger shuttle hasn't released its lander yet. I'd say three hours. They'll want to come down by daylight if possible, since our landing area lighting's substandard."

This would be another terribly long day. "Wake me if anything develops," he told the night aide. He hurried back to the housing corridor to catch a few hours' rest.

· · ·

Meris stumbled out of bed early. Annalah lay on her bunk, curled toward the stone wall and snoring softly, so Meris made an effort to dress quietly and went looking for kass. She claimed a mug in the commons and then stood leaning against the railing, wishing she'd slept better. Slanted sun rays filtered down through the skylights to give the pool's surface a pale turquoise cast, with pure white flickers that appeared and vanished. From the kitchens came a sweet, yeasty scent. At the pool's far end, a lone Sentinel stood guard outside the defense corridor.

She sipped from her mug. Watching Minster Wind's vital signs yesterday had given her nightmares. Bereavement shock was medically unique, and she wouldn't wish it on anyone.

Someone emerged from the medical corridor. Meris recognized the posture. It was Tavkel, but he wore clean grey shipboards for once. He'd probably come from Minster Wind's bed of grief, but as he approached he gave Meris a smile that looked almost mischievous. "Good morning, Meris. And it will be good."

Unimpressed, she wrapped both hands around the warm mug. Had she just been favored with one of his supposedly infallible predictions? "So you don't just foretell death and catastrophe?"

"I tell people whatever love requires. I need some help, actually."

He needed help? It felt good to be asked. "Sure. What with?"

"A medical problem."

Meris contained her curiosity. She assumed this concerned Minster Wind, but as she followed him past the Chapter room and back up the med corridor, he stopped short of that tightly shut door. He turned right instead, into the big triangular general prep room across from Stasis. "We'll need," he said, "seven sets of surgical scrubs and the bacteriology kit."

Puzzled, she dug into a gowning rack. Bacteriology implied a communicable disease, but no one was sick here. And didn't he claim to be able to heal anything?

Patience, she reminded herself. Or as Chancellor Gambrel had written, *Time passes. I endure.* She found the scrubs and bundled them into a cloth carry-bag, then it took her a few minutes to find her test kit. Finally she located it—a substantial black case—at the bottom of a second gowning rack. She backed away so Tavkel could see it. "It's heavy," she said. "Would you mind?"

"Certainly not." He lifted it easily and slid its strap over his shoulder. "And you'll want walking shoes."

She glanced down at her hall slippers. "You aren't headed back to Tekkumah, are you? I'm not sure I'm in shape for a long hike." And the Shamarr would want her to check out on the roster in Minster Wind's office, not that she really cared.

"Not that far." He took the bag of scrubs too. "While you're there, wake Annalah and ask her to come along. I'll wait in the commons."

• • •

After a brief nap, Kiel breakfasted in the office. Fielding was tracking the shuttle's lander by then, and a monitor on Wind's desk put him directly in touch with the scan. Only five of the seven Sentinels who had arrived in the Procyel system on that cross-space shuttle had boarded its landing craft: Jorah, Colonel Kirck Spieth, his wife Gini, and an elderly couple who'd been vacationing on Tallis. Two active duty Sentinels had transshipped to the larger craft, where they joined six non-Sentinel crew. Was it a hostage situation?

Just one aide had come on duty this morning so far. He was sitting on a side bench, working from his handheld. Soon the office would fill with people. Hastily Kiel laid his small altar cloth squares on the desk: red over green, over blue, reminding him to pray for those in danger.

A voice rose on the general comm. "Lander, correct your altitude. You're low."

Curious, Kiel set down his bread—he'd managed to talk kitchen staff out of another small pot of latchem preserves—and he poked a different link to call up a map.

There weren't any mountains along the approach vector, via the lower Tuva River valley. The lander wasn't in particular danger, but there shouldn't have been any major downdrafts to pull them off course. This could be a malfunction.

Or did someone on board those Federate ships have orders to kill Jorah and his shipmates in sight of the Sanctuary? He must not be paranoid. And above all, he must not look as if he suspected an attack.

He must be ready for it, though.

"They're down," the fielding operator announced. "Hard landing, but within tolerances and in retrieval distance."

Another voice came through, slightly softer. "They aren't responding. There could be injuries."

Kiel narrowed his eyes, unable to remember a shuttle lander going down that far short of the strip.

"We'll send a buggy," said the tech who'd been talking to Kiel. "It'll take just a few minutes to reach them. Sit tight, Shamarr. I'll inform you as soon as we know anything."

Kiel spent the next several minutes staring at Wind's primary monitor. At last, an odd tone sounded. He leaned closer to the desk. "What's that?"

The tech sounded puzzled. "Quarantine beacon, sir."

They were quarantining themselves? Kiel raised his handheld and asked for Meris. She didn't respond. She was entitled to privacy when treating a patient, and she might be with Wind.

But he must send someone. Annalah? No, she'd been up late. She needed her rest. And where was Tavkel?

He activated the desk's tracking function and used it to locate the man. The answer startled him: Tavkel had already reached the self-quarantined lander.

Infuriated, Kiel jabbed a control to speak to Fielding. "Put me in touch with that lander."

"Still can't, sir. Apparently there was transceiver damage when they landed."

Kiel wiped his palms against the sides of his tunic. He would not lose Jorah the way he'd lost his own parents! "Then pass an order to that retrieval group. They are to board, using force if necessary. Stun Tavkel if he won't leave the area. Then find out whether that beacon is genuine."

CHAPTER 23

Jorah unharnessed on the landing shuttle's copilot seat. Lieutenant Colonel Kirck Spieth had brought them down from the Federate craft, five of them equally eager to see Procyel again. For some reason it had been a rough short landing, and four damage lights gleamed red. Colonel Spieth pushed up out of the other forward seat.

Something clanged against the hatch.

Jorah frowned. Downside hadn't talked much during descent. Was something wrong at the Sanctuary? He definitely needed to report Tallis's new hostility. He'd kept to himself shipboard, reviewing the Boh-Dabar files. Now he understood that he couldn't be that person, not seriously. It would be a relief when Gambrel sent an ITD disk here. With the Whorl fully in synch via ITD, soon there'd be less confusion on all kinds of topics. Less delay, fewer misunderstandings. A lot less unnecessary travel too.

On the other hand, it would be easier for Gambrel to manipulate people. Instantaneous communication, Whorl-wide—was that what the prophecies meant? Was *Gambrel* the prophesied one?

He couldn't be. That just didn't align with what his people expected.

Colonel Spieth flipped the manual safety switches on the hatch, and Jorah caught a whiff of clean outdoor air. He spotted a young-ish man already standing atop the ladder. He was nobody Jorah recognized.

And Jorah ought to know everyone here in his age group. Colonel Spieth backed away, angling a hand to use Sentinel voice command.

"I'm sorry to startle you," the stranger said, "but it's essential that none of you leave this shuttle."

Jorah backstepped all the way to the comm board. He wished he could probe or otherwise help the colonel.

"Who are you?" Colonel Spieth still held his hand cocked. "What are you doing at this Sanctuary, and who authorized you to give orders?"

The stranger stretched both hands forward, keeping his palms down in a position that couldn't be used to direct ayin energy. It also showed that he didn't have a handheld clipped to his belt, though he carried a square black case over his left shoulder. And was someone lurking behind him?

"What's in that box?" Jorah asked sharply. Distracting a potential assailant was the only way he could assist, if Colonel Spieth needed to take action.

To Jorah's amazement, the man smiled at him. "It's a bacterio-logical test kit, Lieutenant Caldwell. My name is Tavkel." Still holding his hands out, he asked, "Permission to come aboard, Colonel Spieth?"

"And you know us from where?" Jorah lowered his chin to glare.

"I'll explain. But listen." The man's voice had such an authorita-tive tone that Jorah half expected Colonel Spieth to obey him, even though this wasn't voice command. "You've all been exposed to a deadly infection—which," he said, looking straight at Jorah, "has caused those headaches of yours."

Jorah felt sucker-punched. En route, his fellow passengers had tried several kinds of pain management on him. Nothing had helped. Even now, he could scare up a wispy but painful aura if he let himself think about it.

Tavkel, whoever he was, continued, "I brought a medical specialist. May we come aboard?"

Colonel Spieth answered, "Yes, but you're both going to be watched. Who authorized your presence here at Sanctuary?"

"Minster Wind Haworth-Caldwell. Lieutenant Caldwell's mother." The stranger squeezed into the lander's cabin, between the crew seats and the passenger chairs. "First, let me prove that you're in danger. Jorah knows, but he can't remember." He turned one hand over, palm up. He wasn't a large man, but his arms and shoulders looked solid. "Jorah, you've been trying to recall something whenever you're hungry, haven't you?"

This was getting more bizarre by the moment. Jorah nodded.

"Remember it now." The man didn't angle his hand, but abruptly Jorah heard voices, saw faces, felt himself clamped to an examining table. Zeimsky. Gambrel.

Plague!

Gasping, Jorah backed farther away from the other passengers. It was too late, of course. He'd already exposed them. His head bumped the overhead control board, and he ducked before asking, "Who are you? Are you a medspec? Can you—he's right," Jorah exclaimed, fighting panic. "Nobody leave this lander. We're on a plague ship!"

"Plague! You aren't authorized to give orders either." Colonel Spieth sidestepped away from Jorah and the newcomer, toward the front seats.

The hatch darkened again. A young woman stepped onto the platform, wearing shipboards that fit stunningly well. Jorah felt his eyes widen. He didn't know her, either. She had the aggressive posture and unique facial planes of the Elysian upper caste, with broad temples and fine cheekbones and long, straw-gold hair.

He'd met only a few of these Elysians, and they usually sneered at his kind. Still, the haunted intelligence in her eyes was obvious. What else was it about her? Something about her made his insides spin as she walked into the cabin.

Forget that for now. Plague . . . Gambrel . . .

His head whirled.

Then—finally—came someone he knew: his non-gifted, strait-laced cousin Annalah. Seeing her made him less uneasy about the two strangers with her.

He raised both hands. "Stop, Annalah! Don't come one step closer. Back away—" No, wait. Annalah had no ayin. Wasn't she safe?

Colonel Spieth angled his right hand again, as if he meant to voice command the Elysian woman. "Annalah, who are these people?"

Tavkel, whoever *he* was, spoke again. "Colonel, this is Meris Cariole, a Federate medical student and friend of Annalah's. She was en route to Tallis aboard the *Daystar* when it diverted here. Minster Wind has authorized her presence at Sanctuary. Meris is the only person on Procyel with no ayin at all. That makes her safe from the plague bacteria, doesn't it, Jorah?" He turned toward Jorah again. Oddly, smile wrinkles formed around his eyes, as if he saw something he particularly liked.

"Oh," Jorah said solemnly. That weird feeling came back, nudging him toward the Elysian woman. "Yes. But then, okay. Annalah, I guess you're safe. But she—I—Annalah, the Feds just did it to me. Too."

Annalah slipped toward the crew chairs, her expression unreadable. "Hi, Jorah. Just listen to Tavkel."

All right, he would. First, though: "Wait. Let me talk. I just remembered. I've been inoculated with some kind of bacteria. It only infects people with an ayin, and it's deadly." He talked as quickly as possible, needing to get it all out. "Gambrel. Chancellor Gambrel. He and his people mean to kill us all."

The Elysian woman, Meris, frowned at him. Recalling something else he'd been told, he flung open an overhead compartment and dug out a message roll he'd been given back at Tallis—moments before he'd departed—"For a woman you don't expect to see there." Gambrel's cryptic message suddenly made sense.

He turned around. Colonel Spieth's wife Gini, who'd pulled on a lightweight jacket to disembark, looked slightly pale, maybe from hearing his story. "We've breathed the same air all the way here from Tallis. Jorah, are you sure?"

Meris also looked pale. He handed her the message roll anyway. "Here. Chancellor Gambrel asked me to give you this."

Meris's eyes widened. "Chancellor Gambrel?" She seized it and spun around, cracking the seal.

"Meris," Tavkel said softly, "you'll need to take breath samples to confirm this infection. Start with Lieutenant Caldwell. And please, Colonel Spieth, secure that hatch."

• • •

Breath samples. Right. First, though—*from the Chancellor himself. For me. Me, personally!* Sure enough, her name appeared right beneath the Collegiate crest as recipient. A terse, elegant greeting preceded the oddest request she could have imagined. *The man who gives you this roll will make some unexpected spiritual claims. For the moment, please act as if you believe him.*

Her arm went limp. She looked hard at the dark-haired young Sentinel. He had startlingly long lashes for a man, and oddly, they didn't make him look any less masculine. She didn't dare let the others sense that under normal circumstances, with no telepaths nearby, she'd be practically swooning with envy. This man had spoken with Chancellor Gambrel! Still . . . spiritual claims, really? Him too?

"Meris," Tavkel said softly.

"Oh. Breath samples." As the big metal door clanged shut, Meris took the test kit back from Tavkel and hooked it over a seat. Tavkel had said she'd be needing it. As she dug for aerosol collecting slides, Annalah stood doing nothing. Tavkel had said she was coming along just to witness.

Meris stole another glance. So this was the Jorah Caldwell she'd seen in tri-D? Then it was a terrible likeness. It made him look too young, just like her own mother's favorite tri-D of her. His face was an exotic mix of Shuhr, Sentinel, and something else she didn't recognize, and his thick black hair needed to be detangled. He was slim and agile-looking, and judging by the way her whole body tingled, her hormone levels had to be surging. *Stop it,* she commanded herself. She'd never reacted like this to the sight of a man.

And he had to be lying—or mistaken—about what Chancellor Gambrel had supposedly done to him.

Chancellor Gambrel never would stoop to the acts Jorah Caldwell had claimed. However, she was asked to cooperate with him for the moment. Here, maybe, was her chance to bring one Sentinel into the Collegium with the Chancellor's advance knowledge. They would be coconspirators.

Yet there stood Tavkel, the man who'd emptied Hesed House's med center. What did he need breath samples for? It would have been nice to feel a little more informed.

She pulled out a screening slide. "Here." She stepped closer and opened its hinge. "Exhale slowly onto this."

• • •

As if he'd just woke up, Jorah remembered. "Zeimsky did the exact same thing. He used a hinged slide. He made sure I was going to spread plague with every breath." He backed against a bulkhead, cracking his knuckles. It was a miracle they'd had to land so far from the Sanctuary. Colonel Spieth and the other passengers were doomed, though, unless this young med student could come up with a specific treatment within just a few hours. Not likely!

And was he exposing this stranger, this Tavkel . . . did Tavkel have an ayin? He still hadn't said who he was, or why he was on Procyel where no outsider ought to be. Maybe he'd arrived on the *Daystar* too.

At least Annalah ought to be safe from him. Jorah wanted to melt to a liquid and seep down into the floorboards, if that would spare these people from contagion. Instead, he squared his shoulders and puffed onto Meris's slide.

Meris. What *was* this sensation? Surely not . . . Some of his friends, back at Sentinel College, had said that the moment they met their connatural future spouse, even before mentally probing, they'd known. They'd felt it.

But Jorah didn't have an ayin anymore. That was impossible.

And this was no time for that kind of thinking. He glanced back at the others—the Spieths, and the older couple on board. "Are they all infected?"

"I'll test everyone." Meris Cariole's voice had the slightest waver. Either she felt the same bizarre attraction or else she wanted to bolt. And what had been in that message roll? Not that he had any business asking.

As she strode toward Colonel Spieth, there was more clanging on the hatch. "Open," someone shouted from outside. "Sanctuary Security. Colonel Spieth, is this craft's communication disabled?"

Colonel Spieth waved Meris aside. She shuffled aft, and he stepped toward the hatch. "This is Spieth. Confirm, our comm was disabled on landing. We've got a medical emergency underway. Stand by."

"We're under orders to enter, sir, and to use force if necessary."

"Then I'm countermanding those orders. We have a *communicable* medical emergency."

"Our orders are from the acting Sanctuary Administrator."

"Sentinel." Colonel Spieth raised his voice. "You understand the word *communicable,* do you not?"

Meris shoved more slides at the older passengers. She had slender hands.

Jorah gave himself a fast shakedown. He shouldn't be staring, but thinking about how to thwart this new catastrophe. How to save his shipmates, for starters.

Gambrel!

Jorah had been used and manipulated. Betrayed. Coached to tell people he was Boh-Dabar, and meanwhile sent to infect and kill all his family. Fury, fascination, and fear pulled him so hard in opposing directions that he felt like he might rip apart.

He stepped closer to Meris. "How long do those slides take to read?"

"Just a few minutes." Meris closed up the last one, raised an eyebrow, and shot him a look he didn't understand at all.

"And how long to find something that'll kill the stuff?" he asked. Colonel Spieth and the others might fall ill within hours, even if there was a long incubation period.

For some reason, this time she looked at Tavkel instead of answering.

There was more clanging and shouting from outside. "Colonel, Shamarr Caldwell still wants this lander opened."

"No!" Jorah cried.

To his surprise, Meris stepped to the hatch. "Listen," she shouted back, "this is Meris Cariole, and I don't care who ordered that. In a medical emergency, the ranking med takes command. That's me, do you understand? Shamarr Caldwell's nephew has raised the suspicion of plague on board. A plague specifically engineered to wipe you people out. Tell that to the Shamarr. And tell him I've got diagnostic slides running as we speak."

She paused for breath. "Then if you really want to open this hatch, first go back to the med center and suit up for hazardous materials. Or else you can just wait ten minutes for these slides to read out."

Jorah gaped, liking the way she took charge. Maybe she *could* do something about the plague. Was that what this bizarre feeling was trying to tell him?

Tavkel stood leaning against a bulkhead, dressed in the grey shipboards they sometimes used here for indoor occasions. "This test," he said drily, "is simply to prove that you're actually infected."

Colonel Spieth turned around and leaned against the bulkhead next to the hatch. "Aren't you exposed now too?"

Jorah kept as much distance from the stranger—from Tavkel—as possible. "Who are you? And what are you doing on Procyel?"

Tavkel stared back. Lines appeared on his forehead. "I was born here on Procyel. Your aunt Tiala is my mother, which makes me your cousin. Did you even know," he added, "that you have an aunt named Tiala?"

Jorah did have cousins outside the Sentinel kindred. They lived on Netaia. He never would've thought he would appreciate confusion. Right now, being distracted was a relief. "My Sentinel aunts are Dad's half sister, Saried, and Uncle Kiel's wife, Hanusha."

Gini Spieth pulled off her jacket. "Actually, Jorah, Tiala was your father and uncle's younger sister. I'd almost forgotten her myself. She left Hesed House thirty years ago to go live at the prayer retreat at Tekkumah."

Jorah never thought about Tekkumah. Nobody ever talked about it. The last time he'd heard it mentioned, actually, was during his first sekiyr rotation to Sanctuary, during a tour for wide-eyed second year students.

Tavkel nodded. "I was born there. I have an ayin, but I can deal with infections. Normally, I would ask permission to heal your illness." He glanced at Meris. "This time, too much is at stake. So I won't ask." He closed the distance between them in two steps and raised both hands.

Jorah stared into clear brown eyes in a prematurely weathered face. Callused hands covered his ears. For some reason, he decided not to defend himself against the uninvited touch.

"Father." Tavkel's voice came through muffled. "Take the plague and its spores out of Jorah's body. Open his eyes."

The headache's whispery remnant vanished. Jorah shook his head, startled. For one instant, the man standing in front of him looked like someone who'd haunted his dreams for the last two weeks. Someone he'd hoped he would recognize if he ever encountered him. This ordinary-looking man, wearing indoor work clothes and claiming to be his own blood relation—

"*You're* Boh-Dabar?" Jorah whispered loudly. He almost felt silly asking it.

But Tavkel glanced over his shoulder at Annalah and grinned. "Yes. Well done, Jorah. You have a quick mind."

Colonel Spieth and Gini gaped. The elderly man still seated in the passenger area struggled onto his feet. His wife did too.

Outside, there was more clanging and shouting. "We need to hear Jorah Caldwell confirm that claim too, Med Cariole."

Jorah had the strangest sensation, as if he'd been transported momentarily to a peaceful reality and yanked back home to confusion. He took a step sideways. "This is Jorah Caldwell, all right?" he shouted. "I was deliberately infected at Tallis by Federate medspecs. There's someone with Meris Cariole who says he can deal with this. Stand by, will you?"

Colonel Spieth edged between Jorah and Tavkel. "If that's really who you are, and if you can keep us from dying, then heal me too."

"Of course." Tavkel turned away from Jorah and wrapped his hands around Colonel Spieth's head for a moment.

Colonel Spieth backed away.

Tavkel addressed Gini. "Will you be next?"

"I think you'd better, if what you're saying is true . . . I mean . . ." Gini's voice faltered. "Did you . . . Are you really Boh-Dabar? Were you the one who brought us down way out here, this far from the Sanctuary?"

Jorah stared. There'd been no explanation for that sudden altitude loss.

"It's all right to doubt." Tavkel shot Jorah a sidelong glance before he turned back to Gini. "I've told you very little and shown you even less. If you would like to be sure who I am, you may probe me. I warn you, though. It will leave you temporarily ayin blind."

She touched her temple, eyes wide. "I want to know."

As Tavkel stepped in Gini's direction, Jorah looked aside at Meris Cariole. She stared down at her slides with the kind of concentration he'd seen in people in combat. Again his insides did that odd flip.

Gini gave a soft cry. Colonel Spieth, her bond mate, gasped. They stood side by side staring at Tavkel. Then the two elderly passengers also accepted Tavkel's offer to let them probe. Jorah stood back, leaning against a bulkhead and fighting off deep pangs of jealousy. He couldn't probe anyone now.

Maybe that was his punishment for trying to grab a title that he'd known all along he couldn't claim. Probing this man might have been a taste of the truly supernatural.

"Okay." Meris cleared her throat. "This is for real. It's a dangerous pathogen, a bacillus related to . . . Well, the genus and species might not mean much to you. But the closest genetic match is a respiratory disease that swept Federate Caroli two centuries ago." She lowered her voice. "It's a bad one, a famous one. It killed several million people."

"They're all right now." Tavkel waved a hand at Jorah and the others.

"Are you sure?" Jorah caught a pleading note in Meris's voice. She added, "And what about me? Are you sure this won't affect someone without a functioning ayin?"

"Run another set of slides," Jorah suggested. "This was Chancellor Gambrel's strategy, to kill Sentinel families without endangering anyone else."

She scowled and straightened her shoulders, then pulled another one of those test slides out of her kit. Thrusting it at Jorah's face, she practically snarled, "Exhale."

"What did I say?" he asked.

Instead of answering, she snapped the slide shut. "Now that I know what we're looking for," she said, staring down at the slide, "I can key this to pick it up much quicker. If it's still here." She shot Tavkel a suspicious look. "Should I test the others?"

"If you like," he said.

They all stood in silence. Meris just kept staring downward. "Seven minutes this time, people," she said. "If Jorah's cured, you probably are too. You might as well do . . . whatever you need to do. Gather your belongings. Get ready to debark, if I give the all-clear."

• • •

Meris waited long enough, and then she waited another minute for good measure. He'd actually been infected with a terrible disease. Surely he'd been mistaken about the Chancellor's involvement—or maybe he misunderstood the Chancellor's intent. Still, just like the first slides this second was incontrovertible. Rather like High Commander Caldwell's instant recovery.

She glanced back up at Jorah, wondering how he would respond when he sensed her relief that the plague was under control. After all, these people generally unshielded under pressure.

He didn't respond. Was he using full shields? She frowned at him, and finally he widened his eyes.

That was a perfectly normal response, like someone who didn't have mind powers! What was going on? And when was he going to make the "unexpected spiritual claim" that she needed to support, on Chancellor Gambrel's behalf? "You're all clear to disembark," she said. "There's nothing growing on these second slides that's out of the ordinary. Tavkel took care of the infection. There is precedent." She looked over at Tavkel. "The man can do things I've never seen before and can't explain."

"Maybe I can," said the middle-aged woman standing behind Jorah, one of the other shuttle passengers. She gazed up at Tavkel with a smile so broad that it puckered her cheeks.

For one moment, Meris wished she were a telepath. Whatever these people felt when they touched Tavkel's mind, it convinced them. "No, thanks," she muttered. Her loyalty remained elsewhere. The Chancellor had asked her to support Jorah Caldwell, not Tavkel. Everyone, everywhere, carried his or her own spark of divinity. Perhaps Jorah needed help finding his own. That would be a calling worth her best effort!

And, she realized, he'd brought her a treasure worth saving for the rest of her life. She tucked the Chancellor's personal message back into the roll and dropped it into her kit bag.

"You'd best leave your clothing onboard." Tavkel gave a good imitation of med-in-charge. "It could be full of spores. We left a bag of surgical scrubs at the foot of the ladder. Take a pair each, but don't put them on yet. Head straight for the river, rinse your hair, and put the scrubs on. Get a pre-op bath in the med center. Meris, please tell the people on that buggy to keep a safe distance, and to call ahead for those disinfectant baths."

"I certainly will." She stepped out through the hatch.

• • •

Jorah was getting ready to follow her, but Tavkel caught his arm. "I need to speak with you."

Behind Meris, Colonel Spieth stepped out of his clothing. Meris paused at the top of the ladder, showing him a striking silhouette. If their landing was one miracle, she was another one. How many times in Hesed House's history had there been someone present who could safely diagnose these bacteria?

And he was going to have to strip naked right in front of her. His blood heated. Med student, he reminded himself. She'd seen it all.

Yes, but not *his* all.

He turned back to Tavkel, glad to give someone else his full attention. After the others' reactions to probing him, Jorah didn't have much doubt. Someone who could bring down a lander out of the sky and do instantaneous healings was no ordinary Sentinel. And Tavkel was his cousin, his own grandparents' grandson. It made perfect sense.

"A bit of good news first," Tavkel murmured. Annalah lingered close to them, but Tavkel waved her toward the ladder. "Grandfather's alive and well."

"What?" Jorah wouldn't hear a Shekkah funeral service after all? And Tavkel had said "Grandfather" instead of "your grandfather." Tavkel was a Caldwell. Pieces were falling into place.

Tavkel's smile winked out. "I can cope with radiation damage as well as bacteria. But you will have some lingering headaches, while your brain tissues mend. And I can't heal bereavement shock. There is also bad news."

Jorah rested a hand on a passenger chair and sat on its armrest. "Who? Oh, no." Tallis had shipped his father back here in stasis, after all. As soon as Aunt Saried had revived him, he would've— "Father went back to Tallis for me, didn't he?"

"Yes. Your mother went into shock yesterday."

Jorah clenched both fists, freshly furious at Gambrel, his paid researchers, and the treacherous SOOC committee. They had created this mess—maybe even deliberately. Betrayal after betrayal! *Always suspect a trap,* he recalled. *One of the last things Dad ever said to me.* Black ribbons of grief wrapped around his heart. He slammed a fist into a padded seat back. "He went back to try and save me, not knowing that Gambrel—Gambrel—" Jorah's voice dropped to a lower pitch as he repeated that awful name.

Meris Cariole stepped back inside. "Tavkel," she said somberly, "the retrieval crew has backed off. But they told me you've just been ordered to stay topside. You, specifically. By the Shamarr."

Jorah barely heard. He'd been duped. Deceived. Infected, and sent out to kill his family and friends. He hated Chancellor Piper Gambrel with a clarity that almost brought back his headache. Gambrel had set a deadly trap for Dad too. Who would he betray next?

"You must not hate Piper Gambrel," Tavkel murmured, and to Jorah's surprise, Meris's head whipped around. "You were just part of a much larger plan. He also is part of a plan that reaches beyond his understanding. I do grieve with you, Jorah. I loved your father from a distance. At Tekkumah, we often held vigils for his protection."

"I bet," Jorah muttered. "Too bad it didn't work this time." *My dad!*

Tavkel touched his arm. "You'll see him again, Jorah. I promise."

Jorah stared into those dark eyes, desperately missing his ayin.

"Jorah," Tavkel said, "I want something from you."

"What?" He felt dull inside. Those moments of craziness had exhausted him. He just wanted to sleep.

"Your loyalty. I can heal you without your permission, but I can't recruit you." Tavkel backed away from him and glanced toward the hatch. "You'll find the Sanctuary in some confusion. Your Uncle Kiel has just banned me."

That perked him up. "He what?"

Tavkel nodded toward Meris. "Not everyone here has accepted my claims. Have they?"

"No," she said firmly. "The Shamarr's obsessing about launching a shuttle—"

"Even after seeing what you can do?" Jorah demanded.

Tavkel sent him a sad smile. "But your father committed himself to me, though he didn't ask for certainty."

"What does that mean?"

"He preferred to keep his abilities. I do know yours are already gone."

Jorah dug his fingers into his hair, and he sent Meris another glance. Her eyebrows shot up. It occurred to him that she might be sick of Sentinels. What had she thought of his father . . . what had his father thought about her?

My dad . . .

"Listen, Meris. I told you: Chancellor Gambrel's people destroyed my ayin. I was supposed to bring the 'happy news' here to Sanctuary, that people could be ayinectomized without surgery."

She curled her lip in obvious confusion. Another thought sprang into his head. Obviously—from the message roll—she was already one of Gambrel's low-ranking followers. Jorah wasn't the only one who'd been duped. He needed to talk with her. She could be in danger too.

First, though, he had to deal with Tavkel. His head seemed clear at last. "My father decided in your favor?"

Tavkel barely nodded.

Jorah took a deep breath. "Then in his memory, I do give you my loyalty."

Silence fell in the narrow cabin.

"Give me the right to own all the darkness inside you."

That was easy. Why would anyone want to hold onto darkness? "It's yours."

Tavkel's eyes widened with what looked like affection. "Do you mean that, Jorah?"

Suddenly his own willingness to pose as Boh-Dabar looked dark indeed. He grimaced. "Of course I do."

Tavkel still smiled. "Don't feel humiliated about Gambrel having trapped you and used you. He's a brilliant strategist, with supernatural help of his own—"

"That sparkling thing!" Jorah saw it clearly in memory. Saw it looking out of Gambrel's eyes, at the last. Remembered that he had asked it to save him at one point. He'd had a terribly narrow escape. He shivered.

Tavkel nodded curtly. "For you, Jorah," Tavkel said, "the only way home was through Gambrel's manipulation. I did warn your father," he added.

Jorah turned toward the passenger compartment, swallowing bitterness. "Didn't he believe you? On second thought, Dad has— *had* a history of ignoring orders."

"Tavkel warned him, all right," Meris Cariole put in. "The whole Sanctuary heard him."

Jorah frowned. Would Meris ignore his own warning about Chancellor Gambrel? Gambrel had killed his father.

His father had gone back to try and save him.

Well, I never asked him to— Jorah picked up his duffel.

Meris thrust out a hand. "No! Leave that on board. We have to consider it contaminated."

"Oh! Right." He dropped it again. Then he thought of someone who would have been hit even harder by this awful news. "Have you seen Mother? Is she bad?"

Meris's expression softened. "She's sedated for now. I spent most of yesterday evening with her."

"So it did just happen."

"Yes. Last night."

Jorah guessed where he'd been when the stroke fell: onboard, decelerating into the Procyel system. It seemed unreal. It would become real, he guessed, when he saw his mother in bereavement shock.

Gambrel would pay for this.

"Meris." Tavkel stepped between them. "Jorah and I will go to the river first, and he'll ride back on the retrieval buggy. You'll have privacy."

"You aren't—" Jorah began, confused.

"Out of respect for your Uncle Kiel," Tavkel said, "I'm going to stay outdoors—in exile, so to speak. Meris, be sure to seal the hatch when you follow us." Jorah felt Tavkel's hand grip his shoulder once more as he added, "We won't look back."

Jorah finally understood. Picturing Meris descending that ladder, gloriously naked in the spring morning, he felt his body respond instantly and predictably. He left his musty shipboards in a pile and hurried down the ladder, then hustled straight to the river.

CHAPTER 24

Kiel had sent a sekiyr up to the med center to fetch Jorah, but oddly, it was Meris who escorted Jorah into Hangar One. No ayin shields dimmed his agitation. Kiel frowned, concluding that Tavkel had taken down yet another Sentinel's abilities.

He embraced his nephew anyway, savoring the sensation of holding his brother's son. From now on, this was the closest he would come to touching Kinnor. One of Kiel's workers, carrying a sheet of metal toward the shuttle's extended ramp, smiled sadly in their direction and set his eyes forward again, guiding the metal sheet around a portable maintenance display.

The hangar was littered from inner wall work area to the big door's catchfield projectors. Parts cabinets, tanks, and welding equipment sat at floor level, while above his head a tangle of hoses hung from adjustable component shelves. The dual-tread tow vehicle stood parked to one side, and a tall metal cabinet hung open, closest to Kiel.

He let go of Jorah and drew away, keeping a hand on Jorah's shoulder. Through his lowered shields he felt Jorah in a horrific confusion of shock and rage—undoubtedly over his father's execution—and something else, something harder to read. Something Jorah was trying to suppress. "It's good to have you here." Kiel turned quickly to Meris. "It's true? The quarantine beacon, the plague report. There's proof?"

The glance that passed between her and Jorah startled him. Connaturality . . . *them*? Impossible. If Jorah could no longer use his ayin, then he wouldn't be able to tell whether Meris was a potentially connatural mate. In his grieving, his nephew might cling to whoever offered comfort.

Or was the Sentinel culture's familiar *pair-bond-now!* response a separate and distinct holy gift?

Kiel hastily brought his mind back to the moment and the young people standing in front of him. Jorah needed counseling. And more.

"I can show you proof slides." Meris crossed her arms over her lab tunic. "But you'll need to examine them in the med center if you want to see them. The transmission vector was supposed to be exhaled spores. I don't think you could catch it by handling slides, but this is nothing to take chances with."

"I believe you." Kiel thought back to that first meeting with Meris. To the anguish he'd sensed in her, though she had declined his offer to counsel her. Having lost her parents' support, she too might be reaching out for comfort.

To Jorah, whose loyalty must be to his own people.

"I'll run some susceptibility tests and check what they used against it in previous outbreaks." Meris paused with an odd little frown. "After encountering Tavkel, this group did stop exhaling bacterial spores."

Kiel rolled his eyes. Tavkel, Tavkel. What would it take to make other people understand Tavkel could be deluded? It was time for Meris to be on her way too.

Jorah stood close to her, simmering with agitation. "But there are still people up in orbit who've been exposed," he said. "They traveled on board our cross-space shuttle. So she needs to get back to the lab, unless you want to send Tavkel up to them in orbit."

There was a tempting thought, but not right now. "Thank you, Meris." Kiel put a dismissive tone on his words and crossed his arms. "Please notify me when you've confirmed a conventional treatment. For now, I'll simply alert the orbiting ships."

She slipped between that tall metal cabinet and the portable maintenance display, and she hurried back out the hangar's inside door.

"Intelligent woman." Jorah clasped his hands and cracked his knuckles. Kiel remembered that nervous gesture. "Full of herself, though."

Jorah sounded so much like Kinnor—rather, so much like Kinnor voicing his early impressions of Wind—that Kiel managed to laugh. "Jorah, it is good to see you."

"She doesn't believe what I told her, what happened back on Tallis." Jorah leaned against the metal cabinet. "But her hero, Gambrel, betrayed me. He turned me into a biological weapon. He sent me here to wipe out the whole Sanctuary. I wonder who he's sending to Thyrica. To the College."

This fit what Kiel had just heard. He needed to calm and counsel his nephew. "The College is on alert, Jorah. Aunt Hanusha's parents are there. We'll help them if we can." Kiel kept his shields diffused. Jorah was in real pain—and there was a toxically strong sense of guilt.

Another pair of workers strode past. Kiel subvocalized, *Let's find someplace more private.*

Jorah's head came up. "I heard that," he exclaimed. "I wasn't sure I could even do that anymore."

It was possible to subvocalize even to outsiders, but Kiel did not remind Jorah. "You need a deep healing. Guilt and anger can make you essentially ineffective. Hateful."

"A healing would be such a relief. Yes. Please."

Kiel led out the big hangar's door, glad to know Jorah would not sense his pity.

The weather was holding clear. Livestock noises echoed downhill from the barns, bleats and baas and the occasional *whack* of a hoof hitting the side of a stall. Kiel and Jorah sat down on a wooden bench at the landing strip's edge. Jorah plucked a long grass stem and then let Kiel do a long mind-access. Soon they were both letting tears wash away anger.

Apparently Gambrel, not Tavkel, had taken Jorah's ayin. That comforted Kiel for a few moments, until he grasped the extent of Gambrel's scheming. He'd glimpsed the man briefly, traveling with the Mikuhran, Tamím—but at the time, he'd thought Gambrel seemed sympathetic.

Now, Gambrel had apparently taken aim at the entire Sentinel kindred. He might even be angling for a spot on the Regional Council. In this web of intrigue, had Kinnor been singled out as a particular threat, to be trapped and executed before Gambrel made his next move? "What happened after they locked you up?" Kiel asked.

He'd threaded a probe into Jorah's memories. Now they took an eerie turn. Jorah's sparkling visitor appeared, and Kiel had a horrifying moment of recognition. This uncanny presence could be the same shadow who had used Tamím to kidnap Kiel on Mikuhr. When it entered Chancellor Gambrel, Kiel gasped.

Tavkel and Gambrel . . . could they be linked, shadow to shadow?

Yet that suspicion felt tainted, as if Tamím's touch really hadn't left him. He also recalled Tavkel's description of the damned soul, turning away from the Eternal Speaker's might and beauty. He feared that fate more than anything else.

Gathering Jorah's memories, Kiel drew them together. He shaped them for Jorah to see, helping him make sense of the coercion and deception that Chancellor Gambrel had thrust upon him, and strengthening the conviction that he'd resisted as well as possible—organizing the memories without altering them. Most of all, Jorah needed to feel sure he wasn't to blame.

Jorah sighed deeply. "Thank you."

A breeze drifted across the landing strip. It carried the odor of sun-warmed metal and lubricants from that row of parked shuttles and landing crafts. "Chancellor Gambrel," Kiel told Jorah, "used a logical, powerful temptation. We did wonder, when you were born, if you might be . . . that one."

It had seemed ironic that Kinnor, the perpetual rebel, had produced the only male heir in the next generation. And apparently the prince of shadows was looking for Boh-Dabar too. It was ready to create its own imitation, using Jorah.

As for the attraction to Meris, Kiel had not forgotten the moment when his lifelong friendship with Hanusha had become something entirely different. The Sentinels maintained a chaste culture partly because they spent so little time in courtship. It always happened suddenly, if it happened at all.

"I hear," Jorah said, staring ahead, "that you decided against Tavkel."

Kiel looked left, uphill. Beyond the landing strip and around the amphitheater, several makeshift tents were going up. Whole families had already joined Tavkel in voluntary exile. This was good camping weather, but the schism was a storm gathering strength. "I haven't denounced him."

"Not yet?" Jorah wore a pleading expression.

Kiel sat silently for a few seconds.

Jorah lowered his voice. "He saved us all. Meris says that this plague was deadly. And Grandfather . . . he's alive, when he ought to be dead. Even though Dad really is . . ." His voice sounded painfully young.

Some animal bleated up in the barns. Kiel shifted his seat on the bench. "Jorah, that's all true. But there are prophecies Tavkel clearly doesn't fulfill. He's trying to circumvent them by claiming they aren't Boh-Dabar issues. And you know that redefining scripture is a sure mark of an impostor."

Jorah twisted the long grass stem into a knot. "But look what he's done, Uncle. I won't pretend to be an expert in your specialty, but it seems to me Tavkel acts like . . . Well, there's a . . . a *something* about what people say he's done, like he has some sort of authority over people and things, and that he's entitled to take care of them."

"It's an interesting thought." Kiel spoke as blandly as possible. "But leaping to an observation like that, without factual foundation, is setting a course for false dogma."

"Why don't you just arrest him, if you think he's a fraud?"

Kiel shook his head. He'd certainly been tempted. "The Holy Path forbids it. Remember, in Third Siyach it says, 'The Eternal Speaker makes clear to his children the voices of truth.' Our freedom is an enormous part of our faith. And as that verse teaches, all true believers will turn to the truth, if only in the nick of time."

Jorah returned a shrewd look. "You can't think almost everyone here is deceived, then. Can you?"

Kiel could not bear to accuse one of his nephews to the other. "On the Holy Path, we do not dictate to others the choices they make. It's part of the same discipline that was imposed on us when—"

"When the ancestors altered our genes," Jorah chorused with him. After several seconds of silence, Jorah tossed the grass stem away. "When will you hold the Shekkah service for Father?"

Kiel sighed softly. "As soon as the bodies are returned. Please discourage your mother from looking at his remains. Shipping coffins disfigure the dead in terrible ways."

"Right." Jorah gripped his knees with both hands. "Did you say *bodies?*"

Oh, Holy One, will this never end? Kiel leaned forward and spoke gently. "We also lost your Aunt Saried. She went along with him. They accused her of collusion, and apparently she confessed."

Jorah groaned. "Oh, no. I liked her. A lot. She was the best med I ever consulted too. But," he added, furrowing his forehead, "she always seemed to be sad, and she never would say why."

This, Kiel observed, showed how well the kindred had accepted his half sister. Even after Saried had died, he couldn't explain to Jorah all the pain she'd confessed to him privately down the years. Her maternal grandfather had been one of the cruelest, most murderous Shuhr leaders of all. Whenever she had heard another story about her Shuhr ancestors, she'd felt that she too fell under suspicion. He'd heard that latter confession from other Mikuhran Sentinels. They never completely assimilated. Not even Wind.

Poor Wind—

But at the moment, his job was to comfort Jorah.

And to convince Jorah to leave Procyel aboard the College shuttle. "Saried is happy now."

Jorah narrowed his eyes. "I wonder how many cruisers they'll leave in orbit when they bring Dad and Aunt Saried home."

Kiel nodded, wondering again why the *White Squall* was parked in geosync. The Federates had devastated Mikuhr with shiploads of deadly dust. They could strike here in the same way. Dust barges could already be on a collision course, in fact. This exquisite world could be ruined, especially if a demonic, creation-hating shadow were giving orders at high levels.

He hated the thought of surrendering this planet—the entire Whorl—to the enemy, but he was responsible first to his people. He would have to grieve the Whorl later. "Jorah, we're refitting the College shuttle for a long-term flight. I can use all willing hands."

"Meris told me you're planning to evacuate." Jorah sat straighter. "To do the Mattah maneuver, rather than stand and fight. I want to hear more. Later." He stood. "But right now, I need to see Mother."

Kiel also stood. He straightened his tunic, shaking off disappointment. There would be other chances. Even if Jorah didn't agree to board, the Caldwell name wouldn't die out if they used gene bank technology. And his daughters were heiresses of the bloodline.

His people had always shunned technological methods, though. Those robbed humankind of dignity.

"Yes, go to her." Personally, he needed to be in the Minster's office. "But don't hesitate to come talk to me. I can't be your father, but I'll be all I can for you."

"Thanks, Uncle Kiel."

• • •

After an hour's work, Meris rapped on the arch leading into the Minster's office. Shamarr Kiel sat at Minster Wind's desk, again leaning heavily on an elbow. The office aide sat on a bench and studied her handheld.

Meris stepped inside. "I found it," she said. "The drug susceptibility."

The Shamarr looked up. The circles under his eyes looked darker than she remembered. "I had no doubt that you would, Meris."

It felt good to hear those words. She stepped closer. "Everyone who traveled on that shuttle—and anyone who had contact with Jorah pre-landing—needs to be treated. Everyone, even if Tavkel apparently healed him . . . them."

She still couldn't believe Chancellor Gambrel had plotted genocide against Sentinels. The others must be cared for, but there had to be a better explanation than Jorah's.

So she had to get Jorah alone. In her lab, she'd realized that he and Chancellor Gambrel must have come up with some kind of plan—together—something Shamarr Kiel and the rest of these people wouldn't be privy to. Hence the private message roll, telling Meris to go along with Jorah's claims.

The Shamarr glanced down at his command board. "It would be simplest if you would transmit whatever information is crucial straight to the cruiser's captain."

That was what she'd hoped. "Immediately."

"They've ignored all my hails, though. And you'll have to explain why you diagnosed a disease before anyone showed symptoms."

She smirked. "I've actually thought that through. The Chancellor and his real followers will be delighted to know that lives have been spared. But if some minor officer up there really is hostile to you people—afraid of you—" and she still had some sympathy for that viewpoint— "well, I don't object to telling a lie based on truth. I am in training, so I can honestly say I was practicing routine health checks and stumbled upon the infection."

He pursed his lips. More lines appeared across his forehead. "I assume you'll also ask to be evacuated to Tallis." Before she could speak, he added, "You'll do so with my blessing, Meris. I want to know when those Federates intend to depart, as a matter of fact."

"The thought had occurred to me." She didn't mention that she'd been told to cooperate with Jorah. Chancellor Gambrel might need her to remain here a little longer. Still, Shamarr Kiel had probably seen that she was attracted to his nephew. He'd probably be glad to get rid of her now, and save Jorah from her.

Well, that was none of the Shamarr's business.

He waved her to a stool near the end of the desk. She sat down. Spotting a desktop transceiver set up to record text, she reached for the touchboard.

"Attention," she keyed, "Federate cruiser orbiting Procyel II. This is Meris Cariole, daughter of Senator Brisbane Cariole and Doctor Clementia Moor, both of Elysia. I am an Elysian citizen, a member of the Collegium of Human Learning, and a medical student at Elysia General, student ID 608367, temporarily housed on Procyel II, having arrived aboard the damaged shuttle *Daystar*. First, I formally request that I be evacuated to your passenger shuttle now in orbit, and then to Tallis, which was my original destination." She could cancel that request if Chancellor Gambrel communicated again, asking her to stay here.

"Second, as a medical student continuing my training, I ran some standard emigration tests on the passengers who arrived via your cross-space shuttle. Unexpectedly, I isolated a dangerous bacterial infection. All your crew and passengers remaining in orbit should receive treatment. I will attach antimicrobial sensitivity information to a second transmission, so you may begin synthesizing treatment immediately."

She skimmed her message, found its clinical tone satisfactory—really, her parents' names ought to be all the password she needed—and gestured toward the monitor. "There you are," she told the Shamarr. It was time he knew what he'd never bothered to ask. He wasn't the only one who could point with pride to his family.

As he read the screen, he raised an eyebrow. "Tell me more about your parents, and what happened."

She shut her eyes. Other people might come to this man for comfort, but the last thing she wanted was to feel that kind of vulnerability. "My mother's research is in peripheral neuropathy. Most of Father's work is in regional planning."

"You didn't enter any of this on the *Daystar's* records." His voice sounded compassionate. Was he subliminally urging her to say more?

"Annalah told me to just enter the fact that she and I were friends." And what had happened to that friendship? she wondered. She barely saw Annalah anymore. "If that wasn't good enough for the *Daystar's* screening officer, nothing else would have been." She created a second document, containing the antimicrobial data. Pointedly she asked, "Will you send it, Shamarr?"

He reached down and keyed a long code sequence. The screen went dark, and he sent Minster Wind's office aide out for kass.

They sat in uncomfortable silence.

Several minutes later, the incoming transmission light came on. Meris sipped from her mug as Shamarr Kiel keyed in another code. Text appeared.

She leaned toward the monitor and read aloud, "'To Meris Cariole, currently listed among Procyel II's resident population.' Ah! 'Acknowledging receipt of medical alert. However, no—'" She faltered. "'No evacuation is possible at this time.' What?"

It was one thing to consider staying voluntarily. But to be told she still couldn't leave was intolerable! If only there were regular flights to and from this world!

She jumped off the stool. "Tell them I'm not a resident, sir. Not even a relative. Tell them I'm here by special exemption. No, wait." She tried to imagine what her father might have done. "May I DeepScan Elysia, or at least Tallis? Obviously, we're dealing with some minor officer who thinks he's on a special mission. For both our sakes, I think we should go over his or her authority."

The Shamarr sat shaking his head. "The power expenditure for sending a DeepScan transmission is enormous, and it could take four or five transmissions just to reach the right bureau. We've always prohibited nonofficial transmissions." He fidgeted with something on the desk before adding, "If you urgently want to leave Procyel, and if you're willing to travel in tardema-sleep, you would be welcome to leave with my group."

But he was obviously headed out-Whorl! If she traveled with him, she would never get home. And how did he think he was going to launch anything if the Federacy turned on these people and started a shooting war?

Maybe she'd rather not know. She'd heard whispers about their defensive fielding and RIA technology. "That's a generous offer," she said stiffly.

He rested both elbows on the desk. "I've spoken with Jorah, you see. He thinks that you two are connatural. He has no way of knowing, but I believe he'd like to be wherever you are."

She felt her face flush. Connatural? But Jorah had no Sentinel abilities . . . So he claimed, anyway.

And so this was the Shamarr's take on their potential relationship? She stood still, heart bumping. If this man couldn't separate her from Jorah, would he use her to manipulate him—to make sure Jorah got on board the shuttle? He wasn't even trying to recruit her for her own sake. Just Jorah's.

"Do think about it, Meris."

"Hmm." She spun around and stalked out the arch.

She still was fuming an hour later, sitting under a tree on the island in the middle of the underground pool, as she spotted Jorah striding toward his mother's sickroom. She'd seen pity in the way people had greeted him. Some of that was because of his father, of course. Still, it infuriated her to see people feel sorry for him just because he didn't have unusual abilities anymore. Did they pity all normal people?

Frankly, she pitied them right back. It had been horrible to see the Sanctuary's capable Minster collapse in on herself. Only the psi-med ministrations of some newly arrived Sentinel had enabled Minster Wind to sit upright and take a small meal.

If half of all pair bonded people eventually went through this, then the pleasures they claimed to enjoy carried a hideous cost. Bereavement shock had to be like losing your sight, your hearing, or your dominant hand.

If the Shamarr's lectures had truth behind them—just imagining it, for the moment—and if there were such a thing as a supernatural creator, then it was no wonder the temporary bliss of pair bonding hadn't been in the original plan. Its ending was too terrible to contemplate.

Saried had survived it. But come to think of it, Saried had been a sad person.

Meris stared down into the water, not wanting to interrupt Jorah's time with his mother but more impatient than ever to talk with him.

Connatural? It was tempting to smile. Instead, she shook her head and flattened her lips. Back home on Elysia, the next step would've been simple. She was overdue for her first lover, after all, and she found Jorah appealing enough. The thought gave her insides a pleasant little flip.

On the other hand, Jorah had been raised in what looked like a very chaste culture. He might be offended if she suggested comforting him that way.

Still, he wouldn't be committed for life by one sexual encounter, not with his ayin gone. She understood that much about pair bonding and how it happened.

Come on, Jorah. Finish in there, would you?

And what about his uncle's manipulative offer? *Did* Jorah mean to leave with the Shamarr? Surely not. He'd made a commitment to Tavkel, right? In memory of his dead father. But he hadn't been here long enough to see what that generally meant.

Well, for now, he was distracted taking care of his mother. *I should just tell him I want to talk with him whenever it's convenient.*

She stood and strolled up the bright medical corridor, into Minster Wind's room. Only Jorah sat at the bedside. He held one of the Minster's hands. She lay quietly, staring at the ceiling.

If it had to end this way, pair bonding was *not* a good thing.

"Jorah?" Meris murmured, "I want to talk, when you can spare an hour. Maybe out on the island."

"Will someone be bringing her something to eat?" Jorah stared at his mother.

She'd expected more of a reaction to her entrance. Still, that was easy enough to answer. She backed toward the door. "I'll make sure." It took only a few minutes to find a sekiyr, who promised to feed Minster Wind a few bites of dinner.

Finally, Jorah appeared out in the corridor. His shoulders sagged.

The poor man. Suddenly the island didn't seem private enough. "Can we go outside?" she suggested. He shrugged and came along wordlessly. She strode to the elevator, and they rode up to the surface.

It would be best to get him away from prying eyes and sensitive minds. She silently led him along the familiar trail down to the Tuva River and its little bridge. From this vantage, looking upstream from the bridge deck, she'd previously seen a clump of gorgeous blue flowers close to the water. She leaned against the wooden railing and peered down, trying to spot them.

Jorah still didn't speak. It felt peculiar to stand in his presence, distracted by each angle of his face and body. A new sensation, definitely pleasant. She hated to raise a difficult subject and spoil the mood.

But she had to.

CHAPTER 25

"I'm truly sorry about both your parents." She knew that had to be said.

He stood beside her, so near their shoulders almost touched. The sun had gone down behind the peaks, and a breeze blowing upstream rippled the water below.

Meris decided to bring up the message next, not the accusations he'd leveled against Chancellor Gambrel. Maybe it all was an awful mistake. "That message roll that you brought me," she said carefully. "Did Chancellor Gambrel give you any idea what was inside?"

"Message rolls are confidential." He stared down at the flowing water. "It's illegal to tamper with them. I assumed it had something to do with your Collegium."

"Actually, it had something to do with you."

"It did?" He spoke levelly, giving her no idea whether he expected something good or bad. Maybe he was still thinking about his poor mother. Or his father. What a terrible loss for the whole family. Whoever had dreamed up pair bonding . . . Hadn't they realized what bereavement would do to the offspring?

She gripped the rough bridge railing. Its weathered wood scratched her hands. "Essentially, he asked me to fall in with your . . . well, your religious position. But you didn't say what that was, and then everything went crazy with Tavkel on board the landing craft."

"Oh?" He raised his head and laughed shortly. "Oh," he repeated, this time drawing out the word about three times longer. "Oh, Meris. It's . . . it's ridiculous. He was grooming me to come here claiming to be Boh-Dabar. Can you believe it? But—you know what Boh-Dabar is supposed to be, don't you?"

"It's . . ." She shook her head. "It's what half the people here are saying Tavkel is."

"It's what Tavkel *is*. He's really Boh-Dabar, Meris. Not me. But Gambrel almost had me believing it. So you see, that's one more scheme gone astray for him."

She squared her shoulders. "Couldn't you be?"

He spoke without hesitating. "Absolutely not. Hey, I know you think a lot of Chancellor Gambrel. But he used me and betrayed me and tried to wipe out everyone on this whole planet, and I—"

"There has to be some kind of misunderstanding. Has to." She stared at him, hoping for a positive answer.

He furrowed his forehead but said nothing.

Very well, then. She faced upriver again. Leaves rustled on the tall bushes. "So tell me . . . more about what you think happened," she said. *Information removes doubt. When in doubt, gather information.* That had been one of her favorite litanies when school work had confused her.

Standing on the bridge with dark water rushing beneath them, he spun an appalling story. It made the Collegium's upper level and some of his own superior officers look like criminals. Still, she understood that as a Sentinel he would have to resent the Collegium. It also empowered people, but it didn't put them under the kind of all-consuming regulations he'd spent years memorizing.

After listening to him explain, she also understood why he couldn't claim to be Boh-Dabar. Apparently it was more about fulfilling prophecy than having unusual powers. To Jorah, at least.

She had to make him understand about Chancellor Gambrel. "My Collegiate experience," she said, "was completely different. Entirely positive. They sent recruiters to University when I was a first year. Their techniques for focusing the mind, improving learning, and regulating unpleasant emotions gave me mastery over my own destiny. There are litanies for everything—against known and unknown dangers, against stress and confusion . . ."

She faltered, abruptly remembering what a narrow cosmic frame had held that picture. She'd found that out on board the *Daystar*. Up to the very day Sabba Six-alpha had blown off that mass ejection, people on board had been living normal lives: being healed of ordinary diseases, dealing with parental problems, planning next term's studies.

She'd lived in a stable era. Not every human born had that privilege. She couldn't call Jorah's culture invalid, either, if she wanted him to respect her own. "The Collegium brought me to adulthood," she went on. "I finally felt capable and independent. I went home during the next break and told my parents. By the end of the year, they signed on too."

"I see."

Had the Collegium empowered her parents . . . to disown her? The thought slammed her.

No! She shoved it aside.

Jorah stood motionless and stared over the guard rail, so she too looked upstream. On one side, drooping bushes hung over the darkening banks. Along the other bank, the blue flowers had fallen into shadow. The water made eddies as it swirled around stones in the shallows. And had she spotted some kind of nest in the stream bank, that pile of twigs that was a little too organized? There was so much to look at it was almost overwhelming.

She pointed. "You wouldn't know what those blue flowers are, over there? I realize it's getting dark, but—"

"Mira lilies. They were bred here not long after the Sanctuary was established. I'm told they were a 'fortuitous sport.' That's what it's called when a mutation—"

"I know what a sport is," she answered, amused. Apparently he had no idea what a medical education involved. "So this is the only place they grow?"

"I think so. They actually depend on a different plant species' roots, if I've got it all straight."

It was a sweet thought, that this place had an unusual ensign flower. She gazed down into the river. An early star's reflection shone up at her out of a smooth stretch. How long had they already been talking?

"Your . . . uncle Kiel," she said, still facing away from him. "He's being something of . . ." *Careful, Meris,* she warned herself. "Something of a recruiter. On your behalf."

"What do you mean?" His voice sounded warm.

Meris turned around so she could see him again. In dim light, he looked rather more broad-shouldered.

"He said I'd be welcome to leave Procyel with his group. Headed out-Whorl. He freely admitted that it wasn't because he wants me to go. It was because you . . . Well, we . . . Hmm." She cleared her throat. "He used the word *connatural.* That you might think we are, anyway."

Out of the shadows over his face came the quick gleam of a smile. "What?" he asked. "It surprises you that a man would find you attractive?"

Being admired was a lovely sensation. Being admired by a man she already found herself drawn to—even better. "That's not what I think he meant. But thank you."

"The connaturality idea . . . Well, we don't spend years or months or even weeks risking our virtue and sanity in courtship.

We know almost immediately whether someone's a suitable mate. So if Uncle Kiel can tell that . . . that we're well matched," he finished softly, "then please don't be intimidated."

This was no time to laugh. She kept leaning against that rough rail. "Actually, I thought I was going to be the one who intimidated you."

"Oh?" The word came out halfway between a laugh and a grunt.

"Back on Elysia, I simply could have walked up to you and said, 'Jorah.'" Shifting her voice into a tone that she hoped sounded flirtatious, she continued, "'do you have a lover at the moment?'"

He stood up taller, and this time there was no laugh in his voice. "That sounded like you meant it."

Relieved, she took a step closer. Apparently he'd forgotten about accusing Chancellor Gambrel. If things worked out between them, maybe affection would bring him around. "I did," she said. "You come from an antiquated world, my friend."

He raised both arms out to the sides, pointing one hand back to the Sanctuary and the other out into the wilderness. "And you know nothing about my world, my ways. My upbringing. Ask what's important to me, Meris. Even if I could have taken mental advantage of you, I wouldn't have. We have those 'antiquated laws' for good reasons."

"And I don't need to be afraid of you. Because you don't have an ayin anymore."

For almost a minute, she heard only the chuckling stream. Suddenly she realized—it was the strangest sensation, almost like chest pain—that she must've hurt his feelings. She stepped away from him. "I'm sorry. To me, that's just stating a . . . medical issue."

His voice dropped lower. "You forgot I had a heart? It's a little raw right now. That's a really personal thing. And I just lost my father. Not to mention that my mother's suddenly disabled too."

She shook her head, deeply embarrassed. She knew just how terrible losing a parent felt, and hers hadn't even died. There were litanies for comfort. She'd used them. She longed to share them with him and show him the power of Collegiate ways. "Do you . . . miss it?"

"Of course I do. My whole life was based on something I'm not anymore. I'm starting over."

He couldn't have given her a better opening. "Can we start over too, Jorah?"

"How far back?" he asked curtly.

He'd offered to answer any question. "Well." She stepped back to his side of the bridge. "Did you grow up on Thyrica, or was your mother already stationed here on Procyel when you were born?"

They talked until billions of stars made a gleaming second bridge far overhead. He answered all her questions—even about the fielding defense that kept everyone else off the world. Mentalic technology, he called it. "It keeps the place peaceful," he said. "Secure. And since everyone else knows about it, no one's really at risk of being harmed unknowingly. We only ever wanted a place where there wasn't conflict. It wasn't supposed to be a fortress. Except from the Shuhr."

"That makes sense."

A cloud bank drifted across the starry sky, the breeze eventually died, and a flock of jabbering night birds roosted in the riverside bushes.

• • •

Late the next morning, she entered her name on the task schedule as Minster Wind's primary caregiver. She and Jorah stood watch over her as she slept. For long shifts that day, and the next day, they kept talking, pausing only to comfort their whimpering patient.

On the third day, the Minster opened her mouth and spoke clearly. "Would you take me uplevel, please? I want to see Tavkel."

Delighted, Meris helped the Minster wash and dress. She walked alongside as the Minster plodded to the elevator holding onto Jorah's arm.

They emerged and headed up the path to the shearing barn, following two sekiyrra leading wooly kipreta. Beyond the barns, people had made peculiar tents out of landing craft covers around the hillside amphitheater. Several small children chased a larger one across its sloping bowl, shrieking in the sunshine.

Jorah found Tavkel inside the largest building and probably the oldest, its boards weathered grey and punctuated by round holes where pieces had apparently fallen out. An oddly sweet animal smell hung in its woody darkness. Straw lay unevenly on the wood floor, here a bunch and there a bare swath. Tavkel greeted Minster Wind with an embrace, clasped Jorah's hand, and gave Meris a nod and a smile as the sekiyrra led those two kipreta into side-by-side stalls. Tavkel's shirt had sweat rings under the arms. She wanted to avert her eyes from such raw physicality.

"Will you be teaching this afternoon?" Minster Wind sounded eager.

"No. But stay awhile." He crossed the central room's floor with two long strides and brought back a stool, kicking straw litter ahead of him. It probably kept this place from stinking.

They sat down in a stall. "I grieve with you, Wind," Tavkel told her. "I loved Kinnor too."

"I feel stronger today." Minster Wind looked around and heaved a long sigh. "Jorah," she said, looking up with grief in her eyes, "you know your father wasn't an easy man to live with. But we'll both miss him until we die. I'm going to be here for you. I'm going to get better."

"Of course you are," Jorah muttered.

Meris decided that the best thing she could say was nothing. But the Minster's statement made her wonder whether the woman had considered suicide when she was at her worst.

After several awkward seconds, Wind turned back to Tavkel. "Would you have been shearing this week over at Tekkumah too?"

Meris had expected a theological discussion. Instead, these people talked for an hour about herd animals. Maybe it was their way of dealing with grief.

Meanwhile, Tavkel sheared several kipreta. First he called to a young assistant, who led a kipret to him. Two other shearers were doing the same thing in other stalls. Tavkel nudged each creature into the stall with that walking stick. Some of the unattractive, blunt-headed creatures kicked the ground, ready to bolt, until he covered their eyes with his hands and spoke a few words. After that, they stood still or willingly lay down for him. One even craned its neck to watch as he slid primitive metal shears around its body. He lifted off each pelt like a blanket and dismissed the kipret with a pat on its cleanly clipped rump, all the while discussing breeding records, what grasses made the best hay, and evil rams they'd both known.

Minster Wind's eyes looked markedly brighter when a bell rang outdoors, and Tavkel and the other shearers hung up their tools. As they emerged from the shed, three older women stood ladling stew out of small kettles to campers near the amphitheater. Tavkel still wasn't talking theology—not that Meris could tell, anyway—and Minster Wind seemed content to walk outdoors with her son. Jorah seemed glad to escort her.

Meris joined them for a bowl of stew, then slipped away and went indoors looking for Shamarr Kiel. She wanted to stay on his good side, now that he'd decided she might be useful to him.

Where that would take her situation with Jorah, she had no idea.

• • •

Kiel stood at the waterside the next morning. Two empty wooden caskets, hand oiled with intricate carving on the ends, lay upon a raised platform out on the large island, prepared for Kinnor and Saried's return. A wide hatch also lay open in the midst of the island. Through it, Kiel could see the stone stairs that led down to the Sanctuary's catacombs. His brother's death was becoming reality.

Meris had worked tirelessly for him last night, prepping hundreds of gene samples. She'd even donated a few skin cells, in case outsiders' DNA might improve the genetic pool.

It was a generous gesture, but it also told him she hadn't committed herself to make the journey. Jorah remained a question mark on the roster.

And until Kiel left this place, he couldn't stop trying to save just a few more souls, which required him to head uplevel for one more painful confrontation. He would not violate the commands of Third Siyach if he lovingly offered the choice once more. *Help me,* he prayed as he turned toward the elevator. *Let me be loving but firm and true. Save Annalah, please. Let my daughter live.*

Sunlight shone down as he left the elevator and took the right turn, toward the barns and amphitheater. Beyond the odd little campground, nearly a hundred people sat in the hillside bowl and stared at Tavkel's familiar figure. Tavkel called out a question, asking where in scripture there was any specific reference to disembodied life after death. Someone called out a reference Kiel knew well.

"Implied," Tavkel called back, "and possible. But what about resurrection?" Now a chorus answered. Kiel wondered where Tavkel intended to lead his congregation, starting with such basic concepts.

He spotted Annalah seated a short distance uphill. He strode forward. Heads turned around him.

"Exactly," Tavkel called. Apparently seeing the crowd react to Kiel, he too turned around. Something in the way he gripped that walking stick made Kiel think of a herdsman defending his flock.

Kiel strode on until he also stood within the amphitheater's focal point. He dispersed his epsilon shields. To his surprise, he felt affection streaming off Tavkel. The man honestly loved him.

He hesitated.

Tavkel raised both eyebrows.

Glancing sidelong, Kiel saw his parents sitting close by, and he sensed that they were afraid. Tavkel's awful prediction sprang to mind, that if he chose Tavkel he chose martyrdom. On the other hand, if he opposed Tavkel he chose a long, permanent exile out of the Whorl, leaving nearly everyone here behind.

But what else—what lies—had this man been telling? Kiel let his shields spring up again. He planted his feet on the dirt and focused energy into modulating his voice, willing it to carry his love for them all. "My friends, my people. I must interrupt. Hear me, please. I speak for your sakes, though it breaks my heart. We all are impressed by Tavkel's abilities and his persuasive personality.

"However," he said, trying to make his voice even more compelling, "Tavkel does not fulfill Melauk's third prophecy."

"That's not relevant!" Kiel didn't recognize the voice. He turned too late to see who'd spoken.

He addressed the crowd again. *Third Siyach,* he reminded himself. Those who were truly loved would recognize truth. "He even denies our forefathers' wisdom in applying it to the coming of Boh-Dabar. I am forced to conclude that he is not the Word to Come." Several people murmured. He raised a hand for silence. "Remember, a true prophet cannot err in any way, not even a small issue. I'm truly sorry, but we still are waiting for that person, in whose service I would gladly give my life."

The murmurs broke out again. "He healed me, Shamarr!" A woman spoke up. It took Kiel a moment to recognize Lieutenant

Dijka Gardner, who'd been aboard the *Daystar* with his father. "This man is no impostor. If anyone's in danger, you are—"

"Peace!" Tavkel raised a hand. "Show your Shamarr the respect that his office deserves!" He glanced sternly at Kiel.

Kiel spared him a nod, then turned back to the crowd. He eyed his parents near the amphitheater's front. "Further," Kiel cried, "since the Federacy now rejects our service, which can only lead to them attempting to destroy us all, I beg you all to leave the Whorl with me, as our ancestors left Ehret with Mattah and his family, narrowly escaping annihilation. The Holy One called a single faithful priest to lead that emigration. He will guide our flight now."

Utter silence answered him. More than a hundred solemn faces stared back. There wasn't even the usual crowd rustle.

Tavkel raised his walking stick with both hands and stepped closer. Kiel stood his ground. *Here I must stand,* he prayed. *I am at your mercy, not his!*

Instead of cocking the latchem-wood stick to strike, Tavkel stared another moment. Through Kiel's shields seeped a swirl of loving fury. Tavkel whispered, "My father does not change, but he also never does things the same way twice. You are not Mattah."

He shifted his hands, gripped his stick like a hoe, and cut a furrow in the dirt between them. "Shamarr Caldwell," he shouted uphill toward the crowd, "from this moment, if you cannot support me, you are opposing me. If you cannot lead people to me but try to carry them away, you condemn them to grief. Here, soon, you could learn how love and justice will actually balance."

Balance, his voice echoed off the hillside.

"Here, soon, you could respond to divine love in faith. If you wait," he said more softly, turning back to Kiel, "until after you leave this life, you will acknowledge the same loving justice." His voice caught as he lowered it again. "But having turned against me, you will find that clear understanding an agony."

Kiel stared numbly into the crowd and picked out Annalah. He shook his head. "Please," he mouthed. "I love you." She was an adult, though. He couldn't force even her obedience, not and remain true to his priestly calling. He turned slowly and walked back toward the elevator.

Behind him, Tavkel raised his voice again. "Do not criticize that man, aloud or in your hearts. He is a great lover of scripture, treasured by the God he still longs to serve. He is the beloved son of faithful parents, the beloved father of gracious daughters. . . ."

Kiel walked faster. The uneven path blurred through his tears. Tavkel was due to be dosed again. Meris needed to call him in.

He slapped tears off his face.

"Pray for him, all of you—"

The elevator doors slid together and shut out that heartbreaking noise.

CHAPTER 26

Kiel spent the rest of that afternoon in the fielding station. Techs still hadn't been able to thoroughly scan the Tallan cruiser *White Squall* in orbit. Besides keeping its distance from surveillance satellites, it remained opaque to mentalic technology. That suggested that Special Ops had supplied it with a RIA unit.

It could also explain why two Sentinels had remained aboard. Had they been duped, or drugged, or were they serving under threat?

Weary and hungry, he found a meat pastry in the commons and made his way back to the Minster's office. He expected to find some word from College too.

He found his parents sitting at Wind's desk. Startled, he scattered his shields. "What are you doing?"

His mother's emotional state hummed with angry pain.

His father, calmer, reflected Kiel's own grief. "We're trying to use whatever pull we still have to convince Tallis to send one of the new ITD disks. Our service contract with Regional Command, Tallis, grants communication rights with the full Federacy, and disks are starting to be distributed."

Father was hunkering down for the siege, then. Kiel couldn't challenge him about the expense of using DeepScan. It was actually becoming absurd to worry about financial resources, since he couldn't take Federate gilds shipboard. "Why not just wait for Regional Command to invade?"

"Your father also just managed to simulate a RIA circuit from groundside." Feeling his mother's anger was like being raked with a sharpened fork. "Looks like it is a RIA unit up there."

"Doing what?" He rested a hand on the desk's corner.

"They went inactive the moment we transmitted." His father swept a hand over the desktop. Another panel lit. "Those are our people. I must do what I can for them."

"I'll give you some time." Kiel retreated to the poolside and stood staring into the water until his parents emerged from the office.

His mother walked on, but his father joined him, placing both hands on the white railing near Kiel's. "She's not angry, son. She's devastated to lose you. Have you heard Tavkel's explanation of that Melauk prophecy?"

Kiel shook his head. "I've been trained to defend beliefs we have passed down for eight thousand years. I am trained in spiritual discernment. Besides," he added bitterly, "I know a shadow when I see one."

He thinned his shields again and felt his father's unease. "Perhaps your vision is smudged."

Something angry and hateful clawed out of Kiel's heart. He turned away, glad that his father couldn't sense others' emotions anymore. "Fine. Tomorrow, I'll confess publicly that I know what a shadow looks, feels, and sounds like. I'll admit publicly why I'm more sensitive to deception than anyone else here, and I'll accuse Tavkel of shadow possession. Is that what you want?"

"No." His father seized his shoulder. "Your original instincts are better. Emphasize the doctrines of free choice. And if you must speak, at least wait until Kinnor and Saried are buried. Don't tear the kindred apart as we sit here waiting for that."

Kiel clenched the railing. "All right." He stared straight ahead. "After the burial but before we take off, I'll address everyone once again. There's still room for you and Mother onboard. Leaving the Whorl is our last chance to escape extinction."

Father shook his head.

"Then will you—at least—help the fielding team defend our shuttle when we launch, if the Federates pursue us?"

Although his father's face sagged, he spoke firmly. "Of course. We think that could be what the *White Squall's* intending to do, anyway—use our RIA technology to try and prevent a major launch. I'll do all that I can to circumvent that kind of activity."

He turned and walked away.

● ● ●

The next evening, a few of the campers dined indoors, though they did not converse with Kiel. It felt like an uneasy truce had settled. Kiel slipped back into the office to check on events out in the Whorl. He switched on the Thyrian news feed first, filtering for *Sentinel* and *College* related information. An ordinary text page appeared. The College's next Vesting ceremony had been postponed. A memorial stone for his father, recently set in the main garden, would not be removed despite the good news that High Commander Caldwell remained alive.

Kiel decided to transmit a fresh message to his in-laws, so he reached for the touchboard. But the page blanked, and in its place appeared an aerial view of the red-stone Sentinel College campus. Grey smoke and a running mob belched out of the main building. An androgynous voice spoke. "Thyrian military forces responded swiftly to violent vandalism . . ." The building vanished in a cloud of red rubble.

Kiel clenched his hands. This wasn't live news. Newsnets often used recorded imagery, and the date under this horrific image was several days ago. His insides crawled as his mind sprinted forward. When had they last heard from Hanusha's parents?

Several days ago, discussing that gene bank technology. Why hadn't Tallis informed the Minster's office about this attack?

Had Tallis actually ordered those troops to attack the College instead of defend it? Ellet and Damalcon would have DeepScanned a warning if they could have. They might be . . .

Holy One, no! Let them have gotten away! He sprang to his feet. Surely now, his people would see that they must flee this hostile Whorl. There was no going back, not even to Thyrica. He would accept anyone who asked for passage, even Tavkel. He sprinted toward the hangar, wanting to pray a blessing on that shuttle, that ark of their own next Crossing.

Lights glared in the silent hangar. An odd smell drifted out of the shuttle's open hatch. Uneasy, Kiel followed the odor into the cockpit.

Raw-edged metal twisted back from a hole blasted into the main board's surface. Thick black mist drifted out of it. Black sludge dribbled onto the deck beneath the damaged console.

Sabotage! He stood listening with all his senses. Was the saboteur still aboard?

The silence told him nothing.

He made a circuit of the cockpit and found nothing else damaged, so he knelt beside the console. This could be repaired—but Tavkel, the likeliest troublemaker, couldn't be mind-accessed by security personnel to confirm that he hadn't suggested sabotage.

Everyone else could be accessed, though, including the one man Kiel hated to accuse. The one who had helped Kinnor escape house arrest.

Kiel paused on his way out of the hangar and checked the hangar doors' subtronic monitors. They showed no intrusion.

Whoever had passed them unseen, it couldn't have been one of Tavkel's disempowered followers.

Unless they too had supernatural help. Or—his mind leaped to the possibility—Special Operations training.

Heartsick, Kiel strode down the shuttle's ramp. His shoes clanged on metal.

• • •

In the Security-Fielding installation's vaulted chamber, deep in the defense corridor, seven evening shift Sentinels sat their stations. They wore close fitting caps that linked them to an amplification system and satellite uplink far older than the RIA units of his father's generation.

The overhead dome displayed a map of surrounding space, surrealistically extended to include the view from the world's far side. Colonel Harris stood at the back of the chamber as Kiel stormed in. "Colonel, there's been sabotage in the main hangar. I need the location of every person here for the last six hours."

Colonel Harris was fortyish and straight-backed, a modest, conservative man who hadn't deserted to Tavkel. He turned to the nearest station. One of the sekiyrra, a young woman of maybe twenty, sat there. "Sara, how quickly can you give Shamarr Caldwell that information?"

"I'll do what I can to hurry the process, sir." She swept a hand across her display.

Kiel leaned over her shoulder. On her monitor, a map of the world's surface zoomed in to display the underground Sanctuary. The hangar area seemed to grow until it filled the monitor. He peered at it as her left hand danced over a control surface.

"I see no intrusion, sir." She craned her neck and looked up at him. "But the Sanctuary is so crowded that at any one time we have up to two dozen individuals who are not under surveillance."

"Two dozen?" Kiel tried not to shout. "How could you lose that many people?"

The sekiyr looked over Kiel's shoulder.

From behind him came the colonel's voice. "Shamarr, as Sara said, we have more than twice as many residents here as usual. Sara is doing phenomenally well on groundside tracking."

Kiel pushed upright, realizing he'd had leaned too close to the fielding tech and also challenged her commitment to duty. "Forgive me." He stretched out a hand. "Your colonel is correct. However, there is a saboteur among us."

He faced Colonel Harris again. "Plainly, we need more technicians on groundside tracking. Would you please assign two stations to that task?"

Colonel Harris rested one hand on the back of a chair. "Do you feel that's wise? We have a RIA unit orbiting that might be in use against us."

An outside attack could also come from any of six spatial quadrants. However, sabotage could come from much closer. "For just a few days," Kiel suggested, "just long enough to protect that shuttle in the hangar until we get on board and fly away." He faced the fielding tech again, keeping a respectful distance this time. "Give me, please, a list of the people who were not being tracked during that time. Is that possible?"

"Certainly, Shamarr. I'll need two minutes."

Kiel scanned the quiet room. The fielding operators sat motionless at their stations, eyes closed, focusing their minds on the various approaches to this world. Traditionally, the oldest and most experienced tech was tasked with monitoring the Tallis approach. His own fielding experience, decades ago, had been unspeakably tedious . . . but rewarding. Each Sentinel in Federate service spent a rotation here every few years.

"Here, Shamarr."

He bent toward the groundside watch station again. Unfortunately, six people on Sara's unaccounted-for list were Special Ops.

Including Kiel's father.

"Thank you." He turned away, rubbing his chin. It would be best, he decided uneasily, to question him immediately—and personally. "Colonel Harris."

"Shamarr?" Colonel Harris still stood close by. He spoke softly.

Kiel glanced at the door. Two Sentinels stood there, on guard duty. "Would you please send someone to ask my father to come down and speak with me?"

Colonel Harris hesitated several seconds. Was he hoping Kiel would change his mind?

Kiel waited him out.

"Very good, Shamarr." Colonel Harris strode toward the door arch.

Kiel sat down on a stool near the wall, observing the team at work while he waited. The overhead display cast a dim glow on the room, brilliant blue instead of space black. The color had apparently been chosen to make Fielding duty less onerous. Kiel could have called up the same view from the Minster's desk, but he loved this display. It reminded him of the universe's vast beauty, and the beauty of the eternal heart, hand, and mind that had imagined and created it.

Constellations looked slightly stretched on the underside of that dome. Kiel squinted up at The Cat, one constellation that was so distant that from both ends of the Whorl, it looked almost the same.

Where he was going, there would be entirely new stars. *Is this what you want me to do, Holy Speaker?*

His father strode in. As always, the man seemed to effortlessly dominate a military environment.

"I'm sorry to disturb you," Kiel said, "but someone has sabotaged our outgoing shuttle. I need help."

His father lowered his head. "Kiel, I have not been bending the law again. I'm not responsible, and you're welcome to confirm that."

Father had never been one for evasion! And his fearless gaze, straight into Kiel's eyes, was utterly convincing. Still, Kiel led up three steps into a side room. Four metal stools looked down into the fielding area through a viewing wall. The side room itself was narrow and bare, with metal walls. That was unusual in this refuge.

His father looked directly at his eyes. "Go ahead."

Kiel's mind-access skills were adequate for the job. A fast scan of his father's memory proved that his father had been in a small classroom near the Chapter room, helping several military Sentinels—and Kiel's mother!—develop their returning abilities. In the man's emotional savor, Kiel also tasted confidence and utter calm, despite an awareness of imminent danger.

And was there also a flicker of epsilon shields? Distant, as if dropped or scattered for access, but naturally, the High Commander's abilities were also coming back. He'd been one of the first to lay them down.

The first, actually.

Kiel withdrew the probe. "Thank you."

His father smiled faintly.

"Now, I need your advice for a repair detail. I want a team that can transfer a control board from one of the other ships, parked groundside, with no mistakes, the first time."

His father mentioned several names. They got to work together, eventually sending out crew assignments via handhelds.

After they finished, his father sat flicking his left sleeve's cuff, a gesture Kiel recalled seeing all his life. "The problem remains," Father said, "of your saboteur. We have a RIA ship orbiting

Procyel under outside control. It wouldn't surprise me if they were involved."

"Turncoats, do you think?" Kiel glanced through the side room's viewing wall. Down below in the fielding station, the team sat motionless. Even Colonel Harris stared down at his monitor.

"Buying their lives, or in fear of them." His father sat more casually, both elbows on the arms of his observer chair. He laced his fingers over his lap. "I'm working on it. Meanwhile, I suggest you ask Colonel Harris to post armed guards clock-around. Make sure there's always at least one on watch who isn't . . . who hasn't given up his or her abilities. That will reassure you, won't it?" He shot Kiel another knowing look.

"Your epsilon shields." Kiel barely smiled. "They're coming back."

His father stood. "Yes. It's like learning to walk again, but with four legs instead of two. Steadier, once you know how. The new guidelines will be—"

"I don't need that information." Still, Kiel scattered his shields as he reached the door. Instead of irritation, he sensed his father's deep affection.

"Be sure," Father added, "to assign Jorah a watch. He needs to feel useful."

"Agreed."

"Shamarr, High Commander," a voice called across the vaulted room. "There's another subspace wake coming in."

Kiel spun around and scanned the main chamber's ceiling. About halfway up the dome, near the ecliptic, an elliptical zone had filled with rapidly changing numbers.

"Just one ship this time," the tech announced, "but it is the Tallis vector."

Kiel stared. This couldn't be Kinnor and Saried's bodies being delivered for burial. With a funereal detail, there should be at least one escort ship, carrying Sentinels who wished to attend the Shekkah service. And wasn't this too soon? No matter how he counted transit days, he could not make the calendar turn out right.

He also checked the time and was startled to note that it was nearly midnight. "Could Tallis have developed a faster drive?" he muttered. His father had just retired from a level where such things were known.

"Not even in the design stage." Father's voice came from close to his shoulder. "Maybe the same irresistible force that brought Jorah down short, away from the breakaway strip, hurried Kinnor and Saried's arrival."

Kiel brushed aside cause-and-effect. He turned around. "If it is, we should hold the Shekkah service tomorrow morning. I want to load and leave the moment our repair crewers complete the refit. Before any more sabotage can be committed."

"May I offer a suggestion?" His father's voice sounded sad. "Mind-access everyone who's going on board with you. Make sure you don't carry your saboteur along."

"Yes. But these are probably more refugees." Kiel glanced up at the ceiling again and down at that nearest tech. "How soon before your team will be able to ID that ship, Sara?" He was careful to speak respectfully.

She kept both hands on her instruments. "Less than an hour, sir."

• • •

In fifty-two minutes, the ship left slip state. Colonel Harris's staff quickly identified it as yet another old *Brumbee* messenger ship, declaring two shipping coffins as cargo.

Flabbergasted, Kiel brushed aside the notion of miracle, along with all speculation of how or why. Even *Brumbees* couldn't cover such distance so quickly.

Apparently this one had. His father went off to bed.

Kiel sent alerts to all Chapter room personnel to prepare for services tomorrow morning, shortly after sunrise. Still wide awake and abuzz with adrenaline, he walked to the med center and stood silently at his sister-in-law's bedside. She slept peacefully, her features relaxed in childlike peace. He quashed the temptation to wake her. When she heard all the news from an aide—the attack on the College, sabotage here, and the coffins' early arrival—she would need to be well rested.

So would he, if he meant to make his public confession and a last plea for passengers. He hurried to his own bed, where Hanusha lay deeply asleep, and he used ayin energy to quiet the cacophony circling in his mind.

CHAPTER 27

Jorah stood on the big island between the kirka trees' planters, keeping a distance from the yawning hatch. That hatch had always spooked him. Looking down those stairs inevitably meant someone had died.

A low-ceilinged vault beneath the reflecting pool received most of the Sentinel dead. The pool itself, lapping and whispering around him, usually symbolized the kindred's unity. But on occasions like this, the waters stood for separation—between those sleeping below, waiting for another creation, and those still alive and struggling in this one.

Jorah cracked his knuckles and stared down at the island's white flagstones. He wore his dress whites today, and so did all the other military people. Non-military also wore mourning white. Rafts of freshly plucked, multicolored flowers floated on the pool's surface, and as he glanced aside, a sekiyr bent down to toss another handful.

On the platform close to the hatch, those painstakingly carved coffins had been closed. They looked almost like boats with their arched lids, or miniature cross-space shuttles. Uncle Kiel had always

347

called them *arks*. Inside lay two leathery mummies, desiccated and crushed to save weight and storage space while they were shipped. Jorah had just helped transfer them out of the cheap metal crates they arrived in, and to anchor the ark lids with special permanent bolts.

As a soldier, he'd expected to see death and disfigurement. Still, this had been a hideous way to get a last look at his father. The leathery object might have been almost unrecognizable, if it hadn't worn his father's midnight-blue uniform and Sentinel's shoulder star.

Jorah narrowed his eyes and directed a thought toward the coffin, *I never asked you to go back for me. Things should've turned out differently.* His father had been executed. The Federate Whorl was no longer a friendly place. He wished he could make the Feds pay—Gambrel and SOOC in particular. And what about Madam Kernoweg, the woman they'd been trying to protect when they'd been arrested? Had she no sense of gratitude?

Uncle Kiel beckoned with an upraised hand. "Come closer, everyone. I'll give you your places for the mourner's procession."

Jorah walked closer. It was good to have the rest of his family here.

Uncle Kiel's formal white robes had long, loose sleeves like his regular tunic. He nodded in Jorah's direction. "Jorah, as the only offspring, you must lead."

"I will." He nodded.

Uncle Kiel turned toward a group of non-family members. Eight of them, of course. Four bearers for each ark. "Med students, you will carry Saried into the Chapter room. You military . . ." His voice caught. "Carry Kinnor."

As father to them both, Jorah's grandfather would walk between caskets. Jorah noted that Uncle Kiel didn't have to tell him so. Grandfather stood staring out over the water, hands clasped at the small of his back. Jorah didn't want to imagine how he felt.

Grandmother sat on a stone bench, staring fixedly at the coffins. At the pool's west end, beyond the stepping stones, people streamed silently up the waterside and into the Chapter room.

Meris had already escorted his mother inside, since a bereaved spouse never joined the ceremonial entry. He wondered whether Meris had litanies for days like this.

At the moment, his grandmother wouldn't even look up at Uncle Kiel. Grandfather bent to speak with her. She shook her head and said something Jorah didn't catch. Grandfather walked back across and beckoned to Jorah. "She needs to go inside now," he murmured in Jorah's ear. "But this is terribly hard for her. She and your father parted with hard words. It's the worst kind of grief."

Jorah nodded. Really, his grandparents were losing all three of their remaining children today. Aunt Tiala—who was Tavkel's mother, so he had to believe there'd been such a person—had already "died" to them as a child. But Uncle Kiel meant to depart this afternoon or this evening.

Jorah hadn't told Uncle Kiel, but he'd decided to stay here for whatever happened. Whether it was a renewal of the universe or a Federate invasion, he wanted to be here. He stepped to the stone bench. "Grandmother," he murmured, "Grandfather asked me to escort you inside. I'd be honored. And I'll stay here at Sanctuary with you and Grandfather and Tavkel, wherever Uncle Kiel goes."

She glanced aside with a slack face and slowly stood, straightening as if every vertebra hurt.

He steadied her as they crossed the stepping stones from island to waterside walkway. Hoping to comfort, he reminded her, "Rena, Perl, and Annalah will sit with us."

She halted at the water's edge and snapped, "I have five grandchildren. Not just Kiel's girls and you." She glanced back toward the island, where Uncle Kiel had circled the bearers for what looked like final instructions. Then she added tartly, "They won't start without me." To his surprise, she turned and marched toward the elevator.

Jorah hustled to catch up with her.

● ● ●

Kiel finished reciting the preparatory prayers and opened his eyes. His father stood staring out over the pool again. Kiel turned around. His mother was headed back toward the island, trailed by Jorah . . . and . . . by the one man he did not want to see on this already bitter morning. Tavkel's deprecating shout still rang in Kiel's ears—"Pray for that man"—but today of all days, Kiel knew he ought to show mercy. To his mother, if not to Tavkel.

Pale cheeked, she clutched a bunch of small crimson flowers. Tavkel held a matching bunch. He dropped them into the pool and came the rest of the way, stepping into the circle of bearers as if he belonged there. For several seconds, no one spoke. Tavkel was the only person in all the Sanctuary who wore work clothes instead of mourning white. He turned left and slowly looked around the circle to the right. At the end, he faced Kiel. "I grieve with you," he said.

Kiel crossed his arms over his chest. Everyone said that. "Thank you." He turned away, thinking, *Do not push my grace any further, Tavkel. I will let you attend.* He motioned the bearers toward the arks—the ones in which they would wait for resurrection, while he traveled away in an ark of his own. After the Shekkah service, Tavkel must go back outdoors . . . and he must not join the mourners' procession.

Kiel always had to shield himself during these services. Such farewells were too much for the human heart. For him, this was evidence that the Eternal Speaker had created those hearts for more than a few short years of existence—that these partings weren't the original plan.

Kinnor, he wanted to wail. *Could we have saved you from this, or is it what you were born for?* He glanced at the other long, glossy box. *Saried, are you glad to be with Nebb? We loved you, though you had a hard time believing it.* Still, he couldn't think about Saried for long. His memory kept wandering back to Kinnor and growing up together on Tallis. Shared pranks and rivalries, and the empty hole in his life when they had sent him so early to College—just like Father. To Kinnor, who'd . . . who'd been so blazingly willing to lay down his life for his son.

"Wait." Tavkel's voice turned Kiel back around. "Shamarr, I have a question."

More theology? *Not now, Tavkel,* Kiel wanted to say. Staring toward the Chapter room's open door, he straightened his back. He didn't feel like arguing. He had a service to conduct, his brother and half sister to bury. Mourners to comfort, and then—quickly—a painful confession to make. Hopefully, there would be more passengers to mind-access and bring aboard.

Still, most of the bearers had joined Tavkel's camp—all but Colonel Harris, in fact. If Kiel impressed them now, he might win back a few later. He decided to challenge whatever question Tavkel asked with a question of his own. *Guide me,* he prayed. *This could be my last chance.*

He turned around.

"Kiel." Tavkel rested a hand on Kinnor's coffin. "If you could awaken your brother from the long night, would you?"

Kiel clenched a fist. "How dare you—you ask that in front of our parents? Why would anyone want to return from rest and safety to danger and grief?"

Tavkel opened his free hand. "Are you hinting that life is not a great gift?"

Plainly, Tavkel had understood Kiel's challenge. It was to be a duel of questions. Smiling, Kiel raised his chin . . . and the stakes. "Are you claiming power over life and death, young man?"

"How old do you think I am, Shamarr?" Tavkel turned to Kiel's mother, who stood gaping, still clutching her small bouquet.

Before Kiel could ask another question, Tavkel spoke again. "Saried is at peace." He nodded solemnly toward the four medical people who would carry her inside. "But Kinnor sleeps restlessly. His son still needs guidance. So does his beloved Wind. And his mother made no such peace with him."

Kiel gaped. What possessed this man? The Adversary, lord of death, never gave up his prey. "How dare you?" Kiel muttered again. "What deceit will you not stoop to?"

Tavkel paced to the platform's edge, hands at the sides of his rough work clothes. "You can do kinetics, can't you, Shamarr? Because of your love for a child."

And so they returned to questions?

An instant later, Kiel gasped. Tamím had enhanced Kiel's ability to move inanimate objects so that Annalah would not be accidentally killed in surgery. Kiel had made it a spiritual discipline to refrain from using it.

But Tavkel knew! Not just what Kiel could do, but why. He knew, and he was threatening to expose Kiel.

Kiel's cheeks heated. If he asked either one of the next logical questions—*Why do you think I can?*—or—*What do you mean?*—he would fall into Tavkel's snare. On the other hand, if he accused Tavkel of receiving dark knowledge from Tamím and his ilk, he would disrupt this already terrible morning.

"Your question is inappropriate." He glared back at the young man.

Tavkel smiled slightly, acknowledging his triumph in the duel, though his eyes remained soft with what looked like pity.

Behind Tavkel, Kiel's mother took a step forward. Her face was almost as white as her mourning dress. Kiel shielded himself. Judging by the hope in her eyes, she was thinking the unthinkable. His father laid a hand on her shoulder. She seized it.

"Pull the bolts, Shamarr," Tavkel said.

Kiel eyed the nearest coffin bolt. These expanded into their sockets when driven home. It would take Sentinel kinetics to recompress the expansion sectors and remove them again.

He stood tall and looked down into Tavkel's eyes. For the first time, he sent Tavkel a thought on his carrier wave. *Don't you dare give our parents false hope. You're torturing them!* He re-raised his shields instantly. He had no intention of looking into that young man's mind, of exchanging his gifts for Tavkel's deception.

Tavkel returned his stare. "Please."

Kiel turned to his parents again. He imagined poor Wind, already sitting in the Chapter room, held upright by Meris the outsider.

And there stood Jorah, who couldn't pull permanent bolts either, thanks to the Federates. The soldiers and med students were all Tavkel's, except Colonel Harris. Kiel was one of just two people present who could do such a thing.

He glanced at Colonel Harris and swallowed bile. He would not evade Tavkel's request by passing it on to someone else. But he didn't want to see his brother's crushed mummy again. He especially didn't want their mother seeing it. "Do you realize," he said, turning his back on Tavkel to address the rest of them, "what he's doing to you? The false hope, the agony—Mother, let go. Please. Father, Kinnor is at rest. Today's services will help us begin to find our own peace."

His father stepped forward and laid a hand on the casket. "Kiel, if I could pull those bolts, I would. My abilities haven't returned enough, though. Do it under my authority, if you don't want to take the responsibility yourself."

"You would do it," Kiel said dully.

"If Tavkel gave the order, yes." His father nodded, but his eyes drooped sadly. "Kiel, you know who he is."

Kiel glared at Tavkel, standing there with his herding stick—a young tree, cut down without bearing fruit. Kiel shook his head and stepped to the wooden ark. *Forgive me,* he prayed. *Forgive us all for going along with this charade. It seems like a cruel way to expose the lie. But the lie must be exposed.*

He rested his hand on the first bolt and reached inside himself for energy, focused it in the palm of his right hand, and made a calling burst. He compressed the far end, closing his hand as if gripping the bolt. Under his hand, the bolt head rose. He closed his fingers on it, pulled it free, and turned aside.

His father stepped up beside him, palm outstretched. Kiel dropped the bolt on his father's palm. Its inner end had already expanded again, giving it a club-like appearance.

Kiel moved down that side of the casket, pulling the rest of them. He rounded the foot and came back up the other side.

Finished, he stepped away. The soldiers and med students kept a respectful distance, but everyone—family and coffin carriers—stood staring at that ark.

"Help, Jorah," his father ordered. They raised the lid and carried it aside. Vaguely stale air stirred. Kiel edged closer to his mother. She would need more comfort than ever.

Tavkel laid down his stick. He stepped up to the long box and reached down a hand. "Kinnor Caldwell," he said, "good morning."

Then he stepped away, and a hand gripped his forearm. A rounded, fleshy, intact hand. It was followed by a midnight-blue sleeve, an arm, and the top of an uncrushed head.

Kiel's blood turned to ice. Barely aware that the crowd broke ranks and plunged forward, he stared as his father, Tavkel, and Jorah helped his brother—his living brother—climb clumsily out of the ark, drop his bare feet onto the flagstones, and stand upright. Their laughter echoed across the water, off the walls and the skylights.

Kinnor tossed his head and shook dust out of his hair. He cleared his throat. "Those idiot colonels. What did they do, blow the execution?"

Kiel's mother finally shrieked. She dropped her flowers and rushed forward to fling her arms around Kinnor's shoulders. Kiel's father instantly engulfed them both.

Kiel stared over their heads at his brother. His brother, alive. He felt paralyzed, nearly blind to all else.

Kinnor looked back, blank-faced. "What?" he mouthed. He gazed around slowly. Finally his long sweep caught on the coffins—one empty—and the opened underground vault. His eyes widened.

Rarely had Kiel experienced the twin link everyone seemed to expect. In this moment, he counted two heartbeats before Kinnor's blast of horror echoed his realization that he'd been successfully executed.

Kin turned to Jorah, who was talking rapidly. He shouted, "What? Slow down, slow down."

The bearers plunged into the huddle, leaving Kiel and Tavkel standing alone.

Kiel felt naked, horrified while everyone else celebrated, devastated when he ought to be leaping for joy. The herdsman had either robbed death using life itself, or else he was entitled to reclaim one of his own victims.

Which?

Beyond Tavkel's shoulder, Kiel's brother and father embraced. Both of them were alive because of Tavkel. Indeed, they all were alive because of Tavkel, who'd prevented the plague from spreading.

Kiel backed away from the crowd. He faced a decision. There was no other way forward: Either he must give himself irrevocably to Tavkel too—and the power that had captured the rest of his family—or else he must walk off this island alone, this symbolic boundary between one life and the next, rejecting a man he'd waited his whole life to meet, to conduct his half sister's Shekkah service—

Wait.

Kiel re-ran that penultimate thought. *A man he'd waited his whole life to meet.* Some part of him was already convinced, and had lain waiting for some inexplicable act to stun his scarred heart to silence.

He'd always believed that faith based on miracles had little value. Otherwise, the Holy One would've granted thousands of them, out of love for his people. It was mercy that stayed the almighty hand, mercy that preserved human freedom. True conversion was an act of the free will—but most often, the free heart led. Occasionally the eyes also gave evidence.

His own heart felt shrunken and cold. It belonged in a mummy. It struck him then: It was darkness, not wisdom, holding him back.

Desperate to shed his tainted abilities, he prayed, *Give me discernment, Holy One. Give me strength.* He sank down like a consecrant, squeezing his eyes shut. He swallowed more bile. "Show me," he said, folding forward over his knees, "who you really are."

He knew the voice that answered. "I hide from no one. Come and see."

Kiel focused the probe that would cost him everything. He opened his eyes and glanced once more at his father's back.

Tavkel had also sunk down on one knee. He knelt beside Kiel on the white stone. "Is this what you truly want, Kiel? Do you come to me freely?"

"Your mercy is eternal." Staring into clear, deep brown eyes, Kiel inhaled and plunged in.

PART THREE

. . . *He shall cry to all peoples,*
and in His hand shall be power
to unmake all that His hand once made;
unmake the universe and form it again,
perfectly, as in the beginning.

. . . *A new song you shall sing,*
though the stars themselves fail.
And He shall be a flame to the frozen and a feast to the famished,
a hymn for the deaf and true light for the blind,
but death to the placid and proud . . .

MELAUK 72, 74, 75

Tavkel went through the pantries again this morning, and two kitchen staffers
followed him this time, but they still didn't see anything happen. The fact remains
that we now have more than enough to feed everyone for at least another week!
And it's much too early for garnetberries, but three big bowls of them turned up
in the main cold unit. We feasted on fresh berries with cream at midday meal.
Just being with him is a feast—but most of what he does, he seems to do secretly
and quietly. We only notice if he calls attention to it for his own reasons, or if
we're paying extremely close attention to "before" and "after."

"Esthenn on Bishda," I greet you again. Tavkel says you are correct, and
Siyach I, 5, 16 is a prophecy that has been overlooked! Only Tavkel and

the Eternal Speaker know how many others we'll understand only in hindsight.

He also says that everyone will receive enough information to make a choice. He says it's important that we decide to trust—but he won't ever overwhelm us with evidence. He never will take away our power to choose.

Here's what he says today: "Your greatest freedom is to love. Love the Eternal One, and love those whom he created. The Collegium tells you to believe in concepts, but no concept will carry you into eternal peace. Only I can do that. The one vital concept is faith. Bring me your darkness by that faith, regardless of the distances. These are the only gifts I can accept."

FROM *Procyel Eyewitness Report* #61
DAY 20 OF OUR DAYSTAR'S WALKING AMONG US:
ANNALAH CALDWELL

I am the spark of undying light. I shall see. I shall know.
I am the spark of undying light. I shall see. I shall know.
I am the spark of undying light . . .

LITANY I, AGAINST CONFUSION
PIPER GAMBREL, CHANCELLOR
COLLEGIUM FOR HUMAN LEARNING

CHAPTER 28

The stone felt cold under Kiel's knees as he touched the unknown. First he sensed a priestly compassion, a staggering awareness of rejoicing and suffering all over the Whorl. It blasted his last resistance away.

Called deeper, he circled the supernova of love that had created and still contained everything—he tracked his people's past back to the first man and first woman, coming to wondering consciousness in a fruited garden—and back farther, to the first illuminating explosion of light, a moment pregnant with all that would follow. A passion for each atom and element touched every flickering and unforgotten life for thousands upon thousands of years.

Here also was the determination to end the evil that had entered the beloved creation and spoiled it, the evil that ensured even a well lived life never escaped suffering and darkness. Destroying this evil, he saw, would extract a hideous cost. If anything could have been too much for the Infinite to bear, it was this: this agonizing separation of godhood from godhood, this virtual dismemberment.

Then came a startling, specific memory, passed directly from Tavkel's mind. Hard stone pressed against twelve-year-old knees as Tavkel knelt to be consecrated into Tekkumah's faith community. Kiel had to be seeing the scene from Tavkel's perspective. He glanced first at an auburn-haired woman there in the prayer retreat's stone chapel. Kiel's sister, seen by someone outside Tekkumah for the first time in forty years, was slender and greying, and she looked remarkably like Kiel and Tiala's mother. She clasped her hands in front of a magnificent blue-green brocaded robe.

Behind her, another presence hovered. To Tavkel's memory it was also familiar, but Kiel wanted to gape. There stood personality embodied in light, a Bright One, an angelic messenger.

They're real, Kiel exclaimed silently. *As real as the shadows.*

Yes, but Bright Ones are still true to their maker, the Eternal Speaker. Tavkel's reply resonated between them like the strings of two kinnora, as if one ringing harp had set the other vibrating.

An elderly man stepped close, also wearing brilliantly colored robes. Kiel somehow understood that Tavkel had requested this formal consecration, over the protests of Em'Gadol and Av'Gadol, the retreat's elders.

Why did they protest? he wondered.

By way of answer, he felt his probe nudged deeper. Beneath Tavkel's conscious memory, instead of the usual tangle of will and intention Kiel found a complex but ordered awareness. Young Tavkel had known who he was from the dawning of self-awareness.

Besides, Mother was warned who I would be and what I must do. She was commanded to tell the others. In that mental orderliness, along every thread of thought, pulsed the warmth of absolute love received and given, and the willingness to face mental, physical, or spiritual anguish to restore creation to its Creator. It would look like—

An explosion blasted creation clean, lighting every dark corner. From that depth where suffering and love mingled like fuel and flame, the suffering universe seemed to turn inside out.

Kiel instantly realized his peril. This power could vaporize him merely by redirecting a thought. Still, mercy and love remained inseparable in Tavkel's mind. Knowing what lay ahead beat down even the mighty heart that upheld him now. *But there is no other way,* the Presence assured him. Like rolling chords from those two harps, a hopeful joy swept dread away. The bent universe would be straightened. Kiel would be restored to the image he was intended to wear. He would see the dawn of a purified Light.

Overwhelmed, Kiel folded inward to bow in submission . . . but he was gently caught and returned to Tavkel's consecration memory. *One more thing, Kiel, beloved,* he heard. *To endure what's ahead you must see this, though you need to keep it secret for now.*

Back in Tekkumah's light-washed chapel, the robed elder laid both hands on Tavkel's head. Kiel had done this for many young Thyrian consecrants. This was the sacred moment, when the priest passed down a memory that had been preserved since the kindred had fled Ehret. A last sacrifice had been offered in their temple.

Kiel saw the memory begin in his mind, but something seemed wrong about it. Before, Kiel had always seen and given this memory in the way that an adolescent named Timarah Gall had originally experienced it. Usually, when the sequence began, Timarah had been helping to lead a sacrificial kipret down the abandoned temple's stairs toward the altars. But something was different in this version. Had Kiel ever seen the temple from so close to the ground?

They reached the altars. Kiel found himself looking up at *three* young Ehretans—consecrant and both priests—

The priest held a knife down at his side, almost hidden against his forearm. Kiel bent his head toward a curl of rippled carpet, but a rope seemed to tighten around his neck. It tugged his head up. He did not flinch as the knife sliced his neck.

Kiel wanted to jump back in terror and pain, but Tavkel's memory—could this be real?—included no sense of struggle. He crumpled . . . and incomprehensibly, his consciousness seemed to flow through that opened throat into a wooden bowl that caught the kipret's warm blood.

Then Kiel realized that Tavkel had experienced the vision not as a person but a kipret, through whose eyes Kiel had been seeing.

Impossibly, Kiel felt his consciousness flow again, out of the blood into the consecrant's living hands, which were plunged deep into that bowl in confession of guilt—and finally, preposterously, he was fleeing the Sanctuary as priest and consecrant ran for their lives. *No, not that door. This way!* he urged, and the runners obeyed his voice.

Kiel breathed raggedly, trying to comprehend. Tavkel . . . He was present then, as the sacrifice . . . present still, in its life's blood . . . and also present in spirit, helping the new consecrant flee . . . Was that what Tavkel was showing him? *Was that how this memory survived, Tavkel? Did you make sure Timarah reached the evacuation ship, so we could pass on this memory?*

No verbal answer came this time. Still, Kiel believed he had finally comprehended a great mystery.

But what does this mean, Tavkel?

He felt a vast waiting, as if the One whom he served wished him to find his own answer.

Surely . . . you aren't going to be slaughtered—here on Procyel II, like the kipret was there—and go with us in spirit, into exile? Not again, if you never do things the same way twice!

Now an answer came: *Just trust me. And follow.*

Water lapped softly nearby. Kiel wasn't aware of having withdrawn his mental probe, so it must have evaporated along with his ayin abilities, which Tavkel had just taken. Apparently Tavkel had finished communicating.

Now he knew how he would spend the rest of this life. He knew how privileged he had become, to look through these brown eyes into that mind that transcended ayin abilities and the starry Whorl.

And how close he'd come to throwing it away. He shivered at a puff of breeze and opened his eyes.

Tavkel knelt before him. Knelt like a servant, ready to do what he must.

Kiel shuddered with dreadful joy and stared at the face that had come from outside creation. It was now made up of cells that carried the very chromosomes Tavkel had personally created.

Kiel understood with sudden clarity that he would follow this man to his death. And it was fine. Whatever happened now, he wasn't in charge. He'd seen death defeated in Kinnor. He could not be afraid of it now. The awe he'd known as a child—a sense of deep, perilous mystery—was back, and it felt wonderful.

"Welcome," Tavkel murmured. "I will be glad for your help."

Struggling to his feet, Kiel looked around an island that seemed oddly still. His tainted powers were gone, and that felt good. Clean. The epsilon silence he'd dreaded sounded restful. Peaceful. He looked up at the stone ceiling. Morning sun still streamed through the skylights. On the island's other side, several people—his parents, his formerly dead brother, the coffin bearers—had gathered beside Kin's open coffin, as well as Saried's closed one. Saried, who had made her peace.

Apparently, only minutes had passed.

But those minutes had changed everything.

Kiel squared his shoulders. *Holy One, forgive me for doubting so long.* He would have to humble himself in front of his people and admit he was the one, after all, who had seen the truth in the nick of time. But he had seen. They would face the coming cataclysm together. "We still have Saried's Shekkah to hold. Will you speak to the congregants?"

Tavkel straightened his work shirt. Kiel no longer sensed the man's emotional state, but he thought he still saw joy behind those hot brown eyes. "I will," Tavkel said.

Kiel took several steps toward the other group. Kinnor looked up at him again, shrugged, and tried to step away from the others.

But their mother was having none of that. She clung to Kinnor as Kiel walked closer, her white mourning dress pressed against Kinnor's rumpled midnight blues.

He thought he might understand how she felt, even if he couldn't sense her emotions. So he threw his arms around them both. *Thank you, Holy One. Thank you!*

• • •

Something finally rustled outside the Chapter room's door.

Meris sat in the back of the crowd with the Minster, gently holding her hand. Minster Wind seemed to have calmed during the last few minutes. There'd been no chest clutching since shortly after they'd come in and sat down, which was a relief. These people didn't force a widow to sit in front where everyone could watch her suffer, but they'd shown Wind and Meris to seats in the last row, next to the aisle. Also, the Chapter room wasn't as cavernous as the great poolside. If the Minster wanted a good view of whatever happened up front, she could simply stand up.

Meris didn't expect her to do that, though. Her own chest hurt in sympathy. She'd never sat this close to a bereaved person. Making things worse, there'd been an unexplained delay of a quarter hour. Maybe the rest of the family was saying private farewells. She would probably need to drug this poor woman again tonight.

She glanced left. The idea of waiting to say an eternal good-bye suggested a sort of pain Meris hadn't considered before, and the delay was giving her plenty of time to think that through. It seemed unfair, that human beings would live just a few short years—and would be young, and strong, and able for so few of those years—

Abruptly the Minster sat straight. Her head whipped around. Before Meris could react, there was a shriek and a flurry, and the Minster dashed out the door arch.

Meris sat befuddled as heads turned in front of her. Two more people with aisle seats jumped up and stared toward the door. Meris shifted to scoot along the bench, closer to the aisle.

Shamarr Kiel strode through the arch that Minster Wind had fled through, looking tall in his white formal robes. "Sit down, please. Do sit down. Join me, please, in a prayer of gratitude."

Like a flock of their kipreta at feeding time, most of them lowered their heads. Meris slid into the place Minster Wind had vacated. She slowly, silently turned around. Someone stood behind the Shamarr. It had to be Tavkel. He looked as if he were talking with someone.

Wait, hadn't the Shamarr exiled Tavkel outdoors? Was his return what had excited those people? Had there been a reconciliation?

Shamarr Kiel raised his head and took a long breath. "Oh, my people. I have been terribly wrong. And you would not—could not—believe the lengths to which our Dabar will go to prove himself. My friends . . ." He shook his head and spread his hands.

Meris braced herself. Shamarr Caldwell hadn't been convinced by Tavkel's supposedly supernatural healings, had he? She had a good theory, that Tavkel's mutant abilities included a grasp of bio-electrical phenomena. If the Shamarr *had* been convinced, something spectacular had to have happened. It had raised poor Minster Wind right up off of her bench.

Raised . . .

Don't even think that, Meris. It's preposterous.

Shamarr Kiel gestured behind him. "My friends," he repeated, "today we sing Shekkah for my beloved sister Saried. But not, it seems, for my beloved brother." With that, he began the Qavah song for the dead. Meris had read the text in preparation for this service.

He stepped forward, striding down the aisle beside Tavkel. Both of them sang lustily in that throaty language. Behind them came four military people in uniform—she'd seen them practice the coffin-carry together, but now they walked unburdened.

And then, with the wide-eyed Minster clinging to his left arm, came Kinnor Caldwell. The supposedly dead man walked through the door with his head held high, grinning and making shushing gestures as people greeted him with cries of shock and delight.

What? Was Tavkel re-animating dead bodies now? Meris swallowed on a tight throat. She'd shivered at horror stories about dead people who had been shot with some kind of energy that made them get up and menace the living—unthinking, inhuman. The Air Master looked rumpled and pale, but not frightening. And plainly, his wife wasn't afraid. *She* thought it was him, moving that body around.

And . . . Meris's thoughts galloped . . . these people buried most of their dead right here, under this Sanctuary. If Tavkel could bring back the dead, might he re-animate a veritable army?

No! The whole affair stank of fraud. Meris stared at the couple's backs as they pushed through a cheering crowd, and she wondered whether any real proof existed that it had actually been Kinnor Caldwell's body that had arrived in that coffin. Could he have been smuggled home in some other part of the messenger ship?

But everyone here believed the Minster had gone into bereavement shock. *Everyone, including me!* Minster Wind would have had to be an extraordinary actress, to have carried that off.

Well, these were extraordinary people, and she mustn't forget it. Jorah's grandparents—beaming—followed Jorah's parents up the aisle, followed by Jorah. His grin lit the Chapter room.

Last came another group, carrying just one of the hand-carved caskets. More shushing noises swished around the room. When the second little group reached the front, everyone went silent again.

The Shamarr in his white robes stood beside the younger man in brown work clothes at the long altar table's end.

Meris peered uneasily over the crowd. The Shamarr's wife, Hanusha, sat in the front row, slowly and rhythmically shaking her head. If these spouses really were emotionally linked, she would probably see Hanusha Caldwell kneeling in front of Tavkel as soon as this meeting ended.

Could that really be a dead man, standing at the table's far end?

I fear what I only imagine . . .

She understood nothing they said or sang for the rest of the hour. Afterward, though, Shamarr Kiel took center stage in front of the altar. "Forgive me." He spoke softly into a room that had fallen so quiet that Meris could hear the pool lapping outside the open rear door. "I was wrong. Wanting to see, I was blind. I hindered you all instead of helping. But now we walk forward together. Not into darkness, but into the dawning day."

And finally, Tavkel asked Kinnor Caldwell and Minster Wind to stand in front of the congregation. The Minster never looked away from her husband. Not once. "In the sight of you all," Tavkel said in a triumphant tone, "I give Kinnor Irion Caldwell back to his people."

The room rang with cheers.

Tavkel raised a hand. "But most of all, back to his wife." Now his voice was tender. "Wind, you have graciously kept the privacy suite vacant for special needs. For the next few days, go and enjoy it. Those who love you will make sure the Sanctuary doesn't stop running."

Right in front of men, women, and children, Minster Wind and Air Master Caldwell kissed each other—and it was no mannerly peck. Meris hoped she didn't look as pink as she felt.

The congregation stood and cheered as the Air Master and the Sanctuary Administrator hustled back up the aisle and out of the Chapter room.

Now what? Meris turned to face the front, where the whole Caldwell clan seemed to be exchanging embraces, laughing, talking. Apparently there would be no further announcements. Tavkel . . . where had he gone? Meris narrowed her eyes and searched the platform for brown work clothes. No one else had been wearing them—

There. Backed against the far wall, edging away from the platform, passing underneath one of the wall sconces. Not smiling, though. *He looks guilty* was her first thought, followed by *No, not guilty. But sad. Why in the worlds* sad?

And what would he do next?

CHAPTER 29

Each year during midwinter holidays, Piper Gambrel hosted a reception for the leaders who were making the Collegium for Human Learning a vital cultural force. This year, his planners had hired a gravidic platform. An expert pilot timed today's slow flight. Sunset found them floating over table-lands far from city limits. Dozens of people—the crème of Tallan society, resplendent in decorative winter tunics and gowns—stood on risers near the platform's west edge. The crimson sun sank behind purple and grey clouds rimmed with orange fire.

Really, this view was available anywhere, at any time, on a view wall. But seeing it personally was a reward for his best employees, his most valuable contacts. The god-voice within him had not responded to the view. It guided him from group to group, occasionally suggesting conversational topics. Most of his guests either fawned on him or obsequiously left a wide berth. He would send compliments to the weather control committee, he decided as he wrapped two fingers around a cylindrical toasting goblet. He turned his back on the risers to address a pair of guests near the refreshment table.

Before he could speak, someone tapped his shoulder from behind. He took a deep breath and turned slowly, making it clear he interacted only on his own terms.

The intruder was Madam Kudennou Kernoweg. He let out that breath in a long "Ah, Madam."

Her tailored black gown swathed the accumulated weight of four-plus decades as a Regional Councilor. Despite the smooth skin and dark hair that her youth implant maintained, she stood with a stoop and tottered when she walked. Zeimsky had whispered that her sleek jaw resulted from continual surgeries.

"Good evening, sir." Her voice creaked. How old was she now . . . ninety?

"Good evening." He bent forward, deferring to her position. Besides, she had assisted the Collegium over the years, publicly endorsing his philosophy.

Someday, *he* would sit on that council. Maybe in her central chair.

"You made excellent use of our little assassin group." She raised her own toasting glass. "It was worth the inconvenience."

She was referring to the Lenguan trade delegation. Her own people had suggested the ambush. Lenguad was a Federate world where Sentinels were particularly unwelcome. "Thank you again," he said. He would have liked to withdraw from this party—to let his new god-voice take over his social duties so he could float over the hovering platform. He disliked personal rituals.

To his relief, a tone sounded in his cutaway coat's breast pocket. "Please," he murmured. "Forgive me. I'm having calls screened tonight, so this must be vital."

Her lips pursed for an instant. Years ago, she probably would have controlled every impulse. Obviously, her years at the top had made her equally intolerant of whatever piqued her.

He backed toward the platform's empty east side and raised the handheld to read. *DeepScan from Major Preston on board the* White Squall *in Procyel orbit. Content will follow upon acknowledgement.*

Inserting Major Preston and his observer group on board a RIA ship, as escorts to young Jorah Caldwell, was already bearing fruit. Thanks to two Sentinels under Collegiate control, the enemy's technology could be used against them. Those RIA operators had been taken off duty in the Elysia region and offered the humane cure for themselves and their families, or else this RIA mission as an alternative.

Gambrel tightened his thumb on the ACKNOWLEDGE panel. Here came the report: *Unexpected voiceprint on Procyel's defense frequencies. Positively IDd as Air Master Kinnor Caldwell. Request further orders.*

Startled, he read the display a second time.

The god-voice blasted back into conscious contact, reading through his eyes . . . and he watched as his right hand clenched in semi-divine fury. Those SOOC idiots had botched the Sentinel's execution! Either that, or—could it be?—SOOC had deliberately deceived all observers and sent the Air Master back to Procyel Sanctuary alive, instead of executing him. Maybe in medical stasis. The corpse could have been someone else's.

He addressed a whisper inward. "Can you confirm that? Is the man alive? What happened?"

He had no idea how long it might take to get the god within to answer. Its silence infuriated him. Still, the situation had potential. He hurried to rejoin Madam Kernoweg. "Madam, forgive me, but we must further discuss the Sentinel problem."

• • •

The next morning, the SOOC colonels produced medical records from Sentinel Caldwell's alleged execution. The records looked authentic, which meant they had to be falsified. To Gambrel's satisfaction, Regional Command locked up both colonels and ordered Colonel Zeimsky to *cure* them. Regional called in Covert Operations' best interrogators and put a Covert Ops man in charge of the interviews. By nightfall, both colonels had been disempowered, questioned, and executed—and confirmed dead. In Collegiate terms, they were now "dispatched to rejoin the Infinite Divine."

But they had provided no new information.

The next afternoon, Gambrel appeared before another subcommittee in a bare white room. Madam Kernoweg wore her robe of office and sat centrally behind the data table, three civilians to her right and two military personnel to her left. The civilian next to her kept fiddling with control surfaces next to his inset data monitor.

Gambrel had been assigned a chair slightly away from the long table's other side, between his ally, Zeimsky, and a pair of military men he didn't recognize.

"So Kinnor Caldwell was not executed after all," Madam Kernoweg opened the meeting, her voice echoing slightly in the room. "Obviously, they have stopped respecting even their own laws. This is all deeply disturbing. That clemency request from the Sentinel College plainly was their signal for a pre-planned rescue operation. We must act quickly. And decisively."

"Surely that College is no longer a concern." Gambrel sent a glance to his left. Seated beside him, the balding man in Tallan grey nodded crisply. His uniform nameplate read URNOCK. "I am told they are no longer holding classes but have taken a purely defensive position . . . and they're calling it 'training.'"

One of the military officers behind the table clenched his hands. "We will be taking appropriate steps on Thyrica. First, we will discuss the mission for which we have called you three."

Gambrel listened carefully. Were they including him personally? If this subcommittee asked him to do anything that other staff could accomplish—to drop his vital business to go somewhere else for no good reason—he would need to speak privately with Madam Kernoweg.

"The most culpable persons are at their Sanctuary," the committee member continued, and Gambrel started to smile, "harboring the Air Master. They must be brought to justice." He waved a hand at Gambrel and Zeimsky, and at Urnock, the Tallan on Gambrel's left.

"Yes." Madam Kernoweg coughed. "Interfering with a capital case at this level can be construed as treason. We will require that these actions be investigated and every perpetrator prosecuted, so we are sending a multi-level mission to Procyel."

Gambrel looked left and right again. *Ah. A good command team. Zeimsky for the cure, Urnock for the force, and myself for the authority to implement both.* He smoothed his coat and addressed Madam Kernoweg. "I will be glad to be deputized, however I may serve the Regional Council."

The god-voice, which had been rather quiet today, seemed to wake up. *You should have expected to be sent.*

Oh? he answered it. *Did you arrange this?*

Another committee member interrupted his internal conversation. "While you're there, we want a full report on the so-called Dabarite phenomenon. The reports are obviously exaggerated."

Gambrel gave a curt nod. This morning's newsnet had sizzled with rumors about a rival philosophy now allegedly competing with his Collegium. If only he'd intercepted that Sentinel woman, Saried Kinsman, before she'd been able to visit the local Chapter.

Apparently, her so-called martyrdom had raised her personal interest rating, taking her "Tavkel" and "Dabarite" stories into the "most read" category—along with several reports of alleged supernatural healings on Procyel II, which were appearing in the new *Procyel Eyewitness Report*. These reports were signed "Annalah Caldwell." As far afield as Netaia, a young monarch was apparently spreading these *PER*s using official resources. Remote nodes such as Netaia could unfortunately control a vast network.

Further, he'd learned that "Annalah Caldwell" was not a pseudonym. She'd been an honors student on Elysia, and her name appeared on the *Daystar* passenger list. Plainly, she needed to be brought under Collegiate influence. He'd sent Zeimsky a quick message, suggesting that if unusual healings were taking place, their local plague might not amount to much—not that anyone expected reports from the isolated Sentinel Sanctuary. Still, he had faith in Zeimsky's work. Also, Lieutenant Jorah Caldwell was on site while Major Preston awaited orders aboard the *White Squall.*

The other committee member was still speaking. " . . . spreading too quickly to control. The most threatening rumor predicts another cosmic catastrophe. Supposedly, people are being asked to 'gift' their 'personal darkness' to this Boh-Dabar entity before that becomes impossible."

Gambrel sat back and crossed his legs. "Speculation is the excreta of inferior minds. Also, any philosophy that requires instantaneous lifetime decisions is suspect."

"Emotional manipulation. Right." Zeimsky spoke from beside him. He didn't look at Gambrel, though, and Gambrel continued to act as if he barely knew the man. This subcommittee need not know about their confidential discussions.

Madam Kernoweg made a swirling gesture over her tabletop station. Gambrel recognized the motion: She was transferring data to the handheld in his breast pocket, and probably Zeimsky's and Urnock's. "Chancellor, you will either squelch or absorb that Dabarite movement and investigate the Caldwell family's offenses. Colonel Urnock, you will enforce whatever steps must be taken, as new head of Special Operations Oversight."

Gambrel smiled to himself. The Sentinels weren't going to like this Covert Operations man's posting. Special Ops and Covert Ops rarely got along.

"Colonel Zeimsky," she continued, "you and whatever staff you require will go to Procyel and stand ready to implement the treatment of all its residents as your primary mission." She extended both hands, indicating all three of them. "If they will not allow you to land, along with a defense group of appropriate size, they will become liable to military reprisal."

"I don't think there'll be trouble." Gambrel waved a hand. He disliked bloodshed. "They have been begging the Collegium for an ITD platter. As a significant people group, technically they are entitled to one—in return for services rendered."

"And payment." A civilian committee member with a closed, careful face spoke for the first time, pointing down at his glowing station. The man probably had to authorize funds for this mission. "And we thank the Collegium, again, for transferring the proceeds from this particular ITD sale into this subcommittee's affairs budget."

Gambrel smiled. The Collegium could have used those funds. Now, however, the investment he'd made in that splendid invention would fund a shift in Federate policy. Above board.

Someday, though, Regional Command would be under his control. "I shall bring it to them personally," he said, "along with your invoice."

"Now, Admiral Vellis." Madam Kernoweg spoke to the man beyond Colonel Urnock, and he straightened his back. "You shall assemble and deploy a second force—an authorized force, this time—to Thyrica. Order the Sentinel College complex to impound all surviving staff and students and await your arrival. You will escort a medical group, to be provided by Colonel Zeimsky. There too, we authorize the use of overwhelming force if they do not cooperate. Given their abilities, we have no option but striking preemptively, from safe distances, if there is any doubt regarding their cooperation with disempowerment."

As the older man saluted, Gambrel finally felt himself start to float over his body. Calm, confident. He could let the god within him take charge.

"Those people were granted that Sanctuary under specific terms." Madam Kernoweg's voice creaked again. "Plainly, some of them are now choosing to overstep those boundaries. Proceed with the investigation, Chancellor . . . Colonel . . . Colonel. Normal humanity must not be menaced or dominated by a post-human race of offenders. On Procyel as well, their abilities require us to maintain safe distances, reasonable numbers and adequate armament."

On Gambrel's left, Urnock folded his arms and leaned back on his seat.

"Chancellor Gambrel," she continued, "in addition to your specific mission, you will ensure that all reports leaving Procyel show that we have acted fairly and appropriately. We will be publicizing the humane Zeimsky Cure as widely as possible. These two elements should counter those wild *PER* stories."

He watched himself nod. Carefully managed publicity would be vital. Most Federates secretly supported ending the Sentinel era, but they didn't like thinking about what it would take.

He didn't, either. If he'd been down there, in charge of his body, he might have said something compassionate. Ending that era meant making a temporary sacrifice, overriding his lofty ideals for the sake of a better future.

Madam Kernoweg kept speaking below him. "Nominally, Chancellor, you shall oversee the mission. However, Colonel Urnock stands on equal footing, while we hope Colonel Zeimsky's work will prove the most important of all."

Again, he watched himself nod. He would've liked to argue for the right to give orders to both of them—officially, not nominally. Zeimsky would be no problem, but he couldn't count on this man Urnock.

Madam Kernoweg turned her head. "Colonel Urnock, upon arrival you shall immediately prosecute whoever is found to be responsible for this act of defiance regarding Sentinel Kinnor Caldwell. You then shall present Procyel with a roster of persons who shall surrender into custody within twenty-four hours, all of whom are to be preemptively stunned for your safety and then transported here in medical stasis. Air Master Caldwell is to be included, if he has not by then been efficaciously executed. We particularly wish to examine and interview the individual called Tavkel.

"Chancellor Gambrel," she said, glancing his way again, "shall choose up to nine additional individuals for that roster."

Gambrel brightened. Below him, his head nodded. Theoretically, that did put him in a strong position over Urnock in at least one respect.

"If they don't cooperate?" Urnock asked. "If those individuals aren't brought to us immediately?"

"Then we authorize full use of antipersonnel ordnance on that site." She shook her head slowly, as if she regretted giving that order.

Gambrel knew better, though. Surely at the back of all their minds, they were thinking the same thing: Leave fewer to breed another generation of altered humans!

"Colonel Zeimsky." Madam Kernoweg raised her voice. "We wish you success in helping as many as possible of these unfortunate people regain normal and healthy humanity. You will begin with the individuals on Chancellor Gambrel's list, after they are stunned and before they are stased for transport. Then you shall continue processing the entire site." She paused and looked down at them all. "If there are no further questions?"

There were no questions. It was obvious what must be done. Gambrel just would have liked to make a short speech, showing that he accepted responsibility over the others.

"Then this committee is in recess." Madam Kernoweg ran a hand over her gleaming tabletop station, and the table went dark.

CHAPTER 30

Jorah plodded uphill with his grandmother clutching his left arm. Ahead of them, Tavkel took short steps and leaned on his walking stick, though Jorah was pretty sure he didn't need it. He'd asked eight followers to join him at a rocky knob where Jorah had once attended a bonfire party.

Besides Jorah and his grandparents, the group included his uncle Kiel and cousin Annalah, plus a couple who'd been kitchen supervisors here for at least ten years, and a psi med specialist who had just arrived from Caroli. Tavkel hadn't explained why he included any one of them, but they made up an interesting group—different occupations, different generations—and it felt like an honor to be here at all.

Grandmother sighed as they rounded the last switchback and headed left. Up on the knob, yellow flowers hunkered among arrow-shaped leaves. "Haven't been," she puffed, tightening her grip, "up here, in twenty years. Or more."

"Worth the hike, isn't it?" Jorah stared down the long slope. The crop fields lay below like a set of grids, each furrow perfectly straight. Mountains sliced the western horizon like a serrated blade, receding into a hazy distance. The U-shaped valley divided the forbidding Tuva Teeth from the slightly less angular south range. Jorah kept to the path's edge, so she could walk on the smoothest part. "Even Meris admits those mountains bowl her over."

"So when are you going to get serious about bringing her inside? Onto the Path?"

"There isn't time."

She planted her feet and held on to his arm, letting the kitchen supervisors pass them. "Don't tell me there isn't time. You're just being cowardly."

"Grandmother!" She wasn't the kind to use that word lightly. Still—

"That's just what I see." She let go of his arm long enough to pull a strand of hair out of her eyes. "The girl's prickly, of course. Who wouldn't be? But I have a feeling . . ."

Jorah spotted the fire circle up ahead. Tavkel was already sitting down. *Come on, let's go,* he wanted to urge his grandmother.

But she stood her ground. "Meris is important. I've always thought so. I know what it feels like to look in on this people from outside. She's being kept very much on the outside, here. Even though she knows nearly everyone on the command staff, Wind's treating her like a sekiyr. And she's human, and . . ." She pointed at his chest. "Jorah, just talk to her."

"It wouldn't be appropriate to let her in on certain things—"

"Of course not. But talk to her. What would it cost you to just be a friend? We don't want her here as a snake in the underbrush."

Jorah frowned. Meris might already be such a snake. Maybe she was the one who had sabotaged Uncle Kiel's ship. Besides, Jorah was too busy to deal with a self-important Elysian, even if she did speed his pulse up. Better to concentrate on defense work. "Come on," he murmured, "please."

They reached the hilltop together. The site was dished around a central pit and ringed with sun-bleached logs for sitting. White little spring eyes bloomed in clumps along the seating logs, even between the stones lining the fire pit. It was the only wildflower whose name he knew for sure.

Jorah guided Grandmother toward a low log, sat down beside her, and stretched out his legs. The ground up here was soft, full of pebbles that were just the right size for tossing into a fire. Annalah had claimed one end of a log on the downhill side, next to the kitchen staff. Afternoon light shining through her hair made his cousin's head look like an orange corona. Uncle Kiel sat beside Tavkel, clasping his hands around one knee.

And did he ever look different! In the hours since Jorah had watched him get up off his knees beside Tavkel, Uncle Kiel had lost his haggard droop. Now, he looked . . . what was the right word . . . stately. Aunt Hanusha hadn't wasted time, either, but had gone to Tavkel as soon as Aunt Saried's body had been committed to the catacombs.

A high, whistling cry came from directly overhead. Jorah craned his neck to look up. Across the hill, straight as a beam of light, a red-tail kiel soared with its wingtip feathers splayed.

Jorah grinned at Grandmother. She bumped his shoulder and then stared across the fire pit at Uncle Kiel. It had been her family that started all the bird names. But his dad had been named for a small, triangular harp—

"Father." Tavkel's voice broke into his thoughts. "All glory to you for the creatures who fly, hunting the prey you provided. All glory for those that bloom in the soil and declare your beauty. All glory for those creatures who adore you without question.

"And all glory for those with the perilous gifts of freedom and faith. All over the Whorl and beyond, glory to you."

Silence fell. Even the breeze seemed to be quietly listening.

Uncle Kiel straightened. "Amen."

Jorah shifted his seat on the log.

Tavkel looked around the seated group. "The family is growing, my friends. You have sisters and brothers on seventeen worlds, and Chapters even on Elysia."

Jorah's grandmother bumped his shoulder again. Gently, though.

"The kingdom is like a low but powerful wave, sweeping onto the shore at ebb tide. People are beginning to hear of it." He sent Annalah a smile, and she blushed attractively. "That wave will reach all over the Whorl, creating an eddy around this very center. Then I will speak to them myself. Then . . ." He stared straight ahead, seeing over Jorah's shoulder. "Then comes the cataclysm."

Nobody asked *What kind of cataclysm, Tavkel?* so Jorah didn't feel comfortable raising the question. And . . . "Kingdom"?

Well, yes. The Boh-Dabar prophecies spoke of a king. It was just hard to imagine Tavkel wearing a tiara and sitting on a gold throne, like Aunt Rinnah.

"Meanwhile, the Enemy will keep trying to reclaim every one of you. Any of you could be tempted to betray me—or," Tavkel added, turning to Uncle Kiel, "be lured away. Your Adversary can use even the sacred teachings. So be on your guard."

Uncle Kiel nodded at the ground and picked up a pebble.

Tavkel kept talking to him. "He mistook you for me, years ago. Didn't he?"

"Yes." Uncle Kiel raised his head, cradling the pebble in one hand.

Jorah leaned forward. What was that about? Some family story Jorah hadn't heard?

"He will not make that mistake again," Tavkel said. "Still, he especially hates you, since you freed Tamím from him at the last possible moment."

They smiled at each other, as if remembering an old conversation. Jorah made a mental note to ask somebody who might know that story. *Dad. I bet. Or Mother . . .*

Tavkel reached left and right with open hands, as if indicating the whole circle. "I brought you eight away to tell you something no one else needs to know yet." Hearing that, Jorah sat up straighter. "You know that Chancellor Gambrel and his Collegium threaten everything I mean to do. Still, I must deal with him. He intends to come here in person."

Jorah felt Grandmother's gaze resting on him. *Yes,* he thought at her. *Meris will be ecstatic. So that's it. I can't compete with her Chancellor Gambrel.*

"His excuse will be that he is bringing the ITD disk that you have been requesting. I will use that disk. But my doing so will come at a high price, and you all will be asked to pay it."

Jorah grinned. If Tavkel was about to wipe out the Federacy and change the Whorl, that debt wouldn't matter. Meanwhile, Tavkel would use Fed technology to force the Feds to give back the honor that Sentinels deserved.

The arrangement sounded perfect.

Seated on Grandmother's other side, closer to Tavkel, Grandfather folded his hands. "A high price, yes. Chancellor Gambrel won't come here without a strong military presence."

Tavkel dug a small spiral in the dirt with his walking stick. Jorah noticed there wasn't anyone here from the new defense force. Dad would need to know about whatever was said here.

"I must tell you," Tavkel said, "my friends—you all are my friends—that although I will win the victory in the struggle that is to come, my victory will look like defeat. Exactly like defeat. You'll need to tell the others that I expected it."

Annalah gave a soft little cry.

Tavkel reached down and picked a white spring eye from the south side of his log. He twirled it between his fingers and spoke toward Annalah. "Courage does not mean fearlessness, sweet one. Courage does what it must, even when it is terrified. Be sure to tell them that." He looked straight at Jorah.

Jorah's arms prickled. Was that a prediction—that Jorah would need all his courage? He thought he felt a headache coming on.

"And remember the holy promises." Tavkel rested a hand on Uncle Kiel's shoulder. "There will be a victory over the last enemy—victory for some who thought they had been defeated, victory for others who did not fall. For some, a victory within hours—and for others, only after millennia. A victory of joy for some, and a victory of mourning for others." He raised his voice. "The dust of your body will breathe spirit again. Death will not hold you. It cannot hold me. Remember Kinnor, and don't be afraid. Do what you know is loving and right, even when it seems like the worst thing to do."

Jorah caught Grandmother's hand before she could poke him again. Grandmother grinned. He frowned and looked away. Two birds flew past the knoll, chittering as they vanished.

Unmake the Whorl . . . He'd heard that prophecy, but he hadn't thought what it might look like. Now he considered it. This world—those mountains, that shed down below, the spring eye blossom in Tavkel's hands—would Tavkel somehow destroy them? What would that take—solar fire, radiation, gravity waves?

Tavkel folded his hands between his knees. "For I am your true sun, around which you orbit. And I am your daystar, reflecting the sun's light as dawn approaches. Trust in the light, even when everything has gone dark. Show your friends—and yes, even your enemies—what faith looks like. Your Holy One prizes that kind of faith, since it demonstrates love. His love, reflected in you."

"Help us." Uncle Kiel sat tall. "Better yet, make it easy for the holdouts to join us before it's too late. I feel responsible for them. I held them back. I kept them away from you."

Tavkel stared into the cold fire pit. "I can only prove myself. Communication is easy, and proof is easily broadcast. After that, the choice becomes theirs. The longer they wait, the harder it will be—but even at the very end, there is freedom. You were created for it." He raised his head. "Even now, I tell you again as my friends that any of you could freely turn against me. Be faithful, and your choice will be easier. But I must make even your codes harder to follow. From now on, merely *wanting* to use your gifts selfishly—or capriciously—is worthy of death."

Thought control. Right. It had been part of Jorah's training.

His head seriously hurt now.

• • •

There had to be some way to prove Kinnor Caldwell had never really died.

Meris slammed her hoe at the ground alongside a seemingly endless furrow. The breeze cooled her forehead, but her thoughts boiled. For three day shifts—since the Air Master's stunning appearance at his own funeral—she'd kept busy, trying to shut out her coworkers' chatter as they swapped speculations or sang eerie hymns. An idea was growing at the back of her mind. Just a thought at first, but soon it became consuming.

There had to be a research protocol no one had invented yet, even in her field of stasis technology. It must be possible to prove whether death had actually occurred. Inventing such a test could put her name on the scientific map. Less than a percent of patients died in stasis—far fewer than she'd heard about who had died in t-sleep—but even that added up over the years. She had once heard a professor complain that there was no test they could do *before* working through the entire revival process.

And it seemed—didn't it?—that there could be a way to examine the human body for effects so subtle that they could be used to differentiate viable stasis patients, who were practically dead, from those who really had died. There were theoretical limits to how long a person could be kept in full stasis. So what if . . .

These thoughts circled in her mind as she worked the ground. At least this hoe was a tool she'd heard of. Here in her isolation—*whack*—unable to get to Tallis for that practicum year—*whack*—she might actually accomplish something—*whack*—something career-building—*whack*—if they would let her.

Sunshine and warm days seemed to have settled in, and the ground had dried hard enough that hoeing the weeds up roots and all just wasn't working. She and a half dozen sekiyrra and refugee youngsters stood in a line this afternoon, each one hoeing his or her own row, working toward the western peaks.

At the end of her row she straightened, leaned against her hoe, and stared out over the compound toward those mountains. Imagine! A research lab with her name on it, on Tallis or even Elysia—publication in significant journals—her parents *proud* of her.

She'd knotted her hair today, but it came to mind now that her father had actually complimented her on it the last time he'd seen her. Apparently she owed her life to this natural blond color. When it had come to a final choice among four *in vitro* embryos, all pre-tested for potential intelligence and physical health, her father had selected the one with genes for fair hair.

Tossing her head and facing the breeze, she frowned. She needed authorization. And she needed to get taken off this never-ending task rotation as soon as the Minster reappeared. According to her coworkers, that pair's second honeymoon could last another day or even a week.

I'm learning patience. The last sekiyr reached the end of her row. Meris trudged a few meters up the gravel path. She turned east to face the near hillside and leaned back into the killing of weeds. She tried to recall a litany she had never much cared for. *Form habits of peace and patience, and they will form you . . . to . . . to do . . .*

What was the rest of it?

Jorah never came looking for her anymore—which stung—and even Annalah seemed too busy to bother with her. She needed to re-immerse herself in those litanies. Litanies never turned their backs on her.

And there always were weeds to hoe.

• • •

The next day, a woman—apparently a military aide, since she came in uniform—finally fetched Meris. Meris brushed dirt off her scratchy work pants, left her hoe in a rack, and rode the elevator down to the cool commons, where she paused for a drink of iced water and recited a litany for focus she'd reviewed last night. *Clear the mind, still the heart. Let the eternal shine through me.*

Her own thoughts kept breaking in. What if the Minster said no? *Clear the mind.* Meris might have to compromise. *Still the heart.* Or back off, if stasis were suggested. *Let the eternal—* They all insisted they didn't deceive people, partly because they couldn't be deceived, right? So she would be doing them a service. Offering to help them prove that Tavkel had really resuscitated the Air Master.

Except that he hadn't, of course. *Let the eternal shine through me. Right. Here we go.*

She set down her drinking glass, straightened her work shirt, and headed up the waterside.

The Minster sat tall behind her broad desk. Her whole face seemed to be smiling—wrinkles surrounded her eyes, and a dimple puckered one cheek. She looked a decade younger than she'd looked four days ago, waiting for the Shekkah to begin.

Off to her right, Annalah sat at the desk's end. Her fingers danced on a touchboard. She looked up. "Good morning, Meris."

"Hello, Annalah." Was *this* where she'd taken to spending all day and night?

"Please sit down." The Minster gestured toward a chair. "I do apologize for keeping you waiting so long. I'm sure they told you Kinnor and I had to renew our pair bond."

"Well . . . yes." Had the Minster's hair always had that bit of curl, or was she trying a new style? Meris remained standing. "Congratulations."

The grin showed teeth now. The woman might be full-blooded Shuhr, but Meris couldn't imagine one of *them* radiating delight like this. "Thank you, Meris. And since you said your business was urgent, I bumped you up the list for today. How may I serve you?"

Despite those gracious words, Meris braced herself and stayed on her feet. She honestly didn't want to offend—and that would be easy, since essentially she was suggesting *I think you're all lying to me.* "I'd like to serve you, actually."

"Yes?" The Minster's eyes barely widened.

Clear the mind, still the heart. All right, then! "I'm requesting a release from the outdoor task rotation, plus authorization to conduct some medical research. With MedSpec Saried gone and all her top aides working in the crop fields, I'm suddenly one of your senior medical people. And there's an important job to do. Someone needs to investigate and document what happened to your husband, biologically speaking. If he really was dead, and is alive now, we need to—"

The Minster shook her head, laughing softly. "Believe me, Meris. He was dead. I felt it the moment it happened. You spent time with me when I was in shock, didn't you?"

"Of course." Meris flicked another bit of drying dirt off her pants. It didn't surprise her that the woman didn't remember who had sat with her. "And I do see that everyone here calls your bereavement shock proof of death. But out in the Federacy, other people won't take that for granted. Some will be saying it didn't actually happen, and that he was smuggled back here alive. You . . . and Tavkel . . . you all want the truth to get out, don't you?"

If he hadn't been smuggled back here, maybe he hadn't actually left! In any case, someone should try to prove something. Thank goodness the Minster had lost her powers and Annalah never had any, so they couldn't see how very exciting Meris thought this could become.

Or could they? Annalah chuckled. The Minster tilted her head and said, "What is it you'd like to do, Meris?"

Meris spoke carefully. "I'd like to start with a thorough physical exam. As soon as your husband finishes whatever he needs to catch up on today, of course."

The Minster picked up a stylus and fingered it absently. "Do you truly think you can tell by examining a man whether he has been dead?"

When conscious patients died, it was obvious: Heartbeat and brain activity ceased, along with muscular reflexes. "I don't know yet. I'll start out looking around in the dark, but surely something will turn up. Maybe a non-growth ring in all his fingernails, or a skin abnormality. Maybe something odd at the cellular level." That might be especially applicable in a stasis lab. "He wasn't just dead, you know."

If it really had been him in that crate. Had anyone gotten a tri-D image? Surely his loved ones hadn't wanted to remember him that way, but an image could be topologically examined.

"What do you mean, not 'just' dead?" Minster Wind asked.

"He was also . . . I'm sorry, it's an ugly word, but . . . desiccated. That must have left some kind of evidence."

"Isn't it marvelous?" The Minster spoke so softly that Meris almost couldn't hear her. "I would have called it impossible. Anything can happen now. Anything at all."

Annalah paused, hands poised over the touchboard. "Yes. Anything. He's using the physical to show us the true divine."

Meris shifted her feet. There it was again, their confusion of physicality and spirituality. She was tired of it. "So don't you want the physical truth proved? Whether Tavkel's power to heal actually goes so far as to revive a dead body?"

"Oh, that's not—"

"Unbiased empirical tests should make it plain," Meris interrupted Annalah. "That would be pure gold to you as believers. Because on the surface, this looks like a genuine . . . miracle." She disliked the word. Really, there was no such thing. There were natural explanations for everything in the universe.

She wanted the truth. So would these people, unless they all were complicit in fraud. She eyed the Minster closely.

The smile lines around her eyes didn't go away. She didn't look the slightest bit guilty.

If Tavkel's previous healings had been bioelectric—due to some kind of unusual energy in his enhanced brain—maybe their blocking drugs just hadn't affected him. Still, she wasn't about to call *him* in as a research subject. She liked the man. But he would know what she was up to.

She shrugged and kept talking. "If I can prove that Tavkel's abilities really are miraculous, well . . . that'll matter, won't it? You need the kind of evidence that will convince people. I've got the right kind of training. MedSpec Saried left plenty of equipment. Minster, I can't just stay topside with a hoe when I'm qualified for a more important job."

"I think I can see that." The Minster tapped her desktop with the stylus. "I do have some new personnel to run the med center, by the way. You could focus on your research, instead of being interrupted."

Very good—or would someone be keeping an eye on her, with stasis in mind?

She'd remained standing beside an extra chair. Now she sat down. "I already proved that Tavkel decontaminated and disinfected Jorah, as well as the people who arrived with him. Those slides are documented well enough to hold up in a law court." Meris smiled at the memory and straightened her shoulders. "Minster, I'm well qualified for this task, an objective and neutral observer—"

"Stop." The Minster laughed, and Annalah smiled broadly.

Feeling outnumbered again, Meris shut her mouth. Really, all she would need to prove fraud would be to turn up another body, the one that had actually arrived in that coffin. They had a whole planet at their disposal, though, and they would have hidden it well. Besides, she wasn't that kind of investigator.

The Minster set her stylus back down. "All right. But I can't imagine why Tavkel would leave any proof of death on my husband. When he heals people, he does more than we expect, not less."

"Yes, that seems to be true . . . but . . ."

"I'll ask Kinnor to speak with you as soon as he can. And—" The Minster reached for a touchboard and made a few strokes. "There. You're officially off the field task rotation. I'll need daily reports on your project."

"Wonderful." Meris pushed out of her chair. "I'll go straight to the med center and set up for a basic examination. Then I'll create some additional files. Thank you." She stepped toward the doorway that led back out to the poolside.

The Minster's voice halted her. "I do hope you find what you're looking for, Meris."

Meris turned around. She'd heard an odd note in that voice.

The Minster spread her hands. "What you're *really* looking for. Truth."

Meris stood tall. "Yes," she said. "I believe I will."

CHAPTER 31

The Air Master seemed delighted to yank off his work shirt and let Meris scan his heart, lungs, liver and other internals. Nothing seemed abnormal. She reached down and passed a UV beamer over his toenails, holding a spectrometry slide at the correct angle. "Do you remember," she asked casually, "what it was like? Anything?" She'd heard the usual stories—bright lights, tunnels—but had he invented something new?

"No." His dry tone told her she hadn't fooled him. He knew what she really thought. "I don't remember a thing. One second they were coming at me with the crystace. The next second, I was looking up at skylights. And Tavkel."

She straightened and took another look at his bare chest. If he'd really been stabbed, it had left no scar. Minster Wind could be right about Tavkel not leaving traces. *When he heals people . . .*

What if this man really had been shipped home dead? She shuddered, thinking of all those dead bodies down in the catacomb. *I fear what I only imagine . . .*

Yet she wouldn't find any execution evidence on this man if there'd been someone else in that coffin. Was it possible that Tavkel had done the unthinkable? "Hmm." She kept her emotions bland. Unlike his wife the Minster, this man still had formidable abilities. She had no emotional privacy in his presence. "It's interesting," she said, "that you've still got all your, ah, powers. Doesn't he usually take them away?"

"I didn't ask to get into his mind. I didn't even ask to get healed. People usually are conscious, you know, when they go to him. He's big on choice and freedom."

"Hmm." Meris set her slides on the countertop. "Well, these tests could yield some useful information. On both fingers and toes, your nail beds will have undoubtedly shrunk during desiccation."

"Maybe," he said cheerfully. "But I still have them all, don't I?"

"Ah . . . yes." And *that* could be evidence of fraud. Not proof— not by itself—but a step in that direction.

She'd gotten blood, urine, hair, and skin samples, and done a whole-body scan, but so far the automated diagnostics hadn't flagged a single abnormality. Other than those extra organelles in his brain, he seemed to be a healthy man in non-youth-implant forties. She'd be looking closely at those cells, though—especially the nail slides. She wouldn't give up hoping for that research lab of her own, on Tallis or even Elysia. "That's all for now. Thank you."

He slid off the examining chair and reached for his work shirt. "You know where to find me. Just send a sekiyr."

"Right. Thanks again." She slipped the nail slides into the spectrometer, keyed them to run, and sat tapping her finger against a countertop.

Another thought occurred to her. It was forensic, not medical, but it was something she could actually see herself looking into. She dashed into the corridor. He'd vanished. "Sentinel Caldwell?"

Booted footsteps approached again, and then came the Air Master, refastening old-fashioned buttons on his shirt.

"I'm . . . still thinking this through," she said. "Do you still have the uniform they sent you back in?"

He twisted his mouth into a thinking pose. "Probably. It's unwearable, but I haven't bothered to dispose of it. Unless the wife did that for me."

But Minster Wind had been busy. Meris was willing to bet she hadn't. "That would be perfect." Then she realized what else he'd said. "Unwearable?" Hope tickled her heart. "What do you mean?"

He shrugged. "Damaged, of course."

Better and better! "The same uniform . . . they, ah, executed you in?"

"Isn't that what we're talking about?"

Oh, perfect. Perfect! "Not necessarily. I mean, yes, please send it down with a sekiyr. Thank you, Air Master."

He leaned against the door arch, smirking. "Anything else?"

She caught herself smiling back at him in spite of herself. He seemed fearless, which wasn't something she'd admired in the past. This place was changing her. "That should be all, sir. Thank you again."

She checked her instruments. A green light blinked atop the spectrometer. The first set of nail slides was already finished, the scatter pattern analyzed.

No Abnormalities gleamed on the readout panel.

When Tavkel heals people . . .

Nonsense. The man hadn't died. Couldn't have.

She loaded the next slides anyway.

• • •

That night, it wasn't her fault that she dreamed about research grants. Right after breakfast—the fifth day since Tavkel had become Shamarr Caldwell's personal god—rain was pouring down on the skylights when the Minster's aide brought a musty, midnight-blue bundle into the med center.

"He said you wouldn't want the pants," she said. "Anyway, they were burned before the Shekkah service."

"This will do. Thanks, Shari."

The aide left, and Meris pulled on her lab coat. She opened all the new files on the research station she'd claimed and donned a pair of sterile gloves and a breath mask. Gingerly she spread the tunic on the exam table. It certainly had been damaged. Most fabric—normal fabric, not the homespun stuff they apparently wove here—maintained a smooth surface regardless how it was treated. But this tunic was a network of wrinkles. Almost certainly, it could be considered the right garment.

Her glove snagged on something mid-chest on the tunic. She bent closer. A small rip had been opened slightly to the left of center. Excellent! If the wearer really had been stabbed in the heart, there could also be minute bloodstains. Barely breathing, though the mask should prevent contamination with her own genetic material, she sprinkled a reagent over the tear. She waited the requisite five seconds and then picked up the UV beamer she'd found in Saried's small equipment locker.

The fabric glowed uniformly. It was unstained.

She leaned away. *Well, that doesn't prove or disprove anything. But it's interesting.* If he had faked this rip, wouldn't he have bothered to add a bit of blood to make it look more convincing?

She set down the beamer and made a note, determined to document everything she found. After all, she needed to make an honest attempt to find evidence *against* fraud too, to make the inquiry valid. Maybe she should ask to see one of those mysterious hand weapons that had allegedly been used. Maybe they created a deep, thin wound that made death instantaneous and even bloodless.

She smoothed farther up the tunic's shoulders. There—was that a dark hair? She plucked it off and mounted it on another slide.

DNA evidence could prove this had been someone else's tunic, possibly stripped off another body. Or—matching the hair with Kinnor Caldwell might suggest evidence tampering.

And what was this? A longer, more significant rip had been opened in the left sleeve. She held it up to the examining light. Stuck to the lining, near the big rip . . . this narrow brown strip . . . could it be desiccated flesh?

Holding her breath again, she took her forceps and delicately worked the strip free. It looked no thicker than skin. Still, it might have been thicker before . . . heavens, was this rip made by *clamping* the body inside the coffin before desiccating it?

She made another mental note. *Check for standard desiccation procedures.*

Instead of dropping the strip on another DNA test slide, she hesitated. During the desiccation process, any nucleic acids present would've been degraded. She should culture this specimen for best results. Then she could run standard tests on this tissue strip, plus the hair.

She found tissue culturing supplies in a cupboard out in the general prep area, where a man she hadn't seen before sat reading something on a glowing monitor. Back at her own station, she gingerly laid the sample in a small round dish and pulled out a tube of sterile medium.

If this turned out to be muscle, damaged severely enough to indicate desiccation—and if she could reconstitute enough DNA to prove it matched Kinnor Caldwell's blood sample—then she might at least be able to prove whether the man had been dead. It wouldn't be a beautiful, useful new research protocol. And unfortunately, it wouldn't support her own theory—but if she wanted the truth, she had to eliminate the most obvious impossibility.

Because it simply couldn't happen. A spark of life dissolved. That energy rejoined the Infinite. Life ended. That was all.

So what kind of counter-spark would it have taken to make a dead body function again—to set all those neurons firing, the heart pumping? And by definition, a desiccated body had had all its fluids removed—so where would the fluids have come from, to restore it to functional health?

Another thought struck her. Minster Wind might also let her look down in that catacomb. If a body had been clamped into place, she might find similar evidence inside the shipping coffin.

And what if that coffin weren't empty? *That* would be proof of a different sort.

Meris looked over at the strip of flesh in the culture dish. She'd better not tell anyone she wanted a look in the catacombs, not yet. Not until the very last moment, when she was ready to walk down that big burial hole.

She went to work on the tissue culture.

● ● ●

Jorah found his mother sitting in her office—not at her desk, but on one of the stone benches attached to the wall. The familiar streamers fluttered over her head, and a uniformed woman he didn't recognize sat talking to her. His cousin Annalah sat in the chair behind the big desk, talking into the air: " . . . seems perfectly healthy, and . . ."

"Jorah." His mother smiled. "Over here."

He pulled a wooden chair toward her bench, but he didn't sit down yet. It felt wonderful to see her smiling again. It had taken three aides to keep the office of Minster Wind Haworth-Caldwell running while she was gone. Now, Annalah seemed to be recording some sort of message, maybe to send via DeepScan. Besides the recording unit, two of the flush inset monitors were lit.

"Jorah." His mother called his attention back to the bench. "This is Captain Mel Anastu, last stationed on Netaia."

"Netaia?" Jorah saluted the captain and shook her hand. Other worlds were in turmoil, but he wouldn't have thought they'd be evacuating Netaia yet. "*They* aren't dismissing us, are they?" Sentinels were actually honored there.

Captain Anastu had about ten years on him, with dark hair and a defiant tilt to her chin. She smoothed her midnight blues. "Not at all. But a group of us asked for leave to come here. Good thing too. Wait 'til you hear about Thyrica."

"What?" He caught a fast breath.

The sun of his mother's smile set quickly. Her mouth and eyes drooped. "We've just gotten a detailed DeepScan from people with access to orbital images. The College was attacked by an allegedly spontaneous group of rioters. It looks like they gathered in Arown outside city limits and surrounded the campus, and then they moved in, setting fires. We lost both classroom buildings and the admin complex. One dorm's damaged too badly for use. Another source says they're double-occupying Lene Hall until they figure out what to do, and classes are canceled until further notice. There's loss of life—"

"Inside job?" Jorah asked. Someone plainly wanted the College closed. Obviously, local police hadn't defended it. "Do you think somebody put down the shields and just let rioters in?"

"We may never know." His mother spread her hands. "Worse, they're claiming the survivors suffered trauma of a particularly nasty kind. Tallis is sending a specialized medical team—"

"No!" Jorah pointed toward his head. "*This* is what Gambrel wants to do! This . . . this so-called cure—"

"We know." His mother lifted a hand, sounding weary. "They're trying to scatter some survivors. We can't get many offworld, not with the spaceports watched, but there are places on Thyrica where they might live quietly and wait this out. Especially those of Mikuhran ancestry."

He swapped glances with Annalah and Captain Anastu and shook his head. Awful questions sprang to mind. "You said . . . loss of life?"

His mother shut her eyes and gripped the stone bench with both hands. "Your Great-Aunt Ellet and Uncle Damalcon's bodies were pulled from the rubble last night. And Uncle Ze'en's. We did hear from Uncle Zeph—he's hiding somewhere in the Belfords. Ze'en's boy Jace is with him, but the so-called rioters probably wiped out the rest of Ze'en's family."

Jorah groaned. He was seeing the run-up to Tavkel's renewal of the Whorl, and life as he'd known it was ending.

But that only meant something better was coming. He squared his shoulders. Annalah was talking into the raised DeepScan pickup. " . . . He only asks for the gift of our darkness, if we are willing to give it."

His mother shook her head. "Tavkel has come just in time."

"Makes sense." Reassuring her felt odd, as if he'd grabbed the adult role. "Things have to get really bad before we can ethically strike back, defend ourselves from the Federate power structure that we're supposed to have been obeying. The people who supposedly valued us. Well, doesn't it look like we're almost there?"

"Tavkel doesn't talk about striking back—"

"He wouldn't." Jorah glanced past her. Captain Anastu wasn't showing any sign of getting up off the bench. His mother must have kept her on as an aide. "You've met him, haven't you?"

"First thing when I arrived." Captain Anastu shot him a crooked smile. "I took the keep-your-powers option, but he's the real thing. Finally. Her Majesty Rinnah would have loved to be here."

"Right. The real thing." Jorah decided he liked the new aide. "But defense isn't his job. It's ours, those of us who took the military option."

The captain raised her head and nodded.

"Tavkel is like Uncle Kiel and the whole priesthood," Jorah said, warming to his topic, "but amplified about ten thousand times. Even Uncle Kiel can't see the whole picture." Again he glanced at the desk, where Annalah silently fiddled with a desktop control. "Praying and studying and hoping—that's the heart of all our hopes. But other than Uncle Kiel, our family isn't priestly. We've always been more military."

Instead of answering, his mother glanced at Annalah. "Do you see much of Meris?"

Where had that come from? Maybe she'd been talking to Grandmother. Jorah widened his stance. "As little as possible. She could have been our saboteur, even if Uncle Kiel isn't planning to launch anymore." Work had ceased downlevel in Hangar One. With his dad resurrected, there was no one left who wanted to leave the Whorl.

His mother lowered her chin.

Captain Anastu said, "I agree, she's a likely suspect. But does she know enough about how ships are engineered to carry it off?"

Jorah shrugged. That was the weak spot in his theory, and it bothered him that she'd spotted it so easily. It was time to switch subjects. "How soon will we be able to tell how big a group took off from Tallis, headed here with Chancellor Gambrel—and when they'll arrive?"

She shook her head. "Special Operations still hasn't DeepScanned us—right, Annalah? Nothing from the new SOOC people?"

Annalah glanced across the desk at another lit monitor.

"Oh, SOOC!" Jorah crossed his arms. Hadn't his mother heard anything he said? No, of course not. In bereavement shock, she couldn't have. "SOOC is the other side now, Mother. We're on our own."

"He's right," Captain Anastu said.

Jorah stepped to the big desk's edge and turned around. "Mother, we're all behind you. You and Uncle Kiel and Tavkel might be all the leaders we have left. Unless Dad takes command of the defense."

That woke her up. She pushed off the bench, pursing her lips. "We'll take that suggestion under advisement. Thank you."

Smiling quietly, Annalah vacated the big chair. His mother reclaimed it. "Tavkel asked to speak with you this morning, Jorah. Please greet him for me."

Jorah saluted his mother and Captain Anastu, converting the end of it to a wave at his cousin as he strode out. He remembered too late to ask what had happened to the old SOOC people. He hadn't known Aunt Ellet and Uncle Damalcon well, but they'd been family. Things were definitely falling apart out there.

As he emerged into the rainy morning, he spotted Tavkel just uphill, standing in a covered holding pen and tossing a ball with Thyrian four refugee children. Jorah hustled up the graveled trail as the leather ball came sailing in his direction. He snagged it midair and held it a moment before he sent it toward one of the taller boys, who spun in place and sent it on.

"Good one, Rex." Tavkel caught the ball and handed it to a tiny girl, who seized it two-handed and went toddling out into the rain shower. "Now, off you go. Cousin Jorah and I need to talk."

A bigger girl intercepted the toddler. She flipped up the little one's rain hood and steered the group down the gravel trail toward the compound. On the breakaway strip below, crewers in rain suits gathered around three small craft. They looked like they were prepping to launch. Because Gambrel was coming, Jorah guessed. Naturally, command staff would be ordering families to flee. He wondered where they would go. Netaia, maybe.

He stepped closer to Tavkel, whose hair stuck straight up on one side. His nose had started to peel too. "Underfoot, aren't they?"

Tavkel kept watching the little ones dash down the graveled trail. "Never. They know they depend on us. In any encounter, the most valuable things they bring are their joy and freshness—and gratitude. Most of them, anyway."

"Where you grew up, there weren't other children. Right?"

Tavkel ran both hands over his hair, smoothing it back down. "Sadly, you're right. They are delightful. And if you can't be child-like in that way, I can't use you." He peered into the grey sky. "Let's go in."

Jorah followed into semidarkness that smelled of fresh hay. Tavkel backed into a small, strawy holding stall and skewered him with those penetrating eyes. "How is Meris?" Ayin skills or no ayin skills, he had a look on his face that suggested he knew everything that had been on Jorah's mind.

Jorah had actually dreamed about the woman last night, to his embarrassment. "Sir . . ." Then he didn't know what to say. He didn't even know whether "sir" was the right form of address. Should he salute? "Haven't seen her much. She's busy. I'm busy."

Tavkel turned to watch a pair of sekiyrra lead a furry ewe into the broad shearing stall. "Yes, but when a stranger comes to your home, do you welcome her? Do you offer to help with her work, if she needs assistance?"

He'd last seen Meris on a hoeing team. She definitely needed help with that. That probably wasn't what Tavkel meant, though. He cracked his knuckles. "You, uh, want me to help her? What with?"

Tavkel rested a foot on a low slat. "Her larger search. Chancellor Gambrel's Collegium has encouraged her to look in the wrong directions. Today, she's trying to accomplish something more dangerous than she knows. Things could go terribly wrong for her. I would like to save her the pain." Tavkel lowered his voice. "Tell her that Chancellor Gambrel is coming. She has to find the truth, but she also needs to know that someone here is for her—not against her."

That sounded ominous. Jorah dug his boot into the straw on the floor. "Could you explain, sir?"

"I want you to see for yourself. It'll mean more that way." Tavkel took a pair of shears off a wall peg. He wrapped his hands around them and squeezed idly. "It's not too late to reach her. Harder now, though. Harder every day."

"Sir, I actually want to spend time with my dad." It couldn't hurt to say so. "That's where I thought Mother would send me today. Things are terrible on Thyrica. And actually," he said, trying to make it sound funny, "I'd rather go off on a life-and-death mission with Dad than talk too much to Meris." He raised his head and tried to smile. "She's just a distraction. We need to defend ourselves." Why wasn't Tavkel helping with that? Why did he shake his head now? "And Meris isn't one of us, not really."

Tavkel lowered his foot and frowned. "In all ways but one, Meris is one of us." He accented that last word, *us*. "I don't fully understand why she is here. But I can guess, and my heart breaks for her. I tell you, this is life and death for her. I am her daystar too."

Jorah crossed his arms and stared down at the straw. His insides squirmed. This wasn't the kind of heroism he'd thought Tavkel would ask of him. Everyone's plans were changing, though. Especially his uncle's, which reminded him . . . "Sir, the other day at the fire pit you said something that confused me. You said something about how Uncle Kiel had once been mistaken for you. What did you mean? Gambrel wanted me to play-act your part, to behave like I thought I was Boh-Dabar. But what was Uncle Kiel supposed to be doing?"

"Your uncle will tell you that story, if you ask him privately." Tavkel turned and looked over into the next stall. "If you want to assist Meris today, your mother will authorize it."

This new chain of command was confusing. Had Tavkel asked Mother to make this morning's assignments? "You don't need me for shearing." And why were they bothering to shear at all, with a war about to start? Who'd take the time to spin this and weave it?

"You may stay and shear if you prefer. One thing is vital, but every facet of life under your Creator is important. Right up to its final moment."

Stay and shear—and feel guilty every time Tavkel looked at him, knowing he'd been sent to Meris? No chance. He pushed away from the wall. "If I'm heading out to help her, I'm going now."

"Don't go reluctantly. Go joyfully."

Feeling dismissed and—despite Tavkel's last words—down-right sullen, Jorah strode outdoors. Meris might at least give him something for this faint, plaguing headache.

• • •

She was easy to find, and she looked busy—sitting with her back to the med center's door, bending over some sort of metal box. He rapped the edge of the door. She looked up.

Her eyes widened for a split second and narrowed again.

Jorah almost wished he hadn't been trained to see people's emotions. She'd been glad to see him—at first. He decided to take it as a good sign. That would make it more pleasant, at least. And really, even with her hair pulled back so severely, she was a lovely woman to spend time with.

"I suppose your grandmother sent you." She shut the box.

Jorah stepped into the room. "What, she's been pushing you too?"

Her shoulders relaxed. She shoved the box aside. "She and I had something of a friendship on board the *Daystar*. Why do old people feel like they have to push us together, just because we're close to the same age?"

"But worlds different." He sat down on a stool, keeping one foot on the ground. "Too different, I think."

"And much too busy." She returned a curt nod of agreement.

Vaguely disappointed—she might have at least argued—he said, "Yes. Truce?"

"Truce." Now her smile looked genuine. "So am I right? Did she send you?"

No, Tavkel did. He decided not to say that. "Actually, I've been having headaches since we landed. Nothing as bad as I had en route. I think Tavkel healed those." And Tavkel had said they might linger, right? "But I'm sure Aunt Saried kept something effective in here."

She glanced into the corridor. "General health care is well stocked. Come on." She led across the passageway.

They seemed to be alone, so he decided to launch the G-missile right away. Then he'd have more time to see how she reacted. "I heard Gambrel's coming."

"What?" She whirled around, holding a jar in one hand. "What, here? Did he contact you? Wait, he wouldn't be allowed . . . What are you talking about?"

That wide-eyed expression, that smile exploding all over her face—was that how he looked when he talked about Tavkel? The people who had mind-accessed him sure did. "No. Actually, it's Tavkel who said so. I don't know how he knows."

"Hmm."

• • •

Could it be true? Chancellor Gambrel, coming here? Surely they wouldn't refuse to let him land. He was the Chancellor! Imagine, sitting in on a discussion between him and Tavkel—

Mind, be still, Meris told herself. *Just because Tavkel predicts something, that doesn't mean it'll happen.* But this made it imperative to finish her project. A "well done" from Chancellor Gambrel would mean more than any award. "Hmm," she repeated, turning back to the cupboard. A general painkiller wasn't necessary. Just something for intracranial pressure. She put the jar back and pulled down another one.

Chancellor Gambrel in the flesh. Oh, my.

Instantly, she reprimanded herself. There was nothing special about flesh! These people were getting to her. She already knew the Chancellor spiritually, through his teachings. That was all that mattered.

Furthermore, Jorah was obviously falling ever deeper under Tavkel's pseudo-spiritual spell. Jorah had become a normal human back on Tallis, and not at Tavkel's bidding. Now, sitting right there—she eyed him as she turned around, holding the jar of cephstyp and a dispensing vial—he so resembled his father, with that sharp chin and those bold, direct eyes. "Here." She held up the jar. "I can make it time-release if you'd like."

"I would. Thanks."

And he could probably get her into that burial cave! The other med assistant had gone out for kass. Meris set down the vial. "Jorah, I need something, and you can help me."

He pushed away from the counter, as if she'd startled him.

She wondered at his response but pressed on. "I need to see the shipping coffin they sent your father back in. I assume it's down in the . . . what do you call it, the catacomb? I need to see it. Right now."

His raised foot slid off a stool rung and hit the floor. "What?"

"Research. It's important."

"That's a sacred place." With his arms folded, he *really* resembled his father. "You can't just march down there and have a look around. Not even for research. Not without the Minster's approval, for sure."

How much should she tell him? She took a cup off the shelf and filled it with water, which gave her a moment to think. Why not tell him everything, and just not let him out of her sight until he led her to that coffin? That way, he couldn't send out some signal to hide the other body. Once more, it was a relief to know that he was only a normal human.

That fact shouldn't make her so delighted inside. She always found herself smiling when he was around, didn't she?

Irked, she gave him the water. She cleared her throat and told him exactly what she wanted to look for.

And why.

CHAPTER 32

Jorah listened to Meris's explanation, thunderstruck. How could anyone not believe his father had been dead? Still, she was right that nobody had made tri-D images of the corpse. Also right, that even if outsiders didn't understand, you couldn't fake bereavement shock. Two for two. And she didn't know—yet—what her people had incited at College.

"So you see," she finished, "I'm stymied for a few hours, until that culture grows out. Then I'll know if there are any DNA strands long enough for analysis." She poured something out of her medicine jar into a piece of machinery and reached for an opening on the front. From it she took four capsules, which she dropped onto his palm.

"I really want the truth, Jorah. Whatever it is." Her voice sounded almost too sincere. "And I want it proved in a way anybody with a mind can understand. This business with Tavkel is too important, too cosmic to keep to yourselves. If it's real, it has to get out. Right?"

"Like the news from Thyrica." He couldn't hold that in.

"What news?" She put the jar back on its shelf.

"Rioters just destroyed our college. I've got relatives dead. Your Chancellor wasn't personally involved, but it's his people killing us. He means to wipe us out—but he's going to keep his own hands clean."

"No!" She pushed away from the lab counter. "Oh, Jorah, I'm so sorry. Chancellor Gambrel would never approve—"

"Not publicly. But that so-called cure he subjected me to is just one more way to make us helpless. To take us down."

She lowered her chin. "Don't tell me your people don't have secrets. Big ones. There are reasons you frighten people. All those things you can do. And . . . what happened at your college?"

He clenched his teeth, not wanting this to escalate. Tavkel hadn't sent him to fight her or talk about the College. She'd said she wanted to prove that his dad's death was real, but she wasn't fooling him. She really wanted to prove it a fraud.

The only positive spin on this he could think of was that since he really *had* died, her search might actually lead her to the truth. And if it hadn't been his own dad, and if Tavkel hadn't been Tavkel, Jorah might have been suspicious too.

He swallowed the pills, which gave him a moment to focus himself. "I'll get Mother to show you the newscast. And . . . I think I could clear it with her, after the fact, to take you down into the catacombs. Just be respectful down there, all right?"

She lifted her head.

Didn't expect me to cooperate, did you? Warming to his mission, he set down the water cup. "Come on. Right now. If it turns out we shouldn't have, I'll take the fall." And if she tried snooping around down there, looking for more things to sabotage, he would see.

She flung open another cupboard and dug inside. "I'll pack a sampling kit. Then there'll be no need to bring the coffin topside. That's respectful, right?" He heard the irony in her voice.

Instead of challenging her, he waited for her to drop items into the kit box. A minute later, they strode out over the stepping stones.

Two of his military colleagues sat on the big island's stone bench, probably snatching a quiet moment.

"We'll need their help," he told Meris. "The hatch can't be operated by just two people. They don't know why you want to do this, so you'll believe nobody tampered with the coffin. Right?"

She spoke softly. "Unless they already did. Tamper."

He rolled his eyes. No wonder Tavkel didn't want her doing this alone. She suspected everyone. Or maybe Tavkel knew she was really their saboteur! "If you already found tissue on his tunic," he said, trying to sound reasonable, "and if either that or—or anything else you find inside the shipping coffin—can be proved to be Dad's, do you think that'll convince other Federates?" He watched her eyes.

"It might." She glanced down.

It was just what she hoped not to find. That was good to know. They stepped together off the last square platform onto the island.

He saluted the military Sentinels—a major and a second captain, if he remembered correctly. "Med Cariole is conducting some research . . . with Mother's approval." That ought to be vague enough. "She needs access to the catacombs for a few minutes."

The second captain shot the major a startled look, and the major frowned, but they stood up from the bench and walked clear of the section of the island that could be elevated.

Jorah flipped the control panel cover and touched its single sensor. A six-by-four meter section of stone rose up enough to slip a hand under it. He got Meris's attention and pointed at its nearest corner. "There are two grip rods just underneath. We'll all lift together. Just guide it. It's counterweighted."

She crouched and set down her kit. Her hair dangled over one shoulder in a long coil, which looked fetching. *She's one of us*, he reminded himself. *Thank you, Tavkel.*

When all four of them were in position, he gave a nod and pulled on his rods. The panel swung upward and aside, re-creating the raised platform where the wooden coffins had lain and simultaneously exposing the catacomb stairs. "Thanks." He smacked dust off his hands. "We'll take it from here."

The others headed back to the bench under the island's big kirka tree.

Meris headed down the stone steps with a bouncing gait that showed she didn't care whether this was a catacomb or a food cellar. He followed more reverently.

Dim everburners gleamed in the walls, and he gave his eyes a moment to adjust. From this point, an aisle led east toward the hillside. Both sides were lined with bunk-like shelves. The narrow ends of hundreds—maybe thousands—of beautiful wooden boxes faced the aisle. How many of his people, for fourteen generations, had been laid here to rest? Each permanent casket had a name boldly carved, inlaid, or mounted on the near end. It was a musty-smelling, silent city.

He turned. Behind the steps, numerous shipping coffins had been stacked against a stone wall. Even these were treated with respect, since they'd been used to bring people home. Older models were silver or midnight blue. A newer model, always black, had been in use for several years. Cheaper, he guessed, another sign of his people's diminishing status.

She wrinkled her nose. "Can you tell which one?"

He frowned at the pile. These weren't labeled plainly, and he'd better get the right one. Tissue from the wrong coffin could suggest they hadn't really executed his dad. "There's a code on the end." He touched the top unit on the stack, which should have been either Dad's or Aunt Saried's. "Give me a minute." It was hard to read the small engraved plate. He leaned closer and squinted.

She stood close by his shoulder. He caught a breath of her herbal soap, or something—something nice, like springtime. Nicer than the still air down here, anyway. "I don't think . . ." He didn't recognize any part of the code sequence on the top plate. Surely the label for his dad would include a military serial number, which Jorah ought to recognize. "You've got medical data for him, right?"

"Oh, yes. He has records on file. The tests I ran yesterday show no statistically significant difference."

"Huh?"

"At the cellular and biochemical level, your father is the same man he was ten years ago, the last time he was treated here for anything." She went on in an odd tone. "Proving he died wouldn't win me any awards in my field. But it would be interesting."

That was just too much. Jorah straightened up and looked her in the eye. "Think about it, would we all be acting like we believed he'd been dead if we faked it? We're supposed to be the undeceivables." Though they *could* be surprised, obviously. Especially by people they thought were their allies. People wearing Tallan uniforms . . .

"There would be a few people who knew." She looked straight back at him. "The rest of you could be deluded."

He tucked his thumbs into his waistband. "What would it take to prove this to you, Meris? What, really?"

"If you people are so convinced Tavkel brings back dead people, why do you care if anyone died at Thyrica? Why not just send Tavkel to raise them all?"

He bit back a furious retort. Whether or not this woman was looking for things to sabotage, she had arrived here with preconceived ideas about his people. She would be glad to report her own assumptions to Gambrel as unbiased observations. No wonder outsiders weren't allowed here—and, he realized soberly, no wonder Tavkel didn't want her left to her own devices. Tavkel had sent Jorah here not to watch her, but to win her. What should he do . . . go with his grandmother's suggestion, and talk sweet?

No! No Sentinel would "willfully use a personal relationship to enhance a mission, even when gathering intelligence." That was the memorized version of a rule every Sentinel knew. In plain language, even Special Ops weren't allowed to engage in sexual espionage. He'd had a long talk with Grandfather about how tricky that could be.

Right, then.

"Tavkel says some confusing things," Jorah said, realizing it was true. "But what he *does* proves who he is. To me, anyway."

"Don't you think his teachings could be reconciled—some-how—with Chancellor Gambrel's?"

"No." Hiding his disgust, he bent toward the next coffin. To his relief, the first few digits created an echo in his memory. "Here it is."

She helped him lift the other unit off, and he opened it. A stale smell drifted out. *My dad lay in here. Dead.* Already it seemed unreal.

Meris reached into her little kit and pulled out something stylus-shaped that proved to be a small beamer. She bent over the left side. Something dangled there, a nasty-looking clamp. She sprinkled something on it, shone the beamer, and stood waiting. Plainly, if she expected to find anything, it should be here.

"Well." She leaned in with a little metal scraper and slide.

"Found something?"

"Mm-hmm." She straightened up, holding the slide. "Bloodstain, and a bit of thread. This location corresponds to the tear and tissue I found on his tunic. This is the coffin that tunic arrived in."

Her confidence made him feel contrary. "Either that, or they all rip right there. Want to look inside two or three more, just to be sure?"

This time, her slightly raised eyebrows conveyed respect. "That's a good idea. Would you help me?"

"That's why I'm down here." He opened three more, including Aunt Saried's. Each time, Meris bent in with the beamer.

"Clamp," she exclaimed the first time. "Same place." A short sigh. "But it's clean." She examined the others in silence. Finally she tucked her tools back into the kit. "I think I'm done."

"Then let's put these away." He took care to align the shipping coffins properly and then he waved her toward the stone steps. He half expected her to hesitate, or even ask if they could explore a little more.

Instead, she plodded directly back up into the skylit noonday. The other Sentinels still sat on the bench.

Nearby, however, Colonel Harris stood glowering. "Jorah, what is this?"

Since Meris was within earshot, Jorah decided not to mention that Tavkel had suggested he assist her. "I am helping Meris with research." He faced her. "Go on back to the med suite, and good luck with it. I'll stop at Mother's office and explain."

Jorah stood in a dignified military brace as she walked away, hair swinging down her back. Softly he told the colonel, "Tavkel sent me down, sir. And I will speak with Mother. Straightaway." As he spoke, he saw Meris leave the step-stone path at the far waterside. He would have liked to go with her, just to see the look on her face when the samples matched.

"Good, Caldwell." Colonel Harris gave his tunic a tug, straightening it. "I don't see any need to accompany you." His frown said more than his words, though. The catacombs weren't to be entered casually.

"No, sir. I'm going right there."

"First you will help close this door."

"Of course."

• • •

His mother sat beside Annalah, both of them leaning over Annalah's corner of the desktop. "Hello again," Jorah said. "Sorry to interrupt, and I'll keep this short. I couldn't get to you before I took Meris down into the catacombs, but you were right—Tavkel wanted me helping her. And wait 'til you hear what she's up to. She wants to prove Dad didn't actually die. She's got a long, fancy explanation about research protocols, but I know that's what she's after."

His mother's smile didn't fade. "Wonderful. We don't need to be afraid of the truth."

"We certainly don't," Annalah said.

He wanted to gloat. "The only person who needs to fear the truth is her precious Chancellor Gambrel. She simply will not believe how evil he is."

"We've just gotten official word." His mother slid her chair back to its usual position. "From Tallis. Gambrel is en route, bringing an ITD. They're requesting we actually let him land, along with support staff."

"Land?" He stood straighter. "That's ridiculous. We'll shuttle it down, right?"

"Colonel Harris is in charge of defense. It's not my decision." She flicked something on her desktop, and the light reflecting off her chin darkened slightly. "Please don't antagonize Meris. But tell me what she does when the DNA matches."

"And now that I've spoken with Tavkel and done what he needed, would you assign me to Dad?"

"I think that would be good for you both." At last she really smiled. So did his cousin.

• • •

Jorah found his dad on board the College shuttle. A crew appeared to be cannibalizing supplies from on board, since Uncle Kiel no longer intended to launch it. His dad wore a new uniform tunic, even though technically he'd been dismissed from service. "How's your mother?"

"Smiling." Jorah remembered witnessing some spectacular fights over the years. But when his parents were working together, the universe seemed friendlier. "And it looks like she's got a competent new aide."

His still-gifted dad must have caught his unspoken thought. "Believe it or not, Jorah, it's good that your mother stands up to me. I'm not always the Whorl's easiest person to live with. And she isn't the kind to lie down and let me do what I want, unchallenged." Two people walked past, carrying crates.

"Huh." Jorah had heard there was more to connaturality than making you stellar in bed, but thinking about his parents in that light was strangely embarrassing. He was glad when the others called his dad aside, ending the discussion.

Jorah bent down and got a good look at the sabotaged control panel. Really, whoever did this had known precisely what she—or he—was doing. The ship's main control lines ran through a constriction right over the greasy smear on the deck.

Maybe it hadn't been Meris. She didn't seem to know much about much, other than medical things.

"Anyway," Jorah's dad said, stepping close again, "they made a mistake, attacking the College. Once we get rid of Gambrel and SOOC, and put some competent people back on the Regional Council, things are going to be different. Somehow, Tavkel's going to get it all done. But until then, we need to dig in and defend ourselves."

"I just heard," Jorah said. "It's official. We're going to be visited by Gambrel and his team—or so they hope. And what's this about a new SOOC colonel?"

From outside the hatch came a metallic roar, plainly some other craft being serviced. The air blowing onboard smelled good. Like fuels and cleaning solvents. Familiar.

Jorah's dad ran a hand over the ruined command console. "The old ones got what they deserved. Removed from office and executed." He gave the console a pat and leaned away. "Well, we're getting an ITD out of it. And meanwhile your grandfather's working on tweaking fielding circuits, to see if we can look *out* through the RIA unit they've put in orbit. See what they're doing up there."

"Mmm . . ." Grandfather had been involved when RIA had first been developed. "Good luck to him."

"So you want something to do here with me?"

Jorah nodded. "If you can use me."

His dad reached over and flicked the main communication monitor. "The crew rosters are filled right now, but I'll give you some legwork."

"Wherever I can help." *Crew rosters* probably meant prepping some of those small shuttles. He'd heard that several more family groups had been ordered to scatter. "I'd sure like to look for that saboteur." It could still be Meris. What if she knew more than she was letting on, about spacecraft in general? "He—or she—"

"No, we've got that covered too." His dad frowned at the pale orange fuel indicator panel, and Jorah wondered if fuels and lubricants were running low. Uplevel, the pantries supposedly were miraculously full. Couldn't Tavkel fill these fluids too? "But here's something else I want done." His dad pointed back outside the hatch, roughly toward the poolside. "Walk through the whole installation—this time, your mother will get you a *pass* to enter the private level—and look for weak spots. Especially downlevel. I want to know where to deploy guards. Guards who can still listen for other mental presences."

Jorah nodded. He was glad that his dad was still treating him like a Sentinel, even if he had no ayin anymore.

"Try to see this place simply as a physical base. Pretend you have no idea what any of the rooms are for. Just imagine how you might get in, if somehow you got past the fielding net."

Jorah laughed shortly. He nearly bumped his head on an overhead panel. "That won't happen. Not for Gambrel, not for—" He stopped himself.

"Right." His dad glowered. "Your mom let Meris in. Didn't she?"

Jorah barely nodded. That was exactly what he'd been thinking. His mother didn't always follow the old rules. "Tavkel says Meris is important, though."

The metallic roar died. "Tunnels." His dad cuffed him on the shoulder. "You've got an order, Sentinel."

"I'm on it." He turned toward the shuttle's boarding hatch.

No, first he had to say something. He pivoted again and cleared his throat. "Dad. I'm glad you're back. Really glad. Ever since the Feds ambushed you at Tallis . . . I mean, sometimes we *do* have to disobey our superior officers. And I don't think I would have balked if I'd have known you were doing that."

His dad laughed quietly, sounding relaxed. "I'm glad I might live to see Madam Kernoweg taken down off her perch, her and the other Lenguans. Whatever Tavkel's got in mind, it's going to be good."

Jorah stared aft, toward the shuttle's passenger cabin. Several rows of reclining seats had been removed. "Dad . . . Tavkel hasn't pushed you, has he? You know, to . . . give it all up?" Jorah just couldn't imagine his dad without Sentinel abilities.

"He knows some of us need to stay as we are. We can serve him this way too." His dad glanced down at the handheld. "Dismissed, Sentinel. Good hunting."

Jorah saluted again. He strode down the ramp and back up the public tunnel toward his mother's office, to get that pass and a map.

CHAPTER 33

Meris took a deep breath, dropped the first of her new DNA slides into the analyzer, and touched the *compare* key. The samples she had recovered from that tunic, and from the coffin's bloodstain, had grown opaque cultures overnight. There should be enough intact strands to get a definite negative—or an assumed positive—match with the man's data file. Something ambiguous, between thirty and fifty percent matching of the strands' nucleotides, would mean she should let the cultures grow another day.

He means to wipe us out. Jorah's accusation echoed in her mind. She had never heard such an unfair assumption. Chancellor Piper Gambrel was a good man. A great man.

Dark letters appeared on the data readout, just a few of them on a pale background, but they made her breath catch: 95% MATCH.

Time passes. I endure. Only a shipped corpse would've left that shred of fully desiccated flesh. There was nothing more to prove.

Kinnor Caldwell had been executed. People had clamped his non-metabolizing body into that shipping coffin and pulled every bit of moisture out of it, then crushed it. Yet now he was walking around, convincing the people who knew him best that he was the same man who had died at Tallis.

She withdrew the slides half-heartedly, labeled them and started filing them. Halfway through the third one, she slammed a hand down on the counter. So why hadn't Tavkel gone through the catacombs and brought back to life everyone there, the way he had cleaned out the med center? Why hadn't he raised Saried? Why wasn't he creating that formerly dead army she'd first imagined at Kinnor Caldwell's funeral service?

Or—she shivered—was that still the plan? Would Tavkel teach his followers to empty other Sentinel coffins as their powers returned, here and on Thyrica, to challenge Chancellor Gambrel and the entire Federacy? The idea made her want to vomit. She leaned both arms against the lab counter and took a deep breath.

Saried had sampled *his* DNA, right? What had that looked like? She scrolled back through the record—didn't have to go far—and found another file labeled CALDWELL with a question mark and the name, in quotes, "Tavkel."

She stared first at the maternal mitochondria. A side note confirmed he was descended from Lady Fi, along with a cautioning symbol she didn't quite understand.

Then she found images of his chromosomes. She'd never seen anything so strange, with those bizarre long telomeres at the end of . . . were they half?—yes, precisely . . . half of them. Those unnaturally elongated ends should enable the cells to replicate almost indefinitely, protecting him from cell death, cancers, even aging itself. Maybe he was the result of another genetic experiment, such as the Minster's Shuhr ancestors had infamously performed. Maybe the Sentinels were trying for immortality too.

A nearly immortal mind reader? Horrified again, Meris stared at the white ceiling. *Stop,* she ordered herself. *Think. Recite.* Deep breath: *I fear what I only imagine.* She let it echo through her mind several times.

Clear headed again, she sat down on the stool. She clenched her hands and tried to make incongruous thoughts fit together. The mitochondrial DNA from Lady Fi's family looked normal, despite the ambiguous warning sign. So . . . had something coded in that odd nuclear DNA given Tavkel the ability to bring back some people who'd been recently killed, by reconstituting their chromosomes? She still didn't know where the new fluids would've come from.

And to bring back Kinnor Caldwell, not just his body but his personality, Tavkel would have had to reconstitute a human spirit too. What kind of mutated energy would that have required?

That was actually a much larger question.

She stared at the wall. Collegiate teachings had given her confidence and stability, but even they didn't rest on empirical proofs at the crucial level of first causes. The Sentinels' belief that the spirit didn't dissipate upon death was a primitive notion, but "primitive" didn't always mean "wrong." They would probably say that Kinnor's spirit had simply reentered his revived body.

She shook her head. She honestly believed that the body was disposable—essentially trash—partly because it replaced and repaired each cell countless times, using molecules that had been part of other bodies—other animals—plant and stone and soil.

Did Tavkel's potentially immortal cells factor into this? Was there some kind of connection between a potentially immortal body and a possibly immortal spirit?

She scowled at the analyzer. So much for her great discovery. Apparently there would be no research lab with her name on it. No protocol contributed to her field. No paeans from her parents.

But one man had reversed death. So—again, why just once?

Maybe to prove that he could.

But Kinnor Caldwell didn't seem central to any of Tavkel's teachings, nor any plan she could imagine—

Unless—oh, this had to be wrong!—Tavkel really did plan to launch a re-animated army, and it needed a commander!

She paced to the lab's far end and back again. Tavkel had . . . he really had brought back a dead man. That suggested powers beyond anything she'd ever heard of these people possessing.

Could he really be everything he claimed to be? She stood and stared at a wall. If Tavkel Caldwell really were a divine—even a semi-divine—being, did that mean everything she ever believed, all she'd studied under the Collegium, even the facts of re-absorption into the Infinite Divine after death—was false? All of it?

I am the spark of undying light. I shall see. I shall know. She pushed the thoughts back into whatever wounded, rebellious part of her spirit had birthed them. If she had not just lost her relationship with both parents, she would not be even considering such things. A weak part of her mind was just looking for another authority figure. She needed no such thing. *I am the spark of undying light,* she repeated.

She was an adult. It was time to act like one, time to ask pointed questions. And if they wouldn't let her take the answers to Chancellor Gambrel, at least she would know for herself.

Meris walked out of the med center without waving off the lights and made her way through the crowded commons, where the morning shift was sitting down to midday meal. She rode the elevator, crowded shoulder to shoulder with ten other people. A boy standing in front of her backed onto her foot. She pushed him off. Her mind roiled. *Telomeres. Desiccation. Indissoluble. Eternity. Kinnor Caldwell. DNA . . .*

The other passengers dispersed at the top: planetside. After the rainy morning, the afternoon looked to remain cool. To her relief, no one else headed for the shearing shed.

Inside the shed, she heard a faint, rhythmic swish and squeak. "Hello?" she called.

"Over here, Meris." Tavkel's voice came from the uphill east side.

She followed the swish-squeaks to a stall and found him strad-
dling a fat ewe, gripping its head between his knees as he sheared
its furry belly. Oddly, the animal wasn't struggling. After focusing its wide-set black eyes on Meris for a moment, it turned away.
Tavkel smiled at her and looked back down at what he was doing.
The shears moved swiftly, peeling dense, curling fur away from the
belly's center line.

"I'm not bothering you, am I?" She didn't want to stand too
close, knowing now what he could do. Still, he hadn't harmed
anyone, had he? She should be safe here with him, alone, for a few
minutes. "May I ask you a question?"

"You just did." His voice had a teasing note. "Two of them. No,
you aren't bothering me. And yes, ask whatever you need to know.
Want to sit down?" He glanced at a wooden crate near one end of
the stall.

She kept standing. "Why him? Why Air Master Caldwell?" She
might as well start there. "Why not Saried? For that matter, there's
a hall full of bodies under the Sanctuary. Wouldn't Saried have
been more useful?" she added hastily, lest he feel threatened by her
suspicion. "I mean, you can heal people, and there are trained psi
medspecs among the refugees who've arrived, but—" She'd never
felt so clumsy with words. "And how did you do it?"

"You found your proof, didn't you?" He kept looking down,
still apparently giving the animal his attention.

"You brought a dead man back to life." It felt good to admit
this.

"For your sake, I'm glad." His voice suddenly sounded as if
something hurt. "The truth brought you here, to ask questions. I
won't harm you, Meris. The worst I could do—the very worst—is
simply send you away. And I won't do even that."

She looked at this baffling man, this super-Sentinel who spent
his days dealing with animal fur while everyone here thought he
was about to destroy and re-make the universe. What would he

actually do if he traveled to Tallis or Elysia? She didn't dare ask what he planned for the future. No, she'd better stick with the past and present. "Who are you? Who were your biological parents? Why is one set of your chromosomes . . ." She searched for the right medical term. There wasn't one. " . . . Bizarre?"

He made a soft sound that wasn't quite a laugh. "I'll tell you, Meris. But you must agree to tell the Federates later, when . . . after . . . when it has to be said." He looked up into her eyes, so she nodded. Maybe she would figure out what he meant when the time came.

He opened his knees with a bowlegged gesture. The ewe rolled onto one side, as if she'd done this many times and knew the routine. Tavkel dropped the hand shears onto the stall's wood floor. He folded his hands. "My mother was the Shamarr and Air Master's younger sister, Tiala Caldwell."

"Right. I heard that. You're maternally descended from Lady Fi."

"Yes. And my father is the Eternal Speaker—the Holy One, the creator God—and please don't imagine something inappropriate." She felt herself flush. The first thing that had sprung to mind was, in fact, a lewd myth. "My father created the human form. He has mastery over it."

And he'd prayed to his *father* when he'd healed Jorah. She'd caught that. "Mastery over reproduction as well as aging?" This was ludicrous, but she needed to hear it. "As well as death? What does that make you, half human and half god?"

He shook his head. "No. One hundred percent."

"Which?"

"Both."

She laughed shortly. "That's not possible."

"Is light a wave or a particle, Meris?"

She thought a moment, startled by his answer. People said it had all the characteristics of both. And she could not deny the existence of light. "Oh." So . . . if the comparison applied, she stood talking to a god? Incredibly, to *the* God?

He was still insane to claim it. "And that . . . gives you the power to re-animate dead people? You can just . . . call them back from some other place and slap them into dehydrated bodies, and they can get up and breathe and eat and sleep with their wives and . . ." She stopped, hoping he wasn't taking offense.

He actually smiled again. "It's more complex than that, but essentially, yes."

She had to try once more. "Why Kinnor Caldwell?"

"Short answer?" Was he laughing at her?

"The shorter the better."

"Four words, then: My father said to."

His father the deity. So *he* wasn't the light-particle-wave deity? Still, being told by a god to do something would be reason enough, except for one thing. "I don't believe in gods." She tossed her head. "Calling the Infinite a person would be like calling an ocean a person. Or a star system a person. A thing that enormous just doesn't have personality. Doesn't have volition. Doesn't *do* things."

"You're wrong," he said, though his voice was gentle. "In every aspect that defines personhood, he is. He is aware—more aware than anyone you know. He has intentions, and he carries them out, and he calls them good. More than any other person is, he *is*. He loves you, Meris. And your honesty."

He loved her? When was the last time anyone had used that word to her face? And how strange that Tavkel had used it. He barely knew her. How could he claim that his absentee father even knew about, much less *loved* her? "And this . . . request you keep making. To take people's darkness. You're collecting it? Why doesn't it affect you—or does it?"

"A perceptive question." He nodded. "I'm only collecting deeds of ownership. Later . . . Well, you'll see. You will see," he repeated.

The ewe on the floor bleated. Tavkel reached down and scratched it behind one ear. It shut its eyes, apparently enjoying his touch.

"Frankly," Meris said, "I don't think I have any such deed to offer you."

"Well said. You never were asked to live by a holy standard, so you don't know how many times you . . ." Then he stopped and seemed to switch thoughts. "Meris, like everyone else, you fall short of perfection. Most people learn to scoff at the idea, or else they make excuses."

She laughed. It sounded harsh in the narrow stall. "Who defines 'perfect'? You?"

Tavkel kept scratching the drowsy, half-shorn creature at his feet. "That's exactly the kind of excuse I mean. My father does. Because he is."

"Perfect?"

He nodded and shifted his hand, scratching the ewe under her chin. "And as for the body—watch this."

He picked up the shears again, repositioned the ewe, and swiftly finished peeling back its fleece, which he lifted off like a winter jacket. Amazingly, the thick, curly fur hung together. He draped it over the stall's far edge. "Think of your body as something like this fleece. It grows out of who you are more deeply. If it's sheared away, it will regrow—exactly as before. It's not your essential part, but while you wear it, it's part of you. Through it, you interact with creation. That's what the new universe will be like." He shrugged. "It's not a perfect comparison, but it's not far off."

"Hmm." She rested her shoulder against a rough board. "So why do you think your father, the god, told you to restore Kinnor Caldwell, instead of my medical supervisor? Does he want soldiers instead of healers?"

Tavkel stroked the fleece absently. He sat back down. "Let me tell you a story."

Now they were getting somewhere! Tavkel's stories were cleverly crafted puzzles. She'd enjoyed solving the one about water sources, over at the amphitheater. She'd heard about others secondhand. "Please do." She grabbed the crate he'd offered and sat down across from him. *Tell me a story, Super-Sentinel.*

He tipped his stool against the opposite wall. "Some time ago, at Avillan Hospital in Jerone City on Elysia, in the occupational therapy wing, a husband and wife were admitted for treatment." He sent her a somber look and reached aside. His walking stick rested in the corner. He gathered it in and laid it across his knees.

Meris raised an eyebrow. She had been born at Avillan Hospital. It startled her to know he'd heard of it. Maybe he hadn't been raised in total isolation after all.

"Both had severe spinal injuries after a hovercar accident. The prescribed treatment was arduous, but the wife followed the therapist's instructions to the letter. She recovered eventually and was discharged. The husband, on the other hand . . ." He rolled his eyes. "He was an independent man. He made up his own sensible protocol and stuck to it faithfully. He actually worked twice as hard as his wife.

"When she was discharged, he was no longer in pain, but to his shock, the medspec refused to discharge him. The medspec insisted that the underlying problem had not been addressed, that he had only worked on the symptoms. The medspec could not in good conscience discharge the man."

A door slammed nearby, causing a soft commotion among the other animals in the shed. Tavkel turned toward the walkway between stalls. A curly-headed boy stood gripping another kipret by its neck rope, digging his fingers into the creature's fur.

"Just a minute, Pieters," Tavkel called.

"Okay." The sekiyr had a cheery voice that Meris thought she recognized. "I'll leave her over here." He tugged the kipret into the next stall.

"And?" Meris asked. "Go on."

"That's it. Simple."

Right, then. Now to decipher the story's meaning. "The wife . . . That's Saried. She was 'discharged,' to whatever afterlife you people expect."

He nodded.

"Because she lived the right way, I guess? According to the teachings of the Sentinels?"

He nodded again.

So . . . the man in the story had to be Kinnor. And to make it fit the story, she had to assume that Kinnor still had his underlying problem, whatever that meant. He wasn't ready to stay dead—to be discharged—so he had to come back, to finish his healing, but to do it right this time. Was that it?

Well, of course he wasn't ready to stay dead. Who was ready to die, really?

"Want another?" Tavkel grinned.

Meris leaned toward him. "Go ahead. I'm ready."

"Once there was a little girl," he said, "years ago. On . . . let's say Luxia. She had a little pet that she loved. You had a pet when you were young, didn't you?"

"I did." She must've smiled when he said the word "pet." Or else he was reading her emotions, blocking drugs or no blocking drugs. Or maybe he had just guessed. Many children had pets. "So . . . this little girl . . . what did she do?"

"It was a kind of creature she'd never seen. It had been imported from . . . Bishda," he decided. "She called it her 'LittleBreath.' It had four stubby legs, a big head, and sharp little teeth, and she played with it and brushed its silky fur. Her parents even made it her job to feed it. She opened the bag of pet food the dealer sold them, she put the food into LittleBreath's bowl, and she stroked it while it ate with those sharp little teeth."

The shorn ewe made a weird noise and started chewing something, rotating its lower jaw around and around and around.

Tavkel half-smiled at it and went on speaking. "After a few days, the girl noticed something. Her pet wasn't getting any bigger. In fact, it looked thin. She was old enough to worry, so she tried to find out more about what kind of creature it was. She found out that LittleBreath's species was strictly herbivorous—but the pet dealer had sold them dried meat pellets by mistake."

"The sharp teeth must have fooled them," she muttered.

"As you say. It looked like a carnivore. So she asked her parents to buy the right food. She filled LittleBreath's bowl and called for it to come.

"And it sniffed the good food, but it wouldn't eat. It walked away from the bowl and looked up at her with desperately hungry eyes. It had learned to like the wrong food. It refused to eat what would nourish it, because that food seemed strange and mysterious. One day it lay down at her feet, looking up at her with those hungry eyes, and it died."

Meris pulled herself out of the story's spell. *It's just a story. A children's story, at that.* "There are too many irresponsible pet owners," she said brusquely. "And dealers." After she'd gotten old enough to focus on her studies, her parents had given her pocket-dog to someone else. She'd cried. She'd gotten over it. Still, she didn't want to linger over that story.

Tavkel pressed on. "It had never eaten any other food after its mother's milk, you see. It was so hungry that it learned to eat what it couldn't digest, but then it couldn't learn all over again, even when someone gave it the right food. It broke her heart to realize she had helped kill it."

"Obviously." Where was he going with this? "And?"

"End of story," he said, arms still crossed. "I wish it were happier. That one isn't a perfect analogy either, by the way."

"At least tell me the moral." She didn't want those images roll-ing around in her mind. She wanted some closure. *She helped kill it . . .* That was the most unsettling thing she had ever heard the man say. She would have nightmares tonight. About food, and little sharp teeth, and desperately hungry eyes. What in the Whorl did those symbolize?

Instead of telling her the moral, he said, "A blind woman and her guide were traveling a hard, stony path—like the trail to Tekkumah."

Relieved, Meris crossed her arms to mirror his position.

"She was pulling a wagon filled with everything she owned. Every now and then, her guide would pick up a rock and—" he uncrossed his arms and made a tossing gesture— "pitch it into the wagon behind her. Nothing so big that she would notice the added weight right away, but as she walked, the wagon got heavier and heavier. Eventually it became so heavy that she was simply walking in place, not getting anywhere—but she didn't know, because she was blind.

"Another traveler came down the path. 'Toss the stones out of your wagon,' he said. 'Give them to me.' 'I have no stones,' the blind woman answered. 'I packed that wagon myself. It's full of impor-tant belongings.'

"But since she walked in darkness, she couldn't see the stones." He shot Meris a glance. "She didn't know about the stones. In fact, she didn't even know about the darkness, because she'd always been blind."

Darkness. Right. I get this one. "I see."

"Yes, you do."

"So you're the second traveler, the one she meets. I'm the blind woman. And who's my guide, Chancellor Gambrel?"

His eyes had always looked shrewd. Right now, they seemed to see through her. "If that's what you hear when you hear it, yes. Maybe your education."

She sniffed. Neither Chancellor Gambrel nor her education had thrown stones into her wagon—and she resented the accusation that she was blind. She had half a mind to walk out right then. But she didn't. "You're good at inventing personal stories, Tavkel. What are you going to tell the whole Whorl, simultaneously, if you get the chance? One of these tales?"

"When the time comes, I'll know. I do need to speak with all my lost children. Not just you."

She was not lost. She was just stuck here. And she was not blind. She had one more urgent question. "How did you find out that Chancellor Gambrel's coming? Do you have some unusual way of . . . intercepting DeepScan transmissions?"

"My father tells me some things ahead of time. When it's important for our people to prepare for them."

She reached down and picked a bit of shorn fluff off the floorboards. "Jorah thinks the Chancellor means to wipe you all out. He's imagining things, of course, getting ready to fight a man who only wants peace. He's frightening people!" Shredding the fluff absently, she frowned at Tavkel. *Give me your darkness,* he'd said . . .

"People fear what they only imagine," he told her. "But they fear more than that, Meris. They also fear what they don't understand."

She nodded, unsettled. How could he . . . But she hadn't taught him any litanies. "Of—of course."

"But Chancellor Gambrel is dangerous to my people. Also to you," he added. "He's afraid of us, just as you are afraid. But what you fear is your only real hope. And the things you cling to must be tossed away. They can't help or save you. Not now, not later."

"He isn't coming to harm anyone!" It frustrated her that she hadn't understood the second story. What did it mean that the girl had helped kill her pet? But looking down at that contented creature lolling on the floor, she just didn't want to imagine animals dying—especially because of someone's honest mistake.

Besides, if she really were "clinging" to anything, it was good solid teaching. She dropped the bit of fluff she'd picked up. "Well, I can't take in one more idea just now. Let's talk again later."

He stood, brushed bits of wool off his work clothes, and used his stick to guide the creature out of the stall with a few gentle-looking touches. "I wish you would let me show you what light looks like."

What? Oh—how it would feel to give up any claim to alleged darkness. He didn't sound hostile, just sad. What harm would it do, just to say the words—

But the Chancellor was coming! Wouldn't it be amazing to listen in on a conversation between those two? When that happened, she wanted to stand where she stood now, intellectually and spiritually. The Chancellor would know how to deal with Tavkel's wild claims and unusual stories.

She sidled out of the stall. "I'll be back."

● ● ●

It surprised her the next evening to see a crowd gather around the reflecting pool as sekiyrra whisked the dinner dishes away. She thought she spotted Jorah, standing at the white railing near the elevator doors, so she wandered his way, wondering if this would be the night when there was going to be some sort of concert. She'd lost track of days.

He stood talking with someone she didn't recognize. Eventually he turned her direction and shot her a surprised smile. "Meris, hi. Are you a music lover or just curious?"

"Curious, mostly." All around the waterside, people were setting up chairs or just standing, staring out at the island. Apparently it *was* concert day. Out on the largest island under the kirka trees, several people sat or stood in a small arc that would let them all see one another.

With the sun down, the skylights were starting to fade—but there would be a longish natural twilight. She knew that now.

She needed to say something. He stood at the railing, obviously waiting for her to explain her curiosity. "Sound usually carries well across water, but not down here. Why is that?"

He shrugged and moved aside, making room for her in front of him. "Don't know."

She edged into the space he'd opened. Silence fell abruptly. A few seconds later, she realized what had happened: She'd stopped hearing all those rushing and splashing noises. Obviously, they normally provided some sonic privacy within this tightly contained community. Now they'd silenced it, probably for the concert.

On the big island, someone she didn't recognize stepped out from under the broadest kirka tree. He introduced himself and several others—including Lady Fi, who sat on a white chair, balancing a skinny, stretched-out wooden harp on her lap.

They started to play. Meris didn't recognize most of the instruments, but she thought they blended well in a light, slightly wistful classical composition.

She didn't realize she'd rested against Jorah's chest until he shifted his weight slightly. "Oh!" she whispered, leaning forward again. "Sorry."

"It's all right," he whispered back, right against her ear. "I won't take it personally. Be comfortable."

So she did. The musicians played for most of an hour. Once, the announcer—Kirck Spieth—sang a ballad that wasn't in that strange prayer language but Old Colonial, so Meris understood it. He'd written it, he said, for his wife, Gini—he gestured for her to stand, and it turned out she'd been the one playing some sort of thick, back-curved flute.

There was more applause at the end of that piece. Jorah's breath tickled Meris's ear as he murmured, "So that's what she was so protective of, in the hand luggage. They were on my shuttle here from Tallis."

"I remember. She was one of the people Tavkel healed of the plague." Lost in the moment, fully relaxed for the first time since she left Elysia, Meris sighed. People were still applauding and talking.

It still made no sense to blame Chancellor Gambrel. Somehow, Jorah had picked up a deadly disease in the crowds at Tallis.

And she'd heard no more about it from Tallis . . . Why not?

Because—of course!—because there were no Sentinels left there, and it killed only Sentinels.

Jorah pressed one hand to his head.

Alarmed, she spoke quickly. "You all right? Need anything?" Could the disease have come back?

He pulled his hand down and shook his head.

She'd better keep an eye on him. If he needed more headache medicine, he knew where to find it. "You'll let me know if you have any respiratory symptoms, won't you?"

"I won't. Tavkel healed me."

Fine, then. "Your grandmother's not bad," she murmured as the applause stilled.

He laughed softly and shifted his weight behind her once more. Then he rested a hand on her shoulder.

It felt good. He left it there for most of the next musical number, another instrumental piece that Jorah's grandmother dedicated to "Tavkel, our daystar."

Whatever that meant.

When the concert ended, he walked her back around the waterside toward the housing corridors. "Is anyone in your family musical?" he asked.

"We never took time for it. Too busy pursuing excellence. Are you sure you're all right?"

"I'm fine." He laughed. "My mom and dad and I don't do music, either. I guess Cousin Perl does, but . . . Well, there are different kinds of excellence, aren't there?"

Where was he taking this conversation? "Of course."

"Meris." He sidestepped out of the waterside crowd, toward the dining commons. She followed. "Just in case you had any doubts—about pursuing excellence—I think you chased it down pretty successfully. I wish we'd met . . . well . . . before the whole Whorl came apart for me." Those dark eyes seemed to be shooting sparks at her.

Her stomach did an odd little flop. She wanted to back away from him. No, she wanted to get close again. Which? "Maybe it isn't. Coming apart, I mean." Normally she had better control of her tongue than this! "Maybe it's really just starting to come together."

Her pursed his lips and nodded, smiling crookedly. "Yeah. You're right. Maybe it really is."

She stood waiting, wondering if he might say more. Wishing he would. The kitchen doors hung open as usual, and several couples had sat down at dining tables. Sekiyrra scurried to and fro, carrying pottery mugs and plates. They could sit down together and—

What was she doing? She forced a yawn. "I'd better—"

"Right." Jorah strode on. She turned off at her own corridor, and he kept walking.

Annalah wasn't in the room, and Meris fell into her bed with the strangest sense of contentment. She was not falling for that man, or so she told herself as the bunk warmed around her. That just had felt . . . nice. He really could say kind things.

And he had beautiful eyes. That too was merely an objective observation. Still . . .

Only the light is real. And I am the light, and I go to rejoin the brilliant light.

Only the light is real . . .

But if I weren't merely a spark of light, Meris added, *I think I might have loved that man.*

She smiled and rolled toward the wall.

CHAPTER 34

Two days after the concert, Jorah hustled up a narrow stone tunnel toward his mother's office. With her permission, he'd been prowling the private tunnels since his dad had asked him to look for weak spots. He still couldn't imagine invaders actually landing and trying to enter. All he had found so far was a thin exterior wall in the pantries, on the uphill side.

He was still determined to catch Uncle Kiel's saboteur, even though Uncle Kiel no longer was leaving. Jorah had always known the Minster's office was connected privately with the hangar area. After all, he'd lived here during his early teens. What he hadn't known was that there were so many other passages. A route led from the hangar to the Chapter room. An even narrower space vanished uphill, bringing water lines down from the spring. He'd patrolled them all in a randomized pattern and reported to her four times daily.

Now he listened carefully just outside the thin, almost invisible secret door to her office. Hearing nothing, he rapped three times.

"Yes?" Her voice had a faint note of alarm, as if he'd startled her.

He pushed through. His mother sat at her desk, leaning heavily on an elbow. Lights flickered from the desk's surface. To his chagrin, she wasn't alone. Her new aide, Captain Anastu, stood near the opposite wall as usual—but his grandfather was also close by.

"Oh!" Jorah hated his disablement more than ever. He should've sensed them. This could have been a grave tactical error if she'd had other guests, people who didn't already know that the private tunnels existed. "I'm sorry! I didn't mean to interrupt, and—"

"It's all right." His mother braced both arms against the desk's edge and pushed her chair out. "Anything today?"

"No. Quiet as usual." He suspected she asked for reports simply to keep watch over him.

"Good," she said. "Carry on."

Grandfather came around the desk, "Jorah, are you all right?" He had a peculiar tone in his voice, not voice-command but something Jorah didn't recognize.

"Mostly, sir." Jorah didn't want to talk about the headaches. He could get more of Meris's remedy if they got too bad.

Meris . . . did he like her, or did he distrust her?

Both! And when he was with her, there were feelings shooting off inside him that he didn't trust at all. He was best off avoiding her.

Grandfather stepped closer and peered into his eyes. Jorah quickly banished Meris from his thoughts. The lightest flicker of what might have been a mind-access probe touched him, but Jorah didn't get any of the usual nausea. Its weakness also felt weird. Grandfather's abilities had once been amazing.

"What, sir?" Jorah was slowly getting used to seeing his high-ranking grandfather simply sit in the commons or classrooms, helping people work with their re-growing abilities. Today, he wore a troubled look.

"Nothing." Grandfather stepped away. He must have been looking for something else. Jorah turned back to his mother's desk.

Footsteps approached from the waterside. Colonel Harris strode through the arch, followed by Jorah's dad and two other military Sentinels, Major Heryld Ryken and Lieutenant Willin Prescott. Jorah snapped to attention. So did Captain Anastu.

Colonel Harris saluted Grandfather and stepped aside.

Tavkel followed the military group into the office. Startled and curious, Jorah stepped out of his salute and backed against the stone wall, hoping nobody would dismiss him. His mother's aide returned to the opposite wall.

"Minster, High Commander." Colonel Harris remained at attention, looking sharp in his midnight blues. "The new Federate group's subspace wake has been detected. They should arrive in two days, and I am sorry, but I must confirm a request Tavkel has made."

Jorah's dad cleared his throat.

"Oh?" His mother glanced up at his dad, but he said nothing. She slid her chair toward her desk and sat tall, looking official. "If Tavkel requested it, I will approve it."

Tavkel stepped forward, between the major and the lieutenant. Jorah recognized them as second circle people, who'd never given up their ayin powers.

Tavkel spoke softly. "Wind, I asked Colonel Harris to deactivate the fielding net."

Jorah gaped. His father glared down at his mother. Dad had been right, asking him to check for weak spots. They might actually end up with Feds on the ground!

"And—forgive me." Colonel Harris looked from Tavkel to Jorah's mother and back again, as if asking them both to excuse him. "But for something so grave, I do need authorization." He turned to Grandfather. "We all follow Tavkel, but we follow him freely. And your advice would be welcome, sir. You have decades more service than I do."

Jorah snapped his mouth shut. His mother eyed Grandfather, whose face looked somber. Obviously the second circle believers were having a hard time buying this. Even Grandfather, who had looked directly at Tavkel's mind and so lost his ayin abilities, plainly came up against a point of doubt here.

Jorah shot a glance across the office at his mother's aide, Captain Anastu. She was second circle too . . . right?

She shrugged instead of joining the conversation.

Tavkel kept his hands at his side. "The Whorl has to see and hear me. My father has waited millennia for this moment, and now even those people who could mean you harm are doing his will."

Jorah spoke up. "He's right." His elders' heads turned toward him. "Chancellor Gambrel and his force think they're coming to destroy us, but they're actually helping us. They're bringing the technology Tavkel will need to transmit to the whole Whorl."

"So you'd deactivate the fielding net," Captain Anastu said, "to let them land? So our forces can storm their ship and take their ITD?" She grinned at Tavkel. "And then we would set up their Instantaneous Transceiver Disk here, and you would beam out your message . . ." she lifted a hand . . . "to the stars?"

"Not in that way," Tavkel said, "not at all. My father's word will go out. And so will your message—your example—of service. But if you mount the strong resistance that tempts you now, they will not deliver the ITD. Their greatest fear is of being manipulated. Your abilities terrify them."

His mother folded her hands on the desk. "But must we let them *all* land? As much of a force as they care to bring?"

"Yes. For centuries, your people have been tested. Your ancestors' great disobedience made you a people apart. The great service I ask now will end your generations of separation." Had Tavkel always spoken that confidently, or were the others' doubts making the contrast clear?

His mother shut her eyes. She did that when she was totally undecided. "Tavkel, I believe in you. I trust you. I've seen who and what you are. Still . . ." She opened her eyes, and they looked haunted. "Would anyone else care to advise me?"

"Yes!" Jorah's dad swept out both arms. "Tavkel's a man of peace, and that's admirable. But we've got to defend him." He turned toward Tavkel. "Yes, defend you. You know the future. You brought me back—I was dead!—but do you have any idea the kind of force these people could aim at this place? They could smother us with Ostian dust. They could burn us out. They could—"

Tavkel raised a hand.

Jorah's dad shut his mouth.

Colonel Harris remained at attention. "I would suggest—respectfully, Tavkel—that we negotiate the smallest possible landing party while keeping the fielding station operational. As an alternative, we could suggest sending a freight shuttle up to orbit to receive delivery."

Standing near the desk, Grandfather rubbed the old scar on his cheekbone. "Colonel Harris, I agree—at least I would, under any other circumstances. Wind, remember I owe Tavkel every breath I take. So weigh my advice accordingly. But I cannot advise you to refuse his request—for precisely the reasons Kinnor just reminded us about. Tavkel knows things that we don't. Including the motives behind others' actions. If he orders us not to resist, we do not resist."

Tavkel stared down at Jorah's mother.

"Colonel Harris?" She kept her eyes shut. "Do you have any further advice?"

Colonel Harris compressed his lips. "The Federate ships that arrived with Jorah are still in orbit, just out of fielding range. They also constitute a threat, especially when combined with this new force that will shortly arrive."

"Yes, they do. And their onboard RIA team? Our own people?" She sat very still.

Colonel Harris answered in a quiet voice. "Still active, according to the scan team. But we haven't been able to confirm what they're up to, or whether they could be rescued."

Should they shut down the fielding net? Jorah didn't know. Surely the answer was yes, if both Tavkel and the Feds were going to want it. Still, the conflict in Jorah's mind felt spooky. Assuming his further thoughts weren't wanted, he kept silent.

At last, his mother looked straight at Tavkel. "You ask us to simply trust you."

"I do, Wind." Tavkel locked eyes with her.

"Even if it means dying for you?"

Tavkel glanced at Kinnor and then down again. "Why should you be afraid to die?"

Jorah's breath caught. Tavkel was going to split the Sanctuary's leadership right down the middle.

Tavkel looked at each one of them—Jorah's dad, the other military Sentinels, Grandfather, Jorah, his mother. "I will never— never—take away your freedom to serve me as you see fit. But if you cannot obey, your reward will be harder won."

Mother shut her eyes again. She leaned both elbows on the desk. "Very well. I would do this for no other person, but we have no one else to follow and certainly nowhere to run."

Tavkel stayed at a sort of relaxed attention. "No one else would ask you to do this. But it has begun. The renewal is at hand. Remember, I told you all to be ready for what looks like a defeat. You will not be in real danger, even if you die. I have proved this."

Jorah's mother kept staring. Colonel Harris furrowed his forehead so hard that his eyebrows almost met in the middle. Grandfather clasped his hands behind his back. He'd gone into service back in the glory days. How did all this look from his perspective?

"All right," his mother said. "Colonel Harris, you are ordered to power down the fielding station. There is . . . there's a way to do it, isn't there?"

Jorah felt his eyes widen again. Everything *really* was about to change, and he was going to see it happen!

Colonel Harris made fists at his sides. "Yes. There are master circuits. Then, unless you have other orders, I shall release the fielding operators to either scatter along with the civilians or else stay here, in case a defense has to be raised . . . at some point." He sent Tavkel a sidelong glance. "If that force is actually coming to wipe us out, we've still got to get you that ITD."

"I told you. If you fight them, they will not deliver it." Tavkel swept out an open hand. "Remember that you're doing this for the sake of your brothers and sisters on twenty-three other worlds. Not just Sentinels, but the unaltered humanity you're all sworn to serve. This, my friends—my family—this is the service you are called to give them."

"But it's all right," Jorah's mother said, "if we evacuate nonessential personnel. Isn't it? At least scatter the families with children, until our fuel runs out?"

Tavkel clasped his hands in front of him. "Yes. Please do that."

Jorah's mother's eyes lit with purpose.

• • •

For the next two days, every time Jorah stepped out of the narrow tunnels he saw someone scurrying, carrying a duffel or hoisting a backpack. More than once, the ground vibrated as a civilian craft blasted off the breakaway strip.

His task felt more vital than ever. He reported back to his mother in the early hours of the second day. A thirtyish couple and three older kids stood in front of her desk, dressed in warm-looking coats. "No," his mother said, "we've already sent five groups downstream. Just a little way east of here, over the hill, you'll strike easy going. Go that way, with the Holy One's blessing."

The group hustled out. No one else remained with his mom but Captain Anastu.

Jorah strode forward.

"Good morning, Jorah. First report of the day?"

He nodded. "I don't think there's anything else to find. Really, the Sanctuary's main weakness is right at the hangars. Any one of those four entrances could be blasted open, and we've got two routes from there into the main chamber."

The College shuttle was still down in H-1, what was left of it. Crewers were taking it to pieces to get smaller vessels up and running. And Colonel Harris's crews had prepped the four light fighters in H-3, whether or not Tavkel approved. That hangar's concealed launch doors had never been opened.

"Good work, Jorah. I've sent nearly half the families on their way."

"Good work to you too, then."

She smiled. "It's slower than I'd like. But it has to be organized. If your dad's right . . . well . . . they need to be spread out, and they all need food and survival gear. In fact, supplies are running low for the first time since Tavkel arrived."

"Hmm," he said. "Well, shall I convert my mission to police-and-patrol?"

"Yes. You'll see others on guard." She raised her head. "I love you, Jorah."

He wasn't used to hearing that. He just knew it. "Oh. I, ah. I love you too." He hustled across the office toward the door arch.

Behind him, his mother cried out. "There!"

Jorah wheeled around just short of the arch.

She pointed down at one gleaming desk panel and lit another one. "Colonel Harris, they're here!"

Colonel Harris's voice spoke out of the desk. "Confirm. Leaving slip-state. Big cruiser-carrier, four support ships. I'll get you an ETA. Probably just a few hours."

Jorah's mother raised her handheld, still ignoring Jorah. "Father?"

The answer came a few seconds later. "Yes?"

"They're breaking slip-state. Would you hail them? You're our elder statesman. When they speak to you, they won't see the face of Mikuhr—my face—looking back at them."

His voice was clear. "You're our Administrator, and we support you."

"Please, Father?"

Jorah rested a hand on the door arch, torn. He wanted to stay and listen to what his grandfather told Piper Gambrel. But that wouldn't happen for awhile—and he had orders.

His mother glanced at him. "Thank you for patrolling, Jorah."

"Yes, ma'am." Chastened, he turned toward the door again.

• • •

Piper Gambrel stared at a cabin monitor as the big carrier decelerated out of slip-state. A well-earned biokinetic rest had refreshed him. Now he could get a first look at where he was going.

By his own preference, he'd traveled inside a landing craft on board the big cruiser-carrier. He always found the self-important scurrying of bridge crews distasteful. Besides, this very module would become his planetside headquarters. He'd kept his staff busy, preparing it for arrival.

Now, on his main bulkhead monitor—his systems were synched with the carrier's sensor suite—he eyed a magnified view of the surface of Procyel II. Tactical schematics overlaid the main compound. He ignored those. Military maneuvers would be Urnock's concern, if they proved necessary.

Small crop fields, pastures, and tree plantings surrounded his target like a set of simultaneous messages. Day was breaking down there, and to his satisfaction, the Sentinels' allegedly impenetrable fielding net would be no problem. Urnock's task force commander had simply requested landing clearance. It had been granted by the retired high commander himself.

Strange that High Commander Caldwell looked and sounded so healthy. Perhaps the reports of radiation poisoning had been false.

We'll see. The god-voice had not controlled his body for awhile. He missed the exhilaration of hovering above himself, watching and listening.

A sharp tone sounded, and a black square appeared at the center of his monitor. It was immediately replaced by the insignia of Regional Command, Tallis—and then a rotund face that he didn't recognize. This was undoubtedly a recording, sent via DeepScan II.

"Good day, Chancellor. I am Lieutenant Lulea, speaking for Madam Kudennou Kernoweg of the Federate Regional Council." When the man dipped his head, two more chins appeared. "There have been no significant changes to your orders while you were en route. You, personally, are to either squelch or absorb the Dabarite movement. Colonel Zeimsky will subject every individual on site to the humane cure. In that respect, his mission will be secondary to yours."

Gambrel nodded. It was good to hear that Zeimsky would be taking *his* orders. There'd been a bit of jockeying, en route.

"If there is resistance," the lieutenant continued, "especially resistance using their mind powers, the Sentinels will become subject to military reprisal, under Colonel Urnock. If no such reprisal proves necessary, his force will also support yours while the humane cure is implemented. You may ask him to take any disciplinary action that proves necessary."

Excellent! It was beneath Gambrel's dignity to smile, but he smiled anyway. Effectively, Regional Command had given him command of the mission after all. He touched the *record* panel at the bottom of his monitor. "Thank you, Lieutenant Lulea. It is my hope that it can all be done with minimum bloodshed. The Instantaneous Transceiver Disk appears to be payment enough for their submission." Provided, of course, that he used it cannily. "We shall alert you if hostilities arise."

He flicked another panel and relayed the lieutenant's message—and his reply—to both Urnock and Zeimsky. They too were on board the landing module: While Gambrel had enjoyed his rest, Zeimsky had claimed nearly half the craft's main level and spent the passage converting it to a twelve-bed med suite. Colonel Urnock had been assigned the main level's remaining quarter. His guard complement occupied an upper level.

The big carrier's engines made Gambrel's form-response chair vibrate and hum. He finished updating himself via the bulkhead news monitor, and he requested hourly reports on Sabba Six-alpha from the carrier's command deck. The Whorl's Dabarites were predicting that Tavkel would use its final explosion to bring about his cataclysmic, so-called renewal. The next Sabba Six-alpha update would arrive in forty-six minutes.

However, according to a file that had been waiting for three days while he was en route, Regional Command had countered those rumors by enlisting a Tallan astrophysicist. His prominently posted article explained that Sabba Six-alpha's recent blast was not pre-catastrophic and was well within normal parameters for this stellar era.

Good, good. Gambrel shifted, and his chair shifted under him. Another report was less satisfactory. Federate Caroli's ruling council had split, citing an argument regarding the latest *Procyel Eyewitness Report*. During the DeepScan silence en route, Gambrel had wakened occasionally to work on a list of persons who must be silenced, even if they all submitted to being cured. The *PERs'* persistent author, Annalah Caldwell, was high on the list. Newer *PERs* displayed a tally of supposed healings and several more monologues, supposedly quoted verbatim, by this same Tavkel, their alleged Boh-Dabar.

Below each *PER* entry appeared the annotation, "Approved for redistribution by her majesty Rinnah of Netaia." Naturally, Netaia's non-Thyrian "Path" priests had their monarch well in hand. Reports were being disseminated there. To quash the Dabarites, Tallis would need to send representatives—assassins, if necessary—to Netaia as well.

Interestingly, nowhere in the *PERs* was Jorah Caldwell mentioned. Perhaps the young lieutenant had learned a lesson about keeping his head down.

Gambrel touched another armrest control. "Colonel Urnock, what's the status of Major Preston on board the *White Squall*?"

"Standing by." Urnock's face appeared at the monitor's edge. "I'm going to transmit groundside to Procyel."

Without waiting for Gambrel's orders? Well, permission was easily given, and Zeimsky could commence his medical program after the locals understood their precarious status. "Proceed, Urnock."

Gambrel kept the news reports scrolling. New Dabarite Chapters had apparently sprung up on several worlds. Meanwhile, Collegiate numbers had kept dropping. More and more people were throwing in with the countercultural upstart, Tavkel.

A temporary setback. Soon to be reversed.

A white frame appeared around Urnock's image. He was transmitting. Gambrel pointed at the white frame. The sound came up.

● ● ●

Kiel rushed into the office. He spotted his sister-in-law standing beside his father, who sat in the command chair. "Wind?" Kiel murmured.

She raised a hand for silence.

Kiel had come on behalf of a young refugee family. They'd decided to flee offworld, if it still were possible. After all, the *White Squall* had not interfered with previous launches—but apparently, this group had waited just too long. Kiel stepped aside and took a seat on the bench beside Captain Anastu, Wind's new aide.

As a desk panel brightened, his father sat straighter. "Colonel Pelson Urnock," Kiel heard someone say, "on behalf of Special Operations Oversight. Good morning, High Commander. We are en route to a landing site eight klicks north of your location. We shall commence negotiations upon our arrival."

"Good morning, Colonel." Kiel knew that tone of voice. His father was masking displeasure. "We request that you—" The panel darkened abruptly, indicating that Urnock had ended the call. Kiel frowned at the disrespect.

His father pushed away from the desk. Eyes narrow, he was no longer hiding his anger. "Urnock! Pelson Urnock, speaking for SOOC? That's monstrous."

Wind looked puzzled. "I . . . haven't heard of him."

Kiel's father stood. He spun the empty desk chair to face Wind. "That's because Regional Command has put a Covert Ops man in charge of a Special Ops matter. A hostile one at that. It's a deliberate insult. Covert Ops always resented Sentinel abilities. Here and now, they're taking charge."

Captain Anastu stood up off the side bench. "It isn't too late to scramble those fighters, sir. Tavkel said we were free to—"

"No." As Father glanced back down at the desktop, the lines on his forehead shifted in parallel. Kiel thought he faintly felt the man's alarm. "Wind." His voice rose in pitch. "Everyone. Look. From Thyrica."

Kiel sprang off the bench and hustled closer. The last signal from Thyrica had been a code—he'd prearranged it himself, months ago—to scatter and hide in a final emergency. Could he hope the alert had been canceled?

No. This text reported another genuine catastrophe. People were being rounded up and subjected—willingly or not—to Tallis's new medical "cure" for being born with an ayin.

Kiel turned to Wind's aide. "Captain, would you please find my wife and bring her here, if she's able to join us?" Whatever happened next, they should be together. And where was Annalah? This new outrage had to be relayed to Cousin Rinnah, so she could declare it to the Federacy. Perhaps it was not too late to remove whoever was in charge of these events. Most Federates would oppose anything that looked like genocide. Tavkel couldn't disapprove that, could he?

The aide glanced aside.

"Go," Wind murmured. "In fact, if you can find all our spouses, please do. Have everyone gather here."

The aide nodded. She saluted the High Commander and hurried out.

Even with Boh-Dabar among them, this was terrifying. Kiel looked around. "Where's Tavkel?"

His father gestured toward the waterside. "He's been in the fielding station. You heard that he asked us to deactivate the net?"

"Of course. And . . . you concurred?"

"It goes against the grain, even knowing who he is. But yes, I supported the decision."

Did Tavkel mean them harm after all? The thought flickered through Kiel's mind before he could stop it. *We are called to serve and obey,* he reminded himself. Still . . . "Does he know about Urnock, the Covert Ops man?"

His father backed toward the far wall. "We just found out. But maybe he does know. We don't know all the Holy One shows him."

Wind drummed her fingers on her desktop. "Our guest—Meris." She reached toward the controls along another monitor panel. "She's in the med suite. Her handheld is there, at least."

Kiel had known for years that subtronic items could be tracked from this office. "Yes. I had been sending families there to pick up aid kits. I'm authorizing one to launch," he decided aloud. "Right now."

"Then let's keep Meris there for the moment."

"Why?" Kiel asked.

His father shook his head. "I agree with Wind. We don't want her in here, not yet. Not until we know whether she would help us or hinder us."

Kiel waited for Wind to speak again, but for several seconds she only sat staring at the desk. Finally she said, "Father, something alarmed you when you spoke with Jorah the other day. What was it?"

Father rubbed his old scar again. "Nothing I could say for certain, so I said nothing. I don't have the abilities I used to have. For the first time, I miss them."

Wind sat stiffly. "He was in Federate hands for some time. We still had Sentinels in charge of SOOC back then, the same ones who ordered Kin executed. Could Jorah have been . . ."

"Watch-linked?" Father murmured. "Put under surveillance?"

Kiel heard the chill in his father's voice. Watch-link was illegal. Only the Shuhr had used it indiscriminately.

"If that were so," Father continued, "wouldn't Tavkel have already healed it?"

Wind covered her eyes. Kiel rested a hand on her shoulder. She was Jorah's mother, as well as being Sanctuary Administrator. "We assume he would have," she said. "But . . ." She trailed off, then seemed to remember Kiel was there. "Maybe we make too many assumptions. Pray for us, Kiel. We can't afford a mistake now. This is the hour when we must show the Whorl who we really are—and Who we serve."

CHAPTER 35

The landing craft set down softly on marshy terrain, and Urnock's staff scrambled to expand its stabilization legs and push-out bulkheads. Urnock went uplevel to take charge of the glass-domed command bridge, while Zeimsky and his staff headed outdoors to set up a water purification rig. It could take weeks to treat everyone here, after all. Since the Sentinels had allowed this craft to land unhindered, maybe they all would cooperate and be cured.

All but the ones on the list, naturally.

Piper Gambrel cocooned himself in the chair on the main level and meditated on the frailty of human existence. Urnock would handle enforcement details from that pop-out command bridge, his temporary SOOC HQ, but Gambrel's section included the boarding ramp. Anyone coming aboard would pass under his scrutiny—and his god-voice's. It would help him maintain authority over the mission, particularly during the risky opening moves.

After precisely two hours of comm silence, as per Urnock's request, Gambrel headed up to Urnock's bridge via the module's central lift. An unfamiliar female voice filled the bridge as he settled in the left chair.

On the monitor, he was pleased to see a head-and-shoulders image of the local administrator. Black and grey hair surrounded her face. Her personal history, displayed beside the communication screen, confirmed her Shuhr heritage. The High Commander apparently had gone elsewhere. This woman—a descendant of pure and powerful evil, aligned now with the Thyrian Sentinels—was everything Federates feared.

No one would blame Gambrel's team for taking down any operation she headed, at the slightest hint of resistance.

He pulled his handheld off his belt and made sure Wind Haworth-Caldwell's name appeared on the list for elimination.

"Yes," Urnock said to her, "the ITD you requested will be shuttled there shortly. Please be patient. Stand by for further announcements."

"Oh, Chancellor Gambrel." She raised her voice, apparently spotting him. "We would like to discuss—"

Gambrel flicked a finger at the comm tech, who obediently cut the connection. "You were finished, I assume." Gambrel raised an eyebrow at Urnock.

"Want to ask for volunteers yet? Or are you going to give me enough time to set up a defensible base here?"

"I'll wait." Gambrel saw the wisdom in Urnock's request. He would demand their cooperation after delivering the ITD.

Part of it, anyway. "Anything from the *Squall*?"

Urnock had a bland face and a high forehead, and his Tallan greys made them look florid. "A RIA burst sent to our ground contact was confirmed effective. If you need him, he's ready."

Gambrel smiled sadly, wishing he could have recruited Jorah Caldwell to serve voluntarily instead of having to use him unawares. Still, alternate plans were necessities of war—and he would see that Urnock used Jorah humanely, with a minimum of collateral damage.

Actually, by fleeing here the Sentinels had guaranteed the isolation of this encounter, minimizing collateral damage to every normal human being. Others might have been put at risk if they'd had to be hunted down world by world.

Urnock eyed the main monitor. "It still would be simpler to wipe them out from orbit. You're risking my troops. And for what?"

Gambrel bristled. "The Federacy, like the Collegium, was founded on humane principles. We will persuade them to cooperate, if at all possible. This is for their benefit as much as ours."

We have to find Tavkel first anyway, the god-voice reminded him.

Gambrel formed an answering thought. *Today.*

As if in reply, satisfaction flowed through him like warmed honey.

A monitor several places to his left lit with unintelligible data— military, no doubt. Urnock swiveled toward it.

"Your hovercraft's up and running," Urnock announced. "And the *Squall* will be standing by. Go grab yourself some volunteers."

"Not yet." Gambrel eyed the time lights at the monitor's edge. They were almost due for another astrophysics report. "We want them to ask for that ITD again before we agree to deliver it. Make it clear we're in charge." First, establish authority. Second, deliver the disk itself—and promise the rest of it in exchange for a first group of twelve volunteers.

Then start to end the Sentinel menace.

• • •

Wind's office felt crowded as they waited out the silence. Kiel stood close enough to Hanusha to feel her warmth, though he barely sensed her presence. After all, he had declined retraining his ayin powers. He gripped his bundle of prayer cloths in his left hand. His brother Kinnor stood with their mother against the far wall—how strange, to see them getting along so well after all those decades of arguments—while Colonel Harris occupied a stool on Wind's right side, apparently watching her desk displays.

Their final mission would be simple: Get Tavkel the ITD, so he could send out his full declaration to the Whorl. Everyone must see and hear him.

Of all the people in Wind's office, Tavkel looked the most relaxed. He sat on a side bench, eyes lowered as if praying. Annalah had claimed the touchboard at the desk's far end again. She was writing rapidly.

Kinnor cleared his throat. Kiel noted that he'd changed out of his unauthorized uniform into a work shirt. A grease spot on his shoulder suggested he'd been in the hangar when Wind's aide had summoned him. "What if Urnock sends down more than just one module?" Kinnor frowned at Father, who sat on Wind's left. "That hauler's capable of carrying three or four landing crafts of that rating. We have the same right as any other Federate people to defend ourselves."

Kiel nodded. Colonel Harris's scan had shown fifty-one people on board the lander. A second or third module might bring additional troops, not to mention whatever weaponry remained in orbit.

Father glanced aside without answering.

Tavkel leaned on his walking stick. "Don't show force. Don't show fear."

"Well." Kinnor glared. "We've still got power in Hangar Three. But if we're going to get one last transport away—or maybe a squadron—we want to launch now, before they can target the whole complex from low orbit."

Kiel's mother nodded. She wasn't in uniform, but she seemed fully alert, even edgy. And today she stood with Kinnor, apparently supporting him.

Kiel clutched the prayer cloths. Tavkel didn't want a battle. But it would take the crews very little time to prep those fighters in H-3.

Wind snatched a handheld off her desktop. She'd been in touch with a refugee group fleeing on foot. Kiel braced for bad news, but she kept her voice steady when she spoke into it. "No. Don't keep any other record of who's going with you, or where the other groups might be. If we're attacked, I will not hand Colonel Urnock a directory of our people."

Kiel pursed his lips. Some of the College youngsters he'd brought here from Thyrica might be their families' last survivors.

The handheld blatted again. This time, Wind handed it across the desk to Tavkel.

"Good idea," he said. To Kiel's surprise, he set down the handheld and left without another word.

Kiel stepped toward the desk. "What?"

Wind shifted on her chair. "One of the children just mentioned finding some caves down the valley. Pieters suggested moving as many animals there as we can."

And Wind had just approved of Tavkel, the trained herdsman, taking charge of that instead of staying in this office? Did Tavkel really feel that this little command team could handle Chancellor Piper Gambrel, a Special Operations Oversight Committee under Covert Ops control, and whoever else the Federacy had sent?

Apparently so. Especially if his victory was going to look like defeat.

It took all Kiel's self-control to stand his own bit of ground, knowing what Tavkel had predicted for him personally, and the implied threat to everyone else here. He had warned Hanusha. Still, if death itself couldn't beat Tavkel, no one and nothing could truly harm his people.

He closed both hands around the prayer cloths. *Keep us all calm, Eternal Speaker. We live in your hands. Every day of our lives.*

"All right." Wind reached toward the desk. "Obviously, they're waiting for us to ask again before they'll discuss the actual delivery."

"Don't," Kinnor said, almost growling. "Urnock's playing dominance games, and we still don't know for sure what Gambrel's up to. Don't play along."

Wind raised her head, looking calm. "We aren't playing. But I'm open to suggestions." She glanced in Kiel's direction.

Kiel shook his head. "We need an ITD. They hold the monopoly. That gives them the right to name the price. It's likely to be steep, so don't even ask. Just agree to whatever they want to charge. If we can get Tavkel a disk, this universe might not last long enough for the bill to come due."

"Right." She touched her desktop and cleared her throat. "This is Administrator Haworth-Caldwell, asking again to speak with Chancellor Gambrel."

Lapping noises flowed through the open door arch. Out in the Sanctuary's heart, the water still made its calming music.

"He's making us wait," Kinnor muttered. "Manipulating us."

Standing beside Kin, Mother nodded.

Kiel impulsively slid his right arm around Hanusha's waist. She wrapped her arm around him in return. She'd never been a demonstrative woman, and he'd never needed public affection. Today felt different.

"Administrator." A voice out of the desk startled him. He heard arrogance in that tone. As he glanced around the circle at shoulders that suddenly bent forward, he knew he wasn't the only one. "This is the Chancellor."

Wind settled her posture. She fingered the transmission control and addressed the inbuilt pickup. "Sir, we would gratefully take possession of the Instantaneous Transceiver Disk you have brought, and we would be pleased to confer with you regarding the future of this Sanctuary, preferably at a neutral location."

She ended her transmission but kept the connection. Again, the first response was silence. "He won't do that," Kinnor snapped.

Wind raised her head. "Of course he won't. He wants to get inside. But I'm willing to concede that request for a parley on neutral ground. So if I back off from that request, he's likelier to concede us the ITD, don't you think?"

Kinnor frowned. Kiel wasn't sure whether his brother disagreed or just didn't follow.

"Tell me." An odd tone overlaid the disembodied voice this time. Startled, Kiel listened closely. He'd heard several of the man's recorded lectures. Underlying the obvious arrogance, he now heard an odd, striking harshness as the voice spoke again. "Where is this person we've been hearing about? This Tavkel Caldwell—do we have the name right? Put him on the transceiver. Still better, a visual monitor. Now."

Had Tavkel ever actually used that surname?

A second observation blasted that one out of Kiel's mind: He'd heard that vocal tone before. He stiffened.

Tamím! The Mikuhran who had kidnapped him, decades ago, had spoken with the same odd edge. The demonic shadow possessing Tamím had mistaken Kiel for the Holy Speaker's Boh-Dabar. The same shadow might still be looking for Boh-Dabar, wanting to destroy or corrupt him—

And this time, it had found him! "Wind, wait! Gambrel is—"

"I'm sorry." Wind leaned toward the desk and spoke steadily. "He's not here at the moment."

. . . Miraculously! Wind could answer honestly, and the orbiting RIA team would have to tell Colonel Urnock that she'd told the truth. Tavkel had left in the nick of time. It felt like one more small assurance that they remained in capable hands, one more reminder that Kiel wouldn't always understand the things Tavkel did . . . until later. Maybe not even then.

Hanusha's arm tightened around his waist. Kiel silently prayed again, *You are in charge, Holy One, even if they overrun this holy place. Protect your children. Give us courage. The courage to lose, if need be—to give back everything you've loaned us, including our lives.*

Still, he needed to tell Wind—

But Captain Anastu, Annalah, and Colonel Harris didn't know about Tamím. He hesitated.

Wind kept speaking. "We do, however, have another guest at Hesed House. Meris Cariole, an Elysian citizen, has offered to serve as liaison between our two parties. She is a non-Thyrian member of your Collegium for Human Learning. Would you find that appropriate, a way to open our talks, if she remains willing?"

Kinnor turned to Wind. "Don't send her alone. I'll go as a bodyguard."

The other voice said, "Stand by."

Wind looked up. "Good idea, Kin. But you're the last person I want to give to the new SOOC. You were executed on SOOC's orders. They'd lock you up the second they saw you."

"They could try." Kinnor tilted his head. "But I can still—"

"I'm not bodyguard trained." Wind's aide pushed up off the stone bench. "But I can handle myself pretty well. And I agree, it's a good idea." She glanced across at Kinnor. "I hate to think they would hurt Meris, but they might. Send two of us. Send a sekiyr," she added, brightening. "Chancellor Gambrel is supposed to be excited about the learning process, isn't he? It's the *Collegium for Human Learning* that he heads. So let him prove it."

"Maybe." Wind frowned. "But only volunteers . . ."

Kinnor stepped away from the desk and strode deeper into the office, toward the private inner door. "I've seen all I can take."

Kiel braced for another confrontation between his brother and sister-in-law.

Wind raised a hand and turned to her right. "Colonel Harris, go with Kinnor. Get ready to launch whatever you can. Kinnor's right. And Captain Anastu, thank you. You'll go with Meris to speak with the Chancellor. We have to protect her, after all. But you know what they're doing to our people at Thyrica. They could well be getting set up to do it here."

Captain Anastu squared her shoulders. "Yes. I know. And I—"

Kinnor paused just short of the private door, raised his chin, and—to Kiel's relief—saluted his wife.

"Yes." The disembodied desktop voice finally spoke again. "Meris Cariole is approved as liaison."

Colonel Harris stood and followed Kinnor into the private tunnel. That left a smaller group: Kiel and Hanusha, Wind, his parents, Annalah, and Captain Anastu.

"Thank you, Chancellor." Wind spoke toward the pickup and then finally cut the connection. "Annalah, please go tell Meris I'll want to speak with her. Have her wait about an hour."

Annalah left through the main door arch.

Now! "I have to tell you something." Kiel spoke quickly, hoping his nerve wouldn't fail. "Years ago on Mikuhr, the man who abducted me was shadow-possessed. His voice changed whenever the shadow took charge. And I just heard that voice again. Chancellor Gambrel is under a shadow's influence. Perhaps even the same one."

"Here?" Wind looked slightly frantic. "On our Sanctuary world—do you think Tavkel knows?"

"He must." Kiel glanced up at the streamers. Years ago, Wind had told him that her earliest memory was of looking up at such streamers inside her clan's home on Mikuhr. "And the shadow—if it's the same one—has been here before. It brought me here from Mikuhr . . ." he turned to eye Hanusha . . ."to spy on you and Annalah."

Hanusha nodded. He'd told her about that too.

"So . . ." Kiel stepped to Wind's desk. "Maybe this is why Tavkel warned us not to resist, or risk losing his chance at the ITD."

Captain Anastu shook her head. "I don't see the connection."

He couldn't expect her to understand. She'd never seen a shadow's power to deceive.

Wind shut her eyes. "I'm no strategist. All I can do is obey Tavkel."

Kiel walked closer. He rested a hand on her shoulder. "Perhaps that's exactly why he put you here, now, in this position. Maybe you were born for this hour. Maybe we all were."

"And do we tell Meris? About the shadow," Wind added.

"You can try." Kiel shook his head. "But she will not believe you."

"What, Captain Anastu?" Wind looked past him, toward her aide. "I'm sorry. We interrupted you."

"I just know who else you should send with us. Piet Keeson. He'll risk it in memory of Terza Shirak."

• • •

Chancellor Gambrel had landed?

He's here!

Meris read the news in the med center via her handheld. She dashed to her quarters and changed into one of the nicer outfits she'd brought from Elysia, a med-yellow blouse with soft grey slacks. She re-read her old, personal written message from the Chancellor: . . . *unexpected spiritual claims . . . act as if you believe him.* Jorah had been ordered to play Boh-Dabar, hadn't he? Oddly, things hadn't turned out that way at all.

She ventured into the commons for a quick cup of kass. Sekiyrra scurried in all directions. One little group—three adults and five who looked to be in their teens—dashed toward the hangar area, carrying duffels. She would have liked to stop and reassure them, but she'd promised the Minster she'd wait in the med suite.

Back inside, she slipped her lab tunic over her blouse. They matched perfectly. *He's here!* To occupy her time, she double-checked Saried's cabinet inventories. She had given general aid kits to several more people who had arrived dressed to travel. Some of them had terror in their eyes.

Of all the inexplicable things she'd seen here, their negative reaction to Chancellor Gambrel's arrival grieved her the most. She should have explained more of his teachings. She should have told more people about his desire to lead humankind in better directions. Anything to prevent this.

Yet apparently Tavkel disagreed. Meris hoped their fears wouldn't lead to aggression. *Fear cannot conquer. I walk past it and through . . .*

She especially should've tried harder to communicate with Jorah. If only they'd been on the same side in all this, they could have had a future together—maybe—mightn't they?

As she stood distributing antivirals into another set of empty tubs, some of Tavkel's eeriest words meandered through her mind. *Once there was a little girl, years ago . . .* What had that second fable meant, the one about the girl who had inadvertently killed her beloved pet? Was it significant that the pet had looked like a meat eater? Or was it central that the girl had trained her own pet to eat the wrong food? *It broke her heart,* she heard in Tavkel's voice, *to realize she had helped kill it.*

That man's voice stuck in a person's memory. It had to be one of his gifts.

And food had to be the key. They didn't eat as much meat here as back home. Looking carnivorous symbolized . . . what, the rest of the Federacy? Maybe Chancellor Gambrel was the pet? These people thought he was a carnivorous monster, but she knew he really wasn't. Maybe the people here were symbolized by the girl in the story.

She snapped a lid on another aid kit and added it to the stack on the examining table before she continued rechecking Saried's general operating inventory. She immediately turned up a discrepancy. The inventory showed twenty-three units of immune system tonic on hand, but a visual count turned up just twenty-one. Overcrowding and panic had apparently made the Sentinels careless.

Still—she sipped from her kass mug—she had *liked* most of these people, these folks who were now panicking. She'd eaten with them and joined them at that waterside concert. Again, Jorah Caldwell's face appeared in her mind. She recalled how good it had felt to lean against him. Warm. Comfortable.

Yet he'd claimed that the Chancellor . . . *means to kill us all, Meris.*

She pushed the thought away. Jorah should have known better. He'd actually met the man!

And he'd given his heart to Tavkel, while Meris's loyalty remained Collegiate.

Really, she couldn't wait to get out of here. She could catch her long-delayed ride to Tallis now, with Chancellor Gambrel and his people. She'd hoped to impress Chancellor Gambrel with a small flock of Collegiate converts, but she hadn't made one. All of her possible converts had turned to Tavkel instead.

Including Jorah. How sad for them both. Still . . . *I am the spark of undying light. I shall see. I shall know.*

Another set of light footsteps approached in the corridor. *This family sent the mother,* she guessed, reaching for the closest aid kit.

Instead, Annalah hustled through the door, hair loose over her work clothes. "Where've you been?" Meris exclaimed. Then she looked at the clothes again. "You aren't leaving too, are you?"

Annalah eyed the stack of aid kits. "No, I have work to do. My family's staying, all of us. But Aunt Wind asked me to tell you the

Chancellor's shuttle is down. They're working out how to talk to each other."

"Yes. I offered to—"

"Right. To liaise. They've all approved it. But Aunt Wind wants you to stay right here for an hour, please. There are all kinds of . . . preparations going on out on the poolside."

Meris wanted to dance. She would meet the Chancellor in person! "Annalah, there's nothing to be frightened of. Nothing! Doesn't anyone believe me? The Chancellor is an outstanding human being. He isn't here to harm anyone."

"I know—that you believe that," Annalah said, apparently seeing Meris's momentary hope. "How could you think any differently? You're you, with your background and heritage and . . . well, your illusions."

Meris bristled. "And you don't—"

"Of course. We all have them. But we've chosen Tavkel's wisdom over the Chancellor's, and Tavkel has warned us to expect some frightening things. He does know the future, sometimes—"

Meris folded her arms. She'd learned a great deal on this planet. "But if he can predict the future, that's *keshef*. Sorcery. Right?"

Annalah cringed. "Well . . . yes, for us normal people. But—"

"You? Normal?"

Annalah ignored her. "But the future is *his* to know. Not ours. Meris, go to him. We don't know what Chancellor Gambrel's here to do. Uncle Kinnor thinks he'll attack us, and he isn't the only one who thinks that. There are others who think he wants to make us all like Jorah . . . or worse. But even if we aren't attacked, nobody's going to live forever. Tavkel has beaten death, and anyway, there are things that are worth dying for."

"Annalah, he'll never—"

"Listen to me! We've always been servants, my people. And now I've found somebody really worth serving. Look what he did for

Uncle Kinnor, and before that, for Grandfather. And you've heard the things he says. The things he teaches."

Meris shook her head sadly. Annalah had once seemed such a hopeful prospect for Collegiate wisdom. She had passed beyond its reach. "Good luck, then. And thank you for an amazing experience here. Maybe I'll see you later, when this all blows over." She didn't want to have parting words that would leave Annalah too embarrassed to come back later, admitting she'd been wrong.

Annalah stood for a moment, looking as if she wanted to say more. "Thank you," she mumbled. She hurried out.

Almost an hour later, Saried's message board gave off a shrill tone. Letters appeared: *Meris, please report to the Minster's office.*

Meris spread the remaining aid kits on the exam table and covered them with a hand-written sign that said, "Take one per family of four." She hung her lab coat on the peg and paused in the freshing room to knot back and smooth her hair. Satisfied, she headed out. *He might even be here, right here at the compound.*

Out on the waterside, far to her left, two uniformed Sentinels stood near the Chapter room door, looking as if they were standing guard. Although it would soon be lunch time, the dining commons was strangely empty. She didn't spot anyone else on the poolside walkway or out on the stepping stones, either. Those who were scattering must've all gone.

She swung into the Minster's office and looked for Jorah amid the small crowd she found there.

He was obviously elsewhere. Minster Wind, three Sentinels in uniform, and the Shamarr stood together near the data desk. Even the Shamarr's wife was present, standing with her arm around him. Normally, that woman showed all the warm affection of a stasis patient. Maybe in Hanusha's case, it was possible to be improved by fear. Meris half-smiled at the woman and stepped closer to Minster Wind.

A surface panel gleamed on the desk. There could be a conversation ongoing.

Meris cleared her throat anyway. "You called me? Annalah said the Chancellor has arrived, and I'm approved as a liaison."

That panel faded to dark. Meris held back a second wave of disappointment. Besides having missed Jorah, she wasn't going to see the Chancellor yet. *The eternal is in me. I cannot know defeat . . .*

"Yes, Meris." Were those new worry lines on Minster Wind's forehead? "He asked for you."

"He?" she squeaked. She deliberately lowered her voice. "You do mean Chancellor Gambrel, don't you?"

"He's here with a force of fifty. We did inform him some time ago that you're here." Minster Wind gestured Meris toward an empty chair. The others stepped back a bit. "Remember, we DeepScanned Tallis when you arrived. Under normal circumstances, we would have evacuated you to Tallis much sooner."

Meris recognized an apology when she heard one. The Minster was making sure Meris took a good report to Chancellor Gambrel. She sat down. "Minster Wind, I haven't forgotten. You've been as gracious as possible, considering . . . our natural differences." She looked around the office again, noting another conspicuous absence: Tavkel. "Chancellor Gambrel asked for me, specifically?"

"Yes. We allowed him and his party to land." The Minster emphasized the word *allowed,* and Meris got the point. Trying to land here had always been forbidden. "They're a little ways upriver. Your offer to serve as liaison sounded good to both sides. I wanted to make sure your offer still stands."

"Yes!"

"We'll send you with an escort, of course." Minster Wind touched a spot on her desktop, and the light reappeared. "Chancellor Gambrel's party, this is the Sanctuary Administrator. I've spoken with Meris Cariole. She would be pleased to serve as a go-between."

Meris craned her neck and tried to see the monitor. She sat at just the wrong angle, so she got up and strode around the desk.

The young man who looked out of the desktop seemed to be a low-ranking aide. "We're sending a hovercraft downriver to your landing strip."

The Minster answered quickly. "Wait! We have ground rovers. They don't tear up the terrain so badly. I'll send one—"

The aide shrugged. "The hovercraft just left. It should be there in six minutes." The desk went dark.

Hanusha Caldwell groaned. "They're going to destroy a whole swath of natural growth—either that, or our crop fields!"

Meris turned to head out, but Shamarr Kiel touched her arm. "Meris, they came here to deliver some advanced new communication technology for Tavkel to use. A large disk, something they call an ITD. Are you familiar with it?"

"Only what I've heard here." How many days had she been isolated? Thirty, at least. Was this "ITD" old news out in the Whorl?

"We're counting on you." The Shamarr leaned toward her. "We need one of those disks, to plead our case to the Federacy. We're being attacked on other worlds, and some of us believe we'll be attacked here too. Please help us. After all, the Federacy was founded—"

"On open communication and mutual respect among all peoples." It irked her that even Shamarr Kiel seemed to think he needed to plead. "We learned that quote as children, Shamarr. Of course he's bringing you an ITD. And of course, he's honoring you by bringing it himself. The riots on Thyrica were an unauthorized rabble. He'll prove it. It's going to be fine." She turned to Minster Wind, who still looked appallingly desperate. "You'll see. Finally, things are going to be settled between you people and Tallis."

The Shamarr stared at her for several seconds. "Meris, he . . . he could be under the influence of spiritual beings. Ones who are hostile to humanity. And especially to Tavkel."

She resisted the temptation to laugh. He looked so serious, standing there. He honestly cared about her. "I know what you believe, Shamarr. Please respect my beliefs too."

He nodded slowly and raised a hand. "Go with the Holy One's blessing, then. May he guide and protect you."

Minster Wind raised her hands to waist level. "Yes, go with all our hopes. And two escorts. Follow me, please."

CHAPTER 36

Meris strode out the access door and across the landing strip, barely containing her excitement. A silver-blue hovercraft had already landed. It looked big enough to hold about twenty people, a snub-nosed transport with a transparent cockpit. It stood with its hatch wide and welcoming. A Federate crew had arrived to take her to Chancellor Gambrel, and she couldn't help thinking of this hovercraft as her ride back to all that was familiar. To her left, on the hillside that she'd so often seen dotted with task teams, only the tall grass moved back and forth. On her right, just a few cross-space shuttles remained under their shrouds. Overhead, clouds were blowing in.

It felt bizarre to be walking with bodyguards—young Piet and Minster Wind's aide, Captain Anastu—but on the other hand, how wonderful that they'd volunteered to be the first people here to actually meet Chancellor Gambrel. They walked close behind her. She turned and gave them an enthusiastic smile, and as she did, she caught sight of the peaks once again. How marvelous that the Chancellor was getting to see this magnificent valley!

They'd almost reached the hovercraft when Captain Anastu came up behind her. "Meris." She spoke softly. "Let me board first."

"All right." Meris gave the woman high marks for courage, but she knew what Captain Anastu plainly didn't: There was nothing to fear.

So she slowed down and let the Sentinel pass. Two heads peered out from the cockpit, but no one debarked. Obviously Hesed House's sanctity was being respected, although the Federates had been given clearance to land on Procyel II.

Positively lightheaded with delight, Meris wanted to gloat. *See? They're honoring terms. There is nothing to be afraid of.*

As if answering, a strange voice spoke at the back of her mind. *Don't be so sure, Meris.*

Startled, she whipped around and eyed young Piet, the sekiyr who was coming. He was the same curly-headed young man who'd looked familiar in the shearing shed. She opened her mouth to reprimand him for reading her thoughts and even subvocalizing to her. But just then, Captain Anastu reappeared at the boarding hatch.

"Come on up," Captain Anastu said. "Meris first. Then you, Piet."

Meris hustled up the short ramp and into the hovercraft's main cabin. It had seating for about twenty, with cushiony folding seats and a wide aisle. It looked like she and her escorts would be the only passengers. She took a window seat on the aisle's far side. Captain Anastu sat down behind her, Piet in front of her. Now she remembered: Piet had been the one who had wanted to study with MedSpec Saried's mother, Terza Shirak.

It seemed like months ago.

"Please be sure your restraints are secured." The disembodied voice came from overhead. Meris checked her seat and shoulder harnesses as the hatch slid down to shut them in. Interior fans whooshed. There was a leap that made her stomach lurch as the craft rose on vertical thrusters. It steered straight downhill toward the river, to her surprise, tearing a path through tall bushes.

"Hey!" Captain Anastu shouted. "There's no need to destroy this much greenery. Hey! Can you hear me up there?"

The craft turned sharply north. Looking out her west-facing window, Meris realized they were following the Tuva River. Its other bank had already been reduced to a muddy swath by the hovercraft's flight out here, and she couldn't help remembering the patch of lilies Jorah had identified. They wouldn't bloom this year.

Still, there weren't any roads in this direction. The river probably was just the best route. Aloud, she asked, "Why do you suppose they brought an air-cushion craft instead of gravidics?"

Piet turned around in his seat. "Lighter to transport? Or maybe just because they cause more damage."

"Piet." Captain Anastu spoke sharply. "No provocations."

They had to be terribly nervous, to argue when there could be strangers listening from the cockpit. Meris spoke up. "Well, the ground's probably soft, so I suppose they have to use the opposite bank until the first side dries out. And plants grow back." It was just vegetation, after all. Part of the physical world, and therefore meaningless. She couldn't wait to talk Collegium with people again, to honor the eternal spark in those other spirits without being constantly reminded by Thyrians that "physicality is important . . ."

Yet in a way, they'd been right. It had strengthened her spirit to taste fresh food, to guhsh the brown dirt, and to lean against Jorah's warm chest—

"These things can travel over water." Piet sounded huffy. "They don't need to use the riverbank at all. And some of these species don't grow anywhere else. What if we're blasting roots away?"

Simultaneously, Captain Anastu's subvoice tickled her brain. *The driver hasn't been told any details at all about you, Meris. I think they're afraid Piet and I might mind-access them en route. We terrify them. That's why they're here, you know.*

Meris hastily refocused her thoughts on the moment. She formed a careful response, thinking deliberately in words instead of concepts. Now, she realized that the lightheadedness she'd felt on the walk out to this hovercraft had actually been the odd prickly nausea they'd told her about. *So you actually mind-accessed the crew? Through a bulkhead?*

They're sitting close to it, Captain Anastu answered. *We're assigned to protect you, as well as the Sanctuary. They're hiding things, even from you.*

Meris twisted around in her seat. She sent Captain Anastu a furious frown, then faced forward again. *Get out of my mind.* She thought the words distinctly, even though she hoped Captain Anastu had already stopped listening. The lightheaded sensation had dissipated.

But had Captain Anastu been listening a few moments earlier, when that memory of listening to the concert with Jorah had flitted through her mind?

Outside the window, those jagged peaks had shifted visibly under the clouds. The hovercraft had picked up impressive speed.

Meris tried to settle in and enjoy the ride.

● ● ●

Jorah had stood beside a shed and watched Meris stroll out the hangar door between those two volunteers. He'd offered to escort her, of course. His mother had kept him back—needed him here, she'd said, but Jorah guessed that she also knew how badly he wanted to smack down that new SOOC colonel.

Based on your previous experience with Chancellor Gambrel, she had added, *we think you should be protected from the man. So please keep out of sight while they're here. Major Ryken will stay with you. See if they can use your help in H-3.*

So he was getting a bodyguard too—just one more frustration of having a mother in charge. At least if Major Ryken had seen how badly it hurt to watch Meris walk away, he wasn't letting on. Major Ryken—one of Tavkel's second circle people—hadn't shown any sign of listening in on his unshielded thoughts, either.

The hovercraft soared away, but Jorah stood there a little longer and stared downhill. He had to admire Captain Mel Anastu and Piet Keeson, who were walking knowingly into enemy territory. Each had swallowed a lifesigns transmitter. They hoped to send valuable data concerning the Federates' treatment of them.

Jorah could guess what they were in for. As Meris had stepped through the hovercraft's hatch, he'd shifted from one foot to the other, still unable to believe that she thought the Feds meant no harm here. She would find out the hard way, when they attacked— or started grabbing people—or both. If only he'd tried harder to show her how wrong she was about the Collegium. She was a good person, deep down where it mattered.

If he'd meant to get serious about her, that should've happened at least a week ago. Tavkel had warned him. He could've shown some compassion, instead of brushing her off.

Well—he shoved away from the weathered wooden wall— it was too late for that, and he couldn't wait to see what Tavkel pulled off, now that the enemy was here. Meris might come back to Hesed House for her belongings, but he might have seen the last of her. "Time to head indoors?" he asked Major Ryken. "Grab some lunch?"

He'd just learned that Major Ryken was forty-something, a friend of his dad's, and had been serving on Caroli. Major Ryken raised a hand. "Wait 'til they're out of sight."

The hovercraft slid away, snapping branches and tearing up ground. It looked deliberate. Jorah smacked the shed's wall, wishing he could do some damage to that hovercraft.

"That won't help. Let's get back to the hangar."

Jorah led downhill. The Sanctuary seemed quiet and empty after so many weeks of overcrowding. The main hangar's small access door stood open, so they went in through it and passed through H-1. Amid the crowd in Hangar Two, he caught a glimpse of his dad hurrying somewhere. Jorah pressed on into H-3, where those four FI-221s—small, nimble fighters often transported aboard carriers—were being re-prepped despite Tavkel's . . . had he called them "orders"?

Brilliant lights burned overhead. Several people pushed a blocky service unit alongside the craft parked in lead position. This hangar lay concealed under several meters of dense stone, and its launch door had been planted over with grass, a foresight that had seemed redundant just a few days ago.

Jorah snatched a ration bar from a side table—imagine, eating shipboard food at Hesed House!—and scrambled back up onto the slot fightercraft's wing. He'd been helping check ordnance circuitry when Colonel Harris had sent him and Major Ryken outdoors. He needed to finish that job now.

Major Ryken went back to work in the craft's cockpit; Jorah had been issued a gravidic probe that had to be applied to both ends of each onboard ordnance-related circuit, linking cockpit controls with its weaponry. On his handheld he checked the data he'd already entered. The hangar smelled like nervous sweat. Maybe he did too. He polished off the ration bar and went back to work.

He pressed one probe end against the wing's base and one to a surface laser cannon, and he touched the "check" control. Unexpectedly, a red zero flashed on its display as he checked the first circuit. "Hey," he muttered.

He'd probably missed one of the sweet spots. After all, he hadn't been trained as a crewer. "Come on, come on." He pressed the probe's ends down again. He fired the circuit. He got another zero.

He stared, wondering if he should send his dad the data. These ships had sat for years, serviced by military-option sekiyrra but rarely flown, since for secrecy's sake they were routed outside via H-2.

It was possible that the probe itself might be faulty. Jorah worked back up the wing, holding one end at the wing's base and sliding the other along the hull. He didn't want to screw up by rushing.

The circuit he'd checked a few minutes ago had also gone dead.

Major Ryken stood up in the cockpit. "Jorah, I'm getting some odd readings. I need to double check—"

That was actually a relief. "Me too."

His dad came running into H-3. "All techs, step down and stand away from your ships. We've suddenly got malfunctions everywhere."

Jorah slid off the wing and stood at attention. So it wasn't just him! The saboteur—what *was* he up to, and had he been caught at last?

At least he could stop suspecting Meris. She'd been under close watch all morning, and now she was gone.

Gone. But innocent. He clenched a fist in frustration.

A uniformed woman dashed in, Captain Jamee Mattason. He recognized her as another recent arrival, like Major Ryken. Without wasting a moment, Captain Mattason reached toward the first crewer's forehead for mind access. She moved down the line quickly. Jorah's turn lasted just a few seconds, and she moved on.

He spotted a third person standing at the door arch. Someone in brown work clothes.

Tavkel—down here in military country? Jorah hung his head, vaguely embarrassed. Tavkel had said they were *free*, right? Free to be ready to offer resistance, at least.

"Sentinel Mattason?" Tavkel called.

The intelligence woman turned toward him, frowning.

Tavkel stepped the rest of the way into H-3. "There's no need to look for a saboteur. All weapons in the Procyel system are inoperable now. It's my doing."

She whirled back. "What?"

Jorah remained at attention, impressed beyond anything he'd previously seen. So that was what Tavkel was up to! When he put down the Federates, he wanted it clear that he had done it all by himself.

Colonel Harris hustled in through the arch. He stopped beside Tavkel, his uniform tunic showing sweat stains. "What?" he echoed Captain Mattason.

Tavkel spread his hands, looking unflustered and unhurried. "All weapons. From shipborne ordnance down to hand weapons. Both sides. All parties. No one's weapons will operate. There'll be no open conflict."

Colonel Harris raised his handheld and keyed rapidly. "All right. If the Feds can't shoot either, we're scattering another group of Sanctuary staff. A few volunteered to stay—but they're gone now. Crewers, get out there and prep those last shuttles."

Jorah nodded, liking Harris's decisive action.

Colonel Harris walked with Tavkel back into Hangar Two, conversing softly.

Jorah's dad clapped his hands. "You heard him, people. They're going to need two more atmospheric shuttles. Get outside. Make yourselves useful."

Jorah headed out with the others for H-2 and its open door to the landing strip.

• • •

Meris.

She was hearing voices again. This time, she didn't turn her head at the freakish sensation. It definitely arrived without nausea. *What?* she thought hard, wishing she'd asked more questions about the abilities of her two escorts. This voice felt like Captain Anastu's again. Firm, cocky.

Let's test them. Order the driver to turn around and take you back. Say you forgot your handheld or something. See how he reacts. Now, she felt lightheaded. The weird subvocal voice added, *Please?*

Meris touched her grey trousers belt. The handheld was there, a lump at one side of her waist. *Of course they don't tell their staff everything!* Irked, she wondered how many times her thoughts had been monitored while she was here on Procyel II, despite everyone's assurances. She didn't remember feeling this kind of oddness, but . . . still. *No. We'll talk with the Chancellor himself. He's an amazing man. You'll see.* She clenched her tongue between her right molars, wondering whether Captain Anastu would now demonstrate voice-command and try to make her speak to the driver.

After several seconds, Meris relaxed. Apparently they wouldn't be allowed to do that. Didn't they spend literally years memorizing those Codes, and didn't they spend the rest of their lives enslaved to them? She wished she'd sneaked a look at one of those Code books. She'd like to have known what they should and shouldn't do around the Chancellor. Surely, they would respect his mind's privacy. He was no one to be trifled with.

She'd never heard anything so ridiculous as Shamarr Kiel's accusation. Hostile spirits, of all things? Plainly, he was getting desperate. Grasping at straws in a last bid for her loyalty.

She smiled and stared out the window.

Abruptly the craft turned left toward the river, and the ride got smooth for a moment. Then the nose tilted uphill. She clutched her armrests and craned her neck, trying to see where they were heading. After half a minute they halted and seemed to hover, rotating in place. The bushy edge of another stretch of forest slid to the left. She hunkered down to peer out the windows on the far side. Not far away, in a biggish clearing, stood something that looked like it had been built for a frontier world. Four stories tall, it had long, gangling support legs protruding from all sides. Was that a Federate landing module?

And the Chancellor had to be inside! Meris smoothed her blouse. He'd traveled all the way from Tallis. It would be her job to make him welcome, to represent the Sentinels fairly but accurately when negotiations began. Even to mention her fears, regarding the intentions Tavkel might have toward the Federacy.

Something flashed into her mind—not that queer "other" voice, but the memory of Tavkel's. *Chancellor Gambrel is dangerous to my people. Also to you.*

How could he have said that? Chancellor Gambrel was a pillar of learning, of peace and empowerment. Unlike Tavkel, he wasn't positioned to muster a formerly dead army! Furthermore, the biological injustice that had been done to these people's innocent ancestors could be undone now, thanks to Collegiate research. Just like Jorah, they all could become normal human beings, free from their Codes, their uncanny powers and their archaic "path." She and Jorah might still pioneer a cross-cultural relationship, blessed by Chancellor Gambrel as well as Shamarr Caldwell . . .

The craft dropped a meter and rocked side to side. Its engines fell silent. Meris unbuckled. She smoothed her blouse again and waited for the hatch to open.

That took several minutes. After staring out her window until her neck hurt, she heard something whir behind her, right there in the cabin. She turned quickly. A man wearing the Collegium's dark green-grey stepped past her, headed forward down the aisle. "Please follow me, Meris. Your escorts may come if they like, or they may remain on board."

She looked around. He hadn't entered through the hatch. Apparently he'd been traveling in the tail section, probably to protect her from the Sentinels, who had thought they were protecting her from people like himself.

She smiled at the silliness of it all and followed him to the hovercraft's hatch, where she saw the reason for the delay. A walkway had been laid down between this craft and the tall landing module.

The module was so big that for a moment, she wondered how large the spacecraft had been that the Federate force had traveled in.

That did not matter. Within moments, she would meet him in the flesh. *I guess the flesh does matter . . . emotionally, anyway.*

She stared across to the landing module. The walkway had a slight undulation. It had been laid atop unleveled wet ground. They wouldn't muddy their feet, and she appreciated that too. She turned around. "Coming?"

Captain Anastu was doing something to a weapon in her holster. How rude, to carry weapons so openly. Still, she was trying to act like a bodyguard. "I'll be right there. Something's . . . odd . . . with this . . ."

Meris smiled and shook her head. Captain Anastu and Piet the sekiyr could do as they liked. She inhaled a deep breath and followed the crew member onto the walkway.

At its other end, a sloping ramp rose toward the module. The stranger stopped at the base of the ramp and let her catch up. "This way," he said. "Chancellor Gambrel will speak with you immediately. And your escort is welcome, of course."

Meris didn't turn around, but she felt vaguely odd again. She thought words at Sentinel Anastu: *See? Chancellor Gambrel is absolutely honorable.*

Tell that to my stun pistol. It's malfunctioning. They're using some kind of disruption field to disarm us, Meris. We're probably walking into an ambush. We can't do you much good with our bare hands, but we're here for you with those hands.

Now she turned around. Both Anastu and Piet were right behind her. Mentally she formed an answer. *Stop worrying! You fear what you only imagine, you know.*

She turned forward. The crewer paused again atop the ramp. He stepped aside and gestured Meris through.

She took one more deep breath, five steps up and a hard left turn, and returned to the world she knew. Instead of white stone, she stood on tasteful black flooring surrounded by unostentatious grey metal paneling. The room had no windows but narrowed toward the back, where the far wall was black and shining and—

Oh, my. Between where she stood and that far wall, Chancellor Piper Gambrel rose out of a large chair. He walked forward, extending a hand.

She stepped forward to meet him.

She'd seen tri-D images, of course. In person, Chancellor Gambrel looked remarkably young for a man of such importance, beautifully fit for someone who wasted so little attention on physical matters. He wore a formal cutaway coat—she felt honored!—and that broad, famous smile. It made her feel truly welcome.

"Meris Cariole," he said, "thank you for answering my summons. Captain Anastu, Sekiyr Keeson, welcome to you as well." He gave them a quarter-bow and glanced toward her right, where the room opened into a corridor that led off to fore and aft. Might that be an elevator shaft in the middle?

No matter! "May I offer you all a beverage?" Chancellor Gambrel's voice was utterly familiar, like hearing an old friend.

Meris looked over her shoulder at the Thyrians. Again she thought at them, *Do you see how gracious he is? His staff could do that, but he—*

A picture of a giant spider flashed into her mind. Captain Anastu must have sent it. Some sort of warning, about poison perhaps, or about walking into a trap.

Meris stepped farther inside, to where the cabin widened. All the furniture was Collegiate grey-green—the large chair in front of the dark inner wall, a two-person lounger, and three lightweight side chairs. A staffer hurried in from the aft corridor, pushing a cart. A portable ChoiceMaster stood on it, fully loaded with drinkable treats. She selected an exotic tea she'd always loved. The Chancellor himself filled her cup from the spigot, and the aroma surrounded her with comforting memories.

Her body might still be standing on Procyel II, but her spirit had come home. She took the cup. "Thank you, sir. Thank you so much."

Apparently her escorts had declined. The Chancellor poured the same tea for himself, and the staffer wheeled the cart out of the room. Chancellor Gambrel held his cup one-handed and waved her to the lounger, which faced his chair and the dark inmost wall. The Thyrians walked around the lounger to stand behind her, remaining between her and the entry.

She no longer cared if they stood guard. This was a dream in awake-time. "Chancellor, I'm deeply honored to be here, to meet you." She set her cup on one of the lounger's broad arms. As she settled, the lounger shifted to support her weight. Something else she'd missed—form-response furniture!

Those were all physical things, though, as she reminded herself. She was above depending on them. She had done well without them. "Welcome," she said, "and thank you for coming to Procyel. On behalf of the Thyrians and on my own account, I look forward to serving you as their liaison."

He leaned toward her, his expression gravely dignified. "They haven't mistreated you, have they?"

Meris decided not to tell him they'd just been reading her thoughts. She shook her head. "No, sir. They've been quite solicitous."

"As they should be. You have been their honored guest."

She felt warm inside. "They made me welcome. I was frightened at first, of course." She glanced at the dark wall behind him. Near eye level was a workstation with several monitors.

"I can only imagine." His voice soothed, its tone sympathetic. "They are a frightening people." He looked straight at her, not at the Thyrians standing behind her. "You leaned upon your litanies, I'm sure."

"Of course. And I tried to pass them on, as I could."

He smiled, his cultured voice a balm after the Thyrians' odd accent. "With so much of your medical training complete, you were surely a great asset to them in many ways. I'm sure your parents are also proud, back on Elysia."

And he knew so much about her! She wanted to praise him in return, but she didn't want to offend him by fawning. She knew him for a humble man. She glanced down—the black deck had a textured, non-slip artificial surface—and back up at this man she'd admired for so long. "How shall we begin your discussions with them, sir? Would you like my impressions of them and their ways?"

"In time. First, we have questions about this new rising star they seem to be worshipping. This . . . Tavkel."

Feeling bold and comfortable—was it the scent of this luscious tea, or was it his magnetic presence?—she spoke quickly. "Yes, Chancellor. He could be an asset to the Collegium, because he appears to be a remarkably gifted healer, thanks to some new kind of Sentinel abilities. Bioelectric, perhaps."

That didn't explain Kinnor Caldwell, of course.

"He also seems to be the kind of leader who can sway people quickly," the Chancellor said.

How much had *she* been swayed? Her days among the Thyrians already seemed oddly dreamlike, as if none of them really had happened. She stretched a hand toward the Chancellor. "You and he must meet and speak with each other. It would be terrible if conflict broke out now, now that you're so close to making peace with them."

That was why he'd really come here, wasn't it? To keep peace in the Federacy?

Oddly, his smile twisted toward one side of his face.

CHAPTER 37

Chancellor Piper Gambrel's god-voice had returned in an instant, casting him out to hover below the cabin's ceiling. He watched himself raise the cup and take another sip.

From this angle, he had a clear view of his armrest, where a message gleamed from Zeimsky: Both Sentinels had been darted from behind with blocking drugs and snatched away simultaneously. They both showed actively functioning ayins. The procedure that would humanize them was underway.

Meanwhile, the body below him kept its attention on Meris Cariole. "Yes," he heard himself say, "we want to speak with that man. Immediately." The young woman responded with a confident nod. He probably could get a great deal of preliminary information from her. He tried to call down to the god-voice below him. *Is there anything unusual about her?*

The other seemed not to hear. It steepled his fingers. "Where is he?" it asked.

"Back at Hesed House, somewhere on the grounds."

"You're sure?"

Her eyes widened slightly, a startle reaction. The god was forgetting its manners. "Almost certainly. I don't think he's left the place since the day he arrived."

And is there any reason, Gambrel asked the other, *to maintain our little fiction, that young Jorah Caldwell might be their Boh-Dabar instead?*

His body kept its fingers upraised, pressed together. It smiled. "Then I see no reason to delay. Take me there." It lowered one hand and touched another armrest panel. This one would signal Urnock, who was in touch with the *White Squall.* The fingers moved too quickly to follow, though. His next words also surprised him. "And tell us about Air Master Kinnor Caldwell. Is he really alive?"

She hesitated. Was she saying a litany . . . or stalling?

• • •

Meris reminded herself that her job was to tell Chancellor Gambrel whatever he needed to know. Perhaps his sudden abruptness was due to some message he had received. "Yes, Chancellor. He is alive."

He frowned slightly. The intelligence in his eyes was so sharp that it almost glimmered. "Have you heard how they falsified his death, and who might be responsible?"

The perfect question! Meris reached toward her belt and unclipped her handheld. "Chancellor, I ran several forensic tests. I consider it conclusively proved that the man was dead when he arrived."

"He actually was dead?" The Chancellor's voice took on an even harsher note. "You have forensic proof?"

"Let me show you." She keyed up data.

He seized the device and scrolled her file with startling speed before handing it back. "What happened?" He laced his fingers around one knee. "Who is responsible?"

He believed her data. What a marvelous man. "Several witnesses reported that they saw Tavkel pull him from his burial coffin. They all believe Tavkel personally brought him back to life."

Those brilliant eyes widened.

"Sir, you and he have a great deal to say to each other. Quickly too. Because . . ." Should she say it? Yes! She must! "Sir, this is the place where they bury most of their dead."

He bumped his cup and tipped it over, but he ignored it. He probably had staff who dealt with that kind of thing. "What are you implying?"

• • •

Ask her about Jorah Caldwell, Piper Gambrel pressed. *Ask her about that Shuhr woman who's in charge too. And High Commander Caldwell. Do we arrest him yet?*

The other ignored him. He found himself circling his own body, trying to get back in. What good were these thoughts if he couldn't speak? He could see, though. Down on the armrest, he spotted another new message. *S6A, reporting. No new radiation activity.*

Obviously, the new super-Sentinel wasn't doing anything cataclysmic at the moment. Gambrel really didn't expect anything, of course. Maybe he should just cancel . . . No, he would keep the reports coming. All knowledge was potentially useful.

"Well, sir." She shifted slightly on her chair. "Many of those dead people were military. And if Tavkel really can revive the dead, he could be down there right now, bringing more of them back."

"That's impossible."

"He did it once, sir. I proved it."

You proved enough to help us convict Tavkel, Gambrel reflected. *Later, we'll figure out what actually happened.*

Apparently the god agreed. His body stood. "Enough delays," it said.

A whooshing noise preceded Urnock out of the lift. Gambrel did want to talk to the man. Once again, he tried to regain control of a mouth that kept talking. "Colonel," it said, "we are leaving. Begin to—"

The voice went silent. Gambrel's vision shifted suddenly. He found himself blinking at Meris and Urnock, who stood at his eye level again. He was back in his body. Urnock had opened his mouth, but now he just stood there, looking startled.

A stranger stepped into the open hatchway. A medium-sized adult wearing rough brown clothes and carrying a long, straight stick, he strode into the room and walked around Urnock. "We must speak, Piper Gambrel. In privacy."

Urnock didn't move. His eyes looked glazed and vacant. Was this Sentinel voice-command? And the stranger had apparently passed right through their perimeter, which plainly was a demonstration of circuit control at the least.

This had to be Tavkel Caldwell. The Sentinels had found Gambrel, and so he was in grave danger. Coolly, Gambrel looked for his own guards. Then he remembered sending them off to Zeimsky's country with the woman Sentinel and the youngster, in case they were needed.

Before he could shout for them, Meris Cariole sprang forward. "Oh! Chancellor Gambrel, sir, meet Tavkel. Tavkel, this is my spiritual mentor, Chancellor Piper Gambrel, of the Collegium for Human Learning." She stood between them, arms outspread, wide-eyed as if she felt guilty about what she'd been saying when Tavkel had arrived. Really . . . a military force made up of people who'd died . . . How ridiculous.

"Yes." The man offered a hand to clasp. "I know you, Chancellor Gambrel."

Tavkel? This . . . bumpkin, this hick who smelled like livestock . . . claimed to know him? And this was the man people were claiming such bizarre things about? For instance . . . if Sabba

Six-alpha exploded in a grand catastrophe, it would be *this* man's doing?

If I were an inferior man, I would laugh! This job was going to be easier than he had anticipated. *Right?* he asked the god-voice.

The petulant god, its wish finally granted, had gone silent when Tavkel had appeared.

Was that what the bumpkin had meant by "in privacy"?

• • •

Meris stood waiting, eager to eavesdrop on their lofty conversation. At last—finally—they stood together! *I've been fearing things that I only imagined. Now I'll see something wonderful.*

Tavkel stepped toward the Chancellor, still extending that hand but leaning on his stick.

Chancellor Gambrel backstepped. He looked as if he might be sniffing the air. She'd gotten used to the scents of this place. What was he noticing?

"Piper Gambrel," Tavkel said, "you are as welcome here as any other human being. But the spirit you brought with you is destroying you. Its persuasions deafen you." He raised the stick. "I could set you free. You would have to want your freedom, though. Do you?"

Meris frowned. Did he mean the spirit that Shamarr Kiel had been talking about?

Chancellor Gambrel kept both hands at his sides, his clothes and his posture shouting *high culture* compared with Tavkel's working garb. "How dare you?" Apparently the Chancellor understood, even if she wasn't sure.

"I have authority over such creatures." Tavkel raised the hand that Chancellor Gambrel had declined to shake. "I can silence them. I can even destroy them. Otherwise, like human beings, they could be eternal."

Authority? Meris stared. Eternal? Well, he had claimed to be divine.

"Yes. It is a divine spark." Chancellor Gambrel took another small step away from Tavkel.

So what did divine *mean?* Her head whirled. Tavkel could not be a god. Not in the sense *he* plainly meant it. What was he going to do?

Tavkel paced in the opposite direction, shaking his head. "No. It is a conscious being, and it is older than you can imagine. It means to eventually destroy you."

Meris remembered his words. *Is light a wave or a particle?*

Whatever it was, it was *light*. It was inexplicable in simple human language . . .

Tavkel halted several steps away from Chancellor Gambrel. "I will finish what I came to do here, regardless of your actions. You don't need to stand condemned because of me. I bring life, not death. You can choose to be one of the living and joyful."

"What?" The Chancellor backed another step away. Looking thoroughly aggravated, he turned his head in both directions. This time Meris followed his glances. The three of them—plus Colonel Urnock, who hadn't moved and seemed to be in some sort of trance—seemed to be alone. But what about her Sentinel bodyguards? When had they vanished?

Tavkel planted his walking stick. "You can be forgiven for what you did to Jorah Caldwell. And what was just done to Mel Anastu and Pieters Keeson under your orders. Even for what is happening all over Thyrica, as well as your intentions toward Madam Kernoweg."

Chancellor Gambrel stood straight and tall. And silent.

"You can be forgiven anything," Tavkel said, drawing himself up, "except for rejecting me. If you do that, you will have no advocate in the final court of judgment. Your soul is stained. But you can turn back. You may start over. Give your darkness to me."

If Tavkel were actually divine, those words made sense. But only if he were truly divine.

And how could that be?

• • •

Piper Gambrel stood awash in shocked disappointment. He'd expected so much more from this man. For one thing, he'd anticipated an intellectual discussion, not bizarre accusations. Surely Tavkel had taken a shot in the dark, mentioning the Consular Head's position! "If you have been referring to the god who travels with me, it has given me good counsel. If you sent it away, you did so without my permission." It'd frustrated him a few minutes ago, but he felt eerily naked without its presence.

However, he knew now who had interfered with Kinnor Caldwell's execution. Meris Cariole didn't seem to realize she'd just handed him Tavkel of Procyel, who was about to be arrested for treason. Gambrel could take control of this situation in any of several alternate ways—but he would *not* simply let Urnock execute this man.

First, he wanted answers.

The bumpkin rested both his hands on his stick. "You preach human determinism, and human freedom of will. So do I. Determine your own future now, and walk to me freely. There is still time."

Freedom? How droll, coming from someone who would shortly be under arrest. Still, there was no rush to lock him up. With the new force in orbit, Tavkel could not escape this world—and even before quashing the Dabarite movement, Gambrel wanted to see how he could use this man in his equally vital mission to end the Sentinel menace. "How did you get here, friend Tavkel?" Urnock's security perimeter had to be full of holes.

"In a local hopper."

"I'm . . . surprised . . . that my soldiers let you through our defenses."

Tavkel raised a hand again. He kept it upraised, looking eerily like a Sentinel ready to voice-command. "All deadly weapons on and around this world are nonfunctioning. Your forces could not have shot me down. Nor can the Sentinels harm your people. In this moment, physical matters—including battles—are irrelevant."

That felt like a snub, directed toward Collegiate teachings. "Peace in our Federacy rests on enforcing its laws." Gambrel squared his shoulders. "When laws have been broken, consequences must be enforced. Do you not understand that by using his mental abilities for selfish, capricious reasons, Kinnor Caldwell committed a capital crime?"

• • •

The mind rules the body. I choose to continue. Why should I not shine? Meris stared from one man to the other. They stood there accusing one another, when they should have been pooling their wisdom!

Maybe it was necessary, even among greatly gifted leaders, to establish dominance. She sagged a little. Did she dare to step between them, to remind them there was work to finish before conflict broke out?

How odd. Her legs wouldn't move. Was this Sentinel voice-command at last? Didn't Tavkel trust her? She glanced his direction.

He trusts no one. The words seemed to shimmer in midair. Startled, she looked up. Something like a gleaming cloud hovered over Chancellor Gambrel. Between her and the grey metal bulkhead, it pulsed like something alive. It extended a long tendril toward her, pale and beautiful. Was that cloud what Tavkel had meant by "privacy" and "a conscious being"—and by "spirit"?

"Stop!" Tavkel spun toward her, hand still upraised.

Meris ducked, thinking he was talking to her. Then she realized that he was looking straight at the shimmering cloud and that she actually could move. Tavkel's frown, and those narrowed eyes— and the way he thrust out his right hand—startled her. She'd never seen him *fierce* before.

"Leave us."

At his word, the beautiful thing—whatever it was—vanished.

What in the Whorl was going on?

●　●　●

Gambrel glanced up in time to see the shimmer disappear. Could that be how the god-voice visibly manifested? And . . . more importantly, didn't he truly believe that the human mind and will reigned supreme? Yes, he did—but in this portentous moment, Tavkel had sent away the one counselor he trusted. Left to depend on himself, he felt keenly alone, robbed of that extra power of persuasion, the extra confidence—

"You don't need it." Tavkel lowered his chin. "Already, you can do all you were created to do. Wanting more is a facet of darkness. Give that darkness to me."

Gambrel bristled again. This mind reader had no right to tell him what he did or did not need! On this hostile world, he wanted all the spirit power he could wield. Litanies were fine for followers. But as his Collegium's leader, he needed safety and security.

"I am sorry." The bumpkin spoke slowly, shaking his head. "You could have been an example of undeserved joy." He lowered his hand, but he raised his voice. "You walk the path to misery, Piper Gambrel. Wealth and power will not buy back your life."

Tavkel looked aside, at the girl. "Meris, Kinnor was for proof and for mercy, not the first of many. I will raise no army of the dead. I will harm no one. Will you not give me your darkness too?"

The girl stood there, looking puzzled.

Tavkel turned and walked out, leaving a faint barnyard odor.

Still standing next to the lift where he had emerged, Urnock shook his head. He glanced out the hatch, looking puzzled.

"Sir?" Meris Cariole piped up.

Gambrel turned his head and eyed her. He had not meant to let Tavkel slip away—and she must have watched the entire exchange. Would it be necessary to put her on the execution list? She could prove to be a dangerous witness, if the mission went poorly.

"Sir," she asked again, "are you all right?"

Urnock shrugged and got back on the lift. He might also testify if things went wrong.

Gambrel took a deep breath. He'd had Tavkel in the palm of one hand. Next time, he must hold tight.

He gave the girl his full attention. "You aren't one of . . . his . . . are you?"

• • •

Was Chancellor Gambrel asking her to declare that she was no Dabarite, or did he simply need to know whether she was in a position to give him more information, from up close to Tavkel? *Come back*, she wanted to call after Tavkel. *For proof and for mercy,* he'd claimed. What had that meant?

He hadn't even been nearby when she'd thought those things about the catacombs! How had he known she was afraid he would bring back an army from death?

Jorah, she guessed. Jorah must have reported to him. Of course. Or had she said something herself? Yes, she had. In the shearing shed.

But was he really . . .

Plainly, she needed to settle down. "No, sir. Tavkel is an impressive person, and I'm glad you were able to speak with him privately. But I'm a Collegiate, Chancellor Gambrel. And I am a mature, confident woman because of your teachings. I'm free to act as a go-between, and I'm eager to serve you."

"Ah." He sat back down and fingered something on his armrest. He looked oddly disquieted. "Then we have work ahead of us, Meris. And we must move quickly."

The room grew brighter. Maybe the sun had just come out. She could still serve them both, as a liaison. "Tell me what to do, sir. I'm proud to be here for you."

Chancellor Gambrel reached aside, toward the cup he had spilled. He looked startled for a moment, as if he hadn't noticed when he spilled it. He righted it before turning back to her. "I have a number of questions."

CHAPTER 38

Jorah blinked, feeling stupid. He recalled heading outdoors kind of suddenly, to help prep those family shuttles. He vaguely remembered sitting down on the grass with his head between his knees. But why?

He also remembered that his guard, Major Ryken, had crouched beside him and grasped his shoulder, looking at him oddly. "Jorah? Jorah, can you hear me?"

As Jorah took in his surroundings now, he found himself standing alone in the Chapter room's main aisle, halfway between the high altar and the rear door arch. How in the Whorl had he gotten here, and where had Major Ryken gone?

The Chapter room was dim, the candle sconces unlit on the red stone walls. He pushed the heel of his hand against his forehead, trying to think. The last time he'd blacked out, there had been too much going on to bother anyone about it. With Aunt Saried dead and no one but Meris staffing the med center, it had been potentially embarrassing anyway. He'd practically forgotten it.

Once had seemed odd, but twice made an alarming pattern. He needed this checked. This went beyond mere headaches. Tavkel would know what was wrong. After all, Jorah had been under Gambrel and Zeimsky's knife. He'd been healed of the plague, but maybe Tavkel had missed something. Seemed crazy, but he might as well ask.

Jorah headed out through the Chapter room door. As he reached the waterside, the skylights looked dark. It might rain this afternoon.

Something rumbled underfoot. *Thunder? No—*

A deeper, sharper *boom* shook the ground. Jorah grabbed the waterside railing and widened his stance, suddenly sick to his stomach. That had been an explosion—and close! It couldn't have anything to do with his blackout—could it?

Or was Hesed House under attack after all?

• • •

Meris stood aside, awed, as an aide wheeled a large apparatus off the lift and into the room. She was seeing an Instantaneous Transceiver Disk at last. The silvery circle was maybe a meter and a half in diameter, resting upright in a metal frame. To her surprise, the aide unfolded the frame and gingerly lowered the disk to nearly floor level. Two additional sides of the frame unfolded to create an open-ended enclosure with posts that were roughly waist high.

Chancellor Gambrel stepped onto the disk. The man who'd been introduced as Colonel Urnock joined him there. The disk's surface began to shimmer oddly.

Light also reflected from circles along the railing. Chancellor Gambrel touched one of those circles and looked up as if addressing someone on the bare grey wall. "Am I transmitting clearly?"

"Perfectly." The response seemed to come from the handrail, not a pinched sound like DeepScan transmissions, but full and round. "We have a quorum."

He nodded—again, not looking down at the small moving circle on the handrail, but into the air in front of him. Apparently, this was how one could talk to multiple locales—and how people in those places could respond.

It was a vast leap forward from DeepScan II technology, and there wasn't even a visible power source. Meris bent toward the active circle on the railing. All she could see from her angle was a soft, blurred glow.

Someone grasped her arm. She turned quickly. Another man wearing Tallan grey stood behind her. "Miss, Chancellor Gambrel and the colonel should have privacy. Follow me, please."

Chancellor Gambrel raised a hand and shook his head. The guard backed off, to Meris's delight. Judging by Chancellor Gambrel's next words, she'd missed some of the conversation.

"Yes," he said, "she is an excellent witness. Apparently the man has some sort of new mutant powers. For awhile, he seemed to be taking abilities away from the rest of them—but they're apparently regaining them. They're training all over again." He glanced at the lift and then over his shoulder toward the main entry, looking uncharacteristically nervous. "They could prove more dangerous than ever."

Colonel Urnock took a step forward. "Especially since we still don't know whether the Sentinels' plans for domination may have changed, now that their College is under our control. We must move forward. We are experiencing numerous weapons malfunctions, however. The Shuhr woman in charge there could be responsible . . ."

Meris tuned out Colonel Urnock, realizing that Chancellor Gambrel had just used her own words about the people here retraining their powers. She could stand tall today. She hadn't just served the Collegium—she had provided assistance to the Federacy itself, all because of having taken the "wrong" shuttle to Tallis. She could scarcely believe the way things were turning out.

Several seconds of silence followed the colonel's speech. Apparently, a group was conferring on the other end of this transmission.

It was an elderly woman's voice that finally answered. "Chancellor Gambrel, you remain in charge. You are to proceed and prosecute as we previously discussed. Whatever steps must be taken to safeguard unaltered humanity there and elsewhere, you shall take them. If Colonel Zeimsky's treatments can be universally implemented without incident, we shall be pleased. However, we would prefer to interview the Dabarite suspect before carrying out sentence. It appears he could be safely transported in stasis. It would be desirable to conduct further interviews at this location."

"Our . . . feelings precisely." The Chancellor looked somber, though his voice still sounded uncertain.

Carrying out a sentence? Had Meris missed something important?

The older woman continued. "However, in light of some of the DeepScan transmissions that have recently originated on Procyel, we feel it would be best that he not be allowed ITD access. If disciplinary action proves necessary, command must transfer smoothly and immediately to Colonel Urnock."

"Madam, the ITD access in question will simply be a matter of timing." The Chancellor turned toward Meris. "Our Collegiate liaison appears to be an effectively neutral third-party observer. All actions will be reported fairly. This will not devolve into a military confrontation."

"Colonel Urnock," the woman's voice said.

The other man glanced down at the small moving surface before raising his head again.

"You are pre-authorized, if it proves necessary, to use any available force, including our assets that remain in orbit. However, you are to delay until Chancellor Gambrel and Colonel Zeimsky attempt to complete their assignments."

"Yes, madam." Colonel Urnock stood at attention. "The Remote Individual Amplification team in orbit has just activated the local contact. We believe there should shortly be a capitulation. Remember, their water supply has been discussed as a potential weakness. Our hovercrew has already ensured that the river cannot serve as an alternate source. However, I must protest. Chancellor Gambrel, while an admirable—"

"Very good, Colonel."

Meris craned her neck, shocked and wanting to see whatever they saw on the railing. What did they mean, a weakness in the water supply?

The disembodied voice continued to speak. "Gentlemen, that is all. We anticipate hearing from you upon the assignment's completion."

Colonel Urnock saluted. The Chancellor bowed slightly. They both turned and stepped down off the platform, and its surface darkened.

Meris backed away. "Colonel, Chancellor, I am sure you may depend on these people's cooperation. Whatever you meant about their water supply, there is no need for intimidation—"

"Meris." Chancellor Gambrel lowered his head and spoke mildly. Still, she heard the rebuke in his voice. "Of all people here, I did not expect insubordination from you."

Colonel Urnock barely smiled.

Meris shook her head, only half mollified. She did not like this Colonel Urnock. Not at all. "That's . . . a remarkable technology," she murmured. Perhaps she could steer this conversation in a more productive direction. "The Sanctuary Administrator did request an ITD—"

"And as you heard," Chancellor Gambrel said, "we will deliver it. First, though, we have to settle another matter. We'll . . . we will bring them the disk itself now, as a token of our goodwill. That's what we're leaving to do right now." He smiled slightly. "We'll deliver the supporting mechanism after they meet certain terms that have been set by the Regional Council." He beckoned to a staffer. Through an inner hatch came two others carrying another large, flat object. This one was crated.

Chancellor Gambrel and Colonel Urnock headed out the main hatch.

"You brought another disk? Where did these devices come from?" Meris asked, gazing down at the one they'd used.

"Ancient technology." It was one of the staffers who answered. "It was found on a remote world roughly two decades ago. The Collegium unlocked its secrets just last year."

Impressed, she stepped aside and let the bearers pass. Another small group emerged from the corridor, including her Thyrian companions, Captain Anastu and young Piet. They walked unsteadily, arm in arm. Two large men in Tallan grey flanked them, looking ominously like guards rather than escorts.

Alarmed, Meris frowned. "What's wrong? What happened?"

Another man stood behind the little group, faintly smiling. "They've been relieved of their curse, like Jorah Caldwell. Forgive them for not speaking just yet. They're really too weak to be up on their feet so quickly, but it's vital for them to return to their headquarters along with the Chancellor."

They'd been cured that quickly? Then certainly, Chancellor Gambrel must show Hesed House that he could, indeed, offer them all a treatment that would last—like Jorah's—and that it could be done quickly and easily.

Still, she didn't like the idea of performing medical procedures on people who plainly hadn't volunteered. A shadow seemed to fall across her bright vision of the future. She shook it off. Right now, these Thyrians looked wobbly. They needed a word of encouragement. She stepped toward them. "Piet, Captain, I'm here for you." She reached out an arm to help Mel Anastu.

What she saw in the Sentinel's eyes looked more like hatred than gratitude. Like there were things she wanted to say subvocally, but couldn't. Never again.

Meris backstepped.

"You're coming too." Chancellor Gambrel addressed those words to the man who'd emerged behind Piet and Captain Anastu. "We'll need you to supervise stasis, won't we? As I recall, it should be redundantly monitored."

"Listen." The newcomer wore a medspec's tunic and stood with his hands thrust into his pockets. The tunic's pocket crest was the ornate lozenge of Elysia General, and over the crest she read ZEIMSKY. "There's no need. There are surely enough medical people there. Including this one." He jerked his head toward Meris.

"Coward. I'm not sending a minion to deal with these people. Neither will you."

This had to be the end of an ongoing argument. The medsped stepped backward, glaring.

Meris wanted to shrink into the floor. Weren't these high-ranking Federates above arguing and name calling?

Colonel Urnock pointed at one of the muscular guards, who took two steps toward the medical man. Seeing that, the other man—Zeimsky—raised his head and walked toward the hatch. He didn't stop glowering.

Meris let them all pass. Captain Anastu's hateful stare had stung. Really, Captain Anastu had no right to be upset. She'd had no choice about being born "altered," had she? So having had no choice about being cured—that created a kind of symmetry, didn't it?

Still, Meris couldn't escape a lingering uneasiness.

She followed the Chancellor out the module's main entrance, back into the sunshine and onto the undulating walkway. And what had that been about the river, and the Sanctuary's water supply?

Instantly, she found herself distracted. Something like a small, shimmering cloud hovered over the walkway. If this was the thing Tavkel had banished, it hadn't gone far.

Before she could speak, the cloud swooped toward Chancellor Gambrel—who'd almost reached the hovercraft—and it seemed to vanish.

• • •

Gambrel felt it return, and he greeted it with a rush of relief. *We have a star witness,* he reported. *She'll testify against him, we'll have authority enough to convict, and—*

The god-voice cut him off with a shriek. *Kill him, kill him! Tavkel. Guilty, he's guilty enough to die, kill him—*

What had so angered his god-voice? Appalled, Piper Gambrel took a breath. The voice went on shrieking. Years ago, he'd written a litany for focus. His followers often needed such things, but he never had. Now he tried to recall it. *I am the spark of undying light. I shall see. I shall know . . .*

Kill him kill him kill him kill him—

I am the spark—

Kill—

I am the spark of undying light . . .

He kept the litany droning at the back of his mind as he found that he'd boarded the hovercraft and seated himself. Urnock stood in the aisle, giving orders.

The god-voice seemed to have gone insane with anger—or was this terror? Was it the encounter with Tavkel?

What else could it have been? And why, after weeks of demanding to be taken to him, had it now been reduced to incoherence?

Kill—

I am the spark of undying light . . .

Maybe when Tavkel had been tried, convicted, and safely placed in stasis for transport back to Tallis, the shrieking would end. This was bizarre.

Urnock sat down beside him. Gambrel half thought the man might be able to hear shrieking noises spewing out of his brain. "Update from orbit," Urnock said gruffly. "They're still working on those anti-personnel weaponry malfunctions. Shouldn't take long."

"Tavkel said—" Gambrel began, but the instant he said the name, the shrieking intensified.

Kill him kill him kill him kill him . . .

• • •

Meris sat on board the familiar hovercraft as people in Tallan grey plodded up the aisle. Most of them carried heavy-looking weapons. She shook her head, feeling her hopes grow dimmer moment by moment. Why did they think they needed them? What were they really planning to do when they got to the compound? Tavkel had said that all weapons had been disabled. Still, these ugly grey things could be used to club people.

She had expected better behavior from the Federate group. There didn't need to be hostilities! Everyone should sit down and talk to each other. Why bring charges against Tavkel? Surely that had been a misunderstanding. But the obvious alternative—rearresting Air Master Caldwell, whom the Federates had executed—was too awful to even suggest.

Another muscular Tallan sidestepped past her. He hauled a thick tube nearly as tall as he was.

Chancellor Gambrel probably was bringing these troops as bodyguards. Perhaps he was afraid to face so many Thyrians at once. She couldn't blame him—but most of the Sentinels couldn't do bizarre things anymore, thanks to Tavkel. This seemed a bit overblown.

On the other hand, some of the Sentinels would probably fight unarmed, with their last breath, to keep Federates out of their Sanctuary. Air Master Caldwell came to mind.

She'd taken a seat behind and across the aisle from Chancellor Gambrel. Almost as if he too could read minds, he turned toward her at that moment. Something seemed to glimmer through his eyes. His face looked placid, but something in that glance raised hairs at the back of her neck. He stretched his lips in an answering smile, then he gave his handheld his full attention.

Meris made herself sit back and relax. Had she been caught up in Federate treachery after all? She checked her lap and shoulder restraints and looked behind her. Her Sentinel bodyguards had been separated. Piet sat near the back of the hovercraft while Captain Anastu sat on the opposite side, next to the aisle. Captain Anastu looked down at the deck, not at the escort sitting next to her.

Another big soldier took the empty seat next to Meris. Meris scooted closer to the bulkhead and looked out the window. The weather off to the west was turning grey and threatening.

The hatch slid down, and the engine noise grew louder. The hovercraft lurched upward and rotated.

CHAPTER 39

Alarms clanged all around Jorah, echoing off the water and the high ceiling. He walked toward the administrative corridor as fast as he could without running. *What* had happened while he blacked out?

Out through the arch came Captain Mattason, the intelligence woman who'd been accessing crewers and helping Grandfather deploy guards. "Stop right there. Hands where I can see them, Jorah."

He froze, hands stretched out in front of his waist. His eyes had to be huge. What had he done? All around him, people streamed onto the waterside. The alarms kept clanging.

Captain Mattason strode closer. She put a hand on his shoulder, and the nauseating prickle at the back of his throat let him know she was looking deep inside his mind—probing hard, because the walkway seemed to tilt underfoot.

"You have no memory of putting Major Ryken in t-sleep." That plainly wasn't a question.

He answered anyway. "No, ma'am. Wait, he's in t-sleep? What happened?"

"Perhaps you'll tell me."

"How could I do that . . . to anyone? I don't have an ayin anymore."

She scowled and pursed her lips. "You were seen coming back into the Sanctuary through H-2. Alone. And that isn't all." She paused a moment and let that sink in. Then she gestured him to walk in front of her.

He complied, feeling nauseous. What had happened? He'd come back into the hangar . . . While he was blacked out? But that was impossible.

Or was it? His mind flashed back to his time on Tallis. What else had that foul Chancellor Gambrel's medical crony done to him, besides infecting him with a plague? His thoughts sprinted ahead as he walked into his mother's office. There had been Sentinel SOOC people present when Gambrel and Zeimsky's goons had operated on him. They would have known how to . . .

Oh, no.

Both his parents stood inside the office, his mother having pushed back her desk chair. His father looked like he'd just stood up off one of the stone benches . . . And there stood Major Ryken, his expression unreadable. Grandfather sat on the bench behind Dad, leaning against the stone wall. His face looked seriously stressed. Other voices babbled out of the desk. Beyond the arch, the clanging alarms finally shut off.

Captain Mattason remained at his elbow.

"Jorah," his mother exclaimed. "We—"

"Wait." Jorah had never made a habit of interrupting her. But he couldn't bear letting her embarrass herself by accusing him. He had to speak first. "Listen, whatever just happened, I'm pretty sure I'm responsible—but only indirectly." He explained the headaches— that hateful time under Zeimsky's knife—and wondered aloud if they'd done things to him that even Tavkel hadn't gotten out of him . . . because he hadn't been told and therefore wouldn't have known about it. He frowned. "But Tavkel would have known it happened, right? Did Tavkel let this happen?"

Captain Mattason spoke beside him. "Tavkel has never guaranteed our safety. But he—"

"Right." His father stood with arms crossed, glowering. "Your grandfather was also concerned. And when we found Ryken curled up like a rock on the landing strip, we brought him up out of t-sleep and got what we could out of him. This time, one of the surveillance monitors caught the saboteur passing into the private passages."

Jorah remained at attention. "Me."

His mother nodded. The others just stared.

Feeling helpless and just about hopeless, Jorah sank onto the closest chair. "What did I do? Did I sabotage the College shuttle too? What else have I done?"

Instead of answering, Grandfather beckoned. "Come over here, on the bench. I might—maybe—be able to tell. I should have done this sooner."

Jorah complied. He stared straight at his grandfather's eyes and sat simply breathing, waiting. Waiting. Waiting—

The older man leaned slightly forward as he worked. Jorah's neck prickled.

Abruptly Grandfather sat straighter, took a long breath, and shut his eyes. The prickling turned to full-blown nausea before it snapped off.

Jorah got a deep breath. What had just happened?

Grandfather turned toward Mother. "Watch-link," he said simply.

It wasn't lingering mind-access nausea that made Jorah feel sick to his stomach now. "Oh, no. Lock me up. Or put me in t-sleep." He gripped his hands together and clenched them between his knees. "Do whatever you have to do. I should've come forward already."

Grandfather raised a hand, but Jorah ignored it. "Back when I had the first blackout, I should've said more. But everybody was busy. Besides, Tavkel had healed the plague thing. Doesn't he always heal completely? Why didn't he heal this . . . if I'm watch-linked?" He blurted the awful words.

"I just broke it, Jorah." Grandfather spoke softly. "You're not linked any longer. And as for Tavkel's healings—Terza and Saried left us, didn't they? We thought we had Tavkel figured out. Perhaps there are some things he will not heal."

Jorah wasn't really in the mood to discuss theology. All he cared was that he was no longer watch-linked. He hadn't felt any hint of the link, just as they'd taught in the second-year Intel class at College.

He sent his dad a weak smile and got one in return.

"You don't remember where you went?" His mother stood beside her desk. "What you did, under link?"

Jorah shook his head. Why hadn't he guessed this? "But I just heard an explosion. That's why I came running."

"It was the spring," she said softly. "Our water source has been compromised."

He looked up, appalled.

She went on. "There's mud flowing into the main pool. Down the waterfall in the privacy suite. Into the cistern. We're putting people to work bucketing clean water out of the pool's other end. You know we never stockpiled water, and Security's dealing with it, but . . ."

"But there's no purification apparatus." His father's voice was grim. "And the Feds have been deliberately fouling the river with that hovercraft. Haven't they?"

Even the cistern! Jorah covered his face with his hands. "Oh. Oh, no. That's worse than I thought."

Control. His dad's sharp voice cut into the back of his mind. *Don't blubber in front of your mother.*

Jorah pulled a deep breath. His dad was right. They'd taken everything else away from him, but they couldn't take his affective control. He took a moment to get his grief and humiliation under wraps. "This is Gambrel's fault. Gambrel and Zeimsky's. I assume I'm headed for lockup. I'm not safe otherwise."

"No." Mother spoke sharply, sitting down at last. "If your grandfather said he freed you, you're perfectly safe now. And we need every pair of hands and strong arms on outside guard. We'll just double guard you this time."

Jorah squirmed inside. "So you might be up one pair of hands in me, but you're down two pair in my guards. That's a net loss." A thought struck him. "If our weapons won't work but you still need to arm people, there's knives in the kitchens."

"No." His mother tilted her chin. "We will not meet the Federates looking like barbarians."

He shrugged. To his mind, the Feds were the ones acting barbaric.

She nodded at him. She too had to be getting back her abilities, lowering her shields to sense his emotions. "Jorah, just stay with those guards."

Grandfather stood slowly, looking weary. Breaking a watch-link supposedly took enormous ayin strength. "And since you were headed back here to confess and ask for help, we trust your intentions. I agree, though, Wind. Keep him guarded, for his own sake."

"Thanks," Jorah muttered.

His mother glanced down at a tracking panel on her desk. "They're en route now, Gambrel and Meris. With the Holy One knows who else. That hovercraft could hold twenty soldiers or more. But Tavkel left their site first. He'll beat them back here. Maybe he can tell us what's going on."

"I would've been glad to stay with you." Grandfather laid a hand on Jorah's shoulder. That felt good. "But I've been given other work. So Major Ryken and Captain Mattason will both be there. Consider yourself cabled to them."

"Yes, sir." Jorah looked ruefully at Major Ryken. "You're all right with that, sir? After what I just did?"

Major Ryken squared his shoulders. "That wasn't you. But we still don't have working stun pistols. If it turns out you have to be controlled, it'll be with wrist restraints." He rested his hand on a belt pouch.

"Just hit me over the head," Jorah mumbled.

His dad stepped closer, arms crossed. "And if anyone finds you alone, you're headed for t-sleep."

"Understood. Thanks." Jorah saluted them all.

"Better go back out and look at the pool first," his mother said softly. "You need to understand the gravity of the situation, whether or not you consciously caused it."

"Right. I didn't even look down at the water before." As Jorah plodded out of the office, he felt the pair following him. *Guards,* he reflected bitterly. *I have to be guarded now. You owe me, Gambrel!*

They reached the waterside. He rested both hands on the railing and stared down, disbelieving. From a spot between the dining commons and the Chapter room, a brown stain spread into the pool. Along its far left, people knelt to fill containers. Three of them looked like they were setting up a pump.

He closed his eyes on the horrible scene. "All right. We're supposed to be on guard duty? Where?"

Captain Mattason gestured toward the corridor that led down to the hangars. "Landing strip."

"Can't I help them here? Seems like that would be a more fitting job for me."

Captain Mattason shrugged. "I agree, but your mother gave orders. We're going to combine security with some maintenance by the strip."

Smoothing the landing zone? Good. Hard physical labor might be just what he needed right now. And just as much as they could safely trust him to do.

First, though . . . he took one last look at the clouded skylights. "With your permission, sir, ma'am, I'd like us to go back to my quarters so I can get my crystace." Would they trust him to carry the ancient hand weapon? He'd been authorized for it when the College had vested him as a Sentinel.

Could he still call himself a Sentinel?

Major Ryken frowned and glanced aside, at Captain Mattason. "Actually, I want mine too."

• • •

Wind watched the trio leave her office and reactivated the desktop monitors. She'd darkened them all the moment Father had raised the suspicion of watch-link. "Did you find anything else?" she asked him grimly.

Her father-in-law remained on the stone side bench. "Our own SOOC people did the linking."

"That's illegal!" Kinnor stayed at her desk's corner, forearms crossed and muscles twitching. Wind barely sensed his irritation, but she did sense it! "The Codes absolutely—"

"It's over." Father held up a hand. "I broke it."

"Are you all right?" Wind had no idea he'd recovered so much of his abilities. Her own returning ayin strength was barely a flicker.

Had Tavkel healed even the damage that Kinnor's father had done to his ayin back at the Golden City, decades ago? But then why had he not broken Jorah's watch-link?

Father ducked his chin and smiled, sending a silent reprimand. "I'll be fine after I rest a bit. But there's more. It was our people on board the *White Squall* who remotely used Jorah to put Major Ryken in t-sleep."

"Traitors!" Kinnor's eyes went wide. "I knew he wouldn't have done it on his own. Not my son. But they'll pay."

"Kinnor," Father said softly, "that crew has paid in full. Or they will very soon. They sent me a subvocal message, just as Jorah walked in here. Via that RIA unit."

All heads turned toward him.

"Oh?" Wind asked quietly. After Jorah, highest on her mind were Mel Anastu and Piet Keeson, with those lifesigns monitors. Both were alive but plainly weak. This was what Gambrel had in mind for them all—and their children, and their children's children.

Hurry, Tavkel! Put the Whorl back together as it should be!

"Their families have been under threat. But as of this hour, they understand that even their families won't buy their lives at this cost. They're standing down. Refusing to obey their Federate guards anymore. It will probably cost them their lives, but they said they'd sabotage the RIA apparatus if they can."

"A little late for that." Glowering, Kinnor sat down on her desktop's corner. "And I still want to know why Tavkel didn't fix this when he got rid of Jorah's plague."

Father got up off the bench. "Let me say this again: We had thought we had Tavkel figured out. Consider the arrogance of that assumption."

Wind stared at the defense update. "Well," she said, "I'll ask Kiel to sing Shekkah for the RIA crew. And . . . do we need to try and bring down the *White Squall* after all?" She hated to ask, but she'd been thinking it for most of the day.

Surely Kin and Father had too—because the underground blast had also killed Colonel Harris. The Sentinels' former High Commander had reluctantly taken charge of one more planetary defense.

"Or can we assume they'll manage to sabotage the—" Movement on a panel near the middle of her desk caught her eye. Fortunately, Kiel had offered to link his handheld for observation. "Tavkel's back," she exclaimed. "Just landed. Looks like—"Another panel lit. Kiel had just gotten a call. "He's asking to confer with Kiel."

Kin nodded. "Good. Maybe Kiel will talk some sense into Tavkel. Maybe we'll get ordnance again."

Wind shook her head, frustrated. "Kinnor, think! If we do, they will too . . . and they hold the high ground!"

"What makes you say that?" Kinnor slid off the desk's corner. He paced two steps away and then spun back around. "Didn't you hear what Father said? Tavkel can do anything he wants! He could shut down just *their* weapons, and—"

Father stepped toward the desk. Wind slid off her chair. "You have the command center, sir."

"Thank you." He sat down and took a long look across the boards. "No, there's no change in our ordnance status. Whatever Tavkel did, it's still in place. That weather alert looks a little ominous, though. There's a strong storm coming in." He pointed at a side panel. "We might have to send away a negotiating party on board that Federate hovercraft, or else invite them all indoors. Gambrel. Urnock." He spoke the names harshly.

"Okay." Kinnor walked back toward the desk. "Then I suggest the good old-fashioned ramming attack. Maybe not on the *White Squall* but that big cruiser-carrier they just brought in. Just to even the odds a bit. And I volunteer."

Wind's stomach lurched. "No," she exclaimed. "Kin, that would accomplish nothing. They came here to do Tavkel's will. To bring them the ITD. *He* called them here. *He—*"

"I've been dead before." Kin stepped toward her, fists at his sides, chin tilted up. His determination came through with painful clarity. "It was worse for you than me, right? But I still say this place is going to be attacked. They're here to wipe us out. And if it means saving the Sanctuary—not to mention the people we've scattered all over the back country—you'll volunteer to be bereaved again too. Won't you?" He lowered his head.

"No, Kinnor! Tavkel said not to . . . That is . . ." She looked helplessly from Kinnor to his father. It wasn't that she was afraid of going through all that again. But if she had to be bereaved again, it had to count for something definite. Not just her dear Kinnor's impetuosity.

Father stretched out his hands and gripped both corners of the desk. "Wait. Kinnor. You will not put the primary mission at risk."

Wind exhaled, relieved.

"Although . . ." Father tapped a desktop monitor. She recognized orbital tracking. "I do believe we must be ready to defend ourselves, before a clear threat emerges. So." He looked back up. "Kinnor, report to H-3. Finish getting one fighter ready. One." He raised a finger. "And you will stand by for orders."

Kinnor saluted, smiling with his eyes. He strode out the door arch.

Anguished, Wind picked up her handheld. She needed an update on the water salvaging work, just in case their world didn't end when Tavkel spoke to the Whorl. And in case Kinnor didn't die . . . again. "Father, I'm leaving you in charge." She ached inside, but this was no time to lose affective control. This could really be good-bye to Kinnor, and she didn't want the Sanctuary remembering another shouting match. "But I'll be out on the strip when the Chancellor arrives. I'll see you then."

Her father-in-law glanced down at another desk panel. "Eight minutes."

• • •

Kiel stood beside Tavkel, both of them leaning on the railing of the Tuva River bridge. To left and right, tree trunks and bush stems lay bleeding sap into the fouled river. The only mira lilies in existence lay reduced to a muddy hole in the riverbank.

If Chancellor Gambrel were trying to ruin this beautiful place, he couldn't have begun it much more effectively. It was tempting to grieve. To despair.

He stood next to his God, though. Kiel had heard Tavkel's voice at the back of his mind even before his handheld had lit with the call summoning him to this bridge, for a moment of preparation. He'd been glad to escape the chaos downlevel.

And it would end for him soon, anyway. Tavkel had forecast his death. But then, Tavkel would renew all the worlds. Kiel mustn't grieve for the riverbanks, nor for the beautiful pool at the Sanctuary's heart. Not when the entire universe was about to be made new again.

What would happen out in the Whorl? Would there be moments of terror and eternities of regret?

Surely not if Tavkel could speak to the Whorl. Every person on every world would see, and love, and—

No. There would be some who refused. Kiel had nearly been one of them. He must pray for them. Or was that a contradiction in terms? He pulled the small prayer cloths from his pocket. Absently he smoothed them over the rough bridge railing.

Staring upstream, Tavkel smiled gently.

"How long will it last?" Kiel asked. "This defeat you're predicting?"

"I don't know." Tavkel rubbed his chin. "Only my Father knows, and apparently, he isn't telling. Long enough for the word to go out, and for darkness to finish all that my Father has decreed it may do. Then the light will come. Then the victory."

Kiel nodded. "I remember," he said, gripping the rail, "back when I was much younger. The Adversary thought I might be . . . you. The plan was to tempt and corrupt me, before killing me. It seems pointless to warn you, Tavkel, but surely that is coming upon you."

Tavkel shook his head. "It has already happened. When I was walking here from Tekkumah. Remember? I told you. That shadow has contact with the one who now possesses Chancellor Gambrel. I would have liked to have freed him, but he didn't want that. I wounded it, sent it away briefly. I could do that much without his permission. Because I've weakened it for awhile, Chancellor Gambrel still could throw it off and escape. The choice still is his."

"I'm glad." Kiel hadn't forgotten Tamím. So was there anything left to be done in the time he still had? Surely Tavkel had called him here to prepare him for something specific. A last task, perhaps. He pulled out the red cloth and laid it on top. Gambrel and his forces had already violated and damaged the Sanctuary, using Jorah. Kiel took a deep breath. He reminded himself that when Tavkel renewed all things, this world would be included.

He just wasn't sure he could bear to see what would happen before things were made new again. Especially to Annalah, to Perl and Rena, and Hanusha.

Tavkel stared upriver. "I'll speak to all worlds. Then comes the ordained end, and the real beginning. Just think, Kiel." He smiled slightly. "If our ancestors hadn't altered the genes—if DeepScan and the ITD weren't available—I might have needed many more acts of power to prove myself, and more years to bring in all people. But it all can be done quickly now. And your people *know* who I am, thanks to the ayin. Your sweet Annalah has given the Whorl my words and your testimony. Now they are well prepared to hear me speak."

Kiel recalled those intoxicating moments when he'd seen deep into Tavkel's mind, the mind that had imagined the worlds. "Kinnor's story will surely soften reluctant hearts."

"Kinnor's return will be central." Tavkel leaned heavily against the bridge's railing. "I am ready, Kiel." He sighed. "But it will be hard."

Would Tavkel set off Sabba Six-alpha again? Was that what he meant by "hard"—the long-dreaded catastrophe? The Holy One had already used Sabba Six-alpha to assemble the people whose presence he required here on Procyel. He controlled even the stars.

Kiel looked over and was startled to see fear in his Lord's eyes, as dark as the clouds bearing down on Hesed House.

"Pray with me," Tavkel murmured. "Please."

Shocked, Kiel wrapped his arms around the other man's shoulders. As if a storm had already arrived, Tavkel's shoulders shook. Kiel held tight. He'd offered many people the simple human comfort of holding them. This, though . . . this seemed out of place. Backward. Almost sacrilegious.

He abruptly remembered Tavkel's consecration vision, where he'd been the kipret led to the altar.

Oh, surely not! Surely *that* wasn't coming! "Wait, Tavkel. You can't—"

Tavkel pushed away from him, frowning. "I asked you to pray, not counsel me. I will do what I must." He stood straight, seeming in that moment to be just as tall as Kiel. "Do nothing to try and stop me, or you could endanger everyone—everywhere—in all times and places."

Alarmed, Kiel murmured, "I . . . won't . . . but . . ." Deep down, where he'd shoved it, Kiel felt fear lurking sharp-toothed and ready to bite. What if Tavkel died too? How could he have power over death *if he were dead?*

No, they would move forward together. *Follow me,* he heard in memory. *Not too far back, but never ahead.*

He shut his eyes and raised both hands as Tavkel bowed his head. Courage didn't mean the absence of fear. It meant the determination to do what he must, despite his fears. The right thing was to follow. "Eternal Speaker," he prayed out loud, "grant Tavkel courage. He is our daystar. Strengthen his light. Strengthen us all."

It seemed pathetically simple . . . but also ridiculous. Praying for this man?

Still, Tavkel raised his head, the anger gone from his eyes. "Thank you, Kiel. Remember what I did for your brother."

Kiel took a deep breath. The air smelled like distant rain. "How could I forget? Still, how could—"

His handheld blatted. Tavkel nodded toward it.

Kiel raised it and eyed the read panel. It was utterly strange to see a foreigner's message header here on Procyel II. *Chancellor Piper Gambrel,* it read, *Collegium for Human Learning. To Administrator Wind Haworth-Caldwell.*

Wind had willingly linked the receivers, but this still felt like a violation of her privacy. Kiel touched the *receive* panel.

We are en route, bringing the Instantaneous Transceiver Disk you requested.

Then came a second message, addressed directly to him—and it had Wind's origin code, but the wording sounded like his father's. Two more landing modules were being activated up in orbit. Apparently the disarmed Federates were preparing to land a larger force, and the fielding net would not turn them back.

Fielding. That bunker lay under several meters of stone, behind massive doors, probably impregnable . . . but if they ever needed to huddle inside that last defense, it would be a defense without hope.

No, it was better to lay down his life according to Tavkel's timing.

Tavkel too seemed to shake off his grief and . . . had that really been fear? Smile lines reappeared around his eyes. "Come on." Tavkel picked up his walking stick. "We should be there to greet him when he lands."

Kiel gathered his prayer cloths. He pocketed them as he followed.

CHAPTER 40

Something rumbled in the distance, and Jorah flinched. More sabotage? At least it hadn't been him this time.

No . . . Major Ryken kept on raking the muddy landing strip beside him. So did Captain Mattason, working a few meters away. Jorah stood up and stretched his back. The exercise had helped him clear his head. Gather his thoughts.

Meris was in deep trouble. She'd almost come inside, almost understood his people and the truth they served. For the rest of his life, he would remember that brief concert on the waterside, feel her leaning against him, smell the scent of her hair. She'd probably given herself back to Gambrel by now, a hundred percent or more. For keeps, this time. He might have prevented that, if he'd just shown her he liked her.

Tavkel had warned them all that Gambrel was enslaved to dark spirits.

Poor Meris—

He leaned into his mud rake again, feeling guilty and cold.

Before he could finish his swath, Uncle Kiel and Tavkel appeared where the Tuva trail emerged from the trees. The destructive hovercraft pilot had somehow left a few leafy branches standing over the trailhead. They created something like an arch. The Sanctuary's spiritual leaders emerged through it.

His mother walked out of the Sanctuary through the open launch door of H-1. Grandfather, Grandmother, and several others followed. Not his dad, though, and not Colonel Harris. Were they in H-3, still thinking about an attack?

Trees tossed behind him. The sky looked ominously grey beyond the trailhead. Thunder rumbled in the distance.

Tavkel turned around and raised a hand, not toward the people approaching him but to the sky. "Peace. Not now."

The wind died instantly. The trees straightened. Jorah gaped, first at Tavkel and then at the sky. A strip of blue appeared under the dark cloud, getting wider by the moment. It looked for all the Whorl as if the rain had been shut off right inside the cloud.

All Jorah's tension suddenly vanished, and he laughed out loud. What was there to worry about? Look who stood among them! He gave his mud rake a shove, and it fell on the ground. A hovercraft roared not far away. Jorah sprinted off the landing strip along with the rest of the crew.

Most of them had held on to their rakes. *Whoops. We could use those as weapons.* He judged the distance, decided he had time, and dashed back for his.

Now. Right now, whatever Tavkel was going to do, it was going to happen right now! Jorah grabbed his rake out of the mud, got his balance—he didn't want dirt on his face for the big confrontation—and dashed toward the downhill side of the strip under a lightening sky.

The Federate hovercraft decelerated. Jorah noted that they were grounding it near the strip's center, blocking any launches from H-1 or from H-2's closed but exposed launch door.

But not blocking H-3. He tucked his mud rake against his left shoulder and tugged his shirt's left sleeve down, covering his crystace. It felt awkward. He'd never quite gotten used to wearing that ceremonial dagger on his forearm, between his recent vesting and his even more recent arrest.

His grandparents had taken up a position several meters away on his left, between the two visible launch doors. Grandfather had scattered a few second-circle Sentinels, who'd kept their abilities, among about thirty others. Six of them made a solid row flanking Tavkel. If the soldiers who came out of the Federate hovercraft wanted a fight, at least a few of Procyel II's people meant to give them pause—and, after Tavkel used the ITD, maybe a resistance they would remember.

Tavkel stood watching the settling hovercraft. Jorah couldn't read him at all. A few moments ago, he'd looked . . . well, not exactly "amused" but something like it. Now, he furrowed his forehead. It made him look slightly sad. Definitely unafraid, though.

The next hour should be spectacular! Jorah pitied the people who'd fled into the hills or offplanet, or were cowering in the housing corridors. They would miss Tavkel's triumph.

Major Ryken nudged him from the left. "Can't get mine out of the sheath," he muttered. "Can you?"

"What?" After seeing what Major Ryken was doing, Jorah wrapped his right fingers around the protruding section of his crystace hilt and tugged it toward his palm. It stuck in the wrist sheath. He yanked the whole scabbard out of his sleeve. It came off his arm, all right, but the weapon itself could not be unsheathed. He glanced at Tavkel, thinking, *Come on, sir. They're just defensive weapons. Antiques, at that.*

Tavkel looked straight at him and shook his head minutely.

Jorah compressed his lips and buckled the scabbard back on. Sometimes that man baffled him. So did his mother, who—according to a rumor that had spread through the raking crew—had actually locked up the kitchen knives. *Not to worry, Mother! This is going to be Tavkel's victory, not ours.*

The wind had died. Grass alongside the landing strip stood upright. Overhead, the last shreds of that storm cloud were giving way to early afternoon blue sky.

This Tallan hovercraft was a model that could be brought shipboard by an invasion force, capable of carrying a squad of heavily armed ground troops. Its utilitarian lines, like a rounded box, emphasized that sense of menace. Its engines wound down to a bass thrum. Jorah glanced left again.

Major Ryken uncrossed his wrists and called, "Tavkel, we'll defend you with our bare hands, if that's all you'll leave us."

"Trust me." Tavkel planted his walking stick and took a step forward. He turned around to give them all one of those somber eye-sweeps. "The Adversary's victory will be short." He spoke loudly over the engine noise. "Keep your hearts up. Not one will be lost."

Whatever that meant. In Jorah's mind, simply getting here was a victory for Gambrel already. But what could a mere chancellor do against a one-man weather control system, a man who could turn a corpse back into Jorah's living dad?

Tavkel faced Jorah's mother, who stood tall between the launch doors. Still, he seemed to address them all. "For the moment, say nothing about who and what I am, and do not hurt anyone by trying to defend me, especially those on board this hovercraft. Believe me, if I chose to call all the Bright Ones in creation to fight a battle here, I could do it."

That would be something! Jorah glanced up at the brightening sky again, then took another quick look at the group in front of the launch doors. Grandfather had put on his dress whites. The gold star on his shoulder practically glowed. With his hair grown back, he really looked the part of a high commander. Grandmother stood beside him—strangely, she'd changed into a sekiyr's gown instead of her Netaian uniform. She held her head high and looked defiant.

The hovercraft's engines coughed out, and the stench of fuel blew across the landing strip. Grandfather raised a hand to speak. Jorah leaned toward him, wanting to hear every word. "It's not necessary for troops to know their commanding officers' intent. We've always been servants, every one of us, regardless of rank. We obey Tavkel now."

Jorah nodded, but he still would've felt better if he were armed with more than a mud rake. Some angry creature shrilled in the damaged forest.

"There is one thing I ask from you now," Tavkel called, and Jorah perked up. "This is the time. I need to speak with my other flocks." He smiled aside at Annalah, who returned a nod as he continued. "These people brought the ITD, but they mean to keep it on board until you make unacceptable concessions. Also, they don't think it's useable without some hardware they deliberately left behind. But they are wrong. When I signal, a group of you please bring it down off the hovercraft."

Grandfather saluted. Jorah stared across the muddy strip at the Federate craft, sitting there with its landing struts jabbing a world he'd always considered inviolable. *They'll pay,* he assured himself. *Just wait 'til they see what Tavkel can do.*

A ramp slowly extended toward the ground. Meris was probably on board. He still wasn't sure whether to feel guilty that he hadn't been able to stop her from going back to Gambrel. She'd had every freedom to do the right thing. Maybe to her, this had looked like the right thing. Had she liked what she'd seen when she met her hero in person?

And here they came, striding down the ramp. Nine Tallans in grey walked in front. Most of them were armed, but two didn't carry weapons. Neither did a man wearing a green cutaway coat—that had to be Piper Gambrel. And sure enough, Meris walked behind him. Her hair was still tied in that knot at the back of her head. She looked somber but—thank the One—unharmed. Jorah wished he could sense her emotions. Did she feel proud or ashamed? This time, he couldn't tell by looking.

Eight more Tallans followed her. Some carried long-tube energy weapons. To his dismay, others had mortar launchers. Jorah hoped those were as non-functional as his crystace. He saw nothing that looked like new communication technology, though. If they'd brought Tavkel an ITD, they'd left it on the hovercraft. So he eyed Tavkel, watching for the signal. Did he want them to storm the craft or sneak on board?

Gambrel swaggered to a place near the landing strip's midline. "Sanctuary Administrator Haworth-Caldwell. Shamarr Caldwell. High Commander Caldwell. Lady Firebird. On this momentous occasion I greet you all, with the authority of the Federate Regional Command, the Special Operations Oversight Committee, and of course, the Collegium for Human Learning. Today marks the end of your separation from the rest of the Whorl and your persecution as a people apart. I congratulate you on the excellent choice you made, on the precedent set by your honorable decision to power down the unusual defenses you long have maintained here, guarding yourselves against the normal human race . . ."

Jorah hated that kind of talk. He wanted action. He looked at Tavkel—still calm. At Meris—sticking close to Gambrel. Back to Tavkel—flanked by six of their best.

"On behalf of the Special Operations Oversight Committee," Gambrel said, "I present Colonel Pelson Urnock, formerly of Covert Operations." He motioned another Tallan forward, a man with a high forehead and a slack expression.

The new SOOC man! It was a good thing Jorah's dad was elsewhere.

But where?

• • •

Kinnor Caldwell stood behind the concealed launch door inside Hangar Three, next to the FI-221 that had been prepped for launch. And he wasn't alone. His crew chief and half a dozen others hefted long, heavy objects that could double as weapons: cleaning tools, fueling probes, spare parts.

Kinnor's father had ordered him to stay here and await orders. But Kinnor had spent a lifetime ignoring orders he disapproved of. He'd been wrong more than once, and he'd paid for his mistakes. But he could not forget that these people had watch-linked his son. They should pay. It was revenge he wanted.

And his preflight checks hadn't shown a single malfunction. In other words, he had weapons. The Feds weren't even blocking his launch path. Apparently Tavkel was going to let him do it—him, out of every Sentinel here. The infamous loose cannon was armed.

And he could not figure out why. Maybe because he'd been dead, and now his heart was pounding and his forehead sweating, by Tavkel's power. Or maybe because he'd never willingly laid down his abilities for Tavkel's sake.

No, that made no sense. Maybe this was just the very last temptation of a lifetime that Tavkel had extended for him, and a final chance to get it right. It wasn't his dad's last order that now echoed in his mind. It was Tavkel's. If the Sentinels resisted before Tavkel spoke to the Whorl, there would be dire consequences.

But what about afterward? Kinnor rubbed his chin. He knew that his bond mate Wind, the only woman strong enough—or fool enough—to take him as a lifetime partner, stood outside the other launch doors. She was going along with Tavkel's plan, simply trying to talk Gambrel out of doing anything stupid.

But Gambrel *would* do something stupid. Kinnor was utterly convinced that the Feds would attack this place . . . and he wanted it known, by any future generations there might be, that someone had fought back!

He glanced aside. Crew Chief Upsalte stood beside the charging console, ready to give the FI-221 a last shot of launch juice. Kinnor outranked everyone else in H-3. They all waited for his decision.

Launch? Flame the Feds on his way down the strip, and then ram the *White Squall?*

His dad wouldn't approve, of course—but when had that ever stopped Kinnor Irion Caldwell? And naturally, his mother would have a righteous Netaian snit. That had never stopped him either.

And he'd already been dead. It was nothing to be afraid of. Weren't the Feds breaking all kinds of Federate policies all over the Whorl, persecuting his people? Tavkel wanted to claim the moral high ground. Well, that was fine. *And he's going to win. I know he is. Because he's Boh-Dabar. He can't lose.*

So why had he armed Kinnor Caldwell?

Kinnor rested a hand on the FI-221's wing and clenched his eyes shut.

• • •

Jorah watched his mother step forward to answer Gambrel's speech. Like Grandfather, she'd put on her best—a brown formal jacket that she often wore to greet new arrivals.

"Chancellor Gambrel, this is a historic moment." She looked tall and calm. "It is our wish, now as always, to serve the Federacy."

Not exactly "Welcome to Procyel," Jorah observed, but she'd always been a little too cordial with difficult people. Like Jorah's dad. Like Jorah himself.

Glancing right, he spotted Captain Anastu and Piet Keeson, the pair who'd gone off with Meris. They trailed the last of the Federate party down the ramp. Captain Anastu took a bad step as she stepped onto the scarred ground. Piet caught her. What had happened to them?

Chancellor Gambrel raised an arm. He beckoned those two forward. All the Federates stood together in a tight little knot, on the landing strip's center zone. Captain Anastu and Piet ended up between them and the array of Sentinels in front of the hangar doors. More Sentinels stood with Jorah along the strip's downhill side.

Chancellor Gambrel spoke again. "Well said, Administrator. The Federacy has always valued your service. We ask you to serve us now in a new capacity. These two arrived at our landing module as menaces to humankind, as frightening outsiders. They now are normal human beings, reabsorbed by the human race—as the Eternal Speaker whom you claim to worship created it. I have come in his service, you might say. I come with the cure for your centuries of isolation."

Jorah squinted at the man in medical yellow. Instantly, his gut boiled. That was Zeimsky! Tavkel had restored that blocked memory. And since Zeimsky was here, Jorah had no doubt what had just happened to Mel and Piet. *They're going for our ayins right here!*

To Jorah's left and right, Sentinels shifted their stances. He obviously wasn't the only one who had understood Gambrel's threat.

If it came to unarmed combat, they were ready.

His mother was one of the few who still looked placid. "Chancellor, on behalf of all Thyrian Sentinels, I must decline. We will continue to serve the Federacy, perhaps not as originally created, but as the Eternal Speaker allowed our history to unfold. And you made a promise to us." She raised her head and peered toward the hovercraft. "An Instantaneous Transceiver Disk was to be brought here, so we could plead our case to the Federacy in a fair, two-way conversation. We strongly protest what was done to the College at Thyrica—and, apparently, to Sentinel Anastu and Sekiyr Keeson.

"Let me reiterate: We only wish to go on serving humanity—there on Thyrica, here on Procyel II, and wherever else the Federacy sends us. Exactly as we are, Chancellor."

Gambrel made a slight bow. "Minster Haworth-Caldwell, the disk will be offloaded as soon as my party is satisfied with your group's compliance with me, and with my medical officer."

Zeimsky shifted his weight. A chill raced down Jorah's spine. Zeimsky hadn't waited for *his* consent. Why should anyone think they would wait now?

Tavkel frowned slightly. What was he waiting for? It had been one thing to see Tavkel take and renew people's abilities. Tavkel had been one of them, his own cousin. At this Tallan Zeimsky's hands, they'd get what amounted to an amputation. And no promise of eternal mercy would ease the transition.

His mother straightened. "That never was part of the agreement, Chancellor." She too glanced at Tavkel.

Tavkel stood still in front of a hangar door, eying the Chancellor. Jorah couldn't tell whether he was paying the hovercraft any attention. Nor the armed contingent.

Gambrel made a careless gesture with one hand. "Occasionally, an agreement must be altered. Surely you understand that as the developers of this technology, we are justified in controlling its use. We do offer the disk now, as a token of our goodwill. However, we ask in return that twelve of your number return with us now, for treatment. We will bring the rest of the ITD apparatus when we return those people to you and gather another twelve volunteers."

To Jorah's shock, his mother gave a weird little head-shake. "No. No, wait. You didn't develop this technology!"

One of the armed Tallans chuckled derisively. He turned to his partner and muttered something.

Jorah's mother kept talking. "Listen to me. According to your newscans, you developed the ITD based on something that was used by the Ancients. Isn't that correct?"

Gambrel raised his hands dismissively. "Correct, madam. However, you have no more connection with the Ancients than we do—"

"No!" she cried again.

Now the other Sentinels—near the hangar doors, and along the landing strip's edge with Jorah—also turned to stare. Even Grandmother looked puzzled. What in the Whorl was his mother going on about, and why now? Hadn't she heard what the Feds wanted to do to them all?

She took three steps toward the Federates. As she did, she reached into a pocket inside her brown jacket. "Chancellor, I found that technology. *I* found it. At an installation on my homeworld, Mikuhr. Deep in a facility the Ancients actually built."

Jorah stared at his mother. She what?

She spoke quickly. "Furthermore, I gave most of those artifacts to Ellet Kinsman Dardy of the Sentinel College on Thyrica. As a historian, she undoubtedly shared them with other historians, including those at the Federate Regional Capital."

A shiver marched across Jorah's shoulderblades. This was no time to mention Mikuhr! If these people feared Sentinels, they were justly terrified by the Mikuhran Shuhr.

His own ancestors. Through her bloodline! As if seeing a stranger, he looked at his mother's long face, black hair, and considerable height. The guards around Gambrel also stared at her, as if they expected her to attack them.

"Chancellor," his mother said, "my people—the Sentinel kindred—actually have a stronger claim to those devices than yours do." She pulled something out of her pocket and tugged her jacket fronts together again. "Here. Here's proof. Our water system has just been damaged, and a worker who was trying to perform repairs found this. It's one of those artifacts, one I kept for myself. At the time, I'd thought it was some ancient form of data coin. I lost it here decades ago and forgot about it. It probably fell off a railing into our reflecting pool."

Jorah gaped. He'd never heard this story! He squinted across the strip, trying to see whatever the three unarmed Feds were passing among themselves.

His mother kept her hand out, obviously wanting it back.

Zeimsky reached toward his pocket with it. Several Sentinels stepped toward the Federate group.

Chancellor Gambrel growled, "Zeimsky."

The medical officer handed it back, glowering.

Grandfather straightened almost imperceptibly. Jorah hoped he had recognized the medic's name—either from the nameplate or from Gambrel's quick word—and that he recalled the reports Jorah had brought back from Tallis.

Anyway, Gambrel had told them all what he meant to do to them.

Gambrel sweetened his voice. "Madam, naturally I can confirm the disks' origin. They were indeed grown from those so-called coins found on Mikuhr. However, my own people performed the difficult research and design work. To yours, there were nothing more than curiosities."

Not far from Jorah, Annalah muttered, "But it all factored into Tavkel's plans."

Gambrel stared at Annalah for a moment.

Jorah's mother stood tall and unflustered between the hangars and the landing strip. "You force me to insist, sir," she said. "Until you keep the promise you already made, there can be no further discussion. You have asked us to trust you with our very lives. Show us we can also trust you. Bring us the machinery that will make your disk operable. Then, we will discuss our future."

Jorah had to admire her poise. Hadn't Tavkel urged *no resistance?* Not until he'd used the ITD, anyway. After that, Jorah wondered how many of those burly Feds he could take down himself, unarmed, before they got him.

Colonel Urnock flicked a finger. Several uniformed Tallans stepped forward, holding those big energy weapons across their chests. *Not hand blazers,* Jorah observed. *Maybe those are all stuck in their holsters, like my crystace.* Still, the threat was plain. He could end up laid out on the ground, beaten senseless with one of those barrels.

He eyed Tavkel again. *Now, sir? Now?*

To his relief, Tavkel raised a hand. Jorah's mother stepped aside in deference. "Now, my friends," Tavkel said. "We gave them the chance to act honorably. Go on board, but don't hurt anyone."

CHAPTER 41

Jorah expected a fight to break out at those words. But none of the Federate party moved—other than their eyes, many of which widened in surprise. Someone had voice-commanded the whole Federate group! Whose powers had come back *that* far?

Walking with utter dignity, Jorah's grandfather left the hangar doors and strode forward across the soft ground. The armed Federates still didn't budge. "Jorah," Grandfather called, "come on. You've earned this."

Jorah dropped his rake and sprinted out onto the strip. Major Ryken and Captain Mattason followed, of course.

The rest of the Sentinels stayed in their places, but several of them twitched, or scratched, or shifted a hand. Plainly they weren't voice-commanded, even if the Tallans were. The people in grey uniforms all stood with their weaponry across their chests, only their eyes flickering.

Jorah exulted. Things were not going to go Chancellor Gambrel's way! He spared Meris a glance. She still stood behind the Chancellor, and she wasn't moving. Except her eyes.

A voice spoke in his mind—it startled him to recognize his grandmother, since for as long as he could remember, she'd been powerless. *We'll watch your backs. There are still more of us than them.*

Tavkel really had healed her! Grandfather must be training her too.

"Wait." Grandfather stopped in front of the Federate party. In front of Meris. "Meris, please come with us, in your role as liaison. We would like you to witness that we will touch nothing except the ITD we were promised."

Meris gave a little shake and spun around. Grandfather walked on, straight across the open space toward the hovercraft, not hurrying. Meris followed. They passed right in front of Jorah. She didn't look at him.

He fell in behind them, confused. Was it Grandfather or Tavkel who had put everyone under voice-command? He'd assumed Tavkel . . . but . . . Grandfather had looked like he'd released her.

Maybe it didn't matter. Maybe Tavkel and Grandfather were just working in full communion.

Meris paused at the top of the ramp and then plunged in. She led the group into the passenger compartment, its seats folded up and shoved aside. Remembering that they hoped to take prisoners back to their landing module to be ayinectomized, Jorah shuddered.

Meris stepped to the far back of the compartment and pointed at a large crated object. It was anchored to the rear bulkhead with several bolted bands. "But that's just part of it." She sounded troubled. "That's the disk itself. As Chancellor Gambrel said, when he used one back at the meadow, there was also a . . . a frame, a mechanism built up around it." She pantomimed something like a box. "He actually stood inside it, on top of the disk. He said it wouldn't work without the rest of it."

As she looked straight into his eyes, Jorah imagined he felt her sincerity. He couldn't imagine any Sentinels going meekly away to be disempowered, not even to buy Tavkel the rest of the ITD—but if it meant Tavkel could speak to the Whorl, maybe they would.

And Tavkel had said Gambrel was wrong, hadn't he? Jorah gave himself a fast mental shake. This was going to be *good*. "Maybe down in the hangars, there's something we could add to make it work?" he asked.

"This is Tavkel's time. Let's see what he can do with just the disk." Grandfather extended a hand toward the crate. To Jorah's delight, bolts popped loose and a set of metal bands flopped free, releasing the crate from the bulkhead. "Jorah, I'll make this somewhat lighter than it really is. But I want you to carry it to Tavkel."

Jorah pushed past Meris and got his hands around the object. Sure enough, for all its apparent mass it felt as light as a crockery bowl. Still . . . "No, sir." He steered the disk out into the aisle between seats. "We shouldn't take risks with it. What if I slip? What if I'm still watch-linked?"

Grandfather smiled slightly. "You don't trust my work?" Still, he took hold of the crated disk. He turned sideways and stepped up the aisle toward the hatch.

Jorah brushed up against Meris. "Are you all right?" he asked softly.

"I'm fine." She flicked a loose strand of hair off her face. The gesture made him wish she would let the rest of it hang down, just once more. What were the chances he would ever see her again, after today? "But something isn't right, is it?" she asked. "Those two officers with Chancellor Gambrel—they've been arguing with him. Almost the whole time. I'm not entirely convinced that they mean you well."

"Tell Mother. Wait, just tell Grandfather." And maybe it wasn't too late to say something he should've said a long time ago. "I'll protect you if I can, if things get violent. Tavkel's trying to prevent that, but—well, stay close."

She sent him a weak smile and followed Grandfather back down the ramp, talking earnestly.

Jorah hung back with his guards, keeping watch over Meris and Grandfather. Outdoors, the waiting groups stood exactly where Jorah had left them: all the Feds at mid-field, all the Sentinels strung out in front of the hangars and the strip's downhill edge. The last shrouded landing crafts looked forlorn on this side of them.

Only Tavkel walked forward to meet the returning group. The new SOOC man and Zeimsky lowered their eyebrows and furiously puckered their faces.

Tavkel met Grandfather just before he reached the Federate party. He gestured toward a level spot on the uphill side of the landing strip. Grandfather lowered the object there and saluted him. Major Ryken and Captain Mattason knelt down and uncrated the disk, but apparently Grandfather was helping, since they didn't seem to need tools. Soon the disk lay exposed on the grass, gleaming in the early afternoon sun.

Tavkel tossed his stick aside and stepped onto the shimmering disk. Instantly, the surface turned to something that looked more liquid than solid. Jorah felt his eyes widen. For a moment, he worried that Tavkel might actually sink into it.

"Unbelievable," Meris whispered near Jorah's shoulder. "He's doing it. He's activated the disk—without the apparatus."

"Of course," Jorah whispered back. "And now the whole Whorl will see."

• • •

Meris had grown used to seeing Tavkel work wonders with human bodies. But to see him as a master of technology baffled her afresh. Was it illusion, or was she looking through the silvery surface he stood on into some inconceivable distance? A tapestry of faces seemed to shift and melt into each other, as if the transmission were being relayed all over the Whorl.

"You have heard my name," Tavkel said. "Now see my face. Hear my words, in my own voice."

Meris glanced around, at the Federates standing like statues and the Sentinels who also weren't moving—but by choice. The disk cast a faint light onto those who stood close by, but not onto Tavkel. He seemed almost as brilliant as the disk itself.

Did the others think that this was normal ITD operation? Gambrel hadn't shone when he stood on the disk. He'd looked like an ordinary human being.

Tavkel stood with hands low. "You have lived in the stream of time," he said. "That stream has brought you down to the ocean, down to this moment, a moment like no other. You who know you are lost—you have never stepped out of your Father's loving sight. You who struggle and stress, you who feel forsaken—the one who made you is the very fire of peace. Yet you all have betrayed him every day, falling into deep darkness.

"So give me that darkness. While you live, until the Whorl is destroyed and remade, you may come. Come from wherever you sit or stand or lie. Come with your heart beating and your mind awake. Step off your path onto mine. Follow me. That's all you need to know, for this moment. You'll have an eternity to learn more. Choose me," he said. "But choose quickly. The time is short."

Meris shook something out of her mind that felt like dust. Tavkel was making that offer to people all over the Whorl, but especially to *her*. The muddy landing strip faded from view, and she had the strange sensation of looking inside herself.

A flaming and ravenous . . . something . . . burned there, illogically dark. She imagined a figure bound down by black flame, a flickering vision of someone she could have become—a woman who freely expressed the love she had always held back, who cared for people out of compassion instead of a thirst to be admired and accepted, a woman who laughed more and took time to enjoy beautiful things. And in the vision she understood that it was not quite too late to unbind that admirable woman. To become her.

Tavkel's voice echoed in her mind. "Give me that darkness . . . Follow me."

He was a good man, Meris reflected. And maybe he was more than that. She would like to go wherever he was going.

Beyond the hillside, up past the orchard, thunder echoed out of the clear sky. Tavkel's voice took on a harsh edge. The words seemed to blur, as if he weren't speaking to her any longer.

● ● ●

The screaming in Piper Gambrel's head finally tapered away. He heard Tavkel distinctly, each word like a singular burst of fire.

"But you who think you are whole, you do not know your brokenness. You who think you create your own light, the darkness waits to consume you. Give it to me. Come." Tavkel reached out a hand . . . in his direction! "Come with only darkness to give me, but come. Be free of it."

The god within him was silent.

"Or carry it with you into endless misery and our Father's just retribution."

Gambrel thrust aside his sudden fear. *I am the spark of undying light. I shall see. I shall know. The eternal is in me. It cannot know defeat . . .*

● ● ●

Meris blinked. There'd been something about misery . . . retribution . . . No, those words weren't for her. She was loved. She was called.

She shook herself. Tavkel still stood on the glimmering platter, extending a hand. "Chancellor Gambrel," he called. "All of the shadows are silent, in this moment like no other. Even you, and your partners invading this world of holy rest, do not need to press forward with your plans—the spoken plans, nor the secret ones. Not even you, Colonel Zeimsky. I will not be defeated."

Were these words also for her? Confused, Meris clenched her hands to make sure she could feel them. Was she dreaming, or was she awake and hallucinating? To her bewilderment, the Chancellor stood shaking his head. He looked confused. No, he looked frightened.

Finally, Tavkel stepped off the disk. Its surface kept swirling, silvery blue with the multitudinous faces appearing and vanishing. Was it still transmitting? The Chancellor clutched his head with both hands. Colonel Zeimsky took a step toward Tavkel.

Colonel Urnock also seemed to shake free of whatever it was that the Sentinels had been doing to them all. He strode straight up to Tavkel without hesitating. "Sir, I charge you with interfering with a legally conducted execution, not to mention this hijacking of Federate property that you just committed. You, sir, are under arrest."

Arrest? Horrified, Meris spun toward Jorah. He stood beside her, clenching his fists. Near the hangar door, Minster Wind and Shamarr Kiel also sprang back to life. They strode toward Chancellor Gambrel's group. Colonel Urnock's guards shifted their hold on those long energy weapons. At the edge of the landing strip, several other Sentinels hustled forward as if to attack.

Tavkel made the slightest hand motion down at his side. The Sentinels stopped where they stood. All but Minster Wind and Shamarr Kiel, who kept coming until they stood close to Chancellor Gambrel and the two colonels.

Colonel Urnock stood as straight and stiff as a duracrete pillar. "Tavkel Caldwell, you stand accused of selfish, capricious use of your abilities. I remind you, sir, that this is a capital offense. How do you plead?"

Plead? *Wait a minute,* Meris wanted to shout, *are you arresting him, or are you the local judge?*

Without hesitating, Tavkel reached out both hands. "I am no Sentinel. You cannot accuse me of selfish or capricious use of my abilities, because I took no such vows."

The Sentinels who'd gone on alert appeared to relax.

"Hah," Jorah whispered.

Tavkel still stood near the disk. "As to the other charge—bringing Kinnor Caldwell out of death, to demonstrate my power over it—yes. I was born to undo death. Now you shall see what I do with darkness itself. Before long, you will know that I am true light. Not only the sun, immutable and eternal—you could not look straight at the sun—but also the daystar, faithfully reflecting the sun's light. And you may look straight at me."

Follow me. It still rang in Meris's mind, like a bass note below everything else she heard.

"Nonsense!" Colonel Urnock sent a long, triumphant look toward High Commander Caldwell. Colonel Zeimsky crossed his arms. Chancellor Gambrel stood a little apart from them, looking stunned and confused.

And the disk still shimmered, as if it were transmitting. Was everyone else blind to that?

Meris looked around. Chancellor Gambrel and his colonels, and the aides she'd seen back at the landing module, were the only people present—other than her—who knew what a transmitting ITD looked like. And they all stood where they couldn't see it. Tavkel's confession that he'd revived Kinnor Caldwell, and the magnificent declaration that he was true light, along with all the rest of it—had gone out to all the Whorl.

She pictured people on every planet standing spellbound, watching this situation unfold. *Follow me.* How were people back home on Elysia reacting? Were her parents seeing this? Could they see her, standing here as a witness? Might they turn to this man? *Follow me . . .* It rang in her head like a litany. *You who feel forsaken . . .*

"Chancellor." Colonel Urnock spun in place. He faced Chancellor Gambrel. "You obtained proof of that crime, besides the confession he just made. You know for a fact that Tavkel Caldwell interfered with the legal and just execution of Air Master Kinnor Caldwell. Don't you?"

Were they blind? Meris couldn't believe they stood bickering. Couldn't they see—couldn't they hear—that utterly compelling call? Was she imagining things, or did Colonel Zeimsky also look slightly befuddled?

And what had Colonel Urnock meant by "proof"?

Oh . . . An unsettling memory rattled her out of her reverie. Her proof. She swallowed on a suddenly tight throat. She had testified against Tavkel. Maybe she couldn't go to him after all. Maybe she had disqualified herself.

CHAPTER 42

Piper Gambrel stared at the herdsman. The god within him had found its voice again, but it had been reduced to a whisper, repeating three words over and over, to the point where Gambrel could ignore them if he chose. They made no sense, anyway: *Anywhere but here. Anywhere but here.*

I am the spark of undying light, he answered it.

He glanced left and right, toward the waiting hovercraft and then at the Caldwell family in front of the hangar doors. These people would pay. They would pay dearly for immobilizing him, whoever did it and however it was done. Maybe they had another remote apparatus down here. They would also pay for strolling onboard and helping themselves to his possessions. Oh, they would pay. The list was lengthening. Both senior Caldwells were plainly ringleaders. Behind the high commander and his aged little wife, a narrow access door—to the left of the big hangar doors—swung open.

For the moment, he ignored it. Near the senior Caldwells stood the young writer, the troublemaker. Annalah Caldwell. It seemed incongruous that the woman who'd done such damage to Whorl-wide Collegiate causes looked like such a child in person.

And Urnock was talking to Meris Cariole, who lingered close to Lieutenant Jorah Caldwell.

Meris and the lieutenant?

"Yes." She sounded less confident than before. Less Collegiate. "I presented that proof to Chancellor Gambrel. It was medical data ascertaining that Kinnor Caldwell was, in fact, dead when he was transported to this place."

"That man?" Urnock pointed at Air Master Caldwell, who had just walked out through the small access door. He wore a midnight blue Sentinel uniform, as if they needed uniforms in this place. He held his head at a cocky angle that seemed like a deliberate affront to Gambrel and all he stood for. Several other Sentinels followed him, holding empty hands down at their sides.

"Yes. That man, who is alive." Meris smiled oddly as she said it, as if she actually liked the Air Master. Again Gambrel wondered if tragically, she might need to be silenced. "I didn't see what happened to him, Chancellor, but I believe . . ." She hesitated. "If you need a witness who was present, here is Shamarr Caldwell. He—"

"His brother." Zeimsky strode forward. Gambrel took a long look at the Shamarr as Zeimsky kept talking. Unlike his brother, the Shamarr lowered his eyes. "And therefore not an objective witness," Zeimsky said. "I want both brothers under arrest, for immediate treatment. Now." Zeimsky motioned toward the nearest guards. "And him. Tavkel." He pointed toward the herdsman, who still stood near the ITD.

Twins, weren't they? One tall, intellectual-looking, and passive—the other stocky, strong, and defiant—Gambrel had known that, from his files. He plainly was distracted. He raised a hand and ordered, "Wait." Zeimsky had no subtlety. These people had too much power as a group. Maybe they'd all been working together, immobilizing his forces. They had to be separated—but it must be done delicately, without provoking any further displays of ayin energy.

And he did recognize the tall man in the grey ministerial tunic. He'd seen Shamarr Caldwell . . . where? What was wrong with his memory today? Wasn't it time to ask for volunteers?

"I was there." The Shamarr's eyes were serious, his expression calm and controlled. Gambrel recognized another truly spiritual presence. Finally, here was someone he could deal with—though now he remembered the request that the Shamarr had sent, asking SOOC to commute his brother's death sentence. The Shamarr had a tendency to meddle.

The Shamarr pressed his palms together. "I saw Kinnor's body. It had been desiccated for transport. Then, as we prepared to lay him to rest, I saw him climb out of the coffin. That was when I gave Tavkel my loyalty. There were other witnesses." He glanced back at the elderly couple.

Gambrel turned toward Tavkel. The ITD's surface still shimmered . . . wait, was all this being transmitted? Gambrel's people had assured him that it couldn't be activated at all, much less transmit, without the supporting machinery.

Then they had been wrong. He thought hastily. If people were watching all over the Federacy, then he must give the impression of absolute compassion. Of wisdom under pressure.

That shouldn't be difficult. *I am the spark of undying light . . .*

Whereas Tavkel's previous demands, broadcast via those *PERs* and now here in person, had been scandalous. Repugnant. A challenge to independent selfhood. As for darkness: ridiculous! But Urnock and Zeimsky were just making a volatile situation more dangerous.

"Enough." Gambrel spoke firmly, mindful of his potential audience. He looked first at the Shamarr, the Air Master, and the Minster, who stood close together. "That man, Tavkel, is guilty of grave crimes against Federate sovereignty. He has been using extraordinary abilities to gather a following, here and elsewhere. All this is scandalous. For centuries you people have been forbidden to proselytize, haven't you?"

Neither the Shamarr nor the Minster moved. The Air Master took a short step forward, but then he stepped back into place.

At last, he had them where he wanted them. "Any further demonstration of your powers," he said in his best theatrical voice, "and particularly any use of your voice-command on me and my people, will be seen as a hostile act. You claim to be victims, but you act like aggressors."

The answering silence reassured him. Excellent! He still could command attention, even without the god-voice. At the back of his mind, it went on gibbering. *Anywhere . . . anywhere . . .*

"Therefore, I offer all you Sentinels the chance to be healed of the disfigurements that have made you odious to Federate society. My transport can carry twelve—only twelve, the first time. But we will not leave this world until all who wish to be cured have received treatment!"

Gambrel stepped aside, closer to that herdsman in his odorous work clothes. He would be merciful here too. "Tavkel, a sentence has already been pronounced back on Tallis, against whoever had interfered with this man's legal execution. A death sentence. You are that man, as you have just admitted, so you stand condemned to die. Do you still wish to plead guilty? Or will you sensibly retract some of the extravagant claims you just made?"

Zeimsky seized Gambrel's arm. "Just make sure he's on board. I want to talk to him. I want him cured."

Gambrel shook him off. Zeimsky was out of order. Urnock's assignment included carrying out this arrest—and unless there was trouble, *only* this arrest . . . for now. Later, Gambrel would give Urnock the extended list. Meanwhile, Zeimsky's job was to be selecting and curing people.

The herdsman gazed at them all. He glanced aside at the ITD. "I retract nothing, Chancellor Gambrel. Colonel Urnock, I am the man you want to take away from Hesed House. Colonel Zeimsky, let the Sentinels go. All of them. They are my family. If you touch them, you touch me. But—" He looked left and right again, slowly moving his head. A master showman. "For their sake and yours, I shall cooperate with Colonel Urnock."

A storm of protests blew out of the Sentinel group. For the first time, they looked confused instead of confident. Two of them turned and dashed back inside through the small access door.

"So be it, Tavkel." Urnock spread his hands. "By your own confession, you are guilty. And you will face the consequences."

Gambrel let the Sentinels shout and argue. They were growing less organized by the moment. Such confusion put new heart into him. As the hubbub spread, he opened a hand toward Meris Cariole. She still might prove useful. He beckoned her closer. "Well done, young woman. There is a bright future for you on Tallis." Her face remained strangely blank, but he couldn't spare her any more attention. He turned aside. "Shamarr Caldwell, silence your people."

The tall man shook his head. "Sir, that has never been my calling. I am one who listens, not one who—"

You! The god-voice stopped gibbering. A single word rang through Gambrel's mind. It drowned out whatever the Shamarr was saying. Gambrel kept staring at the Shamarr, trying to figure out what had roused the whimpering god. *You!* it repeated.

He couldn't help saying it out loud. "You! Kiel Caldwell!" His own voice sounded strange to him.

The Shamarr backed away, smiling queerly. "So it is you, shadow. We meet again." He spread his hands. "I told you, back on Mikuhr—didn't I? You had confused me with someone else." He looked at Tavkel. "There he is, before you. He is the Boh-Dabar."

None of that made sense, and Gambrel sensed he was losing dignity in front of an ITD audience that should see him as strong. He raised his voice and was relieved to find that he could control it. "Listen," he cried, "Tavkel has been summoned to appear on Tallis for a thorough examination, legal and medical. Therefore, a reprieve is granted to him. Medical stasis will suffice. He will not need to be transported back to Tallis as Air Master Caldwell was transported here." He gave those words a slight, humorous rise.

Not even Meris laughed.

Zeimsky turned toward him, red spots on his cheeks, hands twitching. "You're nothing but a common entertainer, Gambrel. You don't have a big enough audience here on Procyel, do you? Not even with . . ." He jerked his head toward the shimmering disk.

Gambrel's hands twitched too, but he refused to lower himself by answering Zeimsky as he deserved.

Tavkel walked forward and stepped between them. *Brave man,* Gambrel observed. Tavkel finally looked a little grey, though. Maybe it had occurred to him that things weren't going his way anymore. "I will cooperate with you." He spoke clearly, although the hubbub at Gambrel's back kept rising. "You must understand that in what happens now, I allow it. I am in charge. Not the shadows."

Him. The god-voice seemed oddly weak again. Exhausted, maybe. *Him. Caldwell. Kiel Caldwell. Give him to me. Tell Tavkel to give him to me.*

It was easier than ever to simply ignore the disempowered voice. Gambrel repeated—loudly, for all his audiences, "Tavkel, you will come with me to Tallis, in medical stasis. Surely you understand our concern about your unusual abilities."

"I told you." Tavkel extended a hand. Gambrel stepped backward, illogically frightened. The god-voice went back to gibbering. "I am allowing all of this. For the sake of my flocks. This is necessary." He turned to Zeimsky. "Don't try to force these people to cooperate with you, Colonel. They've been holding back on my orders."

Flocks? Herdsman language, used by a hick. Orders? The military Sentinels seemed to be breaking up into small groups, some of them obviously angry.

"Zeimsky," Gambrel ordered, "have your people offload a stasis crypt. Quickly."

The Minster hustled forward, clasping her hands in front of her dress coat. "Sir, we have stasis facilities and supplies—"

"I'm sure you do." Gambrel raised a hand, hoping to keep Zeimsky quiet. The longer the Sentinels bickered, the better. "And we will be pleased to use those facilities. However, the crypt will be ours. Your people may examine it. There will be no trickery." He didn't need to tell her—yet—that she would be travelling in an entirely different kind of crypt.

Scowling and muttering, Zeimsky strode toward a group of four guards between Gambrel and the hangar doors.

Gambrel glanced aside. Did that blasted ITD still look liquid? Yes, it did.

Very well, he would take advantage. As Zeimsky hustled back in his direction, the guards followed. Gambrel walked over and stepped onto the disk. "Surely," he told the Whorl, "this is obvious. A powerful individual, possessed of unknown abilities, must be transported safely. His hearing at Tallis will be full and fair. And public," he added on impulse. Why waste a chance for publicity? "The Collegium for Human Learning will disseminate it via our new ITD technology. The Federacy has always—"

Abruptly, the thing's surface went dark and solid. Almost as if it had a mind of its own— Hadn't some tech told him, years ago, that the things had actually been *grown* from the original ancient stock? Was it alive, an alien life form?

Ridiculous.

Air Master Caldwell, the man who ought to be dead, stepped in front of Gambrel and Tavkel. "You're out of your jurisdiction, Gambrel. You just follow those people back on board that hovercraft, and—"

Colonel Urnock stepped up from Gambrel's other side. "Air Master Caldwell, you will salute a superior officer."

Air Master Caldwell's hands stayed at his side. He glanced toward the big hangar doors. "Don't make me regret what I didn't just do, Urnock."

Urnock raised his chin. "Whatever that is, you, sir, are still under a death sentence. You may also consider yourself under arrest, to be transported back to Tallis—"

Laughing, Air Master Caldwell raised a hand. He looked as if he meant to use that abominable voice-command on Urnock. "You can't kill a man twice for the same crime. Anyway, you heard Tavkel. I'm family. You touch me, you touch him. And I'm going nowhere."

Urnock shook his head and muttered something Gambrel didn't catch.

I am the spark . . . It was time to stop his own people's bickering. They all were anxious, and for good reason. This was supposed to have been a show of force, a demand for volunteers in exchange for what the Sentinels really wanted: a functioning ITD. Obviously, these people had not expected Tavkel to cooperate with arrest.

Zeimsky would get Tavkel into stasis.

Then—after retreating to the meadow with one stasis crypt on board—Gambrel would deliver a much stiffer ultimatum.

• • •

Jorah looked from Meris to Tavkel. Then toward his dad. Urnock. Gambrel. He glanced at his mom. At Uncle Kiel, and then his grandparents. Would someone just tell him what to do next?

Tavkel had used the disk. So maybe he didn't need to *do* anything. Tavkel would show the Whorl what real power looked like. Any moment now.

Jorah glanced at the sky. Would Sabba Six-alpha go nova? Or maybe Procyel's own sun, which was even closer? If any star within the Whorl went supernova, it would incinerate all twenty-three settled worlds. That was his personal guess about the cataclysm. It would happen too fast to hurt. He wasn't the least afraid.

But he didn't want to leave Meris's side. After Tavkel's amazing speech, surely she was ready to give over the deed to her darkness. If she hadn't already.

He eyed the sky again. The storm clouds had cleared. What was Tavkel waiting for? All this talk about cooperating with arrest—it was for show, right?

Nearby, Zeimsky's face had gone red. He waved an arm toward a knot of the big guards. "We are not going back without more people to treat. That would be a waste of time, risk, and fuel. So if no one volunteers, just take whoever's closest."

A big Tallan shouldered his energy weapon. Before Jorah could react, he swung it at Jorah's mother.

She leaped backward.

"You—" Jorah's dad sprang toward her.

"Stop!" Tavkel thrust up a hand.

Before his dad could reach either of them, his mother took another inexplicable leap sideways. The big Tallan's momentum spun him around. One leg slid out from under him. He went down and lay twitching at Mother's feet, clawing the muddy ground with both hands.

It looked like he'd tripped . . . but was Tavkel finally ready to fight? Jorah gathered himself to rush forward. Adrenaline surged through him.

Tavkel lowered his hand and his voice. "Do not touch my family." Every word carried as if it had been separately amplified.

Jorah's dad stopped where he stood, fury in his eyes. The rest of the big Tallans backed away. Slowly.

Tavkel walked over to where the Tallan guard lay twitching. He reached down and grasped the man's hand. He pulled him to his feet.

"Colonel Zeimsky." Tavkel's face looked strange as he turned back to Gambrel and his cronies. Were those pain lines all over it, or was that righteous anger? "You will travel back to your landing module with one passenger. With me."

Jorah ran a hand over his face. Apparently Tavkel had more on his mind than fighting—or cutting straight to the cataclysm. But if he didn't give some orders soon, Jorah was pretty sure he wasn't the only one who was going to do something on his own initiative.

Such as stay close to Meris?

He shot her a glance. Her face had soured. He would have given anything to know what was going on in her brain.

● ● ●

Meris felt like she might explode with conflicting emotions. At last, Tavkel had made it plain that he had mutant powers. He'd had them all along. Maybe he had even more than he was letting on right now, controlling the ITD while voice-commanding a crowd— and then rising to Minster Wind's defense like that. Obviously— obviously!—he hadn't been affected by those blocking drugs they had kept giving him. Still . . .

Follow me. She couldn't shake that echo. She longed to obey it. But she had to stay focused on the moment. They might yet call upon her in her capacity as a liaison.

And she alone, of all the people who'd been living at Hesed House, knew from experience that Chancellor Gambrel was some- one who could be respected. Surely he would save the situation.

Reluctantly she imposed a litany over the echo. *I am the spark of undying light . . .*

It mostly worked. Still, she felt guilty about seeing her research used to condemn a good man. All she could conceivably hold against Tavkel was his having said that the Chancellor was also full of darkness. That, and telling a disturbing story about a girl and a dead pet. Even now, despite her doubt and confusion, she had to admire Chancellor Gambrel. At his insistence, no one was going to harm Tavkel. The Chancellor's reprieve might stretch on for years, thanks to Tallis's ponderous legal system. Her father had complained about it many times.

And—here was a new thought—at Tallis, Tavkel would be able to talk to people right there at Regional Command. Perhaps that was what he actually wanted. He did keep claiming that all this was happening because he allowed it.

Tavkel didn't look steady on his feet, though. He'd picked his stick back up, and he was leaning on it. Maybe all this stress was finally getting to him, or maybe he, like Saried, was exhausted after using his ayin powers. As soon as Colonel Urnock had pronounced sentence on him, almost instantly his face had gone a sickly grey. He seemed to have aged twenty years. His skin sagged along his jaw line. His eyes had become sunken as if in pain. He looked as if all that "darkness" he'd been collecting had suddenly started pumping through his veins.

That was preposterous, of course. In all this confusion, she was starting to imagine things.

Colonel Zeimsky's assistants reemerged from the hovercraft with a stasis crypt on a hovercart. Colonel Zeimsky turned to Meris. "I understand you are trained in stasis procedures. You will join me."

Good. Whatever happened next, she wanted to see it. In fact, she would feel better about what happened to Tavkel next if she could be there. "I will be honored, sir." She turned to Minster Wind. "Minster, you did offer the use of the medical suite."

The Minster spoke with firm dignity. "Only because this is what Tavkel wants. Come. This way."

The Minster walked through the crowd, headed for the small access door. Beside her came the senior Caldwells, arm in arm. Annalah rushed up and joined them. Several Federate guards followed—still carrying energy weapons, which grieved Meris. This had been a restful, peaceable place.

Tavkel came next, flanked by two burly armed Tallans. Meris stepped out beside the Chancellor. Jorah followed her closely. *I'll protect you,* he'd said. *Stay close to me.* Actually, that sounded good.

They walked straight through the hangar, up a short corridor, and into the skylit central area. Here, everything seemed to have changed since she left. The beautiful pool had been partly drained. Sludgy mud lapped at its sides. What had happened?

Uniformed Sentinels stood at all the corridor entries and all four corners of the pool, obviously as guards. At a word from Colonel Urnock, several Tallans stepped out of this group and let everyone else pass. They were probably going to stand guard too, or alert the other Federates if anything untoward happened.

With people like Air Master Caldwell calling it home, Colonel Urnock had to be feeling defensive. Jorah had said something about genocide, awhile ago. He'd claimed that the Federates actually wanted his people eliminated—so they also had to be feeling anxious. Every Sentinel she saw had a weird stiffness to his or her walk, as if they expected something grim to happen—except a few young ones like Jorah, who looked downright exuberant. They were doing this willingly because Tavkel had ordered it. Did they trust him that much?

Follow me. She heard it again.

She raised her head, thinking as if in answer, *I'm right behind you, Tavkel.*

• • •

Jorah marched along the waterside near the back of the group, next to Major Ryken. At any moment, Tavkel would show them all— everyone—exactly what he would do with all that collected darkness. He'd said so, as he'd spoken to the Whorl. The moment was at hand.

Would Thyrica be Tavkel's new headquarters? Or would that be right here on Procyel II? Was Jorah about to die, and would it hurt? In the renewal, would he remember who he'd been and what he'd done?

Jorah glanced to his right. Other than security people, the waterside walkway and dining commons were empty. Tavkel, Mother, or Grandfather might signal everyone who was in hiding to return right now, via their handhelds. They could easily overwhelm the Tallans, especially with everyone's weapons offline. Was *that* Tavkel's plan?

An unsettling thought struck him. "If they stase Tavkel," he muttered, "do you think everyone's weapons will come back online?"

Major Ryken glared sidelong at a pair of armed Tallans and turned his back as they passed. "Could be a nasty brawl."

"But we'd win," Jorah whispered. "More of us than of them."

And they have no idea, Major Ryken's subvoice said in his head, *how many of us have our ayin powers back.*

"Right." An uneasy qualm grabbed Jorah's gut. That very fact, if the Feds saw it, might give them license to shoot first and ask questions later.

No. Tavkel was in charge. This was his moment. Jorah looked around. Meris and Gambrel had passed them. Annalah and Grandmother were already entering the medical corridor.

But when had Grandfather left the group? And where had his dad and uncle gone? "Come on," Jorah urged his guards, and he hustled to catch up.

CHAPTER 43

Meris mentally ran her checklist as she walked. She always followed procedure, but this would be the first time she had worked with such an important patient. Annalah would also assist, of course. Colonel Zeimsky plainly was a medical professional, wearing that pale yellow duty tunic with all those extra decorations.

She glanced over her shoulder at Jorah. Two other Sentinels were sticking close to him. Maybe they were a work team of some sort. She decided not to ask. More importantly, Tavkel walked on her left. He still looked pale. "It will be all right, sir," she said. "I've been stased. You'll feel a little chilly, but that's about all."

He sent her a weak smile. "This is the only way." He caught his foot on something, maybe a loose paving stone. Annalah grabbed for his shoulder. He used his stick to keep from falling. "Understand," he muttered to Annalah and Meris, "no power can take me unless I let it."

Yes, this was his decision. He'd just shown them all he was *not* at the end of his powers. Still, stress showed on his face: the flattened lips, the narrowed eyes. He seemed to wince with each step. "Sir, don't be frightened. It'll be all right. Stasis is—"

"Meris. For your sake."

Perhaps a tranquilizer would help him calm down. He would be perfectly safe once stasis was complete—the safest person here, if Jorah's father or anyone else provoked trouble.

Meris looked away. A Sentinel whom she vaguely recognized stood blocking the med corridor's entrance. "We know all weapons have been deactivated," he said. "But under normal conditions, we don't enter this corridor armed."

The Tallans in the party merely shifted their long energy guns. None of the Sentinels disarmed either.

"Will you never learn?" Tavkel raised his walking stick. Meris abruptly realized that a muscular herdsman could do serious damage with that staff. Sure enough, Tavkel turned and hefted it. The nearest Tallan raised both fists.

But instead of swinging the staff, Tavkel flung it into the fouled pool. "No victory today will be won with weapons."

The Tallan stepped aside. One of his compatriots leaned toward the wall, reaching out with his gun—but when none of the others joined him, he straightened again.

Still holding the energy gun.

Tavkel led up the corridor to the stasis prep room. Meris stopped in its doorway and raised her voice. "Would everyone except Tavkel and Annalah please remain in the corridor? I'll activate the inter-com panel for you. We'll be out of touch several minutes, though, since the prep room is private."

Most of the group stepped back. Colonel Zeimsky pushed past her, straight into the prep room. After all, he was medical personnel.

At the back of the group, the Minster spoke up. "Chancellor, if that man's going in to observe the procedure, we want an observer also."

Before Chancellor Gambrel could respond, the indomitable Lady Fi pushed forward. "That's my grandson, and you can't keep me out."

Chancellor Gambrel looked at the small old woman and laughed softly. "No one's stopping you, madam."

Was Meris imagining things, or had Chancellor Gambrel's glance lingered on Annalah a little longer than it should have? Was he attracted to her? Meris straightened her back and looked around. Was Jorah still close? Yes—he'd edged to one side of the group. "Everyone else," she said, "give us and our patient the privacy appropriate for this procedure."

• • •

Piper Gambrel backed against the opposite wall and took a moment to contemplate his lengthening list. Tavkel, the "Minster," both Caldwell brothers, their parents—the High Commander charged with abetting his son's escaping house arrest, of course. And the tragically deluded young seditionist, Annalah Caldwell. Such a sweet face, such a crafty enemy. A master of the power of a well-told story. In a kinder era, they all might have negotiated their people's future. He might have tried hard to recruit Annalah.

Now, though—no. Such people couldn't be trusted, not even if Zeimsky ayinectomized every last living one of them. Sadly he eyed the image he'd just recorded. With a dispassionate squeeze, he blanked the screen on his handheld.

• • •

Now that it came down to following a well-practiced routine in a quiet environment, Meris felt less uneasy. *I am the spark of undying light.*

She opened the gowning rack. Colonel Zeimsky held up both hands and hurried past her, through the decontamination unit into the procedure room. It was a medically acceptable shortcut in emergency cases, but Meris meant to follow procedure in every detail.

She and Annalah donned sterile tunics and hair tuckers and helped Lady Fi do the same. They helped Tavkel out of his filthy work clothes and into a quick vaporbath with drying fans, then into a medical gown.

She lined everyone up along the spray sink, and then the four of them walked through the decontam unit, pausing under the brilliant lights while she counted to ten. She'd taken to shutting her eyes in here, but this time she couldn't help glancing at Tavkel. She disliked the word "ashen," but there was something oddly burnt-looking about him. "It's a common procedure, sir. Please don't worry." Annalah gripped his other shoulder, plainly supporting him. *Tranquilizer? Yes? No?*

He seemed strangely confused. Looking straight into the lights, he murmured, "Where are you? Where have you gone?"

Didn't they have normal medical facilities at that prayer retreat he had called home?

Maybe they hadn't needed medical facilities, since he'd been there to heal people. Meris reached out to him again. "Everyone's a little nervous at this point, Tavkel. Don't worry. We'll stay with you."

He sent her an odd look, both pained and pleading. "Don't waste drugs. They won't work if I don't want them to."

Just as she'd thought, he still had his powers. She bumped the control panel. The far doors opened. Zeimsky waited inside the procedure room, beside the open stasis crypt. It was the same recent Tallis model she'd worked with before, with a rounded brown exterior and a row of red lights already gleaming on the lid's underside. Judging by the astringent scent in the room, Zeimsky had already run an air purification cycle—and he'd filled the perfusion tank that hung over the crypt.

"We're ready," he said. "I flashed the crypt too."

"Good, sir." She reached for the crypt's side control panel, shut the lid, and flashed it again anyway, since that took only a minute. *Everything by the tutorial.*

She touched one more control, and the massive lid swung up and open. Annalah steadied Tavkel's hand. He climbed inside.

Meanwhile, Meris laid out the cannulas and tubing. She'd gone into this branch of medicine for this exact sort of thing: not to set broken bones, but to help patients through a significant and often intimidating part of their treatment. This very moment justified getting stuck on the *Daystar*. She had been exactly the right person, in the right place, at the right time.

Colonel Zeimsky and Lady Fi took up positions at the room's opposite ends, Colonel Zeimsky near the crypt's foot and Lady Fi close to the head. The red perfusion lights inside its lid gleamed steadily.

Under the lights, faintly lit by the red glimmer, Tavkel lay with his eyes closed and arms at his side. The crypt fit him snugly, its supercooling cradle retracted on both sides of his head. The pale yellow medical gown draped him from neck to knees.

Annalah reached in, down by his feet, and pulled out a pair of slim tubes to attach to the evacuation cannulas. They dangled over the crypt's near side at that end. Closer to Meris, the tubing connected to the perfusion tank hung through a clip on the lid's underside.

Meris took a deep breath of the astringent air. Apparently Colonel Zeimsky would merely supervise. She administered the usual anesthetic with a hypospray as Annalah adjusted the super-cooling head cradle against Tavkel's ears. *All according to procedure,* she wanted to assure him, but that cradle dampened all sound. He was already beyond her words. Anyway, the anesthetic should make him drowsy almost immediately. Annalah moved to his chest and attached the miniature transmitter with a dab of soluble adhesive. Organ functions and chemical readings appeared on the wall display.

Display! Reminded of her promise, Meris hastily turned and activated the wall intercom unit.

A cluster of faces appeared on her own viewing panel, heads turning quickly as if to stare through a suddenly opened window.

"We're almost ready," she told those outside.

Minster Wind stood close to the outside wall. So did Shamarr Kiel. And there was Jorah, at the back of the group. He'd gotten a streak of mud on the front of his tunic, and his hair looked disheveled. She was going to miss him, she realized. Might he consider traveling on to Tallis with her—and Tavkel?

"Meris." Annalah's voice had a frantic note.

She whirled around. Annalah stood pointing up at the wall display. Tavkel's readings were peculiar, as if he were already under considerable physical stress. "We should have recalibrated this for him," Meris admitted to Annalah and the other observers. "His metabolism is unique." But they'd done everything by the tutorial, which was safest. He was the one who was different.

She carefully inserted the perfusion cannulas—external carotids in the throat and ulnar arteries in the wrists—and the evacuation cannulas near his feet, in the anterior tibial veins, properly anchored to the connectors inside the crypt. Tavkel didn't flinch. That meant the anesthetic and pre-cooling cycles were starting to take effect. Correct? Then how could he still be in pain?

She tucked the evacuation tubing back inside the crypt and then glanced up at the board again, making sure. Actually, his pulse wasn't slowing but racing, both systolic and diastolic blood pressures rising visibly. *Unusual metabolism,* she reminded herself. *Don't waste drugs,* he'd said. Maybe that was another one of his mutant gifts, and maybe those blocking drugs never had affected him either, but his system had burned out all meds as they were injected.

She didn't like this. Still, perfusion should go quickly because of that racing heartbeat and rising pressure, possibly as quickly as half an hour instead of the full hour. Could his system handle it?

It should. This was Tavkel, after all. She took a deep breath and repeated the litany for focus one more time. *I am the spark of undying light . . .*

And she'd been through this without anesthetic. The sooner he went under, the less unpleasant his memories would be of the procedure. She leaned close and reached for the crypt's master switch.

He stared down at his feet, as if bowing his head. "Finish it," he murmured.

Startled—was he fully conscious after all?—she responded in calm tones to inspire the observers' confidence. "Initiating perfusion." She touched the master control. Clear fluid started flowing through the injection sites. She leaned over the crypt's edge and confirmed that dark red blood also flowed through the tubes near his feet, into the crypt's fractionation and storage units. "Initial check."

"Initial check." Annalah's voice wobbled. "Confirm."

Meris avoided looking at the intercom panel, which might have made it obvious that she was hoping Jorah admired her professionalism. Instead, she glanced across the room at Lady Fi. Behind the older woman, the prep room/decontam door opened again. A uniformed Tallan guard stepped through, and Meris backed away from her patient. "This is a medical procedure area," she said sternly. "Have you scrubbed?"

"I called him in." Colonel Zeimsky remained against the opposite wall. "Continue, Meris."

She eyed the newcomer. He backed against the wall next to Colonel Zeimsky, well out of her way. So she took another good look at her patient, lying under the still-red perfusion lights. He continued to look stressed. She'd better stay focused on him. His face had gone even paler, but that was normal at this point in the procedure. After all, blood cells were being evacuated from his body.

She took another quick look at the drain tubing and confirmed a steady flow. "Just a few more minutes." She used her most soothing tones. Whether or not a patient could hear at this point, this assurance was recommended. "You'll be a little lightheaded and then rather cold. Then you'll be waking up on Tallis." She glanced up at the monitor once more. Blood chemicals ought to be dropping as cryoserum replaced normal fluid.

They weren't, though. As she watched, one blood-chem indicator actually rose. Some amount of elevated reactive proteins was a sign of stress—extreme stress, in this case—but nothing should've caused that, including his unique metabolism. And where were those chemicals coming from? Hemoglobin especially ought to be dropping, but it wasn't. Inside the crypt, her patient's eyes rolled up. His muscles contracted into knots. Plainly he was in agony. Something was seriously wrong.

She'd never halted a perfusion before. There was some danger, but it could be done. Should she? She studied the board. Bone chemical uptake, another measure of stress, was rising even faster than the reactive proteins. "Annalah," she called. "Neural depressant. Add to inflow. Stat." If those synthetics didn't affect him, they'd have to try something stronger.

Annalah whirled aside, toward the stores cabinet. Meris kept trying to interpret what she was seeing. It looked as if his bone marrow had hyperactivated and was replacing blood cells as quickly as they could be drained away. His cells *could* keep dividing indefinitely—she'd seen the telomeres—but what about fluids? Cryoserum was non-aqueous. It contained the wrong chemical balance for creating blood serum.

Plainly, though, the skeletal system was the source of his anguish. Bone pain was infamously excruciating, and she saw it in his narrowed, anguished eyes. Beyond the crypt, Lady Fi stood staring steadily down at Tavkel. Tears ran down her cheeks. That was her grandson, lying there suffering.

Annalah pressed an ampoule into the injection tubing. Once again, it had no discernible effect. Minutes passed. He continued to bleed without any change in outflow chemistry.

Defeat tasted bitter. However, Tavkel's metabolism simply was too unique to stase—so now she had a patient to try and save. If they couldn't flush his system, they had to restore it. She pushed the hair tucker up her forehead. It felt slick and sweaty. "Abort the cycle." She tried to sound calm. "Annalah, do you know what to—"

"Cancel that," a voice barked. Strong arms grabbed Meris from behind. "Don't struggle," Zeimsky said in her ear. "Then I won't have to hurt you."

"No!" she cried. "Something's gone wrong. Annalah, abort the cycle!"

The other Tallan reached Annalah in two strides and pinned down her arms.

What can I do, Meris?

Meris couldn't tell who was subvocalizing, but the voice felt female—and the queer lightheadedness stayed with her. Abruptly she realized it was Lady Fi, doing a continuing mind-access. Lady Fi had gone to Tavkel before practically anyone else. She'd been born with ayin abilities, and she'd been retraining—no, she'd been training for the first time.

And no one had grabbed her.

Meris kept struggling, hoping to distract Zeimsky as she formed a fast string of thoughts. *Orange handle. Near his head. Pull down. It'll start re-injecting . . . drained blood!*

The weird sensation snapped off as the Lady sprang forward. Zeimsky shouted a name. The big Tallan let Annalah go and lunged at Lady Fi.

The exit door burst open. A crowd surged in, and in that moment, another voice—Tavkel's voice—spoke at the back of her mind. *Right person—right place and time. I needed you here. Please. Your darkness. Give it!*

Tavkel's jaw was set in a terrible grimace, his eyes wide open again. They were the eyes of desperate hunger. *Please,* she heard at the back of her mind. *Let me take it. Let me take it down, down with me.*

"Yes!" she screamed, struggling harder. Zeimsky's hands shifted to her throat. "Help!" she gasped. "Murder—sabotage—"

The hands tightened. The crowded room spun, and she tumbled. A yellow blur that had to be Zeimsky let her go and lunged toward the crypt.

A blur of red lights vanished. Something heavy-sounding thumped. There was a soft whoosh, a snap and clang. A frigid, high-pitched whine.

And silence.

Panting, Meris made it up onto hands and knees. Through the crowd she spotted Chancellor Gambrel standing beside Colonel Zeimsky, both of them next to the stasis crypt's master control panel.

The lid had been closed. The failsafe switch had been thrown under the head end, and the supercooling cycle activated. The indicator had faded all the way to white. Supercooling was *complete.* Perfusion tubing still dangled from the overhead tank, caught and pinched between crypt and lid.

In an instant Meris saw it all: Lady Fi and Annalah, clutching each other and kneeling under the crypt's head end, surrounded by guards. Uniformed Tallans backing toward all four walls, as Chancellor Gambrel waved them away from the crypt. Minster Wind standing in her brown dress coat, covering her mouth with both hands. Shamarr Kiel slowly backing toward Jorah and the doorway.

She couldn't make out the control panel. What had Colonel Zeimsky done?

"What happened?" Close by, Chancellor Gambrel echoed her thoughts in a tone that threatened retribution.

Meris crouched low, but apparently Gambrel hadn't been talking to her. Colonel Zeimsky stood with a hand on the crypt. He raised his voice. "You people. Did you seriously want Chancellor Gambrel taking that man—that extraordinary man—back to Tallis just to make him a public spectacle? A laughingstock? Stripping him of all dignity? Because that's what he would have done. The Chancellor doesn't share his glory. Not with anyone.

"And Gambrel," he added, lowering his voice, "don't even think about threatening me. Or Urnock. I could take you down in front of the whole FRC." Louder again, he said, "And the military here answers to us, not to you. Is that right?"

"Yes, sir." The shout came from a corner.

"What did you do?" Minster Wind rushed forward. She stopped just short of flinging herself onto the crypt. "What's happening?"

"We perfused with normal saline solution," Colonel Zeimsky said. "Not cryoserum. Saline's always on hand. And it has a markedly different effect on the body from cryoserum. Even on a normal body. A human body."

Meris gasped. When Colonel Zeimsky had supposedly been prepping the chamber, he'd actually been sabotaging it. He'd filled the cryoserum tank with saline. She shrank down even smaller. *That* must have made everything go wrong. The saline perfusion had stimulated Tavkel's unusual cells to go on dividing—making more blood cells—more blood—could he have gone on bleeding infinitely?

But then—if his body had been frozen with veins full of saline—Tavkel was dead. Dead! Not in stasis at all.

In an instant, her internal world shifted. Tavkel's invulnerability had made him seen distant and strange. But he had told her he was 100 percent human, and that meant he could be killed.

And she recalled those puzzling words from Tavkel's story, about the girl and her beloved pet: *She helped kill it . . .*

Tavkel, dead? Was it possible? Had he known this was going to happen? Was it possible that he really had foreseen the future, including his own death?

At Zeimsky's hands . . . and her own?

Tavkel! She wanted to wail. *What have I done?*

Colonel Zeimsky reached toward the crypt's control panel. He stroked the brilliant red *end cycle* control. The crypt groaned open with agonizing slowness. Frigid air puffed over its side and washed Meris with its chill. She crawled backward, surrounded by other people's legs and sickened by gasping sounds coming from close to the crypt. She made it to the foot end. She slowly straightened.

Gambrel was talking again. She caught isolated words: "appalled . . . consequences . . . cold-blooded."

She stood up just enough to steal a look. Inside the crypt, softening red shards fell away from arm and neck bones and a network of tendons. Tavkel's pale yellow medical gown was rapidly soaking with red fluid—

Gorge rose in her throat. She had to get away. Swallowing hard, she tumbled again and bounced off a set of grey uniform trousers. People shouted overhead. Her head pounded. Quicker than before, she crawled toward the doorway. She straightened cautiously, bracing herself to run for her life. They'd have to silence her now, as a murder witness—

Someone grabbed her. She spun and dug in her nails.

"Meris!" Jorah held her arm like a vise. Behind him, the shouting continued.

"Call me a coward, will you?"

"That man was going to Tallis. With me—"

"He was too powerful! Nobody was safe with him. Nobody. Get that through your head! There'll be no cosmic catastrophe now—"

Move, Jorah. It was Lady Fi's subvoice at the back of her mind. *We're right behind you!*

She glanced back. Sure enough, the other two women were crawling along after her, apparently unnoticed by Chancellor Gambrel and the others arguing in the stasis room.

"Come on," Jorah muttered.

Meris let herself be dragged into the empty corridor. The guards who'd been out here were gone. Maybe they had rushed into the procedure room.

Lady Fi stood clutching Annalah's shoulders. Annalah kept whispering, "Tears into blood. Tears. Saline, Meris. He turned our tears into blood."

Tears? They flooded Meris's vision. Actually, she deserved to die. She had just helped kill an innocent man. *Guilty. So guilty. Tavkel, could you even want to take that much darkness? But it's yours. It's all yours.*

She let Jorah tug her wherever he was going.

CHAPTER 44

Jorah steered the women deeper into the med corridor. He picked one of the unoccupied patient rooms and got them inside, and then he considered shutting the door—but decided he'd better keep it open. He needed to see and hear whatever was happening in the corridor.

He'd left Major Ryken and Captain Mattason behind, but that couldn't be helped. Everyone here was a murder witness and the Feds would have to eliminate them all, just as soon as Urnock realized what had happened. Urnock was the one who would be tasked with damage control.

Tavkel—dead—how could he be? "You'll see what I do with darkness," he'd said. He'd confronted it . . . and died in the effort!

Half of Jorah's head was spinning. The other half was apparently falling back on his Special Ops training. Whatever needed to be done, he might be the only SO left in this corridor.

And he was armed . . . barely. He had his crystace. Or was it still stuck in its sheath?

He gave it a tug. Still stuck.

How could *that* be? It was Tavkel who'd disarmed everyone. And Tavkel was dead.

Dead.

Well, then. No one here was any better armed than Jorah was, and his mother was out there somewhere. "Stay here," he whispered to Meris. Annalah was blubbering—he couldn't blame her—but Grandmother looked fierce. He'd better leave her in charge, since she'd been military. And to hear her subvocalize, after all these years, was wonderful! He caught her eye. "See if you can get them outside. Uplevel. We can hide in the forest. Is there—"

He stopped himself. No, there wasn't a tunnel entrance from the med corridor. He should know.

She nodded anyway, grim-faced. *No, but there is in the Chapter room.*

"That'll do." He made sure nobody stood outside, and he slipped out.

Tavkel, dead. Impossible! Never, in a million years . . . This was supposed to have been their victory! What about the renewal? Were thousands of years of prophetic tradition invalidated? Had his people survived all that time for *nothing?*

He used the big multipurpose station across from the procedure room to skirt past the mob. Inside that station, a visual interlink displayed the scene of the tragedy. Apparently Meris had accidentally turned on all of the interlinks. His mother was still in there, next to Chancellor Gambrel and the hideous crypt. He hesitated a moment.

Jorah. Hearing another subvoice, he spun around.

Uncle Kiel crouched in the station's darkest corner. Jorah hustled over to join him. For one moment, he let his guard slip and his grief rise. "Tavkel's dead. Tavkel, our—"

"Shh." Uncle Kiel pulled him into some kind of a storage closet. "He knew. Victory that looks like defeat. He was the kipret. I don't have long, either. He said so."

"He . . . what?" And what was in this closet that he could use as a weapon—or at least a club?

Uncle Kiel had a weird look in his eye. "I'm going back in, Jorah. I'm going to ask Chancellor Gambrel for . . . to give me something. As Shamarr, I want to do something. Just a gesture. But I believe the Holy One wants it done, to honor his son."

Jorah nodded, barely paying attention. The cleaning tools' handles looked flimsy. There were such things as surgical knives and saws, weren't there? He could arm maybe half the people in there. What could they do? Maybe extract his mother, and—

"Jorah." Uncle Kiel gripped his arm, and Jorah managed to focus his attention. "We have no idea what they'll do next. They're still arguing."

Jorah shook his head. "What does it matter? Tavkel's gone. We gave up everything for him. There's nothing left. No reason to survive—unless—" It was crazy, the thought that popped into his mind—but did this mean *he* was Boh-Dabar after all? Or did that mantle fall to Uncle Kiel?

Uncle Kiel frowned and straightened. "Sentinel, come with me. I need a guard."

Guard. Sentinel. The halves of Jorah's conflicted mind came together. He'd been given an order, and he would obey. For one moment, the Whorl made sense again. And Uncle Kiel had touched Tavkel's mind. So maybe he, at least, knew what he was doing.

But if death really had taken Tavkel from them—if Tavkel had won the first battles but lost the war—they all were doomed. Forever, maybe. If so, he wanted to go down fighting. He could at least save his mother.

But for what future?

Uncle Kiel's long sleeves swished as he strode across the hallway. Jorah had to hustle to keep up.

● ● ●

Meris trailed Lady Fi and Annalah as they strode up the poolside. The afternoon sun shining through skylights seemed polluted and sickly. She still felt like vomiting. Off to her right, people in Tallan grey rushed into that defense corridor she'd never entered. Lady Fi and Annalah ducked into the first housing corridor.

"Catch your breath," Lady Fi said, panting. "And let me get mine."

Meris had no litanies for such horror. They were all written for life's normal indignities and sadnesses, things that seemed trivial now. She had helped kill a man—a good man—a great man! *She helped kill it . . .* What did it mean, that he'd known in advance? And what would it have changed, if he'd taken her darkness down with him? She'd waited too long, hadn't she? *I want to be one of yours, Tavkel.* She remembered what she'd seen inside herself, out on the landing strip. *I am full of darkness, and I don't want to be!*

"Meris." Lady Fi looked straight into her eyes. Meris felt as if she were being interrogated. "Did you . . . give it to him? Really?"

Have you been reading my mind? She thought it, but she didn't say it. All that mattered was trying to figure out where she stood and what to do next. "I did. But not until—he might have already died when I did, Lady Fi."

The Lady straightened and almost smiled. "What did he say to the Whorl, Meris? To come while *he* lives?"

"No." His words still rang in her mind. "'While *you* live,' he said."

"And he proved he has power over death, didn't he?"

"But . . ." Meris hated how weak her voice sounded. "How could he have died? We were draining his blood for the perfusion, but it just kept coming . . . and coming . . . and . . ." She couldn't go on. At least Annalah had stopped sobbing.

"Well, then." Lady Fi folded her arms, looking birdlike just like back on board the shuttle *Daystar.* "You just wait and see."

Meris stared. Could it be? Air Master Caldwell had been brought back to life from a state just as terribly disfigured.

Yes, but Tavkel had been alive to call him back—

Wait.

If Tavkel's father really were a god—no, these people thought of him as *the* infinite god, something like the "Infinite Divine" Meris had believed in, but a person—capable of actually acting, of doing things. And hadn't the Air Master's revival proved—to her, anyway—that the soul survived death? Death had not changed Kinnor Caldwell at all.

Tavkel was alive, then. Somewhere!

And he had not changed either.

"Oh," she murmured. "Oh . . . my God . . . What have I done, and what am I going to do about it?"

Lady Fi gave a quick, decisive nod and headed back out onto the waterside, quick-stepping toward the Chapter room and its tunnel entrance.

Meris sprinted after her.

• • •

Jorah and Uncle Kiel strode into the stasis room through its wide-open door. Gambrel and Zeimsky still stood beside the crypt. It had been reclosed, but they kept arguing. Jorah wondered if Zeimsky planned to take Tavkel—what was left of him—back to Tallis.

Jorah's mother was close by, on Gambrel's left. Three muscular Tallans surrounded her. He should've grabbed a surgical knife in the other room. Too late.

Uncle Kiel strode straight up to Zeimsky. "Sir." He nodded toward the crypt. "The fractionation reservoir probably is overfilled. May I have the excess? Religious reasons." He folded his arms. His tunic's sleeves hung down in front of him.

Jorah couldn't bear to look at the crypt, knowing what lay inside. Tavkel. As dead as all their hopes. Unbelievable.

So he eyed the three big Feds. They eyed him right back. *Finish it fast and leave, Uncle.* He wished he could subvocalize. And how were they going to get his mother out of here?

"Blood?" Zeimsky's voice was despicably smooth. Gambrel had been going to let Tavkel live! Zeimsky alone—not Meris!—was responsible for killing him. "It's already freeze dried, and it's all going back to Tallis for study. The man was dangerous. We'll be looking into the high probability that you people have been engaging in genetic manipulation right alongside your Shuhr cousins." He shot a dark glance at Jorah's mother.

Gambrel faced her, making formal but insincere apologies while Zeimsky talked to Uncle Kiel. It had been a long time since Jorah had noticed how tall and beautiful she was. Maybe Zeimsky saw danger in that age-softened face, but Jorah saw a lifetime of compassionate service.

One of Gambrel's aides stood talking into a handheld. Recording, Jorah guessed, so he could broadcast a sanitized version of all this to the Whorl. Damage control.

He steeled himself and stared at the crypt. They'd killed Tavkel! Jorah hated them both, Zeimsky and Gambrel.

But he'd attached himself to Uncle Kiel, and if Uncle Kiel wanted blood—*Why?* his mind cried—maybe he could assist. He hadn't missed the animosity between Gambrel and Zeimsky. It was their tactical weakness.

Jorah strode toward his mother and the Chancellor. He edged between them, facing Gambrel. "Sir, the Shamarr has made a harmless request. Colonel Zeimsky wants to refuse." Behind his back, he made frantic sweeping gestures with one hand. *Get out of here, Mother! While he's distracted!* "Would you speak to him on our behalf, please?" Groveling stuck in his craw, but he did it anyway, hoping to help Mother and Uncle Kiel simultaneously. And where was his dad? Had the Feds re-arrested him?

"Jorah." Chancellor Gambrel's voice became almost sweet. "I am delighted to see you. You can't know how glad. I want you to evacuate with me. Get to the hovercraft—Horson," he snapped, beckoning to a guard, "take Lieutenant Caldwell—"

"No." Jorah distributed his weight evenly over both feet. "Sir, this is crucial."

"What is?"

The whole room seemed to go silent.

Uncle Kiel gestured toward the crypt, his eyes as serene as ever. "Please. There was a great deal of excess fluid, wasn't there? For religious reasons, I would like to take some of it . . . as a memorial. Symbolically, if you please."

"Oh, for pity's sake." Gambrel wheeled around and pointed at Zeimsky. "Give the priest his blood. What harm can he do now?"

Zeimsky glowered back at him. "It's ridiculous. What they really want is—"

Gambrel bounced a fist off the crypt's lid. "To clone the man? Here? Tell me, isn't that fractionation chamber full of cells?"

As Zeimsky fiddled with something on the crypt's near side, Jorah snuck a glance between him and the door. His mother had vanished. Excellent!

"Yes," Zeimsky snapped. "Too full, actually."

Gambrel stepped aside. "Good. Reconstitute some." He grabbed an empty glassware flask off a shelf. "And give some blood to the priest." In that voice Jorah heard something evil, something terribly familiar. He looked up in time to see Chancellor Gambrel's eyes shimmer. "Then report to the hovercraft, Shamarr. You're escorting Tavkel to Tallis."

"Very well," Uncle Kiel said.

Jorah wanted to recoil, but he stood his post. Surely Uncle Kiel hadn't meant that.

Zeimsky grabbed the flask and started poking controls on one side of the crypt. He did something Jorah couldn't quite see. Then he lifted the flask up to the perfusion tank and added saline. As he swirled it high in the air, a brown layer at the bottom dissolved. Each brown flake twirled a red comet's tail until it vanished in thickening red solution.

Into Jorah's mind flowed the awful consecration memory he'd been given nine years ago, a bowl full of blood poured out in the ancient temple. This wasn't any less awful, especially as the liquid thickened. Zeimsky carried it to a side doorway and held it up to the decontamination lights, swirling again. It lost some of its redness, darkening toward brown.

Zeimsky's nose twitched as he handed it to Uncle Kiel.

"Thank you." Uncle Kiel turned toward the door, carrying it reverently. "I will rejoin you shortly. I will be honored to travel with Tavkel."

To Jorah's relief, the Tallan trio stayed put, though the nearest one wrinkled his face in disgust. Plainly they thought the Sentinels were subhuman.

Uncle Kiel turned right, left, and strode up the waterside, toward the Chapter room—inside and up the long aisle, with Jorah behind him. He went straight to the altar, where he gently set down the flask. Irradiated blood looked even more horrible sitting on the pure colors of those brocade cloths, just as a bowl of kipret's blood actually would've been more disgusting than lovely. Each vessel represented a life cut off. The idea of sacrifice—of covering darkness with death—seemed abominable.

Uncle Kiel reached out again, hand shaking. He tilted the flask, dipped a finger in, and touched it to his chest, over his heart. Exactly like in the consecration vision, except that this time it was no sacred memory.

But why bother? Tavkel was dead. There would be no renewal.

His uncle dropped to his knees. That looked like it hurt, since today there was no padded bench set up to catch him. "Guide us all, Holy One." His voice wobbled. "You walked among us, and we lost you. We are defeated." His back straightened slightly. "But you aren't. You warned us there would be seeming defeat. But you said it would be short. Guide us. Please . . . what should we do now?"

Shouting erupted out in the commons. Nervous, Jorah turned to look up the aisle, out the Chapter room's open door. He saw no one, but he recognized Gambrel's voice.

"Are we to simply go on obeying you, as best we can? Remembering your words and actions? Your example?"

The shouting grew louder. It was Gambrel and Zeimsky. And the heavy footfalls of armed guards.

Uncle Kiel seized Jorah's hand, startling him. "It's time." Uncle Kiel spoke somberly. "Tell everyone what Tavkel told the first circle."

Jorah blinked. What in the Whorl did Uncle Kiel think to accomplish by—

"What he told us," Uncle Kiel repeated. "Death comes to us all. But we'll never be in real danger. If we have to die fearlessly, this is the time."

Before Jorah could protest, a woman's voice shouted his name. He looked across the curved stage and gasped. Meris? What was she doing up on the platform?

She dashed toward them, straw-gold hair loose behind her shoulders. He couldn't believe how glad he felt to see her. She'd been duped by the Feds. Manipulated. Used. And she knew it, or she'd still be back in that stasis room with that horrible crypt. "Shamarr!" She reached the altar. "Consecrate me. Please."

What? Had Meris actually turned to the faith? But why now, with Tavkel dead?

Maybe she'd just finally seen her precious Collegium for the sham it really was. Jorah wanted to grab her and hold her close. But that had to wait. Right now, he was on guard duty.

He tried tugging his crystace again. No luck.

Uncle Kiel stayed on his knees. "Meris, you gifted your darkness?"

She nodded. Jorah gaped.

"Then you don't need to be consecrated, my child." Uncle Kiel's voice sounded almost like he was singing. "You've already become part of the mystical community, with us and with him—as much as any of us ever will be, on this side of death."

"Oh. But I . . ." She knelt beside Uncle Kiel. "Just let me pray here a minute. Please. I made him a promise, and I . . . don't know how to get it done."

Was she out of her mind? Didn't she see there was no point anymore? And even a few seconds felt too long, with all that shouting outside. Whether Gambrel came out on top or Zeimsky did, this compound was unsafe. There were Feds inside. Tavkel's presence had prevented open conflict.

But Tavkel was dead.

Still, Jorah had to wonder—could this have been the Holy One's plan? They hadn't seen it coming—he hadn't, anyway—but if Tavkel had owned everyone's darkness when he died, was *that* the prophesied immolation? Had he destroyed it at his own death?

Wishful thinking and rationalization! Right now, if they wanted to keep Tavkel's memory alive, they had to survive. Nobody was going to stick around now, with Feds in orbit and groundside too. Their only hope was to scatter.

"Where's Annalah?" Uncle Kiel braced both arms against the Chapter room altar and looked all around, once again acting as if he'd read Jorah's mind. Maybe he'd caught his emotions.

"I don't know—"

Meris spoke up. "She's with Lady Fi. They're trying to get to the Minster's office, or out topside if that fails." Her eyes suddenly brightened. "Minster's office! She's going to tell the Whorl what happened. I'll need to speak too."

"Ah." Uncle Kiel's smile was full of admiration. "Give her my love. He barred us from telling our story for centuries, but the truth will go out now. We can trust him for that."

"But there's no point!" Jorah flung out his arms. "Uncle Kiel, he's dead! He's . . . dead."

"Jorah." Meris grabbed his arm. "Can you get us to your mother's office from over here, through the tunnels?" She eyed the entrance at the back of the stage.

"What? Why?"

Shouting erupted right outside the double doors. It sounded like Gambrel wanted Uncle Kiel under arrest, or something.

Uncle Kiel looked around hastily. "They know I'm in here, but you might have left. Get down there into the tunnel. Now, Jorah. Take Meris out of here and don't look back. I'm going with Tavkel. I offered to escort the stasis—the crypt."

"But you can't—"

"Go, Jorah! They're coming for me. They won't follow you. Or Meris."

Jorah got the message. He slid his hand down Meris's arm to grab her hand. Uncle Kiel could be truly stupid sometimes—but not always. "This way." He tugged her toward the platform's left side. "Hurry!"

"Go." Uncle Kiel stared at the rear doors. "Go in peace."

Acting on impulse, Jorah yanked the crystace sheath off his arm. "Here, Uncle. It isn't much at this point, but if they start firing . . ."

His uncle took the sheath end and gave the hilt a smooth pull. The crystace slid free.

Jorah gaped. Beside him, Meris murmured, "Oh, no."

Uncle Kiel touched the sonic activator stud, and the singing blade appeared. "But I agreed to go with them," he said. "I shouldn't need this."

Jorah clenched a fist. "If everyone has weapons again, the Feds hold the high ground in orbit. Things are about to get much worse. We'll all need more than a crystace." He gave Meris's hand a more urgent pull. "Come on. Get away from here. Uncle Kiel will distract them." This time, she followed him around the altar and toward the far wall. The secret door stood open—was that how she'd gotten in?

They went through, and he waited until she had headed down the stone stair. He stepped inside too, but he stopped on the top stair and stared back through the gap between door and doorjamb.

He couldn't be crying, but his eyes sure weren't working right. *Uncle Kiel, you don't need to do this*—but that Tallan-grey smudge at the doors looked ominous. Careful to stay hidden, he blinked hard. His vision cleared.

Wait—where had his uncle gone?

There he was, standing in front of the altar, crystace apparently sheathed again.

Jorah put his shoulder to the stone door and pushed it closed. It felt like shutting the last light out of his whole life.

"Are you coming?" Meris whispered below him.

Almost the last light. He hustled downlevel to join her.

• • •

Kiel turned back to the altar. The laboratory flask of blood looked like a sacrilege, a desecration. The altar flame cast its shadow across the red altar cloth.

Yet it was surely the holiest thing he had ever held in his hands, second to the living Tavkel.

They had embraced on the Tuva River bridge. He let the memory comfort him. Hanusha, Perl, and Rena were surely far south of here by now. They would meet again, but not in this life.

"There he is!" The shout rang through the Chapter room. Behind Kiel came the sound of heavy footsteps. Kiel crossed his wrists, a little too aware of his nephew's crystace on his wrist. *I am ready, Tavkel. It will be good to be with you again.*

He turned slowly, head high.

Four hulking Tallans marched toward him, followed by Colonel Urnock and Chancellor Gambrel.

Kiel uncrossed his wrists and spread his hands, palms down in the position that couldn't be used to direct ayin energy. These people would not know that he hadn't retrained his ayin abilities. "I'm ready to go with you. With Tavkel's crypt."

Gambrel hustled forward. He halted between Kiel and the others. "Do not kill this man." The voice was Gambrel's, not the shadow's. "He comes with us willingly." Moving with his usual pompous dignity, he folded his arms.

Apparently he and Colonel Urnock had been arguing again.

"Yes." Kiel stepped away from the altar, squelching the temptation to glance toward the secret door. "Is it time to go on board?"

Chancellor Gambrel scowled at Colonel Urnock. This time, Kiel saw the faintest eerie glimmer shine through the Chancellor's eyes. "You will treat this man with the dignity of his office." Gambrel directed those words toward the guards, and the voice was his own.

But that couldn't last.

Not if the shadow wanted revenge.

CHAPTER 45

Jorah felt his way down the passage until his eyes adjusted to the dim everburners. After that, he walked more confidently. The stone tunnel was too narrow for him to go alongside Meris, so he stayed ahead. At the first junction he recognized, he halted and looked back. "Still there?"

"Right here." Meris stopped in place too. Her loose hair framed her face with a kind of gold glow.

"This way." He reached back and closed his hand around one of hers. It was small, cool, and soft—one real thing in the middle of this nightmare. He guided her past the three-way intersection, led on a few meters and let go. "What is it you want to tell the Whorl?"

For a few seconds, all he heard was the soft setting of feet behind him. Then: "It was about Tavkel's father. His biological father."

"Oh." Well, that could certainly wait. Right now, he just needed to keep her away from Gambrel. Odds were good that the Chancellor meant to take her away.

And silence her.

He walked ahead. "We're about to turn—" Another passage opened. "Left. Here. Then a little farther. My mom's office is straight ahead and up some steps—" There they were. "Wait. Listen a minute."

The passage was as silent as the stone itself. He'd been half afraid of hearing a melee up there. It was quiet, though. Dead silent. Maybe they needed him . . . or . . .

Something else occurred to him. He almost felt like he was waking up. "Wait," he murmured again. "Before we go up to the office, I need to know whether the Feds are really leaving." With any prisoners besides Uncle Kiel. "I want you with me. Is that all right?"

"Good idea."

Hearing her say that made the cool passageway feel warmer. "Okay. Don't fall too far behind."

"As if I could lose you."

Jorah heard tolerant humor in her voice and imagined her smiling. He turned right again, heading south.

He wasn't smiling, though. He needed to know whether Zeimsky was grabbing so-called volunteers.

He walked faster. At the passage's end was a lookout, a crack between laid stones that was wide enough for one person to stand and observe the landing area. He pressed close to it and slid his head to the right, trying to see outside and uphill.

Long, late afternoon shadows covered the grassy ground. The ITD still lay near the landing area's edge. Beside it stood his dad, crystace drawn but inactive, with six other armed Sentinels. Plainly his dad had concluded that the Feds would steal back the disk if they could. Federates streamed past the Sentinel group, striding toward their hovercraft—headed back up to the meadow for dinner, Jorah thought bitterly. Several of them kept their backs to their friends and walked sideways, facing the ITD guards. There weren't any prisoners at all.

No, wait. Uncle Kiel walked out of the hangar, alongside a brown stasis crypt on a med sled. Jorah almost wished he hadn't given him his crystace.

Tavkel! Dead! Couldn't Jorah wake up and find that this was actually a nightmare?

At the back of the loose column, Colonel Urnock paused to face the Sentinels guarding the ITD. Jorah imagined he had to be considering whether to attack. Maybe he would order the hover-craft to steer right over them, or something equally craven.

There had to be something Jorah could do, besides report all this to Mother. Had to be.

"What do you see?" Meris pressed against his left side. "Let me look."

"We might still have a pitched battle . . . No."

Urnock turned smartly and headed onto the hovercraft, board-ing it last of the group. The ramp retracted.

Jorah scooted aside so Meris could use the chink. "They're leav-ing." He leaned against cool stone. "I wonder why they didn't grab anyone else." It felt like they'd all been sentenced to die but given a reprieve.

He still meant to go down fighting, though. The Feds would be back tomorrow. He'd like a shot at Gambrel—or Urnock—or especially Zeimsky.

"Maybe Tavkel's still making things happen," she murmured. "Giving us breathing room."

Jorah clenched his teeth. "He's *dead.*"

"Jorah!" Her voice sounded strangely young. "How could it be that I believe now, but you don't?"

He pressed his back against dirt and stone. "Why I don't is obvious. But if it makes you feel better, I'm glad. I mean, you've had an awful . . . That is . . . Right." The hovercraft engines roared. Jorah pushed away from the wall. With the Feds gone, he wanted an update. "Come on. Minster's office."

He led out again. It felt good to keep moving. Maybe something would make sense of all this.

• • •

Meris stepped back into natural daylight through a door she had never noticed before. It led into the Minster's office just behind where the benches ended. The office was crowded. High Commander Caldwell was easy to identify from behind, by that shock of white hair. Apparently he'd been given the command post.

Meris pushed forward, and she saw to her amazement that every bit of the Minster's desk displayed some monitor or another. She'd only ever seen the one screen lit, right in front of High Commander Caldwell's seat.

No, come to think of it, she had seen Annalah sitting at the left end. Sure enough, Annalah had pulled up a stool and sat talking into a raised pickup. Minster Wind perched on the edge of a chair between Annalah and the High Commander. The side benches were filled with Sentinels who hadn't scattered. Between here and the desk, other bodies blocked sections of her view.

Jorah gripped her hand and led her forward. "I'm here. With Meris."

Minster Wind looked up and reached for a panel near the desk's center. Two short lines of text vanished—their names? "Thank you. We're all accounted for."

So they knew Shamarr Kiel had left. Jorah pulled Meris right up close to the desk, so that she stood at the High Commander's left shoulder. Lady Fi was seated on her husband's right side, and she fingered a gold pendant on a chain around her neck. It looked like some sort of bird.

Annalah's face had the blotchy look of someone who'd been crying. She spoke a few more words into the pickup and nodded. Instantly Minster Wind keyed something onto her own touchboard.

Meanwhile, the High Commander stared down at what looked like a map of the planet. Gleaming dots were scattered across it.

"Go ahead," the Minster said.

Annalah started talking again. "But those of us who actually touched Tavkel's mind do not believe that his story has ended . . ."

Meris realized that Jorah had positioned himself behind her. So, just like at the concert, she leaned back against him. "What's Annalah doing?" she murmured.

The High Commander laughed softly, surprising her. "Meris, I think you're the only one here who didn't know. Annalah's ayin gift turned out to be an eidetic memory. She's been recording everything Tavkel said and did—and my niece, Queen Rinnah of Netaia, has been sending it out to the Whorl. His story is going out, Meris—everywhere! There are people on all twenty-three Federate worlds giving Tavkel their darkness."

She nudged Jorah, but he didn't respond.

So she spoke up. "Including me."

"Meris?" The High Commander craned his neck to look back at her. "Well done." He smiled at her, but he quickly bent back toward the desktop.

Annalah kept talking a little longer. She shut her eyes and nodded again. Minster Wind reached for her controls.

"They're transmitting short bits," Meris whispered to Jorah. "Why?"

"Probably in case we lose outsystem comm." Jorah's voice sounded dull and hopeless. "The Feds might target our transceiving satellites at any second. We've just about spent down our subtronic batteries too, sending out all this DeepScan."

And that would leave them truly alone in the Whorl, cut off from anyone who might come to their aid. Even if they could recharge the batteries, with the satellites gone they could neither send nor receive. Meris shivered.

Seeing motion at the main door arch, she looked up. Air Master Kinnor had appeared there.

Well, she'd made her choice. She didn't regret it. In fact . . .

As soon as Minster Wind finished relaying that section of story via DeepScan, Meris edged forward. She gripped the desk's edge with both hands and crouched down. "Minster, when she's finished may I add a transmission? I made Tavkel a promise some time back."

Several people turned toward her, including the Minster and the High Commander.

"A promise?" the Minster asked.

Meris took a moment to compose herself. "He told me some things about his parentage, you see." More heads turned. She kept her eyes on Minster Wind's face. "And he told me he'd told no one else, and he made me promise that . . ." What had his words been? She shifted a little closer to the desk. "When it had to be said, I was to tell the Federacy. It almost looked like he anticipated what we're doing right here." Just as he had anticipated that . . . No, she didn't dare tell people that he'd known she would help end his life. Might they turn on her, even now?

The room had gone still. Annalah stared at her.

The High Commander pushed back from his station. "What would you tell them?"

She hesitated a little longer. What had he said—what, exactly? "You . . . you all know about his strange chromosomes. Well, he told me—straight out—that his biological father was the person you call the Eternal Speaker."

Lady Fi glanced at the High Commander. Jorah made a soft, startled noise behind Meris. Annalah simply smiled.

Meris continued. "He made quite an issue about the Speaker's personhood. I guess he knew that it was what I most needed to hear. He said that . . ."

She pushed her memory harder. "Since the Speaker had designed the human body, he has complete mastery over it. Including reproduction. He told me all this, after . . . after Air Master Kinnor came back." She nodded toward the Air Master. "I went to Tavkel with questions. He . . ." it hurt to say this . . . "he honored me with answers. An outsider. A person partly responsible for . . . his death."

Lady Fi bent forward over the desk and looked at her sidelong. "You're no more an outsider than I am. And we're all responsible for his death. Did you see how different he started to look the very moment Urnock sentenced him? I don't think even Zeimsky killed him. I think our darkness did."

No one else spoke. Meris wondered if they all felt as guilty as she did.

"Let her do it, Wind." Lady Fi turned aside. "Let Annalah finish first, though." She made an encouraging gesture toward Annalah, who bent toward the pickup and resumed talking.

Other conversations started up again too. The High Commander touched several controls on the desktop. Meris couldn't see whether anything resulted. "So what's your strategy, sir?"

"It's important that Annalah finishes," he said. "All along she has been telling the Whorl that Tavkel was Boh-Dabar, explaining prophecies, keeping them updated on what he has done. Including bringing my son and me back from death.

"To tell the truth, Meris, those of us who touched his mind already knew he was the Holy One's son." He rotated the chair, facing her. "But your message to the Whorl will count too, especially to people who don't trust us." He indicated the other Sentinels in the office with a one-handed gesture.

"Thank you for that, sir," she said.

He nodded. "Especially now that he has spoken to them himself."

"But what did he *do* with all that darkness?" Still crouching, she looked him in the eye.

He shook his head. "We don't know. Nor what will happen next."

"We know one thing," Jorah said.

Meris looked up at Jorah, then back over to the High Commander, whose expression had become somber.

Jorah frowned, wrinkling his whole face. "We know Gambrel will lie. We're cooked, Grandfather. And for what?"

She saw reproach darkening the High Commander's eyes. "Yes, Jorah. Chancellor Gambrel will lie to the Whorl. But Tavkel told them the truth."

Jorah just stood there, frowning.

The High Commander took a deep breath. "I'm sorry, Meris, I know you admired Chancellor Gambrel."

"No. I agree." What was wrong with Jorah? Her hair had come loose, and she needed to re-knot it. She refrained, not wanting to be rude to the High Commander. "I only wish I had seen that sooner about him."

"I think you did what you had to do. And now, for the rest of the Whorl, it will simply come down to who tells the more compelling story—us, or Chancellor Gambrel. And I'm afraid he's not too low to stoop to publicity stunts for the sake of regaining his credibility."

"I'm afraid you're right." For the second time in just a few months, she felt utterly betrayed. First by her parents. Now by her Chancellor.

She glanced up at Jorah again.

He stood cracking his knuckles.

The High Commander eyed Jorah too, and then he turned back to Meris. "So you see, it's in Regional Command's best interest to silence us all. It will be easiest to do that by targeting our communication satellites. If they do, no one will be able to contradict their version of what happened here. They can attack this Sanctuary and no one else will see."

She couldn't believe he could say that so calmly. Yet he'd been a military commander. He'd probably been in terrible predicaments before.

Lady Fi rested a hand on her husband's shoulder. "I think that those chromosomes proved more than Tavkel's paternity. I've wondered for years whether our bodies were originally meant to be just as immortal as our souls."

Plainly *she* wasn't fretting about being attacked. But she wasn't sitting in the command chair.

A sharp electronic tone rang out from the middle of the desk. Conversations stilled. "This is Chancellor Piper Gambrel, calling Administrator Wind Haworth-Caldwell. Are you receiving, Administrator?"

Other bodies pressed forward behind Meris, almost pushing her against the Minster's side. The stuffy air was hard to inhale. Over the benches, those streamers hung limp.

Minster Wind reached down and touched a glowing panel. "This is the Minster, Chancellor Gambrel."

"Please record this message."

Minster Wind held still, leaning over the desktop. "You are already being recorded, Chancellor."

"Very well." There was a throat-clearing noise, and Meris recalled thinking of that voice as infallible. No more. Now that voice curdled her stomach. "Having taken under arrest Tavkel Caldwell for interfering with Federate execution order YPN-KIC, and Kiel Caldwell for collaboration, we have been asked by the Federate Regional Council to deliver the following message.

"A list of names will be read at the end of this transmission. All those persons shall surrender to a hovercraft crew that will be sent in twenty-four hours. They will submit to chemical disempowerment immediately and return to Tallis under guard. On Tallis, their interviews will be conducted by the Special Operations Oversight Committee.

"Refusal to cooperate with this order will be taken as noncompliance with a reasonable request, and the destruction of all personnel at that site will result.

"The names are as follows . . ."

Meris listened, horrified. "Destruction of all personnel" was an unconscionable threat. In other words: Give up these people, or we'll kill you all. Sure enough, the Sentinels were to be silenced.

Chancellor Gambrel wasn't even pretending to ask for volunteers anymore. She leaned against Jorah a little harder and shut her eyes.

The Chancellor's voice read off the list of names. Both of Jorah's parents were named, of course. Both grandparents. Several names she didn't recognize.

" . . . Meris Cariole . . ."

Jorah's hand tightened on her left shoulder.

She smiled weakly. Actually, she felt honored to be named on that list.

"Please acknowledge receipt of this transmission, Administrator," Chancellor Gambrel finished.

"That's an execution list," Air Master Kinnor called from the doorway. "Nobody on that list will get to Tallis alive. Guaranteed."

Instead of answering either of them, Minster Wind swept a hand across that section of desk. Silence fell, but it was short-lived.

The High Commander pushed back from the desk. "There they go."

Meris couldn't see whatever he had seen on the desktop, but Jorah groaned behind her.

She pushed up to a standing position. "The communication satellites?"

"All of them, sir?" Jorah raised his voice.

The High Commander nodded. "Every one. We're cut off, except for the ITD, and that won't work without Tavkel or the supporting apparatus."

Meris stifled a cry. Tavkel had asked her to speak to the Whorl—and she'd promised she would! Their water would run out soon too. They couldn't stay here. But where would they go?

"Kinnor, has anyone tried to reactivate it?" Minster Wind reached toward yet another glowing panel.

"We tried. No luck."

Annalah pushed away from the table. "But it'll be targeted next, and we've still got to get the word out. Maybe it'll let us. Aunt Wind, you said you found the seed, right? And the Chancellor said they'd *grown* the disks, didn't he? Well, I think it's acting like it's alive. Let me try—gently—to see if it'll help us. To honor the One who made life."

The Air Master laughed shortly.

"It's worth trying," the High Commander said.

Annalah reached out a hand. "Come on, Meris."

• • •

Up at the meadow, Piper Gambrel had reclaimed his seat in Urnock's upper-level command station. Its view of the western peaks had been improved by the removal of all those bushes. Several of Urnock's staff sat at a second console, exchanging reports with another lander that was now dropping out of high orbit. That one had originally been refurbished as a hospital facility. Zeimsky stood in front of the glass walls on this bridge's north side, watching for it to appear.

However, there'd been another ITD communiqué from Tallis, signaling a significant change of plans.

Essentially, it had contained a promise to publicize his effort to save as many Thyrian lives as possible. However: "We prefer that no prisoners be brought to Tallis. Maintain the twenty-four hour deadline, which will enhance your credibility. You shall report at that time that Sentinels attacked your compound, with Tallan lives lost—"

Urnock, standing on the ITD platform, had sniffed loudly. "That actually gives them time to attack, Madam Kernoweg."

Gambrel had leaned forward to look into one of the small side viewing platters.

Madam Kernoweg pressed her hands together and shook her head. "Our conduct is being closely monitored throughout the Federacy," she said. "Apparently, they have just reactivated the ITD at Hesed House. We are being accused of trying to destroy their communication capabilities—and the scandalous rumor of our actually having issued a death list is being disseminated, along with their attempt to salvage the deceased's reputation by claiming divine parentage. The Federacy's honor must be preserved. I hope I make myself clear, Colonel."

This was bizarre. Their own ITD array hadn't shown any such transmission! The thing seemed to have developed a self-filtering system.

"Unnecessary," Zeimsky shouted across the main deck. "Madam, the cure I developed is highly effective. We can show the Whorl a much better way. We have them where we want them now."

"Colonel," she'd said, "this Council sees the situation differently."

For the half hour since receiving that transmission, Gambrel—with Zeimsky's support, for once—had tried to talk Urnock out of deploying all of their antipersonnel ordnance well before the twenty-four hour mark, even if every living soul on that roster surrendered.

They might as well have spoken to stone. Urnock had plainly been spooked at the Sentinel compound. He simply wanted to finish the job, to protect his forces and the Federacy's reputation, and get back to Tallis with his life. He'd just deployed a troop of snipers in pursuit of the Sentinel group carrying off that ITD platter. After all, it was known that even the strongest Sentinels' abilities were effective only at short distances.

And Urnock commanded the troops, so Urnock was getting it all his way.

Gambrel disliked admitting it, but he didn't want his reputation tarnished either. His own aides were now tasked with drafting various cover stories. He was finished with this assignment. Finished.

The god-voice seemed to be regaining strength now that Tavkel was dead. It evidently approved. *Your people will take less risk this way,* it said. *You can finish sooner and depart. Now take me to Kiel Caldwell.*

It seemed to want his willing cooperation again. It hadn't kicked him out to hover, as before. And it wasn't forcing him to go to Shamarr Caldwell right away. So for the moment—with Shamarr Caldwell detained in one of Urnock's holding cells—Gambrel sat and considered the new ITD transmission.

Included in the new order had been instructions to "make sure no genetic material remains." *That,* the god-voice told him, *was a delicate way to say "burn them all to ash." They don't want any Sentinels lab-creating offspring from their relatives' skin cells. Remember, that's how they made their strange medspec. Saried Caldwell Kinsman.*

Theoretically, he answered the voice, *they're correct. That will include the body in our crypt, won't it? And,* he added, wondering how the voice would react, *Shamarr Caldwell.*

Give him to me. I'll see it done.

As well as everyone we've tagged on Thyrica. Nodding, Gambrel stroked his chin. Zeimsky's arriving "hospital module" would be converted into a crematorium.

Zeimsky paced the command bridge, plainly too furious to speak but now overruled by Urnock, Gambrel, and the FRC itself. Once it was done—the Sentinel threat ended, here and on Thyrica—he and Zeimsky would have to renegotiate their partnership, including their plans for Regional Command. Gambrel wasn't looking forward to that.

Urnock stood up. "Kass," he barked. An aide hustled toward the elevator.

Gambrel stood too. He looked Urnock in the eye. "I would appreciate as little damage as possible to that site. I've started to think of it as a retreat site for the Collegium. Cleanup might be relatively inexpensive."

Urnock smirked. "It will be safer and more economical just to do it with long-range incendiaries. Burning everything for about a klick around it will improve the view there too. It's all stone underground. You can clean up—"

"Cowards!" Zeimsky spun around. "Cowards, both of you! All my work, gone for nothing—just because you two are too scared of those people to back me up. I'm ashamed to be breathing the same air." He stormed to the emergency stairwell. Without waiting for the service elevator to return, he clattered away down the stairs from the bridge.

"What sparked that?" Gambrel said.

Urnock rolled his eyes. "Just temperamental. How'd he get to be a colonel?"

CHAPTER 46

Wind eyed the desktop monitors, already missing Kinnor terribly. Her office had fallen silent when he'd called in at midafternoon, via his handheld. He'd reported that the ITD had come alive once more, displaying Madam Kernoweg and repeating the horrendous new order she'd sent to Colonel Urnock, via her own ITD.

"As if it's trying to warn us," Kin had added. "Letting us listen in. But Gambrel and Urnock may not know we intercepted that call. You'd better evacuate now. Don't follow us. We'll be the first group targeted." There had been a pause. "Go with the One, Wind."

She'd seen in Jorah's eyes that his faith and hope were in tatters. She'd actually felt it in Kinnor, until he'd headed out. The fire within him was all but quenched. And she was tired, so tired.

Her father-in-law sat beside her. He bowed his head. "If I were commanding the Federate force, I would deeply regret receiving this order from Regional—but I'd have to follow it. And if I had to attack Procyel, I'd be inclined to target this location from orbit." A puff of breeze made the streamers flutter behind him.

It blew into Wind's face, and she imagined this Sanctuary full of choking ash, destroyed like Baseline Settlement on Mikuhr, the place she had once called home. Here, though, a more conventional attack was likelier. Probably not Ostian dust nor flash bombs. More likely incendiaries . . .

She glanced at the streamers again. "Kinnor's right," she said. "If anyone wants to head out right now, you're dismissed. Don't wait for us. Take whatever you'll need from the pantries. We don't need to make it easy for them to get us all. Make them work that attack ship's sensor suite."

A few people hurried out through the arch. She tried not to notice who they were.

Wind rested her head on her stacked fists, treasuring these last few hours with so many loved ones. Annalah had already headed out with Kinnor, claiming that the disk showed an affinity for her—whatever kind of consciousness it had.

Maybe Annalah's unassailable faith would help Kinnor find his again. Wind shut her eyes, remembering the ancient chamber back on Mikuhr where she'd found the original . . . was it truly a seed? . . . for the ITD. Kinnor had been with her that day. He'd saved her life. The memory gave her the sense that they had been guided all along.

And she'd lived to see Boh-Dabar. She only wished they'd had longer with him—and that she had the faintest idea what the Holy One wanted her to do next.

One thing seemed clear. Hesed House had run out of options. No one here could count on seeing another sunrise. Meris and Jorah lingered on one of the stone benches, hand in hand, looking as closely aware of each other as a couple newly pair-bonded. It warmed her to think that her son had found love, however late in his too-brief life. Why hadn't they left?

"You two should head out soon." Wind glanced aside again. "Maybe with Father and Lady Fi."

"Minster." Meris let go of Jorah's hand and rocked forward. "Even Chancellor Gambrel could still give up his darkness. Here's what I'm thinking: I'm on his list. If we were to walk up the valley to him, they'd probably let us approach the camp. And then I could talk to him. Maybe offer some kind of negotiations. I haven't been much of a liaison so far. There's time, isn't there?"

Wind pushed away from the desktop, startled and abruptly afraid. "But we have nothing left to offer that they want."

Jorah shrugged. "I think she's right, Mother. I'll put my uniform back on, and we'll do you proud. And who knows. If Gambrel could give his darkness to Tavkel, then maybe . . ." He glanced at his grandfather, the High Commander. "Maybe at least they'll delay the attack."

Wind didn't trust herself to answer. She only nodded. Jorah reached over the desktop and clasped her hands for a moment. He saluted his grandfather and turned toward the door.

Meris followed him. Wind felt sure she would not see either of them again. Not with these eyes. As their footfalls faded off along the silent poolside, she turned her attention back to the desktop. Nothing had changed on the big map.

Lady Firebird leaned hard against her own husband's right side again, and he slid his arm around her waist. "Excellent," she said. "Meris will be his guard now. And they just might succeed." Her smile faded as she also looked down. "That big cruiser will be in firing position well before the twenty-four hour mark. I'd say what, midnight?"

"We'll all be gone from here," Wind assured her. *You will be, anyway.*

Captain Mel Anastu slipped in through the main arch. She wore two backpacks and carried one of Meris's aid kits, and she seemed to have regained her sense of balance. "This is the best I could scavenge."

"Give it to the High Commander and Lady Firebird." Wind pointed at them. She couldn't have said why she wanted to stay here.

But apparently she would be the last administrator of Hesed House. When the fire fell, she wanted to be out at the poolside, standing beside the water.

• • •

Kiel sat on a metal stool in one of the landing module's treatment rooms, absently rubbing a sore spot on his upper arm. One of the Tallans had injected a hypospray full of DME-6 to block ayin activity. Kiel had protested, since he hadn't retrained his abilities. The young man had said grimly, "We've got several hundred doses of the stuff. Some of it might as well not go to waste."

He'd been wristbindered as he boarded the hovercraft. He hadn't protested the wristbinders either, although they made it impossible to reach Jorah's crystace inside his left sleeve. He had the strangest feeling that here, about to leave the planet, was exactly where he needed to be, despite Tavkel's prediction that he would die here on Procyel II.

Metal walls surrounded him, and his stool stood on a textured metal deck. There was not a single natural object in this small, secured cabin. On the metal examination table lay the brown metal crypt that now served as Tavkel's coffin.

The metal door slid open. To his amazement, the medical man—Colonel Zeimsky—stalked through. "Bloodshed and burning," he fumed. "That's what they're resorting to now. I wanted to cure you people. I wanted to rid the Federacy of you, but I didn't think it had to be done this way."

Kiel eyed the crypt. "Damage control," he suggested, though he only understood part of Colonel Zeimsky's tirade. What was the man doing here? "Because of Tavkel's death?"

Colonel Zeimsky's eyes seemed to focus on Kiel. "Yes. Damage control. You understand, don't you?"

"How could I not?" Kiel shrugged, the motion awkward because of his secured wrists.

Colonel Zeimsky strode forward. "Oh, for pity's sake." He unhooked a subtronic device from his belt and touched it to the wristbinders, which sprang open. Colonel Zeimsky snatched them up and set them aside. "You might as well die with a shred of dignity. We're not going to be able to keep Urnock away from you much longer."

"Thank you." Kiel rubbed his wrists. Maybe he should give up the crystace . . . No, he decided. It had arrived in the Federate Whorl with the first Ehretan refugees, and it had been passed down for fourteen generations to Jorah. Perhaps they would burn it along with his body, if he understood Colonel Zeimsky correctly.

It crossed his mind to *use* the crystace, perhaps to take Colonel Zeimsky hostage and see what might be done from there.

No. That was nothing but a temptation, unworthy of the God he loved.

Colonel Zeimsky rested a hand on the crypt, scowling. "This wasn't what I had in mind, Shamarr Caldwell."

Kiel recognized the signs. Here stood a man who needed to unburden a miserable conscience. "You can be forgiven, if you're genuinely sorry." Colonel Zeimsky had committed a heinous crime, killing Tavkel against orders. All darkness was heinous, though, and Kiel had vowed to serve the Eternal Speaker and other flawed humans.

"I am," Colonel Zeimsky blurted. "Sorry. I only wanted to take Gambrel down a notch. And I did think your Tavkel was dangerous. He was, wasn't he? The opportunity presented itself, and I took it. If it's any comfort," he added with a headshake, "the Regional Council still would've ordered full annihilation, eventually. If he were still alive."

"I didn't hear that order." Kiel was still appalled but not surprised. He pulled the prayer cloths out of his pocket and smoothed them on top of the crypt.

"It just came." Colonel Zeimsky thrust his own hands into his pockets. "My hospital ship—I spent days designing the thing, refitting it—it's going to be turned to a crematorium. Cowards," he muttered.

Kiel was again tempted to draw the crystace and head upstairs, but a thought nudged him. "So give Tavkel your darkness. He'd take it."

"Are you sure?" Colonel Zeimsky stared at the crypt. It looked like an altar now. "Anyway, maybe he would have, but it's too late now. In case you haven't noticed, your Boh-Dabar is dead."

Holy One, what is this? He didn't refuse outright. "He still would," Kiel said cautiously. "Still will."

"Oh, that's right. You people believe in immortal souls. That he's out there." Colonel Zeimsky opened his arms. "Somewhere."

Kiel nodded.

Colonel Zeimsky gave a short laugh. He pulled his hands out of his pockets and half-bowed toward the crypt. "Tavkel." He clipped his words decisively. "I apologize. Your priest seems to think you're listening. Have my darkness if you want it."

He turned back to Kiel. "There. Think he heard that? Think it made any difference?"

"Only if you meant it," Kiel said softly. "If you did, it made all the difference in the Whorl."

Colonel Zeimsky grunted and stepped toward the door. "Heard the elevator." He pointed outside. "Probably Gambrel. Or worse, Urnock. So I'm gone. Sorry, Caldwell. Sorry about it all." He touched that electronic device to the door, and it slid open. He walked out.

Kiel expelled a long breath, running the fingers of both hands through his hair—when was the last time he'd bothered to cut it? Before arriving on Procyel, apparently. Just under a month ago. *Holy One, was that why you brought me into my enemy's lair? So one more soul could find rest?*

Chancellor Gambrel stepped in through the door. He looked like he was alone, but a light shimmered in his eyes. His lips curled in a subhuman sneer.

Kiel backed away, heart accelerating. "Chancellor." He spoke as calmly as he could. Might this man also escape the ghastly fate awaiting him? "I am not a man of conflict."

"You belong to me." The voice wasn't Chancellor Gambrel's, of course. "You shamed me once. Never again."

Kiel kept backing, putting Tavkel's crypt between him and the wild-eyed Chancellor—and the entity controlling him.

"Let him go, shadow!" Kiel ordered. "Set him free."

"By your own words!" Shimmering dust flowed out Chancellor Gambrel's eyes, through his nostrils and ears, flooded from his mouth.

Aghast, Kiel laid both palms on the altar cloths. "Tavkel," he whispered, "can you help me?"

The shimmering cloud gusted toward him.

Kiel raised an arm and shouted. "That man's blood immolated *your* darkness, Chancellor. You're his creation too. You can be free even now."

As the cloud circled him, the crystace practically leaped into his hand. Kiel activated it and held it across his body. He hadn't held one of these in what, forty years? "You—shadow—even you were once his child!"

It darted forward. He swept up the crystace. The cloud shrieked again and flowed back toward the Chancellor.

Gambrel's limbs flailed. His back arched. His head struck a corner of the crypt, and he crumpled to the deck.

"Chancellor!" Kiel shifted the crystace to his left hand and knelt down, feeling at the side of Gambrel's throat for a pulse. He was alive, but he'd probably suffered a concussion.

The door slid open. Two Tallans—a man and a woman—rushed in, weapons drawn. Kiel sprang back to his feet. He couldn't tell whether those were shock pistols. Plainly, they thought he'd attacked Chancellor Gambrel. He must defend himself—

No! This time, he kept the crystace low. "Wait!" he cried. "The Chancellor fell. He needs a medspec. Call Colonel Zeimsky—"

Both Tallans raised their pistols. A moment's painful light flooded Kiel's eyes. Then darkness embraced him, as cool and fragrant as kirka trees.

• • •

Tiala Caldwell's eyes ached from weeping. She had been half blinded already, because of the Bright Ones who kept flitting in and out of Stone House more rapidly than she ever had seen before.

She knelt on her prayer bench near the center aisle, beneath Stone House's vaulted ceiling. Under the altar flame, Tekkumah's newest Em'Gadol had laid out the altar cloths for mortal danger once again. Red over green, over blue, they matched the pure colors on Tiala's deeply padded knee and elbow rests.

Vivid memories flooded her heart: two-year-old Tavkel tottering toward her with a fist of weed flowers—ten-year-old Tavkel struggling with his growing realization of who he was and what that meant he must do—at twenty, carrying home a young kipret with an injured foreleg—and the awful morning not long ago, when he had taken her aside to say the time for his leaving had come.

"I won't be able to see you until the end." He had cradled her head against his chest. "That will be hard, Mother. What I must do, I do out of love for you—and the flock at Hesed House—and on other worlds."

Most of these Bright Ones were reporting now from those other worlds, informing Tekkumah's seven remaining residents. One by one, the other Tekkumans had been laid to rest. More recently, the Chapter at Tallis had grown so large they couldn't worship together anymore. Every original member had left Castille City to start a new group on some other part of the planet. The Bright Ones had alerted a few of those leaders today, using waking and sleeping visions. Now those leaders were gathering in vigil. Chapter heads on other worlds were hearing from Tallis and calling for fasting and prayer.

Soon would come the more frightening reports, as Gambrel and the other evildoers tried to explain away her son's death. Might Annalah be able to transmit once more to Queen Rinnah on Netaia?

Probably not. Chancellor Gambrel had nearly blocked outbound communication. He'd use his own ITD, soon, to insist there'd been a terrible accident that had resulted in the death of Tavkel and others. Hundreds of new worshippers would hear and mourn. Many would cling to faith. Some would fall away. Would her brother?

She had always been exceedingly fond of Kinnor and Kiel. She'd prayed them through so many perils.

But now Kiel was beyond prayer. And would Kinnor understand what else must happen? *It must, oh, it must.* The immolation prophecies . . . Who would read them correctly?

I can help that only by praying. She wiped away tears, adjusted her weight over both knees on her bench, and gripped its handrail. *Dear One. Oh, Tavkel, dear son. The immolation is made, and where are you now? Has your own renewal already begun? Is this the new Whorl we will live in, or is it a place only of mourning? How could it go on, now that you're gone from it? Surely not . . .*

She faltered. She rested her forehead on her tear-smeared hands. *We trust you. Holy Father of my son, we trust you.*

Separate out your true people, let them cling to you . . .

Let me *cling to you . . .*

Her forehead slipped on her hands. Sobs shook her shoulders.

• • •

On the Federate world of Caroli, an extremely elderly woman sat in the downstairs common room of the Hazelworth Home for the Aged. Three faded lounging couches almost filled the room, arranged so that residents could sit or lie and stare for hours at tri-D images over the media block. She had tuned the block for newsnet coverage, but there hadn't been a report in two hours. Just mindless talk and unpleasant music.

Rava Haworth kept sitting there anyway.

Her girl—she still remembered the niece who now went by the name Wind Haworth-Caldwell as the young girl who had come home to Mikuhr—for all these years, she'd seemed to have made good. Found a decent man . . . actually married him, the first in the clan to actually settle down with a legal document . . . and over the years she'd become "administrator" over the Sanctuary world of his powerful people. Her girl, made good.

Rava had made sure the staff alerted her any time certain key-words appeared over media channels. That was why she'd spent all day yesterday and most of today on this lounger, elbowing everyone else aside. There'd been a time she could've just voice-commanded them, but people who thought they knew better had taken that ability away decades ago.

She still had her people's unusually long life to look forward to, though.

Didn't she?

After that ITD transmission yesterday, relayed from Netaia—when that man called Tavkel had spoken, though Rava thought she'd glimpsed young Wind at one point—she was less sure about a lot of things. What had all this been about the Whorl being destroyed—or was it going to be renewed—or both? And why were the local netters claiming that news off Procyel II was being censored, filtered by Federate cultural police? And what was this about a human sacrifice?

She didn't buy it. Any of it. She'd liked a lot of what Tavkel had said. At the time, she'd just thought "why not?" and had mentally given him the gift he claimed to be wanting. Her darkness. Just because her girl, Wind, would've liked that.

Wind Haworth-Caldwell, the only person out of Rava Haworth's dim past who had stayed in touch. Who really seemed to *love* her. Rava spent a lot of time asleep these days, but she didn't feel sleepy now. Poor Wind. It looked, now, like it was meaningless . . . that mental gift she'd given Tavkel . . . but she didn't regret it. Just having done something out of love—strange concept, love—made her feel young and warm instead of old and chilly.

And here came Horis again, the resident grump, laughing and pointing at the media block as he clumped along behind the lounger. Anything that wasn't his idea, he hated it.

Well, if he thought he was going to switch this off—if he thought she was really asleep, sitting here—he'd get nothing for his trouble but another good dose of her tongue.

• • •

Federate Netaia was in an uproar.

Prince Tel Tellai was aging into his eighties but looking almost as young as ever, thanks to cell-death-preventing implants. He pursed his lips and stared across a veritable lake of grandnieces, grandnephews, and grandchildren—and even a great-grandchild, thanks to Elspeth and her new husband, Torry. Mostly he could see just the backs of their heads. They sat on an elegant South Continent rug, hunched forward and staring at the palace's private tri-D wall. Most of them were too young to comprehend the unfolding tragedy. Still, it was important they all be together today.

Off to one side, Her Majesty Rinnah—his daughter-in-law—sat on a cat footed chair, conferring with the local Na'marr. Firebird had founded that Chapter house . . . dear, dear, how many years ago? Every Chapter house on Netaia had declared itself Dabarite, of course.

Now, with Tavkel dead but his request for darkness still apparently standing, every believer on this world faced a choice: Cling to that man's declarations, and return to faith in something they could not see daily on Annalah's *PER* reports—or go back to Netaia's ancient worship of the Powers that Rule.

There seemed to be no return to the Path of Faith they'd known. Either it had been completed in Tavkel, or it had been invalidated. Tel saw it that way, at least.

Esme passed him a platter of sweetmeats.

"Thank you, love." He took a nut tart before passing the platter to their eldest son. Prince Brenn sat cross-legged with one of his and Rinnah's twins on each knee.

Imagine . . . if Netaia hadn't outlawed heir limitation, how few of these lovely young people would sit on that carpet today? Life was precious, long life a treasure, and a large family the best gift of all.

Her Majesty Rinnah sat nearest the white-and-gold parlor door, looking like her lovely late mother as she crossed her legs and regally laced her fingers. The Na'marr waved down the tri-D projector's volume and spoke to the children. "He promised to renew the Whorl. He showed he had power over death itself. He will be back . . ."

To Tel's satisfaction, none of the grandchildren—not even Conura, who could be something of a scandal—had gotten up to leave the room, though ITD reports from Procyel were becoming sporadic. Apparently Air Master Kinnor and sweet Annalah were hiking quickly into the hills, convinced that Federate troops would soon find them anyway.

Tel felt as if he were waiting for something, but he couldn't say what. Tavkel had brought Kinnor back from death, unquestionably. But could he bring himself back, as the Na'marr had predicted, or were they waiting for something else? The last tri-Ds sent by Wind at Hesed House via DeepScan had shown a body even more completely ruined than Air Master Caldwell's, with tissue literally melted from the bone. The grandchildren would have nightmares. He wished they hadn't seen it.

Still, Tavkel was a Caldwell. It would be unusual to settle for half a victory.

CHAPTER 47

Daylight dimmed outside the span of windows on the upper-level bridge, and Piper Gambrel rested his head against an inner bulkhead. It ached. Zeimsky had wrapped a cold pack around his scalp.

But it wasn't working. The sound of wind gusting in trees made him ill. In the command chair several meters away, Urnock talked steadily into an audio pickup, probably issuing orders.

Gambrel shook his head and instantly regretted it. Despite the cold wrap, it hurt viciously. He was ready to return to Tallis and his admirers, counting down hours until they could justifiably burn out the Sentinels and depart. He had almost stopped caring about the Regional Council's reputation for mercy.

Between his chair and Urnock's station, Zeimsky was pacing again. After injecting an anti-inflammatory drug and applying the cold wrap, he'd checked Gambrel's pupils several times. Gambrel wasn't at all clear about what had happened. The guards had reportedly killed the Shamarr, downlevel, for attacking him. Kiel Caldwell had been armed? It sounded out of character, but Gambrel honestly no longer cared. *Zeimsky says I'm going to be fine.*

Shamarr Caldwell wouldn't have tried to kill him by hitting him over the head with that weapon, though—and Zeimsky's muttering did not ease the headache. "Stupid waste. All those lives. Stupid, needless . . ."

Gambrel would've liked to send the man away, but until his head felt better, he wanted his medspec close.

The god-voice seemed to have abandoned him. After that mysterious seizure, it had fallen silent. *Have you left me?* he mourned, forming silent words. His unseen counselor used to answer. Nothing came now.

Urnock spun his chair. "Zeimsky," he snapped. "Stand still. I want to talk to you."

Zeimsky paced up to Urnock's station and stood glaring down at him.

"Listen," Urnock said, "the aides' cover-up efforts are ridiculous. You killed Tavkel, and it's on your head that we're dealing with stories of human sacrifice, so this part of the cover story is going to be yours. Write it out if you have to, but get every detail straight. We'll be living with this for the rest of our careers."

Zeimsky pulled his shoulders back. It made him look more military than usual. "Haven't you already approved the excuse," he sneered the word, "for slaughtering everyone here? My part's small stuff by comparison. One death. One pathetic medical 'accident.'"

Urnock scowled up at Zeimsky and then aside at Gambrel. "It would be small, except that thanks to ITD communication, Federate citizens on twenty-three worlds already think we just gave them a holy martyr. They may be idiots, but they're our idiots." Urnock rubbed his chin. "The Federacy pays us to defend them. So give us some medical details, and get them right."

Zeimsky rested a hand on the long console. "You've got a lot of nerve." He paced away again.

Gambrel stayed close to the bulkhead. He simply needed his reputation back. Sending the locals to rejoin the Infinite Divine would be no crime. However, one didn't do that to whole people groups. He'd invested his life in improving humankind, converting them to logic and good sense. Children should be taught the simple truth that the universe was home to highly developed animals. Animals had no intrinsic value, except for those few who acknowledged themselves as sparks of the Infinite Divine.

"Sir?" a young tech called from the command center. "Intruders. Two. Groundside."

Urnock spun back to the monitor board. Zeimsky hustled to the glass wall and laughed. "They've got their hands in the air, Urnock. Gambrel, it's your young friend Lieutenant Caldwell, and the Cariole woman on your surrender list. Looks like you've got your first two already."

Gambrel walked at a creep to the view window. Outside, brilliant flood lamps switched on to illuminate the night. Seeing the young people heartened him. Had she recruited the boy? A small victory, but a sweet one. "Yes," he said. "Yes, that's her. And Jorah Caldwell has been cured, so hold your fire."

"He's probably armed." Urnock poised one hand over the touch-board. "Safest to stun them both."

"Wait!" Gambrel shouted, and the room spun around him. His head pounded. "Urnock! If your people kill that boy I won't be answerable for the consequences. Bring them indoors, keep them under guard, and I'll meet them downlevel."

• • •

Meris peered over Jorah's shoulder but stood perfectly still as four armed Tallans sprinted down the ramp of the landing module. Her eyes had adjusted gradually as dusk deepened. The flood lamps hurt her eyes.

"This would've been my big break," Jorah muttered. "I could've gone on board and taken all three, if I still had my ayin. Gambrel, Urnock, Zeimsky."

"And they would've shot you dead the moment they saw you coming, if they didn't know you were already so-called 'cured.'" Meris stood straighter and raised her voice to shout at the approaching Tallans. "I want to speak with Chancellor Gambrel, please."

One of the Tallans scanned them both with a handheld unit and frisked them for good measure.

Another one stepped away, raising a weapon. "Put your hands on the back of your heads."

Meris complied, and a frisson of fear tugged her shoulder blades. She had no urge to fall back on a litany, though. Never again. *Tavkel,* she silently thought, *can you help us?* He'd certainly known what fear felt like. Walking into that prep room, knowing what was coming—and hadn't he told her that she would see what happened when all that darkness finally affected him?

He'd done it for her. For the all the others too. For Jorah. But just as much for her. He'd also done it for Chancellor Gambrel. *Sometimes courage does what it must, even when it is terrified.* Who had said that? Probably Tavkel. His words had a way of staying in her head.

The guards marched them into the very cabin where she'd first spoken with Chancellor Gambrel. This time, undistracted by hero worship, she saw it as a cold metal place. And she now saw Chancellor Gambrel as a cold, deliberate man. He sat in his special chair, head encased in a cold wrap. Had he been hurt?

Colonel Zeimsky, the medspec, stood behind him. He was taking care of Chancellor Gambrel, but medicine wasn't her focus now. Nor was the fact that if any one person had killed Tavkel, that person had been Zeimsky. They would soon head back to Tallis. This was her last chance to do what Tavkel would have wanted.

She stepped out in front of Jorah and lowered her hands. "Chancellor, may I have a word?"

He smiled at her, and even the smile looked cold. "Meris, I'm glad to see you alive. I had been worried that the . . . dissidents might have harmed you, after what you . . . what *we* did to Tavkel. And Lieutenant Caldwell, how good to see you as well."

She saw right through the manipulation. He wanted to make her feel welcome but guilty. Deliberately she looked aside, at Colonel Zeimsky. "We murdered an innocent man," she told them both. "Absolutely innocent. He would have sat down and talked with you all, regardless of what you thought of him. There are other good people living here too, gentlemen. I came here for two reasons." She paused for breath.

Both men simply waited for her to continue.

Maybe she'd made a mistake, coming here. But now that she was here, there was nothing to do but keep talking. "You still could give Tavkel your darkness," she said. "Even you. Do it now, while there's still time. But also, I . . . Gentlemen, I ask you to show the same mercy Tavkel would've shown you. Don't destroy those people. Even if you've invented some kind of cover-up story, that act would be on your consciences for the rest of your lives."

"Tell that to Urnock." Venom dripped from Colonel Zeimsky's voice. "He just ordered your companion stunned and incarcerated."

Before she could protest, a stun weapon gave off its awful whine behind her. She spun around. Jorah crumpled onto the cabin's deck. The nearest Tallan pressed his weapon against Jorah's skull. Wasn't that lethal range?

The Tallan spoke, but it was to someone who wasn't in the room. "He's down, sir. Finish him?"

No! she wanted to shriek.

"No," Gambrel shouted. "Urnock, that boy is mine." His voice softened. "Come back to Tallis with us, Meris. And the boy will live."

• • •

Wind stood at the poolside, watching muddy water lap against white stone. The pale blue-green lights had come on all around the half emptied pool, and overhead the skylights' edges had vanished. By partially draining the pool, her workers had exposed half a meter of dirtied rock wall. Below the spot where she stood, Tavkel's walking stick floated amidst a small raft of flotsam.

She would've liked to climb down and grab it, to stand holding that remembrance of Tavkel when the Federates fired their first salvo in . . . she checked time lights on her handheld . . . maybe as little as two hours. The High Commander and Lady Fi had led a last evacuation group off down the Tuva River trail at sunset, but as she had told them, she was too weary. She would have slowed them down, even though they were no longer fast walkers. "This is a good place to wait," she'd said, "by the water. With our people in the catacombs."

If Kin fell into bereavement shock—if she were targeted before him—the others in his group would care for him until the end came. She was alone again. Like the old days.

This time, though, it felt right. She wanted to pray, not to run. *Save us, Eternal One. Save your people. You've taken our darkness. Will you let darkness take us?*

She opened her eyes. *He might,* she reflected. The Eternal Speaker had let countless good people die in terrible ways over the millennia. And everyone born eventually died. The story had always ended sadly.

So far.

She raised her face toward the dark skylights. It was the year's longest day, but dusk had ended. *Spare my people,* she prayed. *Spare my husband from having to die again.*

• • •

Meris backed away from the guard. He could kill Jorah with a squeeze of one finger. "Sir," she said evenly, "We wouldn't have come here if we weren't surrendering to you. Don't harm him."

"Shouldn't you be glad," Chancellor Gambrel asked, "if he rejoins the Infinite—"

"We're not sparks, Chancellor. We're eternal, indissoluble individuals." She never would've interrupted the Chancellor in the old days. "It's not too late. For any of you." She tried to look across at the guards and not down at Jorah. "Tavkel died in possession of my darkness. So my darkness is gone. Nothing stands between me and the true eternal. Tavkel proved that we've got it all wrong—the sparks, the dissolving—when he brought back Jorah's dad. Surely . . . surely, 'from somewhere on the other side,'" she said, using a Collegium phrase, "surely he still could take away everything that makes you less than fully human."

"My dear." Gambrel tilted his head and looked down at her. "We *are* all sparks of eternal light. That man has redissolved into the Infinite. He can't take—"

The lander's bulkheads rattled. Thick darkness fell between one word and the next. The module's overhead lights went as black as the clearing outside the hatch. Black as a cloudy night. Black as soot. Someone shouted overhead.

The overhead lights glimmered back on. Faintly, though.

• • •

"What's going on?" Gambrel kept his voice low. "Do we have a systems failure?" Some idiot probably had overloaded a circuit.

"Get to the bridge. Use the stairs," one of Urnock's guards shouted. "Don't trust the elevator. They've attacked our systems."

Who had? The Sentinels? Nonsense.

One of the Tallans seized Meris's shoulder and aimed her toward the stairwell.

Gambrel stood up too quickly. His head spun again. He followed as quickly as he dared in the dim emergency light. "You two," he ordered the other two guards. "Stay here with Lieutenant Caldwell. He's to be guarded and he is to be kept alive. No matter what Urnock tells you."

Painfully he hustled up the metal stairs, trailing the group. Those people had outflanked the Federate presence after all! Maybe Urnock had been right. Hit first, hit hard. The first need was to survive. Only the living could be generous.

He emerged on the upper deck. The windows were utterly dark, and a voice spoke out of the console. He recognized the *White Squall's* comm officer. "The entire ITD net has shut down. And DeepScan's chaotic. Stand by, sir."

Or had Regional Command decreed that *no one* would leave this world alive? Could this be a subtronic hit from the carrier, as it moved into position to flame the Hesed site? A chill started at the top of his head and traveled down his spine. They wouldn't!

Urnock stood next to the unit, bracing his arms against it. "Repeat your previous, *White Squall.*"

The voice spoke again. "This is *White Squall,* repeating. We have what looks like star death. The Procyel sun didn't go nova. It just went out. Its neighbors are dark too. Their mass and gravity are still there . . . just . . . there's no light. And it's spreading, sir. This appears to be the epicenter. There went Tallis. Elysia. It's beyond the Whorl now, sir. Accelerating."

"Are you hearing this?" Zeimsky craned his neck and looked up at him. "They're all—"

"Stay calm. It's probably a trick." Urnock's voice sounded placid. Controlled. "Remember, they defended this world with some kind of madness weapon."

Yes, they did! Gambrel got a deep breath. *Mind, you are calm. Body, you are strong.* He should have thought of this before Urnock did.

"I don't think they've hit us with anything else," Urnock said. "They must've just somehow gotten that groundside fielding suite operational again. They're playing with our minds. I told you not to give them this long. Don't believe anything you see or hear." He pointed down at the console. "We're under attack, but not *that* kind of attack."

Gambrel glanced aside. Meris Cariole stood halfway between the stairs and the windows, peering out into the night. "Kill the lights," Gambrel ordered. As the cabin fell dark, he too edged closer to the big windows. Just a few stars twinkled against utter darkness.

Fewer by the moment.

"Lights on!" Urnock ordered. A room light flickered back on. Flickered . . . and died.

Urnock had to be right. This was madness. Out of Urnock's comm board, voices babbled on top of each other.

" . . . en route from Tallis to Caroli. We have been dropped out of slip-state . . ."

"Regional Council, three of seven members present, emergency quorum . . ."

" . . . Give him the gift. Your time is short . . ."

" . . . reports its power grid is flickering as countless circuits are being switched on simultaneously . . ."

Then those voices died too.

• • •

Meris shuddered in dark silence as she reached the command deck's glass wall. She stretched out a hand and touched its solid, smooth surface. This felt like the eeriest dream she'd ever had. Why wasn't she frightened?

"It's over," she murmured. "It's over, Chancellor. This is the catastrophe." Barely visible overhead, a cluster of distant lights seemed to be moving. The orbiting ships, probably. Before her eyes, those winked out too.

Chancellor Gambrel's voice spoke in the darkness. "No. It's an illusion. Your Sentinel friends are hitting back. We'll get to the bottom of it. Guards," he snapped, "bring Lieutenant Caldwell up to the bridge—"

"No!" That was Colonel Zeimsky's voice. "Someone go check that stasis crypt—"

"Check it for what?"

"I think—"

Abruptly Meris's ears rang. It felt as if something were stretching her eardrums into mobius strips. Her body seemed to be turning inside out—the command bridge, where had it gone—where had *she* gone—where was all that light coming from?

She could see nothing but light . . . and something that looked oddly human.

"Tavkel?" she whispered.

But he didn't look sunburned anymore. He looked like the sun itself.

CHAPTER 48

Piper Gambrel blinked. The command deck's lights must've come back on, along with the daylight. Good—somebody was awake, up on the *White Squall*. Apparently they had destroyed the Sentinels' fielding weaponry by striking the Sanctuary from orbit. After that insane darkness, daylight seemed painfully bright.

He blinked again and turned away from the windows—but the light was just as painful on this side. Fortunately, his head wasn't pounding anymore. He squinted and waited for his eyes to adjust. Where was everyone? His eyes weren't working properly. *Must be the concussion—*

Someone stood between him and the light source, apparently walking toward him. Either that, or the person *was* the light source. And Gambrel could see nothing but light, stretching out in all directions. He squeezed his eyes shut once more, but the light grew so brilliant that blood coursing through his eyelids gave off an unnerving red glow.

He gave up and opened them. "They're at it again," he announced. "They couldn't defeat us with darkness. Now they're trying to chase us away with daylight."

"Be at peace, Piper Gambrel." The words seemed to come from the approaching figure.

He shut his eyes again. It hurt, it hurt. And the voice was familiar, wasn't it? Wasn't it? "Stop it, you people." He turned a circle in place. "You aren't fooling me. Give it up."

"Be at peace," the voice said again.

And he remembered. Not just to whom this voice had belonged, but all it had ever said to him. The offers, the requests, the rebukes. He recalled his responses, and his insides curdled. He wanted to get away. There had to be some way of escaping this . . . this inexplicable, supernatural *thing*. And he saw, to his horror, that he was utterly naked . . .

"No!" he shouted. "This is an illusion. You aren't real. You're dead."

"I am the infinite," the voice said. "I can live this moment an infinite number of times. Face to face, one to one. I am in all good places, Piper Gambrel."

That voice left no doubt. It didn't just speak truth. It was truth.

Gambrel pressed his hands over his ears. "You can't manipulate my emotions, Tavkel. Give it up."

"I never take back the first gift I gave, after life itself." Beneath the voice's explosive power flowed an incongruous tenderness. "Your freedom, precious and perilous. You wish to remain free, forever, of everything beyond your understanding. Never to see my face again. I can grant that wish. But I will never send you away. You will have to leave me yourself."

Gambrel's head rang like a giant bell. How could this man grant that wish, to be away from Tavkel forever, if Tavkel claimed to be in all places? What place was there that someone who was in all places could not be . . . would not go? A corner of his mind cried, *It's an illusion!* Another cried, *It makes no sense!*

"Yes," the voice said. "I delight in all good places, and the joy they give my children. But in mercy, I also made a place without delight or joy. I will never enter it again. I did not make it for you, Piper Gambrel, but you may hide from me there."

"Never . . . again? You've been there?" Gambrel despised the way his voice squeaked. All this reminded him of a childhood instructor who had often confused him. Queerly, he seemed to recall every moment of his life with extraordinary clarity. Maybe he actually did stand in the presence of an extradimensional being.

Or maybe something external was playing with his mind! If so, then he still stood on the command deck, surrounded by Federate staff. "Bring Lieutenant Caldwell to the bridge," he ordered. If the Sentinel boy couldn't silence these voices, at least he could be threatened.

"I have been there," the voice said. "I have just come from there. From offering the last choice, even to miserable souls, that I now offer you."

Miserable souls? So that place already had people in it? "Did they—" The words blurted out before he could stop them.

"That is not your story, Piper Gambrel. You are still free to remain with me. As I am now, I always will be. As you are now, you may hope to outgrow. And I tell you, you do not yet see all there is of me."

Wiping watering eyes, Gambrel tried to imagine how much worse this agony of light—of imagining his own inadequacy—could become. *Stop!* he commanded himself. *This isn't real! I fear what I only imagine . . .*

"The choice you make now," the voice said, "is forever. Yet in the life you recall, your choice is already sealed."

Wasn't that a contradiction? Gambrel longed for his god-voice, the one that had sometimes offended but had made him feel powerful. This one overwhelmed him. He could only hope it was unreal.

"Painful my presence may be now, but you are human. I made you to revel in my presence, not to cower before me. You could have learned to nurture love's small seed planted in your heart. By clinging to darkness, you make real light an agony. Give it to me. Or else keep it as your only treasure."

"Nothing exists . . . in that other place . . . except pure spirit?" That sounded like a hopeful possibility.

"Far less. I also created the spirit."

He wanted a better explanation. Still, he liked the sound of that other place—that place without Tavkel's agonizing presence, without this humiliating effort to contradict all he believed. If it were less than spiritual, it would definitely be non-physical. He'd been right about that!

Whatever the Sentinels were up to, he would wait in that other place until the *White Squall* put an end to them. But if this conversation were real, he'd never have to face another personified spirit. He'd had enough of voices!

I was right about that, he assured himself. A new litany! *I was right—*

"I'll wait there," Gambrel said, turning away. "I have nothing to give you."

"By your own choice." Finally he heard something he knew to be genuine: that voice's deep sorrow.

● ● ●

Ottar Zeimsky shut his eyes and bowed his head. Surely now, that blinding light source would annihilate him no matter what the too-familiar voice had said. He was without hope.

He was dead.

"Painful my presence may be now," the voice continued, "but you are human. I made you to revel in my presence. Now you may learn to love, Ottar. You offered your darkness, but you only half meant it. Will you disown it forever?"

He seemed to be alone with that person—that person who was so full of light that nothing else existed. Anyway, there was nothing else he could see. "Can I?" The words tasted like vomit. "After what I did to you—"

There was nothing foul in that light. It was full of color and incongruous melody. By contrast he felt small and silent, tainted and dull. "You served yourself, a cruel master. My joy would be teaching you mercy. To serve me, and my Father, and others whom we love in the worlds we now remake."

That would be interesting. But he hesitated. He'd have a terribly low status in those worlds. People would scorn him—

"You would be brother and friend. All my children needed to be freed, forgiven, and cleansed."

"But you said *painful*."

"I said *may*." Was that voice laughing?

Oh, mercy. He knew, without being told, that this choice was permanent. There would be pain no matter what he chose. But . . . *oh, mercy*, he repeated silently. Learning to be worthy of that mercy might take eternity. But existing anywhere else—after seeing Tavkel unveiled—would be like starving to death, deaf and blind and paralyzed, when he knew he was made for dancing and feasting.

"Forgive me." He dropped awkwardly to his knees. *How strange that I still have knees.* Hadn't everyone always said that life after death would have to be purely non-physical? Gambrel had said that, anyway. And Gambrel had been the most spiritual man Ottar Zeimsky had known. "And . . . if you still want that gift I joked about—"

"A deep part of you meant it, Ottar Zeimsky. Otherwise, we would not be speaking this way."

"Then take it. Take it. Please, take it."

For an instant, the light was too bright to bear. And then—had his eyes been reconstructed, so he could see clearly again?—a man stood in front of him, stretching out a hand. Tavkel's arms and shoulders looked solid, his face and neck were tanned . . . and were those scars over his external carotid arteries?

Certainly. Those were the scars of a former stasis patient.

Ottar Zeimsky looked into hot brown eyes that seemed to burn with holy fire. Liquid music flowed through him, and a breeze full of scents he had half forgotten . . .

• • •

Rava Haworth wasn't sure where the walls had gone. She did know she felt better, younger than she'd been in about a hundred years. Something smelled heavenly. And standing here before her, somehow, was young Tavkel, about whom she'd heard so much before the nets went berserk.

"So the offer's still open?" She squinted into the miniature sun that seemed to be exploding all around her, wherever she turned her head. "I still could give you that stuff?"

"Because it has happened this way, Rava. Yes." The voice was masculine and alluring, like one of those men she'd taken as lovers long ago, except she believed this man would keep his promises. And that she—for herself, not for anything she could do for him—she was loved. Without hesitation, limit, or condition.

"What's to argue?" She grinned. "Take me away."

• • •

Actually, Meris decided, she hadn't turned inside out. She just hadn't ever known what right-side-out felt like. "You're alive," she murmured against a warm shoulder. "Tavkel, you're really alive."

"And so are you." Tavkel released her, stretching out both arms. He seemed to blaze with internal light, but her eyes kept changing. Now that she could focus on details, she realized that his wrists and throat remained scarred where she'd punctured them. She guessed she would see the same damage on his legs, if she knelt down to look.

She'd scarred him herself, and yet he'd forgiven everything. And he'd felt solid when she'd embraced him. This was no mere spirit, and definitely no spark. He was just as real, just as physical as Kinnor Caldwell had been, walking into the Chapter room after he'd arrived in that shipping coffin. Every molecule of her body and every corner of her spirit vibrated with a holy passion. She had never felt so alive.

She massaged her left forearm with her right hand. "You were right," she said. "Chancellor Gambrel always said that our spirits were all that mattered. But this is a body. There are nerve endings—I see and hear and smell and feel. But it's . . . different. It's more."

Seeing his smile tasted like eating a melody. "You don't begin to know how different. Or how much more. For I am about to renew the worlds. But my children come first."

His children? He had claimed her, as a parent would! Only . . . only much more tenderly than anything she'd ever experienced. She felt cherished, without a single qualifier. It hardly seemed necessary to look anywhere else.

Yet she was also curious. If he were real, and if she were real too . . . She glanced around, wondering where in the universe they stood. She still saw nothing but light around her. Her feet even seemed to be standing on pure liquid light.

"I haven't remade it yet." He lowered his arms to his sides. "For this moment we're alone, you and I. Was there anything else you wanted to tell me? To ask?"

Adoration exploded out of her soul and turned to gratitude. "My parents," she blurted. "Will you speak with them too? Tell them I love them. Are you—already—" What had he said, that he could live this moment infinite times?

"Of course." A universe sang in those words. "I love them even more than you do, Meris."

Something struck her, then. Something else she'd left unfinished. "Tavkel, what about that story? The girl who helped kill her pet, I mean. You . . . you knew what would happen, didn't you?"

"Of course I knew."

"But that story ended with her broken heart. My story seems to have a happy ending."

"Would you like to know how happy?"

"Oh, yes. Yes, please."

"Except that it will not end, Meris." Again the tenderness in his voice melted her doubts. "And now—"

She stood on a familiar hillside. Tavkel . . . she'd thought he stood closer! But he leaned against the same shearing shed she had known, smiling down the same hill. The rough brown work clothes were gone, though. He looked like he was dressed in light itself.

Other than that, he appeared to be one hundred percent human—yet the very center around which the universe revolved. She could have jumped into that center and vanished—or could she? It was no black hole, but the heart of light itself. She had the strangest feeling that she'd been remade just to walk alongside him.

So when he stepped away from the shed and headed downhill, his familiar face astonishingly regal, she followed closely. She did steal a glance aside, though. Down where the landing strip had been, a whole community of shimmering communication disks lay ready for use. Or . . . was she imagining things . . . Were they singing to each other?

And at the hill's foot, not under the ground but over it, that enormous new building complex had to be the Sanctuary, also remade. The red stone valley also looked different. The Tuva River no longer flowed past this enormous place, but out of it.

"Oh, my."

Hearing a voice she loved, Meris glanced left. There stood Jorah, eyes wide. She seemed to know exactly what he was thinking: He couldn't wait to go inside.

Was this shared awareness what Tavkel's divine father had intended when he'd created humanity—was this what telepathy should have been, and had it somehow been lost?

She shook her head to clear it. It didn't matter. She stood on Procyel again. And changed though it was, it was *home.*

Jorah snatched her hand. Like Tavkel, he seemed to be wearing light. "They'll be coming here from all over," he said. "Any minute now, as soon as they discover that they can. They'll realize *he's* here. We're going to be needed, to make them welcome."

Annalah came running up the trail, flaming hair streaming behind her. *Jorah.* Meris heard the voice clearly at the back of her mind. *Jorah, Meris, it's beginning. Finally!*

• • •

Kiel straightened. There'd been blinding pain. Then cool darkness and nourishing dreams—and then that precious private conversation.

He felt elated but oddly shy. He scrambled up off his knees and found himself at the focal point of the hillside amphitheater. Around him fiery light seemed to be singing, blended with more light coming from everywhere and everything. Surely being a newborn had felt like this, a blend of confusion and trust that was the essence of new awareness.

He spotted Hanusha with their daughters among a group of men who had to be his relatives, they resembled his father and brother so closely. Ancestors, perhaps—or could they be some of the clones Jahana had created on Mikuhr? *Tiala,* he thought, starting at one edge of that crowd and sweeping his eyes across it. *Is my sister here?*

As if simply thinking about her brought them together, she came walking toward him amidst another mob. These men and women were all robed in brilliant colors and crowned with flowers. All that had made her Tiala now made her perfectly recognizable: her shining adoration for the One who'd chosen her, the humility in her hands.

"As he said, brother." She pulled off her circlet of flowers and tossed it toward him. It landed precisely atop his head. "Well done, Kiel. Well, well done." Her eyes widened. She turned and cried out in delight.

The woman striding toward them reminded Kiel of a portrait he'd seen in the Angelo palace on Netaia. The man walking beside her looked rather like a young Sentinel priest who used to stare back at Kiel out of his freshing room mirror. Hadn't he been told how much he'd resembled his father? Here was living, walking proof.

They all embraced. Then Mother gasped and pointed downhill. Kiel spun around. The new Sanctuary had above-ground gates that shimmered as if water poured down every wall . . . and they were slowly opening. A group of people stepped out from inside—was that Wind among them, and Sanctuary Master Dabarrah?—and pushed them the rest of the way open. Those people stood aside as Tavkel led the crowd down the hill.

Tavkel. *My beloved brother—my king!*

And those others were the Sanctuary Administrators, Kiel understood. All of them who ever had served.

But Tavkel was going inside. Soon he would pass out of sight.

Kiel dashed downhill.

• • •

Firebird Mari Caldwell linked arms with her husband and hurried toward the gate, following Kiel and followed by Kinnor, who was turning cartwheels on tender spring grass. Brennen's hair was the light, rich red-brown of exotic leta wood again. His glacial-ice blue eyes never had changed, though. Naturally, she *felt* him, deep in that place where pair bonding had been. Deeper, though.

Strangely, she felt the same intimacy with young Piet walking on her other side—and Captain Anastu, beyond him—and stranger still, it felt perfectly natural. They had been made for this kind of communion. And now they were remade, so they could enjoy it without any fear or embarrassment.

Yet after that amazing conversation she'd had, she guessed she would never feel completely whole again, except in *His* presence. He had renewed the universe, just as he'd promised. And she had lived to see it—she, who'd been born with only the hope of dying gloriously.

She pressed in with the crowd through the shimmering gates and then edged aside to stare up—and up—and up. A tree had appeared near the reflecting pool's center, where the kirka trees had been. Red-orange fruit dangled from every branch.

"A latchem tree," she whispered. "It's what his walking stick was made from."

"It *is* his walking stick," Brennen said. "It's been remade too."

"Of course."

Kiel already stood beneath the tree, reaching up for a fruit. He plucked it, turned aside, and gave it to a woman whom Firebird didn't recognize. Maybe Kiel didn't know her either. Abruptly, though, Firebird understood something. *Kiel gives fruit. Tiala gives flowers. Brenn will be a teacher, of course—there will be people who don't understand how to use these new gifts.*

And me? she wondered.

It's too quiet in here, a voice declared, deep at the Brennen-place in her mind. *When the rest of the Whorl comes, it will be full of music.*

The music of all peoples, she answered. *All cultures . . . all times.*

Tavkel strode out across the water, flooding the poolside with his own fiery light. Firebird had traveled the Whorl and met its finest artists and musicians in her long prior life, but never had she seen or heard anything that filled her with such longing—and yet was so utterly satisfying.

She and Brennen went forward together, into a place where undying fire kissed unquenching water.

Author's Note:

This book is rife with the speculations of a theologically underqualified mind, and the last chapter is the most speculative passage I've ever written. Underlying the novel is my theory that God wouldn't do things in the same way if He came in a different time and place—but that His character would be just as plainly revealed (Hebrews 1:3a). This theory suggested numerous "what if?" questions. Instead of listing them, I leave you to find them and chew on them. Like the rest of this series, these are imaginative speculations, not theological predictions or declarations.

Kathy Tyers
Montana
April 2012

CPSIA information can be obtained
at www.ICGtesting.com
Printed in the USA
LVOW13s0406281017
554035LV00010BA/890/P